"POWERFUL . . . SWIFT . . . DRAMATIC SCENE FOLLOWS UPON DRAMATIC SCENE"
—New York *Times*

Taylor Caldwell became a major American writer overnight with the publication of her electrifying novel *Dynasty of Death*, the saga of the ruthless Barbour-Bouchard clan, creators of a mighty armaments empire. In *The Eagles Gather,* she continues the epic of the grand-children and great-grandchildren of Ernest Barbour in the mid-twentieth century. It bears all the marks of a great classic with its prophetic picture of the dangerous military-industrial alliance—but above all with its pulsating story of men and women trapped in a heritage of power, where love serves treachery, and ambition is an instrument of death.

"A novel of palace politics within a great American family. A story, and a moving one, of men and women, boys and girls in an environment of great wealth."
—New York *Herald Tribune*

"*The lofty peaks of best sellerdom . . . are traditionally difficult to scale. . . . But there are three American novelists who have climbed to the top not once or twice but over and over again. In so doing they have established themselves as an elite among U.S. fiction writers. . . . All three are women: Edna Ferber, Frances Parkinson Keyes and Taylor Caldwell.*"

THE EAGLES GATHER

Taylor Caldwell

PYRAMID BOOKS  NEW YORK

TO M. E. PERKINS
*"For wheresoever the carcass is, there will
the eagles be gathered together."*
St. Matthew 24:28

THE EAGLES GATHER

A PYRAMID BOOK

Printed in the United States of America.

Charles Scribner's Sons edition published 1940.
Pyramid edition published January 1963.
Eleventh printing, January 1974

ISBN 0-515-03015-5

This book is fiction. No resemblance is intended between any
character herein and any person, living or dead;
any such resemblance is purely coincidental.

Pyramid Books are published by Pyramid Communications, Inc.
Its trademarks, consisting of the word "Pyramid" and the portrayal
of a pyramid, are registered in the United States Patent Office.

Pyramid Communications, Inc.
919 Third Avenue, New York, New York 10022

LIST OF CHARACTERS

ADELAIDE BURGEON BOUCHARD—*widow of Jules Bouchard*

Armand
Emile   } *her sons*
Christopher

Celeste—*her daughter*

ANN RICHMOND BOUCHARD—*widow of Honore Bouchard*
Francis
Hugo
Jean   } *her sons*
Peter

Etienne Bouchard—*brother of Honore Bouchard*

Henri Bouchard
Edith Bouchard } *great-grandchildren of Ernest Barbour*

Thomas Van Eyck—*stepfather of Henri and Edith*

Andre Bouchard—*father-in-law of Jean Bouchard*

Estelle—*wife of Francis Bouchard*
Annette—*daughter of Armand Bouchard*
Agnes—*wife of Emile Bouchard*

Georges Bouchard—*publisher*
Marion Fitts—*his wife*
Professor Fitts—*father of Marion*

AND Ernest Barbour and his nephew, Jules Bouchard,
though dead, the leading characters.

CHAPTER I

JULES BOUCHARD, of Bouchard & Sons, munitions manufacturers, knew he was dying. He had been dying for a long time, ever since his beloved cousin, Honore Bouchard, had died on the *Lusitania,* while on a secret mission to the Allies. Jules had loved and trusted Honore as he had never loved or trusted any other man in his life. Honore's chief virtue had been integrity, and Jules had had an almost ludicrous affection for this characteristic in his cousin, which seemed to him to exist apart from any of the other moralities, and to be a certain texture of the soul. It had nothing to do with honesty, thought Jules, for honesty was the last refuge of the stupid. It needed only a kind of intelligent personal ethics as its starting point: the refusal to lie to one's self, no matter how one lied to others. It needed imagination, whereas honesty was almost always accompanied by lack of imagination.

Jules had never been one to sit back and meditate for any length of time. He was half English. Despite his Latin appearance, his delicate fastidiousness and exquisite zest in living, his fundamental character was British, which is essentially the driving character. Though he had a tremendous appreciation of all fine delicacies, all intricate perfections and lovely colors and forms and outlines, and loved nothing better than a dainty subtlety or witty paradox, he yet had the most profound contempt for all that was passionately introspective, abstract, melancholy, or sadly metaphysical. He could understand a Faust who sold his soul for youth and riches, which were the better part, but, like the founder of the Bouchard Dynasty, Ernest Barbour, Jules' uncle, he had nothing but a loathing for a Faust that cringed and repented at the end. This loathing did not rise from incomprehension, but rather from a complete comprehension. If a man who repented was twice weak, a man who dissected his repentance was thrice damned.

He was dying. It was regrettable and a damned nuisance, but there it was. But sometimes, as he worked into the night these feverish war days, there seemed to come a stoppage in his thoughts, like a big stone thrown into the neck of a narrow stream. And without a break in his work he would think: I won't see the end of this. Then he would go on, working a little faster, not dejected nor disturbed, but feeling only a fuming impatience, an outraged sense of interference. But lately, after these sudden stoppages, it would surprise him absently that his flesh had a coldness for a little while, an earth-coldness, as if it had chilled in anticipation.

Once he woke up in the middle of a night with a sensation of physical choking, and he discovered that he was sitting up in bed and panting. His consciousness came back very slowly, and then he was horrified to find that a sort of horror had him, a purely physical but most ghastly thing. His mind, reasonable and still calm, was yet shaken and angrily moved by this treachery of his body, this flesh-yielding to something he believed his mind had never objectively considered. This mind was like a cool, well-bred gentleman, poised and ineffably correct, caught in some way in the press of a rude, formless crowd that buffetted him, crushed him, shoved and struggled about him in an impersonal mob-terror. The gentleman might protest faintly, feel disgusted and annoyed, but he would be bruised and bedraggled anyway, and would emerge finally from the mob with a feeling that he had narrowly escaped annihilation. When this horror occurred again, with bad results the next day, he knew that the end was almost here, and he went about his preparations to meet it.

His nephew, Honore's eldest son, Francis, was now thirty years old, and so competent, so much older in manner and appearance, so much more mature than other men of his age, that he had been unanimously elected to the presidency of The Kinsolving Arms Company a short time ago. He had little or none of his father's inventive power, but his business faculty was formidable, his talent for organization, his shrewdness and unscrupulousness, enormous. He was an industrial genius, ferocious, expedient, and sleepless. His marriage had been carefully planned: Miss Estelle Carew was the only child of John Carew, a rising steel and railroad magnate in Pittsburgh, and one of the larger shareholders. of the stock of both Bouchard & Sons and The Kinsolving Arms Company. One quarter of his blood was French, but there was nothing Latin in his tall, angular, frigid blondness, his thin sandy eyebrows, and his bitter blue eyes, like fragments of ice. Neither was there anything English or Saxon about him: he was that new type, the American, already well defined in the South and the West. He enjoyed a large popularity, but this was not because of any fundamental kindness or integrity of character or unconscious charm, but solely because he realized that popularity never hurt any one and helped considerably, and so set himself, as he did in other matters, to win friendship. His agreeable smile, his studied air of sympathy and interest, his carefully worked-out laugh, his speciously frank geniality, his ostentatious favor-granting and candid manner, won him lifelong and loyal friends. His extraordinary talent for acting can be judged by the fact that he even deceived his wife as to his real character, and beyond that no man can have a greater success. If he had any liking for any one at all, it was for his second cousin, Christopher, son of Jules.

Jean Bouchard, second son of Honore, was doing exceptionally well as second vice-president to his uncle, Andre, president of The Sessions Steel Company, and had already married his cousin, Alexa, Andre's only daughter. Andre's own son, Alexander, was first vice-president. Jean was a short agile young man, weighing not more than one hundred and ten pounds, but excessively active and wiry and driving. He had the dark Bouchard complexion, a surprisingly full dimpled face, a wide, white-toothed smile and small sparkling eyes. Francis had contemptuously nicknamed him "the blabber," but it was easily observed that though he talked rapidly, and fairly constantly and very wittily, he, in reality, said nothing at all of importance, or, as he would call it himself, "incriminating." In reality, he was much more intellectual than Francis, and very much more subtle, and, in spite of Francis' power and strength, much more deadly. His popularity, due to his great wit and charming smile and constant good temper, came to him without conscious planning.

Hugo, the third son, had been admitted to the bar. Precise-minded and intelligent, he was one of the number of lawyers who handled the affairs of The Kinsolving Arms Company, and had already been elected to some minor civic post. He had declared his intention of running for the United States Senate within ten years, and was carefully directing all things in his life to that end. Big, bluff, already stout at twenty-seven, hearty and buff-colored, false and jovial, ready-tongued and quick in good-natured repartee, greedy and sly and winning, and a marvelously shrewd judge of human nature, he was well on the way to becoming the successful politician. Like Francis, he had married where it would do him the most good: his wife was Christine Southwood, older daughter of "Billie" Southwood, the State Boss of the Republican Party.

Had these three brothers lived in the early Middle Ages,

9

they would most certainly have plotted against each other, and most probably one would have gathered in the entire fortune of all of them, after disposing of the other two. And no doubt that remaining one, triumphant and red-handed, would have been the second son, the small, dimpled-faced, witty, popular Jean. The deadly Jean. When they had been single they had hated one another monstrously, though maintaining, even among themselves when alone, a fraternal good temper and apparent interest in one another; each of them had hoped with great sincerity that the others would die before marriage. Now that they were all three married, the aversion one had for the others was still there, but less murderous, for the marriages were already producing children. They were all united on two things only: increasing their fortunes and hating their young brother, Peter, whom Jules Bouchard frequently referred to as "Joseph, with his father's coat."

Peter had indeed been given "a coat" by Honore, in the latter's will. Knowing that his three older sons were compounded of all forty of the Thieves, he had provided carefully for Peter, who had "majored in sociology," and had no head for business of any kind. It was a leak-proof will, as Hugo, after ruefully examining it, admitted. Peter was left outright one third of his father's personal estate. This was in the form of a trust, yielding a rich income, half of which was to be turned over to Peter entirely at the age of thirty-five, and the rest when he was fifty. It was most evident to the brothers that Honore had feared that they might rob Peter of the first half of his legacy, but that by the time he was fifty he would most likely have developed sufficient common sense to have separated himself from his brothers. In a letter left to Peter, Honore warned him of their character, and charted for his favorite son the exact steps they would most likely take in their attempts to defraud him. In the event of Peter's death before marriage, the estate was left to various charities.

Peter, who had a talent for writing, was amazingly like his great-uncle, Martin Barbour, of whom he had never heard much except that he had died in the Civil War. He had the same lighted blue eyes and fair complexion and light yellow hair, the same carriage and height and general good looks; he also possessed a similar character, gentle, innocent, sympathetic, and kind. "He weltered in ideals," to quote his brothers, but there were three things about which he had no illusions and no ideals, and those three things were Francis, Jean and Hugo. Honore had underestimated Peter's ability

10

to read character. Everything about his brothers' personalities was detestable to him; he had no scruples about hatred, and so hated them all completely.

Making his preparations for his death immediately after America declared war on Germany in 1917, Jules Bouchard surveyed his cousin Honore's sons carefully, then his brother Leon's sons, and finally his own. Leon's son, Georges, in New York, was not dangerous, neither was Nicholas, who would take his father's place in the bank. But Honore's three oldest sons were very dangerous indeed, and Jules put them in juxtaposition with his own and thoughtfully studied all of them. Finally, in relief, he decided that quiet, apparently stolid, thoughtful Armand was a match for Francis, in spite of the latter's power and cunning, that both Armand and Emile would never be taken in by the charming and talkative Jean, and that Christopher, friendly though he was towards Francis could be depended upon not to trust him. As for Hugo, neither Armand nor Emile nor Christopher was deluded about him.

Another satisfying thing was the fact that Leon's son, Nicholas, was fond of his cousins, Armand, Emile, and Christopher, and was very loyal to them. On the other hand, he disliked Francis, Jean and Hugo and Peter.

Thinking of Honore's sons, Jules thought that Honore was probably better dead, having such sons, who would never have brought him any satisfaction or pleasure. All their lives, they had been a secret affliction to him; without Peter, he would have been completely desperate.

Reassured on his greatest anxiety, Jules then turned to the problem of his young daughter, Celeste. Whenever he thought of the girl, he experienced the only pang he ever had on account of his inexorably approaching death. He loved her as Ernest Barbour had loved his daughter, Gertrude, but with more passion and jealousy. She was a dark, sweet child with a very pretty oval face, and had, Jules said affectionately, all the virtues the rest of the family lacked. Her brothers, Armand and Emile, seemed fond of her; Armand, who had honor, would not be tempted to rob her, but there was Emile, who might not have such scruples. Jules had hated his son Christopher jealously, because of the latter's love for his sister, but now not so oddly Jules was comforted because of it, knowing that no one would dare to rob Celeste of a penny so long as Christopher was there to guard her. Because of this, Jules was showing Christopher much more friendliness than he had ever done before, in spite of the mortal antagonism, born of mutual understanding, which existed between them.

By the time America had declared war on Germany, Jules had made all his preparations for death. No one in the family knew of his condition, though Leon uneasily suspected a little.

A man whose days are numbered usually forgets everything but enjoying himself, and seeing everything, thought Jules. But I have already enjoyed myself, and I've seen everything, and besides, I'm wound up like a top, and I can't stop myself. I'll never see the end of what I am doing now, but I'm running downhill and there are no brakes.

He was in Washington when America declared war, and he heard Wilson's speech to Congress. He looked down from his hidden place and saw Wilson distinctly. He thought: You and I are eternities apart, and we've fought for two opposite worlds, bitterly and to the end, and yet the same thing has done us in.

CHAPTER II

ON NOVEMBER 8, 1918, Jules Bouchard died.
During the days of the sixth and seventh he knew that he had only hours to live. He knew it, though his doctors, specialists from New York, who had come all the way to Windsor, believed it might even be months.

He read his newspapers, but no other news was brought to him. Oddly, he did not particularly care. He knew more than the newspapers, knew that peace was at hand. It amused him a little, that peace which he knew would be no peace. The world would be a very exciting and profitable place during the next two decades. It was too bad that he would not see it. It would be a show too delightful to miss. It was Jules Bouchard's only regret, for everything else had become nothing, puerile at the best.

He was much amused by the expectant faces of his relatives. But he was not amused by the face of his wife, Adelaide, who had loved him passionately, in spite of a good many things. He could not be amused by her, nor by her eyes, so gentle and suffering. He said to her once: "Adelaide, don't grieve for me, my dear. I could die more easily if I thought you wouldn't carry on." Again he said: "I've been fond of you, Adelaide, if that's any consolation."

One night, right in the midst of a casual conversation in the bedroom, his brother, Leon, had burst into tears. He sat there in his chair, a bulky, stocky, almost old man, his broad shoulders heaving, openly wiping his eyes. Immediately afterwards he had quarreled with his dying brother over some trifle, to cover his shame and his despair.

Little Celeste had steadfastly been refused entrance to the room. Jules had a loathing of death, and he knew that his daughter had this same loathing. She was too young to be burdened with the sight of it, he said, though the girl cried outside the door and begged him to allow her to come in. He could hear her cries streaming after her like tattered ribbons as they literally dragged her away.

Two nights before his death he sent for his eldest son, and Armand came quietly into the bedroom with its odor of drugs and starchy nurses and dissolution. Jules was unable to lie down now, and slept upright on mounds of pillows. He lay there, this night, a brown and shriveled skeleton, almost a mummy. His skull glistened through his hair; the bones of his face had become prominent and sharp, his mouth drawn in a grimace of pain. But his eyes, full and brilliant and hooded, were as alive and ruthless as ever, though Armand could see the ridges of his bones under the white silk of his nightshirt as they strained with his tortured breathing.

Armand, moved beyond anything he had ever experienced before, sat down in silence. His father's hands lay on the sheet, brown transparent wax, with knotted veins and delicate bony ridges. They moved restlessly and impatiently, though he smiled quite tranquilly at his son. With no preamble at all, he told Armand of the contents of his will. Armand listened, brooding and immobile, his eyes fixed on his father's face. Jules' voice was fluttering and labored, but his words were quiet and incisive.

All at once Jules laughed feebly. The nurse, who had been banished to a position outside the door, opened it a thin crack and alertly glanced in.

"Emile and Christopher will try to do you in, Armand," said Jules. "But they can't. At least, I don't see how they can. You'll be president of Bouchard & Sons, and they'll support you, or lose everything." Again he laughed, feebly, malevolently. "I'd like to see their faces! I've named you and Leon executors. But Leon won't live long. Hearts run in our family. And another thing: Celeste's share will be managed by

Christopher." He regarded his son with a smile that was almost gloating.

Armand's forehead slowly puckered and wrinkled. "Why do you tell me this, now?"

Jules shrugged; his smile became more enjoying. "It's a pleasure I can't deny myself—seeing, in a small way, the effect of my will before I die."

Armand flushed dully. "Did you think, for instance, that I would rob little Celeste?"

Jules lifted his hands airily, dropped them, looked his son fully in the face. "How should I know that? Money has made devils of men before!"

Armand was silent. His emotions struggled among themselves. He felt elation, a smothering sense of power, a terrible joy and exultation. He had never been sure of what he could expect; he knew how capricious, how malignant, how merciless his father was, knew that he loved a joke, however monstrous. Now, he was sure. But there was also the matter of Celeste; his pride and self-love and egotism smarted. The blood rushed to his head. For a moment or two he looked beset. He stood up, pushed to his feet by his own chaotic thoughts. Jules watched him intently, still smiling.

"You had no right to tell me this just now!" cried Armand, with involuntary and unaccustomed passion.

"But Armand, I've given you something to think about! Besides, you are not really annoyed, are you? It is just that it overcomes you, and you are afraid that you'll be impatient for my death?"

Armand was silent; the blood slowly seeped from his face. Sweat had come out over it. He was visibly trembling. For an instant pity glimmered in Jules' dying eyes.

"Don't be sentimental, Armand. Be honest, always, in your own thoughts. I've always admired a man who could do that. It saves a lot of wear and tear and time, and the necessity of repairing the results of self-deception. Don't be ashamed that you'll be impatient. In your place, I'd be the same."

Armand wiped his face with the back of his hand. (He had never been known for fastidiousness.) He kept blinking; his expressions alternated as though he were being besieged. Finally, through his uncertain passions, he began to see Jules again, there on the bed, panting, smiling, tortured, with the life and brilliance still full in his eyes.

Armand cried out suddenly, sharply, bluntly: "But I don't want you to die!" He made a curiously pathetic and clumsy gesture; his short hair bristled on his head, and a boyish
14

emotion made his lips tremble. "Damn it, I don't want you to die!"

Jules gazed at him; all his distrust, intense cynicism and amusement glistened in his eyes. He looked at his son with gathering concentration, and slowly the smile went from his mouth. An expression of utmost surprise flashed across his face.

Two hours before he died he suddenly realized that death was on him. All the power that had ever been in him seemed to return with his terrific effort of will to conceal the fact from his family. His doctors, as usual, came, and they knew instantly. He saw it in their faces; hardly able even to whisper, he said: "I know I'm done for. But for God's sake, don't tell my wife, or my sons. Give me the last thing I'm asking for: I want to be alone. It's a little thing——"

The doctors withdrew to the opposite end of the great luxurious room and stood in silence near the fire. The rosy light glimmered on their grave faces; once in a while they whispered together. There was no sound in the room but the hissing and crackling of the coals and the frightful sound of his breathing as his body struggled for the last time. He knew that Adelaide, that other members of his family, were waiting in the hall outside, and his one terror was that one of them might enter, might ruin his last few moments alive.

Just before the end, a darkness fell over his eyes and a distant numbness over his body. He felt intensely alive, more alive inside than he had ever felt. Through it he could feel a vague, far-off and bitter cold, a vague distress somewhere off in the eons of space; in some way, some impatient way, he was aware of his connection with that cold and distress. But he, himself, was so alive that all his energies were absorbed in wondering about it. He did not know, of course, that when this happened the doctors admitted his wife and his sons and his brother; they stood about his bed and watched him die, but he did not know they were there.

He was buried on November 11th, 1918. While the funeral services were being read for him, the world was going mad in a frenzy of joy for a peace that would be no peace, that would never be a peace.

CHAPTER III

THERE was an important conference on the second of January, 1919, over which Armand Bouchard presided. President of Bouchard & Sons, he had acquired a greater dignity, a deeper poise and sureness. When he spoke, even Leon, his uncle, listened with respect.

He looked at them all, his relatives, all of whom had large shares in the Company and its subsidiaries. There was Emile, and Christopher, Etienne Bouchard the aged actor, Andre Bouchard, Georges and Nicholas, Francis, Jean and Hugo, Peter, Leon, Alexander Bouchard, and the very young Henri Bouchard, who looked so appallingly like his great-grandfather, Ernest Barbour, and who listened grimly to what was going on. All were here, all the chief members of the formidable Bouchard family, the war-makers, the Dynasty of Death.

Armand had just concluded the conference, which had lasted for hours.

He regarded them solemnly, but now his solemnity, usually so amusing to many of them, did not seem funny.

"Peace has come," he said. He paused. "I am sure we are all grateful for this peace. I am sure we all hope most sincerely that it will endure."

Again he paused. He looked at all their faces.

A curious expression affixed itself to his big pursy face. He bent his head and gazed at the papers on the table before him.

"We hope it is the end," he concluded. "The end of wars. But, if it is not the end, we must always be prepared to serve our country as faithfully, as efficiently, as enthusiastically, as we have ever done."

There was one face he had not looked at too closely, and that was the face of his young second cousin, Peter Bouchard, in his uniform of a private in the United States Army. But he had known all along that Peter had been gazing at him steadfastly, not speaking all the time he had been in that room.

He had known all along that in Peter was his mortal

enemy, that in Peter was the mortal enemy of all the Bouchards.

But Peter went away. No one seemed to know, or care,
just where he went. Even his mother was indifferent. Three,
four, five, six years went by. There were rumors that he was
dead, that he was here, or there, or nowhere. He had been a
stranger in the family, and strangers are always distrusted, or,
if gentle, despised. Peter was gentle. No one had ever really
cared about him but his father, Honore. His enlistment in the
United States Army during the War had been a source of
amusement, derision, amazement, contempt and ridicule
among the Family. But even this was eventually forgotten
in the press of more virile things. Jules was dead. But Leon
was alive until 1923, and he never forgot his cousin's son,
Peter Bouchard, and never forgot a certain evening after
America had declared war against Germany.

It was a Christmas evening, and the usual family dinner
had been held at the home of the Leon Bouchards. After the
dinner, Leon had asked his brother, Jules, to come into his
private apartments with him. They left the drawing rooms,
filled with firelight and candlelight and gleaming white
shoulders and jewels and children and laughter and noise,
and went up the stairway. Some thirty of the Bouchards
had come for the family dinner, not as many as usual. In
one of the bay windows stood a mighty balsam tree, blazing
with lights and tinsel and cotton snow, and heaped about
with mountains of tissue-wrapped boxes and ribbons. Holly
wreaths hung at the other windows. Outside, huge slow flakes
of whiteness fell through the still black night.

A small quiet fire chuckled to itself in the warm dimness of
Leon's suite. The brothers sat down before it and lit cigars.
Jules leaned his head back against the cushions and closed
his eyes. The gray wrinkled mask of exhaustion, so familiar
now since Honore's tragic death, slipped over his dark face.
He said: "Do you think Antoinette would care if I gathered
up my family and went home?" He added: "Or have you
something important to tell me about?"

"It's important, all right! Yesterday, Hugo was in the bank
and told my Nick that Peter was going to enlist."

Jules sat upright, gripping the arms of his chair. The veins
rose on the back of his thin hands. "Peter? Preposterous!
Peter!"

"Well, he's not a child, you know. And you know how
he's always been. As you've said yourself, he's ridiculously

17

like our sainted Uncle Martin. Anyway, Honore's Joseph is off to the wars."

"I don't believe it! No son of Honore's could be that damned silly. Enlist! I never heard anything so stupid. What for?" He threw his cigar into the fire. "What officers' training camp is the young idiot considering going to?"

Leon smiled grimly. "None. He's going to enlist as a private. Put that in your pipe and smoke it!"

Jules regarded him incredulously.

"And he's going to France, too, he says, right in the front line trenches. No soft berths for Peter, and young captain's boots. Heroism and mud and steel helmets. And bullets."

"He's crazy," said Jules, in an almost hushed voice. "I always thought him negligible, but not feeble-minded. However, a telegram to interested parties, and not a recruiting station in the country would accept him."

Leon's face tightened, and he regarded his brother with an odd flash in his eye. "If I were you, Jules, I wouldn't interfere that way. He'd find it out. Peter's not negligible at all; that's where you're wrong. Do something back-handed, and you'll set his back up. Stubborn as hell. The only chance is for you to use some of your well-known eloquence on him."

Jules was silent; he gnawed his lip, rubbed it. Then he said: "If he's still downstairs, will you have him come up?"

Leon rang the bell, sent a servant after their young second cousin. Jules was again silent: Leon studied him thoughtfully; he pressed his lower lip between his thumb and finger, as though he were trying to prevent a sudden smile.

The door opened and young Peter Bouchard came in. When he saw Jules sitting by the fire, and Leon standing on the other side, his questioning smile became cautious and reserved. His handsome and youthful face changed as he approached his father's cousins.

"Come in!" said Leon cordially. "Jules and I were just talking about you, Peter."

"Yes, I thought that," replied the young man, a trifle ironically. His reply was to Leon, but his glance was for Jules, whom he distrusted and disliked. Jules surveyed him blandly, over his shoulder.

"Leon's been telling me an asinine story about you, Peter. I'm ashamed to repeat it to you——"

"About my enlisting?" The young man's voice was abrupt and blunt, and his face darkened and hardened. "Well, what of it? What business can it possibly be of yours, Jules?"

"My dear Peter, none at all, of course! Except that your

18

father was my cousin, and my best friend, and I didn't want to hear any idiocy spoken of his sons. Or watch them doing anything idiotic. However, I told Leon I didn't believe it, anyway."

The young man gazed at him steadily for a few moments in silence. All the lines of his face were naturally amiable and gentle and kind, even when he was angered, as he was now.

"You can believe it, Jules. Call it idiotic, if you want to. But I'm going to enlist within the next few days."

Jules, rubbing his lip thoughtfully, fixed his hooded eyes on the other's.

"Peter, you were your father's favorite son. Do you think he'd want you to do this? You see, I'm not asking you your reason; that is your business. But what about your father's wishes?" He lifted his hands helplessly, let them drop after a humorous gesture. "Peter! My God, Peter!"

The young man's expression changed again, became infuriated.

"My father would want me to do as I wanted!"

Jules' smile became gentle and deprecating. "He would want you to follow your conscience?"

Peter's fist clenched at the tone and the words. But his voice was quiet. "Go on, Jules. Try to make a fool of me. You're an adept at that, making fools of people. But what you're afraid of is my making fools of all of you, of all the Bouchards! Don't worry: I'm enlisting under an assumed name."

"Don't be a child, Peter. Let us talk this out sensibly. You can refuse to tell me, of course, but I would really like to know why you want to do this." He pointed to a chair. "Sit down."

Peter hesitated, then he sat down. Jules smiled at him indulgently. Honore's favorite son. Since Honore's death he had tried to make friends with Peter, for Honore's sake, but Peter had met his advances with reserve and open suspicion.

"Won't you tell me, Peter?"

The young man looked suddenly tired. "Jules, you don't need to put on that fatherly manner. I know you. You always want others to be frank, just so you can snap the trap on them. But I'm not afraid of your traps; I can smell the cheese on them a mile away. (Leon smiled involuntarily.) I suppose part of it is curiosity, and part apprehension, for me (I'd like to hope); but mostly, I am afraid, for adverse publicity, or ridicule. A Bouchard a fourth class private in the rear ranks!" His mouth and eyes became bitter. "But have you thought of the other side? You know very damned well, Jules, that

19

after the war there's going to be an unholy stink about armaments manufacturers; there's a stink already. Senate Committees investigating behind the drums and the guns. Think what an asset it will be for you to point to a relative who enlisted 'humbly and patriotically,' to fight for his country, without ostentatious publicity, and so democratically, too! Asking no favors, and getting none. And think what it would mean to the Bouchards if I get my head blown off! Why, you'll need no better argument than that. The Bouchard blood flowed, too; the Bouchards fought, as well as bought tax-free Liberty Bonds!" He regarded Jules with increasing bitterness. "The American people are the most sentimental and most easily influenced in the world. When they're hottest after you, shrieking for your blood, you can throw them a bone in the shape of me."

Jules was silent; he stared at Peter, still half smiling. Finally he said: "That's a point, Peter, I overlooked. A very good point, too. Frankly, I didn't think you were that bright. Your brothers are such damned villains that they rather overshadowed you. But adding to the Bouchard prestige, and—ah —protecting the name, isn't your reason for enlisting, is it?"

Again the young man regarded him steadfastly. He had become pale. "No, it isn't. But I don't mind telling you. It ought to be good for a laugh, your laugh, anyway, so I'll tell you." He stopped abruptly, then stood up as if his thoughts propelled him. His eyes darkened passionately. "Well, laugh, damn you, laugh! But here it is:

"You, all of you, and what you do, have made me sick! There are some businesses that build up a country and civilize it. Ours doesn't. It pulls it down, makes it barbarous, destroys and mangles it. Because we can live only on death we make death. I've always hated it, and you, and all that you are. Enemies of men. Killers. International gangsters. Why, you're a disease!

"I'm not patriotic, nor sentimental, though you'd like to think so. I don't want to die for anything, or any flag, or anybody. But you, and your friends in Europe, have sent millions out to be torn to shreds and blinded and made idiots, and to die. Just to make money, to run your 'business.' And that's why I'm going: to be torn to shreds, or blinded, or made an idiot, or to die. I'm going to share in what you've brought on the rest of the world. It's the least I can do, to go voluntarily into the thing you've made, and into which you've sent other men involuntarily. In a way, I'm guilty, too, and I haven't any illusions. That's what'll make it so hard: when the others are singing and 'dying for their country,' I won't be singing, and I won't be dying for anything else but to make money for the armaments manufacturers."

"Of all the imbeciles—!" exclaimed Leon. But Peter did not look at him; he was looking at Jules, with contempt and loathing.

Jules laughed gently. "But my dear Peter, you *are* sentimental! I never heard such rot. You really can't be serious!"

Peter flushed.

"Yes, I'm serious."

Jules shook his head with an air of humorous bewilderment. "I suppose you'd call this 'expiation'?"

Peter bit his lip. But he answered quietly: "Yes, call it expiation."

Then he turned and went out of the room.

Leon shrugged. "So, that's all then. The young fool will get blown up, and that'll be the end. But I can't help thinking of Honore——"

Jules lifted his hand and smiled. "Don't be tragic, Leon. You know, I've been thinking. It wouldn't be a bad idea to have that card up our sleeve after all, about a Bouchard enlisting, as a private. The young devil's got a head on him; I wouldn't be surprised if he had the brains of the family, in spite of the showiness of that brute brother of his, Francis. And we can't afford to lose brains, particularly not Bouchard brains. Do you know, this has been the best news in some time, the discovering that Honore's little Peter was worthy of his father's affection. Now, don't worry: I'll have him shadowed immediately, and we'll soon find out under what name he enlists. Perhaps, with careful handling, we can persuade him to enlist under his own name. But no matter. And it will be seen to, that, private or not, he'll never get into a position where he'll be blown up. It'll all be managed discreetly; he'll never know. But I guarantee that he'll come back without a scratch."

He stood up, still smiling, but Leon noticed that he had to hold onto his chair, and then the side of the fireplace, to help himself to his feet. Sweat appeared on his face from the effort.

But in some way Peter had circumvented Jules, and he had gone only as a private into the Army, and had disappeared. There was a vague rumor that he had been wounded or gassed, but for some reason no one was able to verify this.

He disappeared, and was forgotten. Leon was dead now. No one was alive who remembered that Christmas night, except Peter.

21

CHAPTER IV

THE BARBOURS had been close-fisted. The Bouchards had been frugal and thrifty. Wealth had piled up behind them like the waters of a dam or behind the narrow outlet of a bottle neck. Both families had been of good lower middle-class or peasant stock, hardy, strong, disillusioned and toughbodied. Power is not confined to good, but includes destruction also. The Barbours and the Bouchards had had this power in tremendous quantity.

But they had believed in the sanctity of money, and so had dealt reverently with it. The Sessions House had been the most magnificent, but they had fallen heir to that as they had fallen heir to all the good things in this new world, which they had been strong enough to take. The homes they had built, however, with the exception of Robin's Nest in Roseville, had all been as sturdy, strong, heavy-walled and earthy as themselves. Even Jules Bouchard's home, and his brother Leon's, were without exotic magnificence, and inclined to bad plumbing and unreliable electrical fixtures, for all the good colorful rugs and books and massive furniture. They had bought these homes ready-built. In Jules, the delicate, despite his laughter, there had remained the old adoration of money, the realization that money in itself is worthy of reverence.

But the sons of Jules, Leon and Honore Bouchard, had no awed reverence for the huge wealth they had inherited. It represented to them power and, almost as great as power, the things they could buy with it. In spite of the fact that the female Bouchards were busily engaged in building up a mystical and wholly imaginary aristocratic background for their family in France, and were constantly visiting that country and "discovering" ancient birthplaces and distinguished distant relatives, the fact remained that the male Bouchards were still not far removed from the stables and slum streets of England and France. They were not enervated. They were not purged of their peasant blood. They could still, regarding money, feel enormously excited. Armand Bouchard, nearly forty in 1925, had a habit of jingling money in his pockets as

22

he walked or sat, thinking, at his "half-acre" of old polished-mahogany desk. He admitted it "comforted" him, and his friends fondly thought it a quaint and childlike conceit. But it was much deeper than that. His comfort was a true comfort. The sound of the coins soothed anxiety when he was confronted with a problem that meant millions of dollars one way or another. But even deeper than that, much of the soothing was due to the actual sound of the money itself, just the sound of a few silver coins.

Emile frankly admitted he loved to look at money. He kept a locked box of gold coins in his own bedroom, and one of his most satisfactory pleasures was to take them out and pile them up into shining yellow towers.

Plebeians, in spite of their chateaux in France, and their chateaux in America, and their armies of servants and flunkies and parasites, the sight of money, though having lost its power to awe them, excited, thrilled and maddened them. They were still close-fisted—to their servants. (The pantries were locked after meals had been served, and the cooks' assistants had to account for every pat of butter and every spoonful of cold gravy.) But they spared no opulence for themselves, no magnificence, no appalling extravagance. The one exception might be Armand, but his wife was jealous of the other Bouchard wives, and made up for his natural parsimony by building the biggest cheateau of all, right near the Allegheny River. And then there was Armand's brother, Christopher, who had a nervous horror of dark thick-packed rooms and soundless carpets and gloomy tapestried walls: he must have space and solitude, air and coldness and shining bitterness about him. He must have polished emptiness and glass and frosty metal. But these were expensive, and he spared no expense to create about himself an elaborate austerity without the softness and warmth that mysteriously repelled him.

Then there were times, right after the War, when Emile, brother to Armand and Christopher, seemed seized with orgiastic madness. He bought five hundred acres of the choicest land in the environs of Windsor. He had it landscaped into sunken gardens, with conservatories growing delicate peaches and purple grapes and pomegranates, and fruits imported from India, and flowers of more than a thousand exotic varieties. Great ancient trees, like fountains of dark-green fire, were transplanted to the new rolling lawns. In the summer, the peace in this tended forest was too beautiful for description. The roads, smooth as glass, wound desultorily through the grounds, and tremulous gleaming fragments of sunlight fell on them through the trees that lined them. Through the tree-trunks one could see the calm sea-like rise and fall of grass brilliant in open sunshine, and banks of flowers, and distant white stone walls cataracting in blooms. Birds, high in the sky-soaring branches, sang and whistled and trilled and chattered in a silence that had something of holiness about it. Squirrels raced about, and rabbits, and here and there were flashes of wings, red and blue and black and scarlet. As one walked for this long time along the roads, or strolled along a gravelled bridle or by-path, cool and dim and green, one saw the distant glitter of the conservatories, the red wall of an outbuilding, or a tennis court, or a huge outdoor pool, or a golf-course. Then, one approached the many buildings where the army of over one hundred servants lived, valets and cooks and maids and butlers and chauffeurs and gardeners.

But the house itself was the first of its kind in the whole State, and paralyzed the other Bouchards when first they saw it. Containing over one hundred seventy-five rooms, fifty bedrooms and bathrooms, it was a royal palace, indeed. In fact, Emile's wife, the former Miss Fortune, had seen such a palace in France, but that had been over six hundred years old. She had immediately sent for her favorite architect, who had come out, at her bidding, from New York, and he was imperiously commanded to observe it, study it, and reproduce it, in Windsor. After a few weeks study, he announced that he thought it would be best to buy the mouldering old mass outright (as Jay Regan had done with one of his own palaces) and transport it all to America, where it could be rebuilt. The grasping former Miss Fortune had been appalled at first, and then delirously excited. (She did not like Miss Regan, Jay's sister, who was a true aristocrat.) So the whole chateau was purchased, literally en masse, for an incredible sum sufficient to have rescued many of the malnourished and diseased little children of Pennsylvania and to have assured their decent future all their lives. But the plebeian Mrs. Emile Bouchard had, like all plebeians, no love for democracy or the acts of democracy, and if the idea had fantastically occurred to her she would, with hard light laughter, have said something about not "weakening" a race by rescuing its more unfortunate and helpless members. But the idea would not even have occurred to her, for she had never rescued anything in her life.

The palace was set in the midst of the five hundred acres, and the work of reassembling its welter of ancient and hoary stones, and adding to it, and furnishing its interior, took much

24

over a year. Not including the cost of transporting the palace, the total cost was several million dollars.

And there it stood, upon completion, silvery-brown of rough wall, turreted, towered, mysteriously aloof on its green-carpeted terraces. Ivy was trained over it. The terraces were planted with lofty trees. It stood there as sublime and removed as though it still dreamt of its old environment. There was an air of isolation about it and timeless splendor, its slits of windows reddening in the western suns or shining in the flush of eastern skies. Not far from it was a large artificial lake, complete with a little bridge of white stone, like a fretwork of carved ivory, over its narrowest part, and swans gliding over their own reflections in the dark polished water.

A number of struggling universities, four hospitals and ten schools could have been kept open and flourishing with the money that was spent for the furnishings. The dining hall was four stories in height, the ceiling brown-stoned and vaulted. Old, dim-colored tattered banners, Sienese, it was said, hung from the walls Its immense fifteenth-century refectory table was almost lost in the quiet gloom. English silver, centuries old, candlesticks and tureens and platters and bowls and bottles, covered sixteenth-century chests and commodes lined against the walls. The floor was of red tile, almost black with age, and gleaming as though just wet.

Other rooms were famous for their Gobelin tapestries and Rembrandts and seventeenth-century beds and armor and Gothic chimney-pieces. The salons and music rooms, the chambers and the libraries, were furnished with the loot of dozens of European palaces.

A private corps of police were engaged to guard these treasures.

Sunken gardens made their appearance to the west of the palace. Fountains, arcades full of rare statues, grottoes, woodland nooks, made the hottest day delightful. Often, during the summer evenings, Mrs. Emile would have, as her main attraction, the complete Philadelphia Orchestra transported to the grounds for the delectation of her hundreds of guests. (Frequently, each winter, famous orchestras like this were forced to appeal to the shabby populace of their respective cities for dollar contributions, "to uphold a tradition of culture and beauty in America.")

At first, the whole Bouchard clan was stunned and appalled at this magnificence and opulent luxury. The wives recovered first, as is to be expected. Shortly thereafter, the most feverish activity prevailed.

The palace was not to be outdone in beauty and splendor,

however, in spite of the golden rivers poured out, in spite of Mrs. Armand's two-hundred room castle on the Alleghany. One palace after another rose in the midst of exquisite landscapings. Almost in a body, the wives toured devastated Europe for new treasures, each more dazzling and ancient than the last.

In Windsor the Bouchards held the place of a feudal family. There was no activity in which they were not the most prominent figures. Their philanthropies, their office-and-factory buildings, their schools and their hospitals, their music hall and their libraries, their parks and the avenue named for them, the art gallery (an exquisite example of pseudo-Greek architecture), the Museum of Natural Sciences, the beautiful Episcopal church of St. Mary-on-the-Mount, the small but perfect university, the public stadium where free and excellent band-concerts were given in the summer, their big homes and magnificent estates, all amazed and impressed visitors. They owned both of the Windsor newspapers, and controlled their policies expertly; they owned practically all the politicians, and controlled their policies expertly, too. They decided nearly everything, from the most insignificant to the most important, with gravity and consideration. Mrs. Francis Bouchard founded the State Milk Fund for deprived children; Mrs. Jules Bouchard opened three creches; Mrs. Andre Bouchard selected the heads of the Board of Education and expressed her constant opinion on the morals, manners and dress of school-teachers, also their salaries; Mrs. Honore Bouchard conducted all the charity bazaars, most of the affairs of the church, including the selection of the minister. Mrs. Emile Bouchard was active in all cultural matters. Mrs. Jean Bouchard trailed behind, confused, bubbling, bumbling and feverish, for she was not very bright, though handsome.

One cynical young man, elaborately unimpressed by the Bouchard ubiquitousness, had remarked of the church: "That's where the Bouchards, father, son and Holy Larceny, are worshipped." This remark was widely quoted, and though almost everyone laughed, it was a laugh of respect, acknowledgment and obsequiousness. And pride! The city was proud of its feudal family.

The Bouchards, their subsidiaries, and the companies they partially directed, owned (without publicity) the Benson-Winthrop publications, which issued the three most important and glossy fictional and factual magazines in America, eight of the next important and a little less glossy, and controlled eighty of America's foremost newspapers.

It seemed extremely modest of the Bouchards that these

magazines and other publications were not "able" to secure many photographs of the palaces and chateaux of the Bouchards in Pennsylvania, New York, Long Island and Florida. Nor did *Fortune* or *Esquire* publish beautiful photographs of their incredible yachts and race tracks. But the modesty was well publicized, especially Armand's "asceticism." "Mr. Bouchard," sang the New York *Morning Courier*, "lives a life of almost severe simplicity and self-discipline. He is in bed not later than eleven; he is at his office not later than eight-thirty in the morning. An occasional game of golf, or a quick canter or brief swim, are almost all the diversions he allows himself. His summer home is simple and austere, very little more elaborate than the summer home of the average salaried man. The average bricklayer (this was in 1920) has his white silk shirts and silk underwear, but Mr. Bouchard confesses that he never owned a silk shirt in all his life —and as for silk underwear! There are thousands of mechanics and electricians who live more opulently than does Mr. Bouchard, whose automobile is three years old."

Francis Bouchard was proud of his gardens, which, though smaller, were more beautiful than those of his second cousin, Emile. He took a personal and tyrannical interest in them, selecting the new plants himself, and because he had an artistic eye, directing the planting and pruning. *Town and Country* were allowed to photograph these gardens at will, the only stipulation being that they must show Mr. Francis Bouchard in them, clad in old overalls and armed with a spade or rake.

But nothing was said of the renting of as many as four floors of Philadelphia's and New York's most famous and luxurious hotels when the Bouchards gave parties, or sponsored a debutante. Nothing was said of the commandeering of some of the world's most acclaimed orchestras, to beguile them at their banquets and balls. One hundred thousand dollars, or twice as much, was frequently spent on a single night's entertainment, though, in 1921, millions were unemployed, and the dress rehearsal of 1929 was taking place.

(But much was said of "bolshevism" and "normalcy" and "true Americanism," and the hearty bluff character of one, honest Warren Harding, President of the United States. These were subjects, thought the Bouchards virtuously, far more important to the American people than the mere recounting of boring parties, however drowned in champagne they were, and however glittering.)

The noblest party of them all, however, was that given by the thin and vitriolic Christopher Bouchard in honor of his sister's debut. (He was her guardian and the guardian of her fortune.) He chose to present her during the summer, at his summer home on Long Island, which was called "Crissons." The newspapers lyrically sang of the "simplicity" of this party given for one of America's most gilded heiresses. "Only one variety of flower, and that white, with a touch of mauve, was used, and not so lavishly used as at other and less important debuts. No intoxicating liquors made their appearance, for the Bouchards believe in observing not only the letter of the Law, but its spirit, also. Only one orchestra was engaged. The grounds were simply but prettily decorated with old-fashioned paper lanterns and tents. It was a scene very rarely reproduced in these days of workmen's chauffeurs, silk shirts and luxurious motor cars."

But the newspapers delicately refrained from mentioning that the simple flowers "with a touch of mauve" were rare white orchids, costing nearly fifteen thousand dollars. There was no whiskey, to be sure, except that brought in gold and silver flasks by the younger guests, but the finest and oldest champagne had been especially imported from France, at a cost well approaching twelve thousand dollars. The "one orchestra" was the London Symphony, then touring America. The conductor was paid five thousand dollars for the night, and ten thousand was paid to his artists. The lanterns were there, it is true, but they were not old-fashioned, except in shape, and they were not paper at all. The tents were of the brightest, gayest silk, full of the rarest imported food.

There was indeed a sort of simplicity and austerity about that debut, and a kind of sweet ingenuousness. But the other Bouchards were quite accurate in their estimate that the party cost at least one hundred and fifty thousand dollars. They envied Christopher, whose taste was exquisite, and not florid like their own. They thought his summer palace bare and too polished, but were not deceived into thinking that it was cheap. ("Poor little Celeste," Mrs. Emile declared later, "is like a little white kitten in a huge hospital operating room, all steel and white enamel and tile.") But even Mrs. Emile could rapidly calculate the expense of this glittering bareness and shining silver and sharp jetty black.

CHAPTER V

ONE of Christopher's deepest satisfactions was his belief that he and his sister were extremely alike. For instance, they both avoided contact with numbers of people, but whereas Christopher avoided them because of his innate hatred of them, Celeste shrank away because of her intolerable and painful shyness. He suffered in crowds, because of his loathing and contempt for noise and feeding and idiot hot laughter; she, because of hard prying eyes without sympathy or kindness. He was constantly rigid with his fear of a familiar and animal touch, which he felt invaded and insulted him. She was constantly rigid with her dread of being touched by hands and bodies of those who had nothing but envy and malice to offer her.

She was constantly terrified. Terror in some manifestation was almost always present in her, except when she was with her mother, Adelaide, or with her brother, Christopher. She had always been more or less frightened and shy with strangers and in unfamiliar surroundings, but her father's death had precipitated this state of chronic fear and shrinking dread. Jules had been her god, her hero, her protector, her wall of smooth impregnable steel. In some way she had always suspected the predatory world of unspeakable evil and viciousness. The wall once down, her innocence had been brutally assaulted. It took years before Christopher was able to build up another wall of steel behind which she could crouch and hide. She had loved Christopher next to her father; nevertheless, he had played with her in her nursery, and it took a long time before he could emerge from the status of affectionate older brother into protector.

Her two other brothers, Armand and Emile, were fond of her, for who could help being fond of this little creature with her timid gaieties and small trilling voice? But she was afraid of them, somewhat. When they were married, she was more afraid of them than ever. Behind them, she saw the faces of their wives, who alarmed her. Smiles and affectionate touches and solicitude and chaffings did not deceive her. She had had no experience with hypocrisy, malice, greed and cruelty, but there seemed to be a mysterious memory in her of these things. She read them in the eyes and smiles and touches of her sisters-in-law, and their friends and relatives. She read them in the faces of passersby, in the faces of shop-girls and servants and millionaires and actresses and her own few "friends." A threat to her life, some violence, could never have affected her so poignantly, so torturingly, as did the shadows of lies and hatred and envy in the smiling eyes of those about her.

Once, when she was sixteen, she had tried to express something of this to Christopher, but failed. However, she said timidly that she liked "cleanness." This little confidence was one of his most satisfying memories of his sister. He, too, he thought, loved cleanness. He would look about his sterile home, and reflect complacently that there was nothing here where dirt could hide. Why, one could actually flush out his bare and polished palace with a hose! So little Celeste, whose only wistfulness was a desire for the pretty pink and blue fluffy rugs of her girl-friends' chambers, and bed-flounces, and cascades of lace at dressing tables and windows, and bright jars spilling with brilliant flowers, and pastel coverlets filled with plump down, had to endure a huge bedroom all chromium and crystal glass, and black and white tiles, and enormous windows unshadowed by silken curtains. In the spring, the only landscape visible from these windows was acres upon acres of austerely empty green lawns, and a distant ring of tall thin poplars seemingly cut from tapering green wood. In the summer, she had only a view of sparkling white sand and clean blue ocean, or, from the living-room windows, of lawns as rigid and uncluttered as those of her winter home, Endur.

As she grew towards young womanhood, Celeste had the inarticulate feeling that she was beset on every hand by vague terrors too intangible to be expressed but none the less potent and imminent. There was no comfort for her anywhere. There was little comfort for her in her mother Adelaide, for all Adelaide's brown-eyed gentleness and intelligent sweetness. In some way, Celeste felt that her mother was as bewildered and helplessly affrighted as herself, and as in need of protection. She also knew, strangely, that while she had Christopher, Adelaide did not even have Christopher. To run to Adelaide for protection, Adelaide with her gray smooth hair and slender bending body and ingenuous eyes and uncertain smile, was like one frightened child running for help to an even more frightened child. She, herself, could endure Christopher's chromium and glass frigidity, but

30

Adelaide was only repelled by it, and made unendingly apprehensive. The homes he selected and furnished were repugnant to Adelaide, but while they were also helplessly repugnant to Celeste, she kept silent about her aversion, partly because she was acquiescent of character and partly in consideration for Christopher. But Adelaide did not keep silent. Her few rare angers were always close to the surface; she expressed her opinion regularly, her thin colorless cheeks flushing, her voice trembling with indignation and dislike.

Adelaide, being older, had strengthened her original gentle character enough to insist that her own rooms in Christopher's house be as she desired them. "Germ-filled nests of dust and decay and softness," he called them. But here at least there were a few rich rugs, fine old paintings, laces and velvets and silks, and chairs into which one could sink as into clouds. He would never visit his mother in these rooms, not even when she was ill.

Adelaide did not mind this in the least. For between Christopher and herself, since Jules' death, there had grown up a thin but steadfast hatred. Once, before Celeste's birth, he had shown her affection. But now there was no affection, only coldness and silence, broken on infrequent occasions by his icily angry voice, which was like the tap of a steel hammer on brittle glass. He always defeated his mother, but she was never permanently defeated. The battle was endless. Finally, they could not speak without rancor and dislike. Adelaide was afraid of him. She distrusted him as she distrusted all the Bouchards. He was a pillar of salt to her, marking the place where her life had ended and sorrowful bitterness had begun.

Once she threatened to leave and set up a home of her own and take Celeste with her. But Christopher, after expressing his indifference and even desire that she leave, called to her attention the fact that he was Celeste's guardian, not she, and that Celeste would remain.

So Adelaide remained. For Celeste's sake. She could not forgive Celeste for loving Christopher, and so estrangement grew between mother and daughter. But she loved the child dearly, and felt that she must stay to protect her. She felt about Celeste the imminence of mortal danger and suffering; she did not know what she could do to avert these, but at least she could be at hand.

Jules had often playfully called his wife "an innocent." She had received this name with affectionate complacence. But a few months as his wife showed her only too clearly how true the epithet had been, and how true it still was. She
31

remained innocent to the end of her life, for her soul was too transparent and simple to harbour the murkiness of the disingenuous. Violence and duplicity, for all these long years of close association with them in her husband's family, never failed to give her the full charge of the initial shock of her first introduction. Each time she encountered them she felt as naked and cold and bewildered and frightened as she had originally done. They were the smallpox of the spirit, the black plague of the heart, against which she never developed any immunity.

Each time a child had been born to her she had sworn pathetically to herself that this one would remain pure of heart. She would not have him a fool, for she was no fool, herself. But she would teach him that innocence was not necessarily stupidity and blindness. Rather, it was a quality that despised ugliness and lies and cruelty, and refused to believe in a "reality" that accepted all these things as inevitable. But it was no use. Armand had a little integrity, but he was also a realist. There were things he would not do, but they were very few. Then Emile came, and now, when Adelaide thought of Emile, her face turned aside as though she were shrinking from an old wearying pain. Even when he had been a baby, and had lain in her arms, she knew he was no real part of her. Then had come Christopher, a little white baby with brown hair. He had been so small and sickly and slight, he had seemed so innocent. Before he was two years old his mother knew that she had failed again, and she had given him over to the care of others.

Then had come Celeste, a daughter. Adelaide knew instantly that here was one who would always be vulnerable like herself, always unprotected. She would have the singleness of the innocent, but Adelaide, as yet, did not know that Celeste had the strength and power and courage without which innocence is impotent, and a liability rather than an asset to itself and the world. To this little daughter, then, Adelaide, despairingly, turned. She had hoped for a strong innocence which would protect her weak innocence. But now, she still believed that she had one even weaker than herself to guard.

When she discovered that Christopher had developed a passion for his little sister, she was as frantic as though he had threatened the child's life. All the affection she had had for him was shriveled like a green leaf in a fire. Jules had always pretended to misunderstand her when she had gone to him with her "foolish" problems, as he fondly called them. But she knew, at once, when she went to him this time, fumbling agonizingly among words, that he understood immediately, and was, in fact, far ahead of her.

She had said, timidly: "Jules, sometimes I don't think Christopher is such a good influence on the baby—," and had flushed at this pathetic disloyalty to her youngest son.

She had expected Jules to laugh, as usual, and to chaff her. But instead, she was amazed at his sudden tightening, the sudden hard pointing of his eyes. He had said nothing, however. But all at once Christopher found himself doing some pre-arranged task when he returned from school in the afternoon. He had usually spent this time playing with the baby. Now, there was no time. If he hurried, he discovered that the child was out for a walk, or asleep, or "not feeling very well today."

He was a boy in his early teens then, but he was too astute, too mentally precocious, not to understand. And thereafter had ensued the long venomous battle between himself and his father, for Celeste. Jules always won. Then, Jules had died. Now, Christopher thought, he could have his sister. To his outrage and contempt and anger, he suddenly was confronted with his mother. The battle was renewed. But it was a battle between a ruthless and well-armed attacker and an adversary with frail soft hands and no viciousness. Christopher, now, always won. But it was a victory that must be renewed every day; the war never ended, though he won each skirmish. It took very little to defeat the despairing if tenacious Adelaide, but he had to expend that little, and sometimes, he thought, that little was too much. It was like the slow constant dropping of single drops of water on the shaved skull of a Chinese criminal.

There was only one way to end this subtle and invisible psychological war for Celeste. That was to drive Adelaide from his house.

His sisters-in-law liked him, though never trusting him for a moment. Mrs. Emile, especially, coquetted with him, for she liked elegance and fine-strung grace. Christopher, like his father, despised women, but, also like Jules, he knew how to use them.

He went to his sisters-in-law, therefore, and with great frankness and in a humorous voice, laid his problem before them. Adelaide, like all aging women, was becoming pettily despotic in his house. Perhaps she needed a change, a wider outlook. She needed closer association with younger women, who could teach her modern manners and tolerance. Would the dear girls take her for a few months each? After all, she

33

was their husbands' mother. Say, four months in each household? This was only fair.

His sisters-in-law were not enthusiastic. They thought Adelaide a fool; they had no wish to introduce a petty despot into their own households. But they wanted to oblige Christopher, who looked at them so seriously and openly, and talked of fair-play. They consulted their husbands. When Christopher next communicated with the ladies, they had a proposition:

Armand and Emile would be delighted to receive their mother for four months a year apiece. But they knew how fond she was of their little sister, Celeste. They would not hear of separating the two. (Especially not when Celeste was heiress to a monster fortune, thought Christopher with amused bitterness.) So, they would generously receive Celeste, also, for the months of their mother's visit. Armand's young daughter, Annette, was so devoted to her little sister, Celeste, too. (Annette was not actually deformed, poor child, but there was a bend in her back, between her shoulders, which suggested deformity. There was also something very striking in her appearance, which would have profoundly affected any one ancient enough to remember having seen one Jacques Bouchard, brother to her great-grandfather, Raoul Bouchard.)

The wives thought all this exceedingly fraternal. They knew that their husbands were fond of Celeste, they said. They could not understand it when Christopher expressed his regrets, saying that as he was a bachelor, with no incumbrances, he had thought better of the whole matter, and believed it was his duty to keep his mother and sister with him.

When next he saw Armand, the latter flushed somewhat uncomfortably. But Emile had looked full into his brother's face, and had grinned. Christopher had smiled back. However, he did not possess Jules' delighted amusement in defeat. He stored up his defeats in the locked box of his future vengeances.

But he had unfortunately given impetus to an idea which had been growing in Armand's and Emile's minds since the death of their father. The brothers went to their mother, in Christopher's absence, and suggested that she and Celeste visit them for portions of the year. The poor woman was overjoyed. She would escape Christopher for eight months of every twelve; Celeste would escape him!

She knew that Christopher possessed a cold and passionless sort of violence, when fully aroused. But never had she seen him so enraged as she saw him on that night when

34

she timidly told him of her sons' visits. She listened to him speaking to her, so quietly, but with such deadly hatred and fury, and could not believe her ears. For once, she forgot to be frightened, in her appalled horror that he dared speak so to his mother. She merely sat in her chair, looking at him, her face white and disbelieving.

She, herself, could go and be damned to her, Christopher said, without exclamation points. She could go at once, and his house would smell the cleaner for her going. He had always wanted her to go. She was a fool and an imbecile, a drab and snivelling old woman, a burden on him. No wonder his father had amused himself with other women.

Adelaide uttered a cry of pain. Christopher regarded her expressionlessly. He went on, not lifting his voice, that voice so without resonance or emotion, but speaking as though in soliloquy:

But he, since his father had died, had appointed her mistress of his establishments. He had treated her with respect, had interfered in nothing, though her constant complaints and petty oppositions had insulted his patience. He had trusted her, at least, to accord him a little loyalty. But that had been too much for her character. He had only to turn his back for her to attack him to his brothers.

"No!" cried Adelaide, starting to her feet, more appalled by her son's manner, his ability to speak to her like this, and his hatred, than she was by his actual words. "No!"

"Yes," he said, very quietly, almost indifferently. She shivered, and was silent.

He went on for a few minutes more, but she did not hear him. She sat in her chair, her body and head drooping like those of a sick woman. But her eyes looked about the great glassy shining living-room with its indirect lighting and its white rugs and pale polished furniture. A shiver seemed to run over all her soul.

She heard him say: "But whatever you decide to do, Celeste remains here with me. Remember that, always."

She moistened her pale dry lips and said in a trembling voice: "I am her mother. I am her mother, and she is still under age——"

Christopher smiled slightly. "But my father thought so much of your executive ability, and your qualifications as guardian, that he made me the executor of Celeste's estate, and appointed me her guardian."

He took out his platinum cigarette case. She watched him, fascinated as always by his precise and delicate gestures, so full, even in this prosaic ritual, of a refined and sadistic cruelty. Her sick eyes could not help following the gestures of lighting the cigarette, of blowing out the match, of neatly disposing of it in a silver tray. Her lids smarted with tears; a sensation of utter grief and sadness struck at her heart. She stood up, and regarded him for a moment.

He always won the skirmishes and the major battles. But when he looked down into the gentle brown eyes in that small pale face with its aging skin and colorless lips, he saw again that he had not really won, and that so long as Adelaide lived he would never really win. Only death could settle this conflict. He turned away from her. He walked away to a white bookcase and affected to examine some new books. He had a small sleek skull like his father's, but his hair was light brown. His earlobes were bloodless. He held a book in his hand and his mother could see the blue veins on that hand and the bloodless ear.

She sighed. She walked out of the room. But her step was not that of a woman who has been defeated, but of a woman heavy with sorrow.

Christopher heard her leave. When she had gone he replaced the book, took the cigarette out of his mouth. Then he bent his left index finger and bit it delicately and thoughtfully.

CHAPTER VI

EVER SINCE Jules' death, this struggle had continued. The Bouchards, watching maliciously and with open amusement, called it the struggle for Celeste's soul.

They asked themselves facetiously who would win in the end, the powers of light, as personified by Adelaide, or the powers of darkness, as personified by Christopher. They derived considerable merriment from these discussions. When one of them returned, for instance, from Geneva, he would ask the others: "Is Celeste corrupted yet?"

But Adelaide knew there was no danger at any time of Celeste's corruption. The danger lay in a mortal injury to Celeste's heart. Nothing could have destroyed that innocence, but much that Christopher, and all the Bouchards, represented could wound and agonize it. Adelaide, who would always be innocent, remembered her own endless suffering throughout her life at the hands of the disingenuous and the corrupt and the "realists." Her father had been one of these; she could not remember him without a sick turning-aside of her whole mind. Jules had been one of these, and she had loved him, but had always suffered because of him. Her spirit had been incapable of growing scales, like a reptile, to protect itself. It remained soft and naked to the end, as the spirit of Celeste would remain.

Adelaide accepted this vulnerability of her daughter's, but she was determined that she would protect it from the assaults which had unendingly wounded and assailed her own. But she knew that she must give Celeste a species of fortitude; she must make her realize her own innocence, and how precious and beautiful it was, and how true it was, and how it must be cherished and guarded. She knew only too wretchedly that the corrupt and the disingenuous and the "realists" could make the innocent feel inferior and stupid and laughable, until they believed it themselves. Once believing it, confusion and bewilderment and impotence faced them all the rest of their lives. Celeste must be made to realize it was the others who were fools, for all their laughter and their success and their compactness of spirit.

"If we acknowledge the lie that man is only a beast like the other beasts," she told her daughter on one occasion, "then we must know that the things we call law and civilization and progress are illusions. We must follow the argument, then, that law and civilization and progress, which restrain man, and prevent him from enjoying the fullness of his beast-hood, are bad, and must be destroyed." She smiled painfully, "Now, not even our relatives acknowledge that they should be destroyed. In the chaotic society which their brand of 'realism' would bring about, there would be no need for armaments, for there would soon be no men." (Perhaps, she thought to herself, the Destroyers encouraged civilization for the profit there was in periodically attempting to destroy it.)

"There is nothing so realistic, my darling, as a jungle monkey. He has no illusions that he is destined to be an angel, or has a mission to save the other monkeys. He does not believe in the dignity of the monkey, or that he is valuable in the sight of some metaphysical heaven. He has never heard of prayer or beauty or gentleness or mercy, for all these exist only in the minds of the innocent and the idealists, the kind of men who furnish our relatives with much of their amusement, but who make life tolerable, and even lovely, for all the rest of us.

37

"No, our realistic monkey has no illusions. But, he also has no morality. He has never heard of his duty to his fellows; he has never heard of altruism, of justice, of peace, of love, or self-sacrifice. He has never heard of—of—God. If he has heard, he has not understood." (And how like him are the Bouchards; she thought again, drearily.)

"Celeste, whenever you are faced with the sight of monkey-realism, and are frightened and confused by it, you must just ask yourself one simple question: Is this monkey-realism more valuable than the 'foolishness' of a Jesus? Does it make existence more profound, more beautiful, more endurable? Does it give you dignity, or does it degrade you?" And on another occasion, she said:

"You will hear, child, that 'truth' or 'realism' are preferable, even if ugly and vicious and treacherous, to 'silly illusions.' And then you must ask yourself: What is truth, and what is illusion? No one will be able to answer this to your satisfaction, though some will tell you that morality is not an objective fact in the Universe, which is entirely amoral and without subjective values. Perhaps this is true, but in the mechanical and lifeless Universe there is also no 'truth' and no 'realism,' either. They, too, are illusions.

"Your choice, then, perhaps, lies between two 'illusions': the life-giving and the life-destroying, the man-ennobling, and the man-degrading. The illusion which has given us Jesus and Phidias and Galileo and Beethoven and Shakespeare, or the illusion which has given us Napoleon and Nero, Genghis Khan and the Borgias, wars and death.

"You must weigh the value, to yourself, of these two illusions, and you must take your choice. Every man must take his choice. And what he chooses means peace or misery for all those who come near him. What he chooses preserves him or kills him, makes life bearable or intolerable.

"Perhaps in the light of all eternity nothing is valuable. But we do not live in the light of eternity. We live in the light of our own small lives, for just a few moments. We must live for just those few moments. Shall we degrade them and ourselves, or shall we ennoble them, and also ourselves?"

And on another occasion, with what bitterness! she said: "When some one begs you to be 'realistic' he is preparing to exploit you, degrade you or destroy you."

Once Celeste, in tears, declared that Christopher had laughed at her for some innocence, and had called her a little fool.

Adelaide looked at her deeply and sadly for some moments, and then asked: "You love Christopher, don't you,
38

my darling? And he loves you, too, very much. He loves your innocence, which he laughs at. Become like—like him, or some of the—others, and he will detest you, as he detests himself and the others. When he asks you to be 'sensible' he is asking you to accommodate him for a little while, but if you continued to be 'sensible' he would grow to hate you."

She thought to herself: He tells me he despises me. He jeers at me. He hates me. But he does not really despise me. If I could stand in his way, and prevent him from corrupting Celeste into something which he would hate in the end, he would love me as he did when he was a child.

It was Christopher's blindness which caused her such sorrow. She hated this blindness, and not Christopher. Sometimes she forgot her sorrow in anger.

What her mother said to her strengthened and reassured little Celeste. She went to her mother for sympathy and understanding, but she was also shy with her, and constantly growing more shy. Her loyalties were divided. She loved Adelaide. But she loved Christopher more. When Adelaide mentioned her youngest son with a bitterness she could not keep entirely from her voice, Celeste was painfully affronted, and her manner became distrait and uneasy. When Christopher sneered lightly about his mother to his sister, Celeste was uneasy, also, but not so uneasy as when Adelaide spoke of Christopher. At times she tried to act as peacemaker, and was bewildered when she could make no peace. She never fully realized that she was, herself, the territory coveted by both, that she herself, was the battlefield on which they everlastingly came to grips with each other.

Christopher constantly put his mother in the wrong. Unfortunately, little Celeste could uneasily observe that Adelaide, when confronted with the steel smoothness of Christopher's will, became disordered and querulous, pettish and unreasonable. As time went on, the poor woman, feeling that she would grant no victory, even the smallest and most insignificant, quarreled with her son over the most foolish matters. On occasions, so harassed, so terrified was she, that she descended to whining and thin accusations and hysteria. She would attack Christopher, then turn incoherently upon her daughter. Christopher, seeing the effect on the girl, encouraged these occasions. He knew she was too young to understand what caused them. To a tormented animal, the buzz of a fly is sufficient to throw him into a frenzy. Celeste saw the frenzies; she did not see the torment.

But Christopher was satisfied. He provoked Adelaide's nervous and hysterical outbursts, and so shamed her in her

39

daughter's shrinking eyes. Adelaide, poor woman, saw this, and once she cried out to Celeste in her pain:

"He is trying to make you hate me!"

"But Mama," replied Celeste, "why do you get so angry over such little things?"

Christopher was careful to instil in Celeste's mind that she had a duty to her mother. When she asked him about the possibility of buying something without significance, or if she could go to a certain place, he would often say: "Ask your mother. It is her place to decide, not mine."

So Celeste, in defending Christopher one day, cried out protestingly: "He does not hate you at all, Mama! How can you be so unjust to poor Christopher?"

Adelaide saw what was happening, and tried desperately to control herself. But her terror and suffering often got the better of her efforts, and so she played, with her eyes wide open, into Christopher's hands.

When Celeste was confused, she still came, at twenty, to her mother. But she came less and less. For poor Adelaide's nerves and despair were completely wrecking her. She could not keep the bitter strain from her voice; she could not keep the jerk of impatience from her hands and her eyes.

And now, when Adelaide battled for Celeste's soul, Celeste began to see only a nervous and querulous woman, fighting over the most trivial things, gesturing wildly over absurdities, thin-voiced and unreasonable, spiritually disheveled and haggard of face. Almost a shrew.

But still Adelaide fought. The very look of distaste in Celeste's eyes was sufficient to show her how unremittingly, how desperately, she must fight. But how terrible, how heartbreaking, it was to fight to save some one who did not know she was threatened.

Adelaide had never liked the Bouchards. She was what Ernest Barbour had called "a great lady." She had been reared in the traditions of gentlefolk. Many of her mother's relatives had lived in the New England States, where restraint was not thought bloodlessness, and where good manners and civilization were not considered decadent. She had been taught a respect for property, and a belief that it was an evidence of competence. She had been taught to respect money, not for itself, but as an indication of the value of time and the obligations of responsibility. But worldly goods, she had been told, are no indication of the intrinsic man. Florid "show" revealed the plebeian, the kind of individual who was potentially dangerous. Envy, greed, avarice, mean-

40

ness and cruelty were not sins, but evidences of a low-bred person, whom nice people avoided and despised, and did not mention.

She was really too kind to say outright that she disliked, and feared, the Bouchards because they had no "character." She had admired Ernest Barbour, for she had discovered that her husband's uncle had the Englishman's reverence for tradition, discipline, pride and self-reliance. Once she told Mrs. Emile, in a moment of indignation, that whatever Ernest had been otherwise, he had been a Man. Why, exclaimed Mrs. Emile in angry amusement, he had not been even a gentleman! That, replied Adelaide, after a moment's thoughtful contemplation of Mrs. Emile's flushed handsome face, was a matter of opinion. He had had character. Perhaps it was true that he had been a scoundrel. But he had been undeviating; he had had taste, as shown by his love for the old Sessions house. He had hated flamboyance, had despised suppleness and hypocrisy. He had gotten his own way, but had taken no delight in the misery he had caused, nor had he been amused by it. If he had lied, it had not been for the love of lying.

Not one of the Bouchards, she would think sadly, had much character, except, perhaps, Peter Bouchard, son of the sincere Honore, who one never saw nowadays, since his discharge from the Army. No, not one of them had much, in spite of their ladies, heiresses to great fortunes, and their French pretensions, which they laughingly half-believed, due to the assiduousness of their American wives. They affected not to think constantly of money, and the value of the things they bought, but Adelaide knew this was only affectation. Even their elaborate educations had merely taught them the outward gestures of gentility. But gentility was not in their fibre; true aristocracy was not in their hearts.

She was mortally afraid of them. They were ruthless, but it was a Jesuitical ruthlessness, winding, lying, plotting and sinister. She knew they laughed at her, and it took all her fortitude, all the knowledge of her own superiority, to keep herself from being utterly routed by them. She knew they considered her a fool, because she would seem bewildered before contempt, expediency, avarice and selfishness. When Jules had been alive, they had not dared to make fun of her to her face, and openly, if affectionately, deride her. But now they made no pretense at any consideration. From derision, they passed to indifference, and finally ignored her. They knew she was afraid of them, and when they encountered her, there was a cavalier flavor in their speech and manner.

Once she had innocently believed it was because they resented her superiority, but finally she had to admit that they truly believed her inferior to them. She could not be angry or indignant. She could only be sad.

Sometimes, with a trembling of the heart, she thought she detected dim evidences of character in her oldest son, Armand. Detecting these, she would lean spiritually towards him, yearning, soundlessly crying to him to let them have their way. Then she would feel uncertainty in him, depression, confusion; she would cry out to him again and again, trying to catch his eye in desperate encouragement. And then he would sigh, retreat, soften, mass-down, flow away under her hopeless gaze. Finally she came to the conclusion that inherent probity that had no courage was more despicable than no probity at all.

Christopher terrified her more than all the rest of the Bouchards together, for she had no defense against him.

But Emile, her second son, filled her with disgust.

CHAPTER VII

CHRISTOPHER, when Celeste was fourteen, decided that it would be an excellent thing for the girl to go away to school. Postwar Europe in 1921 and 1922 was still in a state of flux. He wanted to send her to school in France, where he had an idea young girls were protected and disciplined and unspoiled. His own experiences in France, especially in Paris, had not made him believe that there was no fastidious morality in that country. He, with his brother, Emile, and his various cousins, had discreetly attended the Peace Conferences, but all without notoriety or publicity. Emile, and their cousin, Jean, and two or three of the others, had had quite a gay time in France. They had sought out Montmartre, fondly remembered from their student days. They had gone to Germany, to Berlin, and then to Vienna and London, and then back to France. There was nothing they had overlooked. Nevertheless, Christopher ("the Rabelaisian Trappist," as Jean cleverly called him) did not believe with the others that women were exclusively rumps, and had a rump-psychology, which precluded them from sexual morality. He had met a number of sincere and decent women (all frumps and homosexuals, said Emile), who were human beings as well as females. Their only trouble, he could see, was that they had a tendency to lean heavily on the human-being side, and too little on the female side. They had not been artful; they had not flirted nor coquetted; in short, they had lacked what Jean called "pretty rump-attitudes."

Christopher had admired them. He hoped Celeste would grow to be like them, though perhaps with a little more femaleness and loveliness. The only drawback was that he was afraid that the sight of the huge devastated areas might frighten and depress the girl. A convent in Paris, convenient to cathedrals and museums and galleries and concerts, seemed the best choice. But even here there were marks of steel-jacketed death, and for some not too strange reason, he did not wish Celeste to see them. He played with the convent idea, however, for some time. He liked to imagine Celeste demurely sitting in her little cloistered room, all white muslin and bare white walls and floors, and walking in sunny old gardens near a green-mossed fountain, and laughing with innocent young girls like herself. The more he thought of the idea, the more he liked it. Black-robed nuns were good companions for female youth. He could vividly imagine the tiny chapel where Celeste would pray and meditate. He could see the sunlight splashing through stained glass upon her little ivory-colored face with its deeply dimpled chin.

He detested the young American girls of the post-war era, with their bare legs and lipstick, their hip-flasks and nonchalant and indecent inanity, their "clear-eyed" imbecility, and their knowledge of contraceptives. He found them convenient and entertaining. The only difference he found, he said, between them and professional prostitutes, was that one paid the prostitutes on a C.O.D. basis. Emile and the others laughed approvingly at this witticism. In manner and speech Christopher might be a Trappist, but they guessed rightly that his vices, if austere, had a sort of cold viciousness about them, and no joyousness.

He vigilantly scrutinized all Celeste's young friends. He did not believe, with his grand-uncle, Ernest Barbour, that a rascal is preferable to a "good" fool. He preferred the fools for Celeste. They kept their skirts down and carried handbags as receptacles for handkerchiefs and combs and perfume, and not for artifices. He was not interested in Celeste being entertained; he was interested only in her virginity and her ignorance of dirtiness. There was much talk these days, among young girls, of sexual knowledge

43

that "made one free and unafraid and uninhabited." (There was much talk of Freud, whom he called a procurer.) Christopher preferred that Celeste should not acquire such freedom and fearlessness. He did not wish her to associate with those who would "enlighten" her in the name of understanding. He wanted her as inhibited as possible, believing that erotic experience was not the most vital necessity for a girl in her teens. He found the new and constant chatter of sex among the "uninhibited" young women of his acquaintance boring when it was not disgusting.

One night, in such company, he said in his quiet but penetrating voice, which was so oddly without inflection: "And now, let's talk about constipation. That's just as important a subject, and very closely related, I believe."

Celeste, at fourteen, had not yet discovered sex. Christopher carefully supervised her reading, and bought her the old classics by the case, after having satisfied himself that they were well expurgated. He liked her to read the great romances; he liked to know that her mind was filling with visions of tenderness and devotion, however much he smiled at them himself, and thought them precious. He encouraged her to tell him about them, and thought there was nothing more beautiful than the sight of her pretty face with the palings and flushings of emotion on it.

Once Adelaide, in one of her struggles with him, had cried out: "You will destroy her innocence!" He had replied, with cold contempt, that he had no greater wish than to preserve it. Then Adelaide had looked at him strangely and had said: "You and I are talking about different things, Christopher."

He had contemptuously affected to be puzzled, but he knew what she meant. But she did not know that he, too, desired both innocences to be kept intact. His whole struggle with his mother for possession of Celeste was for the possession of her love. Adelaide would gladly have surrendered Celeste's love to Christopher, all of it, if it would have kept her spiritual innocence from being violated. But this was the one thing he did not understand.

He discussed, finally, the convent idea with Adelaide. He was not prepared for her sudden delight, and it disconcerted him, until he realized that Adelaide's delight was caused by the thought that Celeste would thus be separated from her brother. "You are a selfish woman," he said to Adelaide, and had immediately abandoned all thought of the French convent. Moreover, when he thought of the separation, which he had overlooked in his satisfaction, something moved painfully in him.

He would not let her go away to school. He engaged the best procurable tutor for her in her own home. He had picked the schools in Windsor which she had attended, and had carefully seen to it that they were exclusively girls' schools. At sixteen, she had never danced with a boy, had never talked for more than ten minutes with a youth, and had never thought of sex.

She had never had more than a dollar in her purse at any one time. Adelaide, with Christopher's approval, chose all her clothes. He would not let her cut her hair. It was very dark and curly and glossy, and did not grow very long. It lay on her immature shoulders in round glistening masses. She was very tiny, and looked, at sixteen, not much more than twelve. Her small face was pointed, and smoothly ivory-colored. She had a tiny full red mouth, almost always smiling, and dark blue, shyly merry eyes. Her white hands and feet were doll-like. Her breasts were just beginning to bud. She laughed and danced and chattered like a child.

Sometimes in the midst of her laughter she would stop abruptly, her mouth still open, her eyes still shining. But a dim and rigid shadow would pass across her face, and she would lift her head as though listening to something that both bemused, interested and frightened her. Christopher would feel something like cold anger and impotence at these times, and he would speak to her sharply. He knew she was listening to something beyond him, some strong secret urging in her expanding life, something which he realized would take her from him for all time. He knew the inevitability of the taking, but he was determined to postpone it as long as possible, and then, when the postponement had ended, to choose, himself, the man who would take her.

Adelaide feared that Christopher would wound Celeste. She never thought Celeste might destroy Christopher.

One day he said playfully to his sister: "One of these days you and I will go away, somewhere, alone, and you shall be my housekeeper and my hostess. Just you and I, alone. Would you like that?"

And she had replied with eager affection: "Yes, yes! That would be wonderful!"

But he had not been satisfied. He had looked into her lovely blue eyes and had seen no passion in them, no understanding. They were the eyes of a child, who knew nothing at all.

45

CHAPTER VIII

FRANCIS BOUCHARD, second-cousin of Christopher, and president of The Kinsolving Arms, said facetiously of the other young man:

"Chris' determination to keep Celeste 'pure' is an objective manifestation of his subjective opinion that he, and all of us, are really 'nasty men.' He's a Puritan at heart."

This description of Christopher as a Puritan aroused long and hearty laughter among the Bouchards. None of them had any affection for him. In all the world, no one loved him but Celeste, and, in spite of everything, his mother. But Francis Bouchard, the angular, the frigidly blond, with his bitter ice-blue eyes and sleepless exigency and unscrupulousness, had a liking for him, and a respect. Nearing forty, Francis was already famous for his ability to smell a victor far off, and the other Bouchards began to take serious interest in his growing friendship for Christopher. There had always been a casual and subtle liking between them. Now it was noticed that Francis had a habit of dropping in to see his cousin (who was secretary of Bouchard and Sons), and spending an agreeable half hour or so with him at least twice a week. There were apparently no secret consultations; the door was always ajar, or their voices were always audible through the glass walls. But Christopher, who laughed very little as a rule, could often be heard to laugh. There was a malicious quality in his laughter, which, like his speaking voice, was without resonance or depth. This laugh, more than his "Egyptian" eyes and immobile smile, warned off honest men.

One of the chief complaints of Christopher's acquaintances was that he was acridly witty at times, vitriolically wry at others, but had no real sense of humor. This was true, for he never forgot the slightest affront, the slightest indifference. These were carefully stored away in his box of vengeance together with great affronts, and even injuries. The pettiest revenge gave him a sense of relief and satisfaction, like the lancing of a small but aching boil. He could wait for years. In the meantime, the unsuspecting offender was treated with usual politeness and amiability. Then all at once he found himself struck or smarting, routed, and when he looked about him, puzzled, he would see Christopher's faint smile and motionless eyes. Many of the offenders, being decent men, were immediately more ashamed of Christopher, then, than they were of the original, and perhaps unintentional, affront. Those who could, kept away from him, partly from fear and partly from the dread of having again to encounter such degrading meanness in another man.

Emile had once called Christopher "that venomous silver snake." Christopher had heard of it, for he, too, like all other men, had "friends." He stored it up. He put the affront far down in his box, however, because he knew that he and Emile had much work to do. Malice could wait on expediency, however it ached to be satisfied, and however almost maniacal vanity throbbed in secret.

Christopher was thirty-seven in 1925, to Francis' forty. Francis was very tall, Christopher only middle-height. But their general build, their avidity, their coloring, their fleshlessness and their expressions, gave them a startling resemblance to each other. Whatever small infusion of French blood they both possessed was not evident in their Anglo-Saxon fairness and American swiftness of thought and objective action. (Francis' coloring and distinctly American physiognomy, a type to be found in profusion in the South and West, was a great disappointment to his wife, Estelle, who had a romantic turn of mind.)

The friendship grew obviously closer. Armand, rubbing his bullet-head, and pursing up his thick sullen lips, felt uneasy. There was a French subtlety in him, which smelled danger. He well knew that both Christopher, his brother, and Francis, his cousin, hated and derided him. He knew how intrinsically evil both of them were. His uneasiness was rooted in his soul, that soul that knew the malaise of probity on many impotent occasions. Often, when thinking of them, his broad sallow forehead would wrinkle up; his scalp, under the thinning graying auburn hair, would wrinkle. He would jingle the coins in his pocket, and feel a momentary comfort. Then his formless misery would return. He would look about for some one to whom he could confide his vague uneasiness. But there was no one but his mother, and she, poor soul, would only be frightened by any of his confidences.

He was president of Bouchard and Sons, and therefore the most powerful of the clan, the final voice in any of the subsidiaries. He tried to take comfort from this. For a time it did comfort him. Then eventually his uneasiness became sharper when he realized that his very powerfulness made him more the object of hatred and envy and greed.

Armand was not the type of man who hates indiscriminately. He hated Christopher and Francis more than he ever had, or would, hate any other men. But even this hatred was eager to be dissolved and reconciled into friendship. He felt some dreary pleasure in his yearning to be on better terms with these watchful enemies; it gave his inner integrity, small though it was, a feeling of virtue and strength and patience. Most of the yearning was sincere, for there was a spot of wistful softness in him; but it was also related to apprehension.

He made an effort to approach Francis on a more intimate basis. To his surprise, and gratification, Francis received his approaches amiably and with open interest. What Armand did not see (for he did not possess much duplicity) was that Francis' attitude was identical with that of a buyer who has already been approached by one salesman and is now approached by another.

Armand was the most powerful, and so Francis listened and watched. But there were some things Armand would not do. In spite of his big swollen body and comical short legs, round red face and little jet eyes, he had a pleasant slow smile which inspired trust. In spite of his role at Geneva, at Locarno and Versailles, in spite of his huge greed and unending rapacity, there were still things he would not do. And these things that he would not do inspired Francis' contempt for him, and his derision. The fact that Armand came to him with a genuine attempt to be friends only increased this contempt and derision. Christopher was activated by no such emotion. He might have a strong liking for Francis, whom he resembled so closely, but that liking would not have prevented him from cutting Francis' throat, if necessary. And Francis, smiling to himself, respected him.

Part of Francis' genius was his ability to make right decisions swiftly. He made his decision, after a short time, in favor of Christopher. It was a long gamble, and would take years. But he could wait. However, he left one small door open through which to admit Armand, should there be a radical change.

None of the clan was at all deceived in Christopher's character. They knew what he was. They knew his silent and deadly ambition, his enormous vanity and capacity for revenge. Therefore, when Jules had died, and it was discovered what had been left to Christopher, and that he would, indeed, be almost a lackey to his older brother, the clan had laughed with huge enjoyment. They had let Christopher see the glittering edges of their laughter, for all their innate wariness of him.

They were not at all surprised by his brilliance in Geneva and in Europe generally. But they were surprised that he showed so little rancor and open detestation for Armand. He had always had a delicately insulting manner towards Armand. Now it was tempered into a pale shadow of amiability. Most of them were deceived.

But Armand was not deceived.

For a time the soft inner spot of integrity and generosity was uneasy. He had tried to make some amends to Christopher. He had doubled his salary as secretary. On his birthday, he had given his brother a block of stock in The American Automotive Company, and for a Christmas present, made him a director in The United Utah Railroad and its subsidiaries, at a handsome salary. Does he think he can buy me? thought Christopher with coldly raging hatred. But he took the stock with much gratitude, and collected the extra salary. His enmity and vengeance grew faster, now, like a malign growth. His natural malignancy stood behind his eyes whenever he thought of his brother.

The others began to watch, with increasing interest and malevolence. Francis' brothers watched intently: Jean (deadly little Jean) and Hugo, the buff-colored and jovial politician. But none watched so intently as Emile, the brother of Armand and Christopher.

Emile, the treacherous and opportunistic, the agreeable and athletic and bulky, the generous and the egotistic, was vice-president of Bouchard and Sons, at a salary twice that of Christopher's, and one half that of Armand's. In comparison with Emile, Christopher was poor.

Emile was watching. He was sleepless in his watching. He never took sides in any family disputes, partly from a natural aversion to quarrels, and partly because he never knew from which antagonist he might want a favor in the future. Too, he was incapable of the slightest loyalty, whether personal or in business. Yet, because he never gossiped about any one, and was never heard to make a malicious or scandalous or nasty observation about another, he had a reputation for loyalty among the clan. He would listen, with obvious amusement and interest, and his laughter would be as loud as any one's, but he would merely shake his head and smile, or leave, if pressed for an opinion. He had no reticence about making a thrusting observation to a man's face, but this was done with so much candor and "frankness," and he had such a reputation for not "talking about any one behind his back," that he aroused little offense. Of them all, only Christopher was not deceived.

Christopher well knew that Emile would join the victor, or a potential victor, with alacrity. But until he was certain that a given man would be the victor, he would do nothing.

Armand trusted Emile more than he did any one else among his relatives. His secret integrity protested faintly, smelling an enemy. But he quieted it. Emile, who never gossipped nor sneered, and who was indifferent to intrigue, surely could be trusted.

And so it was that Armand, growing more and more uneasy and formlessly apprehensive, went one day into his brother's office.

CHAPTER IX

BY THIS time there were already two distinct factions in the Bouchard clan. But Armand did not know it, though his soul suspected it.

On the side of Christopher were Francis Bouchard and his politician brother, Hugo, and all their subordinates, including directors and vice-presidents and other executives, and political lackeys. Hugo, married to Christine Southwood, had inherited the throne of her father, "Billie" Southwood, as Chairman of the Republican Party in Pennsylvania. His salary received from Endicott James of New York (publicity agents and attorneys for Bouchard and Sons) was huge. But his own private fortune was more enormous than the most sanguine of his relatives suspected. This was in addition to three directorships on the boards of the subsidiaries, and his holdings in these subsidiaries. His magnetic personality was no small part of his assets. Jean said of him that he was a club in brown velvet with a gold handle. His wife, for all his genial infidelities, adored him; his three young daughters worshipped him. He was much more formidable than he appeared, a fact which the unfortunate Armand overlooked.

On the side of Armand was the bachelor, Nicholas Bouchard, son of the recently dead Leon, and now president of the Windsor National Bank, and a director in both the Manhattan Merchants Trust Company, and the internationally potent Morse National Bank, which Jay Regan controlled. Nicholas, thirty-five years old in 1925, was short, Napoleonic, in appearance much like his dead father, stubborn, sullen, avaricious, rather dull but tenacious, suspicious, silent, slow to think and act, but dogged and astute. His personality alone would have inclined him more to Armand than to Christopher, whom he detested. He was no asset to any gay party, but was always and assiduously wooed, in spite of his dun coloring, his greenish skin and eyes and hair, and disagreeable grating voice and uncouth manners. (His sisters-in-law constantly tried to marry him off to their women friends, without success. His faithful inamorata was the stout middle-aged widow of a former police chief, a cozy woman who could cook delightfully and who looked like the mother of half a dozen children.) And also on the side of Armand (astonishingly!) was deadly little Jean, brother of Francis, about thirty-eight years old. He was secretary to his uncle, Andre Bouchard, president of The Sessions Steel Company, and married to his cousin, Alexa, a big Wagnerian blond. This smiling little man with his full dimpled face, wide, white-toothed smile and small sparkling black eyes, resembled Emile somewhat, and was great friends with him. His wit, his gaiety, his laughter and affectionate and sympathetic manner, made him a tremendous favorite. But he was far more intellectual than Francis, subtle and extremely dangerous. More than any one else in the family, he looked excessively French.

The subordinates of Nicholas and Jean, their friends and associates in New York, were naturally on the side of Armand, also.

The city of Windsor was soon cognizant of the two factions.

Emile remained aloof from both, but continued his watching. He was wooed surreptitiously by both, but gave encouragement to neither. He maintained his reputation for "loyalty," and was therefore more assiduously wooed than ever. Under it all, suspected only by Christopher, were his resentment and his rage against Armand.

Armand, for all that he was the most powerful of the family, entered Emile's office diffidently. The secret integrity within him always made him diffident in the presence of treachery and duplicity, though he never understood just why it was that he was diffident with Emile. He thought it was because Emile seemed so sure of himself, so compact and flamboyantly forceful.

51

"Come in, sit down!" said Emile cordially, rising and indicating a chair. He smiled. It was a pleasant smile and showed his good teeth.

Armand lowered his big-bellied bulk into the chair and sighed. It was a warm spring day. He looked about the opulent office with inner distaste. It seemed hot and overpowering to him. He pulled out a big linen handkerchief, slightly soiled, and wiped his large round red face, with its pursy and worried expression. He helped himself to one of Emile's cigars, and Emile lit it for him.

Jules had insisted upon his sons becoming as familiar with French as with their native language, English. Accordingly, his sons lapsed into French as easily as American Jews lapsed into affectionate or intimate Yiddish during family conferences. Too, French was closer to the natures of both Armand and Emile than it was to the Anglo-Saxon Christopher, their brother, though he had a greater dexterity with that language than they had, and seemed to understand its exquisite nuances more thoroughly.

Armand began to speak with an absentminded pettishness which led the cunning Emile to believe that he had not come here just to speak of business:

"I still think it was a mistake for one of us not to go to the Locarno Conference." He paused, and fixed his little jet eyes upon his brother and frowned. "This is extremely important. We shall end up short, as we did at the Washington Naval Conference."

"Oh, we did not do so badly at Washington, Armand! Besides, I have it on excellent authority, as I told you the other day, that Congress will soon be asked to approve a new naval program calling for twenty-two ten-thousand-ton cruisers costing about twenty million dollars apiece. You have noticed the groundwork: the insolence of Britain in openly asserting that she still rules the waves—" He laughed. "Or rather, I should say, the insolence of the shipbuilders! A clever but obvious touch, that, was it not? I am still waiting to be congratulated on that suggestion."

"I thought it was Francis' suggestion to the British shipbuilders," said Armand absently, staring at the floor.

"No! It was mine. You remember, it was in 1921. I said to Robsons himself: 'Temperate language never built a battleship. Call in your editors.' He called them in and said: 'Gentlemen, Britain's survival, expansion and welfare depend on one thing: an unsurpassed Navy. As the proposal now stands, the United States and Japan together will surpass us. Our life depends on equalizing that inequality. Britannia

MUST still rule the waves.' The next day, as a result, the Emerson Shipbuilding Company stock went up five points."

"Our stock," said Armand gloomily, "is down two points today, though all other stocks are rising."

"If it does not rise steadily you are inconsolable," answered Emile lightly. "Wait, my farmer with the goose-that-lays-the-golden-eggs! You are too cynical. You know what is coming. See, only this morning Robsons-Strong informed me that they have just perfected an amphibious tank that swims like a steel shark. But they ask an enormous price for the patent. On the other hand, Kronk also informs me he has a small battleship of 10,000 tons, faster than a cruiser and practically invulnerable. For certain patents, he will send us the blueprints. We shall then offer these blueprints to Robsons-Strong for the tank patents. If the worst comes to the worst, we shall have the tank patents and they'll have nothing! But this is old larceny, which good old Uncle Ernest could manage so well. Times have changed. We need goodwill, also. Armaments manufacturers are less competitors these days than partners. I would rather we made a fair exchange with Robsons-Strong. Too, they have a bombing plane that can fly more than 200 miles an hour. We need that, too.

"France has something good also. Look at these outlines: a submarine that makes all others look like middle-aged porpoises. I am not sure this is practicable. However, we shall investigate."

"I hardly believed it when Kronk informed us about the battleship!" said Armand, showing single-minded interest for the first time. "Have we had reports from Russia as to whether they are open to suggestion on them, yet?"

Emile smiled slightly. "Russia, my dear Armand, will buy nothing she can steal. You see, she has learned the lessons of the democracies too well for our profit! However, the Soviet Ambassador to England, Skorsev, gives me hope that Russia is interested. It must be handled discreetly, for France still watches Germany, and one misstep, and Berlin is occupied!"

"Damned bolsheviks!" said Armand restlessly. His face had taken on a deeper tinge, and he moved in his seat as though something had pricked him. Emile watched him narrowly, with a curious drawing-together of all his full and florid features.

"Nevertheless, Armand, they serve an excellent purpose.

"We Americans have a lesson to learn. At times, we are sentimental—and patriotic. Cousin Honore suffered from periodical attacks of honor. [At this, the tinge in Armand's face became thicker and darker, but he stared at his brother

53

with an attempt at a derisive smile at Honore's honor.] Too, he had a maudlin brand of patriotism. He seemed to believe that patriotism was expressed in preserving peace, or at least, in refraining from suggesting wars. Now, we are more realistic: we believe that patriotism is expressed in making our country invulnerable to attack. And we have no objections at all if other peoples are similarly patriotic! Peace, as Christopher says, is the passion of the eunuch.

"But what I wished to say is that we have a lesson to learn, and, as usual, such lessons are to be learned only from dear old England.

"British statesmen are unique. They are entirely without patriotism, though they are unsurpassed in the art of patriotic oratory. They know only too well that emotion is the necessity of the people, but the stupidity of governments. The Briton's lack of patriotism enables him to operate fluidly among foreign policies, like water, surrounding them all. We can, for instance, trust the British statesman to keep hatred fuming in Europe, and to play his ancient game of treachery and hypocrisy. You say this game is obvious? Yes, my dear Armand, it IS obvious. But only the obvious is undetectable.

"It was a good idea, but not a delicate one, of Britain to help bring about an accord between France and Russia. And then, on the other hand, to set about improving relations between Russia and Germany. Communism is going to be an ideology that will threaten the existence of the ruling classes all over the world. Did I say that Britain was playing a good game but one not delicate? I take that back at once! It is most delicate." He clapped his hands together as though applauding, and laughed hugely. "In the meantime, Britain is lauded as peacemaker, trying to reconcile old hatreds."

Armand smiled a little stiffly. He said: "I have always hated the British. But what shall we do if the ideas of bolshevism spread to America?"

"That is the easiest of all to answer, Armand. If we as a class are threatened, it will become our sacred duty to ourselves (and what duty is more sacred?) to invent an antidote. I am sure we shall find it in the churches and American patriotic societies. That should be the least of your worries. But our chief pleasure just now ought to be the spectacle of dear old Britain manipulating in Europe.

"A weak and prostrate Germany, just now, does not appear a good omen for our industries, and our dividends. But as Christopher remarked only recently, weakness inevitably begets despairing strength. Germany will soon demand a strong government when she finally realizes her impotent condition

54

and recovers from the shock. A strong German government (aided and planned by Britain) will emerge from a maddened, wounded and maimed Germany, hungry for vengeance. And vengeance never did the armaments industry any harm at all! A new strong Germany, conservative as only strong governments can be, will then be a fine big gun in Britain's hands. This gun will be used to control an arrogant France and to threaten bolshevik Russia. The balance of power will again be operating in Europe.

"You do not believe me? You think this infamy is beyond Britain? Armand, Armand! You do not believe, for instance, that Britain will castrate the League of Nations? Then you believe in honor, and you are no better than Cousin Honore himself! Surely you have not forgotten that Mussolini could not have seized Italy without, first, the connivance of Britain, and second, her assistance and encouragement and secret promises?"

"Yes, yes!" said Armand testily. "Of course, I know." He did not like this slightly patronizing manner of Emile's. Was he not president of Bouchard and Sons, and Emile only vice-president? "I have not forgotten either that Robsons Strong has supplied Mussolini with arms, and that he has passed along the good business to Hungary, too. I am not yet ready for retirement, Emile," and he smiled, half-diffidently, half-slyly.

Emile regarded him with affectionate seriousness. "Of course not, Armand! Though your nerves are considerably on edge lately." He laughed. Waited. But Armand said nothing. After a few moments, Emile indicated a paper on his desk. "I have just finished making notes on this letter of Robsons-Strong which you gave me yesterday."

"Well? What is your opinion?" Armand moved on his chair nearer to his brother and eyed him impatiently.

Emile pursed up his lips thoughtfully and tapped the letter with his fountain pen. Then he smiled.

"Perhaps my opinion is partly based on the fact that Robsons-Strong, not we, own a third interest in the Japanese-Matsu Iron Works. At any rate, I do not think it advisable for Japan to attack Manchuria yet. We have not yet decided, as you know, as to whether the American people are to sympathize with Japan or with China. Without preparation of the American people it is foolish for Robsons-Strong to give the go-ahead signal to Japan.

"I would advise (but you, of course, must give the final decision), that Robsons-Stong be informed that they must caution Japan not to make a move for at least five years. In

55

the meantime, there can be much propaganda in America about Chinese bandits sabotaging foreign, particularly American, property in Manchuria." He rubbed his nose thoughtfully. "But somehow it is hard these days to arouse anger in America over property. Perhaps that is the bolshevik influence—"

"Of course it is!" exclaimed Armand.

"Then, we must start in where we left off in 1921. We were doing quite well with anti-Communist propaganda in America at that time. Perhaps it was foolish of us to have called it off just because Schultz-Poiret and Skeda bought interests in Russian mines and shipyards.

"We shall have to choose something else besides property to arouse the American people. Francis suggested only last week whenever a strike is called to lean heavily, in the newspapers, on the 'alien subversive influence' among the workers. We can begin it, tentatively, of course. But that is a question, too, that we must not decide hastily without consulting Robsons-Strong, Schultz-Poiret and Skeda. Skeda, especially, must be handled carefully, because of Czechoslovakia's friendliness toward Russia.

"If we could only get a moral grievance against Russia!" He frowned. "Atheism? Yes, that might be good. Then, immorality. Yes! Atheism and immorality are always good for righteous anger among the American people. Nothing can make an American mechanic madder than to tell him his neighbor doesn't believe in God and is having a wonderful time among the wives of the other neighbors. It makes him feel both spiritually hog-tied and physically deprived, and that is always the infallible basis for national hatred."

Armand laughed with his brother. "But you truly believe that Americans can be aroused against Russia by telling them that Russians don't go to church Sundays and sleep with numberless women? A little far-fetched, it seems to me."

"Well, let us get back to the subject. You must make the final decision, of course, but I would suggest that Robsons-Strong put pressure on Japan to delay attacking Manchuria for five or seven years. By that time we can decide with whom we are to sympathize. Perhaps it will be to our own advantage to sympathize with China." He paused and added: "And in the meantime, a little judicious propaganda against Russia can be begun. Just a little, though, for we may want to switch at any time. The Catholic Church hates Russia. Suppose a few anti-bolshevik sermons delivered by Catholic priests were given newspaper space for a time?"

"What are we paying Endicott James for?" demanded

Armand in a surly voice. He made a note in a neat black book which he carried. The book was the only tidy thing about him. His wrinkled vest was spotted, his expensive but badly-fitting coat and trousers were unpressed and baggy. A faint auburn stubble was visible on his jowls. He had a valet, but was intrinsically too much of a plebeian to allow the man to do much for him. Emile, puckering his thick black brows, observed that his brother's short reddish hands were grimy at the knuckles, and that there was a rim of black on each stubby fingernail. He glanced swiftly downwards at Armand's thick short thighs straining at the seams of the trousers, and the dusty boots. Christopher had called Armand "the village blacksmith." Remembering, Emile smiled, put up his hand to hide the smile.

Armand felt, rather than saw, that swift critical glance, and became uneasy again. His expression became more pursy than ever; his tiny eyes irritably betrayed the diffidence of the shy man.

"I don't know what things are coming to," he said, obscurely. Emile said nothing. Under his calm, rather dark and sympathetic exterior a deep subterranean amusement quivered.

"We are still small fry," Armand went on, restlessly. "Old Garrison Burns has got ahead of us again. Why, Father assured me just before he died that Sessions Steel would put The Flexible Steel Company out of business! And what have we done? Let Burns get ahead of us in the Japanese order. We get the leavings, scrap iron! What the hell is Jean doing? And Andre, that fat pink hog?"

"Andre," said Emile soothingly, "is a little slow. But there was pious psalm-singing Arkansas Senator Brunswick to deal with. He doesn't like us. Our father despised him when he was a mere Representative, and used to pray on the floor. There's nothing so vindictive as a religious man. So, when the Japanese deal began to smell, Brunswick began to raise a big stink, too. The stink was all in our direction. In the meantime, Flexible, for a consideration to the Man of God, slipped in with the orders. But you know all that."

"I'm not running Sessions," said Armand angrily. "But look what equipment they have! Flexible is outmoded. We have better patents on gun forgings and armor plate and projectiles. Something should be done. That Japanese order was a crime!"

"But Sessions is certain to get the new railroad orders here. And probably the new San Francisco Bridge. Then, look at The United Utah orders, and the Pennsylvania State Railroad, and the Eastern States! We've got those orders practically on the dotted line. Five new bridges! Flexible is chewing its fingernails over the bridges, especially. And those loco-motives! We can't hog the whole market——"

"Why not?" But Armand smiled a little, somewhat ap-peased. "However, all this is all very well. But we've got to prepare. You know that."

"In the meantime, we've got to get patents. That's important."

Suddenly Armand's big face flushed with ire. He leaned forward towards his brother, and the latter smelt the odor of perspiration. Cigar ashes fell over Armand's bulging vest in his agitation.

"And that reminds me! Parson's Airplane called me not an hour ago! That Russian order which they were almost posi-tive of: it's being held up. And do you know why? Because of that little upstart new airplane company, Duval-Bonnet! With their mythical inventions! A little piddling company which didn't exist five years ago! Bragging about their 300-miles-per-hour plane, and new flexible gun-mountings! Angling for that enormous Russian order for planes which are to be sold to Germany! You know very well that bombers can't travel at that speed and carry sufficient bombs to make them effective!

"It's a pack of filthy Russian lies. And what have you been doing to find out who Duval-Bonnet are, anyway, except that they've got a few rat-sheds near Gainesville, Florida? Who is behind them? Who owns their patents? Why haven't we gotten hold of those patents? Why, they aren't even listed!"

While he had been hurling these questions at Emile, the latter's expression had grown tighter and darker, his features seeming to grow more compact. He picked up an ivory-and-gold paper-knife and was examining it minutely. He replied to Armand, still examining the knife:

"I've told you all we could find out. Where they got the name of Duval-Bonnet is a mystery. I think it is some kind of practical joke. The president is Osborne Goodman, and the patents are in his name. No mystery about that."

"Why doesn't Parson's Airplane buy him out, then?"

"You know why. He won't be bought, and they're skepti-cal about the value of the planes."

Armand snorted. "And in the meantime these little rats are holding up the Russian order! What's the matter with everybody? I'm going to write a letter to Parson's Airplane that'll burn their eyelashes when they read it. My God, must I run everything?"

He lit another cigar with fingers that visibly shook. Emile's
58

head was still bent, but under his thick black eyebrows his needles of eyes were fixed on his brother.

"An army of flunkies, and I must do everything!" went on Armand with gathering and querulous fury. "Secretaries to secretaries and assistant secretaries to assistant secretaries, and brothers who claim to know what they're about——!" He dropped the cigar onto a tray and turned his face full on Emile. The fury left his face, and it became sullen and uneasy again, and crafty.

"How is Christopher these days? I rarely see him. He's got Francis in there with him now, talking and laughing. Business must be bad! Francis has been in there nearly an hour now, and there's a Board of Directors meeting at Kinsolving at twelve."

"I don't run Kinsolving," Emile pointed out. "Christopher is well, I believe. He works hard. That is all that can be expected of him, isn't it?"

Armand fumed. But he said nothing. He regarded his brother with a secretive and hunted expression. An expression of dim distress stood in his eyes.

"I like to be friends with with every one," he said at last.

Emile paused, then he exclaimed heartily, with an affectionate and winning smile: "Of course you do! No one ever denied that, Armand. Don't worry about Christopher. You know his neurotic moods. He'll be swarming around you all at once before you know it. Just now he seems to be amusing himself with Francis."

"I don't like Francis," muttered Armand, and his expression was more uneasy.

He waited. But Emile said nothing further, merely smiling at his brother more affectionately than ever. Armand looked at that florid and smiling face; he saw the wolfish shine on the big white teeth, of which Emile was very vain. He sighed, and got up. Emile rose also, with courtesy. Armand went towards the door, automatically glancing with distaste at the rich furnishings of the big room.

"The best powder in the world, and Robsons-Strong get Mussolini's order for Hungary!" he complained. He shook his head. "We'll be using our powder for fire-crackers one of these days unless we stir ourselves."

He went out.

Emile waited. After about five minutes he yawned, got up, and slipped agilely, for all his bulk, down the carpeted halls to Christopher's office.

CHAPTER X

EMILE found his brother, Christopher, and Francis Bouchard, in the midst of amiable remarks and laughter. The clean and shining steel emptiness of the office was full of cigarette smoke. Christopher was sitting at his desk, a square of pale wood, glass and chromium fittings. He was leaning back in his chair, also of chromium and pale wood and ivory leather, and seemed to be in a pallidly gay mood. The angular Francis, with his long bony limbs, flat body and bitter ice-blue eyes, seemed gay also. An air of rapprochement filled the office like the fumes of good brandy.

Francis raised his thin sandy eyebrows when he saw Emile, and his colorless hollow cheeks filled out with a thin sharp smile. His long fingers, so like flesh-colored bones, took the cigarette from his mouth. "Hello," he said. He raised himself from his lounging position with all the ease and effortlessness of a man twenty years his junior. His voice matched his apppearance; it had a dry hard quality with a grating undertone.

"Come in, Emile," said Christopher. The resemblance between himself and Francis was very marked just now. "Sit down. Have a cigarette."

"What? Those perfumed didoes of yours? No, thanks." Emile smiled affectionately, however, and accepted one of Francis' custom-made Turkish cigarettes. He bent his big round head with its high thatch of black vigorous curls, and allowed Francis to give him a light. He sat down. As he sat there, his big bulky torso gave him a massive appearance, belied when he stood up on his legs, which were similar to Armand's.

He looked from Christopher to Francis amicably, grinning. But his eyes, somewhat rodent-like, darted from one face to another endlessly.

"Just had a session with Armand," he began easily. "He's disturbed about Locarno. Still thinks one of us ought to have been there, at least."

"Nonsense," replied Christopher indifferently. "Haven't we got Sazaroff and Bob Stressman there?"

"Sazaroff," said Emile meditatively. He carefully deposited cigarette ash in a chromium ashtray in the form of a flying nymph. "But events have proved that we cannot always trust Sazaroff. Talk of the phœnix and the harpy and the Gorgons! He's all of them. Look how he blocked the sale of our machine-gun in Austria (after we had gone to such expense and trouble to steal the patent from England!) and wouldn't lift the blocking until we gave him an enormous percentage on its sale. And that's only one instance.

"Bob Stressman? Well, he's excellent as our resident agent in Geneva. But there'll be too many British and French statesmen at Locarno who have big holdings in Schultz-Poiret and Skeda and Robsons-Strong for our comfort and profit. Whatever he is able to do, they'll be watching like hawks to see that their own pet Companies won't be neglected. If he tries to kill anything, they'll fuss and fume about, suspecting a plot which will lower the value of their stock, or possibly bring about a permanent peace."

Christopher smiled faintly. "I give the French credit for doing nothing radical to bring about a permanent peace, Emile. And the British, though less intelligent, know on which side the Bank of England stands.

"Peace! Remember how old Armand steamed and fumed about the Versailles Treaty? Remember what I told him then? That the self-determination provision alone is worth five billion dollars. The Polish Corridor is worth three Kaisers. Military disarmament? Clauses? Metternich would be proud to have composed these! War-guilt? Sazaroff must have had a hand in the 'war-guilt' matter, for which we never did adequately thank him. Though not fully evident as yet, the French occupation has done more for the armaments industries than a Cæsar, five Kaisers and two Napoleons could do.

"Locarno need be worried about no more than Versailles. Vultures have never yet been known to lay doves' eggs. So long as the eminent Dean Birge, three bishops, a former Premier, four bankers, eight peers, fifteen members of the House of Lords, four foremost newspaper publishers, one Chancellor of the Exchequer, and a British holder of the Nobel Peace Prize hold controlling stock in Robsons-Strong, Robsons-Petrillo of Italy, and Skeda of Czechoslovakia, not to mention nice blocks in Schultz-Poiret, we don't need to fear any Locarno or League of Nations, or any other League or Kiss-Mommies and back-scratchers. So long as the British Tories need a dam against Russian bolshevism in Middle Europe, you need not fear that Germany will be completely wrecked. In fact, you can be assured that the new

Germany they are plotting will be five times as formidable as in 1914. The 'backbone' of Britain can be made to wiggle like a charmed snake whenever the armaments flute-player sings his pretty tune. Look what they did for Mussolini!

"I tell you now that the Locarno Conference, like Versailles, is our guarantee of perpetual dividends."

He picked up a paper. "Look here. This was cabled this morning. It is an order for five thousand tons of nitrate of soda for Japan!" He picked up another paper. "And from Robsons-Strong this morning: Nitrates, powder, airplanes and airplane motors! Who do you think all this is for? And on the eve of the perpetual blessing of Locarno, too! Rest thee, Messiah Wilson!"

Francis nodded, smiling. "And that new gun I was telling you about last week, Emile, the machine-gun that can fire five thousand bullets a minute, operated by steam or gasoline or hand or electricity. We've got orders from Britain, France, Russia, Czechoslovakia and Japan for it, enough orders to keep us busy for the next two years or more. Are they going to use it against each other? Perhaps! And are they going to let Germany (all in a spirit of love, of course!) have it also? Perhaps, too. Disarming of Germany? Don't be silly! Britain would no more allow Germany to be really disarmed than she would cut her collective Tory throats.

"Schultz-Poiret and Skeda and Robsons-Petrillo and Bedors will see to it that Germany re-arms, all nice and secret, of course, for the dear people must not be unduly alarmed about the possibilities of any future wars. They will see to it that Germany gets a brand-new and much more ferocious brand of nationalism than she ever had before. They will see to it that the Communists and the internationalists and the peace-makers get bayonets in the neck if they become too noisy."

"Well," said Emile, "I only hope you are right. But please recall that Germany is doing excellently with that radical gang in power in Berlin. You'll have a hard time overthrowing liberalism in Germany now. Chris may be right in saying that a liberal is only a castrated Communist, but Germany is swarming with these eunuchs and they appear to be full of ginger. They'll not stand for militarism."

"You forget," smiled Francis, "that I have just said that the British and French Tories will see to it that all these liberals and radicals and internationalists will have a bayonet in their throats if they don't see reason, and profits."

"A new revolution, eh?"

"Possibly. An anti-Communist revolution, for instance.

This can be done, Sir Herbert Linstone of Robsons assures us. The people of any nation are stupid and sheep-like. They can be made to believe anything. In Germany, they can be made to believe that some group, liberals or radicals, or anything, in fact, caused them to lose the war. They can be made to believe that Russia intends to invade Germany, or Roumania. Or that France is still snarling at them. Once they destroy their liberals and their internationalists (who believe in 'human dignity and peace,' the imbeciles!) our friends in Europe can begin estimating dividends again. A militaristic and nationalistic regime in Germany means the stopping of Communist propaganda in Europe, and the re-arming of Germany.

"The thing is that Britain and France must find a devil for Germany. Communists, perhaps the Roman Catholics, or maybe the Jews."

Emile laughed. "The Germans are intelligent, good Francis de Sales! You fail to reckon with their intelligence."

Francis smiled frigidly. "I have yet to see any intelligent man proof against an offered victim. So, you see, we need not worry about Locarno. Just at present, we are considering more private matters."

A little silence fell. Emile's rodent-like eyes moved slowly, and then swiftly, from one face to the other. His own face changed. He began to smile.

"Ah?" he said gently.

Francis leaned back in his chair and negligently smoked. He seemed to find the bare white ceiling very engrossing, for he gazed at it intently. Christopher did not move, but as intently as Francis gazed at the ceiling so intently did he regard Emile.

"You, Emile," said Francis meditatively, "have an—an uncomfortable reputation for—shall we say?—loyalty. Misguided loyalty, perhaps. You are not a stimulating companion in a gossip session." He suddenly sat upright and looked at his second-cousin. "Are you?" he demanded.

Emile stared into his eyes, his big shoulders humped towards his own ears. He lifted his left hand slowly and rubbed his nose with his knuckles. He spoke slowly, softly, distinctly: "I don't like idle gossip. I listen only to that which is profitable."

Again, there was a little silence. Christopher smoked delicately, as though he were alone in the room and listening only to his own idle thoughts. But Francis and Emile regarded each other like rival hypnotists.

Francis said thoughtfully: "You are vice-president of Bou-

63

chard and Sons. Your salary is commensurate." He paused. "Or perhaps I wrong you? Perhaps no salary is ever commensurate?"

"Perhaps," agreed Emile gently. But his face and features had thickened, become almost brutal. He leaned towards the desk, looked first at Christopher and then at Francis.

"I listen only when it is worth my while to listen," he added with heavy emphasis. "Do I make myself clear?"

"You mean," almost whispered Christopher, "that being 'worth-while' does not mean a possibility that might be dangerous?"

"Exactly." Emile smiled. "I am no gambler. I bet only when the dice are loaded." He stood up. He was breathing a trifle quickly; his fleshy chest rose and fell. A faint film of perspiration had come out on his skin. He waited. Francis and Christopher exchanged glances. But they did not speak.

"Well?" said Emile, again looking from one to the other.

Francis began to study the signet ring on his fleshless finger. "The dice," he remarked, "are loaded. But we need another player. However, even with loaded dice, the game is precarious." He shook his head slightly, and sighed. "No, Emile, the game, I am afraid, is too risky, too involved, for a loyal non-gambler like you. I think you had better maintain your delightful reputation as a non-gossiper and a non-carrier of tales. Particularly as a non-carrier of tales," and he lifted his bright blue eyes blandly to his cousin's suddenly suffused face.

Emile's mouth hardened grimly. "So, you do not trust me, eh?"

Francis smiled as though at an amiable joke. "Emile, my dear relative, I never trust any one. Your own late-lamented father always impressed that on you, didn't he? That no one is to be trusted?" He shook his head as though in denial. "Did you expect me to be loose-tongued?"

Emile turned slowly to Christopher. "I see," he said. "It is you, after all! I might have known it!

"I've been suspecting something for a long time. You can tell me. I'll do no loose talking. You know very well that my tongue isn't hinged in the middle."

Christopher was silent. But Francis leaned towards Emile playfully and touched his arm. "You don't carry our colors, Emile! Perhaps, under your shirt you carry some one else's. Perhaps it might be 'profitable' for you to talk, in the name of your famous 'loyalty.' "

Emile regarded him with black hatred. His lips moved, and then were still. Francis continued to smile.

Then Christopher opened a locked drawer and drew out a sheet of paper. It was the letterhead of Bouchard and Sons and was signed by Emile, himself, and was addressed to the Chamber of Commerce at Gainesville, Florida. In it Emile discreetly asked the Chamber for information, confidential, naturally, about the little airplane company of Duval-Bonnet, and begged to be informed about its officers, its backers, its financial standing, and its activities.

Emile, staring at it, was utterly nonplussed. His eyes gaped; his jaw fell. While he still stared, Christopher handed him the envelope which had held it, and Emile observed that the stamp was cancelled.

"Of course," said Christopher tonelessly, "so many things could have happened to this letter. For instance, it might have been insufficiently addressed, and so returned to this office. Again, I might have opened it by mistake, on its return. So many things can happen to a letter, you know."

Emile wet his lips. Then, very slowly, he lifted his eyes to his brother's indifferent face.

Christopher folded the letter and put it back in its envelope. He proffered it to Emile. Emile took it automatically. But he did not remove his eyes from Christopher. However, he began to smile unpleasantly. His breathing had quickened.

Francis stood up.

"Christopher and I are having a little conference at my home tonight," he said. "At ten o'clock. Nothing very important, of course. Just—gossip. Now, you have a reputation for not caring about gossip. However, perhaps you would like to be present, Emile. As usual, you may listen, and laugh." He thrust his hands deep into his trouser-pockets and glanced humorously at Christopher. "But I think Emile had better bring his check-book, don't you, Chris?"

Christopher smiled. "No one," he said, "is admitted without a check-book."

Emile said nothing. Then Francis tapped him lightly on the chest with his index finger.

"No, Emile, you are no gossiper. Neither am I. If I were, I might have told my wife a funny little tale I heard about you in New York. And Estelle, you know, is such a friend of Agnes'."

CHAPTER XI

NOW THAT she was old, Adelaide Bouchard dreaded each fresh encounter with the Bouchards. Her spirit had acquired no calluses to protect her exposed nerves; rather, any resistance, any fortitude, which she had been able to summon up during past encounters, had exhaustedly disappeared. She felt vulnerable all through her mind and soul. She was like an old woman feebly defending herself with bare hands against arrows tipped with poison. Wherever she turned, the tips were against her heart and throat. And time made them sharper and more poisonous.

Not that the Bouchards were anything else but solicitous and affectionate to the widow of the formidable Jules Bouchard. Yet they could not keep their derision from their smiles, their humorous chaffing from their voices, their officiousness from their manners. No one defended her, not even her sons.

When Estelle, Francis' wife, called upon Adelaide, and invited her and Celeste and Christopher for dinner, Adelaide timidly and immediately refused.

"But, dear Adelaide," said the former Estelle Carew with affectionate protest, "you have not been to dinner since January, and here it is May! What *is* the matter? Have I offended you in any way?"

"No, no," answered Adelaide hurriedly. "But I—I have not been very well, you know. This neuritis. I hardly go out at all." She wrung her withered slender hands in her lap and looked at Estelle with the imploring expression of a frightened child. Her smooth braided hair was almost white now; her face had shrunken, and was deeply lined. Her wide thin mouth was without color. Only her gentle brown eyes were alive, still capable of hurt, still bewildered and ingenuous and sad. She was very thin, almost emaciated, and wore old-fashioned gowns with high lace necks, with a pearl-framed cameo at the throat. On one shrunken finger she wore her broad gold wedding ring, but that and the cameo were her only jewels. Her body always seemed to be swaying forward; her shoulders were bent. Her breast, which had nursed four children, was flat under the old-fashioned gathers.

Estelle, in her modish English tweeds and furs, studied her thoughtfully, and not without some compassion. She, herself, at thirty-seven, was a slender, handsome and vital woman, the mother of two very sophisticated young daughters, Rosemarie and Phyllise. Her carefully waved hair was a glistening copper-color. Her carefully corseted figure was straight and tall, with prow-like breasts. She was excessively fond of horses and had an excellent stable. Her friends amusedly declared that she had the face of a vigorous mare. Certainly it was long and narrow and high-colored; her eyes were big, liquid and hazel, and quite intelligent. Her shoulders were square, her hips compact; she stepped firmly and quickly. When she talked her lips moved more than ordinarily, like the wide mobile lips of a chewing horse. Her more unkind acquaintances asserted that she whinnied when she laughed. For the rest her hands were strong and slender and corded, the brown hands of a born horsewoman.

The only child of the late John Carew, railroad magnate and one of the larger stockholders of Bouchard and Sons and The Kinsolving Arms Company, she was enormously wealthy in her own right. However, she had a number of poor relatives whom she was constantly assisting. She was a shrewd woman, though. She never assisted them beyond bare necessities. The giving invigorated her; almost, at times, she pranced, like a horse who realizes he has been very good indeed. She loathed "pretty" clothes and was dressed invariably in cloth dresses, riding habits and severe silks. Her legs, being excellent, were duly displayed in the current style of short skirts. Officious, arrogant, masculine, not unkind, assertive and vigorous, she terrified Adelaide more than any other of the female Bouchards. She was much amused at Adelaide's obvious terror of her. But she would not have been so amused had she known that part of the terror was due to Adelaide's feeling that she could not cope with the commonness of this granddaughter of Irish peatfield peasants. Adelaide Burgeon Bouchard instinctively fled from earthiness and all coarsenesses.

"Nonsense, Adelaide," said Estelle, not unkindly. "You must get out more. The fresh air is splendid for you. You look positively faded and anæmic. No one ever sees you. Life ends quickly enough without immuring one's self prematurely."

Adelaide was silent, but a look of bitter longing came into her lowered eyes. Estelle regarded her with rising impatience. Heavens knows, she did not particularly relish the idea of this half-dead old woman sitting at her hearty dinner-table!

But Francis had informed her that the invitation must be given, and accepted. There was Celeste who must be considered, Celeste, one of the richest girls in the world. Estelle respected riches more than anything else. She was sorry for Celeste, who, nearly nineteen, was as immature and unworldly as a ten-year-old. It was too bad indeed for the girl. Estelle thought complacently of her own two daughters, Rosemarie, who was fifteen, and Phyllise, who was thirteen. Smart, cynical, sophisticated girls, with knowing airs and blasé manners, and with fine seats on a horse. Rosemarie attended an exclusive school in New York; Phyllise, who had just had an appendectomy, was invalided at home. Rosemarie, however, was also home just now for a few days, for consultations about the possible removal of her tonsils.

"But I shall not take no for an answer," said Estelle, when she became convinced that Adelaide was not going to speak. "Think of Celeste, dear. She never goes anywhere, either, lately, and almost nineteen, too! Is she going to enter a convent, after all? Well, then, she simply must go out. The girls love her; they will do her such good. For her sake, at least, you must forget your neuritis just for tomorrow night." She smiled humorously.

Adelaide lifted her eyes and gazed at Estelle with tired sadness. Her faded brows drew together, not in a frown, but in a motion of exhausted thought. She knew that Celeste was always bewildered and uneasy with the Bouchards, also. Rosemarie, four years her junior, always made the girl feel awkward and stupid and unattractive, though Estelle's daughter was totally without beauty.

"I'll speak to Christopher," murmured Adelaide, with a sensation of relief. Christopher, as usual, could be depended upon to refuse the invitation for Celeste.

Estelle smiled again, this time rather derisively. "But Christopher has already accepted, Adelaide. I spoke to him yesterday. He said he was certain you would accept."

Adelaide was palely incredulous for some moments. She had once heard Christopher call Rosemarie and Phyllise "a pair of little tarts." Adelaide drew in her lower lip in confused perplexity.

She murmured, at last, still incredulous: "Then, if Christopher has already accepted, for Celeste and me, there is nothing more to be said except 'thank you, Estelle.'" The butler brought in the tea-tray and Adelaide poured with a hand that trembled. Estelle again felt compassionate.

"Just an informal little dinner, dear. No one but the family. Just Emile and Agnes, and Hugo, who is in town for a day or two. Don't dress, if you don't want to. I'm not going to dress, and neither is Francis. Emile's boy, Robert, is home from school, you know, because of that scarlet fever epidemic. Celeste hardly knows him, and he is such a clever boy! And he her nephew, too. Celeste doesn't know enough young people. It is too bad that she finds Armand's unfortunate little Annette sufficient company. She ought to have gone away to school. Why, I don't believe she has four friends altogether!"

Adelaide murmured: "Three of her friends have recently married. Christopher doesn't want her to associate with them, now. He believes married women are corrupting." She smiled drearily. Estelle shrugged and laughed impatiently. "So, that leaves just Annette, and the little Schofield girl."

"Both neurotics!" exclaimed Estelle with contemptuous vigor. "Why, I'm firmly convinced the Schofield child is a pervert! You know the story why she was dismissed from Rosemarie's school?"

Adelaide's features expressed her distress and distaste, so Estelle merely raised her eyebrows and went on: "Well, anyway, I shouldn't let Celeste associate with Josephine if I were you. I shall certainly speak to Christopher about it! And there's Annette."

"Annette is a sweet child," protested Adelaide, a dull spot of color coming into her faded cheeks. "She is just not strong. And such a beautiful musician. She looks like an angel when she plays her harp."

Estelle stood up, gathering her furs about her. "I prefer that young girls postpone the harp-playing," she said with a smile. "Well, then, it is settled? Tomorrow night, at eight?"

And she went away, driving her own open car. She had a low opinion of chauffeurs generally. Certainly, she was a competent, if rapid, motorist, herself.

Before she went to bed Adelaide called her daughter into her rooms. It was a warm spring night, full of golden moon and slow heavy winds. Adelaide could hear that wind in the distant poplar trees. They were silhoueted like tapers against the moon, which was enormous. The shadowy grass rippled in light. The windows of Adelaide's sitting room were open, and she could smell the dark night-quiet, the rising fresh incense of the earth.

Celeste came in, her nightgown covered with a long cream-colored silk negligee. Her short curling masses of black hair rolled on her shoulders. She was a young Juliet, and her eyes were unawakened, for all their gaiety. The gown, trailing

69

on the floor about her, gave her height and a new dignity. It had a silver belt, which showed the remarkable delicacy of her waist. Adelaide, gazing at her daughter earnestly, thought that she was an anachronism in these raw and gaudy days of the nineteen-twenties, in which rudeness posed as wit, and obscenity as sophistication. Christopher was wrong! One of these days she must understand rudeness and obscenity, and be well armed against it. Christopher refused to admit this. He refused to insulate her against the inevitable shocks to her innocence. Knowledge, thought Adelaide sadly, knowledge of the external ugliness of mankind will, paradoxically, preserve Celeste's spiritual integrity and true innocence. She will learn to recognize this ugliness, and to avoid it. The only real danger that faces her is the loss of her belief in man's innate capacity for God and beauty.

Celeste had been out for a drive and a moving-picture show with Christopher. (He even picked the shows she attended!) Later, he had treated her to ice-cream. Adelaide thought: It is time she put away the things of childhood. She is a woman, my little daughter.

She said: "Did you have a nice drive, dear?"

Celeste laughed. "Oh, yes. Christopher says my driving is improving. But I still don't understand those awful gears." She sat down, like a child, on the footstool at Adelaide's feet, and laughed again. Adelaide studied her. The little ivory face was intelligent and quick, both with gaiety and thought. The beautiful dark blue eyes shone like polished porcelain.

Adelaide said quietly: "Did Christopher tell you that we are all going to dinner tomorrow night, at Francis'?"

The laughter left the girl's full red lips. A small pucker appeared between her eyes. "Yes. And just when Annette and I had made an appointment to listen to the New York Symphony Orchestra on her new radio." She was suddenly excited. "Mama, it is the most wonderful radio! You don't have to use batteries with it, as you do with ours. Christopher says he is going to get one like it immediately. Such a splendid tone, too. You would think the orchestra was in the next room. It is a direct broadcast from a concert, in New York. They're going to play Beethoven's Fifth."

Adelaide folded her hands quietly in her lap, and lifted her eyes to a point just above Celeste's animated head.

"I remember, dear, the first time I heard that Symphony. I was very sad, for I had just lost my mother. She had always protected me from—everything. Now, I was exposed. I—I learned so many things! I learned things about people that frightened me, and sickened me. I wanted to die, for I had never known that the world could be so ugly, and so wicked." She paused. Celeste was listening earnestly.

"And then, Celeste, I went to this concert. I was visiting relatives in Boston. Such nice people! They seemed to know at once what was troubling me. They took me to hear the concert. I'll never forget it.

"You see, darling, Beethoven told me, in his music, that though there is so much ugliness and wickedness and cruelty and treachery among men, there is something in them which is inherently beautiful and good, too. Beethoven told me that I must not deny the ugliness and the treachery, and refuse to believe them. I must accept them, and be sorry about them. But I must fix my attention and my belief on what man could be if he wanted to be. I must understand man's inclination to evil, and his capacity for nobility."

"But what a paradox!" exclaimed Celeste.

Adelaide smiled her tired smile. "Yes, dear. But the greatest lesson we must learn in living is that only the paradoxes are valid. Consistency is the fundamental of mechanics and mathematics. But we are more than machines, and certainly more than equations."

Celeste was silent; her head was bent. Adelaide desperately hoped, that though Celeste did not fully comprehend now, she would comprehend in some distant hour of danger, and be fortified.

Adelaide began to speak again of Estelle's invitation. Celeste nodded impatiently. "Of course, if Christopher insists! But I don't like Rosemarie, even if it is rude to say it. She is too precocious, but she is clever rather than intelligent. I don't like clever people, Mama. They frighten me. They remind me," and she laughed apologetically, "of some of Christopher's newest chromium gadgets. All bright hard plate, and no intrinsic value." And then she became uneasy. Christopher was a rarely touched subject between herself and her mother, and in hasty loyalty, she spoke of something else.

But Adelaide came back to the subject of the dinner. The details were settled. Celeste again expressed her regret at missing the broadcast. "But Estelle has a fine new radio," said Adelaide. "You can hear the music there."

Celeste shook her head impatiently. "They never put it on, except to hear popular music. And I can't bear popular music; it makes me feel depressed and lonely, and restless. Idiotic love-jingles and braying!"

Adelaide curled a lock of the glossy dark hair over her thin fingers. The ringlet wound itself against the palm of her

71

hand like the ringlet of a child. The mother sighed, shook her head, tried to smile.

"Don't speak so contemptuously of—of love, dear, even if it is expressed in vulgar music and vulgar words. It is the greatest of all the validities. I—I loved your father very much. I never really lived, until I knew him." She released the ringlet, tried to make her voice amused. "Celeste, is it possible you are nineteen! Why, you are a woman! One of these days you, like Elizabeth Darrow, will be getting married and going off to a home of your own."

To her surprise Celeste's lovely small face darkened; it seemed to withdraw. But Adelaide was not disturbed; a sudden lightening flooded her; her heart began to tremble against the walls of her chest. She leaned towards her daughter, her own lips parted.

Celeste flung out her hands and her eyes flashed resentfully. "But how can that ever happen? I never meet any one. I never see any one alone. Besides, I don't like the boys and the young men I know. I never went to a dance until I was seventeen. I—I don't know how to act with men, I can't speak to them. They think I am stupid.

"Just tonight Christopher was asking me if I liked any particular one. I said, no. He said he was glad, for none of them was good enough for me." She sighed with exasperation. "But suppose that is true, which it isn't, really? What am I to do? Christopher says we'll stay in New York next winter and then he'll see that I meet the 'right kind.' But I don't know how to act! I don't know how to dress! I look like a frump; I act like a frump—"

Adelaide drew in her breath. She was trembling all over. She clenched her hands, and was torn with fear and with excitement.

"Darling, Estelle said today that she would like to have you go to Southampton with her and the girls this summer. Then they are taking a cruise on the new yacht. Would you like that? First of all, you would have to get the proper clothes, in New York. You and I could go, next wee——"

Celeste looked excited and eager. Then her expression darkened again. "But Christopher just told me tonight that we would be going to Long Island again for the summer. Oh, I just hate it there! I know that sounds contemptible, for he does everything for me. But I do hate it. I never see anyone but a lot of stupid girls. The boys avoid me, and those who do come around are only fortune-hunters, Christopher says. Or horsy men, who smell of the stables. Or golf-players and tennis-players, and yachters. They make me ill."

Adelaide moistened her dry lips. She could hardly speak for her agitation. "Most men, today, are like that, Celeste. What would you like, yourself?"

The girl blushed faintly. "I—I don't know, Mama. I suppose I sound like a romantic, but I'd like a real man. He could like horses and dogs and games, if he wanted to. I'd overlook that. But he'd have to be interested in the things I like. He'd have to like music, and reading, and walks. Oh, I don't know. I've never met any one I could like. Maybe he doesn't exist, and I'll have to marry a man in tweeds after all." She added, with new bitterness: "Just so long as he meets Christopher's requirements."

Adelaide held her breath. Tears of joy filled her eyes. Celeste got up restlessly and went to her mother's dressing table. She picked up the gold-backed brush. Adelaide could see her face in the mirror. It was the face of a woman, hungry for the natural destiny of a woman, and disturbed. She came back to her mother, sat down on the stool again, and began to brush her hair with resentful pulling strokes.

"Let me have the brush, darling," said Adelaide gently. She brushed the strands back from the white, blue-veined temples. With the hair drawn back so, Celeste's face had purity and a curious strength. The bones were small, the skin like polished ivory. The jaw-line was firm and well modeled, the cheekbones rather prominent, yet delicate. As her mother brushed her hair, the girl studied her mother with somber gravity. "What am I going to do?" she asked at last. "Isn't there any other yardstick for a prospective husband except money?"

Adelaide paused for just a moment in the brushing, then making her voice casual, she said: "Did Christopher tell you that money was the only yardstick?"

Celeste shook her head impatiently. "Not exactly as crudely as that. But he did say that a competent man invariably had money. Lack of money meant incompetence, either on the part of the man, or his ancestors. I can't believe it," she added somberly. "Surely there are other competences besides the one of knowing how to manipulate the Stock Market, or expand a business. I've met a few of Christopher's friends! And I can't bear them."

"Why not?" whispered Adelaide.

The girl shook her head despairingly. "I don't know. That's the worst of it. But I'd never marry one of them."

When the girl had finally left, Adelaide went to bed feeling more at peace, and happier, than she had done since Jules' death.

73

She was not deceived that Celeste was safe, or that she could resist pressure. But she had indicated to her mother that she had the desire to resist. She had indicated that, in spite of Christopher, she was a woman.

Before she fell asleep, Adelaide decided to write to the wife of her husband's nephew in New York, Marion Bouchard. She did not like Marion particularly, but Marion was a lady. And Christopher seemed to dislike her less than he disliked his other female relatives.

CHAPTER XII

ADELAIDE liked nothing about the grotesquely huge estate of Francis Bouchard except the incredibly beautiful gardens. She almost invariably accepted dinner invitations just for the joy of wandering in the grounds. Celeste, too, loved them. They were such a relief to her, after Christopher's austere acres.

It was hot tonight, unseasonably hot, for it was only the middle of May. The immense dining-room was a glitter of crystal and silver and white-satin linen. Estelle had looted a French castle of its chandeliers, and one of them hung over the refectory table like an illuminated mass of stalactites. It was blinding in its brilliance; it threw a hard and dazzling light on the expensive litter of gold-rimmed plates and glasses and heavy silver below. The ceiling above was frescoed; fat nymphs and cupids, decorously veiled with pink at strategic spots, disported themselves in obese attitudes on banks of flowers. (It was a copy of Raphael, Estelle asserted with pride.) Adelaide, who privately thought the Renaissance painters a regrettable mistake, and sentimentally over-rated, never looked at these frescoes without being revolted. The murals along the wall suggested Michelangelo. There was a vague suggestion about them of pregnant infants and goiterous virgins, with here and there a robed man obviously a eunuch. It was all completely without taste, but Estelle was inordinately proud of it. She was proud, too, of her seventeenth-century furniture with its serpentine legs and gilded commodes and sideboards, and of the elaborate crusted silver services and water jugs and handled trays.

All was authentic, and all was hideous. Estelle was envious of Agnes Bouchard's Gothic dining-hall, which she openly declared gave her the "glooms." So, though she secretly liked the bare polished dark tiles of that dining-hall, she covered her own dining-room floor with Oriental rugs, thick and mossy.

The whole house belied her "horsy" character, for there was a plebeian core in her which loved display and richness. Daughter of Irish peasants, who had appeased starvation with potatoes, the price-tag was her yardstick. She seemed determined to convince the world that the rumored gross revenues of the Bouchard clan for 1925 of $500,000,000 was a fact.

She adored flunkies. She had more servants than any of the other members of the family. Adelaide, who liked simplicity and dignity and sparseness in service, was perpetually confused by the number of maids and men-servants. She could hardly eat for them. Her father had always said that a lady was proved by her table, and that one or two excellent dishes were all that were required. Estelle did not believe it. She did not believe, either, that three kinds of wine, and a digestive, were quite enough. The cellars were equipped with enough casks and bottles for a hotel, in spite of Prohibition.

In short, there was, in this palace, a lavishness and a fear of too little, which betrayed almost pathetically the daughter of peasants who had dreaded nothing more than not having enough to eat.

There were comparatively few at dinner tonight. There was old Ann Richmond Bouchard, mother of Francis, all black satin, bare shoulders, jewels and carefully waved hair. She was the same age as Adelaide, whom she privately patronized as "an old dowd, without personal pride." But in spite of the rouge and the corsets and the dyed hair and the jewels and the sprightly nervous manner, she appeared older than Adelaide in her quiet semi-formal silk with the covered shoulders. Ann had been a great beauty in her youth, fashionable, vain and nervous, but the beauty was now painted wreckage, the nervousness had become malice, and only the vanity had remained, stronger than ever. She was reputed to possess "a social conscience," and was deeply interested in a number of charities, on whose boards she was invariably Chairwoman. Estelle, her daughter-in-law, who had frankly no social conscience at all, she despised as a woman unaware of "modern trends and responsibilities." Ann greatly prided herself on her modern outlook. She boasted that her granddaughters were her friends, and that they regarded her, not as "grandma" but as a comrade. It was well for her that she did not know of the intense amusement she gave them. She professed to be unshockable, and had a collection of nasty stories which she had gleaned from Rosemarie.

Then there was Emile, and his wife, Agnes, the former Miss Fortune. Agnes, niece of the Governor, Elliott Graves, was a thin and avid woman of thirty-five, with a narrow white face and violently red painted lips, and black straight hair cut closely on her long narrow head. She had a long bony nose, which she thought patrician, but which at times gave her a slightly harpy appearance. The straps of her dark red gown accentuated the boniness of her shoulders. She had no breasts, for breasts were out-of-date in nineteen-twenty-five; her whole body was lathe-like, very fashionable. She had a manner of constantly twisting her scarlet thread-like lips, and this, combined with her bold black eyes, made her appear predatory, which she was in truth. She had a febrile laugh, and a penchant for Christopher, which he affected to duplicate. He had given her the gold-and-ivory cigarette-holder which she perpetually waved all during dinner; it had been a secret gift, and it unendingly amused him to watch her use it, and to catch her significant glances at him. He usually sought her out, for he liked to look at her and to compare Celeste with her.

Hugo, who had "just run up from New York for a breath of clean air," was there. He had not brought his wife. There he sat, buff-colored and genial and white-toothed and smiling, with his loving manners and politician's false joviality. Armand had once said, gloomily, that whenever Hugo appeared one had only to start looking for the carrion. Just at present he was in an excessively expansive mood, and kept glancing at Christopher with the most intimate and jocose expression.

Estelle, severely dressed in dark gray and smelling slightly of the stables, had already guessed that something was "up." She felt excited, and spots of brighter color roughened her cheekbones. Adelaide sat beside her, and she made unusual gestures of friendship in her direction. Next to Adelaide sat Celeste in a plain dark blue cloth dress with a childish round white collar. What a shame, too, with those eyes and that lovely hair! thought Estelle. And that pure ivory skin! Celeste appeared to be no more than sixteen years old. Dark, thin, knowing Rosemarie next to her, with her sly fluttering eyelashes and streak of red mouth, seemed much older. When

76

Celeste spoke, her voice had a gay freshness about it; when Rosemarie spoke, it was in blasé accents, and in a voice now admiringly called "husky," though only a few years ago it had been usual with chronic drunkards. Next to her sister sat young Phyllise, a more childish edition, but just as knowing and just as vixenish.

Francis sat at the head of his table, spare and frigid and sunken-cheeked. He was the only one of the male Bouchards who wore any jewelry: on the ring finger of his right hand a beautiful diamond flashed and winked. Yet, this did not seem ornate on him, as it might have done on another man.

He was very fond of his daughters, with whom he kept exchanging incomplete and humorous phrases. He was always amused at their flippancy, their impudences, their modern realism. They reminded him, he thought, of little girls dressing in their mother's garments, though he had to admit that Estelle seemed much less competent and poised and finished. He had an old photograph of his aunt, Renee Bouchard Sessions, and considered that there was quite a resemblance between the dead woman and Rosemarie. There were the same dark eyes and Indian-straight hair and hard boniness of face. But Renee had never worn such an expression as Rosemarie wore.

Once Jules had said that Adelaide among the Bouchards reminded him of a rabbit among foxes. There was much truth in this. Adelaide, though smiling fixedly, kept moving her head slightly from side to side, her brown eyes distended and uneasy. She laughed when the others laughed; she nodded and smirked on the appropriate occasions. But her heart kept up the old familiar faint trembling against her ribs, and her nostrils continually quivered and drew in. Estelle seemed especially kind tonight, and solicitous. Adelaide found her own hand clumsily dropping silver in consequence. Once her fingers, grasping a goblet, shook so violently that the water splashed on her dress.

Christopher, as usual, spoke very little. He smiled constantly and faintly, listening. Sometimes his smile was agreeable and acknowledging of some witty remark of Francis'; but most of the time it was secret and inward, as though he heard only the things he was thinking. He had a habit of passing the palms of his small bony hands backward over his hair, like brushes. Adelaide was familiar with this habit; she knew that Christopher was "plotting" again.

Always she watched him more than she watched anyone else. It was like watching a danger which might not culminate if one's eyes fixed themselves upon it. Sometimes she

77

would think: he is my son; I carried him in my womb; I conceived him. He is my flesh. And then she would stare at him unbelievingly. Those were not her hands that moved so lightly and effortlessly among silver and crystal or held a cigarette. There was such a sure and cruel aura about them. Jules had once called them surgeon's hands; he had also remarked that surgeons are sadists who have sublimated their perversion. Christopher, thought Adelaide sadly, had not bothered to sublimate his. Fascinated by him, she watched his motionless "Egyptian" eyes, which never smiled and never revealed anything. When he turned his head the blazing light of the chandelier glittered on his sleek fine brown hair, which always looked so polished, like natural mahogany. His bloodless skin was dry and fine; when he smiled, it stretched and wrinkled like parchment. In company like this, he never said anything that was not tactful or amusing or indifferent or courteous, yet Adelaide always listened with the most painful attention.

Many, besides Adelaide, had often asked themselves, and others: What does he think of? No one knew, not even Adelaide. But she felt his thoughts. They were like bright steel machinery, flashing and gliding and turning without sound. There was not even the warmth of conscious villainy about them, the hot violence of evil. Had there been villainy or evil, she would not have been so afraid, for she knew that sometimes a wicked man can be made to realize his wickedness, but a soulless man can never acquire a soul, a faithless man, faith.

After glancing at Christopher, she inevitably glanced at Celeste. She saw her two children frequently smiling at each other, Celeste with devotion and sympathy, and Christopher with affection. When he looked at his sister a curious thing happened to his face. It did not soften nor objectively change, yet there was a subtle light on it, a gentle quickening, an almost imperceptible lifting of malice, a protectiveness. His toneless voice seemed to acquire a faint life when he spoke to her, but only the sharpest ear could detect it.

In many ways he resembled his dead father, but he had nothing of Jules' true and delightful humor, his impersonal gaiety or warmth. Jules might indeed have been "the Jesuit." No one thought of calling Christopher a Jesuit at any time. Jules had sometimes been intrigued and diverted by his own subtle plottings. Christopher plotted, but he was never intrigued. He would have called it Narcissism, which it probably was. Jules had been conceited, and had admitted it. Christopher was not conceited. To him, conceit expressed

78

some inner morbidity, some self-preoccupation, to be found only in men unsure of themselves. When he had been called a Rabelaisian Trappist he had been called so with startling insight.

Francis had been dilating on the fine qualities of his new yacht, now waiting for him near Southampton. He was an enthusiast, and belonged to the New York Yacht Club. "You ought to get a yacht, Chris," he said.

"I don't like the sea," replied Christopher. "And I don't like the yachting crowd."

"Oh, my dear, you miss so much!" exclaimed Estelle.

"There is," said Christopher, "much that it is pleasant to miss."

Rosemarie and Phyllise giggled. They thought their relative "fascinating." But Estelle was offended.

"After all," she said sententiously, "there is something more in the world than work. You never go anywhere, Christopher, except to Long Island in the summer, and to New York for one week in the winter. You must think of Celeste, too, you know. She is a nun, really. Too bad you aren't Catholics. If you were, I wouldn't be surprised if you locked her up in some convent."

"That wouldn't be a bad thing at all," answered Christopher. He smiled at his sister. To his faint surprise, she did not smile back, as usual. Instead, she appeared restless. She was looking at Estelle.

"I'd like to see the yacht," she said timidly. "I was on one, once. I like the sea, especially when it is stormy. It— it seems so free, as if it is running. Usually it is so calm in the summer."

Estelle smiled at her maternally. "My dear, we don't like to go out when it is storming. I can't say I enjoy being thrown from side to side. But it is really beautiful when it is calm—" She frowned swiftly at her two children, who were silently convulsed by Celeste's naïve remarks.

Celeste saw their merriment; she flushed. She lifted her head and said clearly and simply: "I am so tired of calm things. I should like things to be stormy. Like the sea in the winter. Alive, making sound, running back and forth—living. Even terrifying." She drew in her breath, and her lips parted. For a moment there was a wild and desperate glimmer in her eyes. Christopher put down his glass slowly and carefully. He said nothing; he did not move. But he saw nothing but his sister.

Hugo's eyelids crinkled shrewdly. He looked from the girl to her brother, Christopher; he drew in his chin as though

79

swallowing a morsel he appreciated. Emile, who was usually bored by the girl, seemed interested, and his wife regarded her with a bland and cunning expression.

"I'm taking *Lief Ericson* to Canada this summer, Celeste," said Emile. "You'd see enough stormy ocean up along the coast there, I assure you. And feel it, too, in the pit of your stomach. How about you and Mother coming with us?"

Celeste shone. "That would be wonderful! Mama, would you like that?"

Adelaide had paled. That yacht, with Agnes and her friends on board! But she would be there, to protect Celeste, and there would be the ocean, and Quebec and Montreal— She said, her voice shaking: "I think it would be nice."

Christopher said coolly: "That is impossible. We have already extended invitations to a number of people to visit us at Crissons this summer. You know that, Celeste. And you, too, Mother."

Celeste sank in her chair. But Adelaide looked at her son with new courage.

"We can easily withdraw the invitations, Christopher."

"That is impossible," he repeated, without emphasis.

There was a small but poignant silence about the table.

Adelaide's face wearily darkened.

"However," Christopher went on, "you may go, yourself, Mother. I think it would do you good. You are looking tired. But Celeste must stay with me and receive our invited guests."

Agnes bridled, tossed Christopher a bold look from her big black eyes.

"What's the matter, Chris? Do you think we'd pollute Celeste?"

A burning scarlet ran over Celeste's cheeks. The other girls tittered; one of them eyed Celeste malevolently, and with ridicule.

Christopher smiled. "Yes, Agnes, frankly I do."

Emile scowled, then remembering, grinned. But Agnes laughed heartily. Estelle did not laugh. She regarded Christopher with anger.

"I am sure that I, and Rosemarie and Phyllise, would not pollute Celeste, Christopher." Her voice was filled with scorn, both for him and for his sister.

Celeste uttered a small cry of utter shame and humiliation. The girls stared at her with delight. Adelaide, under cover of the tablecloth, reached for the girl's trembling hand, and was shocked and astounded at the fierce gesture with which Celeste repudiated her touch.

"Christopher," said Celeste in a faint but steadfast voice, "you are making a fool of me."

He raised his eyebrows helplessly at her. "Am I, Celeste? I don't think so. But if you think so, I'm sorry. I had no such intention."

The other girls laughed openly. Celeste was silent. Her breast rose and fell. Tears stood in her eyes, tears of mortification.

Estelle felt pity for her. She said kindly: "Don't be so sensitive, dear. You know how Christopher teases. Perhaps he will change his mind, after all, about your going with us and Rosemarie and Phyllise. Or with Emile and Agnes."

Christopher interrupted. "Celeste isn't a child. Perhaps I had forgotten. Perhaps I had thought she realized her social obligations to those we have invited to Crissons. Perhaps I believed that she knew invitations once extended are not to be withdrawn except in extreme cases. It seems I was wrong. She is a young woman, now, and her own mistress. If she wishes to go with you, Estelle, or with you, Agnes, I am sure I shall offer no objections, now."

"That is splendid, then!" exclaimed Estelle. She reached over and patted Celeste's cold little hand, which lay on the table. "I shall make you a list of the required clothing, my dear. I am sure you are going to enjoy yourself so much this summer."

But Celeste looked at Christopher. He avoided her gaze. He allowed the butler to refill his glass, and then sipped at it appreciatively. Adelaide clenched her hands together under the tablecloth. She prayed silently to her daughter: Darling, look at me! Don't look at him! You can escape now. I will help you escape!

But Celeste continued to gaze at her brother. A tremor like rippling water ran over her features.

"Christopher, will you mind terribly?"

He put down his glass, smiled slightly. "Does it matter so much, Celeste, if I mind or not?"

Darling, look at me! cried Adelaide silently. Celeste did not see her.

"And what will you do, Christopher, if I go?"

He shrugged. "Go to Crissons, myself, of course. It will be awkward, sometimes, but I shall manage, I am sure."

Do not look at him like that, my darling! cried Adelaide with all the desperate power of her soul. You have not wanted to escape before. If you do not escape now, you may never be free.

Celeste was silent. Then she sighed deeply. Everyone
81

watched, with more or less malice and interest, this old, old struggle between Adelaide and Christopher for this girl. When they heard Celeste's sigh, and saw how all the light had gone from her face, they knew that Christopher had won again.

Celeste spoke faintly but steadfastly:

"Of course, Christopher, if you think you ought to go to Crissons, I'll go, too. You can't go alone."

Christopher flashed a humorous glance about the table, which stopped at his sister's chin, and not her eyes.

"Now, why can't I go alone? After all, Celeste, I am of age. I shall be quite comfortable, and quite safe."

They all laughed, except Adelaide and Celeste. The girl continued to regard him fixedly. Her lower lip trembled.

"No," she said. "I'll go with you."

He raised his small bloodless hand protestingly, and again flashed that humorous glance at the smiling others.

"No, no. No, indeed. The more I think of the prospect down there alone, the more it appeals to me. I think I should enjoy myself without a chaperone." He smiled at Rosemarie and Phyllise. "Or, how about you two girls?"

They shrieked with mirth. Rosemarie was smoking a cigarette, in spite of the frowns of her parents. She blew a deliberate cloud at Christopher. "Never mind Phyllise!" she cried. "Take me alone, Christopher," and she languished at him insolently.

Celeste's small face had tightened and whitened with something close to anger and disgust. Adelaide, the old impotence creeping over her, could do nothing. Her head was bent. She hardly seemed to breathe. Estelle caught the expression on Celeste's face, and the dinner being concluded now, she rose and said casually: "Shall we go?"

She and her daughters, Celeste, Adelaide, old Ann Bouchard and Agnes, went into the great drawing-room, where a dull log fire, in spite of the warmness of the evening, was smoldering on the flagged hearth. Phyllise, with the arrogant bad manners of her generation, went immediately to the immense grand piano and began to pound popular music on it. The raucous discord, insistent and vulgar, filled the room. Her grandmother, after the first wincing, began to smile with false enjoyment. She tapped her old foot, painfully squeezed into four-inch-heeled slippers; she tapped the arm of her chair with her knotty and mottled fingers. She kept nodding her marcelled head, and her rouged, seamed cheeks quivered. From under their greased and tinted lids, so wrinkled and sagging, her fagged old eyes blinked, struggling against sleepiness and the desire for quiet. She was proud of her "slim" figure; her neck and chest were mottled and rough and discolored, and her withered breast hung lifeless under the black satin. Adelaide, filled with her own private hopelessness, yet could feel compassion for this old woman. When old Ann began to hum an accompaniment to the loathesome noise, with such a pathetic attempt at young sprightliness and knowing gaiety, Adelaide thought this the saddest of all.

It was even sadder than Celeste, silent and pale, sitting near a widow where she could look out at the dark and blessed night.

Rosemarie stood idly by the piano as her sister played, smoking with ostentatiously blasé gestures. She lifted her reedy and metallic voice and sang. Her flat immature figure was completely without distinction. Her long legs, in their gauzy pink silk stockings, splayed out from under the full short skirt. One long lock of her lusterless Indian-black hair fell over her dark bony cheeks, and her eyes raked the others in the room with an obscene insolence.

Estelle was feeling irritable. She was sorry for Celeste, and this made her uncomfortable and impatient. She could see the girl's cheek and profile; she had always thought Celeste vapid and weak, but now she was struck by the pure strong modelling of that young profile. If Celeste allowed herself to be dominated by Christopher, it was from choice, and not from weakness.

Estelle was altruistically alarmed. This was very bad, indeed! People like Celeste were always being exploited by the cunning and selfish. They were victimized not through their own weakness, but through their integrity and love and selflessness. This was very bad, indeed! But who could help this girl? That weak bending old fool, Adelaide, who did not have the courage of a grasshopper?

Made more and more irritable by her reflections, Estelle became aware of the horrible noise her offspring were creating. She was used to this noise. She thought it an indication of high spirits, which should not be "suppressed," for fear of complexes and inhibitions. But now she could not endure it.

"For heavens sake, Rosemarie! Whoever told you you could sing! And Phyllise: you are being very rude. We can't hear ourselves talk."

Rosemarie said aloud: "That's probably just as well," and went on shrilling louder than ever. Old Ann nodded, smiling her fixed bemused smile, and tapped more feverishly than ever. Agnes shrugged and laughed. "Let the brat alone, Estelle. You were young once, yourself."

But Estelle was fully aroused. Her face flushed with bad temper until it was crimson. "Perhaps I was young, but I was never a nuisance. Rosemarie, stop it at once! And you too, Phyllise." Just at present she did not care whether her daughters developed Freudian complexes or not. In fact, she earnestly desired them to have a few violent inhibitions which would make them "stonily silent." She thought emotionally of the many sharp slaps she had received from her father in her own girlhood, and wondered if she had appreciated him enough. But Francis would be infuriated if she slapped his darlings.

Rosemarie winked openly at Agnes, and continued to sing more raucously than ever. Phyllis sweated with her efforts to make the piano crash more deafeningly.

Estelle's florid face suddenly turned quite white. Her eyes flashed. She strode towards the piano. Reaching Rosemarie, she snatched the cigarette from the girl's painted lips. She seized Phyllise by the shoulder and swung her from the instrument. Amazed, they stared at her, affronted.

She was breathing quickly. "Go to your rooms at once," she said. "Now, I mean it. And don't come downstairs again."

The girls did not move. Old Ann quavered protestingly from her chair: "Estelle, what is the matter with you? The children are only enjoying themselves."

Estelle swung on her. "Why should they enjoy themselves at the expense of their elders, Mother? Did you enjoy yourself like that?"

Ann was taken aback, and then said angrily: "No, I didn't. And I grew up with half a dozen complexes, too! You and I are old, Estelle. But the world is made for youth, and not for us, now."

Estelle was infuriated. She was only thirty-seven, after all. The audacity of this old fool speaking to her as though she were her contemporary! This, more than anything else, overcame her last scruples about the state of her children's psyches. She turned upon the girls, hardly able to keep from striking them. She might have struck them, indeed, enraged at their insolent staring eyes and contemptuous smiles, if a maid had not entered just then with a tray of coffee. So, she contained herself and said again: "I've told you for the last time. Go to your rooms. And to bed. In ten minutes I'm coming up, and it'll be all the worse for you if you're not there."

They saw she meant it. Phyllise, grumbling surlily, stood up. Rosemarie said: "I'll ask Dad."

Then Estelle lost her temper completely. Her Irish temper

was not to be controlled. She slapped the pert Rosemarie fully in the face, not once, but three times. The girl staggered, caught herself, burst into tears. Adelaide, shocked, found herself on her feet, sick with disgust at this display of bad manners. But Celeste, at the window, did not turn. She had heard nothing.

"I say, you're being rough, Estelle," admonished Agnes. But she was smiling. She thought how good her palm would feel against the cheek of her spoiled son, Robert, who, at the last minute, had refused to accompany his parents to this dinner.

The girls simultaneously raised their voices in a howl, and then, terrified, ran from the room. Estelle followed them, and saw that they went upstairs. Rosemarie, reaching the second floor, began to curse hysterically. Her mother heard this. Her anger dissolved. She was filled with horror and dread. She stood at the foot of the stairs, motionless, staring.

When she returned to the drawing-room, old Ann was pouring coffee. Agnes was laughing. Adelaide was silent. Celeste had not moved.

Agnes, seeing Estelle, started on a humorous remark, but stopped, startled at the other woman's hard intense expression. Estelle came to the fire, accepted a cup of coffee, began to drink it. Her hand shook. Her mother-in-law regarded her accusingly.

"The trouble with you, Estelle, is that you are not modern," she said. "No really modern woman would insult the dignity of her children like that."

Estelle put her cup into her saucer with a hard clatter. She said with cold passion: "I've just learned something. There's something wrong. With us. With our children. We let them grow up without values and without restraint. I'm just as bad as the rest of you, I suppose. I'm just as stupid. I've done nothing to make my daughters realize responsibility, and the fact that they are not born merely to gratify themselves. I've never taught them that they owe a civilized duty to other human beings." She regarded old Ann bitterly. "Yes, Mother, you are right. I've insulted the dignity of my children ever since they were born!"

Ann gaped, not comprehending. Her puckered lips twitched. The rouge had dissolved from them, showing the livid skin beneath. Adelaide regarded Estelle earnestly, without speaking. Agnes smiled wryly.

"What do you want of the brats, Estelle? Do you want them to be pious prigs, believing in voodoo?"

Estelle was already sick with reaction, but she said
85

quietly and with bitterness: "I would rather they were prigs than lawless idiots."

She looked at them with stern anger. None of them had ever seen her like this.

"I tell you, there is something wrong with us. With society. I never realized it until now. There is no health in our children. No discipline. We've got to do something about it—" After a moment she added somberly: "Or maybe others will do it for us."

Then Adelaide spoke for the first time. "Life," she said gently, "administers its own discipline, Estelle."

The younger woman exclaimed impatiently: "But we shelter our children from life. We give them false pictures, all in the name of freedom! We pamper their 'personalities,' instead of thrashing them into reason and decency. We forget that the outside world won't pamper them that way."

"Oh, yes, it will," said Agnes. "You see, they'll have such a lot of money!"

There was a silence. Estelle looked at Agnes' cynical smiling face with its crimson thread-like lips. Agnes began to nod. She smiled more than ever. Her lips writhed.

Then Estelle turned away. She stood before the fire. Her hands locked behind her back. Her broad shoulders were bent.

Adelaide regarded her with sad compassion, then slowly regarded the others. She thought to herself how there was no more peace in this rich and lofty room than there was in the drabbest room of poverty. How much passion and weariness and hatred and bitterness and grief and hopelessness there was. There was Agnes, with a faithless husband and a lover, and a spoiled young son, who, at thirteen, had been expelled from three schools for brutality and even for suspected theft and immature vice.—Agnes, who was frankly selfish, and did nothing but dress, sit in beauty salons, shop, play golf, drive and flirt and drink. And there was old Ann Richmond, who had found nothing precious in life but youth. She had not loved good Honore, and so had robbed both herself and him. She was nothing but a miserable old harpy, a vampire, living off the youth and gaiety and heedlessness of others, content with the rags of carnival, grateful for discarded foolscaps and broken bells. There was no dignity in her, no fortitude, no tranquillity. She was old, close to death, and she had nothing at all, not even sadness.

And then there was Estelle, the strong, who had suddenly realized both her folly, and the impotence she had evoked by her folly—Estelle who tried to find surcease from uneasiness in her hounds and clubs and tweeds.

None of them, thought Adelaide compassionately, had a real and vital struggle; none of them truly suffered. None of them had ever experienced real agony, or had known real despair or sorrow. And this was the saddest of all.

Estelle was moving away from the suffocating fire. She was moving towards Celeste, who still sat, motionless, looking out at the dark moonlit gardens. The laden night wind came through the opened windows. Estelle breathed loudly, restlessly.

Old Ann had called for a bridge-table. The maid had come in, and was arranging cards and ashtrays and glasses. Ann picked up a glittering new pack and riffled them in her knotted and jeweled fingers. "Bridge!" she called gaily. She put down the cards, put a cigarette into a platinum holder, held it to the light the maid struck for her. She tapped the holder imperatively on the table. "Bridge!" No one moved. Adelaide sat quietly in her chair, Agnes stared at the logs, and Estelle breathed in the night air.

Ann pouted. She motioned to the maid, who prepared her a drink. "What is the matter with everyone? I said, bridge!"

Estelle turned from the window and made an exasperated gesture. "O God," she said. "Let's not play bridge tonight. Let's go out for a walk or something. Or a drive."

Ann was offended. "I like bridge," she said. She assumed a childish attitude. Agnes yawned. "No, thanks, no bridge. I move we second Estelle's motion. How about you, Adelaide?"

Adelaide hesitated. She glanced at Ann, whose face had grown empty and disappointed under its paint and powder. The old jeweled hands had fallen on the table, and lay there, impotent and faintly tremulous. There was something painfully moving in the sight of this old woman who had nothing in all the world.

Then Celeste moved and spoke for the first time. "Yes," she said, and there was a passionate undertone to her voice, "let us go out."

CHAPTER XIII

THEY went out into the gardens. The wind had fallen. The moon was floating behind silver gauze. Everything, the trees, the grass, the flower beds, the shrubbery, stood still, as though waiting. A dim spectral light mingled with the darkness, and the earth smelled curiously pungent, as if it breathed out, deeply and silently. They walked away from the great house; its windows, behind the Venetian blinds, were ribbed and yellow. A few steps more, and the house had disappeared, and only the rectangles were visible through the trees.

They passed the greenhouses, dark and deserted. The grass felt dry under their feet, and bruised, gave up its strong hot odor. The shadows under the trees were caves of darkness in a ghostly sea of nebulous moonlight. All at once the last coolness was swept away; a gigantic oven had opened, had flooded the earth. The gauze about the moon thickened. From the west came a faint rumble of distant thunder.

"A storm is coming up," said Adelaide. Old Ann had not come with them. There were only four of them, herself, Agnes, Estelle and Celeste.

"I don't think so," replied Estelle. The air became suffocating, all in a few moments. "Look, the moon is coming out again," and in fact, the gauze about the moon was suddenly torn away and she rose up triumphantly, blazing over the trees. But the clouds that raced across her face at short intervals were like black rags blown in a hurricane. It was strange to see that unearthly blowing of the garments of the storm, when down here it was so still, so motionless. Crickets had been shrilling loudly only a few minutes ago; tree-toads had been piping. Now, everything was darkly silent and hot.

The house stood some distance from the river. All at once they became aware of its voice, like the rush of a far-distant cataract. There was nothing, now, but the hot darkness, the blazing spinning moon, the rising mutter of water.

"Let's go for a ride," said Estelle.

"But there is a storm coming," insisted Adelaide in her

low gentle voice. "I can smell it. The earth smells it, too."

"And what about the men? They'll miss us," said Agnes.

Estelle laughed shortly. "They'll not miss us! I know the signs. They have already forgotten us. If we call ourselves to their attention within three hours they'll be annoyed."

Then, thought Adelaide wearily, Christopher *is* plotting something again. She was filled with dull fear.

They walked back towards the house and the garages. A chauffeur, sitting in one of them and smoking and reading by a sharp electric light, stood up and saluted respectfully. "We want a car, Clifford," said Estelle. "The open Rolls. It is so hot. No, thank you, I'll drive, myself."

"It looks like a storm, Mrs. Bouchard," said the young man doubtfully.

"Nonsense," replied Estelle crossly. "There is no wind. And look at that moon. Please, Clifford, get the car out at once."

Estelle drove out towards the river. Even above the deep purr of the motor, they could hear the rapidly approaching voice of the lightless water. The brilliant lights of the car whittled out a vivid path in the darkness. The hot air rushed across the faces of the occupants of the car, seeming to burn their flesh. Now they were on the river road, and could see the flickering lights across the river. Through masses of trees and shrubbery they could see the river, also, restlessly speaking, running invisibly. The air was cooler here. Adelaide glanced apprehensively at the sky. The moon still spun in her own blazing aura, though the mutter of thunder was deeper and more hollow now.

Adelaide sat with her daughter in the rear seat. She could just see the vague white shadow of the girl's face. Her hair was blowing back from it strongly, and again Adelaide could glimpse the pure, almost stern, modelling of cheek and chin. Her heart lightened a little. Perhaps there was nothing to be afraid of, after all. Celeste was not a weakling. She had given in to Christopher tonight, not because he was stronger than she, but that, for a few moments, she had been stronger than himself. Perhaps only the weak were stubborn; perhaps most of the yielding in the world was inevitably done by the strong.

If so, it was sad, but not terrifying. The compromise of the strong ennobled them. Those who accepted the compromise were doubly injured.

There were few cars on the black smooth road, for this road led almost without exception to the great estates in the neighborhood. At times it seemed to those in the car that

89

they were the only moving thing in the universe, for the water could be heard rather than seen.

No one spoke. Estelle was an expert driver. Her big hands were firm on the wheel, and she had the strength of a man. She increased the speed until the speedometer registered sixty-five miles an hour. She seemed to gain some surcrease from this bludgeoning into the night.

The road was becoming more frequented; they passed more and more cars as they skirted along the watery flank of the city. The air, for all its rushing, had a fetid and dank smell, full of the smoke of the day and the exhalations of thousands of human beings. To the left, the city was a tangle of restless lights. Now, just ahead, they saw a huge plume of dull smoky light blowing against the black heavens, and another, and another. They were approaching the tremendous sprawling buildings of Bouchard and Sons.

Estelle abruptly applied the brakes. "How did I get here?" she demanded, helplessly laughing, as the car came to a stop and the burning air stood over them like water. "I wasn't thinking. Imagine coming out here to this nest of ugliness and smoke and furnaces! Well, business must be good. Night shifts again. I suppose that is some comfort."

Agnes made a wry face to herself. An acrid stench rose from the distant buildings near the river. The great stretches of lighted windows showed pigmy black figures leaping about with almost aimless activity. It was like a sudden picture of hell. Adelaide looked at the mighty plants from which flowed the Bouchard wealth, and the death of the world. But Celeste was turning her face to the river, just as her grandmother's brother, Martin Barbour, had turned his, with the same somber wistfulness and inarticulate pain. She left the others standing about the car, and went quickly and lightly down the slopes. They were littered with debris and stones, the grass gone, the trees long rooted up and dead. Her feet struck gravel and pieces of rusted metal. Here her own grandmother, Florabelle, had played as a child with her brother. But surely in those days there was not this barren hideousness, this scarred and ruined earth. Surely there must have been grass here, and flat sun-warmed stones and trees. Surely the air had been clean and fresh, full of the breath of the river and the breath of the brown ground, and pouring sunlight.

Celeste stood on the old towpath by the river. She could see its iron shadow now, moving. Suddenly, from the opposite shore, raw and savage light leaped into the dark sky, from which the moon had gone. A moment or two later the earth under Celeste's feet vibrated with hoarse sound. And after that the hot black air was twisted, spun, torn, with whips of wind.

Celeste ran back up the slopes. Her mother was calling her. They were all in the car. Estelle was still dismissing Adelaide's assertion that a storm was coming. "Heat lightning; heat thunder," she said.

They turned away from the river. Mean narrow streets ran into the road. They could see the endless rows of workmen's houses. Depression hung heavily on Celeste's heart. She had often heard Christopher malevolently speak of the silk shirts of the workmen, and their multitudinous cars, and their two-hundred-dollar radios. Perhaps all these things were true. But perhaps they were gestures of despair, the momentary delirium of the slave. Perhaps, after centuries of living in houses and on streets like these, and working in steaming infernos like these monstrous factories and plants, they could be forgiven for going temporarily mad. "They save nothing," said Christopher. But why should they save? For a bleak tomorrow? Better a starving tomorrow and gaiety today, than an endless procession of bleakness, however guaranteed. Even the slave might love life and want to feel it for a moment.

Adelaide had thought that Celeste acquiesced unthinkingly to Christopher. But Celeste had always had her thoughts. It was because she loved him that she kept silent.

They turned away from the river. They skirted the southern edge of the city. They could see the flashes of lightning through the trees, but the air seemed cooler and fresher, and there was no thunder, or very little. They were out in the country again, and again this road was almost deserted. Estelle increased speed. "We're in Roseville," she called out to Adelaide and Celeste in the rear.

Roseville. It had not been a fashionable suburb for many, many years. Some of the tremendous and beautiful houses had not been occupied for a decade or more, but stood in the midst of ruined gardens and strangled trees, with placards advertising the estates for sale nailed on gates and trunks. They saw empty and lightless walls through tangled foliage. They saw overgrown drives and abandoned greenhouses and stables. There is nothing so pathetic, so sorrowful, as ruined grandeur, thought Adelaide. Stone fountains, dry and full of dust, waited mutely. New young ivy rustled on stone and wall. But everything else was silent.

All at once, without any warning at all, the earth was dissolved in a vortex of ferocious light, and scattered into

91

fragments by the sledgehammers of stunning thunder. Even Estelle was unnerved. She brought the car to a stop. It stood panting in the shaking silence that had followed the thunder, surrounded with a shell of uncertain light. Everything beyond it was deserted and threatening night. The wind had increased to tempest proportions in a moment. A moment before there had been hot silence; now the trees, the grass, the air, bent and screamed and twisted about, and flew upwards. Everywhere was the faint smell of brimstone, the stronger odors of aroused dust and storm.

"Better get the top up," said Estelle. "Come on, everybody. We'll be drenched in a moment." And, in fact, big hammering drops of water were falling with a sucking sound into the thick dust of the road, and splashing into the faces of the women.

But something was wrong with the top. It would not go up, no matter how they strained and tore their hands and panted. In the meantime, the rain and wind had increased. The lightning was a continuous glare, the thunder shattering. They were lost in a universe of blazing light and crashing sound and wind.

"It's no use," panted Estelle at last. Her face was running with sweat. Her hair was blown about wildly. She looked disgustedly at the others. She had to raise her voice to a shout to make them hear. "We've got to go in somewhere! Shelter! Anywhere! Get in the car. The storm's getting worse."

They had a struggle seating themselves, for the wind almost wrenched them from their feet. Estelle started the car. And now the rain, as though the heavens had opened to vomit forth a cataract, came down on the women. They gasped and choked, trying to shield their faces and eyes. It was no use. The car rumbled forward hopelessly. The thunder stunned and deafened everyone. They felt the car lurching on an abandoned road. The lightning was so brilliant and so continuous that it seemed to them that they were driving through a wall of illuminated water. Adelaide had the impression that they drove through gates, past a small lodge, but that was all. She was too busy trying to breathe.

Then, in a momentary lull of rain, they saw that they had driven to the door of a great gloomy house. They could see its blank shuttered windows. The door was protected by iron grillwork. There was no shelter here. The graystone walls repudiated them, ran with rivers of glistening water.

They regarded the place with despair. They were not deceived by the sudden lull in the storm. And then Estelle shouted. They saw a bobbing but steadily approaching light on the drive. Adelaide remembered the lodge. Apparently it was occupied by a caretaker. They all got out of the car and waited earnestly.

A middle-aged man carrying a shotgun came into view in the aura of his flashlight. With him were two police-dogs, growling and showing their teeth. "What do you want?" he shouted. "Nobody lives here."

Estelle tried to assume an air of dignity and competence, in spite of her drenched hair and face and clothing. "I am Mrs. Francis Bouchard," she said, "and these are Mrs. Emile Bouchard and Mrs. Jules Bouchard, and Miss Bouchard. Bouchard," she repeated impatiently, as he stared, his mouth dropping open. "We've got to find shelter until the storm passes."

He stared, and then slowly removed his hat. But he was still suspicious. "Well, ma'am, if you are Mrs. Bouchard, what's this house?"

Estelle was nonplussed a moment, then she cried angrily: "I'm sure I don't know." Agnes giggled. "It's the House of Seven Gables," she said.

But Adelaide had turned and had been gazing at the house. "Why," she said faintly, "it's Robin's Nest. Estelle, you remember hearing about Alice Bouchard? The granddaughter of Ernest Barbour? You remember, she married Jules' brother, François, and then he committed suicide, right in this house, too, and she took her children and went to New York and married Thomas Van Eyck——"

"You mean Alice?" said Estelle, amazed and intrigued in spite of her misery and wetness. "The one who died in England a year ago?"

"Yes, that's the one. And her children still live there, you know. Edith and Henri, with their stepfather. Her parents, Paul Barbour and Gertrude, built this house. Poor woman. You remember, she was hurt in an automobile accident, and then she died. I knew her quite well. But we never heard of any of them after her marriage. They—they never wrote——"

The caretaker now interposed timidly. "The storm's coming up again, Mrs. Bouchard. If you and the other ladies will follow me, we'll go to the lodge."

"But," Estelle cried, "have you the keys? Good! We'll go in and look around. I suppose there are no lights?"

"Yes, ma'am, there are. You see, we just got word Mr.
93

Henri and Miss Edith are coming home, to live. Here. And we put on the power this afternoon."

While they exclaimed about him, intrigued, he opened the grilled door, and then the other. In the meantime the storm had renewed its fury. They were literally blown into the cool dark mustiness of the reception hall. The caretaker touched a switch, and lights flooded on. They saw the dim polished mirrors of the reception hall floor, mirrors repeated in vistas of distant rooms, all glimmering in the lightning. A graceful and delicate spiral staircase flowed and curved upward like a ribbon, losing itself in the darkness of the high upper floors. The ceilings were exceptionally high, almost vaulted, with pale plaster relief work touched with gilt. The wide entrances to the drawing rooms were flanked with slender white pillars. White marble fireplaces were visible in these and other rooms. But the dining room, broad and deep and high, was panelled and beamed with dark red mahogany.

All the great pier mirrors were shrouded; the furniture, shrouded also, looked like misshapen monsters, crouching. The pictures were down from the walls and packed in canvas, on the floor. Gertrude Barbour's beautiful old grand piano, which her father, Ernest, had imported for her from France, was a dinosaur of canvas, lurking in a corner of the immense "music room." The bookcases in the library were glassed and dark. No rugs were on the floors, which echoed gloomily to the tread of the intruders.

And everything was thick with dust and silence and death.

As she walked with the others through the rooms Celeste had a most profound and terrifying impression. She felt that someone else was walking with them besides the caretaker. She could feel the presence of a young woman, restless and despairing, someone, perhaps, who had died a long time ago. She kept glancing back over her shoulder, expecting every moment to see some shadowy figure, some unearthly face. No other house in all her life had impressed her so extraordinarily. The glimmering lightning, the detonations of the thunder, which shook the walls and the floors, the spectral silence, the dust, the shrouded furniture, the waiting coldness and darkness in hall and corner, all contained a somber meaning for her, which she could not as yet translate. She glanced up the stairway and could not keep herself from waiting to see someone descend.

"It was one of the most beautiful homes in Windsor," said Adelaide sadly. "It still is."

"Oh, heavens," said Estelle, shrugging her damp shoulders. "They haven't built such square rooms as this for ages.

Just huge boxes, with no atmosphere, no styling. No imagination anywhere."

"I don't agree with you," replied Adelaide. "This house is Georgian, and built for the ages."

"I don't like middle-age," said Agnes. "A thing, or a house, for me, has to be truly ancient, or right up to the minute. Houses like these are just stuffy. Too formal and forbidding."

But Adelaide was musing aloud: "I came here only twice. It was very beautiful. The grounds were laid out like a park. The furniture is exquisite. Alice's mother, Gertrude, was known for her taste." She added, sighing: "There is a very mournful story about this house, too."

But the others were not interested in the story. So Adelaide, sighing again, went alone up the stairway and glanced down the wide panelled halls of the second floor. Here a girl had passed half a dozen years of torment and grief and despair. She had died in her father's house, not here, and yet Adelaide felt that her death had really occurred within these walls. How many hundreds of times she had gone up and down these stairs, her hand slipping along these very banisters, her small narrow feet touching these boards, her eyes directed somberly ahead. Adelaide shivered. She turned to go down, and almost screamed. It was a moment or two before she realized that the small figure behind her was Celeste, and not some sorrowful young ghost unable to find peace.

"My dear, you startled me," she exclaimed, in a lull in the thunder.

"I don't like this place. I wish the storm would stop and we could go home. I'm soaked," said Celeste, shivering. "I think this palce is haunted."

Adelaide did not smile. She took Celeste's chilled little hand and went downstairs with her again. At the bottom of the stairs she remembered that Alice's first husband, François Bouchard, had killed himself in this house. Yet it was not he who wandered invisibly and so disconsolately through the corridors.

All at once she had the strangest impulse to tell Celeste the story. She stood there at the foot of the stairs, tightly holding to Celeste's hands, earnestly listening to some mysterious compulsion in herself. The thunder was retreating, and the lightning was wide sheets of baleful glimmerings. The others were exploring back-rooms, and Adelaide could hear Agnes' hard light laughter. The caretaker had disappeared.

They stood in the uncertain well of light and shadow at the foot of the stairs, in the reception hall. Through various doorways they saw the hard bright electric light shining on the dusty polished floors and the shrouded furniture. Everything was motionless and silent.

Adelaide began to speak, gravely yet with quiet emphasis, the compulsion growing stronger within her. And Celeste listened as intently, as though impelled to give all her attention.

"It was very sad," said Adelaide. "Jules—your father—told me the story, a long time ago, long before you were born. You see, he had an older brother, Philippe, a very religious Roman Catholic, your Uncle Philippe, who died many many years before you were born, before your oldest brother, Armand, was born. A long, long time ago. Before I even married your father.

"You know that Ernest Barbour, who—who built up the whole family—was the brother of your grandma, Florabelle Barbour. He had just one daughter, Gertrude. They say he loved her very, very much, perhaps more than he ever loved any other of his children. But he was very ambitious. He had a nephew, his brother Martin's son, and he thought Paul a very remarkable young man, fit to continue the dynasty he had begun. He wanted Gertrude to marry her cousin. But Gertrude loved some one else, your Uncle Philippe."

She sighed. She could not tell all the story, it was too cruel! But she said: "I—I'm not certain about all the details, but in some way Ernest Barbour prevented his daughter from marrying her cousin, Philippe. I think he considered the marriage unsuitable. Any way, Philippe went away to become a priest, and then he—he was sent on some missionary work. Gertrude married her other cousin, Paul, then."

"Did she mind, terribly?" asked Celeste, listening with painful interest.

Adelaide hesitated. If she evaded, the whole point of the story would be lost. It seemed terribly important that the point should not be lost. She said in a low voice: "Yes, she minded, terribly. They—they say it broke her heart when Philippe went away. But she married, and she and her husband built this beautiful house. Then, then she was to have a baby—your Aunt Alice.

"Everyone thought she had forgotten Philippe. But she hadn't forgotten, they discovered."

Adelaide's tired eyes filled with tears. She had wept when Jules first told her the story. It never failed to affect her even to this day.

"And then, just when it was about time for your Aunt Alice to be born, Gertrude heard that Philippe had died, off on some island."

She paused. She was silent so long that Celeste touched her arm quickly. "Hurry, Mama. Estelle and Aunt Agnes are coming back." And indeed their footsteps were heard approaching down one of the first-floor corridors.

"There is not so much more to tell, darling. You see, it was such a shock to poor little Gertrude. No one had realized that she had not forgotten, and that she had just been living a life of misery and suffering since her marriage to Paul. Oh, he was very good to her! Your father said Paul was devoted to her. But that was not enough. She did not love him at all.

"And so—and so, when she heard Philippe was dead, she collapsed. They say she never recovered consciousness, even when your Aunt Alice was born. She died when Alice was not more than an hour old."

Celeste said nothing. Adelaide could see her eyes shining in the gloom of the hall. She waited a long time for her daughter to speak, and then what the girl did say astounded her mother:

"I don't know all the circumstances, Mama, but it seems that Uncle Philippe and Aunt Gertrude were very weak. Nothing in the world should have sent him away from her."

"But, darling, he was a Roman Catholic, and it was considered sinful for a Catholic to marry his cousin."

Celeste shook her head slightly. "I don't know. I have never had any real religious training. But I cannot imagine how any superstition could ever truly affect a thinking person. I know it would not affect me. I know that nothing would ever have kept me from Uncle Philippe, if I had been Aunt Gertrude."

A mysterious weight on Adelaide's heart suddenly dissolved. The compulsion had gone. Something beyond herself was satisfied.

"Celeste, dear," she said gently, "superstitions do not come nicely labelled. They come in the most acceptable forms! Even in the form of 'reason.' They have a thousand names, and among their names each one of us finds a favorite. It is almost impossible to live a single hour without believing in some superstition."

Estelle and Agnes appeared, damp but restored to good humor. Their amiability was due to the discovery of the antiquated plumbing system.

"Roseville is such a decayed and abandoned old suburb,"

97

said Estelle. "Why, there's a chemical factory half a mile from here. We opened a window, and the wind was just right. The stench! Not a soul for miles around, and only these old deserted houses. How those two children could bear to think of coming back here!"

"Remember, they haven't seen this place since they were brats," said Agnes. "I give them a month here. That's all. Why, they're immensely rich, aren't they? They own practically sixty per cent of the bonds in Bouchard, Emile told me."

"Yes, they are very rich," agreed Estelle. Her eyes brightened. Young Henri ought to be around twenty-five or six. Now, if Rosemarie— Her florid cheek flushed with excitement. And that dear child, Edith. She was a year or so older than her brother. Strange that she had not married.

"The poor things," said Estelle aloud. "Orphans, too. We must do all we can for them."

Adelaide smiled palely. "I have a feeling they don't like us. I know that Alice and Jules had a terrible quarrel before she went away. She wrote to me, poor girl. She seemed to like me for some reason, and I was always so sorry for her. And then she and her husband and children went to England, and we stopped writing. But she always expressed herself as detesting the whole family."

Agnes laughed. "Bright girl! However, I suppose we owe a duty—to their bonds. Of course, they won't live here a month when they realize what they've returned to."

She walked idly into the drawing room. A very large picture stood against the wall, shrouded like the others. Something about its size struck familiarly on Adelaide's memory. She followed her sister-in-law. "I believe that's Gertrude's portrait, by Sanger," she said with excitement. "Celeste, I'd like to have you see this portrait. Can we get the wrapping off?"

"Oh, let us be going," said Agnes indifferently. But Adelaide and Celeste were eagerly unfastening the canvas wrapping. Estelle, scrubbing her face with her damp handkerchief, scowled impatiently. The wrapping came off. The full force of the raw electric light struck upon the portrait leaning against the wall.

Celeste saw that it was the portrait of a young girl or woman in the grotesque clothing of the early eighties. She was very thin, the smooth gray satin of the basque bodice hardly rising over small breasts. About her throat was a necklace of yellow gold and violet amethysts. In her little ears were smaller amethysts also set in yellow gold. Her cloud of lusterless dark hair was drawn back in a chignon at the nape of her neck. In the midst of this cloud was a narrow little face, the color of pale ivory. There was no red on the somber young mouth, and no smile; its expression was grave and mournful and inexpressibly weary. The delicate nostrils flared above it. Under a smooth low forehead were wings of black brows, and under the brows, eyes so dilated and yet so heavy, that it was impossible to guess if they were dark or gray. It was not a pretty face, but a delicate and patrician one, full of breeding and sadness and spirit.

Agnes smiled at it critically. "I diagnose tuberculosis," she said. "Did she die of it? She looks imminently on the brink of coughing her way to a better world."

"No," said Adelaide sorrowfully. "She died in childbirth. Alice's mother, you know. Grandmother of Henri and Edith." She added in a low voice: "I think someone told me this was painted three months before she died."

"She looks as though the world was too much for her," said Estelle. "What incompetents women were in those days!" And she felt vaguely comforted at the thought of Rosemarie, who at least was competent and knew what she wanted.

"The world," said Adelaide in a still lower voice, "was indeed too much for her. Just as it always is for the innocent and the pure of heart."

But she had spoken so softly that no one heard her. Agnes and Estelle were going towards the door. Celeste was absorbed in the portrait. At last she looked at her mother.

"She does not look weak," she said. And that was all.

When they reached home they found the men seated before the fire in the drawing room. The air had become chilly after the storm. The women entered, shivering and damp, and went upstairs to change into dry clothing. Much laughter ensued because of misfits. Estelle and Agnes were quite restored to good temper when they all went downstairs again.

The men, thought Agnes, appeared as complacent and as pleased with one another as though they had been dining on the proverbial canaries.

"You don't seem worried about us," remarked Estelle, puffing at a cigarette. She stood before the fire, like a man, warming her back.

"Worried?" repeated Francis. "Estelle, I know you can

always be relied upon to handle such things. Christopher was anxious, a little. But not I. Nor Emile."

Agnes said nothing; she smiled a trifle wryly.

Then Estelle began to tell about their adventure. She spoke with strong excitement. "Those two children! And how remarkable it is that we have never known them. Poor lambs. We must make them regret that they didn't know us sooner."

Christopher had said not a word. But he had listened. And as he listened a pale bright spark appeared in his eyes.

Just before they all said good night, Agnes was reminded of something. She buttonholed her husband, who grinned down at her with extraordinary amiability.

"We saw the plants tonight, too. All shifts on, eh? So business isn't so bad, in spite of the complaints? I thought so. So now we can get that Rembrandt before the Metropolitan gets its claws on it."

Estelle was interested. "But who on earth, these days of peace, is buying all those explosives and things? I thought the war was over."

Christopher said smoothly, with a peculiar smile: "Well, they still build tunnels and railroads, you know, Estelle. They still have to blow up obstacles in the way of new bridges."

"Oh, blow up the bridges!" said Hugo.

For some reason the men laughed. The women laughed agreeably, too. Only Adelaide understood.

And only Adelaide did not laugh.

CHAPTER XIV

WHEN they had been left alone in the dining room, Francis had proposed that they, Christopher, Emile and Hugo, go upstairs with him to his private apartments, "where we can be sure of not being interrupted, or overheard."

They went upstairs in the small grilled automatic elevator, and settled themselves in Francis' living room. He ordered a tray of whiskey and soda and a box of cigars.

For a while they smoked genially, and drank, discussing nothing of much importance. Emile had a nose and a passion for scandal. He had no reticence about women, and no natural chivalry. At present he was having an engrossing affair with a certain lady who was one of Agnes' most intimate friends, and he, he said, found the situation very piquant. Agnes believed that Carol disliked him, and was always trying to "make peace" between them. Carol was a fine actress, and had a most engaging sense of humor, as well as the best legs this side of New York. She also had considerable imagination.

Emile talked at length about his various adventures with the lady, digressing when reminded of some new ribald tale or new and shameful gossip. He had an entertaining way of speaking, and his brother and cousins listened with much amusement. Christopher, especially, laughed almost inordinately, for him. Part of his delight was due to the fact that the lady had previously, and secretly, been his own mistress, and even now she wooed him earnestly, and amused him at every private opportunity with tales about Emile's love-making.

Francis, who had a kind of cold fastidiousness, and knew a great deal more than anyone suspected, distended his thin nostrils at intervals with distaste. However, he laughed as heartily as the others. But as he laughed, he kept glancing at his wrist watch. His long narrow foot tapped the rug. He looked at Emile, whose big ruddy face appeared swollen and gross. Emile's eyes, he thought, were those of a pig. But he thought this without rancor. He never wasted time on rancor. He reserved that pleasure for Christopher. Thinking of Christopher, he glanced at him. And listening to that hard toneless laughter, he smiled to himself.

At the end of the laughter following another story, Christopher said: "Now then, shall we get down to business? We did come up here to discuss business, you know."

Emile still smiled with enjoyment at his last story, and kept chuckling a little under his breath. But his amorous-lidded eyes narrowed.

"Ah, yes," he said. "That reminds me, just what is your connection with Duval-Bonnet, Chris?"

"Yes. Let us come to the point," said Hugo, who already knew the point.

Christopher fixed his cold and vitriolic eyes on his brother and said with quiet distinctness: "I am Duval-Bonnet."

There was a silence while Emile stared, changed color, and stared the more. Then he burst out into prolonged laughter. "You!" he cried when he could catch his breath. "You! Why, you snake in the grass! Where did you get the money, anyway?" He shouted again. "You! Where did you get the money?" But for all his laughter, he was considerably jolted, almost stunned.

Christopher carefully fitted the chilly tips of his fingers together, and over the fleshless tent regarded his brother fixedly.

"I had a little. But you, and Francis, and Hugo, are to supply the rest."

Emile stopped chuckling. He stared more than ever, his eyeballs bulging. His thick lower lip thrust itself outwards. His whole expression became more piggish than before, and brutal. His shoulders rose massively. "Oh, we are, are we?" he said sullenly. He looked at Francis and Hugo. But their faces were impassive and bland. "What is all this, anyway?" he cried at last in an irate voice. "What is all the secrecy?"

"There is no secrecy," replied Christopher. He added after a pause: "Between us."

Emile's face darkened and coarsened. "So they both know, except me? Afraid to trust me?"

"Let us say, rather, merely being cautious," answered his brother, looking him full in the eye.

Emile helped himself to another cigar. It fell from his fingers, which were shaking. No one reached for the fallen cigar, nor, when he retrieved it, did Francis offer him a light. He lit it himself, the flame as agitated as though a wind were blowing upon it. Through the smoke he could see them all looking at him, their expressions as smooth and un-yielding as marble.

He tried to make his voice casual and disdainful: "Well, go on. That is what you brought me here for, isn't it? Or have you changed your minds?"

There was another silence. Then Christopher moved slightly on his chair, and said:

"I will make it brief. But first I must ask you a question: How much money, and power, do you want? And how much longer do you want to be Man Friday?"

Emile said nothing. He saw no one but his brother now. Christopher smiled. "Don't bother to answer! Now, I must digress just a trifle. I will remind you of a tale, and point its moral.

"There was a time when makers of ordnance and explosives and arms went humbly, hat in hand, soliciting orders from governments. This was altered somewhat during the World War. In fact, I recall that Father spoke very gaily of 'I and Lazarus.' Our power was rising. However, it was still hampered somewhat, especially in America, where capitalists and industrialists are the most formidable, and at the same time, the most uneasy. The American people still have the illusion that they are potent in government, and to reassure themselves in moments of suspicion, they teach us a lesson. The anti-trust laws are an example, for instance.

"But, through the assistance of government, which has its own reasons for keeping quiet on various matters connected with the last war, we are becoming powerful. Within a few years we shall be the most powerful force in all the world. Our influence is already penetrating into society, industry and politics. Soon we shall control all of these. We shall literally rule the world. And how, in these days of peace? But you know this simplest of all answers. By preparing for war. The war that is to come. The war which will be bred out of the hatred and envy and vegeance of Germany. The hatreds and envies of all the world."

"You," said Emile, "are telling me Mother Goose. I learnt all this in the nursery."

"But my dear Emile. I am merely reminding you. But I am reminding you, too, of many things that are happening in the world, which will be deleterious to us. Unless we hurry. Unless we strike first, and strike to kill.

"Never has there been an administration in America so sympathetic to our interests as the Coolidge Administration. Coolidge, the dunce in cap and gown and eyeglasses! Why, when he was Vice-President, not a senator and hardly a little congressman would speak to him. Don't you remember that time we met him at Harding's birthday dinner? A mean little Vermont storekeeper, spiritually counting out pounds of lard and sugar, and trying to cheat on a box of crackers. But he's a blessing to us, now that he is President. His naïve prattlings about 'normalcy, the American Way, economy, budget-balancing and sobriety' earn the tearful gratitude and admiration of a whole nation of spiritual shopkeepers, and small businessmen who want to be capitalists and hate the unions. They think he has brought this post-war prosperity about, with his bacon-measuring bony hands!"

"I," said Emile, "enjoy these remarks about Coolidge immensely. I remember I wanted to kick him on the backside. But much as I am enjoying all this, I would enjoy, much more, your getting to the point."

"I am merely reminding you, Emile, of what advantages we are having under Coolidge. But now, to speak of a less pleasant thing, I want to tell you that the happy days of

Coolidge, and of Robber Baron Mellon, are approaching their lamentable end.

"Our best-beloved friend, Mellon of the harpy eyes, has been very kind to us. He has given us remissions on our income taxes, which is very gratifying. He has coined the phrase: 'best Secretary of the Treasury since Alexander Hamilton.' You haven't heard it yet? You will.

"Yes, everything is just too sweet for anything. Now. Just now. But this is not going to last. The world is approaching the day of reckoning, when it will have to pay for the next war, while it is still paying for the last.

"There is coming a day, and perhaps very soon, when all this glorious prosperity will reach its peak, and then decline. Humpty-Dumpty, to speak again of your nursery Mother Goose, Emile, will have a great fall. The world will crack its foolish eggshell all over the premises. And incidentally, when it does, it is going to bellow for vengeance. On us. And by us, I mean, of course, all industrialists and capitalists. And that is the day for which we must prepare."

Emile smiled unpleasantly. "And just what is your plan to save our necks in those days? Provided, of course, that you are not opium-smoking just now?"

"My plan? The same plan which Kronk of Germany, and Schultz-Poiret of France, and Robsons-Strong of England, and Skeda and Bedors, are already working out: the control of government. And how shall we get that control? First of all, through armaments."

Emile thought for a moment, and then said with a mocking air: "I see, teacher! But this is an old game. Ernest Barbour thought of it before you."

Christopher smiled. "An old game. But not until today was it the sole game. The nation, my dear brother, that has the biggest and the best armaments is going to rule the world. I propose that the American government, and incidentally ourselves, rule the world. Kronk and Schultz-Poiret and Robsons-Strong also have this idea for themselves. Let them have it. We shall watch their attempts to do it first, and profit by their mistakes. We shall watch them destroy a dangerous democracy in their respective countries, and learn how to do it with dispatch and a minimum of errors.

"For democracy is the only thing that stands in the way of our supremacy. It is the thing which stands in the way of war and nationalism and patriotism. Therefore, it must be destroyed. Before it destroys us."

Emile was incredulous, and also angry at being made to listen to this absurdity. "Now you are going into metaphysics! You and your calm announcement about destroying democracy! Why, parliamentary government is stronger today in the world than ever before——"

Christopher smiled with disdain. "Do you think so? For instance, you would point out the German Republic to me, wouldn't you, and say that this was an example of the falling of autocracy? There you reveal your lack of observation, Emile. Look at Germany quickly! For tomorrow, there won't be parliamentary government in Germany. Communism? No, there won't be Communism, either.

"In fact, Kronk and his soul-mate, Ebsen of the Steel Company, are doing very nicely. We can learn a lot about constructive or destructive propaganda from the pig-Hun. I have just recently been assured that republicanism in Germany, through the efforts of these two, will soon be destroyed. One of the foremost weapons they have is the Versailles Treaty and its 'injustices.' "

Emile laughed contemptuously. "The Versailles Treaty! Why, my God! the provisions of that Treaty have never been enforced, because of British and American sentimentality!"

But Christopher merely raised his eyebrows and smiled again. "Sentimentality? Emile, you don't do us justice! Not our sentimentality, but our farsightedness, our expediency. Catch a Britisher with an ounce of good will or generosity in him and you catch a freak!

"However, let us get back to the subject: the Versailles Treaty was never enforced. Germany was allowed to survive, and live. British bankers financed her after the war. French banks lent her money. Food after the war was our vengeance on the German population, food for starving children. But all this is carefully soft-pedalled in Germany today, and indeed, throughout the world. The world is being allowed, and encouraged, to forget Alsace-Lorraine and Belgium, and zeppelin air-raids and German prison-camps; it is being helped to forget Hun arrogance and threats and general cowardly ferocity. But the 'injustices' of the Versailles Treaty are being brought forcibly to its attention, the Treaty that was never enforced, and never will be enforced."

Emile had stopped smiling. He regarded his brother intently. "Go on," he said after a moment. "Why was it never enforced?"

Christopher replied gently: "I must repeat, not because of kindheartedness or Christian charity on the part of Britain and France. But just—expediency. Britain, for instance, is afraid that France will grow too strong, and combine with

105

Russia. Britain's ruling classes desire nothing less than that their working classes acquire a decent living standard and become full of beans.

"So what is Britain to do? She must encourage German strength in Middle Europe, so that Germany once more would be a threat to Britain's dupe, France, and to Russian Communism. Communism is the biggest bugbear to Britain's horsy aristocracy today. But Britain never acts directly, and with her bare hands, if she can induce a fool to seize the naked sword for her. So, Britain will make a strong Germany. But a German democracy is in itself a threat to Britain. So Britain will destroy German democracy first of all."

"Now who," asked Emile, "has made you their confidant? Or maybe you just have a crystal ball? Or perhaps you know a good spiritualistic medium?"

But Christopher was unoffended. Emile glanced at Hugo and Francis for answering amusement. But to his surprise they did not seem amused at Christopher's words.

Christopher began to speak again, as though Emile had not asked his nonsensical questions. "I must admit that I am not in possession of the complete plans. In fact, the plans are not complete. They just move on from point to point. However, it is easy to see. Straws are blowing in the wind. We have a few, too. Remember those excellent articles our newspapers have been publishing lately, extolling the new Germany, and absolving the German people from any war-guilt? Do you think these are accidental? Just as accidental as the national attack on 'Reds,' whatever they are.

"Emile, we now hold cards in the biggest game the world has ever seen. And we Americans can win the biggest stake of them all. Regan knows, and all the rest of Wall Street. We know. It is just a matter, now, of making the right moves, and profiting by the mistakes of Europe. It is just a matter of watching until the correct European military alignments are made, and then choosing the better. And, in the meantime, as you know, we are helping to bring the day of military alignments nearer, in conjunction with our dear friends Kronk, Schultz-Poiret, Skeda and Robsons-Strong. I don't need to recall to your memory the various orders we have been filling feverishly for Japan and France and Russia and Britain.

"And so, we are now back where we started. We are now back to Duval-Bonnet."

"Which, you say, you are," reminded Emile. He smiled darkly, but his breath quickened.

Before replying, Christopher reached over to a table and lifted a thin briefcase from it. He opened this briefcase, and withdrew a sheaf of blueprints, which he handed to Emile. "The new bomber," he said. "It makes a speed of over three hundred miles an hour by actual test. And we have tested it over the Everglades. Three times the horse-power of present bombers. Observe those gun-mountings. But go on. Study the prints for yourself. And, incidentally, I might inform you that I own all the patents."

Emile studied the prints. And as he did so his dusky skin paled to a curious clay-color, damp and glistening. Why, Parsons Airplane Company's latest planes and bombers were 1915 "crates" compared to this! If they were practicable—"If they are practicable," he said aloud.

"They are, I assure you," replied Christopher.

And then he gave his brother another sheaf of papers, letters this time, from a certain Russian government agent in New York City, making discreet inquiries about the bomber, and cautiously asking when a certain huge number could be delivered, and at what price.

"That," said Christopher, "is the reason Parsons hasn't secured the Russian order. It is practically mine. I need only to secure the necessary funds to start production at once."

Emile handed back the letters. He seemed loathe to hand back the prints. He let them lie on his knee, and his thick fingers fumbled with them.

"I need not inform you, of course," said Christopher, "that Russia is buying these bombers for Germany. And now Japan is avidly interested. Only a week ago we were approached by the Japanese ambassador. The attack on Manchuria is confidently expected by Robsons-Strong within five or six years, or less. Robsons-Strong is already filling huge armaments orders for Japan, and would like to get the plane orders also. But we shall have these orders, and not Robsons. This is making several British bishops, two former Premiers, and three members of the Royal Family, very angry indeed. If Chinamen are going to be killed, they want a share in the proceeds, and the lion's share, too. The Lion with the jackal's soul!"

Emile wet lips that had gone dry. "How did you get these patents?"

Christopher shrugged. "Is that relevant? I'm sorry, but I shall not tell you. I have them; that is sufficient. It cost me practically every penny I had.

"But let us not digress so much. We all know that Germany is re-arming at a furious rate, and that Robsons-Strong's Italian branch is manufacturing armaments for Germany, and Mussolini is gun-running them into that country. We know that Schultz-Poiret are madly competing, and that within a few short years Germany will be the most formidable military power in Europe. The Treaty of Versailles is completely a dead letter. Germany has at least 1,000,000 men under arms, with the furtive connivance and approval of Britain. And only yesterday, *L'Echo* of Paris soberly declared that Germany cannot remain disarmed in the center of Europe, though it did not go into the reasons why not! Schultz-Poiret's other Parisian newspaper openly approves a larger German army. And so, the arms race is on again, and in time there will be another war, vaster and more profitable than the last."

Emile was still shaken, but he shook his head with a derisive smile. "I suppose you have a *casus belli,* too?"

"Don't be childish, Emile." This was Francis speaking, for the first time. He had moved in his chair, and had lighted another cigar. "Let us stick to business. The *casus belli* will take care of itself. Trust the patriots."

"And the clergy, and the press—and the Bouchards," added Hugo, laughing.

Then Christopher went on to tell his brother about the dummy president and dummy officers he had at the head of Duval-Bonnet. The local Chamber of Commerce was coöperating, and minding its own business. However, money, and a very great deal, was needed at once. That is where Francis, Hugo and Emile came in.

Emile, growing more excited every moment, and flushing deeper, was yet suspicious. He kept glancing at Francis and Hugo pleadingly, hoping to exchange covert smiles with them at Christopher's expense. But they did not answer his pleas. Finally he said: "But what about Jay Regan? You were always his pet, just as our father was. Why don't you ask him to finance you? He would do it, on the strength of these prints alone, and then again, for friendship. He and his associates have always been Bouchard's closest friends."

Christopher smiled sardonically. His motionless eyes studied his brother's face with a sort of stony bleakness. "And Regan has always been one of our largest stockholders, too, and incidentally, of Parsons Airplane. Do you think he'd cut his throat with one hand and put on the bandages with the other? If he took such a chance, he would want the controlling stock. You know him. No, thanks.

"Now, this is my plan: Duval-Bonnet, that is, we, will

incorporate for ten million dollars, and issue one million shares of common stock at ten dollars par. I will retain fifty-one per cent of the stock. You three can buy any amount you wish at eight dollars a share, before it is listed on the Stock Exchange. I expect the stock to reach fifteen dollars when the information about our big Russian orders has been released to the press. The present dummy staff will continue to operate. We stay discreetly in the dark."

The storm had come up without their noticing it. Now the same savage crash that had so unnerved Estelle detonated over the great house. The walls shook. A few moments later the windows were streaming cataracts, and the trees outside were groaning.

But the storm was merely background for the storm that went on inside Francis' sitting room.

For now it developed that Christopher was asking that the forty-nine per cent of the stock, to be purchased by the three others, be paid for in common stock of Bouchard and Sons.

Francis and Hugo already knew of this, and had made their agreements with Christopher. The interests of these two were with Kinsolving Arms; they had no particular regret in parting with a portion of their Bouchard stock. But it was different with Emile. His interests were bound up deeply with Bouchard and Sons. He was in a dreadful state. His cupidity, secret but malignant hatred for Armand, and envy, and inordinate lust for power and influence, had been fully aroused by Christopher. His vivid imagination had already ascended the mountain of probability, and had seen the distant and splendid landscape. Nevertheless, he rapidly passed from derisive skepticism to reasoning, from pleading to threats, from offers to counter-offers, and then back to threats again. Christopher, he declared, his face and thick neck a bright purplish red, could go to hell with his comic-opera company. He, Emile, would have no part in this.

Francis and Hugo enjoyed this raving and threatening and shouting very much. They sat back in their chairs, Francis with his frigid half-smile, and Hugo with his jovial politician's grin. They knew very well that nothing on earth could persuade Emile to relinquish this opportunity. They knew what passions the idea had already aroused, what turbulence it had brought boiling to the surface. They knew, too, that Christopher knew all this, and their enjoyment was all the more. For Christopher merely sat quietly, presenting to them his bitter razor-profile, his enigmatic smile.

When Emile would pause for breath, Christopher's sharp and unemotional voice would cut in, repeating the terms.

The daily masquerade of friendship between the brothers had been ruthlessly dropped. Christopher had never been deceived about Emile. But Emile, who had been vastly the better off, due to Jules' will and to his own position as vice-president of Bouchard and Sons, had sadly underestimated Christopher. No one had enjoyed Christopher's humiliation at the hands of Jules more than he. No one had chuckled with more pleasure on learning the terms of the will. Too, Agnes had brought him an immense fortune. All in all, Christopher, in comparison, had been the "poor relation." In consequence of all this, Emile's manner towards his younger brother had always been more than slightly patronizing and tinged with good-natured chaffing. At times it had been positively indulgent, and his voice had frequently had a cavalier undertone in it. When Armand had given those very generous gifts to Christopher, impelled by his uneasy conscience and apprehension, Emile had internally raged. When Christopher made a brilliant suggestion, Emile also applauded with the others, but there had always been a little mockery in his applause, and secret resentment. He never, as was his usual custom, made derogatory remarks about Christopher, but he would always laugh the loudest at the remarks of others. Christopher's coolness and silence, intellect and subtlety, never failed to enrage Emile, for they made his own volubility, coarseness and ribaldry the more offensive. Once Agnes had declared that Christopher was the closest approach to a gentleman that the Bouchard family had produced, and Emile had another grudge to hold against his brother.

Emile had been under the impression that Christopher had a thick skin, or, with reason, had seen his own inferiority and had meekly accepted the results of it. Now, as he sat opposite Emile, unperturbed and enigmatic and full of aloof contempt, Emile saw very clearly that Christopher's skin had not been thick, and neither had he realized or accepted any "inferiority." Emile saw that Christopher despised him, and had nothing but malignance for him, and that he was enjoying this moment perhaps more than any other moment in his life. Instead of this enraging Emile the more, it frightened him, for he was a natural lackey at heart, and servile to those stronger than himself.

His hatred increased with his fright, and his cupidity was greater than both. Nevertheless, he clearly saw what game Christopher was playing.

"You want to get more control of Bouchard!" he shouted. "You slippery little rat! But I won't give it to you! I'll spike your guns; I know what you're up to. And unless you withdraw your unreasonable demands I'll feel justified in informing Armand about the whole thing."

He had got to his feet. His big, but rather short, legs were planted far apart, his massive shoulders bent as though he were about to charge. His arms were long in proportion to his legs, and swung like the arms of an anthropoid in a rage. His short thick neck was thrust forward; his big jowled face was darkly flushed, and his small jet eyes glittered with malevolence and fury.

No one was perturbed; Hugo continued to grin. Christopher merely looked at his brother with his "Egyptian" eyes. But Francis spoke coldly:

"I wouldn't even consider telling Armand, if I were you, Emile. You own quite a lot of Parsons stock, don't you? Yes. You see, if you tell Armand, we'll have to move fast. We own some Parsons, too; we'll dump that on the market. Worse, we'll make our airplane plans public, and you know what news about the superiority of our bombers will do to Parsons stock right now! That little French order, for instance, is in a critical stage. No doubt it will be withdrawn immediately." He shook his head sadly. "Let us see: just how much money will you lose in the ruin of Parsons? Too, too much, I am afraid."

Hugo chuckled. "Whereas, if you are sensible, you will be able to buy a lot more of Parsons stock later. In the meantime, we'll keep ours, and keep up its price, in spite of Duval-Bonnet."

Emile directed all his attention now to Hugo and Francis. He made a gesture of despair. "But don't you see? He is conniving to get control of Bouchard and Sons! I don't know how he will do it, but I have a feeling he will——"

Francis shrugged. "Christopher in control of Bouchard will be an immense advantage for the company. Armand is a tub of lard. But Chris isn't a superman, after all. Don't flatter him," and he smiled.

Emile simmered in his rage and hatred and despair. But he was less panic-stricken now. It was absurd, of course, the idea that Christopher would be able to gain control of Bouchard. Emile gave a short bitter laugh. However, his apprehension persisted. He sat down. He chewed his lips and glowered at his boots.

He was silent for a long time, while the rain roared at the windows. When he looked up, he saw that Christopher

111

had gone to the windows and was looking out at the dark windswept gardens. Something in his attitude reminded Emile of their father.

Emile spoke at last with sullen bitterness: "I see you rats have got me in a corner. All right! Count me in with you."

He regarded them somberly. "But I think it's a dirty trick on old Armand."

The others stared at him unbelievingly for a moment. Then they burst into genuine shouts of laughter. Even Christopher, turning from the window, was convulsed with mirth. And after a few scowling moments, Emile joined them, at first sheepishly, and then loudly.

CHAPTER XV

ALICE BARBOUR BOUCHARD, mother of Henri and Edith, "the exiles," had married the youngest brother of Jules, François, in 1898. Alice was the granddaughter of the "Old Devil," Ernest Barbour, founder of Bouchard and Sons, and a great heiress. The marriage had been manipulated by Jules Bouchard, for the purpose of pirating the control of Bouchard and Sons, which had originally been called Barbour-Bouchard. It had been a clever manipulation, and had made him several mortal enemies, which had not troubled him in the least.

François had always been a "miserable thing," and had passionately believed himself a poetic genius. At any rate, he was nothing else. Young Alice, seventeen years his junior, had also believed in the authenticity of his genius. They had gone to live at Robin's Nest, a beautiful suburban estate built by Alice's parents. There an amazing change had come over Alice, "the starry-eyed little imbecile" (to quote Jules). She no longer cared to sit with her feverish husband, discussing his soul and his soul-malaise. She no longer wrote bad poetry, or any sort of poetry. She became the shiningly wholesome petty bourgeoise housewife. She bore François two children, Henri and Edith, and managed them adequately. She also managed her husband. She managed him so well that when Edith was fifteen and Henri was fourteen, François committed suicide, in February, 1915.

The suicide was a profound shock to all the Bouchards, though they had despised François, and had come to suspect his adequate, hard-eyed young wife. No one, in their awkwardness and resentment, seemed to know just what to do, except Jules, as usual. It was he who managed everything. It was he who plotted everything. And so it was, when he called upon his sister-in-law, five days after her husband's funeral, that he had it all laid out in his mind, all the guns charged, all the maneuvers ready.

He had chosen a time to call upon his sister-in-law when he was certain she would not be receiving sympathetic friends and relatives. It was ten o'clock in the morning. Fifteen-year-old Edith and fourteen-year-old Henri were still at home, and decidedly bored at this enforced absence from their private schools. They had known very little of their chronically distressed and melancholy father, who had lived a somber life apart in his own rooms on the third floor, and who, when he appeared at the table at night, seemed fumbling and bewildered and dimly suffering. He never lectured them or crossed them, as did their mother, though occasionally, when they chattered too much at dinner, or quarrelled (at the instigation of their mother) he would scream at them suddenly and violently, as though they had intruded upon a slowly tortuous pain. At rare times he would speak to them, and question them about their lives and their lessons, but always with that distressed expression on his dark emaciated face, as though he were speaking mechanically over torment. But he gave little evidence of any affection for them; rather, they appeared to frighten him and make him suspicious. He was uneasy and hesitant with them, and knew they ridiculed him. Sometimes they infuriated him when they made a row in their own rooms, and he heard them, and when his blazing eyes and tormented face appeared at their door, and he shrieked at them, they gloated even in their fright and nervousness.

They were sharp children in many ways, mentally and physically. They had sharp cold eyes, sharp lips, sharp bony faces, sharp darting hands, sharp shoulders and sharp voices and manners. At an early age they had discerned that their mother both indulged and patronized their father. Alice had developed a very brittle and authoritative voice, which dominated everything in her household. It was never so brittle and authoritative as when speaking to François, whom she treated like an overgrown and half-witted child. Later, they discerned that she no longer indulged him, but patronized him and despised him. They took their attitude

113

from her, and when in contact with their father, patronized and despised him also.

They knew that he had once written poems. There was a red morocco copy of them in their mother's sitting room, as late as Henri's seventh birthday. But after that they were no longer in evidence, nor was a copy to be found. Once, about a year ago, Edith had asked idly about her father's poetry, and Alice had smiled a little tightly, as though acidly amused. Sometimes, when a maid reported that they were making a great deal of noise in their rooms, Alice would appear with great irritation, and in a loud and meaningful voice, and with a glance at François' doors, would tell them to be quiet, and did they wish to disturb their father, who was no doubt composing a magnificent poem today? Before she was out of their hearing, they would giggle in the hallway, but Alice would never glance back admonishingly, and the giggling would continue until their governess, in despair, would literally drag them away.

The governess, Miss Hathaway, had been dismissed six months before François' suicide. She had been a member of the household since Henri had reached his fourth birthday and the nursemaids had been dismissed. Jules Bouchard had known her quite well, for she was a youngish woman of dignity and breeding, who ate with the family at home dinners. He had admired her very much, for, though she was not at all pretty, and was in her middle-thirties, she yet had a species of beauty. Her skin was a pale clear tan, vibrant and colorless, and she had a wide full mouth, darkly red, firm yet gentle. Her eyes were brown and disconcertingly clear, and very intelligent.

For the rest, she had straight gleaming brown hair, which she wore in a smooth pompadour above a wide low brow. She was tall, too thin for the prevailing style, and invariably wore clothing exclusively of the Gibson Girl type: sleek shirtwaists, high boned collars and serge skirts, and sailor hats. The Bouchard children made much fun of this outmoded dress of Miss Hathaway's, which was very conspicuous in a day of luxuriant hairy puffs and curls and "bangs" and fringes, "peek-a-boo" georgette blouses and satin camisoles, polished kid boots with thin tall heels, slit hobble skirts surmounted by flaring wired peplums, and gay toques aswirl with drooping ostrich feathers. She seemed grotesquely out of date in an era of tangoes, "bunny hugs," "turkey trots," and two-steps, Teddy Roosevelt and big red automobiles, ragtime and Irene Castle, militant suffragettes and "parlor socialism," and all the glitter, the bold rouged faces, the noise and raucous clamor, and intense vulgar fever that had taken possession of America in the first decade of the Nineteen-hundreds. This was probably because she was a lady, and ladies were already going out of style with gay speed. No one could imagine her reading the new "daring" books or attending the new and delicious "problem plays." Neither could anyone imagine her as having (O delightful and naughty and thrilling word!) "sex."

Alice had never liked Miss Hathaway, but everyone assured her enviously that she had a treasure in this graduate of Vassar and daughter of a minister who had died in poverty but with a reputation for great learning. Moreover, Miss Hathaway's ancestors had been among those who had founded Windsor, and though her father's house had been dingy and small and leaking, it had also been firmly fixed in the very center of Oldtown. Everything about her was impeccable, which was partly the reason for Alice's dislike.

She had been dismissed rather abruptly, for Alice explained that the children no longer needed her. They went immediately to private schools in Windsor, and next year it was arranged that Edith was to go to a finishing school in New York. Miss Hathaway had apparently not sought another post as yet: she was in the dingy leaking old house, living with her father's old maiden aunt, reported to be over eighty, whom Miss Hathaway supported, assisted by a very meager annuity left her by her father.

Jules was taken to Alice's sitting room on the second floor, where he found her just finishing her breakfast coffee. Her tray was still before her, and the silver coffee pot and silver service and fine china gleamed in the mingled light of red fire and sun. The large luxurious room, with its white bearskin rugs and pale green damask furniture and gold satin window draperies and rich thick rugs, was warm and quiet and fragrant with the scent of coffee and bowls of roses. Outside, dry bitter snow lay on the window ledges, and there was a view of black trees coated in crystal and snow-patched brown lawns and curving driveways.

Alice, as she drank her coffee and nibbled at her muffins, was dictating to her secretary, a neat small woman with a distinct bald spot on the top of her meek bowed head, stereotyped replies to letters and telegrams of condolence. Alice's maid was already preparing her wardrobe for the day, for the girl kept coming to the doorway that led into the bedroom and respectfully asking questions, to which her mistress replied in a listless and discontented voice.

When Jules entered, Alice brightened visibly. "How nice

115

of you, Jules!" she said with real animation. "I am so dull and sad this morning. Do sit down." Then her expression became petulant again. "I do hope it is not business, so soon, Jules?"

"Not business, my dear," he replied, smiling sympathetically, "though we must have a talk eventually, you know. But I'll try to make it as brief as possible at that time."

One of Jules' most efficacious arts with women was the ability to infuse admiration and devotion into his glance. Under that eye and that glance, Alice touched her dark red masses of hair, which lay on her shoulders, and smoothed the folds of her deep blue velvet morning gown. She assumed a touching and child-like expression, full of bereavement and grief, and then smiled bravely and wistfully.

"I don't know what I'd do without you, Jules," she said with a sigh.

Jules studied her furtively, maintaining miraculously as he did so his admiring and sympathetic manner. She seemed much recovered, he thought, though her eyes were still red-rimmed, her face haggard. But she had touched her cheeks with rouge, which gave her a somewhat hard appearance, and her lips were reddened. Sixteen years had changed her amazingly. In this woman of thirty-four, petulant and demanding, greedy and selfish, fashionable and sharp, there was little of the soft and vapid young Alice who had written and quoted poetry, been concerned over her "soul," completely unaware of the reality that waited outside her cotton-wool existence. At that time, unknown even to the astute Jules, all that she was today had apparently been latent. In certain lights, her eyes lost their dark polished blueness and became quite pale, almost colorless, singularly like the "Old Devil's."

Studying her still, Jules remembered Leon's remark: "Alice has developed into quite a bitch in the last few years." Yes, he thought, there was no doubt that Alice was a bitch. His smile became tender. She touched her eyes with her scented lace handkerchief, sighed deeply, seemed to sink into despondency. However, when her secretary murmured a question, she replied to her with swift rudeness and short courtesy. The abashed woman rose, gathered up the basket of notes and her papers, and crept from the room.

"It is horrible to have to attend to these things, after— after this awful time," said Alice in a trembling voice.

"I can understand that, my dear," replied Jules. Asking permission, he lit a cigar. Alice flipped open a small silver box on the table and took out a cigarette, which Jules suavely lighted for her. She began to puff at it nervously. A little color appeared under the false tint on her cheeks, and she seemed to drop several years.

"Sometimes, Alice," began Jules affectionately, "I've thought, during the last few days, that you had something on your mind, something that affected you even beyond your natural grief and shock. Don't you want to tell me about it? I've heard a woman must always have a confidant." His smile became tenderly amused. "Will you let me help you? Will you make me your confidant?"

At this adroit appeal to her self-pity, and to her own conviction that she had been vilely misused, Alice burst into genuine tears. Jules, cursing her internally, consoled her with such success that she dropped her head on his shoulder and clung to him. She exploded into rapid and incoherent speech, sobbing aloud, wringing her hands, exclaiming, imploring his pity, defending, denying, and through it all, denouncing François with venom and badly suppressed rage and hatred. And Jules listened intently, his eyes glinting over her bent head, his hand pressing hers.

François, he gathered from the ejaculations of his brother's widow, had been "completely impossible, and so very, very strange," for nearly two years. Though, of course, he had always been peculiar, and very distressing, with his absolute refusal to enter into his wife's social life and interests. He had shown no interest in his poor children, who could not help, of course, comparing their odd family life with that of more fortunate and normal families. He had accused her shrilly, and with really terrible violence, of having no "soul," "as if," she added bitterly, "she had not been the president of the Windsor Literary Club for ten years, and one of the charter members, and as if her opinion was not constantly quoted upon a number of artistic subjects! Why, she was an acknowledged authority on Browning and Wordsworth and Longfellow, and whatever small culture Windsor possessed was almost entirely owing to her!"

But François had become worse and worse. Finally, he had made his appearance at the dinner table about once a week, and that only when he was certain no guests were present. When he did appear, he had sat at the table in unkempt and slovenly silence, his face sunken into livid hollows, his eyes swollen and hidden, his lips cracked and dry. The children had had a hard time, in spite of their mother's controlling glances, to keep their faces straight. Often François seemed not to realize where he was, and suddenly, without eating at all, he would get up and leave the dining

117

room. As time went on, Alice saw him less and less, until there would be actually two or three weeks, though they lived in the same house, between the times they met.

One day she had become really concerned about him, a purely wifely concern, in spite of the way he had humiliated her and made her the object of all Windsor's sympathy and derision. At this point the narrative was temporarily lost in a welter of accusations, cries, sobs of self-pity, and only became coherent again after Jules had renewed his murmurs of sympathy and gentle indignation. Well, this day she had gone quietly up to his rooms, which were in a really terrible condition, so untidy and undusted, very much as his mother's rooms had been just before she had died. Alice found her husband kneeling on the hearth stuffing sheets of paper furiously and madly into the fire. Among them she saw the one remaining red morocco-bound copy of his published poems. As he knelt there, doing this extraordinary thing, he had wept and cried out insanely. Alice had stood near by, unobserved, stupefied, unable to move. When her husband had finished, he huddled on the hearth, watching the bonfire, and he had laughed! And such a laugh! It was too terrible to hear.

Alice must have made a sound, for he turned his head and looked at her. She was certain he did not really see her, but he glared at her wildly and screamed: "I never was a poet! I never wrote a word of real poetry! I've been a fraud and a fool all my life!"

Then all at once he had stopped, and appeared to see her, quite suddenly. His eyes had taken on a mad glaze, and his teeth had glittered in his unshaven face. He had uttered one peculiar cry, and jumping to his feet, had sprung at her, striking her full across her cheek. Alice, in great terror, had run out of the room.

He must have gone quite mad after that, for she heard him raving upstairs for hours on end. The servants were terrified, and Alice kept the children below. Finally, he had become utterly quiet, and Alice had tiptoed upstairs to the third floor. And there, on the upper steps, she saw an astounding thing. François was sitting on the top stairs in Miss Hathaway's arms! His head was on her shoulder. She was holding him quietly, murmuring so softly that the sound was almost inaudible. Alice had stood there in the shadow of the stairwell, unable to believe her eyes. The shameless woman was actually rocking him gently in her arms, and he was clinging to her. In a hoarse and broken voice, he would repeat over and over, almost humbly, like a sick

118

child: "But I have loved beauty. I have loved beauty!" And she had gone on murmuring, soothing him. Alice did not know how long this had gone on, but finally François became silent. Alice then went up the rest of the stairs, trembling with fury and detestation. And that woman, that brazen and dreadful woman, had looked at her calmly above François' head, and had said: "He is asleep now. He will be better." And Alice saw that she was crying silently, herself.

Alice had gone downstairs again, without a word, leaving them there. She did not know what happened after that. But François, it was reported to her, had been removed to his bed in some way, and he had slept until the following night.

Alice called the family physician, who, after examining François, said he had had a nervous breakdown and must be kept very quiet.

Now, she must admit she was a tolerant woman, went on Alice, sobbing more and more. She had been willing to overlook what might possibly have been an accident. When Miss Hathaway had appeared at the table at breakfast, Alice did not allow herself to show any expression of indignation or disgust. By her attitude, she allowed Miss Hathaway to gather that the incident was closed. That night there were no guests at dinner, for Alice had been invited to dine out, but had naturally remained at home. To her amazement, as she sat there with the children and Miss Hathaway, François appeared, for the first time in weeks. But the most astonishing thing was that he had bathed and dressed for dinner, combed his hair, cleaned his nails, shaved. He had looked young and relaxed again, fresher than in years, though he was fifty-one years old, and sick. He had actually smiled, looking at Alice humbly; he had spoken to the children. He did not speak to Miss Hathaway at all, but he kept looking at her. Finally, he saw no one else. And she had only smiled at him, in her sly fashion.

After that, things were intolerable. It was shameful. François would go into the children's rooms, just to be near the woman. He would stop her in the hallways; he would go for walks with her when she took the children out. They would meet in the garden, quite openly, but that was just their foxiness. He grew fresher and younger; once or twice Alice heard him laugh. Finally, the servants began to giggle and whisper. It became intolerable. After a month of this, Alice discharged the wretch of a woman.

When François heard of this, he lost all decency, all self-respect, all pride, all remembrance of his wife and his children. He had screamed and raged; he had tramped up and down the stairs for hours. He had shouted his love for the creature; he had wept and blasphemed and accused Alice of all sorts of terrible things. He had called her vile names. And then he had gone back to his rooms, and had become what he had been before. In six months, his wife saw him half a dozen times, and then only by accident, and at a distance.

Then, a week ago, he had done the irreparable thing, the unpardonable thing, to his wife and children: he had shot himself. He had not left a single word, either of excuse or blame, or asking for forgiveness.

Having reached this point in her narrative, Alice's face was blotched and swollen, scalded with tears. How much she had had to bear! Her dear Papa had been only too right in opposing her marriage to François. If she had only listened to him! But this was her punishment. She had married a fool and a madman, and she had never been anything but the best of wives. She had loved him to the last, but now she could not forgive him. She had protected him as much as possible, keeping up a brave front so people might not suspect anything. And he a man old enough to be her father! There was no doubt he had been mad. But hadn't he had a relative or something who had committed suicide ages ago?

Jules was silent a moment. There was a leaden tint under his brown skin. Then he looked at Alice fully. Yes, he said quietly, his father's brother, Jacques, had committed suicide, somewhere around 1850, or so. Alice, triumphant, nodded her head.

Then Jules, holding her eye, said slowly: "But there was quite a story about it. I believe he killed himself because he was in love with your grandfather, Martin Barbour."

Alice's triumph suddenly faded; her expression became shocked, repulsed. Her face wrinkled in disgust and horror. Then, unable to take her eye away from Jules' basilisk stare, her blotched cheeks turned gray with fear and understanding of him.

"You should not have told me that, Jules," she said faintly. She put her hands to her forehead. "Why did you tell me? You must have had some dreadful reason!"

In a surprised voice, he assured her he had had no reason. Again he expressed his sympathy for her, and said that François, poor devil, had always been a fool. But Alice made no

120

reply. Her hands partially hid her face. Once or twice she shivered.

When he had gone, she dropped her hands slowly into her lap.

He is an evil man, she thought, with a sort of terror. He came here to find something out! But what was it? Did he find it out? Was that the reason he flung that—that filthy story into my face?

François' personal estate was valued, after his death, at less than seven hundred thousand dollars, most of which had been his inheritance from his mother. His will was dated some ten years before, and, as was to be expected, it had been dictated by Alice, his wife. Everything he possessed was left entirely to "my beloved wife, Alice Barbour Bouchard, to control, use, retain or dispose of as she may see fit." He named his wife as sole executor. Very little of the estate was in preferred or common stock of Bouchard & Sons or its subsidiaries; pratically all of it was in bonds of that company and its subsidiaries.

In this, was the astute and urbane hand of Jules Bouchard. It had taken him five years of wooing and courting and flattering Alice, of gaining her entire confidence and trust, to get her to accept bonds of Bouchard & Sons and subsidiaries in exchange for her huge and controlling shares of stock. She retained only fifteen per cent of the stock after these careful and skillful negotiations, which Leon and Honore had watched with passionate interest and crossed fingers. Jules had appealed to Alice's greed; by some method or for some reason, the stock of the company had been forced down twelve points two years after Alice had become her grandfather's heir, and Jules had pointed out to Alice the fluctuations that took place in her fortune, and the danger of retaining common stock, or even preferred stock. But bonds! Ah, there was stability, there was security, there was bed-rock! Five years later she had her bonds and fifteen per cent of the stock, and Jules, Leon, Honore and Andre held controlling interest in the great company. In exchange for her reasonableness, François, though never now appearing on the board of directors, still received his salary.

Once Alice had visited her Aunt Lucy in New York, and had told her complacently of the converting of her controlling shares of the company into bonds. She asserted that she would not know what to do without Jules, who managed all her affairs so carefully and expertly, and gave her such splendid advice, practically relieving her of tiresome details in the management of her estate. In the midst of her eulogy about Jules, she became aware that old Lucy was gazing fixedly at a point above her head, and when she petulantly turned to see what engaged her aunt's attention, she saw that Lucy was staring at the portrait of Ernest Barbour.

"Your grandfather," remarked Lucy, "I do declare, looked about to burst out laughing!"

Lucy would not elaborate on this crude remark, but Alice's suspicions were aroused. She investigated secretly, herself, consulted discreet lawyers in New York and Philadelphia, but found that she had not at all been robbed or manipulated, except in losing the controlling power in the company. She asserted, to one attorney, that she did not care about this at all, and would rather be safe. The attorney, shrugging, remarked that probably her son, Henri, might wish differently some years hence. Appalled at this, Alice had returned to Windsor seething with rage and hatred, had called upon Jules and had made a terrific scene, weeping, screaming, calling him a thief, ruining her children, robbing her of her grandfather's legacy. Branding Jules a liar and a cheat and a brigand, she demanded that he surrender his power of attorney, and then she had gone home to rail at a passive and indifferent and numb François. In six months, she responded coldly to one of Jules' many and persistent overtures, and though she declared she would never trust him again, she gave him power of attorney once more. The reconciliation was a tremendous relief to the self-absorbed young woman, for her affairs had gotten into a mess during the period she and her attorneys had handled them. Besides, she was fascinated by Jules, and found his company delightful and stimulating. No one could flatter her so subtly, make her feel so warm and beautiful and poised.

But after Jules' visit to her five days after François' funeral, fear, despair and confusion assailed her to the extent of filling her with dread and panic. Her friend had been no friend: she realized what manner of man he was, and in the appalled and bitter daylight of her realization, she saw completely what he had done to her over a number of years, what he had always been after, how she had been betrayed and cajoled into his hands. But worse than all was the violent fist-blow to her vanity: he had been her friend, not because he was fond of her, or admired her, or really spoiled her, but because he had wanted to use her, had wanted what was hers. Awakened now, she remembered in a sudden lightning flash the day of her marriage, François' ecstatic praise of his brother, who was helping them, and the mysterious manner in which obstacles smoothed themselves out.

Horrified, the poor woman stared in fascination at what had been done so outrageously to her. She had been a lamb led to the slaughter, led to Jules' abattoir. No one had helped her, warned her, though Leon and Honore and Andre and others must have known. But then, by that time, it was too late. The Bouchards! What had her father called them? Thieves, subtle, crafty, plotting Frenchmen! Her poor Papa! How he had warned her, tried to save her, tried so desperately to protect her against these slaughterers, these merciless pirates! But she had defied him, left him, broken his heart, and now she was being punished. The most sincere and abject tears were shed by Alice for weeks after this, and she refused to see anyone connected with the Bouchard family. She took her children and went to New York for a long visit. When François had been dead thirteen months, she became quietly engaged to her honest and tender cousin, Thomas, whom she could trust, and whom she now respected for his long devotion to her. Two months later she married him, and told him frankly that it was a relief to her to shed the name of Bouchard, and that even if she had not been as fond of him as she was, she would have married him merely for his name. When old Lucy died of a stroke while her son and his wife were on their honeymoon, Alice returned to the house on Fifth Avenue and took up where Lucy had left off. Robin's Nest, in the suburb of Roseville, was boarded up and deserted. Thomas made a kind and indulgent stepfather to Alice's children, and was so successful in winning their affection that he became one of the few creatures whom they ever loved.

The enmity between Jules and his family on the one hand and Alice on the other never was lessened. Alice had liked her sisters-in-law, and when they came to New York after her marriage, she entertained them formally and pleasantly. But their husbands never entered her house. She bore Thomas no children. Within a year of her marriage, the society sections of the newspapers spoke of her as "a leading young matron," and her dinners and banquets and parties, even in frugal wartime, were given lavish space.

Alice's hegira was a relief to Jules. He had always disliked her. Had she been a sweet innocuous woman like Adelaide, his wife, he would have been fond of her in a way, though this would not, of course, have prevented him from manipulating her. But she had been vain and vapid, shallow and cunning, greedy and really heartless, all the things he hated in women.

The Bouchards knew quite a bit, but not all, of what had

taken place. Some of them expressed a lukewarm indignation against Jules. But he had been the victor, and in their realistic philosophy, the victor was always virtuous, or at least justified. Besides, no one had particularly liked Alice or François or their children, while Jules was either loved or hated with fervor. Even those who hated him were fascinated by him.

But of them all, Christopher knew the most. He was the most like his father, and he understood things instinctively, for there was much that Jules did that Christopher would have done, and Christopher knew this.

Understanding so much, he knew he had only to wait. And wait he did.

CHAPTER XVI

IT WAS the latter part of June, now, and the air was like lukewarm water. The wide lawns were a dazzle of green, the poplars tapered pillars of moving leaves. The hot sky pressed down over the earth like heated blue glass, and the air under it fumed and danced. But still Celeste and Adelaide and Christopher and the household had not yet gone to Crissons.

Adelaide was puzzled, but secretly grateful. She did not like the seashore very much, for it was damp. She was alternately afraid of and antagonistic to the people who visited Crissons upon her reluctant invitations, which were inspired by Christopher. She had always had a delicate skin, and the raw sunlight and hard salt winds injured it. Being fastidious by nature, she was revolted by the sight of half-naked rumps and wet bare thighs on the sands. She did not consider the average human form something which should be displayed indiscriminately. Once Christopher had declared that most of the women lying on the beaches looked like bloated corpses just washed in, and though she shuddered at the simile she admitted its truth. Then there were the sports which bored and wearied her. She found the summer dull and exhausting, full of noise and sand and boiling blue ocean and heat and uncongenial people.

But what was delaying their usual departure? Adelaide

did not know. Every one else was puzzled, also, for Christopher's household was usually the first to depart.

But discussion of Christopher's unusual delay was lost in the indignation, incredulity and conjecture occasioned by Henri and Edith Bouchard, recently returned to the house where they had lived as children. Days before the two actually returned, the ladies of the Bouchard families had written informal and affectionate little notes to the house in Roseville, expressing their pleasure at the return of the exiles. They knew to the minute, these ladies, when Henri and Edith actually arrived. They waited one day, then called singly or in groups. They were gratified and amazed at the change in the grounds, which had been hurriedly but beautifully landscaped. The French windows of the house stood open on the rear terrace. There was an air of suaveness, dignity and charm about the house and grounds, which had certainly not been there for years. And then the most exciting and amusing thing had already happened: owners of old houses in Roseville, hearing of the imminent return of one of the wealthiest of the Bouchard families, had suddenly taken an interest in their abandoned former domiciles. Several of them, who had luxurious town apartments or houses, had decided to return, at least temporarily, in order to discover if the exiles really intended to live at Robin's Nest. If they did, then the other owners would seriously consider returning. As a result, there was an enormous amount of activity going on in the suburb. Gardeners appeared in droves. Grounds were active. Formerly shuttered and boarded windows admitted new summer breezes. The old tennis courts were put into condition. Real estate values, naturally, boomed. Several families postponed going away for the summer, on hearing a rumor that Henri and Edith would not go away.

But when the Bouchard ladies, and the other ladies of the suburb, called upon the exiles, they were met by cold-faced if courteous servants, and respectfully informed that Miss Edith and Mr. Henri were "not at home." Cards were left by the bewildered ladies. But no word came from the elusive two. Invitations were mailed. After a prolonged delay Edith's secretary wrote polite but cold regrets. The telephone calls were answered as coldly: Miss Edith and Mr. Henri were still "not at home."

Windsor was thrown into the most intense excitement. Those who had returned to the suburb were actively visited by friends from town. Some of them reported having seen Edith and Henri in their cars on the road. Their bows had been returned with slighting coldness and silence. Edith, they said, was very plain and dark and colorless, but quite definitely smart. Her brother was lighter, but a rather sullen young man, stocky and of a brutal if vital appearance. Neither was ever seen in town. And then, at last, visitors were not admitted through the gates, but were met and refused admission by the caretaker.

Excitement gave way to affront and indignation. "Why," asked Estelle, "if they had no intention of resuming relations with the family, and becoming part of the community, did they ever come back here?"

Every one else was puzzled and asking the same question. But Christopher had an idea. The more he thought of the reason the more amused he was. And then he began to think very closely. The result of this thinking was the delay in going to Crissons.

"Don't worry," he told his female relatives one time. "Our young cousin, Henri, is here for a very definite purpose. I think I know what it is. We'll be seeing them one of these days. Perhaps too often."

He began to surmise what sort of man Henri Bouchard was, and to get the relationship between himself and the returned exiles clear in his mind. He recalled that his grandmother, Florabelle, was also their grandmother, and that his dead uncle, François, was their father. They were his first cousins. Doubly his cousins, for their great-grandfather, Ernest Barbour, had been his own great-uncle. The family's practically full of incest, he thought with a smile. But apparently from reports, and from the possible reason for his return, Henri Barbour Bouchard was no weakling.

Indignation was still high when it was reported that the exiles' old stepfather, Thomas Van Eyck, was visiting his dead wife's children. Some of the ladies of Roseville recalled that they had friends in New York well known to the Van Eycks, and they wrote to these friends. They had gratifying replies. Old Thomas, it was said, intended to live with his stepchildren in Roseville. He was a harmless and gentle old creature, very fond of Edith and Henri, who "positively adored him." Gossip became thicker and more active than ever. The older ladies recalled that their dead father, François Bouchard, had been "quite a mess." He had killed himself in that very house in Roseville. Their mother had subsequently married her second cousin, Thomas, in New York, Thomas Van Eyck of the socially prominent Van Eycks. And unbelievably wealthy, too. Hope began to rise in Windsor that the coming of the old man would make the exiles more amenable to social intercourse.

But nothing happened. It is true that old Thomas was driven out by one of the chauffeurs every day, and that when greeted on the roads he replied with evident gratitude and simple pleasure. Once his car had broken down, and a neighbor solicitously offered his home while the vehicle was being repaired. Thomas had hesitated, seemed a little frightened, and then with apparent regret, declined. He seemed eager, however, to speak, and it was most obvious that he was lonely and not very accustomed to easy familiarity with strangers. The neighbor gave a careful description of him. He was tall and thin and bent and shrunken, probably close to seventy, from his appearance. He had thin white hair, gentle brown eyes, and a trustful if shrinking expression that reminded one of an uncertain child. His manners were awkward, but courteous with an old world courtesy. He seemed a trifle vague and unsure of himself, and his hands trembled continuously. While he exchanged remarks with the neighbor, as they both stood by the roadside, he kept glancing uneasily up and down the road like a child afraid of strict parents. Nothing could induce him to speak of his stepchildren, except to remark that he was glad they had come back to their own country to live. He, himself, intended to remain with them. His eyes had a shy brightness in them when he spoke of his stepchildren. He had parted from the neighbor with evident regret.

Then one day Christopher sat down and wrote a note to his cousin, Henri Bouchard. He greeted the other coldly and formally. The note was very brief. He wrote:

"It is possible that the return of your sister and yourself to Windsor is due to your desire to resume life here. But I do not think this is the sole reason. Perhaps I know that reason. If I am correct, you may regard me as a friend. If I am wrong, you need not answer this communication."

He signed himself formally: Christopher Barbour Bouchard.

He waited. A week went by. Two weeks. And there was no answer. But he gradually became sure that an answer would be forthcoming. It was. It came by special messenger one morning, to the office. It was as cold and formal as his own note. Henri Bouchard and his sister, Edith, would be pleased to have their cousins, Christopher and Celeste, and their aunt, Adelaide, drop in for tea at five o'clock on the following Sunday afternoon. That was all.

Christopher held the note in his chill fleshless fingers, and

127

smiled faintly. The pale bright spark grew in his eyes. A clerk came in to ask Mr. Christopher to go into the president's office as soon as convenient. Christopher carefully put Henri's note in his pocket and went to his brother. He found Armand fussily signing letters. Armand wore Oxford glasses, and they slipped on his fleshy nose, which was always of a greasy appearance. His rumpled coat collar and lapels were flaked with white, and he kept scratching his head as he read and signed. Christopher sat down, and waited. Armand, he reflected, looked old and fat and tired and harassed. The sunlight, streaming thorough the windows, showed how thin his graying auburn hair was, for it glistened on his scalp. He needs a bath, as usual, thought Christopher, distending his transparent nostrils with disgust.

Armand put down his pen and sighed. He regarded his brother in gloomy silence. There was something earnest and searching in the eyes behind the gleaming glasses. And something timid.

"There has been nothing more about the Russian order to Parsons, Christopher?" he asked at last.

"No, nothing. Frankly, I think they'd better forget that order. It is obvious that they won't get it."

Armand rubbed his forehead, and pursed up his mouth. "And you can get nothing more about Duval-Bonnet?"

"Not a thing. It is my honest opinion, by the way, that they are not as innocent as they appear. They are evidently controlled by people who stay in the background. When Parsons' man went down there to see them, as you know, he had that same impression."

Armand said irately: "But who? Who? What is all this? After all, there is enough in that order for both Parsons and Duval-Bonnet, if they could only get together— I've been pulling wires on the Exchange, too. We have nothing new, except that they are now listed, and the stock is selling for eleven a share. I don't like mysteries!"

Christopher smiled, but was silent.

Armand continued to complain. There was a time when there was some integrity among businessmen. Now integrity was regarded as something shameful, something to be hidden, like an unclean sore. One could excuse lack of integrity where there was lack of markets, and competition was a game in which a man either killed or was killed. But there was more than enough for everyone, in America. In the world. There was no excuse for skullduggery.

"Not," reminded Christopher gently, "that we are guiltless of skullduggery ourselves."

128

Armand thrust out his lower lip. He smiled uneasily. "Well, not too much. Only what was necessary." He waited. Christopher said nothing. Armand sighed again. After a moment or two he was embarrassed. He knew that Christopher thought him a fool. Perhaps he was. Perhaps Christopher was right when he had said that a longing for integrity rose from a secret impotence. He, Armand, was feeling chronically tired these days. He would like to rest for awhile. But he dared not rest; he could not rest. He glanced furtively but swiftly at his brother. What had Emile genially called him? "That thin silvery snake!" Ah, well. Name-calling might be clever, but he was not one for it. But men like Christopher made it impossible for others to rest.

He said aloud: "We'd like to have you and Mother and Celeste come to dinner next Thursday evening. We leave for Maine the following Saturday, you know."

"Thanks. I'll tell Mother."

"When are you going to Crissons?"

"Probably right after you go to Maine."

Christopher got up to go. Armand said: "No further developments out in Roseville? What the devil do you suppose is wrong with them? After all, they own nearly forty per cent of the bonds in Bouchard. That's a lot of money! Well, if my memory about them is right, they're a pair of disagreeable brats. They made Uncle François' life miserable, they and their fool of a mother. She was our second cousin, wasn't she? The family's all mixed up. Anyway, I remember that they were ugly and black and sharp. Someone said Henri was the image of old Ernest Barbour. Probably a good thing he's got bonds instead of stock."

Adelaide was surprised when Christopher showed her Henri's note. He carefully refrained from telling her that he had written first. She was not disposed, at first, to accept the invitation, for she had unconsciously begun to dislike her seclusive niece and nephew. But Celeste was surprisingly pleased. She would have something exciting and gay to report to her young frail niece, Annette, whom she dearly loved. Celeste was fond of her brother, Armand, Annette's father, but she did not feel so fond of Antoine, Annette's brother, and her own nephew.

For some mysterious reason Christopher was critical about his young sister's appearance before they left for Roseville. Finally he was satisfied. Celeste, he decided, was charming, old-fashioned and lovely in her simple dress of soft blue chiffon, not too short, and fastened at the natural waistline with a belt of linked and twisted silver. She wore a string of luminous ivory pearls about her white throat. A wide-brimmed leghorn hat shaded her face. In its shadow her eyes were dark blue and vivid with life and gaiety, and her lips were moist and very red. Her slender legs were perfect, he decided. He was quite satisfied, and therefore, unusually affectionate towards her.

He even felt tolerant of his mother. Adelaide looked distinguished and highly bred in her gray silk chiffon dress and white gloves and black hat. She would have been amazed to know that her youngest son was proud of her evident breeding, if not of herself, personally. She was feeling distinctly bitter against him today. She did not know exactly why, but her maternal instinct smelled danger, and danger to Celeste. Some prescience was aroused, and in consequence her voice, if low, was irritable when she spoke to him. This antagonized Celeste, who felt that Christopher's extraordinary amiability ought to have been rewarded with greater pleasantness. Whenever he tries to be nice, she thought, Mama inevitably becomes sarcastic and disagreeable to him. Dear me, sometimes I don't blame poor Christopher.

But her gaiety could not be suppressed. The house in Roseville had seized on her imagination. She had not been able to forget the portrait of Gertrude Barbour.

Everything was beautiful to her today. The trees were hot green fountains, their moving shadows thick on the roads. She took delight in everything, in the straight square back of the chauffeur, in Christopher's wry witticisms, in the curve of countryside running beside the car, in the swift wings of birds. She liked to catch the brilliant light in the ring of exquisite opals and pearls and diamonds which Christopher had given her for Christmas. Excitement and joy in living made everything luminous in her eyes. She overlooked her mother's somber silence and averted head.

They approached Robin's Nest. The gates were ajar. The caretaker allowed them to pass. They drove up the curving road to the house. There it stood, Georgian, severe yet beautiful, shimmering with green ivy. There was a stern loveliness about the grounds, something formal and classic. Celeste, feeling disloyal, thought how delightful it was compared with her own home. They were admitted to the cool duskiness of the reception hall. How different it was, this summer's day, to that night of storm and darkness and lightning. The shrouds were all off the furniture. The dust was gone from the dark mirrors of the floors. Everything was polished and formal and waiting. Flowers were everywhere, standing before pier glasses, on round tables of gleaming mahogany, on the shining expanse of the piano, on marble mantelpieces, and even on the sills of the opened French windows. Celeste had an impression of polished formality, of cool dimness, of radiant sun-filled windows, of flowers and leisure and taste. Despite the heat outside, the plaster-and-gilt ceilings and lofty walls and quiet made one feel composed and at peace. There were no heavy carpets here, but small Oriental rugs scattered at strategic spots on the dusky brightness of the floors. Even Christopher could not feel oppressed here, for all that the furniture was old and there were silken ivory lengths at the windows. He particularly liked the dim and delicate winding of the circular staircase of the reception hall.

"It is the same as ever," murmured Adelaide. But no one heard her. She could see the intense green grass and the beautiful trees and the gardens through the windows. A Henri Bouchard to this daguerrotype was incredible. It was no other sound.

A young woman came towards them, smiling reservedly. She laid down a book she had evidently been reading. She came across the smooth floors, which reflected her straight and slender figure like bright shadowy water. Her step was serene, quick yet unhurried, and very firm, and only a certain stiffness and definiteness of carriage prevented her from being extremely graceful of movement. She carried her small head high, with a touch of cold arrogance. Everything about her was narrow, hard and slender, except her thin shoulders, which were broad and level. She wore a dress of a deep blue and white print, which covered the knees of her slim sure legs, and was high in the throat. Her black straight hair, uncut, was wound smoothly in a roll at the base of her neck. Her eyes were nut-brown, without softness, and very direct and disingenuous. There was not a feature in the narrow somewhat Latin face which was beautiful; the nose was too long and too thin and prominent; the mouth was hard, straight and colorless; the cheek-bones, unpowdered, were too high and ridge-like; the chin was square and uncompromising. Her expression was forthright, yet reserved, with no graciousness. Yet, she had breeding and smartness, and a certain magnetism, for all her lines were clean-cut and sharp, and there was no fuzziness or vagueness about her, such as there was about Adelaide, and even about Celeste.

Edith came directly to Adelaide, and extended a brown, veined hand to her, like a boy's. Her smile lessened its re-

131

serve. "Aunt Adelaide? I am Edith, you know." And she bent and kissed Adelaide's flushed old cheek. Adelaide caught an odor of good soap and clean firm flesh. This overcame the bad effect on her of hard disingenuousness and sharp competence, and a well-bred English voice that was too metallic for her ear.

"My dear," she said gently, holding that dry brown hand in her own, "I should have known you again. You have not changed much since you were a child." She turned to her son and daughter. "Perhaps you remember Christopher? And Celeste?"

"How are you, Christopher? And Celeste?" Her more friendly smile, now, revealed big white teeth, which glistened in the darkness of her face. She gave them her hand. Celeste was already afraid of her, and colored brightly. But Christopher smiled into his cousin's face. They were almost of a height, for she was rather tall. "Hello, Edith," he said. "I see you have improved. You were an awful brat."

Adelaide was horrified; Celeste colored more than ever. But Edith, after the first stare, laughed. Her laugh, like her voice, was high and British, but quite unaffected.

"And you apparently are no better than the other Bouchards," she said. They regarded each other with humorous caution. Adelaide was surprised at this mysterious rapprochement. She was always being surprised like this. Her unvarying courtesy and kind thoughtfulness never received much acknowledgment from people like these; in fact, they seemed to arouse their indifference or disdain. Their own kind, however, could bully and insult them, and be bullied and insulted by them in return, and the utmost understanding was the result. She was always at a loss, and always vaguely frightened by this understanding, which pushed her aside as though she were a fool whose opinions could not possibly have any weight, and whose observations could only be futile and silly. She finally was convinced that they despised her sort, which was quite true.

Edith, almost unbending now, turned to Celeste, and kissed the brightly flushed cheek. Celeste looked like a beautiful child in comparison with this compact young woman, for she was much smaller and more delicate, and appeared all softness and sweetness and shyness. Edith regarded her, her nut-brown eyes direct and critical. A foolish little creature, she thought. Probably without much intelligence; but a dear. I can see that: a little dear. She felt quite affectionate towards her young cousin, and candidly admired the dark-blue eyes that shone in the shadow of the hat as though they were newly polished.

"You were such a baby when I saw you last, Celeste," she said. "Six or seven, perhaps. But so pretty."

She led them into the drawing-room, where they sat down. She showed no signs of self-consciousness. Adelaide nervously removed her gloves. Celeste, miserable as she was always miserable (for no reason known to herself), in the presence of people like Edith Bouchard, sat in silence on the edge of her chair. All her pleasure was gone. She wished she were home. She glanced under the brim of her big leg-horn hat at her cousin, and was surprised at her own over-whelming sensation of dislike and fear. Edith was talking now to Christopher; her laugh came with a trifle less reluctance. Her unpowdered dark cheekbones gleamed in the radiant half-light. Her big white teeth sparkled. Now she appeared very attractive and more magnetic than ever. She had small hard breasts under the well-cut dress; all her gestures were decided, yet charming. Her neat slender ankles were crossed, and displayed to advantage the narrow patrician feet in black slippers. Christopher had given her a cigarette, and had lighted it for her. As he did so, their eyes met, and Edith smiled again. Now a faint flush appeared on the prominent cheekbones.

Celeste had never heard Christopher talk so freely to anyone before. He was audacious, she thought, puzzled. Now, with smiling derision, he was remarking on Edith's seclusiveness. Apparently she was not offended, for she laughed, without, however, any comment. Celeste listened to her brother's toneless but apparently sincere laughter, and was more wretched than ever. Now she felt positive aversion to Edith. Adelaide sat in silence, smiling painfully and mechanically. The smile became fixed. Celeste knew that her mother was suffering, and her young heart warmed with sympathy. But she wondered why it was that they both suffered like this when with people of Edith's kind. She wondered why they shrank when cold hard eyes like these glanced at them so piercingly, and so openly scornful. Were they, perhaps, really fools, as those eyes accused them of being?

Adelaide moistened her lips and proffered a timid remark about the regained beauty of the grounds and the house. Edith listened with a faint cold darkening of her face. "But you surely don't intend living here?" asked Christopher. Adelaide colored, for she thought him extremely rude.

Edith apparently did not consider him unduly rude. She
133

shrugged her shoulders. "Why not?" she asked bluntly. "I like it. I was born here. It's better than most I've seen in this city."

"It is my opinion," said Adelaide in a rush of eager placating words, "that Robin's Nest is still the most beautiful house in Windsor. Your grandmother was noted for her taste, Edith."

Edith glanced up at the portrait over the chill marble fireplace. A faint bright gleam lay upon the mournful painted face and somber eyes. "They say I resemble her," said the young woman. Adelaide looked first at the portrait and then at Edith, and murmured something under her breath, and seemed embarrassed. Looking in confusion about the room for a place to rest her eyes she saw another portrait facing that of Gertrude Barbour. She exclaimed involuntarily. She had seen this portrait in the house of old Lucy Van Eyck, in New York. It was that of Ernest Barbour, great-grandfather of Edith. Adelaide had always feared and disliked Ernest Barbour, in spite of his open admiration and fondness for her. He had been dead many years, she reflected, nearly twenty-seven, in fact. Yet she could remember those pale inexorable eyes, the big Napoleonic head, the broad stocky shoulders, the heavy sullen mouth, as though she had seen him only yesterday. The portrait was an excellent one, painted when the subject was less than fifty, and had been a present to his wife, May Sessions. Ernest had looked directly and impatiently at the artist, who had been a brilliant one, apparently, for he had kept the face, with the exception of the eyes, in comparative shadow, and had only suggested the neck and shoulders. And so the eyes looked out of the canvas as though alive, and were so vital, so implacable, so full of power, that Adelaide felt her heart quickening with the old fear.

Edith was speaking. She was explaining the absence of her brother and stepfather, who had been out for a drive. Only a moment or two before the arrival of the guests Henri had called his sister to apologize for being late: there had been a minor accident to the car. However, they were now expected momentarily.

She added that Henri was going to New York tomorrow, Monday, but would return before the week-end. At that time she intended to have a "gathering of the clan," an informal dinner for the whole Bouchard family in Windsor. Christopher raised his pale brown eyebrows without remark; one corner of his mouth twitched. He was thinking of Henri's visit to New York.

134

Celeste had added nothing to the conversation. She had murmured and smiled painfully whenever it was expected of her. The backs of her little white hands were damp with misery. She wished she were sitting next to her mother instead of in this wing chair of mahogany and dark rose silken brocade. The radiant sun that lay along the flowered windowsills and the edge of the polished floor hurt her eyes. She surreptitiously took off her hat, and the dark glistening hair lay in ringlets against her pale cheeks. She seemed more of a child than ever. Edith's thoughts had often touched her curiously. She was not so sure, now, that Celeste was a foolish little creature, for she had caught Celeste's blue eyes fixed upon her with a strange and penetrating expression. She reminded Edith of one of those sheltered and demure young French girls whose very clarity and unmurkiness of spirit enabled them to come to subtle and astute conclusions. She wondered, with some interest, what the girl thought of her, and had a slightly amused but unflattering idea.

There were muffled footsteps approaching, and two men came across the rugs. Adelaide turned and could hardly suppress a cry, for the younger of the two bore the most astounding resemblance to the portrait of Ernest Barbour. She blinked at him, profoundly shaken, her mind in a whirl, time rolling back on itself in her senses. This young man, stocky, slightly shorter than his tall sister, pale and implacable of eye, sultry of mouth, with a crest of thick vital hair springing upward and back from his forehead, might indeed have been Ernest Barbour in his youth. Adelaide remembered, now, having seen a faded daguerreotype of the young Ernest, which had been the most cherished possession of old Florabelle, Jules' mother, and the resemblance of Henri Bouchard to this daguerreotype was incredible. It was grotesque; it was impossible.

He greeted his aunt with grave courtesy but complete indifference. His voice and manners were British and punctilious. Dazed, she listened to his voice, and it seemed to her that she was hearing again the voice of a man dead for a generation. When old Thomas Van Eyck greeted her, she could hardly reply to him. But when his dry old hand held hers she became suddenly conscious of warmth and goodness and kindliness and innocence. She looked up into the old seamed face with the gentle if not too subtle eyes. A good old man, and something tense and bitter in her relaxed, like the coming of tears. She had seen him many years ago, in his mother's house, in New York, and then only once or twice. Life, and the Bouchards, and the multitudinous

135

and predatory hosts like them, had not destroyed his innocence, had not mortally wounded his heart. He spoke to her in his gentle vague voice, and she replied. When he sat down beside her, and smiled at her so gently, so kindly, her tired bent body turned towards him with gratitude and understanding. We are both old, she thought, and we both know what has nearly killed us. I am embittered, but he has been above embitterment.

She missed the meeting between Celeste and her cousin, Henri. Edith had been called to answer a long-distance telephone call from New York, so Christopher was the only witness. For some reason he watched acutely, missing nothing. He saw a bright color run over Celeste's face as she shook hands with Henri. He saw her painful uncertain smile, her aching shyness. She betrayed her lack of contact with young men in her self-conscious stammer, her color, her eyes which seemed to look desperately for shelter and hiding. But Christopher, smiling secretly to himself, was satisfied, for it was evident that she was a great surprise to the sophisticated Henri, who was regarding her with open pleasure and bold curiosity. Her demureness and shyness impressed him; her natural loveliness most obviously excited him. He wanted to see how much of all this was affectation, and how much, real. So he drew a chair close to hers, and began to talk to her in a low voice, bending his big head forward that he might miss nothing of a glance or change of color. The poor girl was in misery; when she was forced to look at him she almost quailed. She wrung her handkerchief in her hands; her face was suffused. When she smiled, it was a smile of pain. Henri was diverted; it was evident, from his greeting to Christopher, and the monosyllables that he had directed at his sister and his aunt, that he was not a talkative young man. Yet he talked to Celeste almost insistently, his eyes fixed on her face.

"If I had remembered that you were here, I should have come back sooner," Christopher heard him say. Celeste laughed; her voice seemed to catch in her throat, as though she were choking. She tried to look directly at her cousin, and blushed more violently than ever.

The girl's lack of coquetry, her lack of knowledge of the art of flirtation, were charming. Her hands lifted to make gestures that were never quite completed, for her confusion was growing.

Thomas Van Eyck was talking vaguely and mildly to Adelaide. She listened more to the sound of his voice than to his words. She kept thinking: how blessed it is to be in the

136

presence of a gentleman again! And then she was curious: how could such a gentleman endure the Bouchards, and be able to live with them? How could he endure Edith and Henri? She glanced at Henri furtively, to discover what it was that made him endurable to his old stepfather. Then her eye quickened, widened with alarm. Her heart rose and shivered. For she saw Henri's face.

She must have started, or moved, for old Thomas looked in the direction in which she was looking. Without Adelaide's start, or perhaps faint exhalation of breath, he would have seen only a young man being agreeable to a pretty guest. But the almost imperceptible gesture Adelaide had made focussed his attention, and he saw what she was seeing. He gazed at the young man and the girl earnestly, and as he did so a dim grave shadow moved over his face.

Edith re-entered the room, calm and dark. She suggested that, as Adelaide had remarked on the beauty of the gardens, they all visit them for a few minutes before tea. Adelaide, trembling with something she could not explain, rose eagerly. The men were forced to rise, also. Celeste lifted her eyes to her mother's face, as though she had been startled from a dream that gave her both excitement and apprehension. There was a bright aloof expression in her eyes, and her mouth had parted childishly.

They went out into the gardens. Adelaide had laid her hand on Thomas' proffered arm. He was explaining something to her; she could not listen. All her senses were centered on the young couple in the rear, behind Christopher and Edith. She heard Celeste's laughter, breathless and self-conscious. Her hand tightened on Thomas' arm as though desperately grasping it for assistance.

"You have never seen the gardens at Versailles?" Henri was asking Celeste, raising his thick, rather light eyebrows. "You have never been to France?" His clipped British voice sounded incredulous. "But you must see Versailles. The gardens, I believe, are the most beautiful in the world. We have tried to reproduce the effect of them here, a little." He glanced about him complacently.

Celeste somewhat forgot her confusion in admiration of the beautiful formal effect of the gardens. Nothing was pretty, but everything was classic and rather massive. The thick green grass was clipped to a plush uniformity, perfectly flat and without a natural rise or fall. They were approaching an artificial terrace, which rose about three feet above the normal level; three broad marble steps, more than twelve feet wide, allowed one to mount the terrace onto

137

another and greater level. On each side of the steps were huge marble pots of oleanders. Once standing on the upper level, one could see formal avenues of trees stretching away on either side. Directly ahead was a park-like grove, in the center of which were a geometrical series of flower beds grouped about a fountain. Marble benches were scattered about at the best points under the trees. Beyond the grove were the rose gardens, at their best on this June day.

The western sun had been wound about with rose-colored gauze, and a cool wind had arisen, pungent with the smell of grass newly wet from hosings. Now as evening began to approach, the multitudes of birds were preparing to sing their last songs. The air was full of chirpings and trills and distant calls and the flutter and brush of wings. The trees murmured in an awakened monotone. Their upper branches were faintly stained with rose, in which the leaves moved restlessly. There were no sounds in this profound and beautiful peace, except the sound of the trees and the birds and the fountain. Behind them, on the lower level, the strollers could see the house, Georgian and formal, the windows standing open, the ivy rippling on the stone walls. The upper windows were slowly brightening into golden fire; a bluish shadow was already rising, like water, on the lower walls, giving the ivy a purple tinge.

The rose garden was more intimate, full of banks of pink, white, yellow and crimson flowers. The fragrance was almost overpowering. Edith had brought a basket and scissors, and proceeded to cut the freshest and most dewy blooms for Adelaide. (She seemed to know that there were practically no flowers at Endur.) They lay in the basket, delicate heaps of colored folded petals and brilliant green leaves, and in their death, already beginning, they exhaled a more exquisite odor. Light seemed to lie along the edges of petal and leaf; globes of quicksilver ran over them. The rising wind suddenly shook the whole garden into a tide of color, and snowstorms of pink and gold and white blew into the air and then fell onto the grass.

"Oh, it is so lovely," said Adelaide. She turned to look for Celeste. The girl was standing with Henri at the other end of the garden. She was listening, holding a rose, and seemed to be absorbed in the odor of it. The young man's voice was almost inaudible; he was bending his head towards her as though what he was saying was of the gravest importance. Adelaide turned away from Thomas, who was prosily discoursing on the newest varieties which his "children" had introduced into the gardens. As she did so, she caught the

138

eye of Christopher, who was standing a little distance away with Edith. Her mouth had already opened to call her daughter, but when her son's eye caught her own, no sound came from her lips. It was as if he had seized her arm and had commanded her not to speak. She could not even move for a few moments; she had the sensation of being struck violently and deliberately, by an enemy.

She stood in silence, a coldness running over her body. "Are you cold, Adelaide?" asked old Thomas solicitously, seeing the faint rigor of her face. "No," she murmured, not looking at him, but only at Christopher. "No." She forced herself to move. "Let us go in," she added, feeling a nightmare weight on her limbs.

Thomas led her out of the garden. They were in the grove again, alone. Adelaide was forced to sit down, for her knees were shaking. Thomas stood beside her, quite anxious. "What is it, Adelaide? But you are really cold!"

"No," she said again, trying to smile. "It is just old age, Thomas."

He gazed at her earnestly before saying: "We are both old, my dear. I suppose we should regret it. But we don't, do we?"

"Regret it?" she repeated. She began to laugh, thinly, bitterly. "Regret it! Who would want to be young, always, or live, always?"

He did not answer. He glanced slowly over the austere magnificence of the great gardens. He looked at the trees, in which a deeper scarlet was caught in the upper branches. The sky was paling to a misty heliotrope in the east. The light was already fading from the earth, and mauve shadows began to fly over the grass. One robin, high in a tree, began to drop slow silvery notes of infinite melancholy.

"Still," said Thomas at last, after a long time, "the world is very beautiful. Isn't it, Adelaide?"

Adelaide lifted her head, and watched Christopher and Edith emerging into the grove. "Is it?" she asked, looking at Christopher. "Is it?"

Henri and Celeste were alone in the rose garden. Henri had picked a white rosebud, and was trying, with exceptional skill, to fasten it in Celeste's hair. She stood still under his fingers, which seemed to burn her scalp. Her face was flushed; she fixed her child-eyes resolutely on his chin. They were both laughing. Finally Henri had finished; the white bud seemed to glow in the dark hair. They laughed more than ever. "You look Spanish," said Henri, taking her hand

and putting it on his arm. A pang, inexplicable and dividing
passed through the girl.

"You don't belong here," Henri said. "Not in nineteen
twenty-five, or in America. Are you real?"

He went on: "French girls are like you. But you are not
French. You are American. An anachronism, too."

The world looked very strange to Celeste. Everything had
a febrile brilliance about it; everything seemed close and
sharp and too clear. Colors burned and the wind seemed
intimate and personal. But she was almost ecstatically excited. Her breath did not seem to fill her lungs. Her forehead felt damp under her hair. When she tried to look at her
cousin she felt giddy, experiencing a confusion which was
both painful and pleasurable. She had read many romances,
the greatest romances of literature, and had dreamt many
dreams. But masculinity had never before impinged upon
her consciousnes. She had perceived it through the distorting
gauze of a protecting veil. Henri had moved aside the veil
and she saw a man fully for the first time in her life. A feeling of utter nakedness obsessed her, a kind of delicious
shame and delight. Henri studied her profile intently. Yes,
she is a virgin, he decided, amused and more interested than
ever. A girl of nineteen, who was a virgin. It was astonishing. Girls like this were to be found only in French con-
vents. He could not forget how she had blushed when he
put the rose in her hair, a silly gesture which could only
appreciated by an awkward school-girl just approaching
adolescence. Yet, there was something more than adolescence
in the young curve of Celeste's breast, and the lift of her
throat.

"Where did you go to school?" he asked, stopping to light
a cigarette. He did not offer her one, for he knew
would be refused.

"I didn't go to school," she answered. "Christopher
thought I should stay home. And besides, my mother
would have been lonely, too."

He shook the match slowly back and forth until it went
out, then dropped it. He regarded her with furtive attention.
Ah, Christopher. Then he smiled. Celeste, for some reason
did not like that smile, though she could not have explained
why. All at once she felt tired and drained, and looked about
for her mother. She and Henri walked back to the grove, and
found Adelaide sitting on a bench, with Thomas and Christopher and Edith standing near her. Celeste left Henri
with sudden quickness and came to her mother. They
looked at her in surprise, wondering at her precipitate move

ments, and their eyes disconcerted her. Then Christopher glanced behind her and saw Henri sauntering up indifferently.

Once Christopher had said that it was the business of survival that forced the "disinherited" to be shrewdest judges of men. Inability to acquire judgment, and the inability to use other men, caused the "disinherited" the final defeat. So he had made it his gravest and most important business to understand men, and understanding them, to use them. Armand had no need of this protection (for protection it was). Of all the family, Christopher alone had need of it.

And so it was that as Henri sauntered up, walking with his firm and deliberate tread, his light inexorable eyes quite indifferent, Christopher scrutinized him more acutely, and with more passionate gravity, than he had ever scrutinized any other man. He missed nothing, from the heavy lips and the short dilated nose, to the eyes and the broad square forehead above them. He read the faintest signals about mouth and eye-socket, in the turn of Henri's head and the mature movements of his body. So intense was his concentration that everything else in the world was shut out from his sight but Henri Bouchard. His own eyes left the mere surface of flesh and insistently penetrated to the mind and the thoughts and the emotions behind it. It all took but a few moments, yet Christopher felt that it had taken an incalculable time. And at the end of it, an almost prostrating sense of elation possessed him.

Adelaide rose, and they all turned towards the house. Celeste showed an inclination to stay near her mother. Christopher maneuvered it skillfully. Edith, with disappointment, found herself walking with her stepfather. She wanted to turn back to Christopher, but when she paused at the edge of the grove and looked back, Christopher and Henri had disappeared.

The two men had turned back to the rose-garden, silently, as though by a mutual consent arrived at a long time ago. They sat down on a bench and smoked without comment for some moments. They appeared to be at ease with each other. Beneath this ease they faced each other, negotiating for position, studying and watching.

Christopher, who was never one to underestimate another, knew that this was no inexperienced young man, who had played about in the capitals of Europe and who snobbishly despised the mighty industries which supported him. He was more than twelve years older than Henri Bouchard, yet he understood that this was no advantage to himself, and no disadvantage to the younger man. Christopher could spare a

141

moment or two to be amused. Jules Bouchard had made the children of his brother impotent; he had made helpless the great-grandson of Ernest Barbour. Yet, out of this impotence and helplessness Ernest Barbour, resurrected like the phœnix, appeared to have come back for vengeance and final victory. For now Christopher knew quite clearly the truth which he had shrewdly suspected a few days before.

To have come back with this idea postulated a plan, or at least, an outline. It meant that Henri Bouchard's first efforts must be to discover all he could, and to understand his adversaries first of all, and thoroughly. This is what Christopher himself would have done, and had been doing since his father's death. Not underestimating Henri, he knew that the young man had been pursuing precisely this very plan. But how much did he know? And how well-formed was his plan?

And all the time Christopher was thinking this, he knew that Henri was following his thoughts and understanding them. Between them, he realized, there could be no deceit, for they could not deceive each other. There had been no "exclusiveness" on Henri's part, Christopher acknowledged with delighted admiration. He had come back, had allowed it to be known that he had returned. But he had made no move. He had sat in this great Georgian mansion, patiently waiting. He had seemed to know that there was some one in this formidable family who would see it was to his advantage to approach Henri Bouchard. For this some one he had been waiting, making no first move, not knowing who the one waited for would be, but sure that he would soon identify himself.

He had had to wait longer than he had expected. But he had not been uneasy. In the meantime, from a thousand intangible sources, he was learning everything there was to know about his relatives. He had received much information in New York. While he waited, he analyzed all the information. Just before Christopher had written to him, Henri knew he would be the one who would come.

And simultaneous with this enlightenment came the conviction that Christopher knew what his cousin was waiting for, quite clearly. Behind the wall of silence and distance, they both waited, hearing each other breathe, aware of each other's movements. Then, at last, Christopher had opened the door in the wall, and had spoken.

They had looked at each other piercingly over conventional words. They knew they could never be friends, in the real meaning of the word, for neither was capable of true and disinterested friendship for any one. They had looked at each other, searching for a weakness which would give one of them an advantage over the other. So far, they had not found such a weakness. This inspired mutual respect, but had also increased their wariness.

They sat and smoked in silence, watching the mauve and heliotrope light of the evening deepen and grow more dense in the rose-gardens. The air was full of the lonely evensong of the robin and the rush of the fountain in the grove beyond the gardens. The sky was a delicate lavender, against which the lofty trees were already blurs of dark and moving shadows.

Then Christopher said coolly: "Do you think you will remain in Windsor, to live?"

Henri did not look at him as he replied: "Yes. I think I'll remain. After all, it is really my home. I'm fed up with the British. I don't like the French." Now he turned his large head and regarded Christopher fully. "I spent quite some time in France. Arnaud Poiret is an old friend of mine. He was a year at Oxford, during my senior year."

"He is the son of Eduard Poiret, of Schultz-Poiret, isn't he?" Nothing could have been more politely interested than Christopher's voice.

"Yes. When I visited France I met every one of importance connected with Schultz-Poiret. M. Poiret is a far cleverer man than M. Schultz. He is also the more powerful. He is a director, now, of the Banque de Paris; only a year or two ago he became President of the holding company he founded—the Union Financière et Européenne Industriale, which is now capitalized at 150,000,000 francs. It is due to him that Schultz-Poiret is the real power behind the Comité des Unions et des Demi-Produits, which, I don't need to tell you, is the world's greatest organization of steel and iron manufacturers." The young man paused, then continued: "I am convinced that Schultz-Poiret overshadows Robsons-Strong in Europe. In fact,. as you know, it is the most powerful of the directors of Skeda. That is why I have already purchased three million dollars' worth of common stock in it."

Christopher was astonished, but he did not reveal his astonishment. He merely listened intently, facing his cousin with his immovable eyes.

"Compared to Schultz-Poiret, you Americans are children," said Henri. "And yet, you, we, could be greater. We could control all the armaments industries of Europe. It is a matter of foresight, of planning. And we had better move

143

fast. Schultz-Poirct is already storing up nickel, aluminum, chemicals and glycerin for sale to Germany in the next war. French iron mines and smelters are working madly day and night to supply Kronk with iron. After all, before Germany can do a good job of re-arming and violating the Versailles Treaty, she has to have iron and nickel and aluminum and glycerin." The young man smiled slightly. Christopher smiled in return.

"And when do you—think—Germany will be ready?" he asked, as though indulgently.

"Don't you know?" Henri appeared surprised.

Christopher shrugged. "First of all, the present government of Germany must be destroyed. Under this government propaganda doesn't seem to make much headway. Schultz-Poiret, Robsons-Strong and ourselves, and Skeda, have spent millions of dollars—literally millions—to stigmatize the government as Communistic. Mussolini has been active; you know he owns a lot of Robsons-Petrillo stock. Britain— good old Britain—has refused Germany a loan, though old Hindenburg has begged on his knees. But in spite of everything, the government seems fixed in Germany, and the damn country seems to be pulling itself up by its bootstraps." He said thoughtfully: "And so long as the present German government is in power Germany won't re-arm—can't re-arm —sufficiently to pay profits to Schultz-Poiret and Robsons-Strong, and Skeda—and ourselves. With this government, there will be no renewed militaristic spirit in Germany—no militant nationalism. And without this nationalism there'll be no re-arming, and no future wars."

Henri looked before him and said meditatively: "Have the damn Germans no pride? Have they no regard for our profits?" And he looked at Christopher and burst out laughing. Christopher joined him. He had challenged the younger man, and Henri had given the sign and the countersign.

Christopher offered him a cigarette, and again they smoked. Pleasurable rapport grew between them. Then Henri said in a lower tone, yet still an indifferent one: "You know about Byssen?"

"Byssen? The German steel manufacturers? Yes, of course. But they are interested mainly in rails and bridges."

Henri regarded him with derisive astonishment. "Is it possible you believe that? My God, you are all more in the dark than I thought! Why, Byssen is expending a fortune to overthrow the present German government; it is practically subsidized by Schultz-Poiret and Skeda and Robsons-Strong and Robsons-Petrillo."

144

Christopher's face tightened. He looked at his cousin narrowly. "How do you know this?" he asked, almost in a whisper.

Henri smiled. "I told you Arnaud Poiret was my friend."

There was a silence. Then Christopher said in a low tight voice: "Thanks. You won't regret this. I'll put my order in for some shares in Byssen tomorrow. You don't intend to tell any one else?"

Henri smiled, still derisively. "No. But I never give without a return. When I come to market, I carry the price with me," and he regarded Christopher with the same expression in his eyes which was depicted in the eyes of his great-grandfather's portrait.

They faced each other for a long time, and understood each other. Finally, they got up together. Nothing in Christopher's thin narrow face revealed the exultation he was feeling. When they reached the grove, they found that it was empty, and full of vague darkness. They left the grove behind. Across the dim colorlessness of the lawns they saw the other four almost at the doors of the mansion. They descended the terrace. At this point Henri spoke again, very casually:

"Have you heard of a man called Adolf Hitler, in Germany?"

"Hitler? Isn't he that Austrian clown, a sign-painter or something, who was thrown into jail for inciting to riot? Or treason? Or something else? Why? Of what importance is Adolf Hitler?"

Henri replied: "I don't know, yet. But I can tell you this: Byssen is interested in him. And behind Byssen——"

Christopher digested this in silence. But he was rather sceptical. He was not given to scepticism, as a rule, knowing that the sceptic is usually a fool. And yet, he could hardly credit any connection between an imprisoned maniac and Byssen, and through Byssen, Schultz-Poiret and Robsons-Strong. However, he knew the probabilities of the improbable, and his scepticism began to seep away.

"You think—Hitler—" he said.

Henri shrugged his big shoulders. "I know nothing, myself. But it is enough for me, and good enough for me, to know that Byssen is interested in Hitler. I have that from Arnaud, too. Pressure is being brought upon the government to release him. And you can be sure that if he is released it is by order of some one greater than Byssen."

They had reached the door of the house now. Christopher

145

would have entered, but Henri touched him on the arm. He turned, gazed at the young man, waited.

Henri did not speak for a moment, then Christopher saw that he was smiling. "I like your sister. Celeste."

They went in.

They were almost at the door of the drawing-room when Henri spoke again, smiling more than ever: "I saw old Jay Regan this week. He sends you his regards. Do you know, he seems to think a lot of you." And then he added: "I told him you and I might see him in a week or so."

CHAPTER XVII

JEAN BOUCHARD, brother of Francis, entered the Bank of Windsor, smiling amiably and affectionately at every one, from the doorman to the old guards and the tellers and the clerks. He was adored by them, for his air was unassuming, his sympathy ready, and his interest in them invariable. The women, especially, worshipped him. He never seemed to be in a hurry nor in a bad temper. When he smiled, it was with candor, and dimples. His agility never unnerved the observer, for it was not erratic, but smooth and well-timed. The greatest egotist of all the Bouchards, his voice was never domineering, hasty or contemptuous. He spoke deprecatingly, patiently, humorously or frankly, as circumstances dictated. Moreover, there was a childlikeness about him that endeared him to women, a deliberate attitude of defenselessness and honesty which had deceived scoundrels to their everlasting discomfiture. No one recalled having been insulted by him, treated cavalierly by him, or having had to endure contempt, haste or impatience. His friends were multitudinous, for most men ask nothing more of their acquaintances than amiability, wit, charm, interest and intelligence, and all these Jean Bouchard (deadly little Jean) possessed in extraordinary quantity. Potential critics forgot his short stature, his tendency, now he was approaching middle age, to plumpness, and the opaque expression in his small sparkling black eyes. Even subtlety was blinded by him, because he was so very subtle himself; caution was disarmed by him, because he knew all the methods of disarming it; intellect was seduced by him, for his intellect was so brilliant. The evil were as easily deceived by him as the good. He wore the uniforms that appealed to each man. He made himself the alter ego of any associate, of any woman, any foe or friend, and even of any child or priest. A mountebank was delighted to discover another mountebank, a thief another thief, a reasonable man another man of reason, the tender-hearted one more tender-hearted, the kind, one still kinder, the ruthless, the most ruthless of them all, the evil, one who surpassed the worst.

Christopher called him Amanita Phalloides. And surely nothing could have been so apt as naming him for the deadliest of the fungi, which yet has no sharp color, no acrid taste, to warn a man of its deadliness.

Like most of his family, he knew no loyalty, except that which Jules had designated "rogues' loyalty." And no one of his family was entirely deceived by him except his big blonde wife, Alexa, of Wagnerian stature and extraordinary stupidity, and his pompous, pious, entirely stupid cousin and brother-in-law, Alexa's brother, Alexander. They were deceived by him to the end of their lives, for he was grateful for their deception. Alexander was vice-president of The Sessions Steel Company, of which his father, old, rosy, blond Andre, was president. Yet Jean, who was only secretary of the company, was paid a salary much higher than that of Alexander, Andre being a clever man in spite of his resemblance to a "pink scrubbed hog."

On this particular blue-and-white December morning Andre had called his nephew, Jean, for a consultation. (He rarely called in Alexander, who usually sulked in bewilderment over this, without, however, subsequently feeling resentful towards Jean.)

Andre was sitting at his desk, when Jean entered. He was corpulent and old now, with huge round belly and thick round thighs straining at the seams of his immaculately creased trousers. His bald scalp was rosy and polished, his blue eyes glittering behind his Oxford glasses. In the gray silk of his cravat was a large pinkish pearl. As usual, he appeared to have stepped only a moment ago from a hot bath lavishly full of soapsuds.

"Come in, Jean," he said. He took off his glasses, rubbed them with a huge square of the finest white linen, replaced them. He smiled. A faint odor of eau de cologne emanated from him. Jean sat down. His manner, towards his uncle, was always one of fondness, respect and attentiveness, which Andre found very soothing and flattering.

147

"Jean," said Andre, "bring Alexa and the children to dinner tomorrow night. Your aunt is much better, and would like to have all of you."

"Thank you, uncle," said Jean, smiling his pleased and affectionate smile.

"Has Bertie got over his grippe?"

"Yes. And Dorcas didn't have measles, after all." When he spoke of his little daughter Jean's expression changed subtly into one of authentic tenderness. Andre smiled. He was extremely fond of his little granddaughter, who he believed resembled him remarkably. On each of her birthdays and on Christmas and other holidays he bought her a beautiful rose-tinged pearl, of fine size and unsurpassed luster and value. So far, at five years of age, she had fifteen of these pearls, strung on a platinum chain. It was calculated that when she reached the age of twenty-one she would possess a necklace of exquisitely matched pearls whose value would be beyond price. Jean, who had no aversion to having his little daughter remain the favorite of Andre, did everything in his power to confirm his father-in-law's belief that Dorcas resembled him amazingly.

There was a fine photograph of little Dorcas on Andre's desk of polished ebony. The silver frame enclosed the face of a small blonde angel with an expression of infinite sweetness in its blue eyes. Andre beamed at it sheepishly. Then he turned from it with a gesture of paternal dismissal, and regarded his son-in-law, who was also his nephew.

"Jean, I've got something for you to do today of the utmost delicacy, and importance. Nicholas has just called me from the bank. He has asked me to have you call on him at once. I have an idea what it is about, but I would rather that you handled it."

"I see." Jean became thoughtful. He exchanged a steady look with his father-in-law which was a mixture of cunning and caution.

"Not," Andre went on, "that there is anything we can really do, you understand. But forewarned is forearmed. It is always well to know what one's adversary is doing, isn't it?"

So Jean called for his car and was driven to the bank. All during the ride he hummed under his breath, a habit he had when deeply engaged in thought. Once arrived at the bank, he was admitted immediately into the office of Nicholas Bouchard, president, and son of Leon. He glanced up at Jean, grunted, thrust out his thick underlip. He seemed much older than his thirty-six years, for there was no coloring of

148

youth about him, and only thickness, solidity, and a uniform tint of greenish eye, skin and greenish-brown hair.

"Come in, come in. Sit down. Are you busy? This won't take long." He sat stockily and sullenly behind his great ornate desk with its glass top. He regarded Jean with his customary dully belligerent eyes. But these eyes were less antagonistic to Jean than to any other of his relatives.

"I am busy," said Jean, smiling. "But not so busy as to disregard the importance of anything you have to tell me."

Nicholas grunted, and then smiled his unwilling and entirely unprepossessing smile. "Have a cigar. Go on; these won't hurt you. They're not as strong as the others, which you don't like. Go on. I won't keep you long."

Jean took a cigar, first lit Nicholas' and then his own. The pale bright December sun struck through the high cold windows and lay across the desk. Nicholas puffed, leaning back in his chair, his hands thrust into his pockets. He surveyed Jean unwinkingly, his cold stare full of calculation. Then abruptly he leaned towards his desk, took up a paper, and thrust it at the other man. Jean took it. It was a confidential report from the offices of Jay Regan.

Jean read, then whistled softly. He put down the paper, and again met the unwinking stare of Nicholas Bouchard.

"Now why," he said thoughtfully, "should Emile and Hugo and Francis turn over that amount of Bouchard stock to Christopher? Why? And where did he get the money?"

"Don't ask me. I ask you. That is why I called you here. To ask you."

"Does Armand know?"

"No. No use telling him. Yet. Why should we tell him? We don't know anything. No use telling him something we don't know the answer to. Is there?"

"I don't know, Nick. Sometimes I don't always agree with you, you know. There is an answer to all this, and somehow I believe it intimately concerns Armand, and all the rest of us. But, naturally, if you would rather I wouldn't say anything——"

"You always talk too much. You've got that reputation." Nicholas' voice was surly. He regarded Jean with harsh deliberation. "Well, have you any ideas? That's why I called you. Ideas."

"Have you?"

Nicholas grunted. "Plenty. But none of them tangible. You know what that white snake has always wanted. You know he'd like to cut Armand's throat. But where does that get us? Nowhere. Facts are facts; we've got to get more of 'em. Why did the others give Christopher that stock? I know his financial standing down to the last penny. I know that, besides the Bouchard stock, he's suddenly deposited money in the Morse National in New York. A fortune. Where did he get it?" He spat out a scrap of leaf. "And another thing: checks have been drawn on that account. All to cash. What's the answer?"

"He couldn't have borrowed from Henri, could he?" mused Jean.

Nicholas' eyes narrowed to greenish slits. "No. The stock was transferred to him a week before he got friendly with Henri and Edith. The money was deposited before, too. I happen to know that Emile, Hugo and Francis withdrew tremendous sums of money from the banks, which were subsequently deposited to Christopher's credit."

"Then," said Jean, frowning in concentration, "he's sold them something. Something very valuable, too, for I can't see them lending him money or giving him anything! Not even if it was to sink old Armand a thousand feet in hell. He's sold them something!"

Nicholas' thick lips curled outwards with contempt. "Now, then, aren't you bright! Did it take all that effort to think that out? Bah. I thought it out myself. I didn't ask you to agree with me. What has he sold them? It must be good. And where did he get it? And another thing I've found out: Henri's bought something from him, too. And paid for it with a flock of Bouchard bonds. Which Chris is keeping very carefully tucked away. Well? Well?"

Jean shrugged. "I don't know riddles. But there's one thing very certain: they know very well that they couldn't keep transactions of this size a secret from us."

Nicholas laughed his harsh reluctant laughter. "Again, aren't you bright! Of course they know it's not a secret. But where does that get us? Nowhere. They know we don't dare ask them. It's confidential business. Bank business. Not supposed to be broadcast. Now then: are you going to ask them?" and he grinned derisively.

Jean exhibited no rancor. "Whatever it is, it smells bad for Armand, and all of us. And Regan can find no answer? Christopher hasn't bought anything on the Market?"

"Nothing we can find, of any importance. The Bouchard stocks and bonds are in Christopher's boxes in the Morse National. They haven't been touched for months. He's hoarding them. Why? Hell, haven't you any ideas?"

Jean was silent a moment, and then replied frankly: "Not an idea. But there's danger in it, and it's up to us to find out.

150

There's another thing I don't like, either: Christopher is very intimate with Henri and Edith. Alexa and I have tried to be friends with them, but we get nowhere. And Christopher is evidently going to marry little Celeste off to Henri. Alexa said only this morning that she heard they are going to announce the engagement at Christmas. The whole family has toadied to Henri and Edith until it is nauseating. But though they are pleasant and agreeable in return, the intimacy is all between them and Christopher." Jean's face quickened. "I've noticed, too, that they seem more friendly towards Emile's and Francis' families than they do to us. And they've just got back from visiting Hugo and Christine in New Rochelle. This is interesting! There's a conspiracy, somewhere!"

Nicholas grunted contemptuously, but made no comment.

Jean went on: "And whatever the conspiracy is, it smells very bad indeed. I know Christopher! We've got to find out what it's all about." He mused intensely for a few moments. "I've found it very important not to overlook anything. And somehow, I feel it's of the utmost importance to Christopher to marry Celeste to Henri. I remember speaking of the possibility to old Armand last week, and I noticed that the idea upset him a little. At any rate, he rubbed his backside uneasily on his chair; you know, that way he has. And he changed color, though he made no comment. Why wasn't he easy about Celeste? I've never caught him showing the poor little thing much affection. Is he uneasy because old Adelaide has been getting after him? I notice she doesn't particularly care about Henri and Edith. This is something we ought to look into."

Nicholas stared at him incredulously.

"You think we ought to get in a plot to keep that girl from marrying Henri? Do you see lots of movies? That's your trouble. Movies and plays. That's what you get for hanging around the theatres in New York. Plots! My God, ain't you got any better ideas than that?"

But Jean only smiled. "The old plots, used from Aristophanes to Shakespeare to Bernard Shaw to Hollywood, are still valid, otherwise they would have died out long ago. They're based on human nature. However, I don't think we could do much about it, anyway. She plays Trilby to Christopher's Svengali. Yes, I admit it's all very fantastic, and that we can't do anything about it. We've got to concentrate on increasing Armand's antagonism to the marriage, though I doubt it'll do much good. We might even work on old Adelaide, though I don't know how. Alexa isn't much

151

good at being subtle, though old Adelaide seems to like
her. Yes, the more I think about it the more I am sure that a
lot depends on that marriage."

He got up to go. "Anyway, we do know there's a conspiracy. We do know a lot of cash and bonds and stocks
have changed hands. We don't know what was given in return, but you can be sure it was good. Very, very good. And
what it was, we've got to find out."

CHAPTER XVIII

A DELAIDE had never been in the offices of Bouchard
and Sons since Jules' death. Now, as she was driven up
to the doors of them, she could see the outlying factory
buildings, the chimneys seemingly extended into the sky
through the medium of straight columns of reddish smoke.
She thought to herself that the business of Bouchard and
Sons must be extraordinarily good. She recalled that the days
of the War had not been busier. Adelaide was not a woman
to question existing facts very acutely, especially when
those facts did not concern her intimately. But now she
wondered, anxiously. Why should the business of war be so
active in the days of peace? Who was buying the powder
and the guns and the steel and the ordnance and the chemicals and the gases which Bouchard and Sons and their subsidiaries manufactured?

All at once, even as she was about to get out of the car,
she was assaulted with a nameless apprehension and fear.
In some way all this seemed to concern Celeste and herself.
The sight of the great fuming buildings frightened her.
In times of peace, Jules reminded her, one must prepare
for war. War with whom? Who in the world threatened any
one else? Of course, these days, there was a lot of talk
about war debts, but who went to war to collect debts? Such
a course was insanity. There was a lot of talk, too, about
Germany's resentment about the occupation of the Ruhr,
and the Versailles Treaty. But one did not again go to war
with a foe already prostrate. Then who was the plotted victim of all this manufactured death?

"Why haven't I given these things thought before?" she

152

asked herself accusingly. "I've been a foolish old woman, without any sense of duty or justice beyond the walls of my own house." The problem and despair which had brought her here became a universal problem and despair.

She was admitted to Armand's office. He rose on her entry, surprised at this invasion. She smiled at him nervously as he gave her a chair.

"Armand, dear, you can be sure I wouldn't have come to your office except that I thought I had to. You see, we are never alone, when you visit us, and I can never speak to you privately in your own house. I hope you aren't too busy?"

He returned her smile diffidently, yet with affection. "Not too busy to see you, Mother. I am going to lunch soon. Will you come with me?"

"No, no, dear," she answered hurriedly. "I won't stay long. And Armand, you—you will not tell Christopher, or Emile, that I was here to see you?"

He was puzzled. "Of course not, Mother." And then his chronic uneasiness sharpened. Part of this uneasiness was a vague but constant feeling of guilt. He dared not analyse why, but whenever he came into contact with his mother, or spoke to her, that feeling of guilt was always present. He sat down. He regarded her with an apprehension that made him squirm on his chair. "But what is it I can do for you? You know I'll do anything——"

She looked at him with sudden and passionate gravity. "Will you, Armand? Will you?"

"Of course, Mother." But he was alarmed at her earnest voice, and the way she leaned towards him. He stared at her with the fixity of his alarm.

She continued to gaze at him with that grave and penetrating passion. Then she sighed, as if hopeless. Her tense thin body relaxed with the deflation of despair. Nevertheless, she said: "It is about Celeste, Armand."

"Celeste!" Whenever he was nonplussed, and was sparring for time, he had a habit of repeating what his opponent had last said, causing that opponent to reiterate his last words.

"Yes, Armand. Celeste." Her voice was despairing. She studied him. He had flushed darkly. He was staring at her intently, and thinking to himself, amid his confusion, that his mother had failed greatly the last few months.

"You see, Armand," she said quietly, "Celeste mustn't marry Henri Bouchard. No, the engagement hasn't been announced yet. But it soon will be, I am afraid. But she mustn't marry him!"

153

"Why not, Mother? It will be a good catch for the girl."
He wet his lips. His heart had begun to thump with a
sensation of dread, as though he were being cornered.

"Armand! Don't you see—it will really kill Celeste—! I
know my child. I know what a marriage like that would do
to her!" Adelaide's voice rose to a cry.

"I think you are being unreasonable, Mother. So far as I
can see, Henri is the most eligible young man in America
at the present time. Doesn't Celeste like him? Please, I am
trying to help you."

Adelaide's head dropped. She answered quietly: "Yes, she
likes him. But that is because she has never been allowed
to associate with other young men. She can't make com-
parisons. You say it will be a good catch for her. And I say,
when she finds out what he really is, it will kill her." Now
she looked at her son directly and said with bitter emphasis:
"You see, all her life I've tried to prevent her from finding
out what you are all really like. She couldn't stand it. It
would ruin her whole happiness."

Armand's flush grew darker, and his eyes shifted. He said
coldly: "I don't know what you mean. It sounds foolish and
sentimental, to me. This is the twentieth century, and Celeste
isn't a child. I don't know what you mean!" He got up and
went to the window, presenting his thick shoulders, broad
body and short thick legs to her. He thrust his hands deeply
in his pockets and jingled the coins in them. The sound
must have comforted him, for he glanced over his shoulder
at his mother: "Anyway, what could I do?"

She got up and went to him, putting her mottled hand on
his arm. He looked down into her face sullenly, glanced
away again.

"Armand dear, you can find out why Christopher wants
her to marry Henri."

She felt him start perceptibly. She saw his jowls tighten,
though he stared obstinately out of the window. "Don't be
sentimental, Mother. It sounds like the Bride of Lammer-
moor. If Chris wants Celeste to marry Henri it is because
he feels as I do: that the match is a good one." He paused,
then turned swiftly to his mother. She was startled by the
change in his face. His eyes were hard and glittering. "What
makes you think he wants this marriage? And why should
he, particularly?"

Adelaide regarded him steadfastly for a long moment or
two before she spoke, and then she said: "I don't know,
Armand. But you can be sure that it is more than just a
'good match for Celeste.'"

154

She went back to her chair and sat down. She watched him standing at the window, his back to her. She thought: Perhaps it was wrong of me to suggest treachery from Christopher. Perhaps it was wrong to sow suspicion between brothers, when there is no ground for it. But I would do anything to save Celeste.

Now Armand came back to his desk. He stood beside it, nervously fingering the paper knife; he would not look at his mother.

"The only thing I can do is to find out if Celeste is unwilling to marry Henri, or if she really cares about him. All I can do is to point out the advantages of a longer acquaintance—after all, she has known him only a little while, barely six months." Now he looked at her with harassed eyes. "She is having dinner with Annette tonight, isn't she? I'll talk to her, if I can find an opportunity."

After his mother had gone, Armand sat in deep and uneasy thought for some time. He gnawed his lips. He took up his pen a dozen times, laid it down. His secretaries came in, and he ordered them not to bother him for a time. Finally he got up and went back to Christopher's office. Just as he was about to open the door he heard his brother telephoning:

"Francis? I've tried to get you all morning. Can you spare an hour tonight? I want to talk to you about something of importance which has just arrived. Yes. That's right. At your club? All right. At nine, then."

Armand closed the door silently, and went away. His heart was beating thickly. He said to himself: Nonsense; I am a fool. What could they do to me? I shouldn't have let Mother poison my mind. It's all nonsense. Probably some speculation they're both in on. If I go on like this, I'll be an old woman, too.

Then all at once he seemed to see his younger brother's face.

He went into Emile's office. Emile was dictating letters at his dictaphone, and he nodded pleasantly at Armand and indicated a chair, not stopping his flow of dictation. Armand sat down. He put his fingers together across his big belly and began to twiddle his thumbs. His eyes were more harassed than ever. Finally Emile had done. He turned to his brother and smiled affably. "Well. What's on your mind? You look worried."

Armand did not know what to say, exactly. He pursed up his lips. Then he said: "It looks as though Parsons are going to lose that French order, too. Duval-Bonnet is after it. What are we going to do?"

Emile compressed his mouth and shook his head somberly.

"I don't know. It's the devil, isn't it? Bob Stressman writes from London that they're interested in Duval-Bonnet, too."

Armand moved restlessly, crossed his legs. "But we can't sit back and do nothing! Can't we hamstring them, or something? Can't we investigate the patents, and find them fraudulent? Surely to God there are ways! We've tried to buy them out; we've tried to find out who is behind them. It's come to nothing. But it's never been our way to accept defeat, especially on anything as important as this. I tell you what: I'm going to New York to have a talk with Endicott James. We'll have patents investigated. That's always a good way to hamstring a new company."

Emile regarded him seriously, and again shook his head. "I'm sorry, Armand. We've just tried that. Christopher wrote to them last week. Didn't he tell you? Here is Endicott James' reply," and he opened his drawer and withdrew a letter. "You see, they admit they can do nothing, though they've searched all the records."

Armand read the letter gloomily, then flung it aside. He stared at his brother. "Then, let's compromise with Duval-Bonnet. Get them in with us. After all, we can offer them a lot."

Emile smiled oddly. "I'm afraid that's impossible. We'll just have to increase the quality of Parsons' own craft, that's all. It's the very devil!"

There was a pause. Neither spoke. Armand gloomily studied his boots. Then he looked up, unexpectedly. He caught the most secret and most inimical expression on Emile's face. It all happened in a flash. The expression changed to one of sympathetic interest and smiling humor. But Armand was profoundly shocked. Something seemed to drop in his chest, then turn over. He thought: He's in it, too, with Chris. But what, in the name of Christ, is it?

He heard himself saying: "There's a rumor around that the engagement between Celeste and Henri is going to be announced soon. Is there any truth in this?"

Emile answered pleasantly: "I don't know yet. You know as much about it as I do. It will be a fine marriage for the little girl, won't it? Keeping everything in the family."

"I'm not so sure," replied Armand slowly, feeling his way through words as through brush. "Celeste hasn't had much experience knowing other men. She's been too sheltered. I think she ought to take her time. I'm going to advise her about it tonight. She's having dinner with us."

Emile said nothing, but Armand's sharpened eyes saw a subtle change in the smile. It had become less pleasant.

156

He got up. "Well, anyway, Emile, don't fail to look into the Duval-Bonnet matter more, will you?"

He went to the door. He had just reached it when it opened from the other side and Christopher entered. When he saw Armand he smiled, but did not speak. His transparent nostrils distended just a trifle. He backed away.

"Never mind, never mind," said Armand, shouldering through the door. "It's nothing important. I'm going, anyway."

The door closed after him. Armand stood outside, against his will. He tried to move away, but could not. He heard nothing inside the room. There was the most complete silence. After a few moments he colored painfully, observing the interest with which Christopher's secretary was regarding him. Stiffening, he walked away from the door, and went back to his own office.

Once there, he sat down heavily, his lip thrust out. He put his hands in his pockets and jingled the coins. He sat in thought for a long time. Then he picked up his telephone and called his mother. She answered almost immediately, and he thought her voice sounded agitated and weak.

"Mother, I've been thinking over what you said. I'll surely talk to Celeste tonight. Don't worry——"

She answered faintly: "Christopher just called a minute ago. He said that he wished Celeste to stay at home tonight, as Henri had mentioned coming after dinner."

There was a short pause, then Armand said: "Ah. I see. I almost expected that. You were right, Mother. Never mind, never mind. What did you tell him?"

"I told him that Celeste was not at home." Her voice dropped almost to a whisper. "But she's upstairs, having her music lesson. I told him she was away at lunch with some friends, and would probably not return until late tonight, as she would probably go on to your home. So he has left word with your wife, Mary, to tell Celeste to return to Endur immediately, when she arrives."

Again there was a pause. Armand spoke again, clearing his throat: "I see. I see. Mother, will you please tell Celeste that Annette is not feeling well today, and would like to have her come over this afternoon? Then she can remain afterwards, for dinner. In the meantime, I'll call Mary, and explain that it is all right for Celeste to remain."

He hung up. He felt quite sick.

It had been pure fiction, contrived by Christopher, of course. For Henri knew nothing of the alleged invitation

157

to call at Endur that night. Had he known, it would have been impossible for him to have gone. The reason for this was that at that precise moment he was in the offices of Washington's richest and most unscrupulous patent lawyers. He was having a very confidential and interesting interview with Mr. Thomas Burke, senior member of the firm. On the table before them were spread all the blueprints of Duval-Bonnet's marvelous bombers.

Later that afternoon, the uneasy Armand called Nicholas Bouchard at the bank. His cousin's harsh voice changed to one as friendly as possible. Armand hardly knew what to say at first. Then he said abruptly: "Nick, I've heard that my sister Celeste's engagement to Henri may be announced very shortly. My mother thinks the marriage unsuitable. She—she implied that Christopher might be interested in the marriage, without regard to the little girl's own happiness. She implied he might possibly be engineering this marriage—. What do you think?"

There was a considerable pause. Then Nicholas spoke, roughly and cautiously: "Jean was here this morning. What we said might interest you. I advised him not to mention it to you yet. Until we knew more. I think, though, you ought to know all we know, now. Don't say anything more. You can't tell what sneaks you've got there in your office."

CHAPTER XIX

ANNETTE BOUCHARD was playing one of her own compositions for her young aunt, Celeste. The big quiet room was all gray shadow, except for the dim scarlet of the fire. The reflection of the snow outside lay along upper wall and ceiling. Little Annette herself was only a small shadow. But her delicate moving hands seemed to catch the spectral reflection of the snow on themselves, and they shone with a pale luster in the indefinite gloom.

Two young girls were sitting in Annette's own sitting-room on the fourth floor of the great mansion on the river. Annette had a suite of four rooms, in which she lived like a recluse with her personal maid. Her mother, a pinched, busy, acid little woman, had nagged and complained for years about the solitary habits of her daughter. But without any appreciable results beyond Annette's occasional surrender at a dinner party. However, even Mary Bouchard had been forced to see how the girl had suffered at her own debut, and so, beyond fixed social obligations, she let her alone. Annette had furnished her apartment herself. For some strange reason this frail little creature, who looked like nothing else but a small hurt bird, liked massive dark furniture about her, furniture solid and heavy and cumbersome. Her huge bed had mahogany carved posts almost as thick as her fragile body, and was topped with a canopy of lace and velvet. Her footstools were as high as her knee, her chairs built for men. She moved amid this ponderous splendor like a child in an adult world.

Annette was not deformed, though that was usually the first impression of strangers. Rather, she was undersized and underdeveloped, and walked so diffidently and so shyly that her little shoulders were always a trifle bent. Her poor little body was flat as a small board, and as fleshless. Her limbs were infantile, her hands like a young child's. She had a sweet reedlike voice, and an embarrassed laugh. Congenital ill-health had stunted and withered her body, but had not touched her mind and spirit. Her tiny triangular face, white and somewhat worn as with suffering, was only the background for her large and beautiful light blue eyes. Her other features were delicate as transparent porcelain. Her hair was a very light color, almost ashen, and streamed down in ripples on her shoulders like the hair of an Alice in Wonderland. All her movements, however, were quick and resolute. Beside her, Celeste, small of stature herself, appeared robust and full of vital color. Annette had always been her father's darling. She had not walked until she was four years old, and Armand had carried her in his arms whenever he was at home. In all the world, he loved no one but this fragile little creature, not even his handsome young son, Antoine, who resembled Jules Bouchard, his grandfather, quite astonishingly.

Annette had had the finest teachers. Long ago, she had shown a passion for music. She played many instruments, but preferred her gold-and-ivory harp. On this she would play for hours, improvising, humming an accompaniment, composing. Armand knew nothing about music, and cared much less. Yet he could sit by the hour watching his little daughter as she played, and found nothing more fascinating, nothing more delightful. At these times the heavy, somewhat brutal, more than merely ruthless, expression of his face would lighten, soften, and something would replace it, something somber, melancholy and tired. He could forget everything, from the hatred and envy that surrounded him, to the exigencies and sleepless anxieties that were his by virtue of his control of Bouchard and Sons. When he would watch the little fingers of his daughter feeling their way through the murmuring strings of her harp, and shaking out thin and airy drops of sound on the air, he would suddenly believe that nothing in the world was important at all, nothing except tenderness and protection and peace. Sometimes he would ask himself the ancient, world-worn question: Why do I do what I do? Of what value is it? Who wants what I have? Let them have it.

Once he asked Annette impulsively: "How would you like to go away with your Dad, somewhere far off, on a long vacation? Just you and me?" She had exclaimed with delight, and had left her harp and had run to him, to climb on his knee like a child. Yet, the next day, almost the next hour, he was embarrassed. When next he saw his daughter, he had been sheepish and uncomfortable, wondering how he could evade his proposal. But she had merely looked at him, and waited. When he said nothing, she had said nothing, either. She never mentioned it. At first he was grateful, hoping she had forgotten. Later, he decided she had not forgotten. Her silence was more painful to him than complaints or disappointment.

Celeste sat by the window, half listening to Annette's improvising and composing. Every note was soft and rounded, fully formed in itself, never blurring into another. They left the strings like silver bubbles, breaking on the quiet air with an almost visible brightness.

Annette spoke, her voice seeming to accompany her music: "What are you thinking about, Celeste? You sit there like Sister Anne. Who are you waiting for?"

"Nobody." Celeste moved the curtain with her hand, and affected to be absorbed in a study of the darkening sky. "It's almost Christmas. What would you like for a present, Annette?"

When Annette did not answer, and the music softened almost to a whisper, Celeste turned and looked at her niece in surprise. Annette's head was bent, the hair falling over her face, which was in complete shadow. Her hands continued to wander among the strings, hesitating, trembling. "Annette! What's the matter? Did you hear what I asked you?"

Annette lifted her head. The spectral light was on her

160

face, now, as it was on her hands. She was smiling. "Yes. I heard. Celeste, do you think I'm too young to fall in love? After all, I'm not much younger than you."

Celeste stared, then laughed. "Why, Annette! Who is it? Do I know him?" She was so intrigued that she left her seat and went to the other girl. She sat down beside her, on a footstool. "Tell me, Annette. Who is it? Of course you're not too young. You're much older than most girls of your age, you know."

Annette still smiled. She looked at Celeste with a sort of gentle light quivering on her face. She appeared almost beautiful. "Yes, dear, you know him. But please don't ask me, just yet. You see, I'm afraid you might laugh. No, you wouldn't really laugh, would you? But I want to keep it a secret for just a little while. Please? You see, when I keep it a secret, just to myself, I don't mind the possibility of his not caring about me. But if someone else knew, and he never could care about me, it would be just like—like making matters worse——"

"But who could help caring about you, Annette? Do you think Armand would mind? Is that the trouble?"

Annette laughed softly. "No, I think he would be glad. He likes—him. At least, I think so." She struck the strings suddenly with a loud but muted sound, so that it seemed like a pang given articulation. Then her hands fell from them, into her lap. She sagged a little, as though tired. But she was smiling. "I'm glad you think I'm not too young. You see, he treats me like a baby."

Celeste was both excited and surprised. She had never thought of Annette as one who could grow up, and marry, and live a normal life. When she had thought of the future, she had seen herself married to a shadowy but worshipped husband, probably with several children. But through all the years of the future she had seen Annette, unchanging, in this room, with her harp, always young and fragile and sweet, waiting to hear Celeste's stories of her children and her husband and her maturing life. Now, it appeared that Annette could have desires and hopes and passions beyond this quiet room with the harp and the old heavy furniture. She decided it would take some time for her to orient this new picture of her niece. But when she tried to conjure up a vision of Annette as a wife and mother, with a home of her own, perhaps in another city, her imagination balked.

Feeling guilty, Celeste curled a strand of the ash-blonde hair about her fingers. Annette smiled at her sideways

161

through her beautiful blue eyes. "You won't, of course, say anything to anybody, Celeste?"

"Don't be silly. I won't, of course. But I'm dying to know who he is."

"You'll know, soon enough."

"But tell me this, anyway: Do I like him? You can surely tell me that."

Annette was silent a moment. She frowned in concentration. "I don't know, Celeste. I don't think I've ever seen you both in the same room together more than once or twice." She sighed, shivered, smiled again.

Celeste marveled. With the instinctive shrewdness of women, she studied Annette's frail boardlike body. The thin short legs ridged her dress. Her feet were tiny as a child's. Her breasts were immature, budding. Celeste felt embarrassed and guilty once more. She was conscious of her own body, warm and vital and rich with young womanhood.

The door opened and Armand entered. He was much earlier today than usual. Annette, with a cry of delight, swooped towards him. He gathered her in his arms and held her to him. Against his bulk she looked frailer than ever, and more than ever like a bird.

"What have you girls been doing alone here, in the dark?" he asked. He nodded at his young sister. She turned on lights, poked the fire into a cheerful blaze. He regarded her with smiling somberness, ashamed that he could covet her young strength and health and glowing vitality, for his child.

"Annette's been playing me her new Spring Nocturne," replied Celeste. She was never quite comfortable with her oldest brother, for she subconsciously recognized in him a betrayal of integrity. "It's very beautiful. Play it for your father, Annette."

"Oh, Dad would be bored," said Annette. Armand sat down, and held his little daughter on his knee. "No, I won't be bored, darling. Play it." He ran his big blunt hand over her rippling hair. He seemed reluctant to let her go.

Annette sat down at her harp. She threw back her hair, and lifted her small pale fingers. They touched the strings gently, softly, meditatively. Armand leaned back in his chair, his hand half shielding his face, his thick short legs relaxed as though he were exhausted. Behind that shield he did not look at his daughter, as usual, but at his sister, who was sitting near Annette's stool. Celeste's head was lifted; her dark hair fell back from her face and temples, and for the first time he noticed the stern delicate modeling of her young face, the strong purity of her cheeks and forehead. He was

162

drearily ashamed of his covetousness, even though it had been for Annette. He seemed to see Celeste clearly for the first time. He said to himself: Mother is right. Now he became aware that Celeste was gazing at him; she must have been attracted by the current of malaise that flowed from him. At any rate she was thinking that her brother appeared much older, much more tired, and much paler, than ordinarily.

The silvery notes were forming on the strings of the harp, and were rising with that almost visible brightness on the warm air. Their melancholy sweetness was nearly unbearable; their poignancy was well-nigh painful. They suggested a spring evening, full of nostalgia and sad beauty. The new greenness they conjured up, the vision of faint dark sky and living air and breathing earth and opening purity, of spring moon and freshening plain and cool running water, was only a background for a dim and mournful suffering that was without words. It was an emotion that both hoped and despaired, that rose one moment on a blowing veil of hope, and then saw that veil dissolve. It was an awareness of life, and the shadow of life, which is death. Armand, who knew nothing of music, and cared less for it, felt as if each of those sorrowful yet tender notes struck on his naked heart. His tiredness and disgust, his depression and dread, his own hopelessness and mental weariness, had stripped that heart of its defenses. He closed his eyes. There was nothing but darkness, in which there was nothing but the singing of the harp. His thoughts were chaotic. It was strange then, that he suddenly thought: It would be better for Annette to die.

He was so startled by his thought that he opened his eyes. The last notes were falling and whispering into silence. Little Annette's head was bent, as though she were meditating. Armand felt a bitter burn along his eyelids, but when Annette looked at him expectantly he smiled at her.

"It is beautiful, darling. Have you-er-got it written down, or whatever it is that you musicians do with your compositions? We'll send it to a publisher——"

She shook her head. "No, it isn't—written down, Dad. You see, each time I play it, it is different. Isn't it, Celeste?"

Celeste started, as if touched, during sleep, by an awakening hand. "Yes. Yes, of course. It is different every time." Her face had a sleeping quality of peace and joy on it. "This time it seemed to promise everything. It seemed to tell me that there was nothing in all the world but beauty and happiness." She smiled shyly at what she considered her own extravagance. "Didn't it tell you that too, Armand?"

He stared at her. She could not read his expression. "No, Celeste. I'm afraid it didn't. But then," and he smiled painfully, "I'm not a young girl. You see, I don't expect anything."

He studied the two young faces and thought: Is it possible that they expect anything? He was suddenly compassionate. Compassion was not a customary emotion with him. He could not recall having experienced impersonal pity before. He seemed to have grown much older in his heart and mind in the last few hours, and much more subtle. He thought again, wryly: Would I have been able to understand all this, and been able to pity, if I were not just cowardly afraid of my brothers? If I had not just come from Nick, and had not heard what I've just heard in his office, would I have found anything else in my darling's music but just a pretty sound? Perhaps all these grand emotions everyone talks about, but which I've never experienced before, are only the products of fear.

Annette was climbing on his knee again. She was putting her head on his shoulder. His arms tightened about her, almost jealously. He remembered his thought that it would be better for her to die, and a pang divided him. He kissed her hair, and gently bit her cheek, a loving habit of his. "You are just a puss," he said absently. Over her head he regarded his sister with heavy thoughtfulness.

"What's all this I hear about you getting married, Celeste?" he asked abruptly.

Annette stirred in his arms. "Married!" she shrieked. "Celeste? Married?" She sat up, her little face brightening with laughter and excitement. "Celeste! That's not fair. You didn't tell me!"

. Celeste was silent. Her face flushed red with embarrassment. But she was smiling. "I didn't tell you because there's nothing to tell. Really. Where did you get such an idea, Armand?"

He scrutinized her for a long moment or two. He saw her warm color, and the way her eyes shone with confusion. Yet, in his new subtlety, he could pause a moment and drearily consider how much self-interest there was in his sudden alarm.

"Someone mentioned it to me, Celeste. But if you do not want to say anything about it—to us——"

Annette slipped off her father's knee. She ran to Celeste, knelt down beside her, laughing. "Oh, you cheat! Never to say anything about it to me! Who is he, Celeste? What is his name? Do I know him?"

Armand, painfully alert, leaned forward, the better to watch his sister. She sat in her low chair, and was turning redder and redder each moment. She did not know where to look. She averted her face from Annette, kneeling beside her.

"It's so silly. There's nothing to say. Honestly. I don't know who could've been telling you——"

Armand felt relief. "Well, then, if it's just gossip, we'll let it drop. But I was given to understand it was practically settled. I might have known, though, that if there had been anything to it I'd've heard, as your brother, my dear."

Celeste said nothing. She rubbed her fingers together. But Annette was becoming more excited. "Oh, even if it's not settled, I want to know about it! You've hurt my feelings. Can't you tell me, just a little?"

Armand smiled at his little daughter. "Don't be so excited, child. You've heard Celeste say there is nothing to it. It was just a rumor that she and Henri Bouchard were about to become engaged. It seems, though, that it was even less than a rumor."

Celeste had blushed again. "I can't think who——" she murmured. Armand frowned. His sister's confusion frightened him. There was something to all this!

"At any rate, Celeste, you're only a child. You've not seen anything of the world. Take your time. Take your time. You've got a lot of time, you know. Young girls can make serious mistakes."

He looked into her eyes gravely. And she looked back, with increasing shyness. Neither noticed Annette, still kneeling beside Celeste. Neither noticed how rigid she had become, there on her knees, and how deathly white her face had turned, and how distended and fixed were her great blue eyes. Neither noticed how her hands had dropped to her side, and how her lips had fallen open as though she had been mortally struck.

"I don't want to make mistakes," said Celeste in a low voice.

"No, of course not," said her brother, with fraternal eagerness. "See here, my dear child: I'm your brother, but I'm old enough to be your father. Almost, at any rate. Perhaps I've neglected you somewhat. Young men are apt to neglect children in a nursery. I'm sorry for that. I've always hoped that you'd be happy, however. I'd——I'd like to help you, some way. And somehow, I don't think Henri could make you happy. You're too young and inexperienced, for him. You see?"

Celeste was silent. But an expression of cold pride and

aloofness settled on her face. Armand regarded her earnestly, and with mounting alarm.

"Celeste, my dear, don't be offended. I don't mean to offend you. I am deeply interested in you. I'd be—sorry—if you were unhappy."

She looked at him with directness. "Why do you think Henri would make me unhappy?"

He could be surprised, even at this moment, that little shy Celeste could exhibit such strength of character. I have underestimated the child, he thought. He stammered when he answered her.

"My dear, I believe he would." And all at once he was no longer hypocritical. He truly believed what he was saying. "Do you remember hearing Father talk about his Uncle Ernest? Do you remember what he said?" The girl did not move; her eyes were fixed upon him darkly. "Well, Celeste, Henri is Ernest Barbour's great-grandson. And from what I have seen of him, I would say he is another Ernest Barbour. Do you think a man like that could make you happy?"

She did not answer. Armand got to his feet abruptly. He began to walk up and down the room. He passed and repassed his kneeling daughter, but did not see her. He was too engrossed with the portentousness of what was happening in this room. He went to the window, and looked out at the dim grays and blacks and whites of the wintry park-like grounds. A wind shook the tall wide windows. In the far distance he could catch the iron glimmer of the river.

"I don't think Henri can be trusted," he said aloud. "If you were my daughter I would say the same thing to you. I wouldn't want to see you marry him. There's something about him that's without integrity—" He paused. His head seemed to sink a little between his shoulders. He twisted his neck uneasily. "He's ruthless. I don't—like men like that. He wouldn't make you happy, Celeste."

Her silence continued. Armand sighed. He lifted his head and looked gloomily at the warm bright picture of the room behind him, which was reflected in the glass of the window. He saw Celeste, silent and brooding. And then a chill struck him. He saw his little daughter's face and attitude. He looked closer, something throbbing in his chest. His lips dried. He moistened them. Then, very slowly, he turned and looked at the picture directly.

And now he saw nothing but Annette, poor little Annette, with her face of death, and her hanging hands.

Celeste began to speak. "He—he's not said anything to me yet, Armand. You mustn't think I'm ungrateful to you—

He's not said anything. I—I like him. I don't think you're fair, in some ways—" She colored again, violently.

But Arnand still saw nothing but Annette. And as he gazed at her a fierce rage of protection came into his eyes, and the grimmest of lines settled about his lips.

CHAPTER XX

JAY REGAN, old and huge and fat, "robber baron extraordinary," knew more about American history than any historian ever did, and more about the history of Europe, too. Only financiers know the true history of any peoples, and as a giant among financiers, Jay Regan was excessively well informed.

He was old, but he loved human nature. He never lost his zest for it. And so, as he turned a certain letter over and over in his hands today, he smiled with an almost childish enjoyment. It was a letter from Henri Bouchard, asking him for an interview within a few days.

He said aloud, musingly, smilingly: "I wonder what this young sprig is like? Is he like his great-grandfather, Ernest Barbour, that glacier among men, or is he like his uncle, Jules Bouchard, the Richelieu of the armaments industry? Or is he a combination of the two?"

Regan remembered Ernest Barbour with the excitement with which one remembers the vision of something extraordinary, and not to be forgotten. His father had often called him into his office to be present during conferences between himself and Ernest Barbour. The younger Regan had found Ernest's face fascinating in its smooth stoniness, its large implacability. Conferences with him present were less exciting than terrible. One had the feeling of something imminent, which did not appear to have happened. It was only later that one felt that it had indeed happened.

But Jules Bouchard! Ah, it was better than all the operas, all the plays and the tragedies and the comedies, to be present when he dominated a conference! It was like watching color and fire, buffoonery in silk and satin. And yet, later, one had the feeling that the thing which had happened was no less terrible than the things which Ernest Barbour had made to

167

happen. But it was all so much fun, and excitement, and color, while it had been happening.

Ah, Jules was a man! remembered Jay Regan. And he remembered this again when Henri Bouchard, a few days later, was announced.

Regan waited with excited interest. He was an old man, now, and he did not think that the heirs of old Barbour-Bouchard were of the stature of Ernest Barbour. He knew Armand Bouchard very well, and had respect for his shrewdness and his executive ability and soundness. But he was also an astute man, and had long ago guessed the uneasiness of the suppressed integrity of Armand, and he had his private apprehensions that some day that integrity might destroy its owner. He remembered Honore Bouchard, and the probity which had well-nigh wrecked a certain conference in his office in 1914. He remembered his own father's story of the uneasy integrity of Eugene Bouchard, father of Honore. "Itching consciences seem to run in the family," he thought. He remembered, grinning faintly, what his father had said of integrity, and particularly of the brand of integrity which cropped up at intervals in the Bouchard family: "It's just a costiveness of the spirit."

Regan knew all the Bouchards. Of them all, he liked only Armand. But he considered Christopher to be the only one possessing some part of the qualities of Jules Bouchard and Ernest Barbour. However, Christopher's apparent lack of human warmth and roundness made him a sterile character in Regan's estimation. To be a Titan, in full, a man must beget with his body as well as with his mind, thought Regan. Steel-colored monks like Christopher must fail at the end for not taking the human equation into consideration. At the end, one invariably bumped into human beings, and if one had no humanness to respond to the humanness of others, one failed, at the inevitable moment. Once he had said to Christopher: "Why don't you marry? Have half a dozen children. You'll be a better man for it, a wiser man. No, I'm not sentimental. But I know what is necessary to success."

He guessed, shrewdly, that Christopher well understood the subtleties or craftinesses or plottings or treacheries of others. But the flesh behind them he did not understand, and therein, Regan believed, lay his inevitable defeat.

Now he was quite curious to see the great-grandson of Ernest Barbour. He, himself, had been a young man at Yale when Ernest had been in his late middle-age, yet the memory of those inexorable eyes, the large head and crest of vital hair, the broad shoulders and virile, stocky figure, the heavy sullen lips and firm tread, was fresh and unfaded. So, when Henri Bouchard entered, Regan was not for a moment amazed; the young man seemed but an extension of his memory into the present.

"Good afternoon, Mr. Regan," said Henri gravely. Regan did not speak. Henri smiled. He was used to this profound transfixion of those who saw him for the first time, and who remembered his great-grandfather.

Finally Regan could speak, and then huskily. "Sit down, please. So, you're Henri Bouchard. Did anyone ever tell you how much you look like Ernest Barbour?"

"Yes. Practically everybody who knew him. They usually end up, though, by doubting if I have what they call his 'qualities.' " And the young man smiled again.

Regan was silent a moment. He continued to study the other. Then he asked bluntly: "Have you?"

Henri lifted his shoulders imperceptibly, the only gesture he had inherited from his Latin strain. He did not answer. But his eyes met the shrewd old eyes of Regan and did not move away.

Finally, Regan pushed his silver-and-ivory cigar box towards the young man. "Will you have a drink?" he asked.

"No, thank you," answered Henri. "I don't care for it."

Regan was in the act of pouring brandy into a small silver container. He finished pouring. Then he said in a peculiar voice: "Your great-grandfather, I remember hearing my father say, did not like the taste of alcohol. But you have lived in England, and in France——"

"I still don't like it," said Henri, smiling. He saw that the old big stout man was considerably shaken.

Regan sipped the brandy thoughtfully. "It's amazing," he murmured, staring at the young man. He finished sipping, put down the container. "I hear you have come home to stay. Is that true?"

"Yes. My sister and I have returned to Windsor, and are living in the old house my grandparents built. We intend to stay."

Regan's eyes narrowed to pinpoints, but his voice was casual when he said: "It must be pretty dull for two young people who're used to Paris and London, and all the rest."

"I," said Henri, "don't expect it to be dull."

There was a long and pregnant pause, while their eyes met and held. Then, under Regan's white clipped mustache a peculiar glinting smile formed.

"Ah," he said richly.

There was still another silence. Finally, Regan said:

"Have you been down the Street? Will you go with me? I would like to introduce you to a number of old-timers who remember your great-grandfather."

"Thank you."

Regan brushed ashes from his vest, poured himself another drink. Henri waited, smoking tranquilly. Regan smiled almost impishly.

"You know, my dear Henri, few transactions take place without the knowledge of old buzzards like me. For instance, we know that there must be great understanding between you and Christopher Bouchard for you to lend him all that money. Considering," and he cleared his throat delicately, "considering the fact that Jules Bouchard did a neat trick of making your branch of the family pretty helpless, when it comes to active participation in the affairs of Bouchard & Sons."

Henri's heavy lips twitched. "The understanding," he replied, "is all on Christopher's part."

Again, the peculiar glint occurred under Regan's mustache.

"You," he said thoughtfully, after a moment, "have been underestimated." He waited. Henri said nothing. Regan continued: "But all that money! Henri, I'm going to enjoy life for the next few years! Things have been pretty dull in the world lately."

"By all means, enjoy yourself, Mr. Regan."

Regan leaned back in his chair, which creaked faintly with his weight. He regarded the ceiling with a pleasant expression.

"There were giants in those days," he said meditatively, as though indulging in a soliloquy. "They did things. They touched things with their hands and moved them with their strength. There was excitement—the personal touch. Now everything is glittering chromium and the click of shiny machinery. No blood. Men don't hit each other over the head with clubs any more and make things exciting for the spectators. They just slip around each other in the dark and use a razor with the utmost courtesy. I don't like it. America wasn't built by dancers on a chromium stage. Have you met old Mellen? Do. He's what I mean. He would never have gotten anywhere eighty years ago. Too bloodless.

"Finance and manipulation and industry aren't roaring in America as they once were. They call their present machinations high finance. I call it decadence. That's why we're soon due for the worst economic and moral collapse we've ever known. That's why capitalism in America is practically doomed. You see, we've left the raw earth, and now we're in the clouds, piling up equations, pyramids of figures which have nothing to do with actualities and with the flesh and blood of America. Wheels turning in a vacuum."

He sat upright abruptly. "Are you following me?"

Henri raised his eyebrows slightly. "I think I am. Go on, please."

Regan stared at him intently for some moments. Then he put his thumbs in his vest and went on, still musingly:

"Even rascality, these days, is oiled and geared. Nothing picturesque; nothing human. There were feuds in those days. Now there are no feuds. It's all done in a financier's office, like this. And then they all go out to lunch. Now, I've no objection to faithlessness. Like your old revered relative's. It's a robust faithlessness, which had, for its result, the industrial rise of America. But I don't like this modern faithlessness. It's poisonous. No one gains by it but the faithless, themselves. The result is toxemia of the body of America. Do I sound metaphysical, young man?" he added abruptly.

"No. Not at all. I understand."

"I believe you do," replied Regan, staring as if in astonishment.

He went on. "I've not talked like this for years. I might say I don't know why I'm talking like this now. But there's something about you that isn't bloodless. You've got flesh; you've got arteries. Like Ernest Barbour. I'm going to enjoy all this! I'm going to enjoy seeing Ernest Barbour operate in these shiny clicking days of high finance and toxic courteous industry. Young man, do you know Wall Street is going to blow up very soon?"

"Yes. I think I do know."

"And do you know the government is going to be blown up with it?"

"Yes. It is inevitable."

Regan leaned back in his chair. "Ah," he said softly. Then, his voice becoming loud and brutal, he asked: "What do you want?"

Henri did not seem surprised at this change of tone. He said quietly: "You've told me a lot of what I wanted to know. But now I want you to tell me your own opinion of Bouchard and Sons. I mean, beyond what you have already told me."

Regan grinned. "I'm a heavy investor in Bouchard, and its subsidiaries. I'd like to be a heavier one. I'd like to get bigger dividends. I like you, Henri Bouchard. I was much interested, for instance, in hearing that you are going to marry Christopher Bouchard's sister, Celeste."

"You seem to know a great deal, Mr. Regan," said Henri courteously. "Nothing has been settled yet. The engagement isn't announced."

Regin's grin broadened. "She's a pretty child. She and Christopher and their mother were visiting us last winter. A very pretty child; very innocent, too."

Henri said nothing. He merely waited.

Regan put his fingers together and regarded them with a pleasant expression. "I don't know why I should want more money. Power? I'm an old man. Why do we seem to want more power as we grow older? Is it to make up for our physical powerlessness? I don't know. At any rate, I can say now, which you probably know, that Bouchard is marking time. There are too many plotters there. Too many plotters stalemate the plot. It needs one supreme plotter. But not a razor-plotter, without blood and flesh." He added brutally: "I like you more and more, Henri Bouchard."

Henri smiled. He continued to wait.

"Armand," said Regan, "is an executive. That's all. And the others! They're bright boys. They know everything that's in the wind of America and Europe. But they're like eunuchs that know all the motions but can't consummate them. You see? I've heard Christopher called a Trappist. Trappists are usual these days. Wall Street's full of 'em. That's why we're going to have the worst damn collapse and confusion and ruin we've ever seen, not only in America, but in Europe, too. We need new blood, the kind of blood that ruthlessly built up this country. The Bouchards don't have it, any more than other industries have it. We've got to have the same kind of faithless and powerful men that paradoxically made the nation powerful and virile, too."

He stopped speaking. Henri said nothing at all.

"Thieves," said Regan softly, after some time had elapsed. "But castrated thieves. The Bouchards."

Henri Bouchard stood up. "Thank you," he said quietly. Regan regarded him quizzically. He did not speak for a moment. He leaned back again, and put his thumbs in his vest.

"You've got to show me," he said thoughtfully. "You see? You've got to show me. And when you've shown me, I'll help you. But not before. I'm too heavy an investor in Bouchard, and its subsidiaries."

Henri picked up his hat. "This," he said, "has been the most profitable morning of my life. Mr. Regan, I want to thank you again. I will be seeing you again, very soon."

Regan smiled. His smile broadened. "I believe you will," he said. "I believe you will!"

172

CHAPTER XXI

EDITH was at her desk this dark early March morning, adding up accounts, and checking off items with sharp decisive motions of her pencil. When her Aunt Adelaide was announced, she raised her eyebrows in surprise and glanced through the French windows of her study. Steel-gray rain, semi-transparent, was a moving curtain between her and the black and twisting trees outside. Edith put down her pencil, and then went quietly downstairs where her aunt waited in the fire-lit morning room.

Adelaide sat on the edge of her chair, her hands in her muff. She looked more Victorian than ever, with her fur tippet about her neck, and her plain dowdy hat set agitatedly on top of her gray soft hair. Yet the sweetness of her expression, the tilt of her head and the set of her body were the hallmarks of her real breeding.

"Good morning, my dear," she said gently, as Edith entered. The young woman hesitated a moment, then came up to her aunt and kissed her coolly on the cheek. "What a beastly morning for you to be out, Auntie," she said. "Won't you take off your things?" She noticed that Adelaide's face was thinner and grayer than it was even a week ago. "You will have luncheon with me?"

Adelaide murmured a gentle refusal. "No, dear, I must go home almost immediately. Well, then, if you insist. But you are busy?"

"Not so very. Just accounts." Edith smiled her dark and chilly smile. Adelaide regarded her earnestly. She accused herself of hardness of heart in that she could not like this reserved plain young woman with her air of competence and hard efficiency and colorless breeding. The thin angular face had a sallow cast, and was entirely untinted. The smooth black hair was rolled in an efficient knot at the nape of her neck. All the coloring, all the smartness of plain black dress and slim silk-shod ankles, were Latin, but the coldness, reserve and severity did not come from that warm and human strain.

Adelaide glanced away, vaguely distressed. She drew in

her faded lips and moistened them. A maid came in to take her coat and hat and furs. She shivered, drew closer to the fire. Edith competently stirred it up into a vivid golden blaze. "Horrible weather," she commented, as she did so.

She wondered why Adelaide had come. The older woman's air of tense eagerness to please, of pathetic supplication, of distress, of abstraction and weariness and hopelessness, intrigued her curiosity, and made her feel a faint compunction.

Whatever it was, Adelaide apparently did not know how to proceed to the object of her call. She asked falteringly about Henri, and a pale shadow of relief passed over her face when Edith informed her that her brother was visiting Georges and Marion Bouchard in New York. Adelaide murmured gently. She liked Georges very much, she said. And Marion, too, she added hastily. They had promised her to visit Crissons during the summer, and then there had been Marion's operation. However, she and Celeste intended to visit them both at Easter. When she mentioned Celeste's name the poor woman's lips trembled, and she bent her fingers against each other in furtive agitation.

Edith had been watching her with sharp attention. So, she thought, it is about that soft little puss of a Celeste that she has come to see me. The young woman's curiosity mounted. Why should she be consulted about Celeste, of whom she was not particularly fond?

Luncheon was served in the warm morning-room, and it was over before Adelaide could again force herself to face the object of her visit. And again, she shrank away. Her eyes had an imploring quality in them when she looked at Edith. Edith also detected fear. She had long ago guessed that her aunt feared her, and was uncomfortable in her presence. But Edith was used to having soft weaklings and the irresolute fear her. She regarded her aunt with a slight expression of pity, mingled with contempt.

Edith had politely asked about all the members of the family she had not seen during the past week. She was becoming bored, and impatient. It was getting along to two o'clock, and this foolish old woman was no nearer the object of her visit than she had been over two hours ago. So she decided to force the matter herself.

"Celeste is almost twenty, isn't she, Aunt Adelaide? You'll miss her when she marries, won't you?"

Adelaide's lips parted in an almost inaudible gasp. Then desperate determination caused her nostrils to distend and her upper lip to quiver rigidly.

"Yes, dear, I'll miss her. But that won't matter. Only

174

Celeste's happiness matters. That is what is so important—Celeste's happiness. She's been so sheltered. She—she doesn't understand people at all." She stopped, unable to continue.

Edith raised her eyebrows politely. "Young girls aren't so sheltered any more, these days, Aunt Adelaide. That is unfortunate for Celeste. Little Rosemarie, for instance, is a woman compared to her."

Adelaide leaned forward in her intense desire to make Edith understand. "Yes, it is unfortunate. It wasn't my wish, Edith. It—it is a little confusing, when I try to explain. I—I wanted Celeste to go away to school. I wanted her to realize that there is so—so much wickedness, and evil, and cruelty in the world, but I also wanted her to understand that while she must accept the existence of these things she must not accept their universality, and their inevitability— Do you understand what I mean, dear?"

Edith was silent a moment. Her expression was a little odd. Then she said: "I think I do, Aunt Adelaide."

Adelaide made a despairing gesture. "I'm not at all clear. Sometimes I am confused myself. The line between hopelessness and hope is so thin that it is almost impossible— But you see, it is that little line that enables men to live at all in the world, and not go mad.

"I know Celeste so well. She—she is somewhat as I was, when I was a young girl. I don't want her to suffer as I did, Edith. You see, for a long time I did not know that there was goodness and kindness and honor in the world, after I saw what wickedness and cruelty there was. I want her to know all of it, right at the beginning, and so save herself years of misery——"

"Aren't you afraid that all this is just a little sentimental, Aunt Adelaide?" asked Edith. "After all, we all have to learn a few fundamental lessons. It won't hurt Celeste to learn them, as well as the rest of us."

Adelaide shook her head. "Edith, you don't know, my dear. The world is full of men and women like Celeste. Evil strikes them down mortally; that is because they were born without scales. They suffer all their lives. Sometimes they commit suicide. I'm afraid I'm not making myself clear," she faltered. Edith's dark face was as smooth as opaque glass, but she said nothing.

Adelaide's face was growing a little wild. "Edith, I'm not very good at expositions. But you remember the stories about one of your great-grandfathers? Martin Barbour? Well, my dear, he was such a one as Celeste. His whole life was a tragedy. His death was a tragedy. I've had the strangest feeling, ever since I heard about him, that even when he died in the Civil War, he believed he was dying for nothing. The conflicts in the soul, Edith, are the most frightful ones."

"Yes, so I've heard. Freud speaks of them quite extensively." Edith could not prevent her lip from curling. "As for myself, I think it is all nonsense. Unhealthy. Celeste is not a child. If she isn't capable of learning things, and adjusting herself sensibly to them, then she has no right to live in the world of today. Forgive me if I sound brutal, but Henri and I have discussed this rather fully. I am afraid we both rather condemned you, Aunt Adelaide. Celeste ought not to have been so sheltered."

Adelaide had turned paler than ever. She uttered a little cry. "But Edith, I've been trying to tell you! I didn't want Celeste to be so sheltered. I just wanted to arm her against —living. But Christopher wanted her to be sheltered from what he calls—dirtiness. And that isn't the thing I mean at all! His sheltering of her has made her more vulnerable than ever."

Edith's fine dark brows lifted. She shrugged whimsically, and smiled with helpless mockery. "Now, Aunt Adelaide, I must admit I'm losing you. This is all so—so metaphysical. Why don't you take Celeste to a psychoanalyst?" She could not help this final cruelty, though she immediately regretted it.

Adelaide did not answer. She sank back in her chair, and averted her face. Edith saw her hands drop on the arms of the chair in a gesture of the utmost exhaustion and hopelessness. A twinge of compunction made Edith's features twitch impatiently.

"I'm sorry, Auntie. I didn't mean to be so rude. But I'm afraid you are splitting hairs. It's been my experience that human beings aren't so delicate and frail as you seem to think Celeste is. They're pretty tough, it seems to me. Celeste looks a robust girl, with lots of fight in her if she gets aroused. You can see that in her face. But you want me to help you, don't you? How can I help you?"

Adelaide's attitude did not change. She did not even look at Edith. She merely said in a dull voice: "By telling your brother that he mustn't marry my daughter."

Edith was astounded. She frowned coldly. Her lips seemed carved out of stone in her affronted face. "But why not? I'm not sure he wants to, really. I've thought he was attracted to Celeste, but young men are always attracted to pretty girls. Heavens knows, Henri is no different from other men. He lived in London and Paris for some years, you know." Now a contemptuous smile stood on her mouth. "But if he and Celeste should decide they want to marry, why shouldn't they?"

Adelaide still did not look at her. She spoke as though from a great and exhausted distance: "Because, if she does, she'll be defenseless. She'll be mortally unhappy. She'll find out what all the Bouchards are. Including Christopher. She mustn't find out. She'll never get over it."

Edith opened her mouth to utter an angry ejaculation, then closed it again. But her whole face was alive with anger and affront and disdain. Adelaide slowly lifted her head, turned to regard her niece fully. "But you won't help me, will you, Edith?"

Edith exclaimed in a rather loud voice: "Aunt Adelaide! How can I help you? I don't know what you've been talking about. It seems so foolish, to me. There, I'm afraid I'm being rude, but I can't help it, really. After all, you've insulted my brother. Strange as it may seem, I'm fond of him! I don't think there is a girl in all the world good enough for him. I had a friend in England, Lady Verity Post-Brian, whom I hoped he would marry. Her fortune is much larger than Celeste's, and I must say, frankly, that her family is far superior to ours. She is the only one I believe is nearly worthy of him. Perhaps he'll marry her, after all; I know he writes to her regularly.

"I'm sorry, Aunt Adelaide," she continued, taking fresh breath, "that you have such a low opinion of the Bouchards. I've heard that Uncle Jules was very devoted to you. No one of us has done you any harm. Celeste will be a very lucky girl if she can catch Henri. But I sincerely hope she doesn't! For his sake."

Adelaide listened, her mournful eyes fixed on the young woman's cold and angry face. Then she said with dreary gentleness: "I'm sorry, Edith, dear. I see that I've offended you. I'm so sorry. I'm afraid that I've blundered dreadfully. Please forgive me. But I thought perhaps you might understand. You are such an intelligent girl."

She rose with the feeble movements of one who has been very ill. Edith rose, also, and stood in dark silence. Adelaide smiled piteously. "You are right, my dear. I hope for your brother's sake, that he won't marry Celeste. It isn't pleasant to be married to someone who—is suffering. I realize, now, that I must have made Jules unhappy, too. I forgave him many years ago, but that was because I loved him. Now I must forgive him all over again, because I finally understand."

177

Edith was touched, in spite of herself. She smiled, and kissed her aunt on the cheek.

"Perhaps we're both too excited. So far, I haven't seen any actual desire on Henri's part to marry Celeste. But I'll do what I can. You'll see!"

After Adelaide had left in the wet and windy semi-darkness of the afternoon, Edith sat down and frowned into space for a long time. Finally, with an air of resolution, strangely mixed with excitement and amusement, she went to a telephone and called Christopher at his office. She was very familar with the number. When she spoke to him her expression became gay and soft and chaffing.

CHAPTER XXII

AT FOUR o'clock Henri Bouchard called his sister from New York, and urged her to join him there. "Take the ten-ten. I'll meet you at the Pennsylvania Station in the morning. Come on. The opera season's about over. No, I don't like music any better!" He laughed. "But Archibald Post-Brian's here for a day or two. Maybe I can get rid of you!"

She refused. Henri seemed surprised. "I thought you were all for old Archie. He's got three million pounds. Besides, I've got a lot of stock in Robsons-Strong now, and we might just as well keep it in the family."

"Well, then, Henri, you'd better marry Archie's sister, and get yourself a little directorship in Robsons-Strong. Old Uncle Strong has hardening of the arteries, and Verity's his pet."

Henri laughed again. "I buy munitions. I don't marry them."

Edith chuckled. "I'm glad to hear that. I thought perhaps you had designs on Celeste."

To her surprise Henri did not speak for a moment or two. Then in a matter-of-fact voice he said: "I have." He added: "Well, if you won't come, you won't. But don't be surprised if old Archie runs over to Windsor to see you."

Edith felt shaken when she hung up. She sat down at her desk and scowled. Something felt hot and sore in her chest. Her nails pressed into her palms. She and Henri had always been more fond of each other than ordinary. When he had first shown interest in Verity Post-Brian his sister had suffered secretly. Finally, she had become reconciled. It was inevitable that he marry. She could think of no one less objectionable than Verity. But now it seemed that there was Celeste.

Something like hatred ran through Edith for Celeste Bouchard. "She wouldn't make him happy," she said aloud. "She will only make him miserable." Then she added humorously and bitterly to herself: "My girl, you must get married, yourself."

She dressed carefully for Christopher. She was edified to see how her thin dark fingers shook. She fluffed her hair softly about her colorless face. She touched her lips with red. Her dark red dress had an old-fashioned air. Her appearance seemed vaguely familiar. Then she smiled, remembering. She went downstairs and walked into the great drawing room. On the wall opposite the portrait of her great-grandfather was the portrait of his beloved daughter, Gertrude, and Edith's own grandmother. She stood under the portrait, and acknowledged, with some amusement, that there was more than a casual resemblance. But the dark living eyes that looked up were not like the dark painted eyes that looked down.

Christopher came just before five. He walked into the room with familiar quickness. Edith came towards him and gave him both her hands. He kissed her lightly on the cheek. "Hello, wench," he said. He glanced about. "Where's old Thomas?"

"Still in bed. There are some troublesome after-effects of the grippe. Do you want to see him?"

"No, thank you. Old gentlemen are very nice, but a little disconcerting. Anyway, I'm in a hurry. We have a dinner tonight, you know. Couldn't you have waited to tell me about this—whatever it is—when I see you at Emile's?"

"No. Sit down, Christopher. It won't take long. I've got to ask you something."

He sat down. She did not. She moved restlessly to the fire, and then turned and looked at him over her shoulder. The red dimness outlined her head. She was very grave and quiet and dark, and her dress, and the fire, and the quietness of her surroundings, gave her a noble and dignified air. Because of the light behind her he could not see her face clearly, but he seemed to guess at her expression. He bit the corner of his lip, and his light fleshless fingers rose and fell on the arm of his chair in a devil's tattoo.

"Christopher," she said in a clear and penetrating voice,
179

"is it so necessary for you to push Celeste into a marriage with Henri?"

He did not move or answer. The devil's tattoo on the arm of his chair did not quicken. Yet she had an impression of enormous tension and awareness.

"After all," she said gently, "Henri is my brother. He's all I've got, I love him, Christopher."

The devil's tattoo slowly stopped. Yet he did not move or speak.

Edith sighed. Then she smiled whimsically.

"Perhaps I'm the only one in the world who understands you, Christopher. But you must think of Celeste, too, besides yourself. Sometimes I've disbelieved what I know about you. As for myself, I can't understand such a passion as yours. I can't reconcile it with you. I want to believe that there's something else——"

Christopher's eyes glinted in the firelight. "My dear girl, you're a little incoherent. What has Celeste to do with all this? 'Pushing her into a marriage with Henri!' I'm not pushing. I have an idea she likes him as much as he likes her."

Edith shook her head impatiently. "Look, Cristopher, it's easier, and less confusing, and more honest, for us just to sit here without speaking, and read each other's thoughts. You never lie in your thoughts, Christopher. That's why I like you."

He laughed thinly. "All right. let's communicate by telepathy." His lips twitched humorously. "Ready?"

She got up swiftly and stood before him. She bent her head a little and looked piercingly into his eyes. His eyes shifted just a trifle, but he still smiled. Her face became more grave, and somewhat sad.

"Christopher, is it so necessary for you that Celeste marry my brother?"

He did not answer for a moment, then he said directly: "Yes." He lifted himself to a more upright position in his chair. His eyeballs had an implacable and inimical gleam in the firelight. "Yes, it is. And Edith, I wouldn't interfere if I were you."

She seemed incredulous. "But Christopher, you wouldn't sacrifice your sister!"

He uttered an impatient sound. "Oh, my God, Edith! Listen to yourself! You're maudlin. I'm not 'sacrificing' Celeste. Look here, if she doesn't want to marry Henri, she needn't. I won't lift a finger to persuade her. After all, the girl's going on twenty. You underestimate Celeste. She

180

can be as stubborn as a mule, and harder to drive than a stone. Good God, you sound like a fool, Edith."

She continued to gaze at him. Then, very slowly, her eyes dropped. She walked back to the fire. Her slender figure had something rigid in its outlines.

"I want to believe you, but I can't," she said musingly.

He laughed suddenly. He got up and went to her. He put his hand on her shoulder and bent his head so that he could look at her profile, rosy with the fire.

"What's the matter? Don't you like Celeste?"

Her thin shoulder seemed to palpitate under his hand. But she answered steadfastly, not turning to him: "That's got nothing to do with it. I told you before: I love my brother."

His fingers pressed deeper into her flesh. Quickened blood rose under the clear dark skin of her cheek.

"Look, Edith, maybe Henri wants Celeste. You don't know what it means for a man to want a woman. He wants her. I can see that. You're a cool piece. You don't know what it is to desire."

She said quietly, her profile still to him: "Do you?"

She felt his fingers lighten on her shoulder. She felt them removed. A dull ache struck her chest.

"Well," he said lightly, "I'm a man."

"Are you?" she asked musingly. "I wonder."

She could feel him standing immobile beside her. She sighed once more, and pressed the slim narrow palms of her hands together as though she were in pain. Her profile sharpened, yet seemed to gain a sort of somber delicacy.

"I've often wondered if you really are a man, Christopher. Sometimes I've thought you are. And then, you do something, say something, that makes me think you are a robot, with chromium insides. I can actually hear you click; I can see the wheels turn behind your eyes. You frighten me, sometimes," she added simply.

He did not stir. She could not even hear his breath. She turned her full face to him swiftly with a sort of fierceness. He was smiling enigmatically, and his eyes were vitriolic points.

"You are a romantic child, Edith," he said. "You make me feel like a Frankenstein monster."

"But you are! You are!" she heard herself crying. She felt the burn of appalling tears along the rim of her eyelids. He was regarding her with surprise. Something rose in her throat, and she was horrified to hear herself give a hoarse sob. "But I still won't believe it. I won't believe you're not human."

He stared, then laughed again. "Don't be a fool, Edith. Of

181

course, I'm human. What is it you want me to say? Women always want men to say things. They'll never take anything for granted. You all love to talk, don't you?"

There were tears on her cheeks. But she was regarding him with dignity. "Yes, Christopher. I want you to say something. I want you to say you love me. You do, you know."

"Do I?" He smiled derisively. But as he looked into her face, into her wet and shining eyes, the derisive smile slowly faded, leaving a sort of rigid fixity behind it.

He walked away from her. He went to a table near the streaming windows. He affected to be absorbed in the confused landscape outside. She waited near the fire, her back to him, her head bent.

He began to speak as though thinking aloud: "I've got no time, I tell you. No time for anything but what I want." He struck the bony knuckles of his hand on the table. "Do you understand? No time for anything but what I want. When I get it—well, perhaps I'll have time for other things. Things that are not so important."

He glanced at her back. She continued to stand before the fire, her head still bent. Suddenly he went to her rapidly. He stood behind her and gripped her upper arms with his hard fingers. He kissed the nape of her neck. A quiver ran over her body. He kissed her again, laid his cheek against hers. Her bruised flesh ached under his fingers.

"I haven't time," he said. "But when it is all finished——"

She stared at the fire. Her eyes slowly widened, until the sockets seemed full of intense and burning light.

CHAPTER XXIII

HENRI BOUCHARD was very fond of his sister, Edith. Both of them had more or less affectionately despised their mother, Alice, whom they had considered a fool. Both of them loved their stepfather; he was also a fool, they thought. But there was a difference between the malevolent and silly foolishness of their mother, and the gentle and honorable foolishness of Thomas Van Eyck.

But though the brother and sister were so deeply attached to each other, they maintained an attitude of respect and reserve in each other's presence. They had no confidant but each other, and there was little they did not discuss frankly together. However, beyond this frankness they did not go; they allowed each other's mind to remain inviolate. Affection, trust and confidence never became humid intimacy or interference or curiosity.

Henri often declared that his sister was the only woman he had ever known who was a human being as well as a female. He did not think her beautiful; but he knew that she was intelligent, and had a curious sort of integrity. It was not the kind of integrity which was above plotting; it was not the kind that would hold her from a sharp double-dealing for her own advantage. But it was the kind that enabled her to keep her mind clear; there was nothing murky in it. She was never dishonorable to herself, nor treacherous to herself.

Everything was candor between brother and sister, except their inmost thoughts. Yet, that night of Henri's return when Edith suddenly asked him the real reason why they had returned to Windsor, she saw, to her sudden surprise, that she had unwittingly invaded the privacy of her brother. This puzzled and quickened her. She watched the smooth dropping of reserve over his face.

"I told you, Edith: we ought to have roots. We've lived all over the world. Just buzzed around from place to place. I got tired of it, as I told you. And you agreed with me that we ought to settle somewhere. And where was better than Windsor, in the house where we were born, and among our own people?" He added thoughtfully, after a moment: "Besides, I'm a Bouchard, too. Our grandparents and great-grandparents started this business. Why shouldn't we have a share in it, or at least a personal interest in it?"

Edith knew that he had spoken the entire truth. And yet, she was dissatisfied. Henri, she felt, was not filling in the outlines. There was something behind all this. She studied him earnestly, and he looked back at her blandly. She frowned meditatively.

He began to smile, as though he were understanding her dissatisfaction and was amused by it. "I suppose I'm not a modern American. I don't like half a dozen houses scattered all over the world. I don't like temporary apartments, no matter how brilliantly furnished. I want a home. Doesn't that sound old-fashioned? But I want roots. An Establishment." He glanced with complacence about the immense drawing room, firelit and lamplit. "Yes, I want roots. Here are roots. I've come home."

And again Edith knew he had spoken the truth. But still, the outlines were not filled in.

They were going to the home of Alexander Bouchard, son of Andre, for dinner. Henri stood before the fire, his back to it, his hands clasped behind him, his strong legs wide apart. Firelight lay on the broadness of his shoulders. The young man had the strong quality of immobility. When he moved his large head it was with the slowness and sureness of power.

"Tradition," he said thoughtfully. "A long time ago someone in the family told me that our great-grandfather had given his whole life to a house. You remember the old Sessions house? A shabby old place, practically in the slums. But it must have been beautiful at one time. Probably fine enough for Ernest Barbour to have sacrificed everything for; probably he did. You don't get such hatred and scurviness in a family like ours without it all originating in hatred and scurviness a long time ago. Well, anyway, I understand what he wanted. And that's what I want."

Yes, thought Edith, that is what you want. But that is not all of it.

She picked up her book and began to read again. Henri watched her for some minutes.

"Edith, are you sorry we came back?"

She did not answer immediately. Then, very slowly, she dropped the book to her knee and regarded her brother with more somberness than he thought necessary.

"No," she said. "I'm not. In a way. Of course, I don't hanker after tradition, as you do." She smiled.

Henri eyed her sharply. He wondered if he imagined that Edith was even more quiet than usual, lately, and if her eyes were really tired and heavy. Her black dinner dress made her dark throat and breast and face more sallow than ordinarily; her cheek bones had become quite prominent, and also her shoulder blades.

"Edith, if you don't like it here, please don't stay on my account. I want you to be happy."

To his surprise, she made a short and violent motion with her hand. "Everyone talks about others being happy! What nonsense. You are never happy after five, and not very often even before that. Don't worry about my happiness, Henri. Take care of your own. Besides, if I went away, what would you and Father do alone together, in this big old house?"

He seemed amused. "We'd do nicely, though we'd miss you. Then, I may get married, you see."

"To Celeste?" she spoke indifferently, but her heart began
184

to beat quickly. She was afraid to look at her brother, believing that he might be annoyed at this second invasion of his privacy.

But he was not annoyed. He added, in a very matter-of-fact voice: "Yes. To Celeste. But you seemed to know long ago."

Edith put her hands together in her lap. Henri could not guess from her quiet voice how deeply her nails were entering her flesh.

"Well, I rather suspected you liked her." Then, all at once, and in spite of her efforts at self-control, she got up and went to him, facing him on the hearth rug. "Henri, have you asked her yet?"

He stared at her. Her face was quite pale under its darkness. Her eyes were full of intense firelight.

"No, I haven't. But I don't have to be so old-fashioned, child. I know she'll have me. Isn't she a pretty little thing? A French damosel, all right. Besides, I think Christopher won't object to the marriage." And he smiled unpleasantly.

Edith put her hand on his arm, and kissed him on the cheek. "Dear, I hope you'll be happy," she said. He heard a faint tremor in her voice. "She is a darling. Be happy, Henri. I'll kill her if she makes you miserable."

He was quite touched by the emotion of his undemonstrative sister. He put his arm around her. "Why all the dramatics? This isn't like you, Edith. What's the trouble? And that reminds me: haven't you found anyone around here that you'd have, yourself?" He pinched her chin, and released her.

She tried to smile. "I'll tell you when I do." She patted the sides of her hair, so like black glass in the firelight. She did not look at him. "Henri, you say Christopher won't object. Of course he won't. He likes you." Henri said nothing, so Edith, thinking he had not heard her, repeated: "He likes you."

He shrugged. "Does he?" he asked indifferently. He turned his head aside.

Something in his voice and manner frightened her. "Henri! Don't you like him?"

He did not speak for a moment, and then said quietly, and yet with such a deadly intonation that she could not believe it at first: "No, Edith. I don't like him. In fact, I hate him. I hate them all. All the Bouchards." He tried to smile a little at her blank face and parted lips. "Except, of course, you and Celeste. And myself."

185

Even then she dimly wondered at this unusual dropping of reticence between them. She saw at once how hypocritical all their former pretenses of candor had been.

"Then why," she asked faintly, "did you ever come back here? You said, 'among our own people——' "

Again, he was silent before answering. "Yes, I said that. And I said I hated them. It's true. All of it is true. It seems paradoxical, but it really isn't, I suppose. We've both seen it lots of times, all over the world: relatives hating each other, envying each other, despising each other, secretly hoping for a chance to strike each other down. Then meeting amiably at family dinners, and giving presents, and visiting sick members, and handshaking, and kissing, and attending weddings and births. The superficial would say it is hypocrisy, sentimentality or suspicion, that brings them together. But I don't believe it is any of these. Perhaps they see memories in each other—I'll be becoming sentimental myself, in a moment! I don't know. Or perhaps it is a relief to be among those who don't have to be fooled—who know all about you. Like taking off tight shoes under the table. Or wearing old clothes."

Yes, thought Edith. That is true, too. But not all of the truth. She said: "But why do you particularly hate Christopher?"

He yawned before replying, and then spoke in a bored voice: "I don't hate him any worse than I do the others. By the way, it's almost time to go. Shall I get your wrap?"

They went upstairs together to see old Thomas, who was convalescing. He was sitting before his fire, reading the evening paper. He glanced over his glasses at them, and smiled with pleasure.

"Hello, my dears. I thought you had already gone."

Edith kissed him, ran her hand affectionately over his white hair. "Not yet, pet. But we're going now. Are you comfortable? Do you mind us leaving you?"

"No. Run along. Have a nice time. Give my love to little Annette, won't you? Didn't you say she was to be at the dinner?"

"Yes." It was Edith who spoke. Henri made a slight grimace.

"Poor lamb," sighed Thomas. "The little girl haunts me. And what a beautiful musician! Tell her I haven't forgotten her Spring Nocturne. Have you heard it, Edith? I know you don't like music much, either of you barbarians," and he smiled tenderly, patting Edith's hand. "But ask her to play it for you."

Alexander Bouchard, son of Andre, and vice-president of The Sessions Steel Company, lived in an ornate house of smooth white stone, grilled windows, iron balconies and bronze doors somewhat French in suggestion. He was big, fair, fat and solemn, his light curly hair thinning, his complexion a delicate magenta. He was known among his irreverent relatives as the Parson, for he was literally a pillar of St. Mary's Episcopal Church of Windsor. Though enormously wealthy, he was, like many religious and church-going men, rather parsimonious and greedy and avaricious. He gave a good sum yearly to the support of the Church, but was not the largest giver. However, his friends and sycophants were induced by him to become members, also, which the minister found very comforting.

Like so many of his solemn-faced and proverb-quoting kind, he was unconsciously hypocritical, malicious, mean, intolerant, reverent of money, small-minded and not particularly intelligent. But his obstinacy, methodical ways and donkey-tenacity of mind had enabled him to acquire the conventional amount of education, which, Christopher often asserted, had done him no good at all. He believed himself to be the only virtuous member of the Bouchard family, and allowed no one to be under the impression that it was a secret. He also firmly believed that he was a living example of the highest probity, good sense, piety, discipline, truthfulness, faithfulness, courage and firmness. Some members of the Bouchard family actually liked each other, more or less. But all of them cordially and heartily hated Alexander Bouchard.

He had no genius, though privately believing that he was the "balance-wheel" of The Sessions Steel Company. But he was so conscientious and so plodding and had such a virtuous and solid exterior that both Andre and little Jean found him delightfully convenient. They had only to send innocent Alexander to do a piece of particulary dirty work, and it was done. Later, the victims howled. But they howled not at Alexander, but at Andre and Jean, rightly seeing the fine Italian hands behind his big fleshy ones. In fact, some of the victims declared that Alexander, too, was a victim of the pirate house of Bouchard and Sons. All this pleased Jean and Andre excessively. They never worried about Alexander's suspecting. He was too stupid. He was sly and suspicious, and believed himself to be quite knowing. However, like his kind, he was always taken in by a pleasant and pseudo-frank face and manner. Those who agreed with him, and attended church regularly, were patterns of rectitude and intelligence, he was convinced. Because of this, St. Mary's Episcopal

Church had more liars, thieves, blackguards, mountebanks and malefactors, who used him, than any other church in the State.

Certain more superficial people called him a rank hypocrite, a psalm-singer who sang his pious ditties to deceive the simple-minded. But this was not true. Alexander devoutly believed every word contained in the two Testaments. When he prayed, he prayed with honest fervor. When he meditated in his pew, his eyes would moisten with tears. At least three times a day he spoke of the "saving blood of the Lamb," and the "grace that saveth," and the careful distinctions to be made by the Lamb between the goats and the sheep on a certain portentous Day in the future. His phraseology was more suited to Methodist revivals than to the well-bred and refined atmosphere of St. Mary's. In fact, the Reverend Edward Moseley was frequently distressed and embarrassed over his illustrious parishioner's sonorous phrases, and was dimly worried as to where Alexander could have picked them up. "Salvation Army extravagance," he thought euphemiously. Mr. Moseley was a gentleman, and an Englishman, and he did not like Alexander. Once, at Communion, he could hardly suppress a desire to dash a glass of wine in that big solemn pious face. He was used to hypocrites and to malefactors in his churches. He had to acknowledge that here was no deliberate hypocrite or malefactor. However, he had seen some number of Alexander's kind. They seemed more repulsive to him than an out-and-out scoundrel frankly using religion as an easy way to accomplish skulduggery.

One or two of the Bouchards had guessed, with Mr. Moseley, that Alexander was a coward and a fool. Naturally superstitious, subconsciously recognizing the flabbiness of his own soul, he had turned desperately to religion, which offered him revenges he dared not take on those he hated, escape from a death that filled him with terror, and which substituted the cheap mumbo-jumbo of piety for a social conscience, that would cost him money. Mr. Moseley, who had a hidden affection for the Roman Catholic Church, always felt more wistfully drawn to that Church whenever he saw Alexander Bouchard. He believed, quite rightly, that the Roman Church was not particularly infested by Alexander's kind, the priests usually being allowed to give way to their lusty brand of humor, and the very tenets of the Church being more earthy, more comfortable, and more human. Alexander, by the way, was a devout hater of "Romanism," and positively declared that part of the "trouble" with politics and international affairs and general godliness was the result of the Roman Catholic Church's "machinations."

He had married rather late. His wife was the only daughter of the president of The Galby Lumber Company. Her hobbies were church work and pottery painting. She sold the pottery at church bazaars, giving all of 33⅓ per cent of the profits to the Missions. A drab, tight-lipped, mean, smiling little woman, with a whining voice, she had long ago been assigned to limbo by the Bouchards. She was childless.

However, the Bouchards did not forget that Alexander was vice-president of The Sessions Steel Company, and that some day he would be president. Moreover, in spite of his wife's meanness and his own piety, he gave excellent dinners, though the conversation subsequent to the dinners was so boring that the Bouchards usually managed to escape within a short time.

Alexander believed he owed a "duty" to his family. He disapproved of them quite openly, but still, he owed them a duty. Tonight he had invited those who aroused his disapproval the least: Armand, Mrs. Armand and young Antoine and little Annette, Henri and his sister, Edith, and Jean and his wife, Alexander's sister. Jean was his favorite; in fact, he had quite a warm affection for him. Jean's frank and winning manner, his open smiles, his apparent respect for proprieties and conventions, and his fairly regular church attendance, all had convinced Alexander that here at least was a soul not entirely unregenerate. Consequently, he confided things to Jean which he never confided to anyone else. The poor stupid man could not see into the future, of course. He could not foresee the day when Jean would oust him from his position, and would consign him to the outer darkness of executive impotence.

Edith did not like any of those at this dinner, and when Henri had accepted the invitation, she had protested when they were alone. "I like to see first one side and then the other woo me," he had replied, laughing. "Aren't you amused, too?" But Edith, who knew nothing of Henri's thoughts, was puzzled and annoyed. She had already noticed that there was some competition for Henri among the Bouchards, and had also noticed that there were two factions. But the significance had escaped her. Moreover, she infinitely preferred Christopher's faction. She admired Francis, liked Emile, was amused by Hugo, and was not deceived by any of them. She liked Agnes, Emile's wife, immensely. Once she told her brother that there was an unhealthy and scurvy atmosphere about Armand's faction, a mean, weasel-like, suspicious air, though she acknowledged that poor Armand was not responsible for it.

Some time ago Jean had lightly mentioned the fact that it would be to Henri's advantage, "provided, of course, that you are interested in becoming an active member of the Bouchard rigmarole," to marry little Annette, possibly within two or three years. Antoine, said Jean, would be nothing more than just a flaccid "flaming youth" in his maturity. Armand had no real heir. Moreover, he liked Henri, and the girl was a nice little creature, who would give Henri no trouble and would not interfere with him.

"No, thanks," Henri had replied wryly. "I'm not in the market for glued-together bric-a-brac."

His open interest in Celeste was naturally causing Armand's faction an enormous amount of uneasiness. Jean had already discussed with Nicholas, himself, the matter of marrying-off Edith to Nicholas, that confirmed bachelor. Nicholas had been terribly alarmed, at first, but Jean's prodding had made him reluctantly promise to "think it over." As a result, he furtively stared at Edith whenever she was about, but when she approached him, he literally fled. But he was really "thinking it over," and found, after a time, that Edith's presence vaguely excited him.

Edith was pale and more silent than usual, tonight. Nicholas approved of the absence of cosmetics. Moreover, when she glanced at him idly with her dark eyes, so filled with light tonight, a thrill ran down his well-padded spine.

Education had so far civilized the Bouchards that they could listen to Alexander's sonorous phrases without displaying too much ridicule or impatience or boredom. Besides, it was an excellent dinner. Most of the Bouchards had French chefs, though few of them liked French cooking. However, as Emile said, they had a certain "tradition" to keep up, or at least their wives had. But Alexander, who did not like anything French, and who listened only to his British blood, went in for huge ribs of beef, joints of succulent mutton, rich puddings stuffed with fruit and oozing with suet, port wines and creamy coffee and tea, soups that were brown and robust, and aged cheeses that filled a room with delicious aromas. The Bouchards laughed at these beefy dinners, but they rarely refused an invitation. Their slight Latin strain was inundated and smothered under a menu that would have been approved by King Arthur's knights.

Their restless minds, which were only stimulated by their own chefs, fell into a state of pleasant torpor at Alexander's house. Some claimed it was his conversation, but it was really his food. They could doze, blinking, over a port that could not be surpassed, and so escape much of Alexander's remarks.

It was unfortunate for Henri that he did not care for any sort of alcoholic beverage. Nor did Edith drink much. Nor Armand. (Armand, however, believing that port "made blood," insisted upon Annette drinking a small glass.) However, the others drank. Bachelor Nicholas, sipping his third glass, found Edith more and more alluring. The thought of marrying her gradually lost considerable of its pain. Edith was not amused at his clumsy attempts to be seductive, but she was polite enough not to be too squelching.

Henri knew it was no accident that he was seated next to little Annette. The girl looked much older tonight. Her long rippling ash-blonde hair, which had never been cut, was rolled softly on her neck in a ball, like pale gold. Her small colorless face, like a delicate triangle of flesh and fragile bones, was tinted faintly. Her beautiful blue eyes were bright, as though with tears or laughter. She wore a dinner gown of thin dark blue velvet, soft and flowing, and a string of rosy pearls hugged her white child's-throat. Everything about her was so frail, so dainty, so small, that she resembled nothing so much as a tinted Dresden figurine. A figurine which had been broken, but had been cunningly "glued together," thought Henri. Nevertheless, he was touched by the girl's sweetness and beauty; her voice was clear yet firm, like crystal tapped with a fingernail. The thought of marriage with her, however, was both repulsive and grotesque. Her place was on a shelf in a glass closet, he thought, glancing at the tiny transparent hands. Her father had given her a diamond bracelet for a Christmas present, and it slipped heavily up and down a wrist that looked as though it would snap between a man's finger and thumb. Tubercular, thought Henri, with some pity.

Henri had lived long enough in France to lose the Anglo-Saxon's aversion for a woman who had some intelligence. He knew the conventional patois of those who understood music. Therefore, he was able to talk to Annette with ease and even interest. He had discovered that she had a light wit and a gaiety that reminded him of Celeste's. A translucent fever seemed to run in the girl's veins, making her flesh radiant tonight. Her pretty mouth was scarlet; her eyes glittered with blue fire. Her father, watching, was amazed, and a little frightened. Intuition told him that despair and love were behind this vivacity and this laughter. Annette was fighting for her life with every gay word, every eager gentle smile, every birdlike turn of her Dresden head. A color like a faint flame kept running across her face. Even her pauses seemed to throb, like rosy wine in a thin glass. At these times she looked at Henri in silence, her heart pulsing in her eyes.

If I married this little piece of porcelain, thought Henri, amused, I would save a lot of time. A short cut. He smiled at Annette, and felt a cool thrill of repulsion zigzag down his spine. He glanced furtively at the poor small boardlike body, almost breastless, and again the thrill turned him cold. God! What an idea! His pity was dried in his aversion. His interest in her intelligent and witty remarks blew away. He could not keep from averting his head. But he could still see the tiny transparent little hand resting idly on the stem of the wine glass. He thought of it touching him intimately, and literally turned icy. The poor child wore lily-of-the-valley perfume, and for the rest of his life it was the most repulsive scent in the world to Henri Bouchard.

It was Alexander's belief that after a host had dined his guests to stupefaction, they owed him the duty of listening attentively to his conversation. The Bouchards did not agree with him at all, but they were stuffed with food and sweltering with the fumes of remarkable port. It was less trouble to doze with the eyes open than it was to flee. Jean often said that Alexander weighed down his victims with food so that they could not escape. At any rate, it was only on the occasions of his dinners that anyone ever listened to him.

Just now he was inveighing against the "lack of discipline and morality and responsibility in the world today." "Where is our pioneer blood?" he demanded, glaring at them with pompous accusation. "Where is our restraint and sobriety and sense of duty?"

They regarded him with dull and bulging eyes, and did not reply. Armand, turning a spoon over and over in his hand, kept glancing somberly at Henri. He knew, now, all about the huge loan which Henri had made to Christopher. But why? What did it mean? Armand had eaten very little; he was too gloomy and depressed. Only when he looked at Annette did he feel any comfort. There were moments, though, when he hated his younger cousin, Henri. But with his hatred came the Bouchard scheming and the Barbour determination. Some way must be contrived to prevent a marriage between Henri and Celeste. And some way must be contrived to consummate a marriage between Henri and Annette, not only for the sake of Armand, himself, but also for his little daughter. Sometimes Armand felt confused. His own welfare and peace of mind appeared less important than Annette's happiness. Finally, her happiness was the only thing that mattered.

He heard Alexander's booming voice roaring dimly in the background. No one was listening much, except his big handsome blonde sister, Alexa, and his mean little wife with the sliding pious eyes. He struck the table a suety blow and glared at them all.

"The trouble with all of us is that we no longer have the saving grace of the Lord Jesus Christ in our souls. We aren't satisfied with frugality and simplicity and humbleness any more. We're effete, that's what we are! We want our bodies to be pampered and our minds to be amused. We're loose-fibered and morally decadent.

"What's happened to us Americans? Once we were clear-eyed and heroic and patriotic. Now our people don't care a bit if Europe doesn't pay back our financiers the tremendous loans it borrowed during the war. No sense of responsibility! Wall Street practically beggared itself, and do our farmers and our workers care? Not a bit! They run around in their cars and go to the movies, and think they oughtn't to work ten or twelve hours a day, as their ancestors did, and they don't care whether our patriotic financiers get their money back— with interest," he added. "And then those who fought in our armies think they ought to have pensions and bonuses and disability allowances for fighting for their own country——

Henri had been eyeing him with contempt. "Maybe they think a wooden medal isn't sufficient recompense for a wooden leg," he said.

Alexander glared at him. "That's the whole thing! You've expressed their sentiments exactly. Glory and duty and patriotism aren't enough for them. They want——"

"A share in the profits, perhaps," interposed Henri.

Jean, who had been slumbering gently in his chair, was aroused. He sat up and surveyed the two antagonists with a grateful expression.

Alexander struck his hand passionately on the table again. "Why should they want profits? Eh? Who are they? They ought to be grateful to God that they live in America!"

"I imagine," said Henri, smiling, "that it's just as uncomfortable to starve in America as it is to starve anywhere else. But don't mind me. Please go on."

Alexander regarded him with bloodshot and bulbous eyes. "I didn't think I'd hear such things from you, Henri. But I suppose, like a good many other people, you've been infected with Jew-Communism."

Henri assumed an expression of bright childish interest.

"Communism? I never heard of it. What's Communism, Alec?"

Alexander fumed. He reddened. "What's Communism? Why, it's—it's—I tell you what it is! It's the damned working class thinking it's as good as we are—and thinking it ought to have—what you said—a share in the profits. And besides, Communists believe in free love, in sleeping with every woman that catches their eye——"

Henri laughed. "I didn't think that was peculiar to Communists. But you interest me. Please go on. Have we any Communists in America?"

"Have we! Just about every damn mechanic and shopgirl in the country is a Communist. First thing you know, we'll have all our churches blown up, and private property confiscated. By 1930, we'll all be ruined. Government ownership of everything and the Red Flag of Moscow flying from every public building! I know! You are all just sleeping with your eyes open, and refuse to see. And the Jews are the cause of it all."

"Now that is very interesting. My information was that there were practically no Jews at all in the Soviet government——"

Alexander snorted. "Just lies! Russia is all Jews. And Mongols."

Edith moved restlessly. She wished Henri would stop baiting this old fat magenta-faced fool. It was boring. The night was pleasant, and the room was hot, and she longed to get out. She glanced about the table. The women were dozing with open glazed eyes. But the men were listening with pleased faces and chuckles.

Henri was already bored. He eyed Alexander with a stuffed expression. He yawned. But Alexander was just getting into his stride.

He asserted that Jewish bankers were ruining the world. When Henri blandly expressed surprise that Jay Regan and most of the important others were Jews, Alexander glowered at him, and continued his tirade.

Suddenly he was back at his old plaint that there was no discipline or stability in America. The people were getting fat and lazy, and impudent. They formed unions. They lacked respect for property. They lacked morality. For some reason the subject of morality was one to which Alexander kept returning, like a fat avid fly to a jam jar. He licked his lips; he moved his bloated belly. Henri, quite interested now, leaned his chin on his clenched hand, and watched intently.

It seemed to Alexander that lack of morality and Com-

194

munism were linked up with big wages and peace. Just how, he did not explain. But like all his kind, he believed what was nearest his desires. The only time the people were orderly and disciplined and meek and patriotic and moral and clear-eyed was during war. War brought them strength and humility and self-sacrifice. They didn't talk about sharing the profits then! It was enough for them that they were given a uniform and a band.

Henri laughed. He indicated Jean and the others with a wave of his hand.

"Then, you have very little to worry about, Alec. The boys here are already cooking up some more wars."

Alexander paused. Jean laughed; Nicholas grunted some pleasantry. But Armand smiled a smile that was more a grimace. Then Alexander smiled. "Yes," he said, "we've just got a new order, as you know, from Japan. Well, it's about time they got after those Chinese Communists!" He became gloomy again, however. "But what about us? The American people are too selfish and unpatriotic to fight Japan."

"Don't worry," said Henri. "The boys will get together with their patriotic pals in Europe, and they'll find a devil for the people to hate and destroy. I don't know who it will be, unless they can build up Germany again, and get a crackpot German leader to threaten the world, or democracy, or something else."

Alexander scowled. "You talk loosely, Henri. But that's because you aren't connected actively with us." Jean glanced at Alexander with warning dismay. Nicholas glowered. Armand bit his lip. But the stupid Alexander went on, oblivious.

"You're just a rich young man. You don't know the responsibilities we carry. You would, if you would only take an interest. But that's neither here nor there. We were talking about something else. I like Germans; I always did. But I hate Britain and France. They're riddled with Communism, and they induce Russia to destroy Germany. What? Nonsense? How can you know, Henri, when you have no active part in anything? We don't foment wars. In a way, armaments manufacturers are really the protectors of the people's morality; they keep the national backbone stiff and virile. They're the physicians who administer purges to sick nations. They inspire manliness and keep patriotism alive. Germany was always a warlike nation, that's why Germans are so superior to the effete French, who like peace. That's why we've got to help Germany, which is a moral nation. And that's what we're doing. We'll make Germany strong! And then——"

"We'll fight her again, eh?" asked Henri, yawning.

Alexander smirked. "Perhaps. The people need to be stimulated to patriotism, in America. Perhaps when Germany gets to talking about her mission in the world, and they commit a few more atrocities, and threaten other nations, our lazy people will see their danger, and forget their unions and their profit-sharings and movies. We'll make Germany so strong we'll have to fight her!"

There was a slight movement next to Henri. He glanced up and saw that little Annette was standing. She stood, all tremulous, like a frightened creature preparing desperately for flight. She looked swiftly about the table, her lips parted in a smile of pain, her eyes distended. The men rose. She pressed her hands together. The women, aroused from their lethargy, rose too. There was a mass migration into one of the drawing rooms.

Annette sat down, not near her father, as usual, nor near Henri. She sat alone, her hands pressed together on her knee. All the color had gone from her face. She looked ill and frantically lonely. Yet, when someone moved towards her she rose and sat down again at some distance. Everyone forgot her. She sat there in a corner, white-lipped, her eyes staring ahead. But Henri, across the great room, watched her, intrigued, more than a little moved, and full of pity.

Henri heard Armand speaking to him. Armand was asking him if he would come into the library for a few moments. When they were alone in the library, Armand, in silence, offered Henri a cigar, which he refused. Armand seemed ill at ease and unable to open a conversation. He sat down, crossed his knees, his expression more and more apprehensive and uneasy. Then he said hesitatingly: "You mustn't listen too much to Alec. He's the family clown."

"You mean, he doesn't know when he is telling the truth?"

Armand flushed. He stared at his boots. "He's a fool," he said. He examined the end of his cigar minutely, while he continued: "Henri, would you like to take an active part in Bouchard and Sons?"

Henri smiled. "My great-grandfather founded the whole business. Yet I can't stir up interest, I'm afraid. Not in a petty position, at any rate." He watched the other man closely.

Armand colored so deeply that his face was crimson. But still he did not look at Henri.

"I wish I had a son like you," he said simply. "Antoine will never be a business man. His pet relative is old Etienne. I

196

shouldn't be surprised if he'll turn out to be a damned actor, eventually. He writes to chorus girls. I've got only Annette——"

Henri was silent. Armand sighed. "Come to the office tomorrow. We'll talk it over." He stood up, met Henri's eyes gravely and steadfastly. "My little girl is a woman now," he added.

They went out together. Annette, in her far and dimly-lighted corner, was weeping.

CHAPTER XXIV

ADELAIDE knew that she had been utterly and finally betrayed by everyone.

She was no longer frantic. She was merely hopeless. After a few attempts, she made no more efforts to approach Celeste. Between herself and her young daughter a wall of ice had arisen, through which they glanced briefly at each other's distorted images.

Adelaide knew that nothing but a miracle or death would prevent Celeste from marrying her cousin, Henri Bouchard. Celeste had taken on a rich maturity; all her soft features had become definite and sure. The pure strength of her face was more in evidence than ever. She did not avoid her mother, physically. In fact, she was gentler, yet in some way, harder. She spoke of Henri, when she had to, quietly and decisively, and refused to discuss him with Adelaide.

Now that it was early spring, Henri called for Celeste almost every morning to go riding with him. She would appear at breakfast, trim, slim and lovely in her riding clothes, the crop on the table beside her. She would eat her breakfast with her mother, speaking very little, and smiling amiably whenever Adelaide spoke. Her hair, pushed up under her hat, allowed, by its absence, the firm modelling of her cheeks and chin to show to great advantage, the steadfast cool light of her blue eyes. Before that reserve Adelaide could only endure silent despair. She watched her daughter's every gesture with the sharpness of sorrow and hopelessness. When Henri was announced, and Celeste would rise hastily from the table, Adelaide saw how she colored, and heard her light laugh, quick and breathless and eager. Henri would come in easily, in his riding clothes, his crop in his hand. He would greet Adelaide politely, but hardly seemed to see her. He saw only Celeste, standing beside him, her cheek bones suddenly stained with fresh scarlet, her mouth smiling, her eyes confused.

Adelaide was sure that Celeste was in love with Henri. But Henri himself was not so sure. Other women had never kept him in doubt. At first, he thought it was natural coquetry on Celeste's part. But later he knew it was complete innocence.

Sometimes Christopher would join them on their rides. But lately he had not. Henri did not seem surprised. He only smiled to himself. He knew a great deal more than anyone suspected.

He had not gone to see Armand at his office, giving as his excuse that he must have time to think certain matters over. However, some deep sadistic impulse in him drew him to Armand's house and Annette. Annette did not repel him as she had done originally. He liked to talk to her, and listen to her play on her harp. He thought it a very pretty sight, and he was amused at the girl's betrayal of passion for him. But he also pitied her. If it gave her pleasure to see him, and talk to him, then he would not deny her, he told himself reasonably. But under it all was his bottomless hatred for all the Bouchards, and even for Celeste, in spite of the fact that he was in love with her, and in love for the first time in his life.

He was having an excellent time among his numerous relatives. He was much wooed and sought after, for he could be charming when he wished. His female relatives, particularly, betrayed a touching solicitude for him and his sister, though they secretly disliked the dark and reserved Edith. But it was the relatives of his blood, the male Bouchards, who interested him most. He knew their intrigues, their envies and malignancies and greeds and plottings. He allowed them to believe he knew nothing. He enjoyed, enormously, their attempts to secure him. He listened to their whispered stories about each other, their innuendoes, their unfinished and jeering phrases. Edith, suspecting much about them, was sometimes appalled. She could not understand Henri's private laughter and enjoyment or baitings. She did not hate her relatives; there were a few she liked. She had acquired quite a fondness for poor little Annette, for instance. And then, when she finally understood what had brought Henri back to Wind-

sor, and what hatred prompted his every action, she felt re-
vulsion, and even horror.

She admired Celeste's beauty, but she saw more than that
in the girl. She saw a firmness and integrity which was also
at rock bottom cold and immovable. Everyone spoke of
Celeste's shyness and innocence. Edith saw them also, but she
saw under them a layer of pride and reserve greater than her
own. The intimacy of marriage would do away with the shyness and the innocence, Edith thought, apprehensively. And
then Henri would discover a wife who would oppose him if
she suspected him engaged in opportunism or double-dealing. She would oppose him grimly and unremittingly, and
would always find him out. Henri, a man, would soon adjust
himself to it. Celeste would never be adjusted, or reconciled,
and therein would be her endless misery. She would, through
the stripping of her defenses, expose herself to a thousand
wounds from every side, and would see at last the faces of
all her relatives, and the face of the world.

And yet Edith knew that her own happiness was bound
up in the eventual marriage between Henri and Celeste.
Therefore, against the prickings of her own conscience,
she aided and abetted Henri in his courtship of their cousin.

One morning, in April, Henri decided that he would ask
Celeste to marry him. He called for the girl later than usual.
They rode away in silence towards the park, which was em-
bellished with the bronze statue of his great-grandfather,
Ernest Barbour. It was their usual riding-place.

A soft green mist floated in the trees; blades of brilliant
green were pushing through the brown earth. The sky was the
color of polished silver. There was no fecundity yet, but the
air had a warm and overpowering smell of life. The statue
of Ernest Barbour, bronze and formidable, shone in the bright
pale sunlight. Henri and Celeste rode to the base of the statue,
and then dismounted. They sat negligently on the railing around it and stared contentedly through the brown
tree-trunks and across the freshening grass. No one but
themselves seemed to be in the park this early morning.

Henri smoked. The horses stood by, lifting their heads,
sniffing the air. The sunlight made a brown moire pattern
on their sleek bodies. Beyond the gates of the park cars were
beginning to glide towards the city. Birds fluttered and
scolded and chattered among the thin trees. The sun was
warm on the faces of the silent young man and girl.

Celeste seemed to dream. She sat lightly on the railing,
her slim knees crossed in their riding breeches. The pure

strong modelling of her cheeks and jaw was almost aggressively revealed. Her lips were parted, and her eyes stared ahead. Her hands gripped her riding crop, not loosely, but competently. The collar of her shirt was open, and Henri could see the whiteness and softness of her young neck.

All at once the young man felt the most overwhelming desire for her, and a tenderness he had never experienced before. He felt his heart beating thickly in his throat; the beating suddenly swelled over his whole body; and his face so like that of the statue above him, flushed darkly. He put his hand over Celeste's, and when she involuntarily tried to draw it away, his fingers tightened. She did not turn to him but color swept over her face, and her lips closed tightly as though she were holding her breath.

"Celeste," he said, trying to keep his voice very light, "when are you going to marry me?"

She did not answer; she still stared ahead. There was an intensity and fixity about her features which intrigued and slightly alarmed him. Her eyes did not blink, and only her dilated nostrils showed the effect of his words upon her.

He kissed her hand, holding it first against his lips and then against his cheek. It was cold and soft, and then, to his surprise and gratification, she pressed it almost fiercely against his cheek, then snatched it away. She was looking at him now, laughing with little catches of her breath. But her eyes were shining and full of tears.

"I didn't say I was going to marry you," she said. Her voice was somewhat hoarse. They looked at each other, smiling, in silence. Celeste was not trembling, yet her slender body seemed to pulse, visibly. With a swift abruptness, Henri put his arms about her, pulled her to him, and kissed her full on the mouth. He felt her resist, and then felt her sudden surrender. A squirrel stopped before them, sat up on his tail, and surveyed them with his little savage eyes.

Henri released the girl. She fell back from him, and began to laugh again, faintly, with embarrassment. "Did anyone ever kiss you before, darling?" he asked, his eyes fixed on her mouth.

She tried to speak, then merely shook her head. She pushed a lock of hair back under her hat. She seemed full of shame and confusion, and could not look at him. He took her hand again, and kissed it. Now he could feel its tremor.

"I love you, darling," he said in a low voice. He rubbed the back of her hand thoughtfully with his finger, then turned it over and kissed her palm. "Don't you love me, just a little?"

200

"I don't know," she whispered. She regarded him imploringly. "But I think so."

He was touched. What an innocent thing she was, to be sure! There was such a pleading and hesitating expression on her pretty face, as though she were asking him to reassure her.

"You don't know?" he repeated, smiling. "You're such a baby, Celeste. Well, when are you going to marry me?"

She tried to be offhand and amused, and failed, delightfully. "I always thought I'd like a change," she said, in a shaken voice. "A girl likes to change her name. I'd only be Bouchard again."

When he kissed her again on the mouth, she leaned towards him with the wild passion of a suddenly awakened virginity. When he released her, after a long time, she was crying and smiling at once.

He knew then, that if she didn't love him at all, no one else would ever arouse her as he had done, and that she would never forget it.

They rode back together, slowly, in a mist of joy and repletion. It was only when they arrived at her home that she turned to him with a quick vehemence. "I'm glad for one thing, Henri," she said, and this time there was no shyness in her voice and face. "Just glad for one thing more than anything else: you aren't connected with Bouchard and Sons."

He was surprised, and stared at her. "But why?" he asked.

She shook her head slightly, and said nothing else.

CHAPTER XXV

NO ENGAGEMENT in the Bouchard family had ever created such a profound sensation as did Celeste Bouchard's engagement to her cousin, Henri Bouchard. It was of sufficient importance to be recorded in every newspaper in the world, no matter how small or obscure. Reporters and newspaper photographers connected with all the great dailies of every city of every nation converged on Windsor, like an army of buzzards, Christopher said. Poor little Celeste was besieged and waylaid, until she dared not leave her home.

The house was thronged with friends and relatives and insistent reporters; the grounds surged. The gatekeeper at Henri's residence was reinforced by a dozen private policemen. Henri, in the meantime, disappeared with his sister, for parts unknown. Edith, who had an ironic appreciation of what she called "human spectacles," had not particularly desired to go.

The President was among the illustrious first to wire his wishes for her happiness to Celeste, and his congratulations to Henri. Cables arrived hourly from every corner of the earth.

Jay Regan sent three telegrams, a paternal one to Celeste, and a peculiar one to Henri. It said: "I and your great-grandfather congratulate you."

But no one but Christopher knew that Jay Regan sent him a telegram, also. It contained only one word: "Congratulations!" Others would have been surprised, but not Christopher. He merely smiled, and carefully tore the telegram to bits and then disposed of it adequately.

There was utter consternation and rage among Armand's faction. One of the complaints of Armand's friends had been that he had not displayed enough rancor and determination in his attitude towards his treacherous brother, Christopher. Now, they felt some satisfaction, even in the midst of their perturbation, for Armand seemed full of a quiet ferocity since the announcement of his sister's betrothal. Never loquacious, he was more silent than ever. When Christopher was mentioned, he would say nothing, but his eyes would glitter.

"This marriage," said little Jean, "definitely puts us in the soup. What soup? I don't know, exactly, but one thing is certain: it is simmering, and it's full of poison. Christopher's own private brand."

It was worse, rather than better, that there was nothing definite to suspect, nothing to lay one's finger on and say: Here it is.

When little Annette suddenly became ill with a nervous breakdown, and her physicians advised a quick change of climate and prolonged nursing, possibly a sea voyage, Armand's faction felt completely desperate. They knew Armand's passion for his daughter, and they believed that he would go away with her, at least for a time, as he had done before during her illnesses. It was very bad this time, too, for Annette was reported to be seriously ill. So Armand, they fully believed, would go away just at the most demoralizing point in the silent and hidden feud between his faction and Christopher's. He had done this before, at the height of an investigation of the armaments industries by a special Senate Committee.

But there was something about the whole situation which they did not know, and which only Armand, suffering more intensely than at any other time in his life, knew.

Annette had become ill, without warning, immediately upon the formal announcement of Celeste's engagement. She had been in failing health for some time, it was pointed out, though she had never complained. Because of her frail physique, she had not been prominent in social activities, and it was an accepted fact that Annette did not care for sports of any kind. Consequently, she was forgotten for the most part by the many members of her family, and the report of her illness did not interest them much, until they were informed that she was gravely ill. Even then, they felt quite resigned, and some even expressed their opinion that it would be "better for the poor little thing," if she died.

They saw how haggard Armand had become lately, and how much weight he had lost, and how suddenly savage his manner became when he was interrupted during his periods of profound and somber meditation. His whole personality seemed to have changed. He lost a certain hesitancy and uneasiness. It was easily seen that he was desperate and determined, and very dangerous. But he did not go away, and even when Annette was removed in a stretcher to a private railroad car, en route to some elaborate sanitarium, he went only a short distance with her, and immediately returned to Windsor.

On the night that Celeste's engagement had been announced, Annette had been unusually gay. Quite a bright color had burned in her face. No one had ever heard her laugh so much, nor had seen her so active. She was everywhere, running about on her poor little child-legs. There was an air about her like candleflame seen through glass. Her flesh seemed transparent, and her eyes shone and sparkled feverishly. When she talked to Celeste and Henri there was a thin sound of incoherent hysteria in her voice and laughter. Everyone spoke of how well she seemed, and how vivacious. No one really saw her at all but her father, who watched her every moment, and who was suffering more concentrated bitterness and sadness than he had ever experienced before.

Then, when they reached home together, he had suddenly picked her up in his strong arms and had carried her up to her room himself. The girl had affectionately protested, with laughter, and then, all at once, she had collapsed on his breast, and had laid her head on his shoulder with a dying gesture, very gently and breathlessly. The servants, and Mrs. Armand, and young Antoine, had watched Armand carry her up, and had not spoken. There was something in this picture of the somber, grim-lipped man carrying the child that made even the most dull feel a vague emotion of distress and pity. They saw his strong, broad black back, and the long white chiffon streamers of the girl's gown floating between his legs and over his shoulders, as he marched up the stairs. They saw her arm on one of his shoulders, a child's frail white arm; the little hand drooped lifelessly, and the other arm and hand swung against his thigh.

He had taken her to her room, and had laid her on her bed. Her bright ash-blonde hair streamed over the satin pillows. She lay with closed eyes, hardly breathing, her face as white as her dress. Her maid came in, and her mother, frightened, and he drove them out. He came back to stand beside the bed and to gaze down at his daughter. He folded his arms across his broad chest, and did not move. He waited.

Annette lay without stirring. At last she sighed, very deeply, as though the sound came from the bottom of her heart. She opened her eyes, and smiled faintly. Armand did not smile. She saw his face, and understanding what she saw, she burst into wild tears, covering her eyes with her little hands. While no one knew, she could pretend. But now she knew that her father understood, and all her miserable little pretenses fell away.

Armand sat down beside the bed. He gathered his daughter in his arms and lifted her to his knee. He rocked back and forth in his chair, and let her weep. He kept smoothing and stroking her hair, but beyond that he did nothing until she had cried herself to quietness. Then he wiped her eyes with his own handkerchief.

He began to speak, very quietly: "There are some things, my darling, which must be endured. This is one of them. You must endure it. I have tried to make life as happy as I could for you. I have tried to go every bit of the way with you. But I can't go any farther. You've got to walk it alone."

She was not crying now. Her head was on his chest. He kept kissing the top of her little bright head. When he finished speaking, she kissed his hand, humbly, but did not speak.

Armand sighed. He held her to him tightly. "But when you come out—the other end of the tunnel—I'll be there, waiting for you, dear." His voice, his manner, made the melodramatic words touching and beautiful.

"Yes, I know, Daddy," she answered. Her face was blotched and stained with tears, but she smiled. The smile was so piteous that Armand turned his head aside.

"When there isn't any hope, you've got to resign yourself—to things," he said meditatively. "We each of us come to the end of hope, sooner or later."

He left her only when she was asleep. As he closed the door behind him, he did not seem despairing. His expression was dangerous.

CHAPTER XXVI

CHRISTOPHER laid his hands, palms-down, on the pile of papers they had all been considering. He looked at Emile, Hugo, Henri and Francis, and smiled unpleasantly.

"So there we have it," he said. "Germany, through Kronk and Byssen, is selling aircraft to South America, Versailles Treaty to the contrary. Bedors of Sweden is shipping her all the armaments she wants to buy. 'Poor prostrate Germany' is doing pretty damn well for herself. We're glad to see her re-arming. Like our good friend, Britain, a strong and re-armed Germany is our best assurance against Labor control of government, and we're willing to help her any time she wants us to. We've not objected to our Companies shipping Germany shells; in fact, we like it! Stresseman did a good job there, and we mustn't forget to send him his bonus. Our subsidiary in Canada is shipping Germany the nickel she needs. Germany, so far, hasn't interfered with our shipments of munitions and explosives and armor-plate to Central and South America, though I haven't the slightest doubt she'll be our best competitor when Britain and France finally destroy the democratic government in Berlin.

"But that's in the future. What is bothering us now is the fact that Germany is getting huge contracts for aircraft from Central and South America. What are we going to do about it? Yelp to the League of Nations or somebody that Germany is violating the Versailles Treaty? And get a polite kick in the teeth for an answer?"

"Well," said Emile, "you've outlined the subject. What *are* we going to do about it?"

Christopher's light gleaming eyes moved contemplatively from one listening face to the other. "You know the answer as well as I do. We've got to start competing in Central and South America. We've got to get busy with propaganda down there. Argentina and Brazil are pretty prosperous, now, and could afford some excellent aircraft, and a few robust hates. That's your Job, Emile. Get busy on it. In the meantime, we're going to sell them all Duval-Bonnet craft." He added, after a pause: "That is, if we can induce someone to lend us twenty-five million dollars, or more, immediately."

Emile said gloomily: "I'm flat. You've got all I could spare. Wall Street's already talking. We've aroused quite a little talk about our money-changing. Besides, you said yourself, before, that twenty-five million is only a starter."

"Quite true. It is. But it will be that. In six months the South American representatives will be here. We've got to show them equipment and men and plans and backing. They're a shrewd lot, those damned Latins. We've done a lot, but it's only a beginning."

"I," said Francis, "am practically broke, too. You're a bottomless pit, Chris. Oh, I'm not grumbling! Don't pull faces at me like that. But there it is."

"As for me," said Hugo, genially, "I'll be standing on the street corner, with a tin cup."

"And I," said Henri, "have lent you three million dollars. You've got a fine mess of building and equipment down there now, Christopher. Nearly as good as Parsons'."

" 'Nearly as good!'" repeated Christopher venomously. "That isn't half good. It's got to be twice as good. Twice as good! Or we're out, so far as South and Central America are concerned. And then, there are Japan and China. They're buying feverishly. In four years, or perhaps less, they'll be tearing each other apart. Robsons-Strong and Schultz-Poiret and Skeda and Kronk are already selling them twenty times what we are selling them. That's because we hoped we could scare them off by advising them not to sell Japan and China for a few years. But they got onto us that our humanitarian concern was only because they were in a better position to do business than we were. I don't want to make that mistake again. We want to be ready." He paused, and then, as no one spoke, he said impatiently: "Well, haven't any of you any suggestions?"

"Don't glare at us," said Francis, smoothly. "You act as though we're a pack of kids who won't play ball with you. We've played ball to the tune of millions. I can't do any more. The directors are going to ask very soon about some manipulations I've been doing. If I can't show them something satisfactory, about Duval-Bonnet, it's going to be very nasty for me. Kinsolving stock will hit rock bottom in half an hour."

Christopher looked at them for a moment before speaking. Then he said without expression: "Every penny I've got in the world is in Duval-Bonnet. Including Celeste's holdings."

At this, Henri stirred. He fixed his cousin with his pale eyes, now so inexorable and hard. "What, Celeste's fortune? You had no right to do that!" He added, with a smile that Christopher found unendurable: "It is perhaps a good thing that I'm only engaged to marry her, and am not married to her, yet."

The others moved, intrigued and delighted. They stared at the two men, whose personalities had met, clenched, and were engaged in a transfixed struggle. Like wolves, who run in packs for mutual advantage, they could form a circle about sudden antagonists and await, with glee, the conflict, the victory and defeat, knowing in the end, that they could devour the loser.

Then Christopher shrugged almost imperceptibly. "You forget," he said. "I'm her guardian. Without bond. She isn't twenty-one. I'll still be her guardian, even after you are married, and I still won't have to show an accounting until she's of age. And that's a year from now."

Henri said nothing. All at once he had become interested in the shape and contour of his fingernails. Then Francis, after winking at Christopher, tapped Henri familiarly on the shoulder. "It looks as though you're in it, not up to the neck, as we are, but right over the head, too. Don't worry. None of us are worried. We just need about twenty-five million dollars more," and he laughed his dry and brittle laugh.

Henri glanced up. His eyes, so like hard agate marbles, moved from one face to another. He began to smile. "I'm not worrying," he said. "I was just surprised, that is all. After all, I'm marrying Celeste, you know."

The others nodded and smiled at him in a friendly manner. But Christopher did not smile. His nostrils flared out as though he were breathing quicker than usual. He smelled danger. He thought to himself: It is only June. October is too far away.

He said, finally: "You'll have an accounting, after your marriage. But it is only a courtesy I'm extending you, and not necessary. You understand that, don't you?"

"Perfectly," said Henri, with an amiable gesture of his hand. Then, again, he fixed his eyes on Christopher. "Let me understand this clearly: unless we can suddenly acquire a lot

207

of money, quite a lot more money than we have at hand, our chances of getting the South American contracts are slim. That is it, isn't it? Well, then, we must acquire it," and he smiled humorously.

"Bravo!" exclaimed Francis. "The Master Mind solves the problem! And now, Sherlock Holmes, perhaps you can tell us where the pot of gold is buried?"

"Well, then," said Henri, "in the first place, I'll lend you four million dollars more. And the rest of you can pinch yourselves in spots, and produce enough to make it ten millions. Now we need about fifteen more. I'll get it for you. I'll borrow it. Personally."

They stared at him in stupefaction. Then, all together, they burst into a shout of laughter. Even Christopher laughed as loudly as the others. But through his derisive mirth his eyes, unmirthful, watched Henri unblinkingly. Henri listened to the laughter. He smiled nonchalantly. He seemed even a little bored, as he waited for it all to stop.

When it finally did he said without rancor: "I'm glad you boys have had your little fun. But let's get down to business now."

Francis said: "In the first place, my child, we don't dare lend any more. As Emile pointed out, Wall Street's already talking about our transactions, and asking itself lots of questions which would be embarrassing to us. One of these days, it isn't going to be so delicate. We thank you very kindly for your offer of four million. We'll take it. We like your spirit of generosity. But you must forgive our vulgar and unkind curiosity if we ask you where the hell you think you can raise over fifteen million dollars yourself."

Henri spoke as casually as though they were discussing a minor transaction. "I'll borrow from Edith, part of it, anyway. If I can get that fifteen million, say within a week or so, I will have a proposition for all of you."

"A proposition?" Francis exclaimed, and so did Hugo and Emile, in chorus. But Christopher merely intensified his fixed regard of his cousin's face.

Henri smiled at them very blandly. "Yes, a proposition. I won't propose it just now. That would be premature. First, I'll try to raise the money."

He stood up. He had an engagement, he said. He left Christopher's office. It was eight o'clock at night. The great mills were vomiting crimson smoke to the black sky. He hummed to himself as he left the building and got into his waiting car.

There was a prolonged silence after his departure. And

then Francis, grinning not very agreeably, said to Christopher: "You know, if I were you, I'd hurry along that wedding."

"Far be it from me," said Hugo, "to disparage a dear relative of ours, who has recently gone from this room, but it is my business, as a politician, to cultivate my nose. And if that isn't a strong odor of snake-in-the-grass trailing in someone's wake, I'm just a bawdy-house ward-heeler."

CHAPTER XXVII

I T WAS Armand who came to his mother, an Armand prematurely aged and gloomy and silent. She was walking around the bare greenly shining grounds when he arrived, and he joined her. He glanced towards the house. It was a Sunday morning, and every polished window gleamed. "There's no privacy in this whole damned place," he said fretfully. He remembered that Jean had said that even the bathrooms had doors of transparent glass, and he smiled, sourly. "Isn't there any place where we could be alone?"

Adelaide sighed. The poplar trees were stiff green wood standing in the sunshine. Every window of the house was uncluttered, and anyone behind them could see everything. No bushes, no arbors, no grottoes, no sheltering trees, no gardens. Just sunshine and emptiness and smooth grass, for acres. Armand, who was not usually sensitive to surroundings, and thought his own huge chateau a mess, felt himself as conspicuous as though he were naked. He had the feeling that every great bare window sheltered a spy. "Where're Chris and Celeste, Mother?"

"They went with Henri and Edith for a canter," she replied.

He was relieved. And yet, it was impossible for him to talk confidentially with his mother, exposed like this, two unprotected figures on a desert of clipped grass. "Let's go to your rooms," he said abruptly. He took his mother's arm. She seemed unusually feeble, and he noticed how thin and bent she was, and how her hair had whitened.

They went into the mansion. Here everything was as brilliant as the out-of-doors, and just as unshaded and unprotected. Armand came here very seldom, for it made him uneasy. He had a weakness for rugs that hushed footsteps, and for rich draperies that added somberness to rooms. Now he blinked in the unsheltered light that glanced back at him from smooth pale wood, bright steel, crystal, white cornices and polished bare floors. They went up white stairways, uncarpeted, with cool marble balustrades. But when he entered Adelaide's room, quietly and thickly furnished, with gilt-framed portraits on the dark walls, and flowers in vases on every table and on Adelaide's old-fashioned grand piano, he felt he could breathe more easily than he could downstairs in that glittering windswept air, which had seemed cold in spite of the warm sun.

Adelaide sat down with a gesture of exhaustion. She waited for her son to speak. She has gone beyond despair, thought Armand, with the new acuteness sorrow and anxiety had given him. He said abruptly: "Mother, everything's settled about Celeste, I suppose? She is happy about this?"

Adelaide's chin had fallen to her chest; she merely lifted her hand heavily, and then let it drop. Armand frowned. "Please answer me. It's important. Is Celeste happy?"

And now Adelaide lifted her head and looked at her son with suddenly passionate eyes. "You're so interested in her happiness, aren't you, Armand? You never were before. Why do you care now?"

He flushed darkly, and bit his lip. "After all, she is my sister," he muttered. He was surprised to hear his mother laugh bitterly, and when he looked at her, he saw that she was rigidly convulsed with her laughter. Her face was contorted; she was leaning forward in her chair as though in intense pain.

"Your sister!" she cried. "What have you ever cared about your sister? You were the only one of my sons who ever seemed to care about his father. You knew how your father loved Celeste. Yet, all these years, since he has died, you have shown no interest in her, and hardly noticed her!"

The dark flush deepened on Armand's cheeks. He said, trying to make his voice quiet and hard: "Christopher is her guardian, not I."

She laughed even louder, and now with wildness. "Your father knew all of you very well, didn't he? He knew, for instance, that Emile would rob his sister, if he could, and that you would probably only stand by. Can you deny that, Armand? He hated Christopher, but he knew he was the only one who would protect his little sister, and that is why he made him her guardian." She stood up; her thin old figure seemed to vibrate with violence. "Armand, you never were a real man. Your brothers are. They take what they want. They

210

never had any conscience. But you weren't man enough to take what you wanted, and think no more about it. You had a conscience, and you never stopped thinking about the awful things you had done. You're a weakling, Armand. You had the capacities for goodness, and you violated them. You aren't even a fine villain."

His face, while she had been speaking so to him, had turned the wet dusky color of a man who is dying of apoplexy. His pale lips shook. He could not speak.

His mother, exhausted again by her brief and terrible passion, sat down. She put her handkerchief to her eyes. "A woman," she said, in a faint hoarse voice, "accepts the man she loves and marries, no matter what he is. But she never accepts the wickedness of her sons. I've done with Emile and Christopher; I don't feel they are my sons any longer. But you were close to me. From the first, I knew you weren't wicked. But it didn't take me long to know you were a coward. And so, at the last, I realized you were worse than they are. You've done violence to yourself all your life. And now you've got to pay for your crimes against yourself with the misery of other people."

She took away her handkerchief, and stared at the stout thick body of her son, and then at his face. She said in a loud voice, as though in wonder: "But you aren't really concerned with Celeste, are you, Armand? It's just yourself, isn't it? You're afraid of Christopher!"

Armand turned away. He felt ill. "No," he said quietly, "it's not that." He was standing by a window; he suddenly twisted a fold of the deep crimson velvet of the draperies in his damp hand. "It's not that," he repeated.

His mother was silent. But he could feel her gaze fixed on his back. Then he heard her approaching him. She laid her hand on his arm, and tried to peer up into his face.

"Armand!" Her voice had changed again. It was the voice of a mother, urgent, pitiful. "What is it, then?"

He looked down into her face, and pain seemed to leap about his heart. He wanted to say: It is Celeste. But he could not. He had never lied to his mother in all his life, though he had frequently deceived her and evaded her. So, he could say nothing at all, his big stout face merely growing darker and colder and more distracted.

She had lived long enough to know that this expression only appeared in the eyes of those despairingly concerned with one who is much loved. She knew it was not Celeste. Then who could it be? Her thoughts ran to Annette. But little Annette had no part in this marriage. However, Adelaide said: "Is something wrong with Annette, Armand? How is the child?"

She knew she had guessed rightly, by the change in his face, the look of misery. "Not very well, Mother," he said, hesitatingly, warily. "No, it's not tuberculosis. It's—it's just a sort of nervous and mental collapse. I've been—upset about her. Don't worry, though. We're going to see her next Sunday——"

They sat down opposite each other, and regarded each other in a long silence. Beads of sweat stood out on Armand's dusky forehead. He kept mopping them away. His fat thighs strained at the seams of his trousers. Moisture gathered at the roots of his graying auburn curls. Adelaide saw nothing of his middle-aged heaviness and grayness; she saw only her son, who was frantic with wretchedness which she could not alleviate.

"Armand," she said gently, "why don't you go away? You have so much money. Why do you want any more? Why don't you go away with your family? Money has never given any one of us any peace, has it? You've got enough. Go away, Armand." She added to herself: Go away, my dear, where you can live at peace with yourself.

He tried to laugh, but it was a painful and smothered sound. "Mother, I don't want any more money. I don't care about that."

And then there was another silence. At last Armand got up to go. He stood before his mother, hesitating. Then he said, speaking quickly, as though hurried: "I don't think Henri is the man for Celeste. You were always right about her; I always knew what you meant even when I pretended I didn't. If there is any way——"

Adelaide smiled mournfully. "There's no way, as long as there is Christopher."

They heard voices outside in the early June sunshine. Armand went to the window. The riders were dismounting from their horses. He could see Celeste's young face, radiant, brightly tinted, shining with excitement and happiness. He saw Henri help her to dismount. For one brief furtive moment the young man held her in his arms, and Armand could see her expression. He turned away, the blackness of complete hopelessness overcoming him.

"Don't tell them I was here. I'll wait until they are inside. Please call my car for the back entrance." He picked up his hat, and hesitated again. "Mother," he said, almost gently, "perhaps we're wrong. Perhaps Celeste will be happy."

And then he went away.

212

Adelaide was alone. But none of them came up to see her, though they must have known she had not gone out. She so rarely went out, anyway. She waited for a long time, though she knew in her heart that no one would come.

At last she began to cry. She was always crying these days.

I have no children, she thought. I am childless. Perhaps, in every mother's life she thinks: I have never given birth.

CHAPTER XXVIII

ESTELLE BOUCHARD was arguing discontentedly with her husband.

"Frank, I just don't know what we'll do! The children will be so disappointed. Rosemarie has already invited some of her friends for the cruise."

Francis replied sarcastically. "That is really too bad, isn't it? Well, the brats can be disappointed all they want. The fact remains that we can't go away on the yacht for more than two or three weeks. After all, Celeste is marrying the latter part of October, and we're invited to Crissons. That comes first, these days. Besides, I can't spare the time."

Estelle was diverted. "Is business so good, then? What wars are you all plotting?" and she smiled.

"Don't be an idiot. We don't plot wars, I've told you a thousand times. We merely supply the instruments for war, if nations are damfool enough to want to murder each other. It's no concern of ours. Anyway, we weren't talking about that. We'll be on the yacht for three weeks, at the most. Then Crissons. I've got to get back here, immediately."

Estelle had been thinking of very little these days but the coming marriage. Her disappointment was profound. What on earth could Henri Bouchard see in that foolish unsophisticated little creature? Rosemarie, the clever child, called her Little Dorrit. Rather bitter, but Celeste truly did belong in Dickens' nineteenth century, and not in the twentieth. She said aloud: "Celeste'll have everything. I don't know what on earth we'll get her and Henri."

"We'll give them a check. I've yet to see the time when money wasn't the most acceptable gift. Though I admit it isn't showy," replied Francis.

But Estelle's thoughts had gone elsewhere. "I loathe Crissons," she said. "The banks of the Dead Sea would be the proper place for it. Why doesn't somebody remind Christopher that there are trees in the world? Lots of trees."

"Take it up with him personally. He likes you."

Estelle smiled. Her leathery skin flushed quickly. "Well, I like Christopher. I only wish, though, that he was a little more human. But I suppose he has quite a lot to endure, with Adelaide. Sometimes I wonder at his patience."

They were eating Sunday breakfast in a room full of June sunlight. Estelle glanced through the windows with satisfaction. The great landscaped grounds swept away to the river. Estelle's attention suddenly focused. "There's a cab, a station cab," she said. "Who on earth——? So early in the morning, too. Are we expecting anyone?"

"No. I hope not." Francis stood up to peer. The cab wound through the grounds. Francis uttered an exclamation, and frowned in his peering concentration. "But it can't be!" he muttered. He flung down his napkin and almost ran out of the room. Estelle followed. Francis was racing down the stairs like a youth. But the butler was already at the door to admit the stranger. Estelle stopped on the stairs, and strained her eyes to see, in the duskiness of the reception hall. Francis was at the foot of the stairs, waiting.

A young man, apparently in his late twenties, was entering. Behind him came the cab-driver, carrying luggage, of which the butler relieved him. But before he could ask the visitor's name, Francis uttered a shout.

"Peter! My God, where did you drop from?"

Estelle ran lightly down the rest of the stairs. "Peter Bouchard! How splendid!" She shook hands with the younger man. She had never had her husband's aversion for his youngest brother, and her smile, therefore, was genuinely pleased. "We were wondering what had become of you. It's been years!"

He had just returned to America, he explained. Upon his arrival, he remembered he had relatives. "So, here I am. For a few days," he added. He had a kind, quiet smile, at once reserved and candid.

It developed that he had come directly from the station, and had not had breakfast as yet. Francis seemed pleased at his brother's return. He insisted that Peter be his guest. And of course, it was all nonsense, he said, about Peter not remaining in Windsor. "Time you settled down here and were one of the family."

He had an amiable if offhand manner of speaking to the

younger man. A patronizing manner. He and Jean and Hugo had never had much of an opinion about Peter's intelligence, competence or personality. Francis knew that regular checks were sent to Peter at a banking address in London. But beyond that, none of the family knew anything more, and cared distinctly less. They knew, for instance that Peter had been gassed during the war, and that he had a chronic cough and poor health; however, none of this had concerned them much. The less he embarrassed them with his "imbecility" the better they liked it. There was something about him that reminded Francis, Jean and Hugo of their father, Honore, and this was sufficient cause for their dislike if they had no other.

He had lived with them as a child in their father's house. But they had had no more contact with him than if he had been a stranger in another country. There had been no point of contact, no small space of ground on which he could meet them. They never knew that he despised, rather than detested them. They had never frightened him with their exigency, their avarice and faithlessness, but they had depressed and saddened and angered him. He felt that there was something noxious about his brothers, something that seemed to devitalize the very air. And so, he had avoided them as much as possible, found their ridicule and dislike not even annoying. At rare intervals he had quarreled violently with them. Before his enlistment he had been strong and athletic, and some of his most pleasant memories were of the times he had whipped his brothers. He remembered, wistfully, what exultation he had felt in punching Jean, particularly, and then in knocking Hugo all about the room. Though he knew Francis liked him little better than did the others, there had been a sort of understanding between the oldest and youngest brother, patronizing and treacherous on Francis' part, but amiable and even kindly on his. Peter knew very well that Francis derided him as much as did Jean and Hugo; he knew that no more than Jean and Hugo would Francis ever help him, if he needed help. And yet, there was a fugitive liking between them, a liking that sometimes approached pale affection. Francis, secretly, sometimes regretted that Peter had so little "sense." He would have liked to have a brother in his confidence whom he could trust, a brother faithful to him but competently faithless to everyone else.

Jean and Hugo had no such weakness. Francis had once said that if they had been women they would have rouged their faces and combed their hair before they looked at themselves in the mirror. They trusted no one, not even them-

215

selves. But there were times when Francis wished he had someone to talk to, someone with whom he could be himself, without being eternally afraid that the confidant was gathering information about his weakness in order the more completely to betray him.

Francis had been subject to these twinges more or less frequently when Peter had been at home. Then he had forgotten them. In the midst of enemies, a man's senses are constantly alert. Now, as he sat opposite Peter at the breakfast table, he was conscious of them again. He said aloud: "It is time you settled down here and were one of the family."

Peter smiled. Francis remembered that in Peter's youth his smile had been either sad, scornful or cold. But now it was both gentle and ironic, tinged with an impersonal bitterness that was without meanness or rancor. Francis thought: It's funny, but I never noticed before how much he resembles me. A curious warmth pervaded his dryness, like autumn sun on dead leaves.

"What inducements have you to offer?" Peter asked.

"What? Inducements? Why, your family!" and Francis grinned.

Peter said nothing. Estelle leaned towards him. "Come on, Peter, stay home. Isn't there a girl? We're a very close-knit clan, you know."

"Are we?" Peter's voice was without irony, but Francis' lips twitched.

"Well, of course you wouldn't know," said Estelle. "You've been away a long time. Where on earth have you been, anyway?"

Peter coughed before answering. Francis noticed that the cough was hacking, and more or less frequent. "I've been in Russia, for one thing," Peter replied.

"In Russia!" Estelle burst out laughing. "Among the Bolsheviks! Now, don't shock us by telling us you like the Communist system!"

Peter answered quietly: "No, I don't. It is built on the premise that human nature can change, radically. It doesn't compromise with it. That's wrong. You must allow for it, always; if you don't, any system, no matter how utopian, must fail. Democracies allow for it, that is why they tolerate capitalism and private property and individual initiative. We don't need bolshevism at all. We just need more democracy, and then more democracy, and justice and peace and mercy. Then capitalism can't do us very much harm."

He added: "In fact, capitalism can do us a lot of good.

216

But not," and he coughed again, "the sort of men that control it today."

Estelle was puzzled. But Francis fixed his eyes keenly on his brother's face.

"I don't think that capitalism can be improved," said Estelle. "It is adequate, in America at least. You have only to look at our universal prosperity and the high standard of living among even the least competent or productive. Our 'permanent prosperity,' as Mr. Coolidge calls it, is the best vindication of our particular brand of capitalism."

" 'Permanent prosperity,' " mused Peter. "Do you think it is permanent? I don't. I think it is over. I think that within the next three or four years it will end. Catastrophically. Don't you, Francis?"

Francis raised his eyebrows. "I? I'm not a prophet, Peter. But I think in a way you are quite right. You must have been visiting Wall Street."

Peter smiled. He said: "But my opinions are not particularly interesting or unique. Before I went to Russia, I visited Germany. I like Germany and the Germans, because I like freshness, and industry, and intelligence, and cleanness. But the Germans are too obedient. They love authority. And the obedience and the love of authority of the German people are two dangers which the rest of the world is criminally overlooking, these days."

He added, looking at Francis: "Have you heard much, over here, of a man called Adolf Hitler, and his 'beer putsch'?"

"A little, yes. Some crackpot Austrian, isn't he? But he's in jail! We haven't heard about him for some time."

Peter said, quietly and grimly: "You will. And perhaps you'll thank him, Francis. You ought to! He'll kick up the biggest stink in Europe you've ever smelt." Suddenly his eye sharpened on his brother, and his voice was louder: "But maybe you know all this, already?"

Francis laughed. "No, I'm not omniscient." He asked, quickly: "Well, where did you go after wearing armor in Germany, and swimming through moats?"

"I went to England. I—I had rather a bad case of bronchitis. I stayed a whole winter in the south. It's funny; people don't know that the south of England is like Florida: white beaches and palm trees. I like England, too. The English are what the Germans will eventually be, when they are civilized. But I hope they'll leave English duplicity and greediness out of it. There's a rotten gang in power in England, just now. They're plotting against the German republic, because they are afraid of Russian radicalism. And they'll

217

destroy it, unless God intervenes, or somebody, and then they'll let loose a pack of madmen on Europe again. One member of the House of Lords told me seriously that democracy was a fungus disease that will eat up the fine old oaks of privilege and class and private exploitation in England and all the rest of the world, unless it is eradicated, and some sort of oppressive feudalism and State-ism rapidly revived. He owns a newspaper, the damned old parasite! His policy is rooted in hatred for the people, and the most enormous greed I've ever seen. He believes in State worship, and sacrifice and discipline, and something he calls 'sturdiness' and respect for authority, all of which, he says, are sadly lacking in the modern English workingman's character. I'd like to see him and the rest of his country-estate pirates and traitors strung up at the gates of London! Maybe I'll have the pleasure one of these days!"

"You," said Francis, "ought to write a book." He winked mockingly at his wife.

Peter saw the wink, and he colored. But he answered quietly: "That's just what I intend to do. But I haven't enough material, yet."

Francis smiled unpleasantly. "You didn't come back home to complete your material, by any chance, did you?"

Peter merely smiled. He coughed again. Francis was interested in the cough. "Where did you pick that up?"

"Gas. In the war. Remember, there was a war?"

"Yes, I vaguely remember. But I thought Cousin Jules arranged all that. I heard he managed to have you kept in the rear lines, out of danger."

"He was under that impression, yes. But I knew what the family would be up to, and I arranged it, myself, that I should be in the trenches. That's where I picked up the gas, and the cough. That was a pretty bad brand of gas you boys put out, and the stench brought back memories of my happy childhood. Oh, yes, it was Bouchard gas; fragments of the shells were stamped 'Made in Windsor, Pa.' "

Estelle was suddenly grave. "You mean, Peter, your lungs —were hurt—with our gas?"

Peter shrugged. "Any other gas would have smelt as bad, and would have done as much damage, I suppose. But don't let that worry you, Estelle. Other soldiers got just as much of it as I did. In fact, lots of us died."

Estelle bit her lip. She knew, of course, of the ramifications of the armaments industry, but only in an impersonal way. Now, it was brought home. "It seems a bit—sardonic—doesn't it? that a Bouchard should be injured by gas-shells sold to the enemy by Bouchards."

"Life," said Francis, "is often sardonic. But what are you doing for that cough, Peter? Not neglecting it, I hope?"

"What could be done has been done. One lung is gone, entirely. But I'll manage. Others have, you know. I've just got to be a little careful. I was in veterans' hospitals for a time; I learned a lot there! Under my assumed name, of course."

Estelle loved her husband, and she felt a warm regard for Peter, who was not only his brother, but resembled him closely. Moreover, she was full of pity. She had sufficient intuition to be moved. Peter, she decided, needed someone to take care of him. She concluded that the look of sadness about his mouth and eyes was due to chronic ill-health. For some reason, she felt relief.

The next night she gave a huge family dinner in honor of Peter, to which every Bouchard now in the city was invited.

CHAPTER XXIX

THE Bouchards were surprised, but not very much interested, at the news of Peter's return. He had never been prominent in family gatherings or business. Though he was possessed of an enormous fortune in his own right, their attitude towards him was that of wealthy relatives towards a poor relation. Moreover, it was the regretful opinion of the family that Honore's youngest son was a fool. "Not very bright," Nicholas said. He had never shown any initiative, any interest in business or invention, or any appreciable activity in sports or other legitimate or illegitimate pleasures. "Absolutely abnormal," said Alexander Bouchard, recalling one of Peter's amused remarks about piety. "A blue-eyed idealist," said Jean, "and entirely disoriented."

Had he shown signs of profligacy, they would have forgiven a young man's high spirits. Had he been "a gay young Bouchard," figuring prominently in the Broadway newspapers, they might have smiled indulgently. But he had never been profligate or gay.

No one in the family had ever loved him but his father.

To the end of his life, Peter never forgot Honore, nor got over his death. He could hardly bear to think of his father; the memory was a pang as violent eight years after his death as it had been the first day. Old Ann Richmond, his mother, had despised him early for his lack of snobbishness and something she called "pride." His brothers had actively disliked him, and had laughed at him uproariously all during his life at home. He had not wasted much love on them, himself; he, at times, had liked Francis, whose temperament was rather congenial and charming, if not excessively brilliant. He had always more or less disliked Hugo, whom he thought false, lying and hypocritical. But his active hatred was for little Jean. This hatred was based on his conviction that Jean was monstrously cruel, dangerous, evil and completely treacherous. He never saw the wit that glittered and tantalized and entertained. He never saw the famed good-temper and affability and real charm. He was always too passionately fascinated by the real man, and too horrified. The mere sight of that dimpled smile revolted him, and struck him into a sick silence. To his youthful eyes, his brothers had been painted in colors too intense for reality. He never saw that a few, if only a few, of Francis' assumptions of kindness and interest were genuine, or that Hugo was occasionally moved to give substantial assistance to the unfortunate, or that even Jean had tact and consideration, and sometimes generosity, and could be stirred to do an authentic favor even for those he disliked.

Once Peter had been afflicted with youthful intolerance and narrowness. Now he had grown more understanding and reasonable. He was even prepared to find some small good in his brothers. He was conscious of some pleasure at seeing Francis again. Much of his temperament was like that of his grandmother's brother, Martin Barbour, but he was more penetrating than Martin, more patient, though equally passionate, and much more tolerant, much less narrow. For his mother, he had had complete indifference. He had become understanding to the point, during the past few years, where he had often sent her cards from various points in his travels.

The surprise which the Bouchards experienced at his return was due mostly to the fact that they had forgotten his existence. However, they were not particularly interested. With the exception of Christopher. He remembered that Peter was very rich. He might be persuaded to invest in Duval-Bonnet, or, better, sell his Bouchard stock. So Christopher, whom Peter had long ago called The Robot, was prepared to be agreeable and very friendly.

Little Annette did not attend the dinner, for she was still at her sanitarium. Henri did not attend, for he was in New York. Nor did Adelaide go. She was too depressed and despondent for family gatherings. The Bouchards, she decided, were bad enough individually; collectively, they were too much.

Most of them had forgotten how Peter looked. But his family resemblance to Francis impressed them vaguely in his favor; they were prepared, after the first glance, to be affectionate. He was tall, perhaps somewhat too slender, and his coloring was fair and pleasant. He had clear eyes, a little too tired and haggard, a firm patient mouth, good features, excellent manners, and an air of grave courtesy which the women found especially attractive. His voice was remarkably like Francis', but somewhat less dry and brittle. Moreover, he seemed pleased to be among his kin, and had not as yet, halfway through dinner, made any of the outlandish remarks for which he was immortally famous. His hacking cough was hardly noticed. "You need building up," said Alexander, with patronizing affection, and with a downward and complacent glance at his own corpulence. He really believed that he found thinness in others objectionable and unhealthy.

Peter was embarrassed because he had almost forgotten some members of the clan. He did not remember Nicholas at all. The children he remembered had grown to young manhood and womanhood. Several of the younger children, too, had not been born when he had enlisted.

Edith came with old Thomas Van Eyck. Old Thomas shook hands with Peter. His vague gentle eyes fixed themselves on the young man with a peculiarly searching expression. He murmured: "You look like your grandmother, I think. I saw her, when I was a child. A beautiful woman—" He moved aside when others came up to greet Peter. But he seemed reluctant to leave. He kept hovering in Peter's vicinity as one who is chilled is wistfully drawn to a fire. He whispered to his stepdaughter: "Now, there is a young man I'd like to see you marry, my dear." Edith, darkly amused, looked at Peter closely. She decided she liked him. However, she was restless. Christopher and Celeste had not yet arrived. She became aware that Peter was standing beside her. "My God," he murmured, "are there any more Bouchards?"

She could not help laughing; her dark eyes flashed at him humorously. "Well, they're great breeders, my stepfather always said. No, I don't think there are so many more coming. A couple of branches live in Philadelphia. Let me see: just what relation are they to you?" She touched her forehead with one thin hard finger with an exaggerated air of concentration. "I give up! I don't know. And then, there is Georges, in New York."

"Yes, I know Georges. I stayed with him for nearly a week. He's going to publish my book—when I get it written."

"Do you write?" she asked, interested.

"Some say yes, some say no," he answered with a smile.

But Edith had lost interest in him. Christopher and Celeste were entering the drawing room. The occupants of the room faded to faceless shadows for Edith. She did not move, did not even smile, but a flash of light irradiated her face. Her eyes met Christopher's, and now she moved slightly as though a passionate current had gone all through her body.

"What a pretty girl!" said Peter. "Could that be little Celeste?"

"Yes," murmured Edith. "She is going to marry my brother in the fall."

Christopher and Celeste came up. "Well, prodigal, the fatted calf was cooked to your taste, wasn't it?" asked Christopher, smiling. He extended his cool fleshless hand and Peter took it. Peter had had much experience with men during the past years; he knew Christopher completely the moment their hands came into contact. Robots, he thought, are hard to kill. They have no heart you can strike.

He turned from Christopher to Celeste, and eyed her whimsically. "You were just a brat in braids when I saw you last, Celeste. But now I can see you are a nice girl."

"I'm very nice," said Celeste, her face dimpling and shining with shy gaiety. "They say I'm the nicest in the family."

"I have no doubt," replied Peter. He held her hand. It was warm and soft and pulsating. He thought: What beautiful eyes! All at once, he saw nothing but her eyes; behind their deep blueness there was a steadfast radiance, a clear pellucid strength. He could not remember seeing this radiance, and this strength, in any other woman's eyes, and it fascinated and strangely moved him. He tightened his fingers on her hand as though it were something precious, and everything and everybody in the room disappeared from his awareness.

Edith was talking with forced lightness to Christopher. Her plain face was lit with beauty. He was smiling slightly; his hand was on her arm, and it was no longer cold, but warm and intimate. She was saying almost in a whisper, above the laughter and conversation in the crowded room: "I haven't seen you for a week. Are you afraid of me? Perhaps you've got just cause. You see, I'm going to marry you one of these days."

222

"Good!" replied Christopher, laughing. "Let me know when it takes place, won't you?" His fingers pressed into her flesh, and a faint color seeped into his dry skin.

"I don't know that I shall," she said, with an attempt at archness in spite of her rapidly beating heart. "If I told you, you might run away."

He did not answer. But his pressing fingers seemed to sink almost to the bone. The pain was bruising, but Edith did not feel it. She stood, smiling into his face, her eyelids tremulous.

At last he released her arm. She sighed. She was conscious, now, of the pain. It seemed to pervade her whole body. She turned to look for Celeste. The girl was standing beside Peter. Neither of them was speaking. But Celeste's face was white and still. She was trying to smile. Over that smile her eyes were remote, and brilliantly blue.

Dinner was announced. Edith walked with Christopher. Behind them came Celeste and Peter. Peter had bent his head and he was speaking to Celeste in a very low voice, and she kept nodding automatically.

Edith sat next to Christopher, but Peter and Celeste were opposite each other. At first Peter was disappointed; now he was reconciled. He could look directly at the girl, and the look was as intimate as a touch. The woman at his left was Agnes, Emile's wife. She had only seen Peter once or twice during her married life, and was prepared, by Emile's amusing stories, to detest the young man. But she was surprised to find that she did not detest him. She thought that he looked far superior to any of his relatives, and that there was something about him not to be found in the others. Perhaps it was a simple integrity, which was also without illusion, and a gentleness of manner which was greater than mere courtesy. Someone in the family, she puzzled, had his same steadfast look, his same purity of facial modeling and refined strength. It was certainly not Emile, nor his brothers! And then her searching eye touched Celeste's face, and she thought: It is the same expression.

Celeste, she decided, must miss Henri and find this dinner very dull, for she seemed pale and tired. She did not listen to anything that was said around the great table. But when Peter spoke, her head lifted and turned involuntarily towards him, and her eyes would take on a curious intensity of expression, as though she were filled with wonder and bemusement.

Christopher had told her a good deal about Peter before they had arrived at the dinner. He made a very funny story of Peter's enlistment. Celeste had begun by smiling; Christopher did not notice that when he had finished the very funny story of Peter's sentimentality and general imbecility Celeste was no longer smiling. "However," Christopher had said, "we must be pleasant to him. He's one of the family, after all."

Everyone knew that Peter was given to outlandish and foolish opinions and some hoped he would edify his relatives by more of them; others hoped that he had acquired "stability" and "common sense." The latter school, of which Alexander was a member, seemed to be satisfied. Peter's remarks were general and tactful; he appeared pleased to be home. Alexander, with satisfaction, decided that Peter had become "normal."

Peter ate and drank and laughed and talked casually. But he saw each face at the table in its entirety. Most of them did not interest him; he did not like the Bouchard women. But he did see his mother, with her jewels and old sprightliness and bare mottled shoulders, and the sight hurt him mysteriously, as though he were ashamed. He remembered that he had kissed her, and had said, his pity making him hypocritical: "You're younger than ever, mother." Old Ann was prepared to be haughtily and suspiciously reserved with her youngest son, and there had been a knowing and very hard look in her eye. But at his words she melted, coquetted, and kissed him with real affection. This made him sadder than ever. And then he saw his brothers. Hugo had come up from New York the day before. His buff-colored geniality struck Peter with embarrassed and embittered remembrance. There was Jean, causing his section of the table to be continually convulsed with his stories and remarks. And then Francis, grinning and angular and dry. Then Christopher, and Emile. From these two his eye fell away with a feeling of mental nausea. And then, Armand.

Peter had had very little contact with Armand in the old days. His remembrance of him was not tinged with dislike and disgust as it was with the others. He had felt that he had some small point of contact with him, though they had seldom met. Wasn't there a little girl—Annette? Someone had said she was ill. This probably accounted for his offguard expression of somber gloom. And yet Peter observed that Armand kept furtively glancing at Christopher and Emile, at Francis and Hugo, and then the gloomy look would be replaced with one of infinite weariness and aversion. He would listen to their remarks, and then when others would laugh, he would just avert his head. Peter felt more drawn to him than ever.

Bouchards upon Bouchards. Peter could not keep his

relationship with them straight. Cousins and second-cousins and third-cousins, and in-laws and brothers and nieces and nephews and aunts and uncles and grandparents. The whole formidable Bouchard family. Peter reflected: It is incredible, but much of the fate and history and peace and misery of America is at this table tonight. We are told in schools to be glad that we are no longer ruled by "tyrants." But we are not told that we are ruled by oligarchies of tyrants, much more dangerous and ruthless than the ancient ones, much more intelligent, much more aware of what they want, and much more capable of getting it.

And yet, they were only mortal men, with flesh and blood, with lusts and wretchednesses, with hopes and impotences, with hatreds and loves. Would Armand, for instance, born in a lower middle-class family, and trained only for minor clerical work, have been able to rise out of his class or accomplish more than a small business man? Were the pillars of dynasty than a petty lawyer, or a shopkeeper? Would Francis have been more than a small business man? Where the pillars of dynasty supported only by mediocre men, instead of the demi-heroes of popular belief? How much did power and greatness owe to inherited opportunity?

His glance kept wandering sharply about the table. And inevitably it came back to Celeste. There it would pause, and he would smile. She would stare at him blindly for a full moment or two, and then would give him an answering smile, uncertain and confused and bewildered. Across the table their eyes would meet and hold, and a swift and silent exchange of confidences would pass between them.

After the sixth or seventh such encounter, Peter thought: I wonder what Henri Bouchard is like now? I remember him, a hard-eyed mean brat. Has he changed, or was I merely prejudiced? I hope he'll be good to her, the pretty little thing! After the tenth encounter, he thought: She is not a Bouchard. And after the twelfth, the thought of her coming marriage gave him an astounding pang.

And then he became aware that she hardly took her eyes off him, no matter to whom he might be speaking. He tried to avoid glancing at her; something in her eyes, in her small pale face, hurt him; when she smiled at him, a faint frightened smile, he was inexpressibly moved and disturbed. It was becoming evident that she waited only for him to look at her. And then, that swift fugitive smile, like a bewildered child's, a terrified child's!

Suddenly he was enormously happy and excited. He dared not ask himself why. He heard himself laughing and talking, and was conscious of the approval of his relatives. He hardly coughed at all. He could even talk to Christopher lightly and casually, Christopher whom he had always deeply hated, Christopher, the Robot, with chromium wheels instead of human internal organs. Through all the talk and laughter, and the rich courses of the dinner, and the wines, he thought: Will she be looking at me again when I look at her?

The first disapproval of him occurred when Francis, in a cleverly satirical voice, announced that Peter was writing "a book."

"A book!" exclaimed Ann, with dismay. "But why a book? Haven't you anything better to do than write a book? Nobody in our family writes books. Nice people don't write books."

When Christopher spoke, Peter knew that here was a deadly and unremitting enemy: "Maybe Peter believes that the pen is still mightier than the sword."

Peter regarded them all calmly, before he said quietly: "It is."

Emile laughed. "We have the smallest literate public in all the world. The market for trash in America is unsurpassed and unbelievable. Good writing stands little chance of publication, or, if published, it sells about twelve hundred copies. Or maybe you're going in for love stories, or movie writing, Peter?"

The other laughed their approval of this wit. Peter waited until the laughter had died down, then he said: "I'm going to write only of the things I have seen. And I've seen a great deal. In Europe, and in Asia. Now I shall see America."

Armand, for the first time, showed interest in him. "But what is your subject matter?"

Peter answered coldly: "The things I have seen. The economic and social conditions of every country I have visited and studied, and a forecasting of the inevitable results of the causes now operating."

"Ah, a prophet," said Jean. "Without benefit of astrology, I hope? Don't mind us; we're just jealous. Most of us can't sign our names legibly. But tell me: what's going to happen?"

Peter regarded him thoughtfully: "I wonder if you really don't know? Somehow, I think you have a vague idea. I'm sure you all know that we are on the verge of a profound national economic crash. There's a great deal of pride in modern capitalism, in America and Britain. You think it something new. I tell you, it's old. It's outmoded. It's done with. Its lumbering structure is top-heavy, and nothing you can do can stop it from crashing. We need something new. A new capitalism. The old is as finished as you are."

Everyone exclaimed. Jean smiled, his eyes disappearing in the laughter-wrinkles about them. "So, you think we're finished? I don't agree with you. I think we've just started. As for myself, I don't feel any symptoms of decay."

Several laughed derisively at Peter. But he did not appear to notice this laughter. "But you really are finished, you know. It may take ten or twenty years. But the end is inevitable."

" 'Comes the revolution,' " murmured Christopher. Those in his vicinity shouted delightedly. Now all the approval of Peter was gone. He saw only hostility about him. He glanced at Celeste. Evidently she had heard nothing of what had been said. Her frightened shining eyes were still fixed upon him, as though she were hypnotized. Yet he knew that she was listening to him.

"Why, Peter, you are a bolshevik!" cried Ann, in angry dismay.

He replied to Christopher: "No. No revolution. Revolutions are brought about by mobs. Mobs are never intelligent, but only brutal and vicious. Like yourselves." He smiled slightly. "The thing that will demolish you is known as natural change. You're as outmoded as the brontosaurus. Once you were useful, and necessary. Protestant liberalism created you, and you upheld it. You were, in fact co-creators of each other. Now Protestant liberalism doesn't need you. In fact, you retard its constant progress towards complete democracy and enlightenment."

He added, looking at their angry or derisive or contemptuous faces: "Cheer up. You'll probably do a lot of damage before you die. A very big lot. That ought to satisfy you."

No one spoke for a moment, and then Alexander cried: "I've never heard such stuff! It's—it's Communistic! It's un-American! It's undemocratic! And unchristian!"

Peter turned his face to him and studied him thoughtfully. "Ah, 'unchristian.' It would be funny, if it weren't so terrible, how you have got even religion, the one solace of the wretched and the helpless, to do your rotten work for you. I'm sorry. But you see, though it sounds too strong, it really is true. This isn't the first time the church has played the whore for you, but it eventually will be found out, too."

The scarlet tint of Alexander's face had deepened to purple. The rest of the family were highly entertained. They despised Alexander, and now they hated Peter. It gave them tremendous enjoyment to watch these two "at each other's throats."

227

"Blasphemy!" Alexander's voice was a strangled gasp.

Peter looked tired. "Don't be a fool. I thought you might have had some intelligence; after all, you are a Bouchard." He turned to the others; his thin face was pale and drawn.

"I've been around a lot, in Europe. I've found, for instance, that Britain and France have repaid American financiers for every penny, with interest, that they borrowed. The 'war-debts,' about which there is so much noise these days, are owed to the American government only. And why aren't they being repaid? I'll tell you why!

"I'm only reviewing what you already know. But I'd like to have you know I know. You know, for instance, that the German Junkers hate the democratic German government, but they can't destroy it, and bring back militarism to Germany, without the help of British, French and American financiers. They can't make Germany a good customer of the Bouchards, and the Robsons-Strongs, and the Schultz-Poirets and the Skedas, unless Germany stops paying reparations. And so, one of these days, as you have all already plotted, a 'moratorium' is going to be called on reparations. And then Germany will use the money for re-armament, and the financiers will lend her money to buy more armaments, and all the rest of Europe will have to re-arm against Germany, and then the golden blood will begin to circulate among the whole criminal gang, among all of you."

There was not a sound in the room. Peter's eyes went slowly from one hating or contemptuous or derisive or startled face to another. It came to rest on Armand's. Armand's face was gray. His eyes were fixed. He had drawn in his under-lip against his teeth.

"Yes," said Peter musingly, speaking to them all, and seeing only Armand. "You'll do a lot of damage yet. You'll bring the world to the end of civilization, or close enough to it to be horrible. But this will be the last of you. Maybe it will take centuries to undo what you've done. But maybe this time men will learn that their enemies are not their neighbors, but you. You and your hirelings, and your traitors, and your bottomless-bellies, and your haters of mankind, and your politicians and professional soldiers and clergymen and 'patriots.' "

"Ahah!" cried Alexander jubilantly, in the thick hotly lit silence of the dining room. "There you have it! The way you speak of 'patriots.' Bolshevik jargon, every bit of it. We've got you now."

But now Jean spoke, in his soft reasonable voice: "Peter,

228

you're being unreasonable. The causes of international conflicts and hatreds are not so simple as you make out. Nations naturally hate each other. Oh, I know, you'll talk about propaganda. But remember this: no nation accepts propaganda which it isn't already conditioned to accept. Propaganda is merely the national prejudices become articulate. You will say we shouldn't play up to it. But let's be realistic: we've inherited this business. If we didn't supply armaments, others would. And besides, the fundamental emotion of mankind is hatred. Personally, I've never liked people," and he smiled humorously around the table. "Personally, I wouldn't mind if every last man and woman was kicked off the planet. They stink. The history of man has been a stench. I can't see any real value in keeping stenches active. Can you?"

"That's right," said Alexander, approvingly. "You've got to look at things from a broad basis."

But Peter replied to Jean only: "I grant you that the masses are fools, and even imbeciles. I grant you that little can be done for them by appealing to reason. But, if they can be taught wrongly, to their death, and be instilled with hatred, they can be taught rightly, to their life, and be instilled with decency. Of course, they will not react, with reason, to good propaganda; they will react emotionally. And, they might just as well react emotionally to goodness as to evil. The world, at any rate, will be a safer place in which to live, especially for the minority which is intelligent, humanitarian and progressive."

Emile, chuckling, said: "But you forget a fundamental thing about the masses: the dears do love their trumpets and their pretty colors, and they do love to kill those they're envious of. How are you going to get around human nature?"

Peter smiled without malice. "By outlawing you. By making it an international criminal offense to dispense racial and religious hatreds. By making greed punishable by the highest penalty. In this way, we'll keep the masses pacific. If they have nothing to gain by murder, they won't murder."

He added: "That's why you are outmoded: the modern world has no place in it for primitive murder. You've got to learn that. But you probably won't, until all potential murderers are killed off. The sad part, of course, is that the intelligent will probably also be killed off, too, in large quantities."

"And you think you'll get around human nature by law, do you?"

"Well, we've gotten civilization by law, you know. Not by natural tendency. For instance, the time will come when men

229

will be sufficiently enlightened to regard the soldier as the lowest form of human life."

Francis laughed. "I can see where your book is going to be immensely popular with the Daughters of the American Revolution, and the American Legion! But seriously, Peter, if you think these things of us, why did you come home?"

His brother answered, smilingly: "A very good question! Remember, in a year or so, I'll be thirty, and I'll have two-thirds of my fortune. Most of it is in Bouchard stock. I came home to sell it to you. Of course, I could throw it on the Market, but that would be showing a lack of family feeling. So, I'm open to offers."

And now indeed there was interest. Christopher, who had been smoking, slowly removed the cigarette from his mouth. Francis and Emile and Hugo glanced at him swiftly. And Jean and Nicholas glanced at Armand, whose eyes were glittering pinpoints. Only Thomas Van Eyck, and Celste, showed no interest in this.

Then Francis said: "Very nice, and we appreciate the family feeling, Peter. But let's discuss business arrangements tomorrow, shall we? There is a time for business, but I was never one to consider it important enough to interfere with digestion."

As they all left the table, Christopher had a moment to murmur to his sister: "Ask Peter to dinner tomorrow night, Celeste. It's important." And he repeated, catching and holding her bemused eyes: "Very important. For me. Don't let anyone else ask him. Try to get him away from the others, if you can."

When they were in the drawing rooms, with the windows wide open to the warm dark night, Christopher manœuvered Celeste into a position beside Peter. He said, smiling at the other man: "You know, there's going to be a wedding in the family soon? Celeste and Henri. It's fortunate, for us, that you are home now."

Peter did not answer immediately, and then he said regretfully: "I'm sorry. But I'm afraid that I won't be here in the fall. I may remain only a week or two." And he looked briefly at Celeste.

The girl's hands closed in a spasm. She would have walked away, but remembered her brother's request. So she stood beside Peter, miserably; she felt a hard sick throbbing in her throat, and a sense of confusion and unreality. Old Thomas came up and took Peter by the arm. "Young man," he murmured, "I'm afraid you are among the Philistines."

"No," answered Peter, smiling at the others, as well as at Thomas, "just among Ali Baba and the Forty Thieves."

"Ali Baba," said Christopher, "came off rather well, if I remember the story rightly."

Coffee was brought in. Celeste, more confused than ever, everything a combination of mist and brilliance before her eyes, and remembering Christopher's demand again, spoke to Peter in a low voice, without lifting her face to his: "It's hot in here, don't you think? We're near the river, you know. Shall we go out?"

He looked down at her in silence. Then he said gently: "Yes. It will be nice." They left inconspicuously. As they walked out onto the terrace the fresh warm air struck them refreshingly. Celeste's soft white chiffon gown lifted and moved in the night wind. Her dark hair blew back from her temples. The light from the room they had left illumined her theatrically, so that she seemed a lighted white statue in the darkness, a heroic statue in a wind that molded white marble about her breast and thighs. She ran ahead of Peter, and was running swiftly down the terrace. Now her dress was only a pale glimmer among the trees. He followed. A strange sense of excitement suddenly hurried his heart, an excitement shot through with pain and a feeling of intense loneliness. Celeste was waiting for him. He could feel, rather than see, the passionate somberness of her eyes, which he knew she had turned on him.

"Christopher," she said quickly, in a somewhat smothered voice, "asked me to ask you to dinner tomorrow night."

He was startled and a little amused at this abruptness. He tried to see her face, which was like shadowy pearl in the dimness.

"Thank you. Or should I say, thank Christopher for me?" She did not answer. He was close to her, but he could not hear her breath. He added: "Would you like me to come?"

Still she said nothing. The breeze moved through the trees, and they began to lift restlessly in the darkness. Behind them, the great lofty chateau high on its terraces was a blaze of yellow lights. Music flowed out dreamily from its open windows. Rain was apparently close, for all at once the moving night air was full of pungency and sweetness, as though a whole flower garden had been bruised.

"Celeste?" Peter stepped closer to the girl. He was not mistaken; he saw the gleam of her eyes, and knew that they were gazing at him intensely.

"Yes," she said at last, in a distant voice, like one speaking in a half-awakened trance. "Yes, I'd like you to come."

Then, abruptly, she had turned again, and was running down the slope towards the river. He followed; once or twice he thought he had lost her, and then he saw the pale shimmer of her dress, leading him. The fresh strong wind told him that the river was close. He could hear its deep rushing sound. Finally, he saw that Celeste had stopped in an open place, and beyond her he saw the dark gleaming surface of the water.

He came up to the girl, and they stood side by side, looking across the river to the tiny yellow lights on the other side. Minute torches ran in the darkness, indicating a motor road. There was no moon; the sky was invisible and imponderable, without light or reality.

They did not speak. They listened to the faint music which seemed to be part of the night wind and the deep rush of the river. Neither knew when or how it happened, but their hands touched, and held. They did not look at each other or move, but stood there, gazing at the water, which gleamed faintly in a spectral light of its own, and seemed to speak in a slowly ascending voice. The wind blew stronger, and the music from the chateau grew louder, or sank, like tides of sound. Celeste and Peter became consciousnesses concerned only with wind and water and music and the contact of their hands and the awareness of pure joy. They felt the beat of each other's pulses, and at last they did not know which pulse was individual and which belonged to the other.

Then, at last, after a very long time, they turned and moved back up the slope, their hands still clasped simply. The pungency of earth and grass increased. They found a bench under some trees and sat down. It was completely dark here. The river could no longer be seen, but the wind brought the passionate rising voice of it to their ears. The limbs of trees bent and clashed, and the tree-tops roared, ominously, in the darkness.

But there was a pit of stillness here, on the bench, under the trees. Peter could hear Celeste without difficulty, when she spoke in a clear soft voice: "I would never have promised to marry Henri if he had been connected with Bouchard."

At the mention of Henri's name, a cold and bitter pang seemed to divide Peter. He said nothing. He shivered slightly. He moved away from the girl a little. But he knew that his movement must have surprised her, for he felt her gazing at him earnestly, though he could see nothing of her but the ghostly and fugitive glimmer of her white dress. He felt her touch his hand tentatively, and again he experienced this pain, only sharper and more unendurable this time. Her fingers closed about his with the simplicity and bewilderment of a child.

"Peter," she said uncertainly.

"Yes, dear," he replied gently.

She did not speak for several moments, and then in the same clear soft voice of grave bewilderment, she said: "I never told anyone. No one ever talked to me about it. But it has always seemed to me that the munitions industry is wicked. I—I never spoke about it to Christopher; I thought perhaps it might hurt him——"

"Hurt him!" thought Peter with somber bitterness. But he said aloud, again, more gently than before: "Yes, dear."

She sighed. "No one ever spoke of it, that I can remember. You were the first. Then all at once, I knew I wasn't foolish; I knew I had been right, when I heard you, at dinner. I knew you were right." She added, "I don't think you ever could be wrong, could you, Peter?"

His voice was surprised and tender: "I? But my dear, I'm often wrong. You see, I set out to tilt at windmills, and fight dragons. But though it is heroic, it is also foolish. There is a system in attacking, and especially when you are dealing with men—like—like—well, faithless men, you need science to attack them. Finesse. And knowing what they are. At first I didn't know, and my foolishness made me impotent. Now, I know. And even then, I'm afraid I'm frequently wrong."

"But not about—this, Peter?" she asked eagerly.

He forgot his pain temporarily in his effort to answer her clearly and justly: "No, I don't think I'm wrong, darling. Better men than I am think as I do. We all know that today, this very moment, hundreds of faithless and irresponsible and vicious men are plotting against the peace of the world, and the happiness of all men. And if they succeed, and they probably will, they will bring about a war and a world-condition which will mortally threaten civilization."

"But—what about the League of Nations?"

Peter laughed shortly and drearily. "The League of Nations? It will disintegrate at the first blow, the first aggression, because all nations today are governed by treacherous and greedy men, without honor or principle.

"Look, Celeste. See how peaceful it is here, now. Nothing more violent than the wind. All over the world, peace and wind and water, and the people feeling safe. And yet, in every capital, in every gathering of diplomats and their masters, this safety is being plotted against, and ruin being blueprinted for South America, for our country, for Europe and Asia."

233

"But, why?" asked Celeste.

Peter sighed. His hand tightened on hers, protectively. "Men have always been greedy, but the conscience of the people, however betrayed, has finally overthrown the oppressors. Today, the peoples of all nations have no consciences. Today, there is little faith and endless evil." He paused. "Sometimes I remember the 24th Chapter of St. Matthew: 'And because of the iniquity which shall abound, the love of men shall wax cold.' The iniquity of universal greed and hatred and perversion and cruelty, the iniquity of faithlessness and irresponsibility and lack of self-discipline and dignity and gentleness and justice."

His voice was lost in the sudden surge of wind, and they sat silently, their hands closing passionately on each other, as though they had heard a threat. The trees writhed about and above them, filling the darkness with fury and violence. Celeste felt the cool impact of heavy air in her face and against her breast; it tore away her breath, leaned smotheringly against her mouth. She averted her head from it; her head touched Peter's shoulder. When the gale retreated, with far-off roars and clashings, her head remained there, and he hardly breathed, that he might not disturb her and cause her to remove it.

"I can hardly believe it," she said faintly. "We're so civilized, now. It seems impossible that there'll ever be another war."

Peter did not answer. He had put his arm gently about her. His lips touched her hair.

They sat like this, without speaking, until the far roaring came nearer again, like a savage and invading army. Celeste raised her head and said quickly: "But what can you do, Peter?"

"I can't do much, dear," he answered sadly. "But what little I can do I shall do."

The wind struck their trees with greater violence than before, and Peter's arm tightened about her. She felt his arm, but hardly heard or felt the mighty wind surging about them and battling with the trees. It seemed to her that the roaring and writhing air was filled with Peter's words: What little I can do I shall do! In the midst of that bellowing turmoil, in which the earth was lost and dissolved, the words he had said sounded as clear as a trumpet, as pure and triumphant as a bell. Exhaustless and victorious, they remained when the wind had gone screaming on in the darkness, giving evidence of the chaos of air and tree and night by distant tempestuous thunder.

In a lull, they climbed slowly up the slope and the terraces towards the chateau. The black clouds were torn into violently twisting shreds, and slivers and splinters of blazing moon appeared among them. They climbed like children, their hands still held. They stopped suddenly. Someone was strolling towards them, smoking a cigar. It was Armand. He was surprised to come upon them, and stopped, taking the cigar from his mouth.

"Hello?" he said questioningly. "Where've you been, you two?"

"A long way," said Celeste. She looked at Peter, and repeated, louder this time, and in a strange excited voice: "A long way, haven't we, Peter?"

He was silent. He tried to release her hand, but she held it tighter. He felt it tremble and turn cold.

Armand said nothing. Peter felt his piercing eyes trying to read his face. Armand had not moved, but there was a sudden tenseness about him which communicated itself to Peter.

Then Armand said absently: "Christopher's been looking for you, Celeste. He wants to leave."

She turned to Peter, and he saw the pale shimmer of her face. She withdrew her hand. They faced each other, and Armand, like a darker shadow in the transparent darkness, watched them.

Celeste did not speak. The approaching wind lifted her dress and blew it about her like spectral mist. Her hair blew back. Her young breast was outlined, and her throat, and her round thighs.

"Good-night, Celeste," said Peter, very gently.

She turned away, suddenly and swiftly, and was gone, running up the final terraces, seeming to be blown by the wind. Peter watched her go. But Armand watched Peter. Side by side, finally, they mounted the terraces. They saw Celeste shining like a white bird on the upper terrace, illuminated by the light from the opened windows. And then she was gone.

Armand said thoughtfully and slowly: "I am a little worried about Celeste, Peter. Men of my age don't usually have little sisters, like this. My own daughter is almost her age, and so," and he laughed awkwardly, "I have a paternal feeling for Celeste, too. That is why I am worried about her engagement to Henri Bouchard."

Peter asked quietly, and without apparent interest: "Why?"

Armand was disappointed, but he said: "I suppose this bores you, but I've got to speak to someone." He laughed with increasing awkwardness: "Celeste has been so sheltered.

I've been talking to my mother. She is sure that this marriage will hurt Celeste. It's a little hard to explain. Henri is—well, he's like Christopher, in many ways. Celeste, Mother believes, will some day find out what he really is, and that will be the end of her. I'm not so extravagant, but I do think the marriage is ill-advised, as far as Celeste is concerned."

Peter was silent. They had reached the upper terrace now. Armand, humiliated, thought that the younger man had no intention of speaking. But just as they approached the French doors, Peter stopped, looked at him straightly, and said:

"What does Celeste think? After all, that is all that really matters, you know. Doesn't she care about Henri?"

Armand hesitated. "Well, you see, Celeste hasn't met many young men. Christopher didn't approve of it; he's her guardian, you know. And Henri's good looking and competent, and knows what he wants. A girl like Celeste might find him masculine and romantic. She seems to like him."

Peter turned his head aside. "That's all that really matters," he repeated. And he went in, and left Armand behind.

*   *   *   *   *

Christopher did not notice Celeste's unusual silence on the way home. He was too amused by his own thoughts. He was usually secretly amused after a family gathering, for his hatred caused him endless entertainment. His thoughts turned to Peter. He said: "Just an amateur Cataline." He glanced at his sister. "What did you say, Celeste?"

"Nothing," she murmured. "Nothing at all."

Christopher chuckled. "Emile's right, of course. This is just pre-publication publicity. I wonder if the idiot can really write?" And again he asked: "What did you say, Celeste?"

Adelaide was sitting up in bed, reading. She was sipping a glass of hot milk, hoping that it would help her to sleep, and obliterate the hours of tormented darkness. Her bedroom door opened and she saw Celeste standing on the threshold. She was so surprised, so pathetically delighted, that her eyes dimmed. "Come in, darling," she said, her voice shaking. "Come in!" She gestured towards a bedside chair. "I'm so glad you came in before going to bed. Sit down, dear."

Celeste sat down. Then Adelaide noticed for the first time the girl's disordered dark hair and white face and shadowed eyes. She noticed how Celeste had fixed her eyes on her mother's face, and how intensely brilliant they were.

"Dear, are you ill?" she cried, throwing back her light silken covers, and preparing to get up.

"No, Mother, please," replied Celeste hurriedly. She tried to smile. She stood up, hesitated, looking down at her mother. Her arms hung helplessly at her sides, like a child's. She moistened her pale lips, tried again to smile. "It's nothing. I—I just thought I'd come in and say good night."

Adelaide gazed at her with intense yearning. "I'm glad, dearest. I've missed you."

Celeste moved her arms restlessly, then walked away. She paused beside Adelaide's dresser, and regarded the simple silver implements on it blindly. Her head was bent. The intense yearning, and now something else, deepened on Adelaide's shrunken and haggard face. "What is it, dear?" she whispered.

Celeste spoke hurriedly, not lifting her head, and speaking as though there were some intolerable pain in her breast: "I don't know what to say. But I can't marry Henri." Now she lifted her head sharply and stared at her mother with startling anguish. "You mustn't say anything! You mustn't tell anyone! I don't know what's the matter with me!" And then she burst into tears and covered her face with her hands.

Adelaide lay motionless for a long time. The room dimmed before her. In the dimness Celeste was outlined with preternatural light. Adelaide heard her own voice speaking, dry and faint: "Celeste, I've wanted you to say that more than I've ever wanted to hear anything else."

Her face still covered, Celeste shook her head passionately: "I don't know! I must find out. I've got to find out, alone. You mustn't say anything about it." She dropped her hands and turned distractedly to her mother: "You mustn't say anything! I've got to find out, alone, all alone. Do you understand?"

Before Adelaide could answer, she had run towards the door. She had half opened it, then stopped. Without turning, she said in a muffled voice: "I almost forgot. I'm supposed to tell you. Peter is coming to dinner tomorrow night." Then she closed the door behind her.

Adelaide did not move. She stared at the opposite wall. The milk cooled in its glass, and thickened against the crystal sides.

CHAPTER XXX

EDITH and Christopher had let Henri and Celeste ride ahead through the sunlit green of the bridle path. Then Edith reined in her horse and regarded Christopher somberly: "Don't you think Celeste looks tired and ill lately, Christopher?"

He looked at her dark smart face under the brim of her brown felt hat. "Yes," he admitted, frowning. "I've noticed that. I was hoping it was just my imagination, though."

The leaf-patterns flickered over Edith's cool colorless cheeks and were reflected in her straightforward eyes. "It isn't your imagination," she said abruptly, and rode on a few feet, then stopped again. He followed.

"What is it then, Edith?"

She shrugged. Henri and Celeste had disappeared.

"It's your fault, in the first place. You oughtn't to have shut her up the way you did. Then she would have had more discrimination. She wouldn't have been taken in by a holy exterior and pious words. She would have been able to recognize a fool when she saw one."

He was silent. His hard motionless eyes fixed themselves mercilessly on her. He was so close to her that she saw the paper-wrinkling of his cheeks and the sharp corners of his set lips. She shrugged again. "All I can say is that my brother isn't going to get any bargain. If he gets it at all."

She uttered an angry cry, for he had seized her wrist in his bony fingers and had twisted it suddenly. "What do you mean? Come on, tell me: what do you mean?"

She struggled to release herself, but could not. She stopped, panting, her face flaming, her eyes flashing fury. "Don't be an idiot. Let me go, Christopher."

He tightened his hold and twisted her wrist again. Her horse lifted his head uneasily, and neighed. Christopher's own horse started and moved away a little, so that the man leaned sideways in his saddle. But his lean narrow face was venomous. "Tell me, Edith," he said, very quietly.

She struggled briefly again, and then seemed to be aware of the indignity of the scene they were creating. She regarded him with cold rage, her struggling halted. "You are a melo-dramatic ass, Christopher. Let me go this instant."

He retained his grasp for a moment. Their eyes struck each other. Edith's nostrils flared out to exhale her affronted breath. Then he let her go. Scarlet marks, deep and bruised, sprang out about her wrist.

"I'm sorry," he said, in a voice as dull as a stone.

She rubbed her wrist, flexed her fingers. Then suddenly she laughed, angrily and contemptuously, but her eyes sparkled. "When we're married, I'm going to teach you better manners, old boy."

She spurred her horse and rode on. He watched her go. Her narrow hard back was as straight and slender as a boy's. She had an excellent seat, easy and light, her legs were trim and slender. At a bend in the bridle path she stopped and waited for him. He rode up slowly, reined in his horse. Blue flecks had appeared about his pinched nostrils. His facial bones seemed just beneath his skin. He took off his hat, for the day was warm. Edith saw that his forehead was wet.

"Of all the emotional fools!" she exclaimed derisively. "Anyone would think I had told you that your sister had been raped, or something. Instead of that she is all tremulous about that imbecile relative of ours, Peter the Hermit."

He stared, unbelieving. "Peter!" And then again, louder, "Peter!"

She laughed at him, with enjoyment. "You look just like a stuck pig, your eyes sticking out that way! Don't take it so serious. Well, it's serious in a way. Young girls like that always get ideas when a Galahad, with white plumes, bursts in on them. They do love Galahads! 'My strength is as the strength of ten, because my heart is pure!' " And her laughter ran out through all the leafy sun-torn silence of the park.

Christopher stared at her grimly. But he hardly saw her. He was thinking rapidly. She shook her finger at him with increasing derision.

"I can hear the chromium wheels turning! Isn't it too bad that the law is so particular about murder? You could commit murder right now, couldn't you, pet?"

His lips tightened until they were merely a pale gash. Then he rode on without her. Edith, still laughing, followed. She caught up with him. They rode out into the brilliant morning sunlight. Christopher's face looked wizened and old and evil.

She spoke lightly to that razor-sharp profile: "You think it's the end of the world, don't you? For you? Well, you are an incredible ass. I know young girls; believe it or not, I was one once myself, but not such a little feeble-wit as Celeste.

There is a time in a girl's life when nothing but a haloed saint with heroic words can make the little heart go pit-a-pat. Celeste has reached that time. I'm sorry if I spoke too seriously about it. I thought you'd be sensible, and understand that something must be done before it's too late. Peter's just as tremulous as she is. But he's full of honor, he is! He won't lay a finger on the gal until the all's-clear is sounded. You've got that to be thankful for.

"Be sensible. You look as if you're about to ride up to Celeste and drag her off her horse and beat the life out of her. That won't do at all. You've got to use the light touch. And humor. Make fun of Peter. Infer things. If they're scurvy things, all the better. But make haste slowly. And for Heaven's sake, don't let Henri know anything."

He relaxed. He could even smile a little, thinly. He reined in, and turned to her. "Thanks, Edith." He smiled even more. "Maybe I'd better marry you, after all. You're a bright girl!" He paused. His smile was almost a grin. "I'll give the matter serious consideration—after Celeste and Henri are married."

She raised her eyebrows quizzically. "Is that a bribe for my assistance?"

"Perhaps."

They rode on. Celeste and Henri had stopped at some distance, and had dismounted. Henri was pointing at something with his crop, and Celeste was listening, a light graceful figure in her habit.

"Remember, move delicately," warned Edith. "Don't let her suspect. I have an idea the poor little thing doesn't know what is the matter, anyway. Don't precipitate anything by words. There's no damage done—yet. Don't alarm her and confer importance on Peter."

Celeste turned her head as Christopher rode up and dismounted. She smiled at him. A moment ago he had been filled with rage against her. Now, as he saw her smile, the first pure compassion he had ever felt for anyone struck him like a physical pain. He realized how much he truly loved his young sister. His rage, deflected, turned to Peter Bouchard, who was directly responsible for this white bemused smile and those tired young eyes. For some split seconds his concern was all for Celeste, and not for himself. This gave him a curiously disoriented sensation, as though he had been disembodied.

Henri had been telling Celeste how much more pleasant the park would be if it were private. Now, the park was no fit place for decent people; it was filled at all hours with infernal brats, the children of the city scum. Barbour Park, he pointed out, had been given to the city by old Ernest Barbour as a magnanimous gift, and a perpetual fund had been established to preserve and increase its beauties. "As if scum appreciate beauty and air and space!" exclaimed Henri derisively. "From what I have heard of my illustrious ancestor, he was not afflicted with Victorian sentimentality, nor with any particular love for the 'peepul.' He understood them only too well. So, this Park remains a mystery to me."

"Maybe great-grandpa had a twinge of conscience," said Edith, yawning.

"Twinges of conscience," said Henri, smiling, "invariably come with twinges of rheumatism."

Celeste said nothing. She gazed at the open vista of brilliant green grass and glittering trees and fountains. Children were racing round a wide marble pool, running about its brim. Their reflections raced darkly with them, gesticulated with them. Christopher was about to add his tart remarks to Henri's, then remembered Edith's clever advice. He put his arm about his sister, and said: "Oh, I don't know, Henri. After all, as you know, the first fundamental of economics is that value is created by people, by the presence of people. This Park, with only a few of us attenuated anemics around, wouldn't have much value, real or sentimental. Besides, whoever told you that the earth, and the fulness thereof, are our exclusive property?"

Henri was somewhat surprised at this Biblical dissertation, and turned to glance at his cousin. Edith, however, smiled faintly in the background.

"What the hell!" said Henri. And then he caught Christopher's narrow eyes, and saw his imperceptible jerk of the head at Celeste. The girl had been listening to her brother; she was smiling. Henri had noticed her paleness and quietness during the last few weeks, and had been silently concerned over them, attributing them to the unusual excitement of her engagement. But he understood Christopher immediately, and he pursed his lips thoughtfully.

"Perhaps you're right," he said, affecting a grudging tone. "I suppose it's just that I've lived too long in bloody old England."

"You've lost a sense of democracy," said Christopher. Over Celeste's bared dark head they exchanged a quick indulgent smile and wink.

Edith's watchful eyes narrowed, her cold expression grew even colder. She was ashamed. She felt that she had witnessed something indecent. Selfish and reserved, she nevertheless had considerable integrity. Her shame extended to herself. She had to remind herself forcibly of Peter's imbecility before this shame receded. "Let's go back. I'm hungry," she said abruptly, and swung back into her saddle. She was well in advance before the others followed.

She felt that Celeste, not Henri, was profiting from the approaching marriage. He could have done better, she often told herself. Whatever sort of husband he would make, Celeste gained. Henri was a man, with something of the early Victorian's solidity and strength and inexorableness. Other young men looked like foxes in comparison. And yet, as she rode ahead, breaking into a gallop, she wondered uneasily about Celeste. Perhaps old Adelaide was right; perhaps a marriage however desirable in point of material benefits needed something else. Henri would console himself; his sister had no doubt about it. But what about Celeste? Once trampled, would she ever revive?

Breakfast was waiting for them at Robin's Nest. It was Sunday morning, and in an hour Celeste and Edith would go to church. They went to church once a month, for it was expected of them. Their ancestors had founded and supported it.

Henri, at breakfast, kept glancing at his morning newspaper and commenting on it to the others. Russia was buying an enormous lot of planes both from France and the United States, he said. "Of course, for Germany. But it'll take years before Germany is thoroughly re-armed, and ready for business."

Celeste, who had been silently drinking coffee, her sole breakfast, asked: "Do you think there'll ever be another war?"

Henri glanced at her with quick humor. How pretty she was, was his private commentary. Her hair was disordered; the deep pallor of her complexion made her large ringed eyes more beautifully blue than usual. He said: "Naturally, my innocent. There'll always be wars, just as there always have been wars."

She put down her cup, and regarded him with passionate earnestness. He was surprised and somewhat puzzled. "But —Peter says that another war will be the end of our civilization," she said.

They all laughed. Henri put his elbows on the table and looked at her affectionately, after the laughter had died down. "Don't believe it, little lamb. There have been many wars and somehow people survived and civilization, too. In fact, they often helped civilization. The Crusades, for instance, with their wars against the Turks, and other nice little enormities, made Europeans realize what serfdom to religion can do to nations. So, out went bondage to the Church. It took centuries, but all our present-day liberalism and intellectual freedom are due to conflict, usually armed and bloody, between the people and religion. So, if we have another war, we'll profit by it, perhaps."

"Don't you mean, you'll profit by it?"

There was a moment's silence. Henri and Christopher exchanged a glance. Henri smiled. "Of course, my dear. But so will the rest of the people. Look at our prosperity."

"But what about Germany, Henri? What about France? Did they profit?"

Henri's voice was patient, the voice of a teacher explaining to a child. "Does one care what happened to Germany? She deserved what she got——"

"Do you believe that, Henri?" To his amazement, the girl's eyes were full of tears, and her mouth was shaken with anger.

Henri's smile faded. He decided to take a serious view of this foolishness. He said gravely: "Look here, Celeste, some idiot has been tampering with your common sense. Let's be reasonable. Wars, like any other business, are run for profit. They're no longer conflicts between ideologies. And we're realistic enough, these days, to understand that profits and economic advantages are the only things worth fighting for. They're the only things we ever did fight for, really, but the people had to be fooled with pretty slogans and such assininities. Now, they're enlightened; most of them, anyway. We've still got tin trumpets for the fools, but the others believe their bellies are more important than their souls. Germany, in the last war, was not defeated on the battlefields. She was defeated in Jay Regan's office, and in the offices of Wall Street and of the Bank of England, and the Bank of Paris, and even of the Bank of Berlin."

Celeste's face was very white, but her eyes were steady and resolute. "And you don't think problems like economics and private profits can be settled by conference and negotiation?"

Henri laughed with returned indulgence. "Don't be silly; of course not. What! Rob the dear people of a chance to cut each other's throats? Rob them of the chance to stop struggling for existence in factories, and to rely upon the government, and wear pretty uniforms and be told what to do? Dear child, you don't know human nature at all. Oh, I've heard Peter's arguments before. But they're highfalutin' and silly.

243

Ask the average man which he would prefer: to negotiate fairly for a profit with an antagonist, or to murder him and take it all."

Celeste was silent a moment, and then she said: "Suppose this is so: are we, then, to be at the will of moron mobs, who prefer killing to negotiation?"

Christopher, with gratification, realized that this was no lesson from Peter, and he was pleased with Celeste's astuteness.

Henri shrugged. He lifted his hands and let them drop. "Why not, honey? Let them kill; after all, as Christopher said just this morning, the people are entitled to their pleasure, too. And our pleasure consists in profits. Everybody's satisfied."

Celeste bent her head. "There is something wrong with your argument, Henri. It seems to me we ought to go to work and eliminate killers from society——"

"We do," he replied, with another wink at Christopher. "We let them have wars, and they kill each other off. It saves the rest of us a lot of trouble."

But Celeste's resolute eyes were lifted to his face again, and she pursued with quiet tenacity: "But what about the rest of us, who aren't killers? And the children who are bombed in cities?"

"That," said Henri with great seriousness, "is too bad. I admit it. But who is the minority, to prevent the majority from having their fun? I'm afraid you aren't very democratic, pet."

Edith's cool laughter filled the breakfast room, and the canaries in their cages near the window responded with excited twitterings. But Celeste did not laugh. She looked slowly from one smiling face to the other. Now she was white to the lips.

"You almost make me believe that the world is composed of feeble-minded killers, and the clever ones who profit by the killings," she said.

"Quite true. It's always been true," said Henri. "You've got to accept things as they are, Celeste. If you don't, you'll never be happy."

Celeste turned her beautiful head and gazed through the windows. Christopher frowned. He had never seen this expression on the girl's face before, so meditative, and so sad, and yet, so understanding. "I've never been happy," she said. "I didn't understand anything. I—I wasn't really conscious. Unconsciousness isn't happiness; if it were, only the unborn and the dead are happy. And I can't accept 'things as they

244

are,' Henri. I don't believe 'they are.' You call it realism; I call it fatalism. I prefer to believe you can make the things 'that are,' the things they should be. If this belief will make me unhappy, I would rather not be what you call 'happy.' "

Christopher thought it time to interpose. "Don't take things so seriously, Celeste. Henri is just teasing you. After all, we are all civilized, and we don't want wars any more than you do. Or Peter does. I hope you haven't believed his ridiculous accusations against us? Celeste?" he added in a louder tone, when she did not answer.

Edith was no longer smiling. She had leaned back in her chair. Her quick dark eyes studied each one in turn. Her expression was somber. When her eye touched Celeste it quickened into uneasy pity.

Celeste replied at last, in her strange meditative voice: "I do believe him when he says that the next war will almost, if not quite, kill our civilization. It will be the most terrible war of all."

Christopher fumed. "But, Celeste, Henri has just told you: war has never ended any civilizations; it has merely replaced outworn ones with new ones. And so far as I can see, the new has been an improvement."

Celeste sighed. "Peter has been travelling ever since the War. He says the next will be the end, because there's something missing in all people now. Even in the Middle Ages, there were some conscience and some compassion and goodness. But now, there aren't. It seems as if all the good men have been killed, or imprisoned. Our civilization, Peter says, has failed, because it has discarded all belief in the progress of the mind, and has lost all reverence for the good. Oh, I know you'll say we're not worse than other generations. But we are, you know," she said simply. "We really are."

The others stared at each other blankly. "Of all the imbecility!" exclaimed Christopher, coldly infuriated. "But that comes of your association with Peter the Dim-Wit! I'm surprised at you, Celeste. You're not a child, and ought to have more intelligence."

But Henri felt that something important, something which threatened him, was working in this young girl's clear and seeking mind. He ignored Christopher's anger, and spoke gently and seriously: "You're so inexperienced, Celeste. Peter's been putting half-baked ideas into your head. You're just like a child who's been drinking on the sly. For instance, your idea that the people today are worse than their ancestors: that's ridiculous. We're not. We're better in some ways. Suppose there is a war; we'll survive. Our civilization will benefit. We don't have racial and religious persecutions, for instance, as we had only a century or so ago. We don't have pogroms and massacres in the name of religion or race. No man is persecuted today, for being what he is by birth. Don't you think that is a gain? And don't you think that past wars for freedom have had something to do with this?"

Celeste gazed at him with passionate concentration. He looked into her eyes, so young, so intense, so beautiful. His own eyes suddenly flickered, moved slightly from focus. But he smiled.

"And you don't think religious and racial persecutions will ever come again, Henri?" she asked.

"Of course they won't, sweetheart. They can't. They've been fought against for centuries, and tolerance has finally won. You've got to thank wars for that, you see——"

Celeste said with merciless and youthful logic: "If this is so, and we don't have racial antagonisms any more, how can you make future wars, then?"

Henri threw up his hands and laughed helplessly. "I give up! You ought to have been a lawyer. Besides, who said I make 'future wars'? I'm not interested in wars. Besides, I'm bored. Let's change the subject."

Edith moved back her chair. "I'm, too. Celeste, if we're going to church, we'd better hurry." She stood up. Henri and Christopher stood up, also. But Celeste still sat. Her eyes still had their passionate concentration as she looked only at Henri.

"Do you know why I said I'd marry you, Henri? Because you weren't connected with Bouchard."

Henri was taken aback. His brows drew together. Then he looked at Christopher. He smiled, laid his hand on Celeste's shoulder.

"All right, dear. I'm not connected with Bouchard— actively. And now, are you going to church, or not?"

Celeste sat with Edith in the family pew in the small but exquisite church which Ernest Barbour had built. It was dim in here, but the handsome stained-glass windows were brilliant with colored light. The upper columns moved in a sort of misty radiance. Few people were in church, for the day was warm and inviting. The minister in his pulpit was a dull figure, without inspiration, and had bored Celeste all her life. He believed ardently in private property and the sacrosanct qualities of those who possessed it. He was their priest, and this church was their altar. He never forgot the family who supported it and himself.

246

Celeste sat quietly. She did not move. Her pale face was an absorbed and saddened disk in the musty gloom. She did not know that Edith was watching her with furtive intentness. Her hands lay quietly on her knee, and she hardly seemed to breathe. She was not listening to the minister but to her own thoughts.

She was remembering how Peter had quoted Voltaire to the effect that if there was no God it would be necessary to create one for the benefit of one's servants, and thus for the profit of the masters. But, Peter had said, if there was no God it was vitally necessary to create one for the benefit of all the world, and the creating could not begin soon enough. A desperate need existed, not for religion, but for religiousness. Religiousness was the way to life; irreligion was the way to death, to wars, to ruin, to the end of the world. Religion which existed apart from men was impotent and sterile. It depended upon churches and priests and ritual, and was without vitality. In times of stress, it had only a dead formula. No formal God was needed at all; in fact, formal gods were the images of hatred. But men most solemnly, in these days, needed a belief in goodness and gentleness and faith and justice. It dared not be an intellectual belief, comprehended by the few. It must be emotional, and the people must share in it. Each man must deliberately will himself to believe, understanding that 'enlightenment' was less valuable than mercy. He must believe in a God who did not need an altar, but only the hearts of the people, no priests, but the souls of men. The brotherhood of man and the fatherhood of God must not be a ritual, dealt out in wafers like Holy Communion, but a fact, a symbol clothed in living reality. Otherwise, there was no hope for the world.

All at once the girl's mind was filled with searing despair. Her face grew drawn with her mental suffering; her lips parted in a sigh of profound pain. She moistened them. A terrible yearning for Peter took possession of her. She gasped in this airless atmosphere of formality and adulation of dead things. The thought of Peter Bouchard was like a door opening in gloom and hopelessness. She suddenly smiled. She sighed again, a sigh of relaxation.

Edith, watching her, was touched. But uneasiness made her scowl.

CHAPTER XXXI

THEY met in old Andre's office, Armand, Jean and Nicholas Bouchard. Jean was chuckling: "Well, at any rate, he listened. I said: 'Peter, Sessions is only a subsidiary of Bouchard. We do what we're told. The Bank obeys Bouchard, too. So do all the other subsidiaries. What information you need you'll have to get from Bouchard and Sons, and Kinsolvings.' "

Armand moved restlessly: "This is all too subtle for me, I'm afraid. I don't like subtleties. You suddenly find yourself in a maze of them, like being shut up in a clothes-closet full of women's filmy stuff, and you don't know which is which, after a while."

Jean spread out his hands and dimpled. "It's really very simple. Peter becomes convinced that the villain in the maze is Bouchard and Sons. He writes it in his book; he talks to Miss Peter Pan about it. A great deal about it. She is horrified, silly little thing. He convinces her that Henri is really a most powerful member of the Company, and will probably actively join it. Presto! It helps get her off Henri, helps convince her that Bouchard and Sons, and, in fact, all of us, are nasty little schoolboys and she shouldn't really have anything to do with us. You see, Armand, with simple minds you must use simple formulae——"

"Phoo! I think this is a schoolkid's plot. It's foolish and complicated, and doesn't get anywhere. You've forgotten, too, that she's bombarded with propaganda at home, which will undo your fifth-form little plottings very completely."

"Well," said Jean, shrugging, "that's only one aspect of our 'plot.' What have *you* done, for instance? Gossamer minds need gossamer plots, a fact you seem to forget."

Armand frowned. He did not like his sister to be referred to as a gossamer mind. Any pricklings of conscience, however, had gone. With vast relief he had finally come to the honest conclusion that Celeste would be miserable if she married Henri Bouchard. He could operate with equanimity, now, because of this conclusion.

"I've done a lot, I think. I've given dinner parties and

other affairs, and invited both Celeste and Peter. I've talked to Peter at length, and frankly, as a brother who is worried about his young sister. I've convinced him that Celeste will be unhappy; I've told him I've begun to think she is in love with a mysterious someone else. I've asked him: who? Has he come to any conclusion, himself? Oh Hell, this is all so childish!" and he moved angrily in his chair. "Why can't we think up man-sized plots?"

"Because we're up against two Babes in the Wood," replied Jean. "Man-sized plots would be like clubbing them. Besides, what man-sized plots? Our only hope is to prevent this marriage. You can't do it with murder or kidnapping. Well, what else?"

Armand chewed his lip gloomily. "I realize the marriage has got to be stopped. I know this Henri is avaricious. I've already been as bald as I could: I can't ram Annette down his throat. He knows what he'd get by marrying the child; I've stopped just short of openly offering her to him. I've mentioned to him a dozen times or more that Celeste looks ill and unhappy, and is he sure she cares enough about him to marry him? After all, I'm her brother, I said—— Hell," he added, with gloomy disgust. "I hate this muzziness of dealing with girls. It's undignified. Everything we have depends on a little girl, and it's maddening to have to admit it——"

"Seeds scattered in the air," said Jean, assuming a sententious expression, "sometimes light on fertile ground. You can't move with a piston; you've got to scatter flowers. The point is: have we made any progress?"

"We've made two young people miserable, at any rate," said Armand bitterly.

Jean winked surreptitiously at Nicholas, who grimaced crudely.

"That's what we want, isn't it?" asked Jean of Armand. "Better be a little miserable now than completely wretched later. I'm sure even you subscribe to this philosophy."

"But it's undignified——"

Jean gave a small screech. "But, Christ, do you have to have dignity to keep yourself from getting your throat cut? Or maybe you think you can persuade those brothers of yours that they'll only be lowering themselves if they attack you, and it's really beneath them?"

Armand was silent; but a dull stubborn look settled on his big face.

Jean raised his eyebrows helplessly at Andre, who began to chuckle.

"This isn't a comedy of the boudoir, Armand," he said. "Nor a sorority skit. It's business. We can't always deal in high finance. Sometimes a great deal more depends on little mean things than on heroic negotiations.

"Things do get out, you know. For instance, it's been whispered to me in New York that Henri has applied to Jay Regan for the loan of twenty million dollars——"

"What!" cried the three other men simultaneously.

"Yes, a fact. I haven't been able to find out if he got it, or will get it. I wouldn't have heard of it, however, if there isn't a very good possibility that he will get it, if he has not already. Is he putting up his Bouchard bonds for it? No, it is said. He isn't. Why not? We don't know. We do know that he's turned practically everything else he owns into cash, and that most of the cash went to your nice little brother, Christopher. And we do know that Henri Bouchard is no fool; if he gives money, it is because he expects much more. What does he expect? We haven't found out. But I have an idea that it won't be so good for you."

Jean grinned faintly; Nicholas grunted a curse. But Armand's color turned from ruddy to a gray tint.

Andre selected a cigar with infinite care, and lit it. His rotund and bloated body sank back in the black leather chair. He smoked meditatively for a minute, and then said:

"What is Christopher doing with all that money, Henri's and Emile's, and even Francis'? We don't know. But we do know all the transactions stink. There's no doubt they know we know all this, and they know we daren't ask. You're in a bad place, Armand. We know only one thing: that a marriage between little Celeste and Henri will clinch the whole matter. How? I—don't—just—know. But whatever it is, a termination of the engagement won't do Christopher any good. And we've got to terminate it."

"We don't even know they're plotting anything," insisted Armand stubbornly. "Everything you say may be true; I'm not disputing it. They may all be speculating together."

Andre regarded the ceiling reflectively. "I remember something my mother used to say about her brother, Uncle Ernest. She said that though he appeared audacious, and apparently took many chances, in reality he was not audacious, and his chances were never long shots. I remember him very well; my mother detested him. Anyway, his great-grandson is very much like him; I got quite a shock when I saw him, after he came back. And I have a good idea that Henri is not being audacious or taking any chances. He is not speculating. I don't like it. Well, it's your affair."

Jean looked at his father-in-law alertly. "Do you think he's doing the lone wolf? Do you think he's grinding a private ax?"

"I've thought of that," replied Andre. "I don't know. For instance, I do know that he visited the offices of the most unscrupulous patent lawyer in Washington, and that he paid fifty thousand dollars for an almost worthless airplane patent whose only good points were two or three outlandish gadgets that were just plain scenery, according to my informants. Why did he do this? If you remember your dinner party last week, Jean, you will recall that I asked him if he had been to Washington lately, and he answered calmly that he hadn't. Christopher and Emile looked interested, and repeated the question, and he lied to them as calmly as he did to me. Why? He's operating with them, and he's operating alone. He knows he can't hide, so he calmly lies, and dares others to prove him a liar. What is the answer?"

"It stinks," said Nicholas. "What are you going to do? Sit on your backside? While you're robbed?"

Armand flushed. "It's fantastic! He's hardly more than a boy. And Emile knows on which side his bread is buttered——"

"Maybe Chris shows him he can have jam, too," smiled Jean.

"And there's Francis," Nicholas informed him. "Have you forgotten? Francis doesn't buy gold bricks. He's stopped just short of big enough transactions with Christopher to make the market uneasy."

"I still have 8,000,000 shares of Bouchard," said Armand grimly. "Let them exchange. I've got it, over 51 per cent. They can't blow me off."

"I'm not so sure," said Andre, regarding him thoughtfully. "How? I don't know. But the boys are up to no good; you're 'no good.' Please yourself."

When Armand returned to his own office, he was startled to discover Henri Bouchard waiting easily for him.

It was a Saturday afternoon, and Christopher and Emile had already gone. His second glance at the young man convinced Armand that he had calculated on this, and had only just arrived. Armand was suddenly excited; his voice was very cordial as he greeted Henri.

"Well, so you've decided to come around and see what makes your bonds good, eh?" he asked. "Too bad the plants are almost empty. But there are a few workmen around. A shift goes on at four; we're working overtime, you know."

"It's three. I'll wait." Henri smiled at him with ease. He

stared at Armand with his light unmoving eyes. "How's little Annette?"

Armand's cordial expression faded into darkness. "Not so well. She's home now, you know. You didn't know. Come to dinner tomorrow, she'll be glad to see you and your sister."

To Armand's surprise, for he had hardly expected it, Henri replied: "Thanks. I can't answer for Edith, though. But we can let you know about that."

They went out into the great echoing plants, which were filled with a penetrating acrid odor and barred sunlight. Henri listened attentively to everything that Armand said. His questions were intelligent and shrewd. After a while, Armand kept his hand familiarly on the other's arm. He even laughed reluctantly. His excitement kept growing.

"You'll be going to Crissons for the summer, I suppose?" he asked.

"For a time. On and off."

"Why not come with us, on your off time?" asked Armand good-naturedly. "Jay Regan thinks his yacht is better than mine; but he's mistaken."

"I might. Thanks."

They continued their explorations. Henri said: "Even Kronk and Skeda aren't better equipped, or bigger. This makes me proud."

"Good." Armand was pleased. He hesitated, then on an impulse, he said: "I've asked you before, and I ask you now: Why don't you come down and learn all about it? I'll fit you in, somewhere."

His surprise was great when Henri said: "That's just what I was going to suggest, myself. How about Monday? I'm getting sick of this prancing around over the country while everybody else is working."

The words were naïve, but not the large pale face and eyes.

Armand's heart was thumping almost painfully when they returned to the office. His hand shook as he opened the door. "Sit down. Will you have a drink? No? It's nearly four. Are you sure you want to wait to see what goes on?"

"Yes. I'll wait.

Their eyes met, Henri's opaque, Armand's furtive but searching.

CHAPTER XXXII

ARMAND found Annette's sunporch full of young girls when he reached home. They filled the warm air with twitterings and chirpings and squeals, and he carefully waited until they were gone before he entered. Only Celeste had remained.

"Well, well," said Armand jovially, kissing his little daughter. She lay on a chaise-longue of gold silk. Her fine hair was tied up with a blue ribbon. Her slight body was so thin and emaciated that she looked hardly more than a child. Her small bloodless face gave him a sick pang. But her large beautiful light-blue eyes smiled up at him lovingly. The warm wind blew her blue silk wrapper tightly about her arms and throat. In repose, her expression was sad, almost grave, but full of gentleness. Today, she informed her father in an effort to lighten his somber anxiety, she had walked down the first terrace, and had not felt the least tired. Tomorrow, she would go down another. Wouldn't that be splendid?

Armand smiled. He sat beside her and took her hands, and rubbed them gently in his palms. They were cool, the fragile bones close to the surface. He regarded Celeste with a perfunctory fraternal smile. "Well, how are things with you, Celeste?"

She smiled in return, but did not answer. She might have been his daughter, sitting there, so young and quiet, her hands folded in her lap. Her expression was aloof, almost stern. She had averted her head slightly; the modelling of her high cheekbones and the curve of her chin were like freshly carved ivory, smooth and well-defined. Armand studied her sharply. The girl was much thinner, and her manner was abstracted and depressed. All at once, very abruptly, she stood up and announced she must go at once. Henri was coming to dinner.

Armand talked brightly with Annette after Celeste's departure. And then he said, feeling his way cautiously: "Darling, is it my imagination, or does Celeste look paler and quieter than usual? As if she were unhappy about something?"

Annette did not display surprise. In fact, she sighed. "Yes, I've noticed it. I—I asked her. She said something about the excitement, and her trousseau—." Suddenly the child's eye filled with tears; she averted her head and bit her lip hard. Armand said nothing. He gazed at her mournfully.

After a while he spoke very slowly and carefully:

"My dear, please listen to me. It is very serious." She glanced up at him, the tears still thick and smothering in her eyes. He wet his lips, tried to find the right words.

"You see, Annette, I think I know what is wrong with Celeste. We both love her, don't we? We don't want her to be unhappy. But she is. We both feel it. And I may be wrong, but I believe I know. I believe that she isn't happy to be engaged to Henri, that she is discovering she made a mistake."

Such a light of uncertain joy flared into the girl's thin white face that Armand could hardly bear it. She sat up, she was trembling. The wind lifted the soft pale tendrils of her hair, blew them about her cheeks. Her mouth parted, shook. She fixed her eyes upon her father with an imploring and passionate look of questioning.

He hesitated. "I'm not absolutely positive, dear, but I think I have guessed rightly. Besides, others are talking, too. You see, I think it's Peter——"

She tried to speak; her lips, suddenly blooming, parted. But she could do nothing but smile, the tears on her cheeks, the passionate look deepening in her eyes.

Armand sighed. A few words, and life had rushed, swelling, into this frail body. He wondered, full of fear, if he were making a mistake.

"We—we mustn't be too hasty, of course, Annette. But, if it is true, then we must find some way to help her."

She could speak now, and in a cry: "Yes, yes! We must help her." Her eyes darkened with intensity, and some of the color left her lips. "But, Daddy, if it isn't true—if it isn't true —then, Celeste's happiness is more important than anything else——"

"Yes, naturally, dear. But perhaps you can find out. Perhaps she is keeping to this engagement because of some sense of honor. That would be wrong for herself, and very wrong for Henri. He deserves someone who cares about him, don't you think so?"

He was surprised and frightened when he saw the rest of the life-giving color leave her face. Now, in its pallor, her large eyes were grave and piercing, almost stern.

"Yes, Daddy," she said quietly, "that is quite true. It—it would be terrible for Celeste and Henri. But I can't find out for you, even though it is so important to you, because Celeste is your sister, and so terribly important for me. I can't ask her; I can't even suggest or hint. Because, you see, just because it *is* so terribly important for me. I, least of anyone, can interfere. I can only wait."

In spite of his bitter disappointment he could not be angered when he met those large and steadfast eyes. All the furtive integrity in him, constantly badgered and insulted and defamed, rose to meet hers in a bursting flame of relief and release. His voice was unsteady: "Yes, dear, I see quite well. You can't ask. But I wish there was something we could do."

She put her delicate little hand on his and smiled at him tenderly. "Dear Daddy. And you've got so many other worries. But I'm so glad that you love Celeste so much; I thought, at times, that you were indifferent to her, and she is so darling and good."

The girl was startled at the sudden dark flush of color that surged over her father's face. He rose abruptly. He did not seem to know what to do or where to go. Annette, confused, stared at him. In an effort to escape her eyes were caught fully by hers. He stammered: "Darling, don't overestimate me. I haven't cared about Celeste as much as I might have done. I'm so much older—and then, I've had you, and your mother, and your brother. It's only lately——"

But his daughter smiled at him more tenderly than ever. "Poor Daddy. Never mind. We've all harassed you so much. But underneath, you were concerned about Celeste's engagement, weren't you?"

He stared at her somberly a long time before he answered, and then his voice was grim and shaken: "Yes, dear, you can believe that. I was very much concerned about it. Very, very much."

She was alarmed, and even when he bent down and kissed her, and laughed at her gently, her alarm remained. It stayed, even in her later contemplative joy.

CHAPTER XXXIII

EACH in his turn, Armand, Francis, Emile, Jean, Hugo and Christopher tried to purchase Peter Bouchard's holdings. They used no finesse in approaching him, and it was this lack, this disregard of the niceties, which awakened his curiosity. This curiosity was enhanced by the way they all approached him within twenty-four hours of his announcement that his holdings were for sale.

Someone had called his grandmother's favorite brother, Martin Barbour, "a blue-eyed idealist." Peter was not such an idealist, in its more ridiculous connotations. He believed sensibly that "wisdom with an inheritance is very good." He knew, too, that the way to combat power is with power, and that to answer a man intelligently one must use his own language, or his own weapons. From his early youth he had been enraged at the monstrous imbecility and wickedness of average men, their lack of values, their malevolence and meanness. He saw how they hated their betters, and the malignancy of their attacks on them. Like his ancestor, Armand Bouchard, he realized that the best defense of a good man is enough money to protect him from other men. He, like Armand, had no desire, by prodigal charity and generosity, to dispose of his own money and thus make himself an easy victim of his species. He saw clearly that a good man, out of compassion and gentleness and simplicity, might make a fortune and give it entirely away to the destitute, and be considered inferior to the scoundrel who victimized many and retained his own wealth. Sometimes his anger dissolved into an appalled paralysis when he contemplated men and the things that men do, the idiocies they believe. How was it possible for any civilization to arise and maintain its vitality, when the majority of mankind was so ghastly stupid, so vicious, so animal-like?

One young American soldier, during his war service, had said simply: "Most folks are lice." Nearly thirty years of life had convinced Peter that there was a great deal more truth than gentility in this observation.

Nevertheless, his awareness of the pediculous character of

his kind did not make Peter a cynic. But it frightened him. He saw that the only thing one could aim for was to delouse the animal-spirit of the people, and at least leave it clean and harmless. Animal-souled they might be, but this did not postulate that they deserved destruction, exploitation, misery and death. Their very lack of discriminating intelligence, their dearth of subtlety and awareness and consciousness, made them just the more piteous, just the more in need of kindly and superior protection. But the most sinister aspect of the whole matter was when unscrupulous and evil men set out to use the huge blundering weapon of the people for private and wicked ends and wholesale death and greed. Even animals, whether enclosed in fur or in human flesh, had a certain fundamental right to a measure of peace and freedom and pleasure and life, and even the superior had no right to deprive them of this right.

Peter believed in democracy, just as he believed in truth or the existence of air. For he saw that the great advantage of democracy was the liberty of all men to protect themselves from each other.

He was no sentimentalist, for he had no illusions and no hardness of heart. Therefore, though he had no particular care for luxury and wealth, he was careful to retain half of his income for himself, distributing the rest among the unfortunate. It was not that he passionately loved mankind; but he did love justice. He had no compassion for a man who got himself horribly diseased through dissipation and excesses; as for himself, he would have let such a man die, and die as painfully as possible. He had no maudlin pity for congenital criminals; such were better and speedily dead, before they polluted other men. Nor did he waste time on the incompetent and malingering; they too, ought to die, for the good of their kind. (He believed that a time was rapidly coming when the superior would realize that it was their duty to inhibit the activities of the inferior, and prevent the births and hasten the deaths of the malformed both of body and mind.) But for children, for the helpless, betrayed and seduced, he had endless compassion, and for their oppressors, endless hatred.

Francis was surprised and somewhat taken aback to discover these things about the brother he and the others had constantly ridiculed, he, with easy indifference, and they with malice. Peter's not such a fool, he thought, surprised. Peter's lack of clear-water simplicity, his lack of trust in anybody, his quick shrewdness and understanding, created respect in him. It was a pleasure to talk to Peter, he dis-

257

covered, gratified. One did not have to be on constant guard to prevent treachery. What a relief this was!

He said, one day: "Pete, why don't you stay here and learn something about the rest of us? I'll make you a place in Kinsolving, a good place. If you can just get over your aversion for the making of national purges."

Peter smiled and answered: "But, you see, I do have such an aversion. If your pleasant products would only kill off the professional soldiers, the old Generals, the patriots and politicians and bandmasters, and, of course, people like you, I'd be all for it. But they don't stop there. They kill off children, and blow up schools and churches, and make men hate each other more than they do normally. This is all very bad, you see."

However, he accompanied Francis to The Kinsolving Arms on many occasions. He was particularly interested in the sanitary condition of the great plant, the apparent healthfulness and contentment of the workers, the short hours and excellent pay. He seemed pleased to hear that most of the men belonged to labor unions.

"Is all this the result of your great heart, Francis, or was it just forced on you?"

Francis grinned. "Well, it was forced on us. What did you expect? Do you think one of us would give our workers a living wage if we could get away with not giving it? But we can't. We fed the dogs, and so they grew teeth, and when they grew teeth, they threatened us and demanded more food. Just a vicious circle."

Nevertheless, as he passed through the shops, the men glanced at him with respect and even liking. He knew as much as they did about the operations of their machines. He had an easy air, and liked guns passionately. Sometimes he would stop and quarrel violently with a foreman or a worker about some small operation, and even when spiritedly defeated, he accepted the whole matter with familiar goodfellowship. How much of all this is sincere, and how much false? thought Peter. However, the results were the same, and he supposed that was all that mattered.

On another occasion, thinking of the Bouchard stock still in Peter's possession, Francis great-heartedly offered his youngest brother a directorship in Kinsolving. "Then," he had grinned, "you might have some legitimate voice in the things we do. Not much, mind you, but some. Reformers like that. Little influence, big noise."

Peter had taken no offense at this, but had laughed. Francis had called in one of his secretaries, and had dictated a formal offer to his brother. Peter gave the matter no thought immediately. The next day he returned. Francis was out. He sat down at the carved walnut desk and wrote a note in answer.

"I've thought over the offer of a directorship, and somehow the idea pleases me. Will I have to buy Kinsolving stock? You see how ignorant I am. I don't want to give up my Bouchard stock, yet, for a number of sufficient reasons."

He went home. It would be a puny directorship, of course. But he would hear a great deal. What he could do with it, he would do. Perhaps he was romantic, he thought, but perhaps there might be just the slightest chance that he could be of some help in the making of policies. Besides, it would be an excellent position to observe everything from. He knew how ignorant he was of a full understanding of the methods of war-makers.

Francis found the note upon his return. He saw instantly what was behind it, and was amused. And then he was thoughtful. He would explain to Peter that his value as a director would depend upon the amount of Kinsolving he possessed; a rather far-fetched explanation, perhaps, but then, Peter was ignorant. He would induce him to sell the Bouchard stock to him, in return for Kinsolving.

He was about to toss the penciled note into his wastebasket, when suddenly his eyes dwindled to hard brilliant pinpoints. He stared thoughtfully before him, turning the note over and over in his lean hands. Then, after some time, he called his secretary and asked him to put this note with the letter he had written his brother and deposit both of them in his private safe.

At dinner that night there were only Estelle, Francis and Peter. The girls were expected home from school the next day. Francis said to his brother: "How about that Bouchard stock? I want it. I've figured how much of Kinsolving you'll get for it."

"That interests me," replied Peter. "What is all this rush of all of you for Bouchard?"

Francis laughed. "Nothing much."

"A rise in the market?"

"Perhaps."

Peter replied jokingly: "Then, I'll keep it. Perhaps. I've got some cash. What's the closing quotation on Kinsolving today?"

Francis told him. Peter glanced humorously at Estelle, and said: "Maybe I'll buy some and keep it. Anyway, I'll let you know. I like money, too."

Francis urged him to come to the office the next day at noon, for a further discussion. When Peter arrived, he found that Francis had been "unexpectedly called away." But there was a note for him, a formal note on the letterhead of Kinsolving:

"Perhaps you're right about your Bouchard holdings, and future profits on them. Perhaps you are in a better position to judge than I. But Kinsolving is going up; we are anticipating a large order for Japan within the next two weeks. I've told you enough to make you realize just what this will mean. Perhaps you'll give more consideration, now, to our offer of a directorship in our Company."

The secretary, who had silently entered the room, then informed Mr. Peter that Mr. Francis had asked for a reply.

"I'll see him tonight," replied Peter, getting up.

But the secretary had had his orders. No, he had replied respectfully, Mr. Francis wished the transaction to be an entirely business one. This was a formal offer, and needed a formal reply. A stenographer was at Mr. Peter's service.

Peter was amused. Even Francis was not above red tape and office etiquette, apparently. He allowed a stenographer to be brought, and dictated:

"From my observations I would say that I believe that Bouchard would be more valuable to me at present than Kinsolving stock. I'm going into the subject extensively. However, I'm not adverse to buying Kinsolving with my spare funds immediately, even if I decide to retain Bouchard holdings. I'll have to talk to you about the directorship, which interests me more and more." He ended, the irony lost on the written page: "The Japanese orders ought to make everybody happy."

At four o'clock that afternoon Francis appeared at Christopher's office with all the correspondence which had passed between himself and his brother. Christopher read it carefully. A spot of color appeared on his cheekbones.

"Movie-ish. And crude," was his comment.

"But pleasingly damning," said Francis.

"But how do you know he hasn't already told Celeste why he wants the directorship, and the reason he is retaining Bouchard is because we've been idiots enough to let him see that it's of considerable importance to us to get it from him, and he wants to know why?"

"It's all ambiguous enough, written down like this. It sounds damning. A little work on our part would convince a saint that there is something stinky in the whole thing, his protestations to the contrary. Show it to anybody, and they'll

260

tell you the same thing. Then, if he hasn't already told Celeste, I'm going to warn him not to mention it to a soul. I don't think he has, personally. He's pretty close-mouthed. It would have to be used in his absence, however, and very, very confidentially, and reluctantly."

"I still think it's crude. Celeste's not a fool. Anyway, keep all of it. We may have to use it."

Christopher then lapsed into somber reflection. He said: "It's slow work. I can't use blunt methods. I was a little rough, and Celeste flew to his defense like an enraged mother-cat. That won't do. I don't know what's the matter with me! I've lost my deft touch."

"Well, it's damned serious for all of us. We don't know whether Henri will back out if the marriage doesn't go through. In fact, I'm sure he won't. He's got too much Duval-Bonnet stock, for one thing. And too large a loan to you. Has he any word about the twenty million yet? Twenty million! And have you any idea of the 'proposition' he mentioned he'd have for us?"

"No," answered Christopher malevolently, "I haven't! But I've a very good notion we won't like it. I tell you, nothing must come in the way of this marriage. We've got him then. Celeste won't let him put anything dirty over on us. I hope," he added. "At least, we've got a lever."

"At any rate," said Francis, "I'd rather have him with us. Do you know, I'm more and more convinced he's a bad devil to cross. And a bad devil to have on the other side. Do you believe in reincarnation?"

"Go to hell!" said Christopher.

Francis went out, laughing.

That night Francis informed his brother of the amount of Kinsolving that he would need to buy in order to become a director. Candidly, he told Peter that he would not consider offering him a directorship unless he turned over Bouchard stock to him and exchanged it for Kinsolving. "A rather unusual demand, perhaps," he said, "but frankly, I've got an ax to grind, myself."

"Aren't you taking all this a little too seriously?" asked Peter, diverted. "I didn't say I wanted the damn thing. I'm not sure I do. There's been a small change in my ultimate plans. How did I get this far in the discussion, anyway? Is the business going to pot? Or something? If I did get myself a directorship, I don't think I'd sell my Bouchard, not for a while, anyway. I'd buy Kinsolving with what I have. How's the Japanese order?"

Francis then advised him, that as the matter was "confidential," and "others might be too interested," Peter must tell no one of the offer of a directorship. He was enormously delighted when Peter assured him, bored, that no one knew or would know.

The next day he dictated a formal letter to Peter, a copy of which was added to the other correspondence:

"We have decided to withdraw the directorship offered you. We know this will meet with your approval, as the Japanese orders have not come through as anticipated. No doubt you will prefer to retain your Bouchard stock, and I would advise you to do so, considering its ultimate value, as outlined by you."

Peter was exceedingly puzzled upon receipt of this letter. But he knew very little of business procedure, and supposed this was all right. He said to Francis, later: "Why all the heavy correspondence? Do you always do this? And how do you get anything else done, if you waste your time writing people involved letters when you've got a telephone and a battery of secretaries?"

"It's customary."

"It's idiotic." Francis laughed. Peter laughed. And when Francis saw Peter laughing, he laughed more than ever, so that when Peter had stopped, the laughter went on and the younger man was puzzled again.

CHAPTER XXXIV

THE household at Endur was preparing to leave for Crissons. The weather was brilliantly hot and still. For the first time, Adelaide, tense and excited these days, longed for the day of departure. She felt that it would be a respite from the fuming dark fever that pervaded every room, a fever which was all the more dangerous because it was silent.

Not a voice had been raised these past weeks, not an angry or furious or wretched word uttered. Everyone dreaded to precipitate a crisis, particularly Christopher. On the surface, everything was as it had been. Henri came in the morning for Celeste, at least four times a week. Sundays, Henri and his sister and Christopher and Celeste were all together, apparently gay and light-hearted these warm June days. Henri came to dinner two or three nights a week. Sometimes Peter was there. He and Henri were scrupulously polite to each other; in no way did Henri indicate that he had the slightest suspicion that anything was wrong, or anything threatening him. They did not argue extensively, and apparently had little interest in each other, beyond a purely formal one. Edith was cordial to Peter, and invited him repeatedly. He dined with her and Henri at least twice a month at Robin's Nest, and relationships there thawed to friendliness. In spite of her fear and her anger against Peter, and her attempts at contempt, she began to like him, reluctantly. When Henri carelessly called him a fool, she was surprised, herself, to hear her denial.

"No, I don't think he is even an idealist," she said. "I think," she added, with an air of surprise, "that he's just an honest man."

Henri did not make any reply to this, and Edith sat back, much intrigued by her own amazement. "Isn't it strange that we should feel such antagonism, or incredulity, whenever we see a really honest man? Nice commentary on us!"

Henri said, smiling: "But really, such men are dangerous. And dangerous men are invariably fools. Or perhaps it is the other way around?"

And now the factions were more active than ever. Armand's faction courted Peter assiduously; Jean, himself, stopped his charming baiting and assumed a reasonable expression whenever he found himself in an argument with Peter. Nicholas invited him to his musty, ill-kept, disorderly old house for dinner, something he would not have dreamt of doing under ordinary circumstances. His old mother, Antoinette, was living in a villa in the south of France. He lived alone in the house where he had been born. Naturally untidy and uncouth, he had no rules to lay down for his servants, and they conducted his household in a raffish and negligent manner. Some of his relatives had told him candidly that the house stank, which did not annoy him. He did not like society, however, and particularly detested dinner-giving and dinner-accepting. He preferred his dank library, where the leather-bound books rotted on their shelves and the room was full of this smell, and of the odors of mice and stale air and strong tobacco, and where the dust lay thickly on the fine old mahogany and in the folds of dark blue velvet draperies, and the windows were opaque with dirt and grime.

Peter went to dinner, against the laughing warnings of his relatives. He went on foot, for it was a fine June evening.

Christopher's household was already preparing to leave for Crissons, and he had received an invitation to spend several weeks there. He had seen Nicholas' house only from the outside, and thought it very depressing, an old unkempt brownstone pile in the midst of frowsy, badly kept grounds. The yellow silk curtains were poorly hung and had a dirty look. The brassware about the door and steps was unpolished and dull, the windows were gray. When the door was opened for Peter he almost stepped back, for hot stagnant air, loaded with a variety of unclean smells, struck him like a weight in the face. The rank odors of dust and mice predominated, he decided, after a moment. The maid was blowsy, also, and poorly trained, for she left Peter standing helplessly in the grimy hall while she went away to announce him.

The carpet he stood on was a priceless Oriental; the walls were paneled in the darkest and finest mahogany; the curving staircase was marble and gilt; the dirty floors were of exquisite parquetry. Magnificent portraits of Bouchards and Barbours were visible on the dim soiled walls of adjoining rooms. All this depressed Peter enormously. All this beauty and pride covered with the greasy film of neglect and decay! Sometimes, he reflected, the wrong done inanimate beauty was worse than any wrong done to a man.

He heard that few visitors were ever invited here, and he did not wonder. The very atmosphere was full of suspicion and dislike, and antipathetic. The whole house seemed to lower sulkily at him; an air of surly surprise seemed to pervade the rooms. Here, he thought, everything is hated, every word is suspected. Perhaps it was not actual dirt that filled this house, but the patina that had exuded from the soul of the man who inhabited it.

The dinner was badly cooked, and worse served. The maids were actually resentful of Peter's troubling presence. Peter could hear their quarrelsome voices below stairs, and the angry slamming of doors. Nicholas did not appear to mind it. In fact, Peter detected a sympathy in him for the disgruntled maids, who had been so unbearably put out by this dinner. Nevertheless, Nicholas put on a heavy heartiness and excessive cordiality, which Peter found more and more embarrassing as the meal proceeded. He liked Nicholas very little. There was something about him, perhaps in his greenish brown coloring, his heaviness, his thick oily skin, his watchful and suspecting little eyes, that contributed much to Peter's increasing uneasiness. He found himself having less and less to say.

There were some who alleged that they liked Nicholas for

his "candor, honesty, and lack of affectation. So blunt and forthright—" Peter remembered hearing this. He smiled bitterly to himself. Nicholas was blunt, without a doubt, and had a habit of reminding his audience that he had little use for what was called tact and pleasant diplomacy. "Just hypocrisy," he would say. "Let a man say what's on his mind. Can't accuse you of anything then, can they? People are always looking for loopholes. To hang you. But if you speak your mind, outright, you've disarmed 'em." He prided himself on saying disagreeable things in the name of truth and "openness." Peter remembered Shakespeare:

> "This is some fellow
> Who, having been praised for bluntness, doth affect
> A saucy roughness. . . .
> These kind of knaves I know, which in this plainness
> Harbour more craft and more corrupter ends. . . ."

Peter had had difficulty swallowing the cool soup, on which had floated half-congealed pellets of grease. He had got through the fish course without any undue casualties, though the fish was not at all fresh. But the meat course was the worst, for the roast was tough and fibrous, the vegetables watery. The linen cloth was of the finest and most delicate, the silver ponderous and beautifully moulded and engraved. But the cloth was also rumpled and stained, the silver black with tarnish. The crystal chandelier that hung from the carved ceiling was so gray and greasy with dirt that the light struggling through it was gloomy and uncertain. Nicholas had inherited the treasures of his father's house, and had grossly neglected them. Antoinette's beautiful Haviland and Bavarian china was chipped and dulled. Near by lay a frowsy hound, with red hating eyes, which were fixed on Nicholas. The latter kept tossing him fragments of meat from the edge of his knife, some of which fell on the rich rug. Catching the meat, the dog would beat the floor with his tail; dust would immediately rise, and then float away in the torpid air. Beyond the clouded windows was the somber and tangled green wilderness of what was once one of the finest gardens in all the State. The pent heat was intense and acrid.

Peter knew, before the meal was over, that he did not hate Nicholas so much as loathe him. Had the older man suddenly displayed talents and virtues beyond belief, Peter's loathing would not have diminished. He wanted only one thing: to get out of here. He knew he was neither wanted nor liked, and that Nicholas had not the slightest personal interest in him. Why, then, had he been invited to dinner? He did not know. But he kept casting about in his mind for the answer.

But Nicholas was shrewd. It was his business to understand men, and he had long ago, probably at the soup course, decided that Peter was no innocent. This disappointed and disgruntled him. He had considered Jean and Armand fools for "beating around the bush. Why don't you come right out?" Now, he felt no inclination to "come right out" himself. However, his conviction of Peter's lack of innocence did encourage him in one respect; disingenuous men always saw which way a profit lay. It was easier dealing with disingenuous men; they never cluttered up the business atmosphere with a lot of foolish and noble phrases. Nicholas hated and suspected nobility, remembering his Uncle Andre.

When coffee was served, he felt his geniality beginning to crack. His face was stiff with unaccustomed jovial smiles. Moreover, he perceived that Peter was both bored and not deceived, and curious. He forced his face into a broader smile, pushed a wooden box of cigars in Peter's direction, thus forcing up a fold of cloth and upsetting a beautiful crystal water-glass.

"How's your mother?" he asked abruptly.

Peter was surprised. He had never heard old Ann Richmond speak of Nicholas at all, but as "that dirty man." Moreoever, he doubted that they had occasion to meet more than once or twice a year. He replied: "Very well, thank you. Of course, she is feeling her age. I don't believe she is going on the yacht with Francis this year. She says she prefers to go to France, and visit your mother."

Nicholas chuckled richly. "Like to see the old devils after a week, wouldn't you? Probably tearing each other's hair out. Nothing like two women, especially two old women, to make things lively for each other. This France business! We —the men—are the Bouchards, not the women. And a hell of a lot of French there is in us! Just about enough to stuff in a thimble. But let them have their fun. Being plain American isn't good enough for the chicken-brains. They've got to go French on us!" He bit off the end of a cigar and spat it out. "Funny. 'The Bouchards.' French-Americans, they say in the papers." He ejaculated an obscene word, and chuckled again. "Ought to sue them for libel. We take our sex straight. Plain American is good enough for me. All those fake illustrious French ancestors our women dig up! Counts and Countesses, and Princes and monseigneurs, and ladies-in-waiting to that fancy Austrian whore, Marie-Antoinette—goddammit, it's enough to make you puke!"

He shook expansively. Peter, in spite of his disgust, had to smile. He remembered Georges' wife, Marion, and how she looked at one with large serious eyes and would say: "Yes, I believe Georges' great-great-grandfather's grandfather was Louis the Fifteenth's most intimate friend—the Duc de Crissons."

Nicholas was still chuckling: "Funny, you get the money, and you immediately get ancestors. What the hell! Didn't they eat and have bowel movements like the rest of us? Didn't they whore around with bitches, just like their lackeys? What's about the aristocracy that ain't human? Anyway, we haven't any ancestors."

Peter laughed. "It doesn't do any harm, and it makes the women happy. What more would you want?"

"Nothing. Nothing!" Nicholas waved his hand with a gesture that magnanimously allowed all sorts of pleasant follies to the piteous human race. "Anyway, I suppose we men should be grateful. It does give us a laugh." He added: "Whatever's good about us came from old Ernest Barbour's side. Nothing like the English for all around piggishness and guts and go."

They went into the musty drawing room. Peter knew immediately that no one had been in this room for months. When Nicholas roughly rolled up a blind, to let in the last beams of summer twilight, rolls of woolly dirt fell off the slats, and made him cough and curse. They sat down. Peter's hands came in contact with the wooden chair-arms, and he immediately withdrew them, fastidiously.

Nicholas still talked. Peter's disgust grew. Why doesn't he come to the point? he asked himself. For by now, he knew there was a point. He was not offended for he had long ago realized that men rarely do anything kind or cordial without the meanest of motives.

Though Nicholas talked on, his eyes were narrowing. He knew that Peter knew there was a point by now, and he was wondering whether he had better be "above-board" and come out with it, and what were his chances of success.

He said, watching Peter's face intently: "Made up your mind yet what you're going to do? I mean, are you staying here? Or going to New York? Everybody who has a book swelling in them somewhere usually goes to New York. I suppose it's just as well. Better pile up the offal all in one spot," and he laughed deeply, disclaiming any intention of offending.

Peter could not help coloring, and he hated himself for his

267

stiff voice: "I don't know where I'll go, yet. I like New York. I may live there. But, after all, Windsor's my home, you know."

Nicholas waved his hand. "That's right. Better stay in Windsor. Settle down. Get married. Or something. Can't say I think much of marriage. Women interfering in everything. Think they ought to run your business. Well. Anyway, it might be the best thing: to marry and settle down." He paused. Grinned. "Better not poach on private property. Lots of good unclaimed ground lying idle."

Peter's slight coloring turned to dark scarlet. "What do you mean?" he cried angrily.

Nicholas studied him thoughtfully before answering with a deprecating purse of his lips: "Tut. Why get excited? I'm not a man to go around sticking my nose into other people's business. Got enough trouble of my own. But others will talk, you know, and I've heard rumors——"

"About what?" Peter had got to his feet. He was thoroughly enraged. But Nicholas shrewdly commented to himself on the fact that the young man's face was becoming more and more suffused.

"About you and little Celeste, the little white bunny," he replied frankly. "She's got a tag on her, hasn't she? Sit down, Peter, sit down. After all, we're family, ain't we? I'm an old bachelor, and perhaps that's why I'm interested in the rest of the family. And do you know something? I wouldn't like to come up against young Henri. He's got a bad eye, and from the look of him, a black soul."

Peter's nostrils flared out; he exhaled loudly. But he said nothing, but only stared at Nicholas with rage.

Nicholas sighed. "I thought you had sense. After all, I'm not a stranger, am I? Well, let it drop. We won't speak about it any more, eh?"

Peter said tightly: "You started it. Finish it, please."

Nicholas raised one hand helplessly, let it drop. "How can I, with you preparing to bite my head off? I try to help, and you rush at my throat. Sit down, and calm yourself. I was only joking. Sorry I started the damn thing. I only heard that you were hanging around the little white bunny too much, that's all. And Henri's beginning to notice, they say. And I repeat: I wouldn't want to come up against him. He's bad stuff, Pete. Bankers and politicians can smell bad stuff a long way.

"I was only about to say, if you had let me finish, that it would be a good thing for you to marry. And stay here. A good thing, if you didn't start messing in other people's soup-

268

pots. See what I mean? Even if the soup is sour, and you think you can sweeten it." He added: "And it is damn sour, you can be sure of that. But then, what can you expect, with Christopher pushing the child into that marriage, probably against her will?"

Peter sat down very slowly; he did not take his eyes from Nicholas' face. He asked quietly: "What is it all to you?"

Nicholas shrugged. "Nothing. Candidly, nothing. I was just talking, like a fool. Ought to have known enough to mind my own business. But I was only making conversation; it's the privilege of relatives, isn't it?"

Peter continued to gaze at him fixedly. The color left his face. He was now exceedingly pale. After a long time he said: "What makes you think Christopher is pushing Celeste into this?"

Ah, thought Nicholas exultantly, we're getting somewhere now! He answered frankly: "I just know. I told you, bankers can smell bad stuff a long way off. I don't know what Christopher's got on his mind, but Celeste is mixed up in it, with Henri. Christopher's dirty weather in any man's language. We were kids together, you see, that's how I know. And from what I've heard and seen myself, little Celeste's up a tree. I'm sorry for the child. My mother would say she was going into a 'decline.' Like Armand's Annette."

Peter averted his head, but not before the watchful Nicholas had seen the expression of somber misery on his face. "It isn't for anyone to interfere," he muttered. Nicholas affected not to have heard.

"The girl's helpless. She never did have much brains. Christopher's always been able to push her and pull her wherever he wanted her. Too bad. A nice little thing, too. Yes, I'm sorry for her. She'll have a hell of a life with that cold-blooded cannibal, Henri. She already looks as though she knows what's in store for her." He shook his head dolefully: "Too bad Jules is not alive. Armand and Emile are no good; they wouldn't pull their little sister out of a fire if they thought they'd burn the tips of their fingers. Old Adelaide's a loss, no matter how you look at her. The girl hasn't a friend in the world. And by God! she looks as though she could use one!"

Peter turned to him again, and again he fixed his eyes piercingly on Nicholas' face. "You've got a motive in telling me this," he said. "What is it?"

Nicholas pretended sudden ire. He pulled himself up in his chair. "Jesus, I haven't any! Why should I? What's it got
269

to do with me who marries who? But you get me to talking. That's what happens when you talk indiscriminately."

But Peter said slowly: "And you think Christopher's pushing Celeste into this?"

Nicholas waved his hand, and glared at him. "Look here, I'm not going to say another word! I've put my foot in it enough. What the devil does it matter to me, or to you, who she marries? Let it drop."

Peter got to his feet again. "Yes. Let it drop." And he went out of the room. Nicholas did not move. He listened, smiling. The door closed. He heard Peter's footsteps in the darkness outside. His smile broadened. After about five minutes had passed, he went to the telephone and called a number. As he waited he hummed hoarsely. Armand answered him.

"Well!" cried Nicholas. "I've found out more in two hours than you half-wits have done in weeks! Pete's been here for dinner. And what I've found out! He's mad about the little girl, but he hasn't touched her because he didn't know that Christopher's behind the marriage. What? Of course I told him that! Who's going to contradict it? Christopher? Hah! Now he's all burning up to rescue the damsel from the big, bad wolves, the wolves being Christopher and Henri. He feels he's got to move very cautiously. It's evident they haven't discussed it, though, and maybe he didn't notice how the girl's been pining away. But he'll look, now!"

CHAPTER XXXV

UPON leaving Nicholas' house Peter walked directly to the nearest telephone. He called Celeste. The butler answered. No, Miss Celeste was not at home. Nor Mr. Christopher. But Mrs. Bouchard was at home. A moment later Adelaide's faint apprehensive voice came to him. Peter spoke quietly and quickly: "I want to see you, Adelaide. May I? At once?"

He hailed a cab and was driven rapidly to Endur. The house was already full of a deserted air, for the next day the household was leaving for Crissons. Peter went upstairs to Adelaide's rooms. He found her there with old Thomas Van Eyck.

Peter was not prepared for the presence of the old man, and hesitated. But Adelaide said: "Do you mind, Peter? Thomas knows everything." She gave the young man her hand and smiled at him gently. Her sad eyes lighted up when she looked at him. Old and tired though she was, there was a new look about her these days, of hope.

Peter sat down and said abruptly: "Adelaide, I want you to tell me something, if you can. You've already told me that you don't want Celeste to marry Henri. You've said that this marriage will make her miserable forever. I—I agree with you. I couldn't help but agree, because it means so much to me, personally."

Thomas Van Eyck regarded him sadly and affectionately. The old man sat quietly, his thin old fingers at his cheek. He listened, almost without breathing.

Peter's pale face tightened; his jaw sprang out. He looked at Adelaide and went on: "Tonight, Nicholas told me that Christopher is pushing Celeste into this marriage, without her knowledge. That he planned it and promoted it, for reasons of his own, the least of which is Celeste's own happiness. Is this true?"

A look of intense fright and fear stood on Adelaide's face. She bit her trembling lips. Her eyes fell.

She almost whispered: "I don't know. Even when I say that, I may be wronging Christopher. Armand would know, I think. I have a feeling that Armand would do almost anything to prevent this marriage. I don't just know why; he's never shown Celeste much affection——"

Peter listened less to her words than to the tone of her voice; he also saw how terrified she was, and how, with every gesture and glance, she was imploring him to believe the things she instinctively knew. He frowned.

"But why? Why should Christopher care so much?"

Adelaide was silent. Finally Peter stood up and began to walk up and down the room, thinking deeply. Some way, he believed, Christopher's attempts to get him to sell his Bouchard stock was tied up in the matter. But then, it was common knowledge that Henri had no actual Bouchard holdings except his bonds. The bonds would do Christopher no particular good——But would they?

He turned back to Adelaide. "Celeste hasn't said anything to you yet, has she, Adelaide?"

"Nothing since that first night. The poor child is struggling. But she won't let me come near her! She won't let me talk to her. I've tried. But she looks at me with such a face! It's no use. She must fight this out herself. Not even you can help her, Peter."

His mouth closed grimly. "I don't know about that," he replied. "I don't know about that! Now."

Thomas Van Eyck stood up and took Peter gently by the arm. He looked into the young man's face.

"I've never been very clever, Peter," he said deprecatingly, with a smile. "No one has ever accused me of being clever, and you know, I'm glad about that. I wouldn't want to be. All the bad people are clever. You're not; you're just good. Peter, we're hoping you'll help Celeste. But you've got clever men against you. It's just the old story: which will win, cleverness or goodness?

"The clever people seem to have everything their own way. That's because the rest of us, most of us, just stand by and let them do it. They also are guilty, who only stand and watch. Peter, you're going to help Celeste, aren't you? You know she loves you?"

"Yes," said Peter in a low voice. "I know. And she knows, too."

When he reached home, the great chateau near the river was silent. Here, too, there was an air of leave-taking and closing. Francis and Estelle were out to dinner with their young daughters. Here and there a dim light glowed through the immense corridors and in distant rooms. A servant brought Peter a message from Francis, which, for some inexplicable reason, annoyed him. Francis requested that Peter go up to his mother's apartments. It seemed that she wished to see him before he went to bed.

Why should Francis leave this message? he thought, as he went up in the automatic elevator. Why didn't Mother ask me to come, herself?

He felt an inner shrinking as he approached his mother's door. His had always been a nature more inclined to love than hatred, and this nature had been continually violated all his life, not by himself, but by those he had attempted to love. He remembered his mother when she had been youngish, a handsome, vain, sprightly woman, whose egotistic self-love and self-importance had made Honore's life one of wretchedness and frustration. There had never been any peace for his father, thought Peter bitterly. He had been assailed in his work, and assailed in his home. He had died, full of wounds. But the impulse, thought Peter, which prevented Honore from making any effort to save himself from death, had been the same impulse which had made his son enlist in the wartime army. Peter never approached his mother without the ghost of his dead father standing before him. And he never saw this ghost without the most passionate hatred for Ann flooding into all the cells of his body and rising in a dark tide to his brain. He had tried a thousand times to overcome this hatred, himself feeling violated by it; he had tried to remember that most of the villainy and cruelty and wickedness of men was due in much part to weakness and blindness and fear. But it was no use. He tried again, tonight, his hand on the doorknob, all his will struggling to beat down the dark tides. And again, it was no use. He knew he would despise himself when he saw her, for he would smile and say affectionately: "How are you, Mother?"

He opened the door. The smile was already on his face, strained and unreal. But old Ann was not in her quiet living room. The door of her bedroom stood open, and he saw the rosy shadows of her bedside lamps. The smile had relaxed on his face; now, with a conscious effort, he forced its return. He walked briskly to the door. "Hello, Mother! How are you!"

Old Ann was sitting up in her bed, which was upholstered in dark rose satin tufts. It was an immense bed, the wood all gilt and dead-white. Though it was a warm evening, a pink silk puff was thrown across the foot. The chamber was luxuriously furnished with rose-and-blue striped satin damask chairs, ivory silk hangings, and pale rose rugs. The lamps were gilt and rose and soft old blue, and the delicate odors of powders and scents filled the air.

Ann's personal maid was brushing her white hair with deft strokes of a gold-backed brush. The old woman leaned back against her gleaming pillows, smoking. Her rings were still on her withered fingers, and they glittered and sparkled in the soft light, as though all her youth and vitality had gone into their hardness and had left nothing behind but this decayed and straining body. Her rouge had been removed, and her skin, ash-colored and shrunken, testified to her age. But her eyes, restless and still vividly bright, revealed what a determinedly selfish and avaricious soul there stood behind this shriveled flesh. Her elaborate silken nightgown foaming with lace, could not, however, conceal the lack of firm contour beneath it.

Peter's entry had been too abrupt for her to slip on an expression of maternal affection, and as he stood in the doorway he saw clearly what his mother's feeling for him truly was. He saw, in one glance, the browned and withered throat rising from the lace, the ruin of her face in which the eyes leapt and burned and flashed malevolently upon him. He was appalled, though he must always have known. But

273

even so, that look, that hating expression, that hidden contemptuous rage, struck on his naked heart.

An instant later she was simpering affectionately: "Hello, dear. Do sit down. Collins won't be more than a minute, will you, Collins? Collins, you hurt me then! How many times must I tell you not to twist the brush on the under hair?" and she snatched the brush pettishly from the maid and flung it in the direction of the dressing table. "There. Do go away. You can bring my hot milk later. No, don't fuss. The bed is all right. I'll ring if I want you."

The girl shrugged almost imperceptibly, picked up the brush, replaced it, and went out softly. After the door had closed behind her, Ann burst out petulantly: "Such a stupid thing! Did you ever see such clumsiness? And she came to me well-recommended, really. But that is the trouble with servants these days. So inefficient, so impudent, so careless, so disrespectful. I don't know what things are coming to. They are treated so excellently these days; they have their own rooms with baths, and good food, and reasonable hours and fine wages, and don't appreciate them in the least. I really don't know! When I was a girl a servant felt she was fortunate to share a bed with only one other servant, and was thankful if there were enough quilts on it to keep her warm in an absolutely unheated bedroom. She was glad to get one good meal a day, and one-half day off every two weeks, and three dollars a week. But now, they think they are as good as anybody else. I really don't know! It's just bolshevism."

She was working herself up. She kept threshing about pettishly in the bed, and withered color had come into her sunken cheeks; her eyes were flashing dangerously, with a sort of fixed malignance. She was breathing quite audibly; her wrinkled, unrouged lips twitched. —She doesn't know how to begin, thought Peter, bitterly. She's looking for an opening, and it maddens her.

He was so tired of people who looked constantly for openings to attack one. Like serpents seeking for chinks in armor through which to strike their deadly fangs. And their rage and hatred increasing during the delay and the seeking. Dreadful people. And the world was full of them. A sudden monstrous sickness clutched at Peter's heart, a loathing for consciousness which permitted one to see what was to be seen.

Ann's petulance had subsided into sullenness. She tried to smile at her youngest son.

"I thought you had gone to the Bests' dinner with Francis
274

and Estelle," he said. He reached out and helped himself to one of his mother's pet cigarettes with the gilt tips. He lit it, grimaced, coughed.

"No, I didn't go," she said shrilly. "I hate the Bests. Such dull people. They pretend to be so musical, and they don't know anything at all about music. Really. And that hideous picture of Paderewski, always glaring and making faces, on the piano, which is actually out of tune all the time!"

Peter was silent. He was remembering that young Mrs. Best was an accomplished pianist, and that Paderewski had, unasked, sent her an autographed photograph after he had heard her play at the home of a London friend. But what could one do before malignance which had never, in all its life, been moved to true kindness or compassion or understanding or generosity?

"I have no patience with people who pretend to be what they're not," went on the cracked malicious voice, which expressed the dartings-about of the mind behind it. "Peter, do you have to cough so? It's very annoying. You smoke incessantly, so it's no wonder. Why don't you go to Doctor Forstdyke? I've asked you a thousand times. You look half-dead."

She began to complain, in his silence. She simply would not go on that awful yacht this summer. Estelle and her stupid friends! No life, no gaiety to them. Always talking seriously, because they were really so empty-minded. She, Ann, had observed that empty-minded people were invariably the most solemn and portentous. Here Peter smiled in involuntary agreement. It surprised him that his mother could be so astute. The complaining voice, always maneuvering for an opening, went on. No, she would not go on the yacht this summer, even if she stayed here and died of the heat, rather than be with people prematurely old and three quarters dead.

"I thought it was all settled that you were going to France, Mother?"

Old Ann twitched her body restlessly under the silken sheets. Her face wrinkled discontentedly, but now her eyes were watchful. "I don't like to go alone, some way. Peter," she added quickly, "won't you come with me?"

He glanced up alertly, his eyes growing intent. "But, Mother, I just came from France. I'm—I'm tired. I've been running around all over Europe——"

She became excited. Her voice rose to shrill piercing heights. She had the most ungrateful and selfish children! Her

275

own wishes and preferences were never considered. Children never thought, these days, that they owed their parents any gratitude or consideration. Her own children, for instance, were quite willing for her to go abroad, alone, unprotected, helpless, not caring if she were ill on board, or suffering, or lonely. It was quite terrible——

Peter listened, trying to hear something behind the rush of hysterical accusing words. He heard a purpose behind them; he knew at once that Ann was acting, and that she was quite cool and calculating behind the external manifestations of hurt and emotion. He remembered that it had always been Ann's boast that she preferred to travel alone; why, only last week, when the trip to France had been mentioned, she had exulted, archly, that now there would be no one supervising her! She was like a debutante, eager to escape a watchful chaperon, she had exclaimed, girlishly.

So, why did she want Peter to go with her? He did not know. But he felt that he would soon find out. In the meantime, he felt his pulses begin to hammer with a sickening premonition.

She was regarding him with vicious excitement. "Well, you can just imagine that I gave Francis a good dressing-down tonight! I told him what I thought of his selfishness, and Estelle's, too——"

That is a lie, thought Peter. You did talk to Francis, and probably in this very room. But what did you talk about?

He said: "Why go to France? Why not stay at home? I'll go with you, to Southampton, or anywhere else. But I can't spare all summer. I—I've got work to do. My writing. And other things. In New York."

She was silent for a long time. But in that silence she fixed her eyes upon him, and they sparkled with malice, cunning, and dislike. The meanest of smiles slowly began to curve her sunken lips. There was something cruel and gloating in that old face between the masses of silken white hair.

"But why New York? In the summer? Such an inferno, Peter." Her voice had suddenly lost its hysteria, and was sly and soft.

Peter began to see. He felt cold. His muscles tensed, as though preparing him for escape. But he answered equably: "I've got an invitation from Georges and Marion, to stay at their country home in Dutchess County. I'm going there, to do my writing. I'm all prepared for it."

She laughed incredulously. "George and Marion! Why, he's the biggest fox in the publishing business! I should have thought he would be the last one in the world you'd care to see, Peter! You, with your idealism!"

Peter flushed. But he merely looked at her steadfastly without replying.

"And Marion! That concentrated essence of the Daughters of the American Revolution! Oh, she's an absolute fool, and you know it, Peter. How can you bear her? How can you bear either of them?"

Peter spoke with painful difficulty: "I think you are unfair to them, Mother. There is much I like about them. They are cordial and hospitable, and sometimes a man likes that. I think they like me, too. In a way. Look, let me call them tonight. I'll tell them you'd like to come."

Ann threw up her arms and raised her eyes to the ceiling. "O my God, Peter! Can you imagine me there, on their glorified farm, gurgling about the cows and the chickens! Why, I'd rather be dead! Dead! You just might as well be dead, anyway, as down there. Peter! I'm surprised at you. With those two old fools."

"They aren't old. Marion's only in her forties. You know that, Mother——"

"Well, they're old and dried-up and sapless, no matter what their actual years are. I'd rather be dead. I'm amazed that you should suggest such an incongruous thing. I want life and fun and gaiety. I'll be dead a long time, you know."

As Peter did not speak, she pulled herself closer to him, and smiled at him wheedlingly. "Peter, dear, please come to France with me. You'll enjoy it so much. I can't understand you, Peter. Paris is so wonderful. You needn't stay down south with me all the time. Go to Paris, if you want to."

While she had been speaking, he had come to the correct conclusion as to what lay behind this, and his face slowly hardened and paled. At the last, she saw his face fully, and was vaguely startled.

"No, Mother," he said clearly and firmly, "I won't go to France with you. You may come to Georges and Marion's with me, if you want. I'll do all I can to make you comfortable and keep you entertained. But I won't go to France with you. That's final."

He stood up. He looked down at her. The eyes of mother and son clashed, assailed each other. The smile had disappeared from Ann's lips, and had left, instead, a contortion of the utmost virulence. She spoke very softly:

"It isn't because of Celeste, is it, Peter?"

She had expected him to start, to change color, to look guilty, to stammer, to deny, to pretend indignation and innocence. But she had not expected that he would just stand there, quietly, looking down at her, with no expression but one of calmness and composure and dignity. She had not expected him to say: "Don't you think that's my own business, Mother?"

She gasped. She fell back against her pillows. She regarded him, now, with open hatred and rage.

"You don't deny it? You haven't anything else to say? It's true, then, all the gossip? Haven't you any shame? She's engaged to Henri Bouchard, who's twice the man you are, a real man, not a whining, psalm-singing fool, like you! Why can't you leave her alone? Or can't you find a girl, yourself? Aren't you man enough to find a girl, instead of creeping in the footsteps of another man, to lick up the leavings?"

In spite of his knowledge of his mother's character, he was appalled at this red and open vulgarity, this vicious lunging, this lack of the slightest maternal and natural affection. With all his knowledge of the lowest in human character, despite all the things he had seen, he could still feel the nauseous plunging of his senses, his first horror. A horrible darkness seemed to grow before him; all his spirit turned away, revolted and torn, from his mother. Something seemed to burst behind his eyes, so that he could see nothing for some moments.

She was raging on incoherently, beside herself. But finally she became aware of Peter's face. The foam of words bubbled to her lips, then died away. She paled. She shrank back on her pillows. A low whimper began in her throat, and for the first time she experienced a shamed pang, a sudden self-detestation and remorse. A ringing silence filled the room.

Peter began to speak, very gently, almost compassionately. She heard with incredulity.

"Francis put you up to this, didn't he, Mother? I thought so. Why did he? What is it to him? I think I'm beginning to see. I'm beginning to see a lot of things, Mother."

He went towards the door. He had almost reached it when she cried out with involuntary alarm, not for herself, not for Francis, but only for Peter: "Where are you going? Peter, you tell me: where are you going?"

He turned slowly. And again, when she saw his face, the pang went through her, made bitter tears rise to her eyes.

"I'm going away, Mother. Tonight. Right now."

"Peter!" Her voice was broken.

He shook his head. "Good-by, Mother."

He closed the door softly behind him. She strained her

278

ears. She heard him go away. And then, with a sob, she fell back onto her pillows.

Three hours later he was on the midnight plane to New York. He had left before Francis and Estelle had returned.

CHAPTER XXXVI

LEON BOUCHARD, even up to the time of his death some years ago, had always admired but distrusted his elder son, Georges. He was brilliant, opinionated, but erratic. However, there was nothing flippant or shallow about him. Neither was he idealistic, or inclined to any artistry or exoticism, or any of the other peculiarities of temperament which the Bouchards would have found objectionable. But he was restless and quarrelsome, not showing any particular aptitude for any particular work, until sometime in 1914, when he had decided, finally and irrevocably, that he wished to go into newspaper publishing. For some months, since his graduation from Princeton in 1913, he had been in the bank with his father. It was impossible for him to do anything shabbily or in a mediocre manner, but it was evident from the first that he found banking unimaginative. Frankly, he admitted it was probably his fault. He did not have, he said, the proper reverence for money, and when his father sardonically said he supposed it was because he had never known the lack of it, he agreed.

Leon was too intelligent to insist upon his own choice as a vocation for his son, and when Georges announced that he would like to work in the office of *The Windsor Courier*, Leon allowed him to leave the bank and begin work as a reporter. It was only a few weeks before Georges' brilliant and powerful articles began attracting local attention, and thereafter national attention. Perhaps part of this attention was due to his name and family, but the greater part was due to his own ability. Nicholas, his younger brother, had just returned from a trip around the world, his father's graduation present to him, and took Georges' place in the bank. His natural aptitude, his sobriety and sullen tenacity, his remarkable insight into character, his native skepticism, his amazing judgment, gratified his father, who felt that he had made an excellent decision in allowing Georges to leave the bank.

Georges had not only been a splendid student, with an extraordinary memory, but he had that attribute which few students possess: a swift and glittering mind. He never forgot anything; words and facts were to him the artist's paints. He made phrases sparkle and compel, paragraphs glow, articles fascinate and stir. He had invented a certain style, terse and explosive, yet fiery, which, being a radical departure from the newspaper style of the past century (which had been involved, ceremonious and ponderous), attracted controversial notice. He used a word where the old writers had used a phrase, a phrase for a paragraph, a paragraph for an entire article. As a result, interest never became fatigued. His clear sentences never puzzled; he hated ambiguity, though he never dispensed with subtlety. He did not believe that subtlety need be ambiguous, as the old writers had believed; delicacy and irony, he declared, shone best through clarified words. He started the style of rapid but descriptive newspaper writing, which eventually found its way into novels, biography and scientific articles. When some of the world's best newspaper writers declared his to be a "bastard style," without polish and urbanity, he laughed and replied that it was better to be a bastard than a eunuch.

His uncle, Etienne, the aging but still potent matinee idol of a nation of sentimental women, had been distrusted by his relatives for his exotic appearance, rich organ voice and womanish temperament. He had aroused in his relatives a healthy and obstinate aversion for all that was "artistic," as had François Bouchard and Godfrey Sessions. The family, therefore, was always prepared to distrust Georges, watching him suspiciously for any tendency to let his hair and cravat flow, his nails become rimmed and his linen dirty, his speech exotic and embarrassing, his temper odd. But he both gratified and disappointed them in this: he was lean and tall and nervous, very much like Jules, his uncle, in appearance, with jerking eyes, a prow-like nose, clipped sleek hair, a hard chin and mouth, and an arrogant, impatient manner. It was very evident that he was selfish and without any softness whatsoever.

Jules had been fond of his nephew Georges. He understood Georges, was indulgent towards him, and liked his company. Georges' appreciation of Goya and Velasquez and Corot excited and pleased him; when Georges confessed to disliking Rubens, Jules was entirely won. Jules often said that he could "talk" to no one but Georges, who was a devil after his own heart. On Georges' birthday, he showed his affection adequately in making him a present of *The Windsor Courier*, the stock of which he owned almost entirely. So Georges became editor.

When Leon sent for Jules one night, urgently, in September, 1914, Jules was surprised. He was afraid that Georges had finally betrayed some exoticism, some tendency to peculiarity, or something disgustingly idealistic. As he was driven to Leon's house in his great Pierce-Arrow, he was apprehensive.

Leon lived upon an ornate estate about two miles from Robin's Nest, all terraces and soft rolling lawns and high walls with iron gates, gatekeepers and stables and garages and artful landscaping. Jules preferred his more austere and gloomy house and estate, but he enjoyed the clever vistas of his brother's property, the studied artistries, the false quaintnesses of stone hall and flagged paths, the very precious turrets and towers, and the French tongue of the imported servants. He enjoyed them all, for they amused him intensely. He was always edified by pretentiousness and affectation, never irritated by them. So few things, he would say, are really funny in life, and when a funniness occurred he was grateful for it.

Antoinette Bouchard, his cousin and sister-in-law, was, at fifty, a tiny but potent grande dame, with silvery blonde hair, passionate and knowing blue eyes, a dimple, a round birdlike bosom, and a very stylish well-preserved figure. She was quick and lively and arrogant, and flirtatious, especially with Jules, whom she not so secretly admired and loved. When he was about she became young and coy and sparkling, and, in turn, he liked her, for her knowledge of wines and her vivacity pleased him. But he found her ancestor-worship extremely hilarious.

Leon was waiting for Jules in the stone library with its stained-glass windows and mighty red velvet draperies. His powerful stocky figure, the way his big head set almost squarely on his shoulders, his slightly bowed legs, were Napoleonic, as were his truculent, violent face and eyes. Jules, in 1914, slim and elegant as ever, with smooth dark face and still black, white-touched hair, seemed supple and youthful compared with his brother.

Leon grunted when Jules entered the library. Jules had hardly sat down when Antoinette, in tears, entered with Georges, who was evidently enraged. Antoinette ran up to Jules immediately, and exclaimed with hysteria: "Jules! You may be able to do something! Georges will listen only to you! I have told him over and over, that in a dynasty like ours, in a family like ours, marriages are so important, and can be so disastrous, just like royal marriages, or something——! Heavens knows how hard I worked to marry Irene and Bertha off satisfactorily—and Bertha with the squint in her eye—but no one can say that I didn't do my duty by my girls. And now, Georges——!"

"Sit down, Antoinette, or get out!" shouted Leon, turning a deep mauve. "Damn women, anyay!"

Antoinette, the tiny and plump, turned upon her husband, stamped her foot with a violence of her own. "It's all your fault, Leon, and I *will* speak, and you can't stop me! You encouraged him to associate with such dreadful people, and never tried to stop him from going to New York to see them, and let him have that horrible newspaper!"

Jules glanced swiftly at his nephew, who had begun to grin unpleasantly. "I take it," he said gently, "that Georges is about to commit a mesalliance."

"Not at all," said Georges, "it's Marion who is going to commit that, in marrying me. Wasn't Great-grandfather Barbour a servant or stable-boy or something like that?"

Antoinette shrieked, and burst into fresh tears. Jules led her to a chair, where she sat down and continued to cling to his hand. Jules disengaged it as gently as possible.

"Impudent young dog!" said Leon, lighting a cigar with fingers that shook. "I thought you had better sense. But you can listen to me: marry that—that girl, and I'll kick you so far you'll never dare come back."

Georges turned to his uncle. "Dad forgets the day of the heavy father has gone out," he said. "But, by the way, what the hell is it your business whom I marry, Uncle Jules?"

Jules smiled in a puzzled way. "I'm sure I don't know, Georges. If you'd rather not tell me, you are perfectly within your rights. After all, you're not a child. But at any rate, I'm interested, naturally. We've been friends, you and I, and I'd be offended if I were not to know."

Before Georges, who had begun to smile at his uncle's words, could reply, Leon said roughly: "I'll tell you. It's Arthur Fitts' daughter, Marion. Arthur Fitts, Professor of Economics in Columbia."

"Ah." Jules raised his eyebrows, and his face became smooth and bland. "A very clever man, Fitts. The only man who can make economics sound like something else besides a hasty pudding of figures. A novelist gone wrong in a jungle of commodities, and met up with a nihilist."

"It's all Aunt Lucy's fault!" exclaimed Antoinette, squirming in her chair in her agitation. "And that awful old bachelor cousin of ours, Thomas. They fill their house in New York with such—such obscene rabble, artists and bohemians and singers and writers and such trash, and it was Thomas himself who introduced Georges to that terrible girl."

Georges was grinning broadly; his pince-nez glittered as he glanced at his mother. "Marion isn't terrible, Mother," he said. "She's a very fine girl, with a mind of her own. Lots of intelligence, even if she's a suffragette. She was to teach at Vassar next term," he added, turning to his uncle, "but her papa made the old ladies and the old gentlemen mad, so they've torn up her contract. She majored in English. If she'll have me, and I'm not certain she will, with our history and so on, it should be an occasion for family rejoicing that someone decent was becoming part of it."

"Ah," said Jules again, in a murmur. He smoothed his lip with his finger, and looked at his brother.

"Fitts!" shouted Leon. "Did you read his last attack on us in the current issue of *American Economics?* We've got a suit for libel pending against him, as you know, Jules. Of all the filthy, lying, scurrilous harangues, this is the worst! And it's that old fool's daughter that my son, my son! wants to marry. There's no loyalty nor pride in him, no self-respect, no decency——"

"Why?" Georges cut in quietly. "Is it loyalty to deny the truth? Everything that old Fitts has said about us is true, and you know it is. You haven't a leg to stand on, and no one knows that better than you. You can't do a thing to him, libel suit or no libel suit."

Jules sighed. "I never had any objection to Fitts," he said regretfully. "There is such a multitude of fools in the world that a wise man, even if he is your enemy, should be appreciated. There is one error he made, however: he presumed to believe the Constitution of the United States.

"It is a strange thing," he went on meditatively, while Georges, watching him with sudden sharpness, paled, "that wise men are frequently naïve. They believe that truth has sufficient vitality to protect its worshippers. It hasn't. Paradoxically, to serve truth is to serve death, even if truth itself is immortal. Of course, I am not speaking of death by auto da fe or hanging or a knife in the back. No, we are too refined, or too barbarous, for that, these days. We do the job more neatly; we, like the Roman Church, don't believe in bloodletting. We kill a man economically——"

"What do you mean?" demanded Georges, his voice shaking.

Jules sighed again. "It was only this morning that I was in-
283

formed that Professor Fitts has been compelled to resign from Columbia University. I am very sorry for that. As I said before, we have few wise men. Professor Fitts was too naïve, unfortunately. I imagine he will find it a little difficult to secure another chair in any American university." And now he looked fully at his nephew with his hooded eyes.

There was a prolonged and intense silence. Slowly, Antoinette turned in her chair and stared at her husband, who was beginning to smile grimly. But Georges, white and still, regarded his uncle, hardly breathing.

Then he said, almost inaudibly: "You did that to him. You cut his throat. You. He's an old man, and he never saved any money; he gave it all away. His work is his life. He——he never harmed anyone in his life. I didn't often agree with him, because he's a dear damned old idealist, but he was so damned *good!* And now you've killed him."

Jules lifted his elegant hand with a pained gesture. "Georges! Not so much melodrama, please! Not at my age. Besides, you are unjust. We are not the only ones poor old Fitts attacked, and I assure you that his attacks on us meant nothing at all. Had we attacked him in return, we would just have centered attention on a——on a matter we'd rather not have noticed yet. But evidently others have not been so discreet."

Georges wet his lips. He said dully: "You're a liar. I know you're a liar."

Jules shrugged, spread out his hands in a resigned gesture.

Georges drew in his breath sharply, and his pale face flushed. "But you can't shut his mouth! I'll help him! You can't hurt me with your sliminess and schemes! How you got your money doesn't bother me, and never would; that's not the point. But you deserve exposure for all this, and I tell you——"

Jules lifted his hand again, and smiled indulgently. "Georges, wait a minute, or I'll be disappointed in you. I wouldn't like that, you know. Now, I'll make you a proposition: I'll use my influence to have old Fitts re-appointed at Columbia immediately, if you give me your solemn promise that you'll marry his daughter as soon as possible."

There was a stupefied silence after his words. Leon's face became almost idiotic in its expression; Antoinette blinked, shook her head slightly, blinked and stared and swallowed. As for Georges, he was so astounded that his face wrinkled and contorted itself into a dozen different grimaces.

Leon finally struggled to speak, and his voice was so

strangled, so thin, that it did not sound like his. "What—what do you mean? What is all this? Are you insane, Jules?"

Jules turned to his nephew, who had stopped grimacing, and who was now looking at him intently, and beginning to smile a little, with unpleasantness.

"If I had known yesterday that you wished to marry Professor Fitts' daughter, Georges, I am certain I might have prevented his dismissal. But the harm is only temporary. But remember: marriage very soon or the Professor starves."

"But what is this?" roared Leon, purpling.

Jules regarded him patiently. "It is so very simple, Leon. Professor Fitts loose, writing inflammatory and disagreeable things about us and our friends, getting them published, as no doubt he would, is a dangerous thing. But Professor Fitts restored to his lost chair, his daughter married to Georges, is a Professor Fitts tamed and made innocuous."

"If you think having a Bouchard as a son-in-law would muzzle the old man, you're mistaken," said Georges. But he was smiling with enjoyment, and he winked at his uncle.

Jules smiled back, stood up. "But, Georges, that'll be your job, you see." He tapped his nephew on the shoulder. "Within a few weeks the wisest men in the country, in the world, will be drooling patriotic imbecilities. We'd like to present Professor Fitts with a bib, too."

When he had gone, there seemed nothing to say. But Georges sat on the edge of the library table and gnawed restlessly at a hangnail. All at once, he looked at his father, and burst into a shout of laughter.

CHAPTER XXXVII

UPON his marriage in 1915 to Marion Fitts, daughter of Professor Fitts, Georges Bouchard had abandoned his former nonchalant and Bohemian manner of living and had leased a mangificent fourteen-room apartment overlooking Central Park. Marion had been reared in austere and dusty shabbiness, and in the years of her young womanhood she had been proud of this, proud of her father, proud of her inherent aristocracy which needed, so she said, no luxuries to prove it. She had desultorily kept house for her father with the help of an indifferent maid in some obscure and gritty section of old Brooklyn, where the ratty and neglected back gardens no longer put up a brave fight against the prevailing codfish smell of the near-by Bay. She had affected, in the mánner of the "new generation," to find something humorous in the large, frame, dilapidated house where she had lived with her father, and spoke of their neighbors, mostly poor Jewish and Italian families, as "amusing." The living room, as she said, was "simply a wild hodge-podge of mountainous books, and old family antiques (Grandma Burnridge cherished this piece of Staffordshire ware, as it belonged to her great-grandmother)." In short, threadbare faded rugs, books, scarred mahogany tables, glass-shaded lamps, dingy curtains, dark oil portraits, hideous Chinese vases, "mission oak furniture," and dirty tapestries, were mingled indiscriminately with dust, cobwebs, paper litter and manuscripts. Professor Fitts apparently was unaware of the state of his house, and in a state of complete and dusty absentmindedness ate the atrocious meals prepared for him by the indifferent maid. Marion, for a time, was secretary to the head of a local Settlement House, donating her services, and finding those who patronized the House more "amusing" than ever. She had a light, gay, brave way of talking, and her stories, only faintly colored and exaggerated, provided endless entertainment for her friends and admirers. She had "jotted" down some of the stories, which, after retailing, seemed quite interesting, and often spoke carelessly and humorously of combining them some day into a book, "which probably won't sell at all, dears, people not being interested in the slightest in segments of Real Life."

Though appallingly sentimental and affected, she unconsciously recognized the fact that she was a mediocrity, and her real affection for her father had in it an element of gratitude that his existence made it unnecessary for her to prove that she was an intellectual. With reason, she was proud of this emaciated, stooping, absent, and fiery man. His theories were her Bible, his ethics her Ten Commandments. Lacking real discernment, never having crashed against reality even in the Settlement House, she would have faithfully swallowed anything her father had told her. He was a radical, a hater of pretense and foolishness and injustice and greed, and she was all this, also, without the faintest idea of what they really were. Had he been the silliest patriot, the most chauvinistic of fools, she would have followed him also, believed all he said implicitly.

Marion had many well-bred poses, chief among them being an indulgent tolerance, an air of sprightly and sensitive sympathy, a clear English accent, a personal fastidiousness that did not extend beyond her person, and which certainly did not object to grimy bathtubs and dusty areas under beds and powder-strewn dressers and dingy furniture and gritty floors. Certain flower-scents made her "quite ill," especially when embodied in perfumes worn by people she disliked; she was quite a martyr, she admitted, to "odors." However, her sensitiveness became oddly blunt in her own home, where the smell of untended drains and grimey and unaired bedrooms was quite palpable, and the stench of the Bay, when the wind was coming from it, quite overpowering to less patrician noses.

She had two classes of friends, which she was careful never to try to fuse together: the Greenwich Village class, and the carefully refined, aristocratic and slightly pinkish Bohemians with which Lucy Van Eyck filled her Fifth Avenue house. These Bohemians were all people of wealth, family, background, or of the more substantial professions, impeccable people, who dabbled in radicalism with the tips of curious white fingers, and liked to discuss forbidden subjects with great tolerance, scientific interest and comprehension. They all disliked "stuffiness" and the middle-class "virtues," but were very careful to adhere to both stuffiness and virtue in their private lives, for all their "reasonable" talk. At their perfectly appointed parties they seriously discussed modern "tendencies in art and poetry," admired the newer and more tawdry young writers with solemnity, dissected sexual abnormalities, affected to despise the Victorian poets and authors, jeered at a suetty Government, all in well-bred and cultivated voices. Occasionally, but very, very occasionally, they invited one of the "new-art" poets or painters or writers or theorists to a party, and found his presence so stimulating, so breath-taking, so utterly confusing, that it was a long time before another invitation was extended to him, or his kind. They could conduct countless parties and discussions upon him, months after, and it was only when his fruity personality began to grow dim that they held their breaths, took the plunge, and invited another young man to disorganize them. They served a good purpose, however; buying, as they did, numerous impressionistic and cubist paintings and statuary and portraits, and hiding these fearfully and hurriedly away in their attics, they kept the perpetrators from city charities or from making public many of their individual atrocities.

Professor Fitts had been an old friend of Percival Van Eyck, and Lucy had become fond of Marion. She had wanted her son, Thomas, to marry her, in spite of the Professor's obvious lack of worldly sustenance. Ladies, she said, were becoming rarer every day, and whatever else Marion was, she was a lady. Lucy, it can be discerned, was not at all deluded as to Marion's real intellectualism, nor deceived by her poses. In fact, the girl touched her; mediocrity trying to grow wings but unable to fly because of heavy mud feet, seemed very pathetic to Lucy.

It was at one of Lucy's parties that Marion met Lucy's second cousin, Georges Bouchard. Of the same type, the same nervous, apprehensive Bohemianism, the same class, the same traditions, they fell in love immediately. Georges' brilliance and truly splendid mind, however, did not detect Marion's innocent affectations; the inability of the masculine nature to judge the feminine nature protected her. He believed her to have "a fine mind," and to possess an extraordinary intellect. Moreover, though he would have denied this himself, the fact that she was a lady, the daughter of a professor at Columbia University, particularly the daughter of the illustrious Professor Fitts, and a friend of Lucy's, were all factors in her favor. He got himself invited to her home, where he met the shy, elusive but passionate old man, the Professor, and was much impressed by his thin but cogent diatribes against his family and what his family represented. The old man was very cautious and distant at first, suspecting and disliking, but he finally came to like Georges and to consider him his friend. He was dimly pleased when Marion told him of her engagement to the young editor.

Once, during a discussion with Georges, he said: "There is a great deal of excitement nowadays about the 'new psychology,' an urge, on the part of educators and psychiatrists and psychologists generally, to cure grave social problems by suggestion, education and comprehensive patience, and by the light of a knowledge of human behavior. The educators and psychiatrists and psychologists are all a-dither over the prospects, quite starry-eyed over it, as if it were something new, this influencing mankind by subtle and understanding methods. Poor innocents! They don't know that politicians, priests and rascals generally have used these methods with magnificent success ever since society first became organized; they didn't call it 'psychology,' however, but they practised it just the same, with lies, propaganda, emotionalism and chicanery. In these days, particularly, the warmakers, the armaments manufacturers, are employing it very nicely. If nothing is done to stop them, we shall be hypnotized into entering the European war." Without a change in his calm, dispassionate voice, but with the fire beginning to sparkle in his eye, he added: "I am to write a series of articles against your family, Georges. Of course, you know they are wholesale murderers. Murder on a large scale gets into the history books, but murder on a small scale ends only in a sordid little note in wardens' records. Your family and their kind have added luster to mass-murders."

When he was dismissed from the University, a sort of blank incredulity fell on him, a stunned state. Georges then saw how really innocent the man was. Only an innocent man could possibly have believed that attacking the unscrupulous strong would not turn apparently honest men against him. Like all idealists, he believed in the fundamental love of mankind for justice; he believed that it was only necessary to show it the truth, and it would inevitably follow it. He was the curious, idealistic schoolmaster type, a quaint and unbelievable combination of sophistication and naïveté, intellect and childish simplicity, having a theoretical knowledge of human nature but unable to recognize it when seen, believing firmly that ills and vices and discrepancies and monstrosities of all kinds could be educated from the minds of men, and revealing at one time both cynicism and credulity, gentle tolerance and the bitterest sort of intolerance. He lived the true academic life, seeing the world in huge and distorted colors, a grotesque and vivid place that existed only in a mind removed from reality. More than he loved his daughter, he loved justice; a lie was the most vicious of all things to him.

(He had met Jules Bouchard once or twice. He told Georges that Jules reminded him of a hooded cobra. Georges had laughed a little, then stared. His respect for Professor Fitts sank a trifle.)

His dismissal seemed to uproot him; he was like a plant that had grown its roots deeply into the soil. Now he was torn up, thrown in the glaring sun; he lay there, withering, parched, dying, his roots in the air. Worse than the loss of his position was the murder of his lifelong beliefs. He would have survived the loss of position, but the destruction of the beliefs was fatal to him. When he was re-instated, he went about in a subdued hushed state; when spoken to suddenly, he would lift bemused and dimly clouded eyes. He wrote nothing more. The plant restored to the soil could not regain its old vitality; its leaves drooped, and its roots had lost their power to extract nourishment from the earth. Georges had no need to exert pressure on the old man, as Jules had suggested. Two years after Georges married his daughter,

Marion, Professor Fitts resigned from the University. Georges, who had believed that the Professor was inherently militant, that nothing could stop his angered tongue, was amazed at this swift decay of the idealist who had not been able to face reality.

Georges, soon after his marriage, had assigned the work of editing his Windsor newspaper to his associate, and had bought a partnership in a third-class New York newspaper. This paper had seen distinctly better days and was on the definite downgrade when Georges became associated with it. He began a series of articles about the causes of the War, economic, political and ethnic. Brilliant, conservative and sardonic, he wrote with irony and wryness, and newly interested readers tried to discover when he was being serious and when contemptuous. He had a laconic but colorful style, a rapid and pungent style, that constantly titillated and challenged, amused and provoked. Within two years the newspaper moved up to second class and was ambitiously negotiating for an opening in the first ranks. Rivals disdainfully said that it was his profanity, his lack of "reverence," his skirting of blasphemy, that caught the attention of impotent fools. More discerning people recognized the solid bourgeois, conservative but tolerant, entrenched but reasonable, under the sharp and bitter bubbles of his style.

Marion found it no hardship to leave her "amusing" neighbors and her dirty old house, and accustom herself to the luxury of her fourteen-room apartment overlooking the park. It is true she mentioned to her friends, with amusement, that she was now among the "Philistines," but Marion and the Philistines seemed to like each other at the very start. Though she had been as violent a suffragette as her well-bred and snobbish temperament would allow, she became less and less an exponent of women's rights, and incidentally of the rights of oppressed and minority groups. Eventually, and still tolerantly, of course, she could speak seriously of the "menace" to American life of "indigestible groups," with "alien ideals, religions and ways of life, inimical to American national health." But always tolerantly, gravely, if a trifle menacingly. A year after her marriage she became an important officer in The Patriotic League for Freedom, which had for its object "the promulgation of American ideals, traditions and ways of life, and the elimination of subversive forces which tend to destroy and undermine the foundations on which the Republic was built." It was probably accidental, but no Jews, Catholics, first or second generation Europeans, with the exception of a few of recent British origin, were admitted to membership. This League, begun in precociously grave innocence, was, twenty years later, to be a dangerous source of Fascism, enriched by funds donated by the Bouchards and similar groups; the American ideals of tolerance, justice and freedom, which it had elected to cherish and disseminate, became the fasces of stupidity and reaction, intolerance and hatred. It proved thoroughly to the intelligent that noble ideals could also wear two coats, and words, fine in themselves, were the mercenaries of any man able to pay. Democracies, it was proved, were, after all, but bought women.

Georges and Marion had gone to England and France and their allies in 1917, and upon his return Georges began another series of articles, entitled: "—and Now?" Brilliant and discerning though he was, his articles were full of elevated nonsense. He apparently realized this himself, for once in a while the reader had the impression that he had written with one eye closed.

The couple had just returned, and when Jules came to New York on a private mission, he decided to visit his nephew and the latter's wife. He liked Georges better than' he did any of the other younger members of the family, his own sons included. A consummate hypocrite himself, Jules liked people who were not hypocrites, though he frequently found them tedious, it being his observation that only hypocrites had color. Georges, who was only infrequently a hypocrite, was an agreeable exception. Jules, however, detested though he tolerated Marion. He was always highly edified by her "being clear-eyed all over the place." Despite her attempts at uniqueness and originality and intellect, she irritated her husband's uncle to the point where he desired to slap her thoroughly. Tall, "rangy," long-legged and thin-hipped and boyish of figure, with lambent serious gray eyes, pale smooth face and humorless mouth, clean scrubbed hands and trim head, she went about with what she believed to be an American air of feminine competence and health. She liked to ride horseback, astride, in breeches that set off her slim boyish legs and trim waist, and her game of tennis, she admitted, was exceptional. She used the phrase "American health-ideal" very frequently, and if she thought at all of her smoky evenings in the fetid atmosphere of Greenwich Village restaurants, it was with a shudder. Firmer than ever in the belief that she was an intellectual, she was chairman or president of several cultural clubs; this, however, did not prevent her from becoming a leader in the Girl Scouts. Totally without humor of any kind, she liked to think of herself as possessing "a gallant and humorous spirit." She had echoed her radical and palely fiery old father; married to a Bouchard, now, she echoed the conservatism, the caution, the aloofness of the family. Her letters to Antoinette had long ago mollified her mother-in-law and won her affection, and though Leon privately thought his son's wife a serious affected fool, he had nothing worse against her.

She was not insensible to the fact that the formidable Jules Bouchard, the head of the mighty clan, regarded her with indifferent amusement, though she did not know the reason. She had been respectful enough to him, when they had met, and had gazed at him worshipfully with her shining gray eyes, and it had hurt her extremely when he had ignored her after bestowing a faint smile upon her. Consequently, the mere mention of his name was enough to disconcert and frighten her. So when Georges announced that he had received a letter from his uncle, who expected to visit them for a day or two, she was paralyzed for several moments with joy, apprehension and terror. In a fever, she began to plan a dinner party in honor of Uncle Jules, and burst into tears when Georges insisted that Jules had expressly requested that his visit be quiet, as he was in New York "unofficially." "Do you want the damned place swarming with reporters and mayors and senators and smelly politicians of all kinds?" he demanded irately. And Marion, who had wanted exactly that, replied "Of course not, Georges."

Her father, the retired Professor, was living with them now, broken in health and spirit. Marion, worried, confided to her husband that "Dad was a problem," and certainly no asset even to a family dinner. Should she dispose of him while Jules was there, by shipping him "to the country," or ask friends to take him off her hands? Old people (though Dad was hardly more than sixty-five) were so tiresome, and Uncle Jules might be so bored. This consultation took place in Georges' and Marion's elaborate Queen Anne bedroom, and Georges, without replying, went to the living room where his father-in-law was sitting reading the evening paper prior to dinner. Unseen by Professor Fitts, Georges stood at a distance and studied him. He sat there, his long emaciated figure slumped bonelessly in the satin damask depths of a chair, his glasses with their black ribbon fallen upon his sunken chest. Evidently he had become engrossed in a maze of vague and heavy thoughts, for the newspaper had slipped from his hand and lay in a heap by the chair. His pointed gray beard, sparse and ashen-colored, mingled with the ribbon of his glasses, for his chin had dropped; his bony knees were on a level with his mouth, which, having fallen open, was a dry dark cavern in his beard.

For a long time, unseen, Georges stood there and looked at his father-in-law. He saw the web of tangled and vaguely tormented thoughts that clouded that gray sunken face, the fixed dull eyes that stared emptily at nothing, the limp lax hand, so beautiful of line and shape and length but so impotent and dead. This was the Professor Fitts who hardly more than three years ago had visited President Wilson and had thereafter poured into the press vitriolic, passionate and loathing diatribes against the "internal enemies!" This weary, beaten, desolate old man, this bewildered and anguished old man, this already dead old man! When Georges returned to his wife, she was surprised to see how pale he was and what a glint there was in his eye.

"I don't think Uncle Jules will object to your father," he said quietly. "In fact, I'd like him to see him!"

He met Jules at the station the next day in his own magnificent Pierce-Arrow, which was decorated by a liveried chauffeur. Jules had taken an inconspicuous drawing room instead of the ornate private car in which members of the family usually travelled. Georges was shocked by the change in his uncle's appearance. Jules' hair was now entirely white, a startling contrast to the dark skull-like face beneath it. The smiling puckered mouth gave him a mummified appearance, and though he moved briskly as usual, there was a sort of tremor about him. To Georges' disturbed comments, he replied jocosely and affectionately that he supposed he was on his last legs, but he had been given to understand that that damned Spanish flu frequently left its victims feeling so. As they drove through the streets, the aspects of a great city gone mad with the ecstasy of war engrossed and amused him.

"War," he remarked, "may have its nastier moments, but it can't be denied that it gives the people something to live for as well as die for. Peace, or monotony, is merely oxen hitched to yokes. If the idealists really want to abolish war, they ought to stop fighting the dragons of armaments makers, ignorance, greed and racial hate, and get after the real enemy, the emasculated dove of peace. What the idealists fail to realize is that people *like* war, for it is adventure and gaiety and excitement, as well as death and iron and blood.

"Now, for instance," he went on, relaxing against the velvet upholstery, and shifting his exhausted body into a more comfortable position, "all the thousands of men in our plants and our mills are exempted from military service. Yet, what has happened? We have had to resort to asking the draft
293

boards quietly to reject men who try to enlist. Why are these men willing to face death and suffering and mud and shells? To get away from monotony, sameness, drabness, the old treadmill. Leisure, peace, extra money in their pockets, a new and higher standard of living, automobiles and security, drive them slowly mad. They want action and excitement, the feeling that they are participating in something important. And peace never made anyone feel important; security never gave a young and eager man anything but the feeling that he was slowly atrophying." He shook his head and grinned faintly. "If Prohibition becomes a permanent law in America, we'll have to have a war occasionally to keep the people satisfied. Remove alcohol and war, and you'll have a people appalled and frenzied by the face of reality. Any calamity can happen, any horror, that will offer them escape."

Georges looked at the buildings smothered in flags, the feverish tempo of the people on the streets. He pursed his lips grimly. "What are you going to give them when the war is over?" he asked. "You've got them all stirred up; they won't settle down for twenty years after this."

Jules smiled. "When the Kaiser is done with, we'll have to find them a new devil, I'm afraid. Finding devils, though, has always been the problem of rulers."

"Yes, I know that. It used to be Jews or heretics or witches, or messiahs."

" 'Used to be'? You forget that we still have Jews and heretics and witches, and messiahs."

"Oh, you can't use that old rot any more. This is America, and the Twentieth Century. The people are more or less literate, and they'll find your fine Italian hands manipulating the silly old devils."

"You overestimate the people, my dear Georges. Stupidity is an inheritance just as is the color of one's eyes. Wise men are never born from generations of fools, and there is nothing so credulous and silly as a literate man whose ancestors burnt books. Given the slightest encouragement, he'll burn books, too.

"Out of the welter and ruin of this war is bound to emerge something we can give the people to hate. What will it be? It is too early to tell yet. Perhaps it will be a new sort of government in one of the countries that is bound, by novelty or originality or boldness or oddness, to be unpopular and suspect. Perhaps we can stir up a moribund Church to new excesses; religions always get new life from blood spilled in wars. This war is going to have profound repercussions. The people aren't going to settle down peacefully, as Wilson so nobly prophesies they will. You can't incite simplicity to rage and hatred, and then ask it to love its enemies and help reconstruct them. That's asking too much of human nature. For a generation or more, we'll have rumors of wars, if not actual wars. We'll have hatred and rages and madnesses and furies on a gigantic scale such as the world has never seen before."

Georges turned to his uncle and smiled cynically. "And the armaments makers, of course, won't exactly lose anything by this."

Jules laughed lightly. "We give the people what they want," he said. "Beyond that, even God can't go."

Georges regarded his uncle for a long moment; his eyeglasses glittered. But he said nothing.

Marion, clad "sensibly" in something vaguely resembling a uniform, greeted Jules with suppressed emotionalism. She had, she informed him, just returned from rolling bandages at the Red Cross. Everyone, she said, must do his bit these terrible days. Georges broke into her speech abruptly and said that Jules was tired and just recovering from an illness. He would probably like to rest in his room until dinner. Georges assigned his valet to assist his uncle, and when Jules, apologizing affectionately to his nephew's wife, retired, Georges firmly told Marion that should anyone inquire if Jules were there, she was to deny it vigorously. He asked about his father-in-law, who was absent, and Marion listlessly replied that the Professor had gone for his morning walk in the Park. "I've told him a dozen times that Uncle Jules was coming," she said, "but he forgets it as soon as I've said it."

"It's probably just as well," remarked Georges. But when his wife demanded to know what he meant by that cryptic remark, he refused to answer.

The Professor was a great trial to Marion. He had been hard enough to keep "respectable" in the old days, and he was worse now. She had to tend him, she said, like a child, almost to dress him, for he wouldn't allow Georges' man to come near him. When expecting friends, she would nervously brush him and pull him straight, scold him for spots on his clothing, would repeat over and over to him that he was only to say a word or two to the guests, and then retire. This was very necessary, for occasionally through the fog in which he lived he would catch a glimpse of the outside world, and would say something that would paralyze or excessively amuse strangers.

Before dinner that night, she nervously rehearsed him

over and over in the things he must say to Jules, and he listened, blinking his faded eyes solemnly behind his glasses, murmuring courteously from time to time. Because of her almost tearful insistence, he consented to allow Georges' man to dress him, and he appeared at the dinner table faultlessly dressed, a white tie decorating his immaculate white, winged collar, a silk handkerchief in his pocket. His beard had been combed and brushed; even his glasses had been expertly polished, and his eyes shone behind them with a vague and childlike brightness. Jules had seen him only once, about four years ago, though he had read everything he had written. He was visibly startled when he was asked to remember that this dead old man was the impassioned, lean, and flaming-eyed Professor he had secretly admired and respected; in fact, he seemed actually shocked, and when he replied to the murmured and formal greeting his voice shook noticeably. Georges saw all this; he smiled to himself and narrowed his lids.

The butler unobtrusively assisted the old man at the table, and by silent nudges recalled him to the fact that he was supposed to be eating. For, from the start, he seemed to be fascinated by Jules, and kept smiling vaguely, and blinking his eyes at him. Once in a while he would murmur something stammeringly, some inanity that was totally irrelevant. Finally, he asked Jules when he thought the war would end, but did not seem to hear the other's conventional reply.

Marion and Georges appeared to forget the old man's presence; Marion was nervously absorbed in impressing Jules with their elaborate establishment and the perfectly cooked and perfectly served dinner. "Of course," she said, in her cheery and humorous voice, so clear-clipped and British, "one is so engrossed these days in war work, the Red Cross, and all the Committees, and the excitements, and canteens, that one forgets that one is a wife and housekeeper. Why, there are days and nights when Georges and I hardly have the time to speak to each other!"

The Patriotic League for Freedom, she informed Jules, had a delegate at all the larger camps, inculcating American ideals and patriotism in the soldiers. They also had a large amusement hall and canteen in New York, where soldiers on leave could gather and be instructed and respectably amused. The soldiers, remarked Jules, must enjoy this very much, and be very grateful. Marion smiled, gratified, but Georges' glasses flashed again, and he smiled lightly. For the first time he began to wonder if his wife weren't something of a fool.

We aren't, went on Marion seriously, really at war with

296

the German people. Some Americans were rather stupid about that, in fact, most of them were, in spite of the President's solemn speeches and pleadings. It was a fine-drawn distinction, no doubt, but one which an intelligent person could readily see, that America had no enmity against the German people but only against their frightful Government. And it was distinctly obstinate on the part of the Germans not to realize this immediately, not to understand that all the Americans cared about was freeing them from oppression and misery and militarism, and inculcating in them——

"The American way of life," suggested Jules, regarding her blandly.

"Yes, that is it!" responded Marion eagerly. An instant later, on seeing her husband's suppressed smile, she flushed a little, wondering if she were being "ribbed." But surely she was not; she was just too sensitive. She had said nothing silly, but only what everyone else was saying.

However, she became a little stiff for a time, and through her fear of Jules, and her gratification at having him in her home, and her excitement, came a small shadow of hatred for him. More and more she became convinced that she had been subtly affronted, but where the affront lay, and what had caused it, she could not tell, though her bewildered mind went round and round. She fixed her lambent gray eyes upon him, and held her chin high and serious as usual, and talked gravely; Georges, with a return of his affection, thought she was infinitely pathetic. But why haven't I noticed before that she is a fool? he thought impatiently.

The old Professor had definitely stopped eating now; he had fixed his empty yet curiously avid gaze upon Jules, who was resolutely not looking at him. His mouth had fallen open; drops of moisture appeared on the beard around the aperture.

New York, said Marion, was a changed city. No one seemed to care for art any longer, or music. Metropolitan stars were touring the camps all over the country, singing for the soldiers. Everything was war; one breathed it, thought it, read it, heard it, slept in it. The theatres were full of war plays; every novel was a war novel. New York was just a huge armed camp. But no one would want it to end; in spite of anxiety and inconveniences and meatless, heatless, wheatless days. One had to sacrifice, as well as "our boys." It could not end, dared not end, until Germany was crushed, and the Allies sat in Berlin and dictated terms. Then, and then only, would the world return to peace, to a new era of joy and happiness; a Golden Age. Why, this was just a purge, a renaissance, portals to a new heaven and a new earth! Her eyes glowed, color appeared in her smooth pale cheeks, her lips brightened. Christ! thought Georges.

"Don't you think so, Uncle Jules?" she pleaded, gazing at him earnestly.

Jules sipped the excellent sherry and inclined his head. "Most certainly, my dear," he replied. "Everyone seems to think so, so it must be so. I haven't the slightest doubt there'll be a new earth after this. And probably a new hell," he added, smiling gently upon her.

Marion seemed a trifle jolted; Georges grinned. But he was infuriated. It was bad enough that Jules saw what a fool Marion was, but it was enraging that he should ridicule her so openly in her home and at her own table. Worst of all was her not realizing it.

Unable to resist the temptation, he said to Jules: "We must have made millions out of this, haven't we?"

Jules smiled with sudden enjoyment as he glanced at his nephew. "Yes, millions—and millions," he replied urbanely.

Marion looked from one man to the other; a fine wrinkle appeared between her fine straight brows, and her mouth opened a trifle. After that she was silent for some time. It was not until Jules informed his nephew that Peter had enlisted as a private that animation returned to her blank face.

"Peter!" exclaimed Georges, edified. "But then, he was always hot-seated about something! He went in heavily for socialism, didn't he? Another Catiline, championing the 'submerged.' But what a jolt this must be to the family! How do they take it?"

"Like castor oil," said Jules, "and with the same sort of faces. Anyway, he is at Camp Brixton, and is being put through his paces, I can tell you! If it doesn't knock all the idealism out of him, I'll be much mistaken. Orders are out not to spare him; he has a particularly tough corporal over him. Outside of that, he'll not be in any danger; we've seen to that, too."

Georges burst into ribald laughter, but Marion, a renewed shine in her eyes, exclaimed: "Peter! Isn't Peter the handsome one, Georges, the youngest one? The son of your poor cousin Honore, who died on the *Lusitania?* How wonderful, how splendid that is! Why do you laugh, Georges? Can't you see how it is? Can't you see he is going to fight to avenge his father?" She turned to Jules pleadingly. "Isn't that the reason, Uncle Jules?"

Jules stopped smiling, and regarded her benignly. "Of course, my dear, that is the reason." She smiled back at him tremulously, satisfied. But Georges gloated over his plate,

298

and looked at his uncle with an expression that became more and more ribald and knowing.

Everyone had forgotten the old Professor. He had sat there in a sunken fog of forgetfulness. Nothing that had been said at the table had penetrated that fog. He had sat in his own enchantment, a corpse that breathed and swallowed, and opened and shut its mouth, and blinked its eyes. It held a glass of sherry in its hand; when Georges had laughed, the hand had shaken suddenly, and the sherry splashed upon the table.

Dinner proceeded amiably to a successful conclusion. It was when coffee was served that Jules felt impelled to look at the old Professor. He was somewhat taken aback to see that the other was regarding him fixedly, with eyes that had turned to fire through his fog. He had become horribly alive; he was staring at Jules with a suddenly aware and terrible face. His shriveled hands clutched the edge of the table, and he was leaning forward a little. Through his bearded and parted lips his teeth glittered.

Marion, following Jules' eye, was alarmed at what she saw. Georges looked, too, and became sober immediately. But the old man saw neither of them; he continued to stare at Jules, and it was like the quickening of flame rising to a frightful crescendo to watch him.

At last he spoke, distinctly, clearly and loudly.

"Murderer," he said.

He had been killed, a little later, while dazedly walking in Central Park. He had been struck by a car, and had died instantly.

As the years went on, no one remembered him, except Georges. It is true that his daughter had a kind of memory of him. But it was a glorified, unreal memory of a man who had never really existed. She quoted him often, and the opinions she alleged had been his were stuffy, platitudinous, portentous and stupid. He was her Scripture. Professor Fitts, thought Georges, would have been considerably surprised at the things Marion affirmed he had said!

But Georges truly remembered him. As year rolled into year, the Professor became a clearer, stronger, more imminent presence for him, his stature increasing, his voice more resonant as it pierced through the confusion of the Nineteen-twenties. It was a prophetic voice, stern yet sorrowful, not bitter, but only sad.

CHAPTER XXXVIII

BUT that had been several years ago, and now Georges Bouchard, this day in 1927, walked slowly with Peter through the immense stretches of his country estate, Southfield. They were talking earnestly. Occasionally they stopped to admire a view, or examine a small field of new young corn. Southfield was one of the larger country homes of the Dutchess County colony, and one of the most beautiful. The two men paused at the edge of the estate, and Georges pointed out the far-distant red roofs of Jay Regan's summer home. They had been talking about matters not much related to Jay Regan, but now Georges said:

"You've met him, haven't you? A real feudal baron. I like him. We'll go over tomorrow or the next day."

Peter was silent. The sun was hot on his shoulders and bare head. He had coughed hardly at all, this morning. The grass was pungent and thick and dusty. Sometimes, through the trees, he could see the hot dazzle of the Hudson. There was an almost imperceptible roll in the land, and a hundred different shades of green, ranging from olive to the palest golden-jade. Behind them, the old white stone house with its latticed windows was buried in masses of warm motionless trees.

Georges liked Peter, and was vaguely sorry for him. Moreover, he had sympathy and understanding for him, which he concealed very well under a dry and quizzical manner. It had not surprised him that his wife, Marion, did not like Peter, and at times was distinctly antagonistic towards the young man. She was not intelligent enough to guess that he was often disdainfully amused by her, but he unwittingly communicated to her his opinion that she was of negligible importance and comprehension. However, he was a Bouchard, and Marion had long ago got into the attitude that she was a sort of earnest "clear-eyed" priestess ministering at the altar of the family. (Peter had guessed that someone had told her that she had "candid, clear-eyed opinions," and was humorlessly living up to the flattery. She annoyed him to the point of acute irritability at times, and he had all he could do to remember her unimportance and feel compassion for her.)

The two men found a seat under a group of hot glittering trees, and sat down. They smoked in silence for some time. Then Peter asked quietly: "So, what am I going to do?"

"I," answered Georges reflectively, removing his spectacles and polishing them with an absent manner, "would advise you not to have a romantic approach. I think you are suffering from it, very badly. I've listened carefully, and I must admit I've come to the conclusion that a great part of your apprehension and excitement is based on emotion, without very much proof." He smiled. "Here and there, we have an authentic romanticism in the affairs of men. But not often. Most affairs are cut-and-dried, and colored a safe nice gray monotone. Look about you: how many lives are there that are exciting and tumultuous? Practically none."

Peter regarded him with something like anger. "That's just the trouble! Here we are, one small island of a world in the midst of universal chaos, ruin, noise, the explosion of systems, mystery, danger, fire and death. And what do we do? We try to level our lives down to the amœbæ, where nothing happens but breeding and eating. We're like idiot housewives determinedly trying to keep house in the midst of earthquakes and tidal waves, and sweeping up cosmic debris with straw brooms. My God!" he added with sudden excitement, "it's horrible to see how our degrading little minds have tried to reduce space and time to ant heaps!"

Georges smiled at him with sympathetic amusement. "Perhaps so. But it's more comfortable that way, isn't it? Besides, it doesn't clutter things up. We can move slow sure inches, if we don't see the chaos outside our windows.

"Let's be 'idiot housewives' while we go into this matter. It boils down to this, sans romanticism and sentimentality: you want little Celeste, and little Celeste wants you. Obstacle number one: Henri. Backing up this obstacle, Christopher. It doesn't look complicated to me. All Celeste has to do is to kick Henri out, and take you on. Now, wait a minute; let me finish before you foam again. I've got something at stake, too, you know. Your book.

"You say you've not spoken to Celeste, and that she's fighting something out. Shucks. Women never 'fight out' anything they really want. They just go ahead and take it. If they don't, they don't want it. Women are absolutely without ethics, dear Peter. Present a woman with an ethic, and she'll honestly wonder what it is. If it is explained to her, she'll look at you with pitying contempt, and wonder why you have such a regard for the goddam worthless thing, which seems to serve

301

no other purpose in life than to make men tiresome and obstructionistic. Sometimes they do suffer, bless 'em; they're like the legendary donkey who starved to death because he couldn't make up his mind which of two bundles of hay he'd eat first. It's probably the only thing which makes it possible to keep civilization going, that imbecile inability of a woman to decide between two equally attractive possibilities. And that's what I think ails our little pet, Celeste."

He laughed at Peter's angered expression and rising color. He wagged a finger at him humorously. "That's it, exactly. Here is Henri, good-looking, bursting at the seams with virility, competent, knowing what he wants and prepared to steal it if necessary (and by the way, don't think that quality doesn't attract women, for it does). He exudes power as a tennis-player exudes sweat, out of every pore. Celeste may think she doesn't care anything about money, but even if she doesn't, consciously, she's been born in a money-atmosphere, and has breathed it all her life, and it's part of her flesh and blood. Henri's got most of the Bouchard bonds, and Celeste's heard dozens of reverent remarks about it, you can be sure. Then, he's new. He doesn't look like the rest of us. He doesn't talk like us. He makes fun of the Bouchards. She likes that. She's used to Bouchards, and probably bored to death by us. Not that I blame her.

"And here are you: a Bouchard, every inch, looking like us, with a voice like ours, and our manners. Even the 'nice' qualities she likes about you are only exaggerations of our own feeble consciences. The only asset you have is a family resemblance to her sweet little brother, Christopher, and a little less bloodthirstiness. She doesn't see, of course, that you're really more bloodthirsty than all the rest of us are, but that you've sublimated it. You appeal to her, for you are like her. Henri isn't like her, and paradoxically, he appeals to her for that reason, too.

"So, there you are. You've got to leave it to little Celeste, herself. Don't be so damned romantic: if she wants you, she'll take you, Christopher or no Christopher. If she finally decides she'd like sleeping with Henri better than with you, you'll just have to make the best of it. That's all."

Peter's thin face had turned grim. He stared before him, and made no answer. Georges chuckled. "It looks to me like a struggle between Celeste's natural human narcissism, which inclines one to love and admire that which is like us, and a natural human curiosity about that which is not like us. Which will win, self-love or monkey-curiosity? I know that doesn't sound romantic and soulful, but that's the fundamental struggle going on in Celeste's wind-swept bedchamber down at that god-awful Crissons."

Peter pulled up a few blades of grass and twisted them about his fingers. "That's all you can see, isn't it?" he commented bitterly.

Georges shrugged. "That's all there is to be seen, Pete. That's all there is to be seen in any human relationship. With no exceptions. But, naturally, you see pink ribbons and postures; that's because you are a writer. If you didn't see the pink ribbons and postures, you'd just be a columnist, or something like us, and just as obnoxious. And that brings me to something much more important than little Celeste's inclination to incest, or disinclination to it, and that is you, and your writing——"

Peter flung himself upon the grass with a violent gesture that made Georges smile covertly, and yet with sympathy.

"My writing! That isn't important to me, until I—until this matter about Celeste is settled, one way or the other."

Georges made a mocking, admonishing clucking-sound and shook his head. But the expression of sympathy still glittered in his eyes. "Don't be a fool. When a man talks like that, I suspect his masculinity. Don't glower at me. But it isn't quite virile, is it? to be so involved about one woman. Or at least, to be so involved about her that you can't think of important things. I thought you had cosmic urges, or something, and a passion to save the world, or something equally damfool; not that it's all gone down the drain because a little brat can't decide whose bed she'd rather occupy for the next few years." He tapped Peter on the arm with a gesture reminiscent of Francis. "Publishers like world-savers. They are usually good for ten thousand copies, and make lots of profitable excitement. How about getting down to business?"

Peter said sullenly: "I'm not in the mood. I thought you'd clarify things for me. But instead, you've smeared them all up."

Georges asked quietly: "All right, then. What do you want me to do?"

"I didn't talk to you about it to suggest something to you! I thought you'd have some ideas. But instead, you talk smartly. Like a half-wit."

Georges chuckled. "Well, I'm a half-wit, then. Hell, I suppose we'll do no business until Celeste decides to wear your favorite color on her nightie, or Henri's. Sometimes I think— Well, no matter. What can I do? We're all going to Crissons next week, for a few days. Do you want me to have

Marion tell Celeste you're much nicer than Henri? Well, then, you see how ridiculous it is. My own advice to you is to hang around Crissons until Christopher either kicks you out or Celeste picks you. Be all around her; don't let her see anyone else. Don't be romantic about her 'struggles.' They're quite primitive, I assure you, and have no connection at all with high ideals, or honor, or other dish-water, even if she thinks they have. Be masculine around her. Swagger. Be powerful. I can see," he added, "that I'm doing no good at all."

But Peter was laughing, involuntarily. "I'm not so sure. You've told me, without knowing it, that I've got to be right on the spot. I will be. The pressure on Celeste is too much. She hasn't had enough experience to decide anything as important as this, herself. Anyway, I'd already decided to fight Christopher."

"But you just thought you'd like to talk it over with some-one, eh?"

Peter confessed: "I'm afraid you're right. I already knew what I had to do, I suppose."

"And you've wasted all this time. And now, about your book. I read it until three this morning. Finished what you gave me, in fact."

Peter waited. But Georges carefully refilled his pipe, and smoked it contemplatively, staring, as he did so, at the waves of light and shadow which were sweeping over the deserted green fields and blowing trees. The sky was the deepest cobalt, hot and empty. The intense shrilling of insects, the low bumbling of bees and the smell of dry heated grass filled all the air.

Georges took the pipe from his mouth. Still staring into the distance he said, without emphasis: "I think it's balderdash."

Peter uttered an angry exclamation of deep offense. Georges smiled tranquilly. "Yes, it's balderdash. The biggest dish of it ever to turn up in this generation, I suppose. Nice, passionate, vehement, tumbling cataracts of mush, accompanied, however, by authentic thunder and some pretty good lightning effects."

"Every word of it is true!" exclaimed Peter, aroused. "I saw these things myself. I spent these eight post-war years in Europe, and I made it a point to go everywhere. If that's balderdash, damn you!——"

Georges' smile broadened peaceably. "I've no doubt you've written down what you saw, or think you saw. But, the trouble is, you saw too simply, too starkly. Life is never so simple and stark as all that. You've seen the crushed and maimed populace of Hungary; you saw Budapest after

304

Bela Kun and his bolsheviks and the rest of the hordes. Your heart bled for Hungary. For Germany. For France. For all the members of the European monkey-cage. Well, I don't blame you. Probably was messy and stinky. But human beings usually are, you know.

"But, you don't know the half of it. Rescue these people; set them up again, like tenpins. They'll stand there, dumb and stupid, and let the iron ball roll down on them again, and knock them flying, and wait patiently to be set up again. They remember nothing, and learn nothing. They can get out of the way; but they don't, and won't. They've got primitive fragments of minds; they could use them, if they wanted to. But still they don't, and won't. Why? Because they like the process of trying to knock hell out of other groups and races, and for the chance of knocking, they'll let themselves be knocked. That's all."

"You don't like people, do you?" asked Peter in a low voice.

"Frankly, I detest them. You see, I've known too much about them, Pete. I know what they are. Among intelligent men there are only two groups: those who see humanity completely, and hate it because of what they see, and those who see just as clearly, and are sorry. I belong to the first group, you to the second. And frankly, I think the first is the more intelligent.

"However, the first group rarely writes best sellers, for people don't like candid mirrors. They aren't pretty, and they aren't heroic. Humanity would rather see itself dressed in velvet tights, and have someone tell it that, though it's really a stinker of a fellow, there's a good simple heart beating under the hair on the baboon chest. Or it especially likes to hear that it's more sinned against than sinning, and all the miseries it's brought down deservedly on its ape-skull are really the fault of someone else.

"Successful writers usually take one or the other of these themes. They're invariably sure-fire. The degree of success, however, rests with the extent of the writer's passion, single-mindedness, colorfulness, gift of story-telling, and sincerity. That's why I think you'll be a marvelous success. You have the two themes: good simple heart under the hair, and more sinned against than sinning. Then, you've a natural gift for story-telling, and passion, and sincerity, and lots of drums and lightning offstage, with here and there an excellent and authentic scream."

Peter was profoundly humiliated. He said angrily: "You

305

say it's balderdash, but I gather you'll publish it, if I ever finish it. I don't understand you."

Georges laughed. "Publishing business, Pete, is just business. We're just like any other restaurateur: we give the people what they want to eat. If we don't, we go bankrupt. If we do, we can put rugs on our office floors and buy lots of chromium, and have size-twelves greeting the customers in the reception rooms." He regarded Peter with laughing incredulity: "You don't think we wanted to save the world, or elevate literature, or something, did you, by God?"

"You must think I'm a fool!" exlcaimed Peter, in a rage.

"I don't. Honestly, I don't. I think you are a brilliant writer. I think this book'll sell a hundred thousand. Look, Pete, we don't take books unless we dream of at least fifty-thousand copies. We make dozens of mistakes. I'll show your our stock-room. But we try to learn from mistakes. I don't think we'll make a mistake with you; but we can't tell ahead of time. It's non-fiction of course, and that's the worst of handicaps. Cinderella is still a "best seller"; you've been unconsciously clever enough to put all of humanity in the Cinderella role, and have conjured up the munitions makers and patriots and diplomatic Judases as the wicked stepmother and her daughters. You've produced the Prince Charming and called him Reason, and the fairy-godmother and called her Brotherly Love. Very good. We'll do it for you. You'll be a success. What more do you want?"

Peter compressed his lips. His expression was bitter, and dark with humiliation. For some devastating moments he felt ridiculous and sickeningly mortified. He saw himself as one of those men who are laughed at in secret by the intelligent, though adored by the people at large. For some of those devastating moments it seemed more desirable to be appreciated by the intelligent, than worshipped by the unintelligent. He even thought that the worship of the helpless and the simple was degrading, and that the savers of mankind deserved contempt and laughter. He thought: I'll throw it up.

Georges was studying him intently. The older man was suddenly disturbed. He put his hand on Peter's shoulder, and said: "Don't look like that. I may be wrong, you know. If you think I'm right, you're ruined." He smiled. "After all, what is the measure of right or wrong? The good is still that which survives. Those who believe as I do don't survive. But your kind does. Therefore, you must be right——"

"Childish reasoning," commented Peter. He stood up. The sun had crept under the trees. "Let's go back."

"Yes. Come into my study. We'll go over what you've written."

Marion had not yet returned from her golf. This was very nice, Georges remarked candidly. He still had a casual affection for his wife, but he could not help disliking fools. He had long ago found out how silly she was. Her father's death had affected him deeply. With his death, Georges and Marion became virtual strangers. Georges did not quite know why, and he had not cared to analyze the matter. Marion was at first bewildered, but she was not intelligent enough to retain her bewilderment.

The study was cool and quiet. Through the drawn venetian blinds Peter could see the smooth green lawns and the great trees sleeping in the sun. Georges sat at his desk, the pile of loose manuscript before him. Peter was suddenly diffident, as well as wretched. Georges was no longer a relative, to be argued with, and fought with, and to be visited, but a formidable publisher who could make a writer's future, or ruin him. There was something of Francis about him, in his angularity and leanness, and the dryness of his thin hands, and his coloring. There was even something of himself in Georges, thought Peter disinterestedly. All the Bouchards resembled each other. Georges was probably right in a good many things. A spot of subdued radiance, seeping through the blinds, glimmered on the top of Georges' bend head, which was narrow and partly bald. It glimmered even brighter on his glasses.

The papers rustled as he turned them. He frowned, chewed the corner of his lips. Peter, in turn, was no longer a younger relative, regarded more or less affectionately, and with sympathy, but one of the pestiferous breed known as authors, a breed so necessary, but so infernal. Sometimes Georges thought of them as putrefactive bacteria, who destroy carrion, and sometimes as the makers of carrion. Either way, they were a smell. Though a profitable smell. Sometimes.

Peter observed that Georges was shaking his head in dissent. "Look here, Pete, you've indicted America's entry into the world war as totally unnecessary, mercenary, financially manipulated, criminal, cynical, and the result of the machinations of—our family—and others.

"That's all nonsense, you know. Surely you realize that while our family, and others, stink pretty badly in the historical mess, there were other factors, some of them quite ethical and civilized, even by your standards.

"For instance, no one, even under the constant pressure he
307

was subjected to, could have been more peace-seeking than Wilson. He was faced with the basic problem as to whether the United States had the right to use the seas in peaceful commerce, or whether it would surrender those rights at the demand of Germany. We fought the War of 1812 against Britain on that very issue. International law has declared that neutral powers are to be free from attack, if not carrying contraband or munitions or other war supplies."

Peter smiled somberly. "But most of our vessels *were* carrying contraband and munitions and other war supplies. To the Allies. And using commercial vessels to do it. That's already been established."

Georges pursed his lips. "Well, that's open to debate. Anyway, in spite of all the pressure, we might have kept out of the war if Germany hadn't declared, on February 1, 1917, 'that any ship, of whatsoever nationality, found in a zone one hundred miles at sea from the British coast would be torpedoed by submarines without warning.' This meant, you realize, that ships not carrying contraband, but any passenger or commercial vessel, bound for any neutral port, would be torpedoed, if passing within British waters. Would you have had us lie down under this outrageous provocation?"

Peter shook his head slowly. "No. When it got as bad as it did, in 1917, and Germany was doing as she did, there was no other recourse for us but entering the war. I realize that. I also realize that surrendering to force, especially violent and inhuman force, is as bad a wickedness as war itself.

"But I think I go deeper than that. My attacks are not against the ultimate entering of the war on our side, but against the war-makers who made the war in the first place. We all know very well that it was they who made the provocation, they who made the war, they who made the conditions that forced us to enter. That is what must be destroyed, the manipulating of wars, the jockeying of nations into war, the creating of situations where war is the only answer, and where not-to-war spells suicide."

Georges frowned, drew a circle in red pencil around a paragraph. "Again, you're being too stark. You avoid fundamentals, Peter. Re-read this chapter, and think about it."

He added: "We know the German character. For instance, it is very hard to force Chinamen to fight, for the Chinese are naturally pacific, individualistic, independent, and thoughtful. But the Germans are none of these. Characteristics like those of the Chinese dispose a man to peace and to tolerance. But the German characteristics of intolerance, belligerence, mass-movement, dependence and sentimentality dispose a

308

man to fight and to hate, and to want to kill. What are you going to do with a nation like this? Gas it off the map?"

"No." Peter smiled. "Gas, instead, the men who cunningly use these unfortunate characteristics to make wars on more civilized peoples. Several eras of peace and understanding between peoples will cause universal intermingling, and we'll breed out the worst traits in the German character, and leave the good ones of cleanliness, order, ambition and intelligence to grow."

Georges read on, shaking his head more and more with denial. He drew another ring about a paragraph. He could not help smiling a little, however. "Marion and her good American patriots won't like this! This, what you say about patriotism: 'the appendix of barbarism at the end of the human colon, which serves no useful purpose, and is a potential danger to life.'" He glanced at Peter, and laughed: "'Breathes there a man with soul so dead——'"

"Nonsense!" exclaimed Peter. "Haven't we anything in our racial characters to be proud of, except our prowess in killing, and our egotism in believing that our particular plot of ground is more valuable than any other, and that the offal we have deposited there is bigger and better than any other offal?"

"Too radical. We've got fine characteristics, mixed up, though, I must admit, with the offal——"

"Then, our patriotism should expend itself in sorting the fine characteristics out, and decently burying the others."

"Nevertheless, even these would lead to war." He smiled at Peter significantly. "Take our own family, for instance. Armand, through good fortune, perhaps, rules Bouchard and Sons. Christopher, through bad fortune, is in the poorhouse soup. They hate each other, Armand out of fear of Christopher, and Christopher out of envy of Armand. There you have the whole international situation at a glance. The question of right or wrong doesn't exist when it is a question who gets the biggest part of the swag."

Peter shook his head stubbornly. "Swag' won't enter into it when we have finally formed a body of international ethics——"

Georges burst out laughing. Ethics, he said, was the cultivated garden of the intelligent man, but the wilderness of the fool. Force, grim hard force, was the only answer to stupidity and aggression.

He continued to read. He began to chuckle with enjoyment, when he reviewed the series of chapters in which Peter gave a frank and comprehensive survey of Bouchard and

Sons, and their multitudinous interlocking subsidiaries. "You've lost no time, have you, Petc?" He remembered that Christopher had written him, and had called Peter "an amateur Cataline." "Where did you get all this information?"

"Observations. And questions. They'll be surprised to find out how much they've told me, won't they?"

"I shouldn't wonder." He whistled softly as he read. "Are you certain of your facts? One small slip and you have a libel suit on your hands. Are you positive?"

"Yes. Bouchard is linked up with Schultz-Poiret, Robsons-Strong, Skeda, Bedors and Kronk, and their subsidiaries. I tell you, I've worked hard for eight years! The information was very easy to get. That's the appalling thing, the cynicism of their operations, and the openness. They either believe that people are too stupid to read, understand and care, or they believe themselves too strong to bother about people. Either way, it is ominous.

"I have many friends in Germany, one or two of them connected with Kronk. I know what's going on. I've seen Sir Charles Carmitchell and Lord Burton Blenfadden in Emil Kronk's Paris home, with M. Alfonse Brenau and the President of France. My friends introduced me as one of the others' dear friends, the American Bouchards, and so, I heard enough! Within a few years, they planned, Germany, with their help and the support of their various governments, would be in a position to threaten Europe again. The Englishmen, however, were more concerned with a strong Germany's preventing 'radical' doctrines from seeping out of Russia into England, and so inducing the English working class to demand enough to eat. Besides, Sir Charles Carmitchell is a member of a well-known and extremely wealthy Manchester industrial family; he, himself, is ardently pro-German. He's got an old brother, Melton, who'd like to be Prime Minister some day, and help Germany along with some real substantial diplomacy. He'll get there, too." Peter paused, and added grimly: "The Carmitchells own one-quarter of the common stock in Kronk, one-third in the Byssen Steel, and a fine share of the Reichindustrie Chemikal.

Again, Georges whistled softly. "Of course, I had some idea. But not as bad as this. Sometimes I wonder——." He shook his head. "But, hell. They wouldn't dare start anything. This is not 1914. People have had a taste of war. They'd better wait another generation, until the war generation is dead. They'll wait, too."

He laid aside the manuscript. "What is your outline for the rest of the book?"

"The future. Don't smile. You have only to live in Europe to see it coming. I was in Berlin during the 'beer putsch.' Ever hear of it?"

"Vaguely. It wasn't important, was it?"

"Very. Perhaps the most important thing that has occurred in Europe since the Russians murdered their degenerate Czar and his perverted gang, and revenged themselves for centuries of bestiality and oppression and torment. For Hitler, the brilliant and demented Austrian maniac, is not just a laughable figure, springing up from nowhere, but the symbol of what is behind him, and who is behind him. The Byssens, the Kronks, the Skedas, the Schultz-Poirets, the Robsons-Strongs, the British Tories, the French Tories, the German Junkers—all the murderous enemies of all mankind, who care for nothing but investments and power. You don't hear much about him just now? You will. For he, Adolf Hitler, madman and genius, is the future of all the world."

Georges laughed. "Now you're being funny. But never mind. Go ahead and write what you have to write. It sounds interesting, anyway. I doubt he'd go far, though. We've got a fairly civilized world, now. Democracy is rapidly spreading. They'll never be able to enslave the peoples again, or arouse much hatred among them——"

"Oh, yes they will! Wait and see. You'll see, yes, within six years. Or less. Within ten or twelve years, there will be the beginning of the end. Don't laugh. I've looked. You see things if you look. Mussolini was the first gun the enemies fired against the world, against democracy, and against civilization."

Georges listened reflectively. Finally he said: "By the way, I have a friend here in New York, a Doctor Adolf Schacht. A German by birth. A really clever man. Maybe you're right! He's told me a little of what you have just said, yourself. He gloats over it. I understand he used to be a member of the Ku Klux Klan, too, an idiotic organization, by the way. I'd like you to meet him. Entertaining and charming as the devil. I've invited him out over the weekend."

He read on, finished the last incomplete page. "Go ahead. But now I've got a suggestion, myself: use a pen name."

Peter answered with quick indignation: "I certainly won't! Why should I? What? Family feeling? Well, anyway, you're smiling, so I won't take that seriously. I'll use my own name."

"I wouldn't. Or, at least, not until little Celeste has finally made her decision. Attack her beloved Christopher, and you'd better go into mourning. And your thumb-nail sketch of him isn't nice at all, you know. Thinking the matter over,

311

from my own point of view, I must insist on a pen name. After all, I'm a Bouchard, too."

"And if I won't?"

Georges shrugged. "Then I won't publish the thing, or even consider it."

Peter was silent a moment. Their eyes met; Georges was tranquil but firm. He pushed the manuscript aside with a delicate, dismissing gesture.

"Then," said Peter, "I'll take it somewhere else."

"Don't be a fool, Pete." He added, smiling a little: 'I thought you were interested in getting these facts before the public, and not in any personal notoriety, or fame. So, what does it matter?"

"It is cowardly."

Georges laughed heartily. "This'll stink just as bad with any name on it, and the consequences will be just as mean. However, Endicott James will go over it with a fine-tooth comb, you can be sure. And, somehow, I hope Bouchard sues!"

"But you're not afraid to publish it——"

"No."

Georges got up. "But now Marion's home, with a flock of guests, so I think we'd better join them. Shall we?"

They left the study together, and went downstairs, where, on the lawns, Marion and her guests were chattering and laughing. "Ha!" said Georges. "I hear the rich voice of old Jay Regan himself. Didn't you tell me he is the biggest supporter of the arms lobby in Washington? I shouldn't wonder. He made millions out of the last war."

CHAPTER XXXIX

MARION greeted her husband and Peter with high-bred British gabblings and chirpings. "My dears, to think you wasted this perfect day! Georges, pet, I did it in eighty-two! Isn't that remarkable? Oh, Peter, do you know Ethel Bassett? Ethel, our favorite relative, Peter. Yes, he does look just like the rest of them, doesn't he? Don't scowl, Peter; I've just paid you the most precious compliment! Mr. Regan, do you know Peter?"

Old Jay Regan regarded Peter with a friendly eye, and chuckled. "Remember me? Your dad, Honore, brought you to my office a long time ago. Around 1912, I should say."

"Yes, I remember you, sir," replied Peter. He shook hands with the huge stout old man, who had the most humorous eyes and the most sincerely genial smile he had ever seen. It was hard to realize the terrible influence this man had had upon the world, what enormous profits he had made from the blood of Europe and America, and what sinister plottings he was even now engaged in, to the further ruin of the world. But, Peter reminded himself sadly, he could not have done all this had not the world itself been so greedy, so ferocious, so full of cupidity and hatred and cruelty. Regan and his kind were merely panderers to a lust which already existed, and which men made no conscious effort to restrain. Even if Regan's kind fomented wars, they could not do so without the enthusiastic response of men. They were the tempters, but they tempted a passion eager to be aroused, hopeful for excesses. To abolish Regan's tribe, it was first necessary to civilize the world.

Regan perhaps might have read some part of his thoughts, for his eyes became piercing, though increasingly friendly. The old man had no objections to good men; in fact, he preferred their company. And if they were intelligent as well as good, a rare combination he believed, he was delighted, sought them out, was proud of them. He said: "I know one of your relatives very well. Henri Bouchard. A very unusual young man."

Peter's lips tightened, but he answered quietly: "Yes. Very unusual." He began to move away, and Regan, interested and amused, followed. They found themselves walking alone. Peter had no desire for this gross old man's company, but Regan, on the trail of the relief that good men invariably afforded him, would not let him go. The others remained behind; they were used to Regan picking out some one and monopolizing him, and they were too reverent of the financier to intrude. They pretended not to notice. But Georges, highly edified and curious, wished he could overhear a conversation that would no doubt be exceedingly interesting. As for Marion, she was amazed that Regan had singled out Peter, who was very dull.

Old Regan found a seat under a tree. Peter, chained by politeness, was restive. He wanted to go away and think. But Mr. Regan evidently had no intention of dispensing with his company. "Sit down," he said genially. "Too hot to be wandering around." He took out a pale lavender silk handkerchief and mopped his huge scarlet face and partly bald head.

Peter sat down reluctantly, frowning slightly. His head had begun to ache; the hot green dazzle of grass, the hot blue dazzle of the sky, tired him. He coughed a few times, with unusual violence. Regan regarded him curiously, and with a furtive concern. He knew the story. He experienced a qualm of uneasiness.

"Marion tells me Georges is going to publish a book you are writing," he said.

"Yes," replied Peter, with some hauteur. Regan waited, but Peter vouchsafed no further information. But the old man's curiosity increased.

"What about? Or is it a secret?"

Peter hesitated. He was not much interested in Jay Regan as a person; he had all the information he needed about him as a condition. But now he looked at the old man consciously and personally. He could not help smiling a little. "About you. And your friends."

Regan raised his eyebrows and began to laugh. "Really? Are we that interesting, eh?"

"No," replied Peter calmly. "You're not. It's just what you do."

"Oh." The smile was still broad on Regan's mouth, but his eyes had pointed a trifle. "My dear Peter, you aren't a crusader or something, are you?" His manner refused to believe such idiocy of such a nice young man, whose father had been Honore Bouchard. He was disappointed.

Peter had flushed. "I hope I'm not a crusader, sir. I don't like that word. Do you call everyone a crusader who doesn't agree with you?"

"Not at all! I detest people who agree with me. They're usually liars, or traitors, or want something I have. For heaven's sakes, go on disagreeing with me. But I would like to know what you disagree with me about. I hope it's something unique?"

His air was so artless, so friendly, so open, that Peter felt himself smiling again, and less antagonistic. "It is unique," he said. "At least, I hope my approach is. But, do we have to talk about the book? It isn't quite written yet. I've got a lot to learn before it is finished."

Regan waved his hand. "Can I help you? If it's about me, I'm sure I can tell you things you don't know."

They both laughed. Regan offered Peter one of his enormous and expensive cigars. Peter accepted; he lit the old man's cigar, and then his own. Georges, at a distance, saw this amiable pantomime. He frowned. He hoped Regan

314

wouldn't disturb Peter too much, or confuse his single-purpose. Regan was ingratiating and disarming, when he wished to be so, and so infernally reasonable and logical.

Georges had acquired the publishing firm of Randorf and James, lock, stock and barrel. He had paid a huge sum for it. He was proud of it, for it had always had a robust and radical reputation, an exuberant and exciting quality. It was eternally new in approach, but had an old and solid reputation, mutual assets unusual in the history of American publishing. He was not exactly sure just why he had bought Randorf and James; his newspaper was sufficient, he told himself. He took up "causes" in his paper, for amusement, and to watch the "crows scream," he said, but, secretly, because he felt some mysterious relief when he did so.

He continued its policy of unusual and exciting and bold and radical publication. He enticed an eminent teacher from another publisher, a teacher famous for his fine and readable expositions of philosophy and history, non-fiction works which had rapidly become international best-sellers. Georges was not interested so much in learned treatment and rigid facts. He asked his famous writers only to be interesting, stimulating, colorful, courageous, cynical and passionate. They responded with heartfelt enthusiasm. He was careful in his editing, careful not to dim a phrase or inhibit an accusation. Some critic had accused him of being a Communistic iconoclast, which amused him tremendously.

He wrote the editorials in his newspaper; his style was sharp and laconic. Sometimes he wrote "elevated nonsense" wryly, for his own amusement.

But no one knew that his paper and his publishing business were his great passions, and that his concern for his authors was personal and unsleeping. From the beginning, he had recognized that Peter had just the fresh and powerful genius he was always looking for; he realized that he had discovered another writer who would go about blowing up the old towers, and splintering the old gates, all to the tune of excitement and profits. He had been accused of "sensationalism," but though there was truth in this, it was not Hearst sensationalism. It was an educated, even profound, subtle and beautiful sensationalism, lavishly decorated with truth and anger, passion and strength. He publicly called it "balderdash," but he knew that Confucius and Buddha, Mohammed and Lao-Tse and all the others of the heavenly company, had spoken only balderdash, great and heroic and splendid though it had truly been. For, was not the impossible balderdash, the beautiful and the magnificent and the true and the

315

holy, only balderdash in that it did not square with man, and had no verity in his works?

Peter was a writer of this thundering balderdash, and Georges, watching him and Regan, hoped that the old financier would not imbue Peter with any devastating "common-sense." Once let an author acquire common-sense, and he was ruined.

But Regan was talking about Honore, Peter's father, and Peter was listening intently, all the habitual tenseness and anxiety gone from his face.

"No man ever questioned his integrity or sincerity," Regan said. "I think, of all of your family, I liked only your father. He was a good man. But he suffered a lot. You wouldn't know why he suffered, would you?"

"Yes. I always knew," said Peter in a low voice.

Regan sighed. "But—you'll forgive me, won't you?—he had no courage. You wouldn't understand that, would you?"

"Yes. I understand."

Regan mopped his face and head again, and mused. "I liked him," he repeated. "His death was a great shock to me." He asked suddenly: "Have you courage?"

He had expected Peter to be affronted, or embarrassed, or to reply quickly, and with annoyance. He was surprised to see how quiet and hard the young man's expression had become, how fixed his eyes. He heard him saying: "I don't know. I don't know. I hope so. But I think I shall!"

Peter, not out of discourtesy, but out of some profound confusion, began to walk away. Groaning, Regan attempted to hoist his huge body onto his protesting legs, and follow. Then he fell back again, and relapsed into thought.

No, this young man was no fool. He would do many things, before he died. Dangerous things, perhaps. But always with an awareness of this danger. That made him the more formidable. Courageous men were usually men without imagination. But here was a man of courage, with imagination, and with a full comprehension of danger. Regan frowned. But for some reason he could not feel annoyed. It was very good that the son of Honore Bouchard was this Peter! It would have been a little dreadful if he had been a man like Jules Bouchard. Honore would not have rested in his grave. It was bad enough that his other sons were so much like Jules. Regan pursed his lips. I'm getting virtuous in my old age! he thought, suddenly smiling at himself. Perhaps my pleasure in this boy is really nasty. Perhaps it's because of that last day I ever saw that rascal, Jules. I'm still smarting. What a bastard he was! He put me in my place, and for that I'll never forgive him. It's pleasant, now, finding a Bouchard who doesn't like his family!

Memories seemed clearer to Jay Regan than the present. He could remember very distinctly every word of the last interview he ever had with Jules Bouchard, in his office, shortly before the end of the war. He had greeted Jules with great affability, for he did not yet know that he really hated this Bouchard with the hooded eyes and the soul of a Richelieu.

He said to Jules: "I was about to ask you to come in. On Monday I am calling a conference of all you boys. I've got something to say. But, you look like hell. I've heard you were ill, and thought of going to Windsor to see you. Are you better?"

Jules informed him that he was visiting Georges Bouchard, and Regan smiled. "Ah, yes, Georges. An exceptionally brilliant young man; he does Leon credit. But your family is noted for its brilliant sons. Francis, Jean, Hugo, and your sons, Armand, Emile and Christopher, and Leon's boys, Georges and Nicholas. By the way, Mrs. Van Eyck, your former sister-in-law, dined with us last week. A charming woman. My wife tells me that her boy, Henri, looks for all the world like his great-grandfather, your Uncle Ernest. I have an idea that one of these days you fellows are going to hear from that young man. He's a Barbour, and a Bouchard, all right!"

"Brilliant!" Jules smiled musingly. "We are a fine pack of bandits, all of us. Except Peter, Honore's youngest. Do you know Peter? He's enlisted. Yes, some sentimental nonsense. But I like that boy. I like Georges, too. Georges would be a rascal if the occasion offered, but he'd not go out of his way to be a rascal. That was a fortunate thing, his marrying Professor Fitts' girl. Fortunate for the Professor, too. The poor old devil was bankrupt."

Jules gazed at him thoughtfully. "Yes, wasn't it fortunate for the Professor? But what seems to be disturbing you so much these days?"

Regan's agreeable expression vanished, and he picked up a sheaf of papers. "I've heard from Sazaroff. He's been around to Clemenceau, Lloyd George, and Kronk. He's of the opinion the war can't last the year out. Germany is done in."

Jules tapped his fingers reflectively on Regan's desk. "Peace, eh? There's no doubt about it?"

"None at all. Patriotism may go on and on, but money is not so self-renewing. So, you'd better pull in your horns and
317

retrench. Propaganda? My dear Jules, don't be foolish. At times, you are quite bright. But you, more than anyone else, ought to know that propaganda is a waste of time in the face of bankruptcy. I tell you, Germany's done in. It's just a matter of a few months at the most."

"Well, your news is not so good, considering the vast outlay we have been put to, and the tremendous preparations we have begun; I expected the war to last at least another two years. What the hell are we to do with our new plants that cover acres? Our new machinery? Our enormous equipment? Manufacture plowshares with them?" Suddenly his eyes narrowed, and his smile widened. He seemed greatly amused. "Who knows? Probably plowshares, after all. But it can be tried! But look here, we aren't going to go into that seriously for a while! It is unthinkable."

Regan smiled cynically. "What do you intend to do? Start a little war of your own?"

"But it is unthinkable. Do you actually believe that peace will come with the signing of peace treaties? Not at all. The world is too stirred up. Yes, I truly believe it. Bankruptcy? My dear Regan, a nation may deny itself bread, but it won't deny itself armaments. Besides, bankruptcy is notoriously a breeder of desperation. Half a dozen, or even less, desperate defeated nations in Europe will be sufficient to keep armaments manufacturers busy for twenty, thirty years. What is the matter with Sazaroff? Has he lost his imagination?"

Regan leaned back in his chair and stared at him in silence. After a few minutes, he replied surlily: "I'm not interested in your damned armaments just now. We've lent billions to the Allies. We've got to get it back. They won't be able to pay us back if they re-arm again. There's got to be an end to armaments for a while, until we get our money."

Jules smiled cynically. "Do you actually believe they'll really pay their debts? For a few years, perhaps, if we're lucky. You've talked before of forcing Germany to pay reparations. Well, go ahead. Do you know what you'll do by that? You'll create markets for armaments such as you can't dream of now. Strip Germany, and you'll let a hungry wolf loose in Europe, against which other nations will be compelled to re-arm. But, go ahead! Go ahead! I'll not stop you by the lifting of my hand!"

Regan turned crimson; he glowered at the other man and gnawed his lip. "Bah. We'll make the Hun's belly so flat that he won't think of anything for a generation or two besides filling it. Hell! Aren't you satisfied yet? Look what you made on aviation alone, or rather, on the airplanes you didn't
318

supply but got a large slice of the billion dollars expended for! Not one damned American-built combat or bombing plane supposedly manufactured by you ever reached the front. You've got no complaint. You'd better listen to your sons. After all, you're not as young as you once were."

Jules laughed goodhumoredly. "Neither are you, Jay. Old age is making you cautious——"

"Cautious be damned! I want my money. You've got yours; now I want mine. That's why I'm calling in the rest of you; you've got to shut up for awhile."

"And I tell you you won't get your money, or at least not all of it. Wait and see. You'd better just play along with us. We're the masters now. You'll do as we say, after this. If we want wars, you'll finance them, and never a word from you. If we want peace, you'll finance that, too, but I tell you it'll cost you more for peace than it will for war. You don't believe all this? Just wait. Desperation creates strange rulers. The desperate nations of Europe will set rulers over them that will take the money of financiers without the formality of asking. You'll be controlled, regulated. Laugh, if you want to; you won't laugh long. We've let out the wild beasts, and your plaints for your money won't shut them up again. Boycott? Threats? Pressure? Don't be silly. You'll just be prodding the wild beasts."

Regan's face swelled; there was an alarming and evil glint in his eye. Jules calmly lit one of his long cigars. Through the smoke he smiled at Regan amiably.

"There'll be no peace. We don't dare have peace. It's a luxury which Europe can't afford, after all this. Let them sign treaties and talk peace. Let the Allies exact reparations and 'reconstruct' Germany and her allies. Let there be leagues formed for peace, and consultations and conferences. But I tell you, the more talk there is of peace the busier will be the armaments factories. We've been just a little too smart in our propaganda, and we haven't the courage to say: 'We were just fooling, children. It was just our joke. Now kiss and make up, and forget all the naughty stories grandpa told you. The little boy next door isn't really your enemy. It was just our joke.'"

He shook his head with mock sadness. "If you try to stop it now, Jay, you'll be riding the whirlwind. You won't retrieve your money by hindering us. But you will make more by helping us." He stood up and laughed a little. "You'll help us, all right. There was a time when we came to you, but the time is coming when you'll come to us. We're your masters now, Jay." He tapped himself gently on the chest. " 'I and Lazarus!' "

Regan laughed contemptuously. "If we refuse to lend governments money for arms, where will you be?"

"Ah, my good friend, we'll put rulers in power who will be able to exist only by our will, and by our arms. Do you think they'll let themselves perish by meekly allowing you to refuse them money? You lack vision, Regan, you lack vision! This war wasn't really to make the world safe for democracy, in spite of what the schoolmasters say. It was a war to destroy democracy. You'll see. I feel quite prophetic today," and he smiled again.

Regan shrugged. "I don't doubt it. You've got one foot in the grave; no wonder you can prophesy. Well, we'll see. We've still got the upper hand. I'd like to have you here when I read the riot act to all the other boys, too."

"But don't forget: the world is ours, now, not yours."

Regan stared at that dying, smiling face, wrinkling and grimacing before him, and a sort of cold horror came over him, in spite of reason, in spite of confidence, in spite of the possession of power. He had the dizzy sensation that something had shifted, moved its base, silently yet frightfully. Something had been let loose, indeed, something deadly and implacable and not to be controlled. And all of this was embodied in this man before him.

His thick nostrils dilated, and he exhaled a deep breath.

Regan, remembering, as he sat under the hot shade of the summer trees, felt his spine prickling, and his blood running, with the memory of his hatred for Jules Bouchard, and his humiliation and anxiety. It was worse, remembering, to see how truly Jules had spoken. Yes, something had been let loose, by all of them. By Regan, and all of them. It was not the nicest thought, on this summer day, just after talking to Peter Bouchard.

"I'm getting old," said Regan, aloud, heavily pulling himself to his feet. "I'll go to England for a little while. It's peaceful there. It's always most peaceful near the volcano."

320

CHAPTER XL

WHEN Peter returned to the lawn festivities, he became aware that Marion was regarding him with slightly affronted eyes. "Where have you been, Peter? You are very naughty, running away like this."

He disliked her, but he was sorry for her, and found her completely impossible. Her figure was tall and youthful, her hair still ungrayed, her fair athletic skin excellent, her gestures all quick and animated. Someone had told her that she was the typical American woman, which had pleased her tremendously. The flatterer, a European, had told her she possessed all the legendary American woman's intelligence, alertness, "clear-eyed honesty," simplicity and competence. As a result, she was careful to have little inanity in her conversation; she sought out "wholesome" epigrams to repeat. (None of these sophisticated, demurely naughty epigrams for Marion!) She secretly loathed the outdoors, but she forced herself to become proficient in golf and tennis and swimming. She was so alert that it was painful to watch her. She was like a rather oldish spring pulled constantly to its last ability to hold together and rebound. She was like to interrupt any subtlety by a clear clarioning: "Do let us be fundamental and honest about this——" And then she would regard the offenders with serious earnestness, widening her empty gray eyes so that they strained at the sockets. She wore tweeds as much as possible, and tailored clothes at all times. In short, she had grown to be an exceedingly dull woman, an officer in the most prominent and intolerant patriotic societies, a bore and a sentimental nuisance, and a person guaranteed to infuriate the intelligent. At the present time she was engaged in "Americanism" (her own peculiar kind), which had for its base hatred of all that had no origin in America before the American Revolution, all "aliens," the Roman Catholic Church, the Jews, liberalism and tolerance and humor, and was ardently supported by many members of the American Legion, the Daughters of the American Revolution, and kindred organizations. Georges' friends loathed her, and even their regard for him could not prevent them from revealing their opinions. He was no longer offended. He knew his wife for a fool.

Peter stood isolated, alone, thinking. Tomorrow, he would go to Crissons. Georges was right, in a way. Celeste could make up her mind, easily, if she wished. He would speak, for the first time. She had only to say yes or no. Whatever she said would be what she desired to say, in the last analysis. He looked up to see Georges approaching him across the grass, accompanied by two youngish men. He seemed to be in high good humor. One of the men, a small plump dark young man, with curly black hair and dimples and dancing gleaming eyes, was laughing quite loudly. The other young man was slight and very fair, with milk-blue eyes, a charming expression, and a quiet, almost contemplative, manner. Beside the dark plump young man, he seemed washed-out and somewhat nondescript, but when he looked directly at Peter, the latter saw how brilliant were the almost colorless eyes, how intense the pupils, how hypnotic their glance. He was actually startled by them, and took a step backwards, involuntarily.

Georges said: "Peter, this is Doctor Schacht, and this, Doctor Weimer. Old friends of mine. Adolf, Wilhelm, my cousin, Peter Bouchard."

They shook hands. Doctor Weimer regarded the young man merrily. "Another Bouchard! Do you grow on trees?" Peter laughed. He decided he liked the little Austrian, with his gay expression and his impudent accented voice. But he did not like Doctor Schacht, who listened to everything, smiled faintly, and seemed to be hearing other meanings under the slightest remark.

"Let's get away from the gabble," said Georges. "We'll go somewhere and talk. Back of the house. We'll have some drinks." Peter was reluctant, but he accompanied the others to the rear. He had no desire for conversation with anyone, and was annoyed at Georges in consequence. His mouth was sulky as he sat down under a great mass of trees some distance from the house. The little Weimer refused a seat, and flung himself full-length on the grass. He pulled up a blade, and proceeded to chew on it as he made comments, or yawned. It was evident that he disliked serious conversation on such a beautiful day, and Peter felt sympathetically drawn to him.

Georges spoke to Doctor Schacht, but looked pointedly at his cousin: "Peter is writing a book. A very somber thing, but very good. A fact. He doesn't think much of the future.

Peter, Doctor Schacht is also concerned about the future. Maybe he can broaden your perspectives."

Peter regarded the pale German with no particular favor, but with polite attentiveness. He thought there was something malignant in Schacht's slight smiles and soft voice, and felt his dislike quickening. Schacht looked at Peter thoughtfully as he said, "Georges tells me you have recently returned from Europe, Mr. Bouchard. I was born in Munich; you see, I'm very interested. Can you tell me what your opinion is, about Europe?"

Peter hesitated. "Do you mean about the prospects of a future war? That's what I'm personally interested in, you know. I don't know if there will be an actual war— But I do think that something terrible is brewing in Europe. I don't know just what it is; it is too early to say. But all the signs are there."

"What signs?" Peter looked at him sharply, expecting ridicule. But Schacht's face was quick and intent, yet secret.

"The signs are vague, I must admit. That is, some of them. In Italy, they are very clear. Tyranny, exploitation, feudal serfdom of the people, the violation of human dignity, worship of the State, no freedom, espionage, brutality, obedience, militarism, nationalism, concentration camps, intolerance. Italy is the European abscess. Unless its poison is confined within the borders of Italy, it will flow out and pollute all Europe. And all the world."

Little Weimer rolled over on his elbow, and stared at Peter over his shoulder. The blade of grass hung from his lips; he chewed the end absently. His dimples came and went in his cheeks, but he was not smiling.

Georges laughed shortly. "That's absurd. We haven't any Mafia in America; no Black Hand. Mussolini has done good work for Italy. He's had to use discipline and force, for the Italians like laughter too much, and are too lazy. Besides, he's an actor. Italians love actors. But can you imagine any other nation loving an actor, a hypocrite, a liar, and a psycopath?"

"Yes," said Peter quietly. "Germany."

Weimer grunted. Georges smiled broadly. But Schacht did not smile. He just gazed at Peter steadily. "Please go on," he said. Peter turned to him. He began to speak; he felt that he was speaking only to this colorless German with the evil eyes and the charming expression.

"I was in Germany a long time," he said. "Germany, within two years, will be more integrated and more prosperous than she was in 1914. She has a great future, for her

323

people are good and strong and healthy. She has a great future, because the Germans love progress and newness, and there's something in the German air that encourages genius and mental clarity." He paused, then continued in a lower but more passionate voice: "Yes, she has a great future. If she's let alone. But—she won't be let alone. You see, a strong and peaceful Germany isn't good business for the bankers and the munitions makers. A liberal Germany, who can be friends with Soviet Russia, is a menace to Tory oppressors in England and France. So, Germany will have to die."

Weimer muttered something. But Schacht said gently: "Go on." Georges said: "Germany die?"

"Yes. They won't call it dying, though. They'll call it 'nationalism,' or 'racialism,' or something equally deadly and virulent. I've seen the signs. I've seen and heard Hitler. And I know who is behind him. I know the identity of those who hate Germany, and who are her deadliest enemies."

No one spoke. Schacht lit a cigarette, tapping it delicately on the back of one of his small hands. Then Weimer said: "Haven't you a tendency to look on the black side? Besides, what has Germany to do with—us?"

Peter shook his head a little. "Germany will have to die," he repeated. "And her death terribly affects not only Europe, but America. Within a few years, unless a miracle happens, every government in the world will be in the hands of wicked and rapacious men, who will use wars, tyranny, murder, persecutions, massacres and brutality to make power and money for themselves. We'll have the Dark Ages again. Maybe they'll even strengthen some religion that is intolerant, greedy and voracious enough to obey them, and we'll have superstition and intolerances again, strong enough to plunge us into medievalism, and make us complete slaves to the men in power."

Weimer regarded him incredulously, smiling. He sat up, interested, wanting to hear more from this absurd fanatic. And yet, he kept glancing furtively at his friend, Adolf Schacht. Georges, for his part, tried, humorously, to catch the pale German's eye. But Schacht was looking only at Peter; his eyes were narrowed.

He said coolly: "And if this is so, what can you, or anyone else, do about it?"

Peter shook his head hopelessly. "I don't know. No one believes anything. We're too prosperous, in America, to see the signs, or care to look for them. Besides, you've got to live in Europe."

There was another silence, then Schacht began to speak,

almost musingly: "I'm not laughing at you. I believe what you say. But I interpret the signs differently. I know, for instance, that Germany is overrun with Communists. I know that she is friendly to Russia, and open to Russian propaganda. You don't particularly admire Russia, Mr. Bouchard? I thought not. Neither do we Germans. That is, the real Germans. We believe that Communism means the disintegration of everything that is prideful in a nation: patriotism, nationalism, racial integrity. You don't like these things, do you? I can see that. But true Germans believe they are the holies of holies. Just as war, aggressive and conquering war, is holy."

Peter interrupted: "I met hundreds of fine Germans who didn't think war is holy. And they believe, as I do, that insane patriotism and banner-flying and drum-pounding are childish and dangerous and stupid. They believe, as I do, that men are men, whether their eyes are blue or brown, their hair yellow or black, and that they differ only in degree. They believe that patriotism is the deliberate poison manufactured by bad men who have something to gain by wars."

Schacht waved his hand indulgently. "Perhaps so. But, you see, I don't call those men 'bad.' I call them adventurers, perhaps. But excellent adventurers, who give nations excitement and glory, and the greatest pleasure of all: murder. You don't think murder is a pleasure? Well, ask a soldier. Not a yellow coward, but a real soldier. A real man. A natural, normal, healthy man.

"But anyway, I interpret your signs differently. I think Germany will soon be aroused against Communism, and against everything which is destroying her patriotism and racialism. Such as the Jews, and the capitalists, and the liberals and democrats. I believe that Germany will destroy democracy, not only in Europe, but in America. For, you see, there are many just like me who believe that democracy is the most abominable philosophy ever to pollute government and pervert nature."

He added, with such a low quiet viciousness in his voice that even the smiling Georges was startled: "Democracy! The doctrine that scum is as valuable as the strong! The theory that every man has the right to say what wars he shall die in, or what sort of society he shall live in! The philosophy that affirms a creature is human just because he has no tail to wag, and can stand on his hind legs! We'll get rid of it, first in Germany, and then in all the rest of the world."

Peter turned to Georges and said simply: "You see?"

But Georges said to Doctor Schacht: "You are quite a realist, aren't you?"

"Certainly. Sentimentality, religion and wish-fantasies have been dominant too long in governments."

Georges murmured: "As my wife would say: 'Let us be honest and get down to fundamentals.' Adolf, I don't think Abraham Lincoln would have liked you."

Schacht smiled. "I don't think I should have liked Abraham Lincoln. He, like so many others, was the prophet of the non-existent. He believed that all men are thinking animals who love freedom. He did not realize that freedom is the thing men fear the most, and hate the most, and that to urge them to think is to make them hate you. They love to be kicked and commanded; they love to be treated like the dumb beasts they are. It's too much of a strain on them to expect them to act like human beings. Therefore, any system of government which affirms that these creatures have a right to vote, to order their way of life, is bound to be secretly hated by them, and easily overthrown. That is why it is going to be the easiest of all revolutions to overthrow democracy in every nation."

Peter said: "There has never been any real democracy in Europe. But we have it in America. I don't think you'll find it so easy to destroy it here."

Schacht burst out laughing. He stared at Peter derisively. "You don't think so, Mr. Bouchard? I disagree with you. Animals are animals, no matter under what flag they live. An American mob is no brighter than an Italian one, or a French or German. See how easy it is to stir up prejudice and hatred right now, in America. The Ku Klux Klan, for instance, was a merciful opening through which you Americans could discharge your natural animal venom. As life becomes more complicated and more intense, you'll have to make other openings, through which your people will be able to murder, torture, kill and destroy when the pressure gets too hard. Otherwise, you'll have the bloodiest revolution in history."

He smiled. "Take your choice: mob murders or war. But if you attempt to stop both, it'll be the end of you. Men must kill. It is their primal instinct, and right. In Germany, for instance, they will soon turn to the Jews. More and more Germans are drawn to Hitler, because he has promised them a general pogrom. A pogrom will lance the suppressed abscess that is swelling in Germany. And is swelling in every other nation."

326

"You draw a nice picture of the human race," said Georges, grinning unpleasantly.

Schacht shrugged. "Nice or not, it's an authentic one. Realists through all the centuries have made wars for the benefit of their people. Now we have idiots who try to suppress wars. So, there's nothing left but the Jews. We can't attack the Catholics so easily, any more. There are too many of them. And few people feel strongly enough about any religion to kill for it. I warn you: if you don't want to be sickened by massacres of Jews, you'll encourage healthy wars."

Georges shook his head: "So long as American workmen can buy silk shirts, and a Saturday-night woman, and a speedy little car, we won't have wars, and we won't have pogroms."

Peter turned to him and said somberly: "But they won't have silk shirts and women and cars much longer. Our family, and their friends, will see to that."

Little Weimer, still on the grass, yawned again and said musingly: "I'm a doctor. I'm going to have a fine laboratory. I hope I can find a virulent-enough bug to kill off human infestation. You know, I don't think the discoverer of an anti-toxin for tuberculosis and cancer and syphilis will be such a hero. The man deserving of God's eternal gratitude will be the man who produces a toxin to destroy his kind in twenty-four hours."

"Don't worry," said Peter, grimly. "The world still has the Bouchards and the Skedas and the Robsons-Strongs and the Kronks and the Schultz-Poirets."

They all laughed. Schacht poked Peter playfully in the chest with one slight finger. "Don't condemn your people. They are really life-savers. They lance the abscesses."

Marion came around the side of the house, briskly. She was evidently annoyed at the disappearance of her husband and guests. "Georges, I must say! Doctor Schacht! There are so many people who want to meet you. And you, too, Peter." She smiled at Adolf Schacht. "We all do so want to hear your next lecture, Doctor. When and where is it going to be, and what is the subject?"

"At the German-American Hall, in Yorkville, Mrs. Bouchard. On August 10th. 'American Communism' is to be the title." He turned to Peter: "Will you come? I should like to have you there."

"I'll come," said Peter. "We Americans can't know too much about our enemies."

Schacht stared at him. And then he burst out into enjoying laughter.

CHAPTER XLI

HENRI listened to the somniferous sound of the brilliant blue water that lapped against the sides of the yacht. The striped awnings made a dim but luminous shade on the white deck, in which the jeweled ring of Annette's little white finger sparkled vividly. His eyes were half-closed; he sprawled in his chair, his feet thrust out before him. The yacht seemed to move as gently as a shadow on a sleeping breast. He could see the intense blue sky which merged with the intense blue sea. It was very hot, but the air was both fresh and strong, and burningly pure. Far off, a pale mauve line, was the coast of Long Island, but here was no sound but the soft creaking of the yacht, the flutter of awnings, the murmurous lapping of calm and glittering water.

The young man was half asleep; the heat and the silence and the gentle motion of the vessel made his thoughts run together and dissolve into mist. He was also extremely bored, and uneasy. Between his partially closed lashes he could see nothing but a colorful glare, and in the midst of it, inescapable, the little dropped white hand with its sparkling ring. He closed his eyes; he could still see it. He moved restlessly against the weight of sleep, and looked at Annette.

She lay in her deck-chair, apparently sleeping. The luminous shadow made her small pale face glow like marble; her light fair ripples of hair were spread out, fanlike, on the deep blue cushions. Her white throat was delicate and frail; her relaxed arms translucent. Henri could see the blue veins in her slight wrists. Her thin white dress hardly rose over her small breasts; her legs were fleshless, though delicate, and defenseless in their relaxation. She was smiling slightly as she slept; her lashes were long and thick and bronze on a cheek that was faintly flushed, as though by a reflection. Henri thought: Poor little thing. He was aware of her sweet and porcelain prettiness, so fragile and piteous. But it was a prettiness which revolted him. The robustness which was his nature turned away from fragility, especially a fragility which had no strong health in it.

Irritation pricked him. The girl sighed, lifted a hand and

put it under her cheek. She sighed again. The bronze eyelashes fluttered a moment, did not part. He was relieved. He had no desire to talk to Annette.

He had long ago come to respect her intelligence, and the white integrity of her mind. Because she was much less healthy and vital than Celeste, she was much more patient, much gentler, much more understanding. There was no strength like Celeste's in her, but there was no sternness, no inflexibility. Celeste, Henri had discovered, could be enormously stubborn. But Annette was never stubborn. He thought it was because she was ill. But he was wrong. Annette was never stubborn because she could always see the other side as clearly as her own, and had come to value compromise as the way to peace and compassion. Sometimes Henri could hardly believe that Celeste was older than her niece. Annette, in her gentleness and patience, and her great comprehension, seemed much older, much less young and vehement.

As he lay there, irritably watching the sleeping girl, he thought: She is almost inhuman. I don't believe she has any blood. Poor little thing. But she is as dainty and delicate as a piece of ivory. She knows too much! She makes me feel embarrassed too many times, for my own comfort. Imagine being married to her!

His face became heavy and gloomy; he thrust out his large underlip. His hands lifted restlessly, fell back on the arms of his chair. Of course, a man who was married to her need not bother about her much. She would always understand, and never blame. And yet, somehow, he felt a sort of shame at the thought. Who could hurt this poor pretty little creature, and not be the worse for it?

He was a realist, and never retreated from a thought. If he married Annette, he would have taken a complete shortcut to everything he wanted. He smiled. He imagined Christopher's face. A shortcut, swift and complete. He played with the thought at length, forgetting Annette. But he knew that he never seriously contemplated it. However, it made him restless and vaguely angry. There was no one, really, for him but Celeste. He was never so completely and passionately in love with Celeste as when he was with Annette.

He forgot Annette swiftly, remembering Celeste. He sat upright, moving his neck irritably in his collar. He stared at the distant shoreline. He was a fool to have accepted this week-end invitation of Armand's. He didn't know why he had accepted, he said to himself. But he knew. It had been to satisfy himself that he could never endure Annette.

Down in their cabins slept Armand and his wife. Young Antoine had not come, for he had gone to a boys' camp for the summer. No one was awake on the yacht but the crew. No guests had been invited, except Henri. Henri smiled sardonically. He felt some pity. He saw through Armand so surely and completely. He knew that it had been Armand's simple belief that if Henri came to know Annette more intimately, he would love her. It was no secret to Henri that Annette loved him, but this fact, instead of touching him, vaguely infuriated him. It was, he thought, as if he had been insulted, his virility and sense deprecated. He was conscious, at times, to his shame, that he wished to hurt her violently. This sadistic urge was sufficient revenge for her daring to want him.

He stretched his short strong legs, his strong muscular arms. His light inexorable eyes fixed themselves upon Annette. A brutal expression appeared about his mouth. She smiled in her sleep; her lips were the color of delicate coral. Henri got to his feet and walked to the rail. The yacht moved dreamily up and down. The mauve shoreline was deepening to a rosy purple. In the west, the sky looked like a golden robe, rippling into folds. A bell chimed softly and clearly in the shining silence. The sea flowed endlessly, blue wave upon wave, with glittering crests. Gulls, with incandescent wings, curved in the pure and brilliant air. Henri folded his arms on the rail and stared at the shoreline. His strong pale profile was sullen.

He heard footsteps. The captain was descending the white stairway to the deck. Henri glanced at him without interest. The man hesitated, then seeing that Henri did not desire conversation, he went below. The awnings fluttered in a rising wind. The gold of the west brightened unendurably. A turn in the course, and Annette's hair, on her blue cushions, became ripples of soft lifting gilt. The delicate tint on her lips and cheeks deepened.

Next week, thought Henri, I will do it. I won't wait any longer. Christopher's a fool. Too cautious. It's now, or never — He thought of Armand's face, when they all struck him down. For some reason the thought had no pleasure in it, as it had had only a short time ago. He preferred to think of Christopher, and now he smiled somberly. Of them all, all the Bouchards, he hated Christopher the most. The robot. The Trappist. The white snake. Henri knew all the names. He repeated them to himself, appreciatively. His hands clenched into fists on the rail.

He scowled at the water. He was angry with himself for
330

the strong flush of longing and delight which came over him when he thought of Celeste. He was angered that anything should seem more desirable, more imminent, than his revenge. He could feel Celeste beside him; he could hear her breath. He was certain that if he turned he would see her face and the strong dark springing of her hair from her white temples and forehead, and the curve of her young breasts. Hot moisture sprang out in his palms; a passionate thrill of desire ran over his body. There was no woman for him but Celeste. His lips tightened. But what was wrong with Celeste these days? She was too quiet, too pale. When he kissed her she colored violently, but she also seemed afraid, not only of him, but of herself. Sometimes he suspected she avoided him. He struck his hand savagely on the rail. There was a sound behind him, like a sigh and a murmur together, and he turned. Annette was sitting up in her chair, smiling at him, her small face framed in blowing gilt, her lips fresh and glowing.

"Hello," he said, somewhat sulkily. He hesitated. Then he left the rail and came back to the girl. He stood beside her. She looked up at him. Her light blue eyes, so large, so radiant, were beautiful, he could not help remarking. She did not speak. But all her love for him was in her face, like a light. He hesitated again, then picked up a strand of her hair and rubbed it between his strong fingers. He smiled at her. She seemed to lean towards him passionately, and yet she did not really move. Her transparent flesh seemed to quiver, to glow.

"You slept," he said.

"Yes," she whispered. All at once there were tears in her eyes. But her smile was more radiant than ever. He gently relinquished the strand of hair he held. His hand lay near her cheek. She gazed at it, filled with an irresistible longing to kiss it, to lay her cheek against it.

Armand had come up on the deck without their hearing him. He stopped, fixed in his tracks. He saw his young daughter's face, saw Henri beside her, his hand near her cheek. His heart began to beat rapidly. He blinked away a mist that suddenly gathered before his eyes. He went towards them, smiling. He bent down and kissed Annette's cheek; she wound her thin arms about his neck and he could feel her warm agitated breath on his flesh. Then he straightened up and turned to Henri. The young man was faintly scowling; there was a flush on his face, an annoyed flush, as though he had been caught in something indecent. But Armand said calmly: "I thought you two were sleeping. It's hot enough to put anybody to sleep."

331

"I was asleep, Daddy," said Annette. She relaxed against her cushions, sighing with a sort of passionate content.

Henri yawned elaborately. "It's peaceful," he admitted. "Perhaps a little too peaceful. Anyway, I'll miss the breeze tomorrow, when I go to Crissons."

All the color suddenly left Annette's face; it became pinched, the lips bluish. But she folded her hands quietly in her lap and her expression was very still. She looked at Henri softly. "Give Celeste a kiss from me, Henri. I want to see her so much." And she smiled.

In spite of himself the young man was touched. He smoothed one of the bright strands of hair that waved over the cushions. "I will," he promised. Her eyes studied his face gently, with infinite understanding and love. But Armand's eyes were hard and dark with pain. Henri added: "You'll all be at Crissons in two weeks, anyway."

He left them. Annette watched him go, still smiling. Even when he had disappeared down the stairs, her eyes were fixed on the spot where she had last seen him. Armand could not bear that white smile, that quiet acceptance, which was both adult and without hope. It reminded him too poignantly of his mother.

"Annette, my darling," he began. She did not look at him. She still gazed at the spot where Henri had been. She still smiled. But she said in a low voice: "Please, Daddy."

And so he could say nothing at all.

But that night he waited until Annette and her mother had gone to bed, and then he went to Henri, who was sitting alone, thinking heavily, on the deck. He sat down beside the young man, not speaking yet. They watched the dark blue heaving of the quiet ocean under the millions of pointed stars. The yacht was in a bell of silence, barely rising or moving. The awnings had been rolled back, and the wind, burdened with salt freshness, rushed over the deck.

Armand began to speak without emotion: "We're sorry you are leaving us tomorrow, Henri. We wish you would stay with us a few days more."

Henri answered as unemotionally: "Thank you. But I promised Celeste——"

"Yes. Yes, of course." Again there was silence. But now Henri had turned his face intently upon Armand in the darkness. Armand lit a cigar; the light trembled in his hand.

"Henri," he said very, very quietly. "I want to speak to you openly. You have intelligence. So, I'll be frank with you. You've been in the plant quite a while now. It interests you. You'd like to be there always. I can see that. I can also see
332

many other things. Your great-grandfather is legendary. From the stories about him, I think you are like him."

He paused. Henri said nothing. He had turned his head, and he was staring at the almost invisible ocean.

Armand sighed, but his voice was steady and deliberate: "I am Bouchard and Sons, Henri. I've always made it a point not to relegate power. That's dangerous. Especially when you are surrounded with—with men like—those I could name. I'd like to think I could turn all this over to a son, a son who was strong enough. My own son isn't. I'm hoping Annette's husband will be the strong one." He added, even more quietly, but as steadily: "Do you understand, Henri?"

Henri answered, without turning his head: "Yes, I understand." Armand could tell nothing from his voice. But when Henri did turn to him, his voice was stronger, colder than the older man expected:

"But, you see, there's Celeste."

Armand was silent. In spite of his frankness, and the openness of his own approach, he was taken aback at this brutal reply. He felt his face grow hot with embarrassed anger. The insult to Annette was almost more than he could endure without exhibiting shameful rage. Henri stood up. He stood close enough to Armand so that something of his indomitable personality flowed out to the other man.

"Thank you," he said. "Good-night."

He walked away. Armand heard him go. His cigar went out in his hand. Then, after a long time, he lit it again. He was quite tranquil.

CHAPTER XLII

WHEN he arrived in New York, Peter called upon his old uncle, Etienne Bouchard, the veteran actor of the romantic school. Etienne lived in an ornate apartment overlooking the East River. He affected red velvet dressing gowns, tied over a rounded paunch with gold braid and tassels. He was an old man, and he wore a toupee over a bald skull like a tonsure. Offstage, he used no rouge or eyeshadow, yet these cosmetics seemed to have ingrained themselves in his skin, giving him a theatrical appearance in a daylight which he loathed. He was fat, with a gelatinous paunch, an excellent carriage, a portentous tread, a rich sonorous voice, stately gestures, and a romanticism which had effectively protected him from reality all of his seventy-odd years. He no longer had any parts, except extremely minor ones. Fortunately, he had a huge fortune, which he expertly administered in spite of his grandiose gestures, and was often accused of buying opportunities to act in small roles. The younger and more ribald members of his acquaintance called him "East Lynne." What rim of hair he had, flowed; his long hysterical face with the brilliant large dark eyes was well known to every theatrical agent in New York. Once he had been exceedingly handsome. He still had a presence. He had never been even a moderately good actor.

His nephew, Peter, was the only one of the Bouchards who did not ridicule the pathetic old man, and who had even the slightest affection for him. Peter was really fond of him. His posturing, he thought, was harmless; it was the play-acting of a child who dared not look in closets or under lonely beds. Etienne had never grown up. The world, for him, was still a place of splendid gestures, of heroes, of pure damsels struggling to preserve their virginity from top-hatted roués, of scheming grand dames, of lords and ladies and duchesses and silk-stockinged leg-makers, of noble poets and tragic murderers, of Macbeth and King Lear, of Lucrece and Mrs. Patrick Campbell, of East Lynne and the Jersey Lily. The Twentieth Century was, to him, just a dirty and noisy newsboy, inopportunely at the back door. He had tried to dramatize the World War, and had been rudely hurt, a hurt he soon forgot in the footlights and the smell of scent and greasepaint and powder and satin.

He had practically no friends. He bored even those who tried to use him, so that even this vermin avoided him. When he spoke to anyone, the latter soon had the unpleasant impression that Etienne did not really see him. He was only a face in front of which the old actor postured. His eyes had a bemused and inward expression, in spite of their restless, egotistic brilliance. He had always been too much in love with himself ever to see a woman objectively, so he had never married. He had had many gallant love affairs, most of which were in his imagination. His courtesy to women, his generosity towards them in spite of a natural avarice, his gallantry, his romantic attitude, aroused the pity of the more discerning, the cupidity of the conscienceless. One had only to admire him to exploit him utterly. A rapturous expression at the end of a period opened his purse without restraint.

Yet, he was a shrewd gambler on the Stock Exchange, who seemed to have an uncanny ability to pick out a low-priced stock a day or two before its startling rise. He had left all his money to a tuberculosis hospital for indigent actors. He believed himself to be a great artist, not a misunderstood artist by any means, but a Figure in the Theatre. His family was ashamed of him.

He received Peter with embraces, rich periods and theatrical exclamations, all of which were sincere in spite of the flamboyance and the dramatic gestures. (He had last seen Peter two months before.) His big apartment, all gilt legs, flaming carpets, flowers, blazing draperies and exotic portraits, was discreetly shaded against the raw sun, which he detested and feared. He called his Japanese servant and demanded refreshments for the guest. Peter, uneasily perched on a loveseat composed of golden wood and purple-striped satin, was served hot black coffee in gilt-encrusted cups and triangle-shaped sandwiches of caviar and anchovies. Etienne sat opposite him in his red velvet dressing gown. He had not yet put on his toupee, and his polished tonsured skull gleamed in the subdued light of exotic lamps. He smiled at Peter with deep affection. The creases in his haunted face were full of greasepaint. Diamonds glittered on his white fingers, which were carefully manicured.

He began to tell Peter of his new part. Of course, it was just a summer theatre, but every experience was "broadening." Manfield, they said, was a tyro compared to him, but this was probably a gross exaggeration. Manfield was his hero. He sighed. The dreadful, mercenary Bouchards had produced no artists save Godfrey Sessions and himself. There was no beauty in the family. He, Etienne, was very tired. It was a hard thing to have to work, year in and year out, in an attempt to convince the world that the Bouchards could produce an artist occasionally. The world was still skeptical; they did not believe that such a family could produce any delicacy or loveliness or refinement. But he would never give in, until the world acknowledged that the family had its quota of richness and elegance and artistry, after all.

He sighed again. He dropped his big romantic head upon his chest. He lifted his hands slowly, let them drop back upon his knees in a theatrical attitude of self-sacrifice and noble heroism. He was a martyr, posturing splendidly before the cynical face of a world that continually accused the Bouchards of only the grossest motivations, and no soul.

Peter sipped his coffee, and panted a little in the intense scented heat of the apartment. He did not smile at Etienne,

335

nor find him ridiculous. He was infinitely compassionate and understanding. He regarded his uncle affectionately.

"Tell me about your new part," he said, and there was no hypocrisy in his mind or his voice. He was sincerely interested. He knew that men in all their phases were the business of writers. He found no man completely contemptible or completely uninteresting.

Etienne talked about his part. He became hysterically enthusiastic. He acted out the most sonorous passages for Peter. He paced up and down the dim room, which was filled, in spite of the blinds, with a sort of luminous filtration of the blazing sun outside. In this luminous dimness his many rings sparkled and flashed as he gestured. His eyes glittered. His voice boomed, soared, trembled, quivered, accused, implored. His tread shook the floor. The Japanese servant came and went silently, with the indifference of familiarity. Peter was infinitely touched. He knew by now that there was no such part for Etienne. But Etienne had forgotten this. He had an appreciative audience, after many barren months.

Finally he had finished. He collapsed gracefully in a chair with the exhausted air of a great artist who had given his all, and who wished, now, only to be alone with his thoughts. He sighed deeply, over and over. He touched his eyes with the edge of a cream-silk handkerchief. He gazed about his apartment with bemusement and mournful gentleness: a great artist becoming conscious of mediocre surroundings, and inexpressibly wounded by them, though forgiving. Peter said: "It was very striking. You made the part."

Etienne flashed his brilliant eyes on his nephew with quick eagerness. "Do you think so? But art is so unappreciated these materialistic days. Even art must be chromium-plated and utilitarian. As though beauty were not sufficient in itself. But it has become a prostitute. It wears a brassiere, and leers. The theatre concerns itself with Sex, and sexual abnormalities and smartnesses. It laughs at lofty gestures and poetry. There is a loveliness even in decadence. But the modern world is not even decadent. It is just dirty."

Peter saw that he did not really believe this, or, at least, he did not believe it permanently. To have believed it completely would have been his death.

Etienne had a deep affection for Peter. All his life he had been wounded; he had not been insensible to the laughter, though he had pretended not to hear it. Peter had never laughed at him. He had always been interested. Gradually emerging from his heroic role, his gratitude made him aware that Peter was troubled and distressed. Etienne might be a fool, but he was not unsubtle. He called for benedictine, and made Peter take a glass. Then he said, with a simplicity that others did not suspect existed in him: "What is it, Peter? Something is distressing you, isn't it? Can I help? May I help?"

Peter answered directly: "Yes. I'm upset. And terribly worried. I think you can help, Uncle Etienne, in a way." And then he told his uncle about Celeste.

As he explained everything to him, Etienne's eyes began to sparkle with excitement and delight. This was delicious! Young love, harassed perhaps, and the cruel self-seeking brother in the background. "Yes, that is so!" he cried, though Peter could not help protesting that this was not the melodramatic case. Etienne sprang to his feet with a lightness remarkable in a man of his age; he began to pace up and down. "Yes, yes, I see it now! I remember that Christopher! A piece of steel, chromium-plated! A dagger with a chromium hilt! Yes, yes, it is so! Don't deny it! Did you not just say it was all Christopher?" He stopped before Peter, his eyes shining with impatience and quickening excitement.

Peter hesitated. "It isn't as crude as all that, Uncle. You see, I doubt very much that Christopher would force Celeste to marry anyone she didn't want. He is too fond of her for that. It's just that he thinks Henri is the man for her, and it is just fortunate that Henri is also the man for him. I don't know just why, but I'm sure of it. And that brings me right down to Celeste again——"

Etienne clasped his hands ecstatically together, and shook his head. "I still believe it is that Christopher. And the child? When did I see her last? Years and years ago. A tiny white little thing with black curls? Ah, yes. What am I? Her uncle?"

Peter frowned, concentrating. "Let's see. Her father and mine were first cousins. I'm her second cousin. My father was your brother— Her father was your cousin— She is your second cousin, Uncle Etienne."

Etienne was disappointed. "I thought she was my niece. Anyway," brightening, "she will be my niece when you've married her. Dear me, how mixed up we are, we Bouchards. One would suspect decadence. But instead, the Bouchards are so coarse. What can I do to help you, Peter?"

"I'm going to call her up right now, and I'm going to ask her to meet me here, in your apartment. I should like you to leave us alone. I've got to talk to her. That's all. Down at Crissons, Christopher will make it a point not to leave us alone a moment."

Etienne was delighted. This was pure romance! "You

337

must elope!" he cried. "You must be married at once! I'll be your best man, Peter. Or, perhaps, I'll give the bride away?" He was overcome. "The Little Church around the Corner! Doctor Benson and I are old friends."

Peter was more touched than ever. "Well, all that is rushing the thing, Uncle Etienne. But I'll call Celeste now, if you don't mind."

He went to the telephone. In a few moments he was asking for Celeste. The butler informed him that Miss Celeste was down at the golf club. But Mrs. Bouchard was there. Peter was soon connected with Adelaide. Her voice came to him, strained, tense, full of anticipation. "Yes, Peter. This is Adelaide. What is it?"

"Adelaide, I'm at Uncle Etienne's. When Celeste returns, will you speak to her alone, and ask her to meet me here? At once? I don't care what time it is. Adelaide, it's very important. I've got to talk to her."

Adelaide's voice, quivering now, came to him: "Peter, shall I come with her?"

"No. Just alone. I think that's best."

He hung up. Etienne had disappeared. Now he was coming from his bedroom, triumphantly carrying a small gold box. He deposited it with a flourish on the table, and beamed at Peter. Then, with great ceremony he opened it with a small golden key. Jewels sparkled inside. He lifted a ring from its velvet bed and dramatically held it aloft, Cæsar selecting a gem for his favorite. It was an antique ring, a radiant opal, full of fire and flame and golden lightning and blue sky, set in a circle of exquisite diamonds. The gold was very old, heavy, and curiously wrought. "Florentine!" crooned Etienne. He laid it in Peter's palm with slow gestures of wistfulness and real emotion. "I bought it for a woman I thought I was going to marry. In Florence. It's a museum piece. She didn't want me," he added simply. "Now, it is your betrothal ring, for Celeste."

"It's exquisite," said Peter. The opal flamed in his palm. It had a heart of fire. "Thank you, Uncle Etienne. Celeste will love it."

Etienne was gratified. He bent over and looked at the gem. "Celeste. Celestial. A heavenly gem for a heavenly maiden."

Peter was much moved. He looked at the theatrical face, which now seemed so old and hopeless, so tired, so eternally seeking. He put his arm about his uncle's shoulder. "You're so good, Uncle Etienne."

338

CHAPTER XLIII

I T WAS seven o'clock that evening before Celeste arrived. The New York sky was a dusky molten color, and the heat had intensified. Etienne had insisted upon remaining until Celeste came. "Young girls are always aware of improprieties," he had said. "To meet you alone here, without first assuring herself that I had consented to this rendezvous, and was willing that my apartment be used for that purpose, and that I considered it entirely proper, would be to injure her sensibilities." To Etienne Bouchard, the girls of the late Twenties were still fragile flowers, whose dewiness must be protected.

Celeste, pale and tired, but smiling, was received by Etienne with great and affectionate ceremony. Her beauty and gentle manners delighted him. Her courtesy towards him flattered and soothed a spirit that had been wounded from its first consciousness. She did not remember ever having seen him, she admitted, but she had heard an immense lot about him. "Good reports, I hope, my dear?" he asked, holding her hand. She regarded him gently. "My mother always admired you, Etienne," she replied.

She hardly looked at Peter. But there was a constant faint tremor about her pale lips, as though she were much agitated. She had not asked him why he had sent for her. But she knew. She sat on the edge of her chair, quietly, her gloved hands folded on her purse; she kept smiling at Etienne. Peter might not have been in the room. When Etienne, with elaborate coyness, declared that he knew the young people had much to say to each other, and that he would now leave them alone, Celeste betrayed a visible fright. To conceal this, she removed her broad-brimmed straw hat, and held it over her hands. Her black upspringing hair made a vivid contrast with her smooth white cheeks and winglike dark brows. Since she had lost considerable weight the pure modeling of her facial bones was very noticeable.

Now Peter and Celeste were alone. A thick silence filled the dim hot room. Celeste bent her head. There were tears in her eyes. The Japanese servant brought in a silver tray of wine and hors-d'œuvre. Peter poured a glass of wine for the girl, and handed it to her silently. She took it. She lifted her eyes for a brief moment, and met Peter's. He smiled at her, and after a moment, she returned the smile. "It's good wine," said Peter. Celeste laughed a little. The tears on her lashes sparkled. They sipped the wine, and the tenseness in the room seemed to relax.

Then Peter began to speak, gravely and slowly and quietly: "Celeste, dear, you know why I asked you to come. I wanted to see you alone. You knew that. Celeste, you've got to decide tonight. Are you going to marry me, or Henri?"

She carefully replaced the glass on the tray. Her hand shook. She opened her purse and drew out her handkerchief. She stared at it stupidly, as though wondering what it was. She touched her lips with it. Peter waited, gazing at her somberly. She began to speak, looking at him, then suddenly burst into tears.

His first impulse was to go to her, then he remembered Georges' cynical observations, and so he did not move. He waited. He let her cry, though the sound hurt him enormously. She looked so like a child, crouched in her chair, her face covered with the silly lace handkerchief, her hair falling over her cheeks.

Finally she became quiet. She blew her nose with the touching frankness of a child. She dabbed at her eyes. Then she replaced the handkerchief in her bag. She looked at Peter simply, her cheeks still wet. "You, Peter, of course," she said. And smiled tremulously.

Then he went to her. He gathered her up in his arms, sat down, and held her on his knee. She dropped her head on his shoulder, sighing. She put her arm around his neck. They sat in the hot dimming silence, at peace, and almost unbearably happy. Peter kissed her hair, her forehead, her lips. She clung to him with a sort of despairing relief, murmuring incoherently. It seemed to them both that a bright glow of ecstasy filled the room, welled about them, became part of them.

After a long time, the girl sat up, perched on Peter's knee. She took off Henri's beautiful diamond and dropped it into her bag. Peter could not help smiling at the childish gesture, and the air of completion and triumph that accompanied it. For a moment he wondered if she were strong enough to face the storm that would follow her broken engagement, and then instantly decided that she was. In spite of her youth and her unsophistication there was a stern strength in the lines of her pretty face. He told her of Etienne's gift, and produced it. The ring was too heavy for her slender little finger, and too large. But the opal flamed in the dusk like a living thing made of fire and glory. Peter kissed the finger that held it, and the ring, and then the small hand. All the tenderness that had never had an opportunity to express itself in his lonely life, all the love which had been waiting for this hour, had their fulfilment now. Celeste was only the narrow gateway through which his passion and rapture flowed; she was only the small island that was surrounded by seas of flooding light. His love for her was release, contentment and peace. Young and inexperienced though she was, she felt this, and was humbled and afraid, wondering if she were good enough, and strong enough, to accept what he had to give her.

When Etienne anxiously returned, he thought at first that Celeste and Peter had gone, for the living-room was dark. He was delighted to find that they were still there, for his own loneliness was a bitter thing. He had, he confessed, ordered that dinner be prepared for all of them, but he had not wanted to make the suggestion before, thinking that perhaps Peter had had other plans. At the table he beamed at them, his foolishness obliterated in his joy in their joy. He found Celeste incomparably beautiful; he colored with rapture when she thanked him for the opal ring. He could not do enough for them. He was disappointed when he discovered that there was to be no immediate wedding, and when they told him that they were going to Crissons that night to inform Christopher that his sister was not going to marry Henri Bouchard, he eagerly and protectingly offered to accompany them. "I've heard of that Christopher!"

He was bewildered when Celeste's face darkened with hauteur at his remark about her brother. Her eyes became cold and almost repelling. But she said quietly enough, while Peter, frowning anxiously, listened intently: "You don't know Christopher, Etienne. He's very reserved; he doesn't make friends easily, so people think he doesn't want them. If you knew him better you couldn't help liking him, I know."

Etienne, more bewildered than ever, and trying to catch Peter's eye, apologized profusely. People did talk, of course. And especially if they misunderstood they were very uncharitable. But mean minds had to have mean fare. He was sorry, but he had spoken too hastily. He hoped Celeste would forgive him. She smiled. The pure curve of her high cheekbones and chin were stronger than ever, and just a little hard.

Peter's own face had darkened. He regarded Celeste with somber thoughtfulness. If she gave in to Christopher, it would not be from weakness. Therefore he, Peter, was greatly afraid.

Celeste had come in on the Long Island Railroad. Etienne insisted that she and Peter go to Crissons together in his own sleek car. During all the drive down the two hardly spoke at all. Celeste's hand lay in Peter's. It grew quite cold as they neared Crissons, but it did not tremble. As lights flashed into the car Peter could see the girl's profile. It was very calm, almost emotionless, the eyes steadfast. Again, he was afraid, though he could hardly have explained why. He thought constantly of Christopher, who must be faced at once. He smiled at his own wincing. The man, after all, was not a monster; he was not inhuman. He was only a human creature. Yet the thought of Christopher was so strong that it seemed to Peter that his personality had invaded the interior of the luxurious car and had poisoned the air. Apparently Celeste was not afraid. Had she been, Peter would have felt easier.

The car swung up the long curving drive to the house. Celeste had already informed Peter that Henri was away for the week-end on Armand's yacht. But Crissons was full of guests, among them Edith and old Thomas Van Eyck. The house was blazing at every window with lights. The grounds were full of wandering and laughing people. The chauffeur brought the car to a gliding stop. Peter prepared to get out. Suddenly he stopped, and looked at Celeste. She looked back at him. He could just see the pale oval of her face in the darkness, and the more intense darkness of her eyes. She must have felt his irresolution, his fear. She softly put her hands to his cheeks and kissed him on the lips, all in silence. She was much younger than he, but all at once he felt that she was immeasurably older and more understanding.

He helped her out of the car, and hand in hand they walked up the steps of the large square white house, deftly avoiding the guests. As they entered the reception hall they saw Adelaide slowly descending the stairway from the upper floor. She saw them; she stopped instantly. Her eyes searched their faces. She clasped her hands convulsively together, and smiled. Her lips shook. "Celeste," she said, and could say nothing at all beyond that. Celeste dropped Peter's hand. She went up the stairs to her mother, and kissed her with complete calmness. "Peter and I are going to be married," she said.

Adelaide put her arm about her daughter and held out her hand to Peter. She still could not speak. There were tears in her tired old eyes. Peter kissed her cheek. "It's all right, Adelaide," he said gently.

Celeste seemed in command of the situation. Something of

342

the Bouchard ability to control events manifested itself in the way she took off her hat and gloves and tossed them upon a table. Adelaide and Peter seemed irresolute and shaken beside her. She could even smile at them with entire poise. "We've got to talk to Christopher right away, Mama," she said. "Where is he now?"

Christopher was outside somewhere, said Adelaide. She had turned pale; she kept glancing about her with a terrified expression. Christopher was sent for. The three stood in the hall and waited. Every room beyond and about them was lighted and empty. Now, all at once, each room, the hallway, the stairs, seemed permeated with menace, full of enemies. Then Peter saw that Celeste was afraid, after all. But he did not touch her. She stood a little apart, waiting. Her mouth was rigid, her eyes a trifle fixed.

Peter wondered who should speak first when Christopher entered. Should he, himself? He had decided on that when Christopher came in, laughing, with Edith. He had decided that he would ask everyone to leave this absurd place in the hall, where the tableau could easily be seen from outside. There would be dignity in a quiet consultation. He was startled when it was Adelaide who spoke first and immediately, looking directly at Christopher with courage and fortitude:

"Christopher, Peter and Celeste have just told me they are going to be married soon."

Christopher had entered, laughing. He was no longer laughing, now. He stood there, a curious smile fixed on his narrow face, his almond eyes motionless. Edith, beside him, gasped once, then was still. Her hand, which had been on Christopher's arm, slipped off. She turned as white as death.

Christopher looked at them all, slowly, without expression. He looked at Celeste, then slowly, at Peter. And then, last of all, at his mother. He still smiled. But now, all at once, the light gray eyes gleamed malignantly.

"Christopher," said Celeste. She went towards her brother, holding out her hand to him imploringly. Peter stepped forward; the gleam in Christopher's eye had become murderous as it turned upon his sister.

But he took Celeste's hand. He smiled at her humorously. He swung her hand a little in his, as he had done when she had been a child. "Isn't this a little—sudden?" he asked indulgently. Her forehead was wet, and wisps of black hair clung to it, curling. With his other hand he gently pushed up the hair, then patted the girl's cheek. Edith, at his side, did not
343

move or speak. She had averted her head, and even her lips were white. Adelaide clasped her hands convulsively together.

Christopher now turned to Peter, his expression amused and amiable. "What have you been doing to Celeste?" he asked. His voice was indulgent, just faintly censorious, and he spoke in the tone of a father reprimanding the little boy playmate of his little daughter for some impropriety.

Peter flushed violently. For the first time in his life he felt the deep and ecstatic urge to kill. His nostrils flared out; his upper lip lifted from his teeth; his eyes were as baleful as Christopher's. But he said very quietly:

"I'm going to marry her."

Christopher laughed gently. He put his arm about Celeste and shook her affectionately. The girl's face was full of fright, and Peter could see the veins throbbing in her temple. She could not take her eyes from her brother's face. She seemed to realize, for the first time, what evil there was in him.

"Well," said Christopher, "don't you think we ought to discuss this in private? Upstairs, in my room? After all, we may attract an audience."

He held Celeste's hand tightly. He went towards the stairway. Adelaide was standing on the bottom step. She moved aside, as though in horror, as her son approached. He passed her without a glance, holding Celeste's hand. After a moment Peter followed.

The three disappeared. Adelaide and Edith stood alone downstairs. After a long time they looked at each other steadfastly, without speaking.

Then Edith, her eyes fixed ahead, passed Adelaide on the stairway. She held her dark head very high. She went up without hurry. She went into her own room.

Adelaide did not move. She leaned against the balustrade and closed her eyes. Her dry colorless lips moved as though she were praying.

CHAPTER XLIV

CHRISTOPHER said: "Let's sit down and discuss this like intelligent human beings."

"Is it possible you can do that?" asked Peter. Christopher

did not reply. He merely indicated a chair for his sister. She sat down. Peter picked up a small chair and put it beside Celeste's. He took her hand. She did not remove it, but she also did not respond to his warm pressure. Her hand was very cold, but still. She did not look at him, but only at her brother.

Christopher sat down. He appeared utterly unperturbed. It was not a matter of importance he was about to discuss. It was some minor affair in which he had been polite enough to exhibit some interest, though he knew beforehand that he would be bored. Peter observed this; his mouth set palely and grimly. He said to himself: the main necessity is calmness.

He had not thought it possible to hate anyone as he hated this thin-profiled and venomous man with the "Egyptian" eyes and vitriolic smile. His values were suddenly confounded. Before the raging of his hatred his passionate belief in tolerance and compassion was shriveled like paper on which had been inscribed the meaningless scrawls of children. He had believed that he had discovered that no man is vile, and no man good, and that the difference between men is only in degree. Now he believed only in evil, and the terrible struggle he must engage in to destroy this evil. Yet, all through him went the dreadful feeling of impotence. He could not attack when nothing was presented to attack. Before Christopher's indulgent and minimizing attitude all hot exigencies and passion became absurd and futile, and not a little ridiculous, and more than a little improper.

Christopher lit a cigarette, then remembering, offered one to Peter. He smiled at Peter, shaking his head slightly. Peter accepted a cigarette; he detested himself because his fingers shook. Celeste was not tense; she sat very quietly, waiting. But every bone in her face stood out under her flesh. She did not look away from her brother for even an instant.

"Now then," said Christopher, addressing both of them with a smile and a casual gesture of his hand. "What is all this?"

He seemed to glance at his sister, but she saw only the glaze of his eyes, a glittering film of glass behind which he surveyed her inimically. He seemed to glance at Peter, and Peter, too, saw the film of malignant brightness.

He tried to keep his voice without emotion as he replied: "It's just this: Celeste has found out that she prefers to marry me instead of Henri. She made a mistake. That's all. Does it need any more discussion?"

Christopher pursed his lips with a tolerant judiciousness.

345

He said frankly: "Yes, I am afraid it does. You see, Peter, Celeste isn't a little shopgirl, of no importance and no name. She is Celeste Bouchard, a great heiress, and daughter of a great family. When her engagement to Henri was announced, it was of world importance. She's not a chorus girl. She can't lightly hop from one engagement to another every few weeks without attracting undesirable attention and notoriety. You see her position?"

It was Celeste, now, who spoke, for the first time since she had entered this room, and there was nothing but tranquil firmness in each word: "None of that is important, Christopher. You see, I never knew many men. Then Henri came. I—liked him. I still like him, no more and no less than I did the day I became engaged to him. But since I've known Peter I know that what I felt for Henri isn't enough. I love Peter," she added simply, her voice dropping to a lower note. Her deep blue eyes, fixed so intently upon her brother, suddenly glowed. She smiled. Now, the hand that Peter held warmed, and he felt its pressure.

Christopher's indulgent expression did not change, except that it became more affectionate. He ignored Peter; he gave all his attention to his sister. In a tone of regret he said: "Do you think this is fair to Henri, darling?"

She pressed her lips together; her nostrils dilated. Peter felt a quick thrust of fear, and he tightened his hold on Celeste's hand. He spoke before she could speak: "Do you think it is fair to Henri for Celeste to marry him, now?"

But Christopher still ignored him. He waited for Celeste to answer him. He still smiled, but there was malevolence in that smile.

Celeste drew a quick breath. "Peter is right," she said, and her hands clenched together as though all at once she was dreadfully frightened.

Christopher shook his head gently. "I don't agree with you, darling," he said. "And I don't understand you, Celeste. This isn't like you. Let's be sensible. You haven't known Peter very long. He is new. He—isn't like the rest of us. You are a romantic young girl, and like all romantic young girls you are afflicted with hero worship." Suddenly he laughed with apparent enjoyment, and his laughter threw Peter into a shamefully ridiculous light, a light of cheap sentimentality and half-witted grandiloquence.

The rage and increased hatred that swept over Peter made him ill. He did not know what to do. Anything he could do or say would make him appear more ridiculous than ever, would degrade him in Celeste's eyes. He said to himself, forcing
346

himself to sit without moving in his chair: He is trying to arouse me. He wants me to make myself contemptible, and shame myself. So he did nothing, though his face was coldly damp and his heart was beating with enormous pain.

Christopher waited. But Peter did nothing. He had made the unbearable reply of silence to ridicule, and it was Christopher who was cheapened. He showed no sign of his inner fury, except that his thin features sharpened with subtle brutality. He did not glance at Peter, but he thought: He is more dangerous, and more intelligent, than I suspected.

Poor little Celeste was white to the lips. But her fortitude kept her calm in spite of a strange terror that had taken hold of her at the sight of Christopher's eyes. Her voice was steadfast but thin: "You make me sound like a fool, Christopher. But I'm really not. I just know I can't marry Henri, and that I want to marry Peter. And I'm going to, you know."

Christopher was silent for a moment. Neither Celeste nor Peter suspected what frightful things went on in him, rage and hatred and murder and despair and deadly determination. They saw only that his face had a curious fixity, and that he had dropped his eyes. He began to examine his finger-nails. The silence in the room became almost intolerable. The open windows brought them the sound of voices and laughter outside in the dark hot night. There were flashes of light on the ceiling from the headlights of moving cars. Someone was calling for Christopher. A telephone shrilled downstairs.

Then tears began to fill Celeste's eyes. Her heart ached, yearned towards her brother, who had become a stranger she did not know and could not understand. Her mouth shook. She said: "Christopher. Christopher!" And now she held out her little hands to him in a gesture that pleaded for both forgiveness and comfort. Peter could not bear it. He put his arm about her; he tried to draw her attention to him. But she looked only at her brother. The tears began to slip down her cheeks.

Christopher continued to examine his hands, palm and back. Then he slowly lit another cigarette. He examined the tip critically. He seemed to be absorbed in thought. Nothing could have been calmer than his manner and his gestures. But Peter saw the swollen veins in his narrow sunken temples, the blue lines at the edge of his lips.

He cried out: "Celeste, don't you see what he is trying to do to you?" He could stand it no longer. He stood up. He faced Christopher, and in a loud hard voice he said: "I know you. I know what you are. I know what you're up to. But

347

you're not going to hurt Celeste. She's going to marry me. You're not going to browbeat her, and poison her; you've got to get past me first." He bent over the girl, who was rigid and bemused. "Celeste, don't let him hurt you. Can't you see what he is doing? Let me call your mother——." His heart was pounding with increasing pain, and he found it difficult to breathe.

Christopher said casually: "Don't be an ass, Peter. Sit down. I hate heroics. I'm not up to them. Like you. I've always conducted my affairs like a mature human being. I'm sorry if you can't meet me on equal ground. Besides, it's up to Celeste, after all, isn't it?"

He flicked off the ash of his cigarette. And again Peter was overwhelmed with a sensation of ridiculous impotence. He was bitterly disappointed in Celeste. She had not replied to him; she had not looked at him. She seemed intent only on her brother. When Christopher had spoken, her lips had parted and her breath had exhaled in a deep, almost broken, sigh. Peter felt thrust out, an importunate stranger who was more than a little insolent, more than a little intrusive, a stranger who had no right to be in this room, involved in any difficulties between brother and sister. He stared at Celeste, shaken to the heart. He could not believe that she could sit like this, ignoring him, caring only for her brother, hearing only her brother. There was a cold dignity in her expression now, since Peter had spoken; she seemed to be rebuking him for his interference in a matter which did not concern him, and in which he had apparently taken part out of sheer busybodiness and vulgar impudence.

The feeling of illness increased in Peter. He was mortally sick with it; he felt that in a moment he would retch. He was humiliated, stricken. All at once he had no desire but to leave this room, and never see either of the occupants again. Celeste was no longer Celeste, the girl who loved him. She was only the sister of Christopher Bouchard.

And then he knew that he was playing directly into Christopher's hands. His vehemence, his anger, his appeal to the girl, had only set her against him. He not only had Christopher's subtle venom to fight, but also Celeste's devotion to her brother. He was overcome with a profound sensation of despair. But his mind was clearing. He sat down again, tried to control the tremors that ran over his body.

Instantly he was rewarded, for he saw by the slight change in Christopher's expression that he had not expected this self-control, that he had felt that he had succeeded in thrusting Peter out, and that Peter had felt the psychic thrust, and would leave. But Peter had both felt the thrust, and had decided not to leave. A sensation of unfamiliar power strengthened him. He had clashed with Christopher, and it was Christopher, struck, who was recoiling. It was Christopher, retreating, who was eying him, and plotting a new attack. So Peter waited, all his senses alert, his mind clarified and cold as ice.

Christopher's eye was caught by the flaming opal on Celeste's finger, where Henri's ring had been. He smiled venomously. "Where did you get that—thing, Celeste?" he asked.

The girl started. Color came into her pale face. She put her hand with a sudden protectiveness over the opal. And both Christopher and Peter saw that the former had been defeated again.

"Etienne gave it to me," she answered. And now her eyes were strong and steady, rebuking. "It was a present. Because I am going to marry Peter."

And she turned to Peter for the first time and smiled at him. Her young face was drawn, but full of courage and love. She gave him her hand. His sense of triumph was so great that he felt weak and dazed. Her deep blue eyes were wide, and welling with light. Rings of black hair curled on her damp forehead.

Christopher looked slowly from one to the other. He did not see them; he saw the end of his revenge, the end of his life. He saw defeat. And defeat was something which maddened him. It was a mortal insult to his vanity, the one blow he would never forgive. This idiot idealist, this imbecile young girl with the foolish smile! These two had defeated him! These two had struck him down and had stupidly walked over him to their feeble-minded heaven. And here he had been left, waiting for the hyenas in his family, the enemies in his family, to gather about him and laugh him into the final ignominy.

He knew that Armand and his faction suspected him, that they were sniffing closely on his trail. Within a few days they would be upon him, knowing everything. For one blinding and horrible moment he thought of suicide, and sweat broke out of every pore in his body. His violent thoughts drove the blood to his heart, and an intense agony radiated through his chest. The cold and virulent Christopher Bouchard was thrown against the very outposts of despair, and driven almost to madness. He thought: I am going to collapse.

Nothing of what he was suffering showed on his face, which except for grayish pallor was quite composed and almost indifferent. He could make his voice strong and firm when he spoke:

"Peter, you understand that I'm Celeste's guardian? Even when she is twenty-one I have control of her fortune for another nine years?"

Peter was not aware of the falseness of this statement. He said: "It doesn't matter, I assure you. I have enough for both of us." He smiled into Celeste's eyes. She smiled back. Their hands tightened their hold on each other.

Christopher sighed. He stood up. He walked up and down the room, slowly and thoughtfully. Celeste, suddenly anxious, suddenly frightened again, followed him with her eyes. He stopped in front of her and regarded her gravely. He forced his gray lips to smile. He made himself put out his hand and smooth the girl's hair. Somehow, in spite of himself, in spite of the terrible hatred which had replaced his love for her, the feel of her soft hair under his hand gave him an intense and intolerable pang. He was conscious of having to make a great effort to remove his hand. He could not understand his pain, so unfamiliar, so disintegrating.

He said: "You can do what you want to, Celeste. I have no physical control of you. I've been your guardian since our father died. I hope I've been good to you, and that you have nothing to complain of—"

Celeste's eyes, which had been full of fear, now moistened. She regarded her brother gently and lovingly, touched and shaken with remorse. "Oh, no, no, Christopher. You've been so good to me." She burst into tears, through which she tried to smile, imploring his forgiveness.

Christopher sighed. Peter studied him alertly and fearfully. What new and dangerous subtlety was this scoundrel about to embark upon? He put his arm about Celeste; she leaned towards him, but still gazed yearningly at her brother.

Christopher spoke again, very gently: "Yes, Celeste, you can do what you want to do. I want you to be happy. But I'm going to ask one thing of you. And Peter." For an instant his light vitriolic eye struck Peter like a lightning flash. "I'm going to ask you to take just a little more time. I'm going to ask you to keep this matter quiet. Until you are more sure. I think you owe that to both Henri and me, don't you?"

"Why?" said Peter with cold directness. "What does Celeste owe to you?"

He cursed himself for this false move, for again Celeste's almost imperceptible withdrawal rebuked him. She gazed at her brother with passionate earnestness.

"Yes, Christopher, that's only fair. I know that. We're sure,

350

though, Peter and I. But perhaps we'd better wait a little while before telling anyone—"

Christopher smiled slightly. Again he put his hand on her hair. For the first time it visibly trembled. "Thank you, darling. You see, your happiness means more to me than anything else in the world. Young girls change their minds. You changed yours, you know!" and he smiled at her with indulgent humor. "Let's be sure this time. Get more perspective on the problem. Be fair to Henri. Compare him with— Peter. Suppose, for instance, that you don't say anything for at least a month? And in the meantime, see nothing of— Peter, during that time?"

Peter uttered a vehement exclamation. But Celeste said, looking into her brother's eyes: "Yes, Christopher, you are right."

Peter could hardly believe what he had heard. He stared at Celeste incredulously. But she was smiling at Christopher, who had put his hand on her shoulder. And again he felt thrust out, and impotent, and hopeless, and despairing.

Christopher had the genius of being able to follow up an advantage immediately. He turned to Peter. Nothing could have been more tolerant, more amiable, than his expression:

"And you, Peter: you'll help Celeste, won't you? You'll help her to be fair?"

The eyes of the two men met. Peter rose slowly. They stood, facing each other, Celeste between them. They looked at each other with mortal enmity and bottomless hatred, and complete understanding. You, said Christopher's eyes, can do nothing. Everything you say will help to ruin you. And in the meantime, I'll do everything I can to destroy you.

And Peter's eyes replied as violently: I'll fight you. I'll never give up. I know all about you, and there's nothing I will not do to defeat you.

CHAPTER XLV

PETER and Celeste left Christopher's room. Peter kissed her good-by outside the door. "You won't forget me, darling?" he asked.

"Peter, how can you say that?" She clung to him, cried a little, smiled. "But a month is a long time, isn't it?"

Yes, too long, he thought somberly. She was tired, she said, and did not want to go downstairs. So he went down alone. She remained at the top until the curve of the stairway hid him, then she ran into her room and locked the door.

The lower rooms were still empty, the guests still outside in the grounds. But Adelaide was waiting for Peter at the foot of the stairway, from which she had not stirred. She looked up at him mutely as he descended, her dry lips moving, her hands clasped convulsively together. He put his arm about her. "Don't worry, Adelaide," he said gently. "It is going to be all right. Go to Celeste; she will tell you all about it."

She cried out: "It's Christopher, isn't it?"

He shook his head. "Christopher has nothing to do with it, Adelaide. Just go to Celeste. She isn't going to marry Henri." He tried to smile. "She's going to marry me."

She shook her head despairingly. "I can't go to Celeste. She shuts me out. She never wants me; only Christopher. She won't let me help her. It's always been Christopher, Peter."

"Yes, I know," he said in a low voice. He pressed her arm. "We can't do anything, you and I. We can only hope that things will turn out for the best." He added: "And I'm going to see that they do."

They heard footsteps descending the stairway. It was Edith Bouchard, pale, smart and composed. "Hello," she said calmly. She smiled at Adelaide. "Do you mind terribly if I take Peter away for a little while. I want to talk to him. Peter, how did you get here?"

"Etienne lent us his car, Edith. But I'm afraid it's returned to New York now."

"Aren't you going to stay over the week-end?" asked Adelaide, in a sort of panic.

"No, I'm afraid I'm not." He pressed his lips together in the cold obstinate Bouchard expression that Adelaide knew only too well.

Edith seemed to take on gaiety. "Then I'll drive you back to the city, myself. Oh, dear no, it's no trouble at all. It's frightfully hot. The air will do me good. May I?"

Peter hesitated. Then he recalled that he would have considerable difficulty returning to the city unless he accepted Edith's invitation. He had no particular dislike for her; in fact, he rather admired her, and knew that she liked him in spite of many things. He also knew that she was not the person to put herself out for anyone; this offer of hers had an ulterior motive. The thought somewhat amused him. She read his thoughts, and could not help smiling, though he noticed that she was unusually pale. Her black-and-white print dress set off her slender agile figure; her black hair was smooth and waveless. Her dark skin had darkened considerably during her days at Crissons. As usual, she was cool and perfectly poised.

"Thank you," he said at last. He turned to Adelaide and held out his hand. "Don't worry, Adelaide, please."

She clung to his hand despairingly; he could feel its rigid tremor. But she smiled through her suffering. "I won't, Peter," she replied.

Peter and Edith went towards the door. Then little Jean and his large Wagnerian wife entered. They stared at him in surprise. Jean's dimpled face beamed with cunning delight. "Peter! Well, this is a pleasant surprise! I didn't think you were coming for the week-end." He extended his hand, shook Peter's hand vigorously. In the meantime his small dancing eyes searched the other man's face shrewdly. What he saw pleased him immensely, excited him. "Well! Well!" he exclaimed again, and there was an exultant note in his amiable voice.

"I'm not here for the week-end," said Peter, amazed at his brother's extraordinary friendliness. "I came only a little while ago. Now I'm going. Edith is going to drive me back to the city."

"Oh, I wouldn't permit that imposition!" Jean beamed at Edith, whose expression reflected her sudden wariness. "I'll take you back, myself."

Edith interposed coolly: "But I wanted to talk to Peter, privately."

Jean stared at her intently, then looked at Peter. Apparently, he was more delighted than ever. He chuckled. "Well, talk to him, then! We'll leave you alone for a few minutes. Until I get out my car." And without waiting for an answer he hurried out. His big blonde wife stood in the center of the hall, blinking uncertainly. Her masses of yellow hair gleamed in the lamplight. Her great bosom and shoulders were as white as milk, vividly revealed by her dress of black chiffon. Edith, vexed, understanding much, frowned at Alexa, who was immediately intimidated. The poor woman had never been distinguished for her intelligence. Peter, uncertain what to do, turned to Edith.

"I'm sorry," he said.

Edith shrugged. "It can't be helped, I suppose." She studied him earnestly. "Then it's all over between Henri and Celeste? Am I to congratulate you?" Her lips twisted ironically.

353

She had spoken almost in a whisper. Alexa colored violently, and almost wept with embarrassment.

Peter shook his head. "I'm not at liberty to say anything just now," he replied. "Suppose you ask Christopher?"

She still searched his face. Her own lightened.

Jean had appeared in the driveway with his car. Without speaking again to Edith Peter ran out and got into the smart red coupé. Soon they were rolling along the broad dark highway towards the city. The air was full of salt and cool freshness. Jean did not speak for some time, and then in a voice of the utmost friendliness:

"Why did you have to run away?"

"I'm staying with Uncle Etienne," replied Peter, somewhat formally. He was still nonplussed at his brother's extraordinary amiability.

Jean laughed. "Etienne! Doesn't he always play the back side of the horse in Ben Hur? Why the hell are you staying with him?"

"I like him," said Peter angrily. "He's decent, which is more than can be said of the rest of you."

Jean was highly entertained. "Oh, I don't know. We're not so bad. Why do you persist in making dragons out of us? Our State wouldn't amount to much without the Bouchard family. We are directly responsible for its prosperity, its fine schools, libraries, museums and excellent hospitals. We're responsible for lowering the tax rate, and reducing poverty. We give employment to thousands upon thousands of men. We've built churches and research laboratories, and have endowed universities. What more do you want? We *are* the State."

In a very curious voice Peter said: "Yes, I'm afraid you are. But perhaps, in the end, we won't let you be."

Jean was puzzled. "What did you say?"

"I was just making a private observation. Please go on and tell me more about how wonderful we are."

Jean grinned. "Well, for instance, the government would be pretty feeble without us. We give it excellent Senators and Congressmen, not to mention governors and mayors."

"And munitions lobbies, anti-labor lobbies, anti-democracy lobbies, and anti-disarmament lobbies," added Peter.

"Dear me, we are powerful, aren't we?" said Jean in a high mincing voice. Peter could not help laughing.

"But seriously," Jean went on, "why don't you stop giving us black eyes? I hear reports. Lots of people are nasty enough to say you are looking for pre-publication publicity. Others say you are a mediocrity trying to avenge yourself on

354

the more showy members of the family. Others say you are just a trouble-maker, a fool, or worse, an idealist full of crack-brained theories. All this isn't very nice for the rest of us to hear. You're a Bouchard, and we have a family feeling for you—"

"Have you?" asked Peter. Jean could not see his flushed face in the darkness.

He shrugged. "Of course we have; don't be a damn fool. Strange as it may seem, most of us like you! We'd like to see you settle down and get married, and be one of us."

Peter was silent. Jean waited, then went on: "You've got a lot of the Bouchard money. We don't ask you to take an active part in any of the subsidiaries, or the Company itself. But we should like to see you take an interest. There's a lot of work to do in the State, if you're social-minded. Housing legislation, better men in public office, boards of education to be supervised, reductions in taxes, and many other things. Why don't you begin with these?"

Peter was still silent. Jean peered at him curiously in the darkness, but could hardly make out the lines of his face.

"Of course," he continued, "these are not as spectacular as fighting 'munitions lobbies,' and other unimportant things. But they have fine results. Yes, Peter, we'd like you to belong to the family in other ways than just blood. Get married."

Peter spoke in a strained voice that he tried to make light: "Find me a wife."

Jean did not answer for a moment; he affected to be engrossed in making a dangerous turn. Then he said casually: "It's best to keep the money in the family. We have a tendency to marry in the family, you know. Makes for dynasty, and all that, though you can't always trust members of your own house. Frankly, we've thought of Armand's girl, Annette, for you."

"Annette!" Peter smiled. "Why, she's only a child!"

Jean shrugged. "Not such a child but that Armand is trying to ram her down Henri's throat. Henri's an opportunist, anyway. I have an idea he's regretting being so hasty in getting engaged to Celeste."

Peter said nothing, but Jean could feel his sudden alertness. He went on, laughing lightly: "Why don't you do him a favor? Snatch up little Celeste yourself?"

The events of the evening had shaken Peter sufficiently to dull his caution. He remembered only that Jean was his brother, and he still had a lurking sentimental conviction that brothers do, or should, make confidants of each other. So he said very quietly: "That's just what I intend to do."

Jean had not expected such a prompt and open reply. The wheel jerked in his hands. He narrowly avoided an accident. It was not until the road was clear again that he said in a voice he tried to make only mildly interested:

"But what about Henri? Does Christopher know?"

Peter was already regretting his impulsiveness, so he said with some reserve and hauteur: "Nothing is settled yet. It is up to Celeste. She is to make up her mind by herself. For the rest, Henri is to know nothing, and nothing is going to be said. I hope to God you can keep your mouth shut? I haven't forgot that Frank calls you 'the blabber.' "

"I?" Jean's tone was offended. "Look here, my lad, I may talk a lot but I invariably say nothing. Besides, it's of no personal interest to me. I only hope you're not headed for a stink. Engagements aren't so easily broken in our family. Christ! what the newspapers could do to all of you!" He began to laugh; he shouted with laughter. Peter did not hear his jubilation; he heard only the laughter, and his anger rose violently.

Jean reassured him as soon as he could get his breath. He would not violate Peter's confidence. But, if Peter needed any help at all, would he remember that Jean would be only too willing to give what assistance he could? In spite of his anger and apprehension, Peter was touched by this open generosity.

The brothers parted with great amiability. It might have disturbed Peter excessively had he seen Jean stop in at the nearest open drugstore and rush precipitately for a telephone. And he would have been enormously surprised to hear Jean put in a long-distance call for Nicholas Bouchard.

CHAPTER XLVI

EDITH, who had not slept well, got up and went to her bedroom window. She thrust out the window, leaned on the sill. The bare open spaces of grass glittered away from her to the edge of the distant blue sea, which hung, a shining blue curtain, between a pale hot sky and the warm morning earth. She could see the strip of white sand over which the lace-edged blue waves slipped monotonously. Gulls, with light on their wings, swept and dived and screamed in the gentle wind. Far off, near the horizon, faint sails shimmered, and a long low cloud of smoke showed the passing of a liner out to sea. Everything was silent, except for the deep whisper of the ocean, and the thin screaming of the gulls. All the guests were still asleep. The sun was hot on the stone sill, hot on the rugged walls of Crissons.

Edith shook out her long black hair. It fell on her shoulders and breast and over her arms. Her dark thin face was somber, and somewhat set. Then her eyes became alert. Someone was leaving the house and going towards the sea. It was Christopher, in a white shirt and flannel trousers. She watched him approach the narrow strip of sand. He stood there, watching the slipping of the waves, the circling of the gulls with their incandescent wings. He did not stand as other men stood, hands in pockets, smoking, idly enjoying the morning. He stood with folded arms, not moving, not smoking.

She watched him for some moments, then caught up a robe, thrust her feet into slippers, shook back her long loose hair, and ran swiftly down the stairs. No one was stirring. Not even a servant was visible. She opened the door, and ran towards the sea. Christopher still stood there, watching the water. He did not hear her coming, but when she stood by his side he did not seem surprised. He smiled. "Hello," he said. He was haggard. His dry skin looked parched. There were purplish streaks under his eyes, which were paler and less human than ever.

She slipped her hand under his arm, and stood beside him. They stared at the ocean. The wind lifted Edith's hair and blew it about her face, and over Christopher's arm. They said nothing at all.

But in spite of her pity, in spite of her deep pain, Edith was passionately contented. Her hand tightened on his arm. She leaned against him. Then, very quietly, she turned her head and kissed his cheek.

He did not move. He did not respond, but neither did he pull away. "It's not the end of the world, darling," she said gently.

He replied indifferently: "Isn't it?"

"I love you, Christopher," she exclaimed with sudden passion. She turned, so she could look directly at him. She took him by the arms. He saw her dark eyes, full of painful light, and the pale sternness of her face. "I love you," she repeated,

357

and shook him a little fiercely. "I don't know why. You aren't human. But there it is!"

He did not answer her for a moment. His expression changed to one she had never seen before. She was amazed when he replied, quite softly: "Yes, I'm human, Edith. Why are you such a romantic fool?" And he took her hands and held them with such pressure that she was aware of hard pain. But she could only gaze at him with grave muteness, the passionate light of her love shining in her eyes.

Then he suddenly threw her hands away. "But I haven't time for that! Not yet. You don't understand anything."

Again she caught him by the arms, forced him to look at her. "Perhaps I do, Christopher. Perhaps I do." He stared at her. She smiled whitely. "But is it worth it? Revenge or anything?"

His stare became more intense. Then all at once he colored violently. "You are a fool!" he cried angrily. "I don't know what you're talking about!"

"Oh, yes, you do! I've been watching a long time. I've seen a great deal, Christopher Bouchard. More than you ever suspected. Everyone is afraid of you and hates you. Except me. I'm not afraid of you, and so I could see nearly everything that went on in your mind. You're not so damned formidable, and obscure! What do you care about Bouchard and Sons? You don't really want a lot of money; you aren't the type, really. You're too austere. It's just your horrible ego, Christopher. You think everyone laughs at you because of your father's will. Perhaps they did, at first. And perhaps it was because you were such a horrid person, anyway, and they liked to see you hurt. People are like that, you know. But they'd forget. If you'd just let them forget. But you keep it in their minds, that you are full of hatred, and want to get revenge, so they watch you to see if you will succeed. And the funny part of it is, you don't care a damn whether you succeed or not. It's just that you hate everybody."

He did not speak. She felt the coldness and rigidity of his flesh, the mortal fury of a man who has been found out and stripped naked.

She laughed a little, with a catch in the laughter. She shook him lightly. "Darling, I'm not your enemy. I love you. Don't look at me like that because I see you and not the frightful-looking thing you dangle before other people. And it's because I really see you that you love me, in spite of yourself. Christopher, I know I'm right! If it was just money you were after, you would have angled for me long ago. You would have married me for my awful lot of bonds."

And now, incredibly, and involuntarily, he smiled. The rigidity slowly left his arms. His light eyes suddenly shone with amusement, not his usual vitriolic sort, but an amusement which admitted disarming. "How do you know I've not been angling for you all the time?" he asked. And then he laughed. "How do you know I'm not after your damn bonds, anyway?"

She put her arms about his neck, and pressed her cheek against his. She did not speak. Her wordless love, her deep sympathy and compassionate understanding flowed out to him. For a moment he resisted, putting his hand on her shoulder to push her away. And then his hand dropped. He stood, without moving, staring over her head at the bitterly bright water, the blazing sky. Self-pity was not one of his vices. At first he felt only shame and anger that Edith had seen into him so acutely; now he was still ashamed, and still resentful. But, in spite of himself, he was touched and strangely moved by her love and understanding, and strangely relieved. For several moments his despair and rage retreated to a distant pain, like an agony momentarily subdued by a narcotic. He felt the pressure of her breasts against him; he could smell the faint fresh odor of her loose, lifting hair. He closed his eyes. He astounded himself by a sudden shaking thought: If I didn't have to go on!

But that very thought brought him back to his terrible disappointment and despair. Now he pushed Edith away from him. His hands stayed on her shoulders. He looked into her eyes. "I can't help it, Edith," he said. "I'm wound up in my own inertia. I've got to go on. I can't give up." He paused. "Will you do something for me? Don't tell Henri about Celeste, and that dim-wit, Peter. She's a little imbecile. She doesn't know what she wants. It's partly my fault; I should have let her run loose, at least part of the time, the little bitch! Then she'd know what she wanted. A normal girl wouldn't look at—him. So I've got to protect her, too. She'll get over this. She's promised me not to see him for a month, and to give Henri every chance. So, I've got to work fast. I want you to help me. Will you?"

She did not answer immediately. Her mouth set with a sort of uneasy sternness. She looked into his eyes, and her own were troubled. Her inner core of integrity was disturbed. Then she frowned.

"Yes, I'll help you," she said quietly.

"Thank you," he replied.

He paused. He waited for her to smile again, to move towards him. But she did neither of these. At last, without another word, she turned and walked away. He was surprised.

359

He watched her go. She walked without hurry, but without looking back. Her hair blew about her shoulders, floated against the dark red of her gown.

CHAPTER XLVII

"YOU," said Henri, smiling coldly at Christopher, "look kicked in the stomach. What's the matter? Duval-Bonnet sunk in the mud?"

Christopher returned the smile. "No. But what about that loan? Did you get it?"

Henri carefully lit a cigarette. He did not like tobacco particularly. He took a few puffs, removed the cigarette from his mouth, regarded it with disfavor, and tossed it away. Then he regarded the long dark-blue swell of the evening ocean thoughtfully. He and Christopher were standing alone at a rather isolated spot, hidden from Crissons and the private beach by a series of high rugged rocks. The sea came in silently, then reaching the rocky coast, it burst into spume and emitted a sound like the tearing of gigantic bales of silk. The evening wind was heavy with salt, and cool. Far out from the coast rotated the monotonous beam of a lighthouse, brightening as the day darkened.

Henri finally answered: "Yes."

Christopher's heart pounded. His head throbbed with excitement. He turned and faced Henri's profile. "Splendid! And just in time, too! You must have performed a major operation on Regan."

Without facing his cousin, Henri replied quietly: "How did you know it was Regan? I don't think I told you. However, it was. I didn't need to perform any operation. I merely talked to him for some time."

Christopher's acute perceptions were those of an adventurer who is an adventurer by desperate necessity. He did not like Henri's cold expression; he did not like the look on the large pale face with its big brutal mouth. His own mouth tightened to a thin white line; his eyes narrowed. But he said calmly enough: "You must have talked very persuasively. Unless you put up your bonds as collateral."

Henri smiled again, bleakly, somewhat cruelly. "I didn't.

Perhaps I was just persuasive. But I have heard that Regan isn't a man to listen to—persuasion. Haven't you? Anyway, I've got the loan. Twenty million dollars."

Christopher was silent. But the perceptions of a desperate adventurer are alert and vibrating. A curious drumming sound invaded his brain, which, oddly, was also as icily clear as a diamond. (He wants something, he thought.) But he was not one, himself, to thrust his chest against a waiting sword. He was accustomed to wait. And so he waited for what Henri would say next.

Henri knew that Christopher was waiting, and why. He smiled again, this time very unpleasantly. He said: "I wonder if it would be possible for all of us to have a little private talk? Hugo, Frank, Emile, you and I? Very soon?"

Christopher's voice was calm, almost indifferent: "Of course. At least, I think so. Hugo's up in Maine, you know. Frank's on his yacht. So's Emile, on his. But I think I can get in touch with them, and have a meeting next week some time. Naturally, now that we have the loan there'll be a good deal to discuss."

Henri did not answer for several long moments, during which the sea obtruded with a loud and ominous sound. Then he said slowly: "Yes, there'll be a good deal to discuss."

All at once he was smiling and affable again. He turned to Christopher, put his hand on his shoulder. "Let's go back to the house. I haven't seen Celeste alone since I came yesterday. What's the matter with the girl? What have you been doing to her? She looks as though she'd been kicked around lately."

Christopher laughed lightly. He and Henri started back along the strip of beach. "I tell you: the child doesn't know what to make of everything. It's my fault, of course. I've protected her, and kept her locked up all her life. She's beginning to realize that marriage may mean something more than an extended wedding-cake existence, all silver candy and frosting. Don't rush her. Leave her alone a little."

Henri said nothing. Then he began to whistle in a low dull key. He kicked small stones out of his path. When he spoke again it was of something else entirely, something quite inconsequential.

It was curious that at dinner that night Henri could hardly look away from Adelaide. She sat at the table as though she were drugged, her sunken face gray, her eyes remote and fixed. She spoke through lips that hardly moved. When her eyes touched Henri they seemed to distend momentarily. Yet she smiled at him. She was the only woman he had ever respected. He had despised Alice, his mother. His pet aversions were female fools. Men, he would say, had other virtues to offset foolishness. Women had nothing. A female fool was merely a female animal which, while convenient at times, was also more than a trifle repulsive. But Adelaide was not a fool. Henri realized that. He realized it more, each time that Christopher spoke slightingly to, or of, his mother. He was also full of curiosity about her. Once he said to her: "You find the Bouchards a little too much at times, don't you, Adelaide?" She had merely smiled at him, and had seemed faintly amused. But after that there was a slight if secret friendliness between them. She was the thing Henri most admired, a great lady. In this respect he was inordinately like his great-grandfather, Ernest Barbour.

Her face and expression tonight vaguely disturbed him. He came to the conclusion that something was wrong, something connected with himself and Celeste. The girl was very pale, not with the luminous pallor of health, but with a certain deadness of color. She was not a voluble talker under any circumstances. Now she was heavily silent. Even when Henri spoke to her she replied only with inclinations of her head, stirrings of her lips, or gestures. Consequently, as the meal went on, noisy with the laughter of women and the clink of glasses, he grew more somber, more sulky of mouth and eye.

After dinner he took Celeste by the arm and said: "Look, dear, let's get away from all this. We'll walk along the beach alone, shall we?" He was conscious, grimly, that her slender muscles tightened under his hand, that a strange rigidity jerked up her spine and set her shoulders. But she said sweetly and clearly: "Yes, let's." And they slipped out together into the darkness, which was all wind and the sound of water and the heaviness of salt.

The moon was rising over the sea. The sand slid away under their feet. The wind was strong. Now a shattered golden path was on the waves. The sky was as black as ebony, and as opaque. The man and the girl walked in silence. In the warm strong light of the moon Celeste's face had the pure and delicate and heroic outlines of a figurehead; the wind lifted and blew back her thick black hair, giving her a wild stern appearance, at once strong and fragile. Her thin white dress flowed backward from her breasts and hips. She walked as though she were alone, with a strange severe expression and carriage. Henri thought: I would rather have this funny child than all the rest of them together. He put his arm about her. She stumbled, as though suddenly agitated, then went on. Neither her expression changed, nor her manner.

They came to the rocks where he and Christopher had talked a couple of hours ago. He helped Celeste climb up on them. She sat down; he sat beside her. The moonlight made her face luminous; the delicate sternness of it was more marked than ever. He felt her quietness and resolution, and an unfamiliar melancholy. He took her hand; for a moment he thought she was going to resist, then apparently she thought better of it, for she let her hand remain in his. He saw that she was faintly smiling.

He rubbed his cheek against her bare shoulder. A quiver ran over her body, but she still looked out over the water, without turning. He kissed her firm flesh. "What's the matter with you?" he murmured.

He was surprised at the strength and clarity of her quiet voice: "Nothing is the matter, Henri. It's just that I have so much to think about."

He laughed lightly. He took each of her fingers separately, worked them, released them. "What are you thinking about?" he asked indulgently.

"You." Now she turned and regarded him gravely. He was leaning on his elbow beside her. She looked down at his face, so harsh in its lines, so powerful and brutal. Her smile became vaguely frightened.

"Me?" He raised his eyebrows, sat up, intrigued. "I hope you think nice things?"

"Yes, I do." Her voice was amusingly grave and determined. "I do," she repeated. And then, a thin wildness breaking through her voice: "I've got to!"

He was no longer amused. He said with some sharpness: "Why have you 'got to'?"

She did not speak for some time. He saw the quivering of her face. She seemed unbearably agitated, and oddly piteous. Her voice was even wilder when she spoke again: "I've got to be fair to you, Henri! It would be wrong not to."

Slowly and grimly he folded his arms about his knees and stared at the dark sea and the shattered golden path on it. He sat like a stone, not moving. She gazed at him, tears almost blinding her. Once she put out her hand to touch him, withdrew it as at the threat of a burn. She said at last, her voice trembling, shaken:

"You remember, I said that I didn't know whether I really loved you? I said I thought I did. Now, I want to be sure. That's only fair to you, isn't it, Henri?"

He shrugged. He answered her in a tone she had never

heard from him before, so sardonic, so inimical it was: "Oh, by all means, be fair to me, darling. But what has made you so uncertain just now? There isn't someone else, is there?"

He thought that she would reply eagerly, instantly, in the negative. But to his consternation she did not answer. He turned his large head and stared at her, infuriated. She was crying, as simply as a child, the tears running over her cheeks. But she said nothing.

He caught his lower lip between his teeth and chewed it somberly. A cold black fury of hatred and rage began to boil in him. His brows drew together, and beneath them his eyes glittered. He could so control himself that he could speak meditatively, without emotion: "I've heard silly tales. But people talk. For instance, I've heard that you've been doing a lot of running around with that foxy idiot, Peter, with his cough. That isn't true, is it, Celeste?" Now there was an unaffected note of incredulity in his words, and a rage that was beginning to break through.

She threw out her hands with the foreign gesture that sometimes betrayed the origin of the Bouchards. "I don't know!" she cried. And he knew she was lying. That infuriated him the more, but he waited in silence for her to finish. "I've got to be sure! I've got to be fair to you, Henri." Now, in her distress, she put both her hands about his arm. "I promised Christopher I would be fair. And I promised him I wouldn't say anything about it to anyone. You see? Now I've told you because I'm so stupid! I didn't mean to tell you. But I did so want to be fair—" She was sobbing aloud. Her head drooped; her hair hid her wet convulsed face.

He stared at her gloomily. He put up his hand and rubbed his chin. He let her cry, until her hands fell from his arm with a moving gesture of complete despair. Then, very slowly, his expression changed. He began to smile. He put his hand on her bent head, and shook it indulgently.

"Don't be a little imbecile, Celeste. Come on, wipe your face and blow your nose. Haven't you got a handkerchief? I thought not. Here, take mine. That's right, blow your nose hard. What a mess you've made of your face! Here, let me help." He took a portion of the handkerchief and wiped her cheeks. She gazed at him with the humble suffering of a child, but with a dawning comfort. She tried to smile at him, and leaned towards him as if for strength and consolation. He put his arm about her, hugged her briefly, let her go.

"Now, let's be sensible about it, you little half-wit. I begin to see the light. I begin to see what all your funny questions were about: your asking me if I ever intended to get mixed up in the family business. You think it's naughty, don't you, you silly brat? You think the world would be a nice pretty place, with everyone cutting out paper-dolls and loving each other and singing gay little songs with each other, if it weren't for the wicked munitions manufacturers, don't you? Celeste, I thought you were a bright girl! But you aren't at all. You think if we were all dropped in the bottom of the sea human nature would change. But it wouldn't, not a bit. We don't make wars. We just make the instruments of war. If men didn't want to fight we'd go out of business in a week. But they want to fight, and they demand the weapons to kill. We make the weapons. It's just a business. If men wanted to build peaceful ships, extend railroads, build cities, we'd have enough to do, and make enough profits, without war. But they don't. They like to kill."

She did not answer. Her dropped head was in shadow. She was as still as though she were asleep, her cheek on his shoulder. He went on, more humorously:

"I know you'll say, after your coaching by our dear Peter, that it's immoral to make profits out of men's 'vices.' But civilization itself is immoral, if you come right down to it. What is immorality? They say it is the performing of acts hostile to the welfare of society. Well, civilization, with its diseases, its neuroses, its laws, its herding together, its unnaturalness, is hostile to the health and welfare of human animals. Therefore, those engaged in building houses that keep out the sun, those engaged in destroying weeds that kill cultivated harvests, those who make profits by the building of railroads and the movement of commerce, those who demand schools and universities and churches, all are immoral. The only morality, the only healthiness, is war, which is a natural manifestation. We ought to be glad for wars. They show us that man is still not completely enervated, completely dead, completely immoral or civilized."

He paused. The moon was brighter. The whole sky swam in milky radiance. The sea was lighted. The lighthouse threw sharp clear beams across the water. Celeste still sat in complete and immobile silence. Then, very slowly, she raised her head and looked at him with intense gravity and sadness:

"But Peter says that men advance only to the degree in which they overcome themselves. Henri, what you say sounds true and unsentimental. Yet in some way I know it is really false. But I know so little. You've got to let me think it all out, myself. I've got to be fair—"

He laughed loudly. "My God, more crimes have been com-

365

mitted in the name of fairness than anything else! But don't mind me, my lamb. Go ahead and puzzle your little brains out of your head." He laughed inordinately, while she sat and watched him dumbly. Then he seized her and kissed her on the lips with violence. "But don't think for a minute that I'm going to let you go, you idiot! I'm not! Not even if I have to wring your Peter's scrawny neck for him and throw him into the garbage."

He stood up and pulled her to her feet. She seemed dazed. She put her hand to her bruised lips and stared at him over it. He took her chin in his fingers and shook it indulgently. "I'm not going to say anything, if that's what you're afraid of. Go on and be fair. But remember, your fairness had better be in my direction."

He helped her down from the rocks. He held her hand tightly. "Come on, let's run. I bet I can outrun you any time."

They ran along the beach. Celeste's hair blew back. Her mouth opened. She laughed, gasped. Her hand grew numb in Henri's grasp.

CHAPTER XLVIII

JAY REGAN leaned back in his chair, smiling genially. He said to himself: Things like this are an oasis in a desert of dry finance. His happiness increased as he saw the face of each man who entered his great mahogany-paneled office.

Francis Bouchard came first, with lean and elegant ease, smiling charmingly, as usual. Then came Emile, dark, stout and brutal, smiling also, but certainly not with ease. Then came Christopher. At the sight of Christopher, Jay Regan sat up in his chair. He had never openly admitted it, but he admired Christopher considerably. Here was a man who had been knocked down, and who was conspiring desperately to get up and sink a knife into those who had worsted him. Jay Regan liked men who did not crawl, even if they were murderous men without honor. Even if they were pale dry-lipped men with almond-shaped inhuman eyes, and full of malignancy.

Last of all came young Henri Bouchard, and Jay Regan experienced again the quickening, the swift amazement, that he always felt at the sight of this youthful man. Each time the resemblance to his great-grandfather seemed stronger, more astounding. He ought not to be dressed in modern clothes, thought Regan. He ought to be wearing somber black broadcloth, a ruffled white shirt, a flowing black cravat. His hair should be longer, and a trifle lighter. He ought to be carrying gloves and a gold-headed cane. (For such was his remembrance, as a very young man, of Ernest Barbour.) He felt excitement again. Time was nothing. It was Ernest Barbour entering this room; it was Ernest Barbour in America again, the lusty America of brigands and feudal barons, who had made her strong and powerful, involuntarily, it is true, but still—

"Sit down, boys, sit down!" he said affably, not rising, and shaking hands with each of them, from his chair. He beamed at them, folded his hands on his great paunch. "It's a hell of a hot day, isn't it? But this is Henri's idea. Business, even if you fry."

The three older men smiled at this witticism. They, thought Regan with enjoyment, would like to fry Henri personally. Henri was sitting beside him. He put his big beefy hand affectionately on the young man's shoulder for a moment.

"Really," he said helplessly, "I don't just know why Henri insisted upon your all meeting here, and having me present. But he is a very remarkable young fellow. Perhaps I, as well as you, am going to be much entertained."

Christopher's gray motionless eyes gleamed for a moment. His thin colorless mouth jerked almost imperceptibly. Jay Regan, watching him keenly, decided that Christopher had aged very much in the past year. He was haggard, gaunt, his dry skin wrinkled like old parchment. But all his malevolence, all his hatred and bitterness and cold rage, flared fiercer and stronger than ever behind the emaciated flesh. He is finishing himself off, thought Regan, with a dim twinge of too open compassion.

"Let's get down to business, eh?" asked Henri, raising his eyebrows humorously. "We've got to get back to Crissons and cool off in the sea. Why does anyone stay in New York in the summer?" He held a slim black leather case on his knee, on which his strong broad hands lay quietly.

"This," Francis reminded him gently, "is entirely your own idea, Henri. If we stew, you're part of it." And his eyes fixed themselves upon the young man with a smile but without noticeable friendliness.

Emile frankly inserted his handkerchief between his bull's neck and his collar. He fanned himself with his hat, and said, simply, "Whew!"

367

But Christopher said nothing at all.

Henri spoke without preliminaries:

"As Mr. Regan has lent me twenty million dollars, I thought it only fair that he should see, for himself, all negotiations. That is why I asked you all to meet me here. Mr. Regan, I must admit, hardly saw the necessity. He," and now Henri's large broad face changed with a wry humor, "has only lent—me—a considerable sum of money, and there, he believes, his usefulness ends. I don't think so. Mr. Regan's father was my great-grandfather's close friend, and there has always been a close communication between the two families."

"Yes," admitted Jay Regan genially, "thieves do like to keep an eye on each other."

Again they all smiled, all except Christopher, who sat like a mummy, and as motionless.

Hugo Bouchard, who had warned them he might be a few moments late, now was admitted, all buff expansiveness and excellent teeth. He shook hands with Regan very cordially, slapped each of his relatives on their sweating backs, expressed himself colorfully about the heat, demanded of Henri the reason for this infernal meeting, and sat down at last.

He lifted his hands, let them fall on his big knees, and laughed. "I'm helpless among fellows like you," he said. "I'm only a politician, not a big-game burglar. But here I am! You asked me." He winked at his brother, Francis.

Francis said: "Henri is new to business. He likes everything to be above-board. That's why we're here. Isn't it?" he asked with lightning-like suddenness of Henri.

But Henri was not caught off guard. "Of course!" he answered frankly.

He resumed: "Some time ago I told all of you that I was pretty certain I would be able to get a loan of twenty million dollars. I also mentioned at that time that when I succeeded in negotiating this loan I would have a proposition for you. That is why I have asked you here: to hear the proposition, to accept it or reject it, as you see fit."

A prolonged silence followed his words. Consternation, suspicion, apprehension, all passed like shadows over the listening faces about Jay Regan's desk. But Christopher showed no emotion at all, except for a more baleful light in his eyes, a grayer shade upon his flesh. Then Francis laughed a little. His lean face was suddenly damp. He wiped it with a fine linen handkerchief. Emile's big florid face had turned purple. Hugo was no longer smiling, but had become exceedingly and nastily alert.

" 'Reject it!' " repeated Francis lightly, waving his handkerchief playfully at Henri before putting it away "How could we reject it? Don't agitate us too much in this goddam heat, my child."

Henri's large heavy lips twitched, but whether it was with contempt or amusement no one could tell. Like Ernest Barbour, he was no sadist. He was merely exigent and opportunistic.

"I'm glad you said that, Francis," he said calmly. "Now, here is the proposition. As you have said, I'm new to business, therefore my proposition may sound somewhat crude. But don't mistake me; I mean it. The terms will have to be met.

"Twenty million dollars have been lent to me. I am to lend it, in return, to you. That was our original agreement. Yet you must realize that I am entitled to collateral. This money will have to be paid out of future earnings, with interest. You can secure permission to issue additional stock to refund this money. But I would not advise it, as it would jeopardize our position. I would suggest, on the other hand, that all of you assign enough additional stock to me as collateral to make my holdings 55% of the common stock. I will deposit this stock with Mr Regan, and promise that I will not sell any of it. But you must appreciate that with the assignment of this stock to me I am to be consulted on the future policies of this organization, so that I may at all times know the condition of Duval-Bonnet. After all, I was entrusted with the twenty million dollars, and Mr. Regan's interests must be protected, too. Especially considering that he will have no collateral except this deposit, which will be in my name."

He added, in the profound silence of the room: "I could have put up part of my bonds as collateral. But Christopher, I believe, will need these bonds in a little matter we have talked of before." And he smiled unpleasantly.

No one broke the silence. Behind his white mustache Jay Regan was smiling peculiarly. He, unlike Henri, had a touch of sadism. The old robber baron was delighted; his ancient pulses were throbbing. He looked at each appalled and hating and infuriated face. He saw murder in four pair of Bouchard eyes. He could not keep his glee decently hid. But no one was looking at him. Each man saw only Henri Bouchard, who sat, quiet and composed, and as cold and motionless as a rock, waiting to hear what his kinsmen would have to say.

Then Francis began to smile malevolently. He touched his forehead in an ironic salute to Henri. He whistled. "Fifty-five percent of the common stock!" he exclaimed lightly. "In

369

other words, you would have the control of Duval-Bonnet."
He added, laughing: "Nice!"

Henri shrugged. "Only nominally, of course," he said indifferently. "Only until Mr. Regan has been repaid his
twenty million dollars, with interest."

"Your tenderness about Mr. Regan's money is very touching," said Francis. "He does not seem particularly apprehensive. But each man's honor is his own, and I wouldn't
for the world violate yours, my dear Henri."

Emile, apparently about to have a stroke, was regarding
Henri with violence and rage. "You're a louse," he said in a
thick strangled voice. He seemed to have some difficulty
with his breathing, and panted hoarsely.

Francis raised his finger with affectionate reproach. "Emile!
I'm surprised at you. After all, as Henri says, this is a business proposition. Business is very sacred, especially when it is
mixed with honor. Let us be calm." He turned to Christopher, who had taken on a corpselike and immobile appearance, so that only his virulent eyes showed life. "Well,
what have you to say, Chris?"

Christopher's nostrils distended, but he said nothing. He
looked only at Henri, and there was something appalling
in that look.

Hugo began to laugh disagreeably. "Remember, Frank,
that I said I smelt a distinct odor of snake-in-the-grass on a
certain day. I was right, it seems. The odor is now a stench;
the snake-in-the-grass is out in the open at last." He grinned
at Henri. "Bravo! The family has now produced a bigger
burglar than the other burglar!"

But Henri was apparently not much disturbed at this display of family affection. His eyes had narrowed. He looked
slowly from one to the other. One might almost have said
that there was a grim satisfaction in his expression, a somber
and vengeful satisfaction, merciless and bitter.

Francis turned to Regan. "Mr. Regan," he said in a
friendly voice, "in the event that we consented to turn over
55% of the common stock of Duval-Bonnet to Henri, he would
deposit it with you. Now, even 55% at the present time is not
worth, by a terrific amount, twenty million dollars. Would
you mind telling us, or would you? why you have lent this
money to our little cousin, Henri, without his bonds? I realize
this must be an embarrassing question, but, you see, we are
in rather an embarrassing position, ourselves."

Regan regarded him for some time with amused thoughtfulness before replying:

"Many, many years ago, long before you were born, Frank,

Ernest Barbour came to my father with what seemed a preposterous proposition. It involved millions, also. The collateral was barely more than half the sum. He studied Henri's ancestor very closely. Then, finally, he lent him the money. Reckless? Reprehensible? Practically embezzlement? Perhaps. Perhaps it was even foolish. But, he lent him the money. And so, I am following in my father's footsteps; he was really an astute gentleman. And," and he stared at them blandly, "Henri is also following in his ancestor's footsteps." Suddenly he shouted with deep rich laughter, slapping his huge thighs, throwing himself back in his chair.

There was no other sound in that office but his laughter, though hatred and murder and rage were there, awful and voiceless presences. Emile was sitting with his hands planted on his knees, which were spread far apart; he chewed his lip savagely, his black brows tangled together. Hugo stared at the floor. Francis faintly smiled, as though meditating. Henri waited, without emotion, his pale inexorable eyes gazing stonily at the opposite wall. Christopher still did not move; his very eyelids were motionless; he did not seem to breathe. He had been still so long that everyone was nervously startled when he did speak, in a low monotonous voice:

"We cannot accept these terms. We must do the best we can without the money. Duval-Bonnet is mine," and then at last he looked from one to the other with the most terrible eyes. A spasm seemed to run over his emaciated body.

The others listened, then, one by one, Hugo, Emile and Francis slowly nodded, grimly but with determination. Then they looked at Henri.

He sighed, shrugged. He opened the case he held on his knee. He brought out a blueprint. He said in a heavy and regretful voice: "Then, I'm sorry I've got to do this. Look at this print. It contains several of the features of your patent, and was patented a year before yours. It is true it is not nearly as practical, and in fact other of its features nullify these important ones. But, you can't use yours without violating at least one of these. And," and he glanced at each one with merciless deliberation, "I own this patent."

No one moved. Every breath was suspended. Every drop of color drained away from the faces of his kinsmen. He extended the print. No one took it; everyone stared at it as at something frightful which paralyzed him. Henri extended it to each man in turn; no one took it. Finally, with a contemptuous gesture he flung it upon Christopher's knee. "I am surprised at you," he said. "Your patent lawyer must be very inefficient."

Christopher took up the print. The others saw, with surprise, that his gaunt hands were trembling. For some reason this disturbed them enormously. They watched him, shaken. He went over each item in a ghastly silence. They could tell nothing from his haggard face.

Henri spoke again: "At the present time, you are violating my patent. However, I shall do nothing, if my proposition is accepted. I'm much interested in aircraft, and I wouldn't mind setting up a plant of my own to manufacture it, myself. I've invested money in Duval-Bonnet. If the worst comes to the worst, I can insist that you turn over your patent to me."

In the following silence the creak of Francis' chair, as he sat back in it, was sharply audible. He regarded Henri with a curious expression. He said, almost with amusement: "I know I'm being vulgar to ask this, but here it is: Why are you doing this to us? After all, though I am afraid you might call this sentimental, we are friends and relatives. You are Christopher's first cousin. You are going to marry his sister. Frankly, between us two, don't you think you are being a bastard, stinker?"

Henri replied to him, but he looked at Christopher as he did so: "Yes, what you say is quite true, in a way. We are relatives. But apparently family feeling doesn't run very high among us. For instance, Christopher's nice papa put my mother into a position where her children are outside the Bouchard pale. Do you think that was very loving?"

No one answered him. Christopher carefully re-rolled the print, and quietly laid it on Regan's desk. He looked more deathlike than ever. Now his eyelids quivered continuously.

Henri continued: "My great-grandfather made Bouchard and Sons. It was Barbour-Bouchard, originally. Everything that it and its subsidiaries are today is because of him. Yet Jules Bouchard, by trickery and mountebankery, by betrayal and misrepresentation, caused the name of Barbour to be stricken out, in spite of the fact that without Ernest Barbour the Bouchards would have amounted to nothing. Don't you think that it is preposterous for you to be sentimental at this late day?"

He laughed a little, roughly. "Yet, really, I am doing nothing to you that any other business man would not do. I am merely securing a loan. The money is being lent to me. In fairness, I am demanding collateral, to safeguard Mr. Regan. I'm sorry I had to put pressure on you, but it was really your own fault. I could have put up my own bonds, as I said before, but I am retaining my bonds for Christopher's use in that little matter with Armand which I understand we are going to take up later. I think I am being damned fair."

He added: "I have already given my word that I'll sell none of the stock assigned to me. I already intend to give half of what I have bought to Celeste, as a wedding present."

Christopher gazed at him steadfastly, and knew what an enemy was this. But some of the corpselike look was leaving his face. There was still Celeste, who was going to marry Henri Bouchard. So, to the stupefaction of his kinsmen, he said quietly: "Perhaps you are right. Perhaps I would do the same. Anyway, we can't do anything, it seems, but agree to your terms."

Immediately there was an uproar. But it was an impotent and raging uproar. The Bouchards knew when they were beaten. This uproar was merely the venting of this fury. Christopher slowly stood up. He had to clutch the back of his chair to keep himself from falling. But his expression and manner were composed. He regarded the others with contempt.

"Shut up. It's done. Stop your damned yelping. You haven't been hurt. Yet." He slowly turned to Henri, and his eyes were deadly. He repeated: "Yet."

CHAPTER XLIX

GEORGES and Peter sat in the former's study, discussing Peter's book.

"It's no use, Peter," said Georges. "I can't, and won't, change my terms. You use a pen-name and keep in the background, or no business between us."

"You own quite a lot of stock in Bouchard and subsidiaries, don't you?" asked Peter bitterly.

"Yes," replied Georges calmly. "I do. But don't get the idea I've got a sinister motive in insisting upon a pen-name. I haven't. It's just that I consider it extremely bad taste for a member of a family to tear the other members to pieces. Maybe I'm sentimental; but I do like a little loyalty, occasionally. Why do I publish this book, then? Ah, but I'm not sole owner of the company! I don't shape the policy, entirely! Besides, it isn't generally known that I am the president."

"Why do you agree to publish the book at all?"

Georges smiled. "I like it. I think it's sensational. I love your style and your enthusiasm, and your goddam sincerity. I believe you have facts. Facts are always violent, and violence sells books."

"Is that all? Is that really all?" demanded Peter, with increasing bitterness.

Georges shrugged. "My dear boy, don't go sentimental on me! A long time ago I was the passionate adherent of my wife's father, Professor Fitts. He had—reverses. He couldn't adjust himself to them. He became prematurely senile, and then, at last, he was killed." He paused, then added almost gently: "You see, I adjusted myself." He laughed: "But don't you adjust yourself! An adjusted writer is a ruined writer."

Peter was silent. He felt ill with frustration and bitterness and despair. For the past week or so a heavy despondency had hung over him, weighing down his body. He had not heard anything from Celeste, and knew he would not hear. Sometimes a sick rage against her rose up in him. He found himself viciously deriding a loyalty like hers, which sacrificed a lover for a brother. There was no one to turn to; his relatives despised and disliked him. His mother hated him. He was a pariah. When he found himself indulging in self-pity he was infuriated against himself, and ashamed. And yet, there was no one who was his friend, except old Etienne, who was never clearly aware of anyone but himself.

He saw all about him men with devoted and loyal friends. As a rule these men were no better than others; some were more greedy, more treacherous, more cruel, more rapacious. Yet Peter had to admit that their friends were sincere in their affection. He found none of their vices in himself; he found no evil in his mind, no selfishness in his desires. Yet, everyone seemed to hate him. Was it because he was "different"? He recoiled in disgust from that thought. The "different" people were invariably stupid, posers, dull, inferior and maladjusted. Was it because he was "good"? He was more disgusted than ever.

He found Georges' affectionate but immovable decision one of the bitterest things in his life. He had convinced himself that there was some cynical decency in Georges. Yet, at the last, his first thought was for the "family." He had the most profound doubts of Georges' professed loyalty, Georges who had an aversion for nearly every Bouchard, and who laughed at them all very heartily. Georges' decision violated some illusion in Peter, and he could not get over it.

He had to give in. He agreed to take an inconspicuous pen-name. Defeated, he left Georges' study and went for a lonely walk. He was suddenly sick to death of living. The world of men seemed to him a horrible place, full of creatures who leered at each other, tore each other to shreds, violated, tormented, hated, murdered, betrayed and despoiled each other. He felt a terrible spiritual nausea, a turning-away of his consciousness. To live in such a world was to live in a humid jungle, where laws were chains of grass about the necks of beasts. There was no gentleness in them, no mercy. Only lust and greed and hatred.

He thought again of Celeste, and even the thought of her was like a spasm of sickness. He turned away from her. Of course, he had not expected her to write or to communicate with him for a month. Yet the memory of her, shining upon her brother, averting her head from her lover, was an agony. As the days went on he slowly became convinced that she would never write him, or recall him, even at the end of the month.

He slowly turned back to the house. A maid informed him that Georges wished to see him. Eagerly, hoping for a reconsideration, he hurried into the library. Georges was sitting there in the dim, leather-cool room talking to a visitor. For a few moments Peter did not recognize the visitor, coming as he did from blazing sunlight into cool dusk, and then he saw it was Henri Bouchard.

All his blood seemed to rush in a dark thick wave to his heart. He could not speak, though Henri was now standing up and smiling at him coldly. Georges still sat in his chair with an uneasy expression, for all his apparent indifference.

"Hello," said Henri. "I came especially to see you, Peter."

Peter still could not speak. In the dusk his face was white and drawn and extremely stern. Georges stood up. "I suppose you two would like to be alone," he began. But Henri lifted his hand.

"No. Please stay. I'll only be a minute. I would like you to hear what I have to say. There's no secrecy about it."

Georges sat down again, more uneasy than ever. He shot a glance of furtive pity at Peter, who had fixed his eyes intently on Henri's large harsh face.

Henri was silent for a moment. He studied Peter without emotion. A faint derisive smile tugged at the corners of his lips. Then he said: "I've got only one thing to say to you, and I think you are sensible enough to listen to it. I want you to keep away from my girl."

Georges' long thin nose wrinkled distastefully. He thought this very bad form, even vulgar. Gentlemen did not speak so ruthlessly.

Peter's features slowly became rigid. He regarded Henri steadfastly.

"Do you mean Celeste? If so, she isn't your 'girl.' She doesn't want you. She is going to marry me."

Henri stared at him incredulously for a moment, then he burst out into contemptuous laughter. "She wants you! Why, you damned idiot, she wouldn't look at you twice, if you'd keep away from her for a week! Why the hell should she want you, you bloodless, cowardly fool? I'm not going to waste words on you. I tell you now, keep away from her, or I'll break your neck. I mean it, now. I'll literally break your neck."

"Look here," began Georges, angered, and sitting upright in his chair. But Peter lifted his hand to quiet him. He still faced Henri.

"I like coming to the point. And so, I'll tell you something now, myself. Celeste doesn't want you. She told me that. She took you only because she was a child who didn't know any better. She was pushed at you, by that white snake of a Christopher. Now she knows better. I know you'd like to tell me that Celeste sent you. But your coming here is proof she didn't."

His voice and manner were quiet, contrasting sharply with Henri's loud harshness and brutality.

Henri laughed again. He looked Peter up and down slowly and contemptuously. "She wants you!" he said meditatively. "Why?"

"Ask Celeste," replied Peter. A gray shade of exhaustion had deepened on his face.

There was a long silence in the room. In that silence Henri's pale eyes narrowed and gleamed. He still smiled that derisive smile. Finally he said: "You want me to take you seriously, don't you? But, you see, I don't. I know what you are! You're a treacherous, sneaking coward who hasn't the guts to fight for what he wants. You're incompetent and fishy and impotent. You haven't an ounce of decent loyalty. You and the damned book you're using to club us with! In a better society we'd be able to hang you for this! But you can't meet us on equal grounds, so you write scurrilous lies about us, you muckraker!"

Peter listened very quietly. His eyelids widened; they were filled with a steadfast blue light. Georges noticed for the first time that Peter had the square-cornered eyes of the martyr and hero. He watched their intense blaze, which seeemed to have something of fanaticism about it. He stood up, and turned to Henri.

376

"You and your kind," he said contemptuously, "invariably believe that restraint is cowardice. It isn't. I'm sorry I let you in here. Go on, now, get out!"

But Peter said to him sharply: "Please don't interfere, Georges. I'll handle this myself." He paused. "Henri's out of date. He likes melodrama too much. For instance, he thought of himself as a strong true-blue Harold charging in here to warn a would-be seducer to keep away from his sweetheart. He belongs in a nickelodeon, with his talk of breaking necks. The-Face-on-the-Bar-room-floor school of acting. I never did like it, even when I was a child. I don't like it now. I especially don't like it in Henri, who ought to know better."

A thick red flood ran over Henri's face. Georges, surprised and delighted, opened his mouth in a startled smile.

Peter shrugged. "Henri's doubling up his fist. In a moment he's going to push it under my nose. Then I'm supposed to recoil, because I weigh about thirty pounds less than he does, and he knows how to punch. I don't. I only learned how to kill." And now the light was blue flame in his white face.

Henri stared; the other man's eyes hypnotized him. He had never before seen the flame of pure hatred in anyone's eyes. But there it was, steadfast, a little mad, but bitterly cold. He had to take pause, singularly disturbed. He had expected fear, recoil, uncertainty, shameful silence. But he had not expected this. He thought to himself: I believe he would kill!

Ernest Barbour faced Martin Barbour again across the width of a century, and again he felt impotence, the inability to inspire fear, which is the most demoralizing experience in men of his type. At the final ruthlessness he would have to stop. But men of Martin's kind never stopped, once they started.

He did not know what to do or say next! He literally did not know! The thick red blood still surged in his face. He was conscious of a horrible embarrassment.

Peter was speaking again, in a very low voice: "You talk about meeting all of you on equal grounds. I can't. Because I'm not a rascal, I think. I'm not a liar and a thief. Perhaps this makes me inferior to you. I don't know. Anyway, I don't want to meet you on equal grounds. I'd have to step down too far. But I'm wasting too much time with you. So I'll tell you just one thing: I'm going to marry Celeste, unless she, at the last minute, decides she wants you."

He went to the door, without hurry, without a backward look, and went out. The door closed silently behind him.

Georges began to laugh uproariously. Henri's suffused face

lighted with rage. He swung on Georges, doubling his fists again. This made Georges laugh with such violence that he fell back in his chair, helplessly. For a few moments it seemed that he would choke. Finally when he could get his breath, he exclaimed: "Go on, get the hell out of here!"

CHAPTER L

CHRISTOPHER, standing by his bedside table, held a small white pellet in his hand. He regarded it with somberness. It was a sedative. He had had to take them regularly, these nights. By nature, he hated a weakness which demoralized self-control. But three nights of utter sleeplessness, during which he had felt that he was going insane, made him take the weaker which was at once the wiser course. For a few hours, at least, he could forget the frightful situation in which he found himself.

He swallowed the pellet, lay down in his bed, folded his arms under his head. The warm summer moonlight seeped through the Venetian blinds. In that hot dusk his fixed colorless eyes gleamed like polished stone. There was no sound but the sound of the ocean, sighing restlessly and eternally in the night. Christopher turned his head alertly. In the next room lay Celeste. As he thought of her, his face took on a pale shimmer.

The sedative began to work upon him, but his thoughts were too terrible to surrender to it. He was enduring agonies. He was like a man surrounded by bayonets, upon which he must eventually impale himself. There was a weight of iron in his chest, which grew heavier each minute. The bed trembled slightly, with his trembling. He could not endure the darkness. He turned on the light. His face was slimy with sweat. He sat up, gasped once, groaned. Then he got out of bed, rolled up a blind, sat on the windowsill.

The grounds were mysterious with spectral moonlight. There was no shelter, no shrubbery. All at once he hated this openness, this barrenness, this cleanness. There was no darkness anywhere, nowhere to hide, to forget. He saw now that his love for sterility, for open places, came not from any desire of his, but from a psychic wish to see his enemies at all times, unconcealed.

In the light of imminent defeat he saw himself clearly, and was infuriated. He knew now that he had no true lust for power, no absorbing greed. These were what others had, not he, and because these others' had believed them valuable, so also believed he, knowing that to obtain the respect of others, one must obtain what they consider valuable.

He was sick to death, of everything, including himself. He wanted to give up. Shamefully, he regarded his desire for defeat. But to accept defeat, one must abolish hatred. He could not relinquish his mortal hatred. Therefore, he could not relinquish success. The answer to his enemies was triumph. He loathed this triumph now, but his wish to answer was still as powerful as ever.

I can't give up, he thought. In that indomitable decision his love for Celeste was shriveled and blown away.

For the last few days, while he, appalled, saw his desire for the valueless ebb away, he had not been able to say anything to Celeste. He knew she waited for him to speak about Peter and herself. But something held him back. He struggled against it, for it was like a large hand upon his mouth. He avoided Edith, for in her face, so pale and tired, in her eyes, he saw her prayer to him that he would not hurt her brother, though she, herself, in spite of her own love for Henri, would not give up, either.

He had tried to speak to Celeste with ridicule of Peter. He had only waited for Peter to get out of the way! But alone with Celeste, he could say nothing. He had tried. But the hand on his mouth had been too heavy. And now a week had gone by.

He hated her for his impotence to destroy Peter. He avoided her. He did not know that his gray silence, his bladelike averted face, were more potent against Peter than any word he could have said. Celeste saw that he was suffering; she thought he was suffering because he was afraid for her. She was frightened; she knew that Christopher loved her, and she had trusted him all her life, believing him wise and good and strong. She had relied upon his judgment. Now, she saw that he was suffering, and it could only be because he was afraid of what marriage with Peter could do to her.

In the imminence of Christopher's love and protection and familiarity, Peter acquired a faint hostile aura. But Henri became more dim. Celeste no longer considered him at all. He had left Crissons for Windsor, which he had declared more attractive than any summer resort. Upon his leaving,

379

Celeste forgot him entirely. His sister remained, but for her Celeste had acquired a fearful aversion.

Christopher knew these things about his little sister, dispassionately. Perhaps, in some curious way, this knowledge was the heavy hand upon his mouth.

He tried to think, realizing the desperate necessity for thought. At each awful vista, opening to his eyes wherever he looked, his soul sweated with despair and violence. Henri Bouchard was to him no longer a young man, and a relative, but a symbol of the hostile and inimical forces with which he had been surrounded all his life. The only hope he had, now, was the marriage between Henri and Celeste. Through Celeste, he would have a rein to hold Henri in check. Celeste was a thin but unbreakable wall of glass through which he could watch Henri, and be safe from Henri at the same time.

He left the window, more distraught than ever. The warm pale moonlight stood on his face, which was like death. He paced up and down the room. Celeste, awake and wretched herself, heard his movements. She felt guilty and contemptible, and lay in rigid misery, listening to him. But as she did so, she was pervaded with the memory of Peter, and it was so sweet, so protecting, that in spite of her efforts she relaxed and smiled with deep contentment, and finally fell asleep.

Christopher opened a desk drawer and drew out a bulky envelope which had arrived that morning from Francis. He re-read the short note: "Movie-idiocy or no movie-idiocy, you'd better use these if nicer methods fail. Send for me if you need corroboration. It's nasty, but it's necessary. We're too deep in the soup to be nice about this."

He re-read the incriminating correspondence between Peter and Francis. He felt disgust and a sense of degradation, new sensations for the merciless Christopher. He sat on the edge of his bed, the papers in his hand. Suddenly the sedative took effect, and he fell asleep, sunken there in a sitting posture, in the warm dim darkness.

He dreamt that Adelaide was standing beside him, in the room, as he sat. He could see her despairing and pleading gestures. He heard the sound of her voice, saw her mouth move. Her hands fluttered in the dusk, urgently. He did not know what she was saying, but he finally gathered that she was pleading, not for Celeste, but for himself.

CHAPTER LI

CELESTE sat in her room, her breakfast tray on her knees, reading a letter from Peter. She kept re-reading it. Her lips trembled. Someone knocked at her door, and when it opened she saw that it was her mother.

The two women regarded each other in silence, Celeste's unguarded expression turning to one of reserve and formality. Adelaide was tremulous and tired. "Come in, Mother," said Celeste.

Adelaide sat down on the edge of a chair. She kept putting her handkerchief to her lips. Her eyelids were moist and reddened. Celeste regarded her with uneasy alarm. "Is anything the matter?" she asked, something fluttering in her throat. Adelaide shook her head. Then she turned in her chair and stared blindly through the window. She began to speak as though she were talking aloud to herself:

"It's a terrible thing for a mother to have to stand by and watch her children destroying themselves, and be thought only an old impertinent fool, if she tries to save them."

Celeste was silent. Her lovely colorless face became cold. Her fingers folded and unfolded Peter's letter. Then, when Adelaide did not speak again, she said formally: "I don't know what you mean, Mother. What am I doing that's so wrong, this time?"

Adelaide said, not looking at her: "I know you have a letter from Peter this morning. I saw it on the tray." Now she turned to Celeste and cried passionately: "My darling, what are you doing to yourself? What is Christopher doing to you?"

Celeste's face was like a stone wall suddenly rising to confront the old woman. Adelaide blamed herself bitterly. She had only to mention her son's name to have this look appear in Celeste's eyes, this maddening look.

"Christopher's doing nothing to me, Mother. That's silly. He doesn't even speak to me—about Peter. He's left it entirely to me." Tears appeared in her eyes. "And apparently Peter doesn't mind so much. He's away up in Canada. He tells me I needn't write to him unless I ask him to come back."

"Oh, the fool!" cried Adelaide, beating her clenched hands

together. "Doesn't he know that he shouldn't leave a girl like you alone with—him?"

"You're being unfair to Christopher!" exclaimed Celeste, angrily. "Christopher doesn't even mention Peter. It's just that I gave Christopher my word that I wouldn't do anything for a month."

"Your word!" said Adelaide bitterly. "You don't know what you're doing, Celeste. You don't know who you're dealing with. How can you use honor in dealing with rascals and thieves?" She stood up and approached the bed. "Write to Peter, Celeste, at once. Tell him to come back to you, that you need him, and that you want him to take you away. My darling," she implored, "listen to your mother. I know more about this than you do."

Celeste regarded her inimically. "Mother, you never did like Christopher, did you?" she asked coldly. "You used to try to turn me against him when I was a little girl, and he was so dear and kind to me. You said unkind things to me about him, and he never retaliated, not even once. He hasn't a friend in the world, besides me. Everyone tries to blacken him, and lie about him. You're his mother; you ought to have been more sympathetic. But you've been so hard——"

Adelaide stared at her, aghast, not at the words, but at her own helplessness. "Celeste! You talk like a fool! Christopher's my son; I'm his mother. What can you know of our feelings for each other, a silly little girl like you? A silly little girl without any experience in living, a foolish little girl who can't even recognize what a fine person Peter is, and how little she deserves him! Celeste, you're a bad impudent girl, and I can't forgive you." She burst into tears, and put her handkerchief to her eyes, stricken, and ashamed that she could not help debasing herself like this to her daughter.

The coldness and obstinacy of the Bouchards became more evident in Celeste's face and eyes. "I'm sorry if you think I'm impudent. I didn't mean to be, really. But you've never been a friend to poor Christopher. You even tried to turn Papa against him. Oh, yes, you did! And Papa listened, and put Christopher into the most awful position, in his will. Anyone else would have tried to revenge himself. Christopher didn't. He just did the best he could, in the position into which you helped put him. He never asked anything of anybody. He's been just and reasonable at all times. He's been like my own father to me, trying to make up for Papa dying. And you've never, at any time, sympathized with him, or encouraged him, or helped him. You've only tried to turn me

382

against him every time you could. So, how can I listen to you now?"

While Celeste had been speaking Adelaide had been staring at her intently. And slowly, as the girl spoke, Adelaide's face blanched to ghastliness. Her lips moved. Her eyes seemed to see things she never saw before. They formed before her, only nebulous still, and beyond a faint formation she could discern nothing. But it was enough. Scenes that had passed slowly reënacted themselves before her. They moved into position, into place. Words she had partly overheard, gestures she had noticed, expressions she had seen. Henri and Christopher! Christopher and Henri! She suddenly cried out. The plottings, still only half-formed, were apparent to her for a few lightning instants. Armand's fear-filled face and gloominess. The many conferences. The tension in the family. And then, Celeste and Henri, and Christopher's face these days since he had known about Peter——

She cried incoherently: "There's something here you don't understand, Celeste! I've got to go away, and think about it!" She seemed to be feeling her way to the door, as though blind. She went down the corridor to her own room. Someone barred her way; she felt her arm hit against a body. She looked up, dazed, uncomprehending. Then she saw it was Christopher, and one bemused glance at him told her that he had been listening.

His fingers closed about her arm, and she experienced intense pain. She felt herself thrust into her room. The door was closed silently behind her. She stood in the center of the room, Christopher beside her. He was panting a little, and grimacing. And now, through the swirling light and shadow of her horror, she heard him say:

"Keep out of this! I warn you, keep out of this!"

Then she was alone. She did not know how he had gone. For a dazed, chaotic moment she thought that he had just disappeared, like an evil specter.

CHAPTER LII

WHEN Christopher came into Celeste's room, she had already gotten out of bed and was standing helplessly by the window, crying. Her white silk nightgown blew about her in the gentle wind, her black hair, rumpled and childishly curling, rolled on her bare shoulders. She gazed at Christopher with wet frightened eyes, and held out her hands to him in a touching gesture.

He laid down on the disordered bed the envelope he had brought and went to his sister. He put his arm about her. His gray face with its sleepless eyes smiled. "Well, what the devil?" he exclaimed indulgently. "Has someone been upsetting you, pet?"

She leaned against him with a sigh of relief, putting her head on his shoulder. Her arms childishly hugged him, she sobbed aloud.

"Mother hasn't been scaring the life out of you, has she?" His voice was still affectionately indulgent. He picked her up bodily, sat down, and held her on his knee. Now his expression was all quizzical affection. "What's the matter now?"

She looked at the face she had always loved and trusted, and tried to smile in answer. But she said nothing, merely wiping her wet cheeks on the back of her hands. Finally she said: "It's just that Mother thinks I ought to send for Peter, right now, though I told her that I'd promised not to see him for a month."

Christopher patted her shoulder, pulled her closer to him. "Well, you've got to overlook things, sometimes. Don't use that tone about Mother, pet. It isn't the thing, you know. I don't want you to be one of those girls who are confoundedly impertinent. Mother doesn't know all the circumstances, so you've got to be patient, you see. Well, do you want to send for Peter, now?"

Her face glowed unbelievingly. She put her hands on his shoulders, studied his face intently. "Christopher! Do you mean it?"

He did not answer for a moment. He regarded her face, her eyes, and felt her trembling. An odd darkness moved over his own face. He looked away. He was still smiling, but it was a fixed smile now, like a grimace. But he said: "Yes, I do mean it, Celeste. That's what I came to talk to you about, you see. And to discuss future arrangements for your and Peter's future."

She did not answer him, and after a while he looked at her. He was taken aback, for in a moment Celeste had become a woman. Tears stood in her shining eyes; she was smiling tremulously. Her breath had quickened, and there was a light about her which seemed to have its origin in her flesh. He saw that she could not speak. But after a little she kissed

384

him gently, and held his hand. He felt its rapid pulse, its tremor.

"Do you—like—him so much, Celeste?" he asked in a strange voice.

She nodded, still unable to speak, and the light on her flesh brightened.

He dropped his head and stared at the floor. His mouth was a mere slit in his face; his jawbone was hard and sharp under his skin. He saw a brilliant flash of hot color on Celeste's hand. He turned his eyes upon it. It was the opal which Etienne had given her. It seemed to burn like a living thing on the white soft flesh, a derisive thing which flashed its scorn at him, its power and immunity.

He moved his eyes away from it, and they fell on the brown envelope on the bed. The envelope seemed to fascinate him. He regarded it for a long time. Feeling his abstraction, Celeste put on a blue wrap, and sat down beside him. She was vaguely disturbed at his expression, the gray lifelessness of his color, the thin compressed line of his mouth. "Christopher," she said timidly, and touched him.

He moved slightly. He looked at her and smiled. That smile increased her anxious perturbation. He put his hand on her shoulder. "Shall we get down to business and discuss how you two are going to live?" he asked.

She was greatly relieved. "Oh, is that so important?" she asked, and laughed.

He responded wryly: "It is considered so, of course. Well, I'll go into this a bit for you, you little ignoramus.

"First of all, you are a great heiress. Do you know that? Do you know what that means? I thought not. It means that you are one of the powerful people in the world. But what do a pair of fluttering innocents like you and Peter know or care about that! But there it is. I'm your guardian, until you are twenty-one. I thereafter have some control over your fortune until you are thirty. But I've told you this before, haven't I?

"Peter is a rich man in his own right, but not a quarter so rich as you. Though he has said nothing to me about this, or to anyone, I have an idea that that is an annoying fact to him. Men don't like to feel financially inferior to their wives. It does something to their masculine ego." He smiled. Celeste smiled also, but with a dim uneasiness.

"Now, lamb, I don't want you to start your married life with this embarrassment between you and Peter. He ought to be put into a position of importance, so that this importance will overshadow your greater financial advantage, and will also increase his own wealth. Francis and I have discussed this previously." He shook his finger at her indulgently. "Yes, lamb, we discussed this a long time ago, only tentatively, of course, as I had only a little idea that you liked him more than you should have done, considering that you were engaged to Henri."

Celeste laughed. She leaned her head against his with deep contentment and happiness. He had a foreshortened view of her delicate smiling face with its peculiar air of strength. "You're so sweet, Christopher," she murmured.

The arm against which she leaned became rigid as wood. This startled her. She glanced up. But Christopher was still smiling quizzically.

"Oh, I'm not so sweet! I'm just careful, pet. Well, I'll go on. You really ought to be in your bathing suit and down on the beach with the rest of them. You see, Celeste, a fortune is a serious responsibility, almost as much as a husband. Peter knows the responsibility. That is why, before he could make any move in your direction, he approached Francis for help."

Celeste nodded solemnly. She was a little bored by this discussion. She wanted to be alone, so that she could write to Peter. At this thought her eyes glowed, her face flushed. She made a chuckling sound, and clasped her hands together gleefully. "Isn't he silly?" she murmured, shining upon her brother. She glanced at the ring on her finger, and with the simplicity of a child she kissed it.

Again the gray rigidity passed over Christopher's face. His lips moved stiffly when he continued:

"You remember, Celeste, that on the night we first saw him on his return to Windsor he mentioned that he wanted to dispose of his Bouchard stock?"

"Um," she murmured, beaming at the ring, and twisting it on her finger.

Christopher laughed goodhumoredly. "Well, as you know, he didn't. That's because he had already met you, and had also heard that the Bouchard stock was due for a big rise."

Celeste glanced up. The color was still soft in her cheeks, but her expression was startled and dimly uneasy. "I don't think that's quite correct, Christopher. He told me he was keeping it because it made him curious why all of you just rushed at him and tried to buy it."

"Is that so?" said Christopher, raising his eyebrows with humorous indifference. "But I don't think you quite understand, sweet. In fact, I'm reliably informed that he bought

386

considerably more Bouchard stock a little later. This might not be true, but my informant had no particular reason to tell me, if it weren't. He sold this stock at a large profit a few weeks later."

Celeste was silent. The color had gone from her cheeks, leaving them singularly pale, as though the blood had left her veins entirely. Her deep blue eyes fixed themselves upon her brother. The sunlight lay in them, so that they had a strong brilliance. Her young body was motionless, but it was the motionlessness of an animal who imminently expects a death blow.

Christopher could not look at her, for some odd reason. He lit a cigarette with immense but casual care. He snapped the lighter shut, replaced it in his pocket. He puffed tranquilly for a moment, squinting at the ceiling. Celeste still did not move.

"Well, anyway, that's not important," said Christopher. "Francis, however, seemed to think that Peter wanted you, and that you had an eye for him, too. Peter's his brother, and naturally, he was pleased and interested in the idea of a marriage like this, though I must admit that I thought Henri the better man for you. So, he offered Peter a directorship in Kinsolving."

A faint painful smile curved Celeste's lips. "That was silly," she said in a low voice. "Peter wouldn't have anything to do with Kinsolving, or——"

Christopher stared at her, as though astounded at her silliness. "Why not, for God's sake? Of course he would! He considered Francis' offer, and they had quite a lot of correspondence and discussion about it."

Celeste said nothing. She was completely white. She shivered; her body seemed to contract as though stricken with intolerable cold.

Christopher continued irately, assuming an air of impatience and affront: "You surely didn't expect Peter to lead a useless life, did you, tagging after you wherever you went, helping you spend your money? Humiliating himself, and being laughed at by your 'nice' friends? Of course, he writes, but this thing he is writing is the first piece of work he's done of that kind. And if you have any illusions that the average writer ever gets rich, you had better disillusion yourself at once, my young lady!"

He paused, as though overcome with indignation at her immature folly. He pretended to be engrossed in snuffing out his cigarette; he muttered under his breath. But Celeste was still silent; she hardly seemed to have heard what he was saying. The deep blue eyes were still rivetted on him in a face as white as milk.

"Well, anyway, Peter's got some sense, if you haven't, Celeste." He got up, retrieved the brown envelope, and with a manner full of stern annoyance, he flung it on Celeste's lap. "Francis gave me this. You'll see that Peter didn't think a directorship in Kinsolving would bring him enough, and that he turned it down for that reason. I've talked it over with Francis, but he can't do any better than what he has already offered. Read it! Don't sit there like a lump of stone. Read it. I tell you, these letters have done more to raise Peter in my estimation than anything else could have done! He's a man of sense, though I admit I didn't think so at first."

With fingers cold and stiff as ice, Celeste slowly withdrew the little piles and notes of correspondence between Peter and Francis. With a sort of awful composure and calm she read them all. Christopher tried to watch her. But he could not. He walked to the window, pretended to fume. But a sudden horrible nausea made him grip the curtains. He smiled at himself derisively. But the nausea mounted.

He heard Celeste replacing the envelope. He turned back to her with a smile, and deftly took the envelope from her. The girl sat absolutely immobile, her hands on her lap, the palms turned upward as though she had been mortally stricken. Her head was bent.

"I'm surprised at you, Celeste," he said tenderly. "But you ought to be glad that Peter's got intelligence enough to realize the embarrassing position he would be in, if he just lounged around and played lapdog to you. Oh, you'll have your honeymoon! Don't be afraid of that. But when you come back, I'm going to see what I can do for Peter myself!" he added triumphantly.

He waited. Celeste said nothing. "What's the matter with you, Celeste?" he asked, outraged. "Aren't you going to thank me?"

She lifted her head. She regarded him with a strange white smile. "Thank you, Christopher," she almost whispered.

"Well, then," he said in a mollified tone. "I don't know just how it can be arranged. But Armand's taken a liking to Peter. He suggested to me only last week that Peter come in with us. But Armand's as cautious as the devil, and a skinflint. I'll have to do some work on him. But I think I'll be successful in getting a better offer for Peter than Francis gave."

388

"Peter will like that," murmured Celeste. She suddenly drew a loud sharp breath, then held it.

Christopher pretended to be amused at his own thoughts. "Of course, there's the book. But it won't do any harm. I understand Peter has consented to let it be published under a pen-name. I've never seen his writing, but I'd like to place a bet that after he's got what he wants, there'll be no more books! I wouldn't go so far as to say it's a form of blackmail, but Peter's a shrewd fellow, and I wouldn't put it past him," he concluded in admiration.

He paused. He gazed at his sister in deep silence. A spasm ran over his face. He thought: She'll get over it. After a year she wouldn't be able to stand him. There's no one better for her than Henri. But the intense nausea and pain which had assailed him remained.

He moved over to her. He rumpled her hair playfully. She did not seem aware of him. There was a muted blank look on her face which frightened him; the lovely firm mouth was carved in suffering.

"So now," he said, "all you have to do is to write Peter at once and tell him to come home. Or get him on the telephone, if he can be reached. And tell him I have something to say to him when he arrives. I have an idea," he added with slow amused significance, "that he'll understand."

She forced her mouth to move in the lines of a smile. But she did not glance up at him. She hardly seemed to breathe. Her body took on the aspect of hopeless mourning.

He patted her head again, bent down and kissed her forehead. It was cold and damp. "Well, go on and get dressed, lazy wretch. Shall I meet you on the beach? And don't forget that golf tournament."

He went out of the room. He closed the door softly behind him. He stood outside, listening intently, for a long time. But there was no sound from behind the door, no sob, no movement, no sigh, no exclamation of unbearable pain.

He went away. He passed his mother's door. He stopped. The long corridor was luminous with seeping sunlight. There was no sound behind this door, either.

When he went downstairs, he discovered that the house was deserted, for all the guests had gone to the beach. Only Edith was there, waiting for him. He descended the staircase; she was at the foot. Their eyes met in silence as he approached her. When he stood beside her, their eyes were still fixed on each other. Then, with a curious smile, she took his hands and turned them palms upward, as though she were looking for something on them.

389

Peter waited in bitterness and hopeless suffering to the very end of the month. He waited for an extra week, and then two. And then at last he knew that Celeste would not call him, that she would never call him.

CHAPTER LIII

PETER wrote Adelaide from Montreal:

"Georges has sent me your letter,—What can I say to you in answer? It seems to me that everything was said when Celeste did not write me and ask me to come to her. She asked for a month, which I had to give her. She said it was only 'fair' to 'everyone.' It appeared that the question of 'fairness' did not relate to me at all. I was the one who was demanding outrageous things, and I was to be dealt with severely, and held in check, in order that an investigation could be conducted as to whether I was invading someone else's rights. It's no use, Adelaide. If Celeste had wanted me, she would have called me back. Her silence is her answer. That's all.

"Besides, her almost psychopathic attitude towards Christopher's infallibility would make a decent married life impossible between us. I would be the half-witted husband, who couldn't be depended upon to make an intelligent decision. She would always be consulting him; such a situation would be intolerable. I detest him. I think he's a vicious influence on Celeste. But I can't help her to throw off that influence. She must do it, herself, or he must let her go voluntarily, for her own good. You ask me to come back and 'help her.' If she really cared about me, she would send for me, experience or no experience. It's as simple as that. She has a lot of character, and can make up her mind for herself. Unless she does, I can't, and won't, make any move."

Adelaide laid aside the letter with a new feeling of utter despair. Pride! Even in a man like Peter, self-love and self-pride could do this disgusting thing, and abandon a foolish child who was being manipulated to her endless suffering. She, Adelaide, thought that when she wrote him in her frantic efforts to save her daughter he would come back. Surely love was beyond pride, greater than self-love, more profound than any hurt, however deep. She was bitterly disappointed, and more despairing than ever. She realized that even at her age she could still believe that selflessness did live, that men might, at rare moments, be nobler than themselves.

She tore the letter to bits, for she could not bear to know that it existed. It was too wounding, to herself. Destroyed, she could imagine that it had never been written or received. The written evidence would preserve, always remain a symbol of, the fact that she was a fool.

There was nowhere to turn. But she made a last desperate appeal to Armand, begging him to come to see her on a night when she was alone. It was now the early part of September, and the wedding between Celeste and Henri was to take place on October second. Armand came. She had not seen him for a month. She was shocked, in spite of her pre-occupation, by his visible aging, his gloomy and despondent air. His clothing seemed neglected, in spite of his valet. He had a distracted manner of rubbing his temples and chin, and his eyes were haggard. Yet his voice and attitude were gentler towards his mother than they had ever been before. She sensed that he was defeated, and that somehow his defeat had lost sharpness in the face of a greater agony.

She could say, in spite of the reason she had called him to her: "Armand, my dear, you are ill. Why don't you go away? Why don't you leave all this?"

"Go away," he repeated mechanically. He smiled drearily. "Maybe I will, one of these days. I'm sick of practically everything." He paused, then added: "But what is it? What can I do for you now?"

She began to cry. "It's Celeste, Armand." Armand's face darkened. "I don't know what to do. You saw her the other night, at that dinner. Did you see how hard and thin her face is? She's always been reserved, but there's something stony about the child now. Something is dying in her. She pushed me away! She avoids me. I haven't seen her for two days. I hear her footsteps, and then when I look for her she isn't there. She clings to Christopher." She stood up and cried passionately: "Christopher, who's killing her!"

Armand said nothing. He sat heavily, chewing his under lip, his eyes directed at the floor. His mother caught his arm, tried to shake him from his apathy: "Armand! You must do something! I have a feeling, and I know it's true, that he is making her marry Henri for his own ends. And Armand, I know that his ends are directed against you, that he is trying to ruin you!"

She expected him to start, to exclaim, to express incredulity or anger, or demand an explanation. But he did none of these. The arm she shook was attached to his body like a heavy lifeless sack, which hardly stirred in her grasp. His face did not change expression, except to become more somber, more abstracted. She let go his arm and cried out, a sound of pure anguish which pierced through his exhausted emotions and touched his heart. He lifted his head, and regarded her with gloomy gentleness.

"Yes, I know, Mother. I don't know just what he's doing, but he's doing it. I can feel danger for me in the very air around him. He's after me." He raised one of his big hands, and let it drop lifelessly again. "But it doesn't matter. I don't care. Well, maybe not a great deal. Maybe I'll care later. Just now, I don't." He sighed, and that sound, in turn, reached her own heart. "I can't think of anything but Annette," he added simply. And now his eyes were fixed on her with the simple suffering of a child.

She looked at him steadfastly, piercingly, and then with a cry from the depths of her maternity she caught his head in her arms and pressed it against her old breast. She uttered soothing murmurs, stroking his gray hair. Her tears fell on it. He was her child again, tortured, turning to her for consolation. But this quiescence was not the soothed attitude of that child, but the lethargy of despair. He let her do what she wanted to do, but she knew that he found no consolation at all, and that it was easier to sit like this, with his big gray head on her breast, than to resist her.

"Oh, my darling," she murmured bitterly, "why couldn't you have been what you were? You were so good, when you were a little boy. So honorable. You never lied. You never twisted around. You were never cruel, or foxy, or deceiving. I don't know what's happened to you! You've done such terrible things to yourself, my dear. And you could have been so happy, if you had only been yourself. You could have made Annette happy, and your poor wife, and your boy—" She stopped, choked with tears, remembering the sick girl, remembering the headstrong, idle, worthless boy, with his extravagance and greediness. "What we do to ourselves, we do to our children. A man who destroys himself, destroys them, too."

He made a motion as though he would push her away, and then his hand dropped, impotently. He thought: It is true. And the thing is that I never really wanted all this, anyway.

He said at last: "Do you think circumstances would have
392

changed me? I don't think so. We really make circumstances, you know. There are as many villains among the poor as among the rich." And then he smiled at her as though she were very young and foolish. "We become what we are, no matter what conditions surround us."

She released him. She sat down. She gazed at him with such passionate gravity that he was touched again. He tried to speak more lightly: "Perhaps I worry about Annette too much. She was never strong. She seems weaker, lately. But perhaps she'll get over it, as she's gotten over other things."

"She's such a sweet little thing," said Adelaide, weeping again. "I think, that of all the Bouchards, she is the only one who is good."

Armand smiled at her with sad gratitude. "Yes, she is good, isn't she? I'm going to take her away for a while, after the wedding," he added with difficulty. "Maybe before."

His words brought back to Adelaide her own misery. She asked in a despairing voice: "Can't you help me, Armand? Can't you help your little sister?"

He stared at her helplessly. "What can I do? I tried to say something once to Celeste, and she looked at me as though I were an impudent stableboy. You know Celeste; proud and obstinate as the devil." He felt his own impotence as he spoke, his will-to-impotence. He thought to himself: If I really cared about Celeste, I could fight for her. But because I don't care, I can't lift my hand. Something of his old integrity had risen up to torment him these days. At every turn it was met with self-interest, secretiveness, selfishness, greed and anxiety.

Adelaide thought intensely, her hands clasping and unclasping each other. She began to speak, as though she were unravelling a complicated thought: "If you could find out what Christopher is doing, and defeat him at it before Celeste marries Henri, he would have no more reason to force her into this marriage. Then he would see how unhappy she is. Yes, yes!" she exclaimed excitedly, "that's it! You must find out what he is doing, and circumvent him, Armand!"

He smiled wryly. "And how am I going to find out? I've tried, for the last two years. He's cunning as hell. He's covered all his tracks. Even the things we know mean nothing, unless we know the connecting links. He, and Emile, and Hugo, and Francis! We know they're in it up to their necks, but what it is that they are in is something we can't find out. We do know that all of them, including Henri, had a conference in July in Jay Regan's office. But why, we don't know."

Adelaide got to her feet. She walked up and down with disordered and feeble steps. She kept putting her hand to her head in a frenzied and feverish gesture. Her white hair streaked across her forehead, her temples. "There must be something to do!" she cried.

Agnes gave a dinner for her young sister-in-law Celeste, and Henri. It was a family dinner, including only a few close friends. It was a warm September evening, smelling of pungent dust, sunwarmed grass, leaves and smoke. The pretentious chateau on its terraces had, as usual, a false and disoriented air. Adelaide often thought that it reminded her of an ancient grande dame in diamonds and ermine, attempting to hide with her skirts the boots of a groom, which she had inadvertently put on. The faces of the Bouchards, sharp and predatory, watchful and fat, amiable and alert, were out of place in this immense gloomy dining-hall with its enormous candelabra ablaze with tall thin tapers. In that wavering and unearthly light, and surrounded by these dim cold walls shadowed with tapestries and banners, the tinted faces of the modern women, the modern dress of the men, were grotesque. The servants materialized out of the stony dusk, and faded again, bearing silver dishes past draped lances and armor, their feet mutely striking on the polished dark stone floor. The tremendous refectory table, lace-covered, glittered with silver and crystal in the moving candlelight. Here and there this light, leaping palely and with a phantom glimmer, picked up a high banner, tattered and motionless, which hung from the distant ceiling or the walls. The faded crimsons and blues were visible for a moment, and then lost again in the fathomless gloom. The effect was somber and melancholy.

Adelaide hated this pretentious place, this embarrassing affectation. The dark splendor of the baronial hall, the grave dim portraits between the banners, the lofty coldness and dignity, seemed cheapened by these faces, these bare shoulders, these gestures and these toneless voices. She kept glancing about her uneasily, half expecting to see some haughty woman in coif and ruff and jewels appear, the candlelight on her pale stern face.

But most of her attention was centered on Celeste, sitting between Christopher and Henri. The girl's silver dress shimmered in the uncertain light. The delicate strength of her facial modelling had taken on coldness and hard pride. Her black hair sprang backwards and downwards from temple and forehead. Of all the Bouchards there at that dinner, she was the only one who seemed to have a right to be in this hall, under the droop of the motionless banners. She wore Henri's ring.

Annette was there, too, for the poor child was unable to refrain from going to those places where she would see Henri. Her thin white silk gown seemed not to be disturbed by the slightest breathing under it. Her childlike face had a feverish whiteness about it, and her dry lips were brilliantly red. She appeared to be wasting away. She laughed softly but continually. Her beautiful light blue eyes, so deep-set but large under the clear broad brow, were full of a sort of haunted radiance. Adelaide, sadly, commented upon the fact that Peter's eyes were startlingly similar to Annette's. They had the same heroic square inner-corners, the same steadfast and luminous quality, the same gentleness and purity. Adelaide thought: Perhaps I haven't been very kind to Peter. Perhaps I've misjudged him. Perhaps he saw Celeste too clearly.

Annette's pale shining hair was rolled upon her neck. Her tiny white hands glittered with rings, her one weakness. As she talked, shyly and softly, she moved her hands, and the rings winked and blazed. Her father sat beside her, and seemed oblivious to anyone else. When she looked at Henri, she took on a fragile incandescence.

After the first or second glance, Adelaide guessed the truth about the poor child, and a sick chill ran over her tired old body, an agonizing compasssion. She thought passionately: Peter and Celeste. Annette and Henri. In this way nature could modify innate ferocity.

She had come here tonight for one purpose: to speak to Emile about Celeste. Emile, who seemed less her son than Christopher; Emile the dark and bloated, the cunning and opportunistic, with his reputation for loyalty, and his treachery to all men. Adelaide had no hope that he could offer her any help, for he was, said Armand, "hand and glove in 'it' with Christopher." But she could leave nothing undone, or unsaid.

It was not until after two hours that she could isolate Emile in the immense drawing room, and then, because he was restless, and was already eying another group at a distance, and because they would soon be disturbed, she said quickly, in a low voice: "Emile, will you help me? Your little sister, Emile. Don't let her marry Henri. She doesn't want to, really."

He was smiling across the room at someone else. He still smiled, not turning to his mother, but the look of his profile frightened her. He said, almost out of the side of his mouth: "Don't be silly. Of course, she wants to marry him. And if she doesn't, she's old enough to make up her own mind." Apparently the person at whom he had been smiling had beckoned to him, for he started away and left his mother.

She stood alone, in this isolated corner, desolation in her heart. She saw that it was Christopher who had called his brother to him. Across the immense space, she watched them talking casually. They were giving the impression of friendly but easy conversation, quite impersonal. But some psychic prescience told her that Emile had already betrayed to Christopher her pathetic effort to save her daughter. Across that space she saw the needle-flash of Christopher's oblique glance in her direction. Then she heard them laugh.

A sense of horror pervaded her, an awareness of something sinister and deadly cold. What enemies were these, which she had riven from her flesh! Her feeling of betrayal was almost deathly. She felt alone, with icy winds about her, for all the many people passing and talking and laughing in her vicinity.

She turned to look for Celeste. Across another space she suddenly encountered the dark grave eyes of Edith Bouchard, who was also alone. Edith was regarding her steadfastly, and Adelaide had the impression that she had been watching her for a long time, unnoticed.

CHAPTER LIV

EDITH BOUCHARD was not surprised when a few days later on a quiet, early fall afternoon, Adelaide came to see her. She had been out in the garden, gathering asters and zinnias and petunias, and came into the room, now, her arms full of rich purple, gold and orange blooms. Above this riot of color her thin dark face was watchful and reserved, but not unkind, when she saw Adelaide. Her black straight hair had become loosened out in the warm blue wind, and this, and her expression, gave her the look of the portrait of Gertrude Barbour, which hung on the sunlit wall, and which confronted that of Ernest Barbour in endless accusation.

Edith put down the flowers. "Well, Adelaide," she said,

almost gently, but with a warning note already cool in her voice. Adelaide had not spoken. One of her gloved hands had involuntarily moved, as though she had intended to speak. She did not stir until Edith had bent and touched her lips to the furrowed cheek. And then, without volition, the old woman burst into anguished tears. She wrung her hands; she tried to speak, but her voice was choked with suffering.

The younger woman was startled, and taken aback. She frowned faintly, glanced at the doors to see if the servants had heard anything of this extraordinary outburst. Her sense of propriety and reserve was disturbed. And then, as she looked at Adelaide with some censoriousness, the frown smoothed out between her eyes, and a troubled expression took its place. Her mouth softened with compassion. She sat down beside Adelaide, she took her trembling, almost convulsed hand in hers, and pressed it firmly. She said, over and over: "Now, please, Adelaide. Please. Adelaide, do try to control yourself. Please."

But Adelaide had no need for reserve and control now. She had gone beyond these petty reins on her agony. Her flat drained figure bent almost double; the tears streamed down her sunken face. Her sobs racked her, twisted her. And Edith saw that nothing could be done until the paroxysm of grief and torment poured itself out on the stream of tears.

She, herself, felt a sort of shame and pain, as though she had betrayed someone helpless and defenseless. She bit her underlip uneasily, as she waited for Adelaide to weep herself into exhaustion. She studied the bent and shuddering body, the white disordered hair, the wet and tortured eyes. She saw the hands fluttering at her wordlessly, imploring. Finally, she could not stand it any longer, but got up suddenly and went to stand under the grave and mournful portrait of her grandmother, who had been so cruelly betrayed and destroyed. From this position, she waited for Adelaide to become more quiet, more reasonable.

Adelaide was exhausted. She had wept herself out. She wiped her eyes. Then, looking across the room at Edith, she cried out brokenly: "Edith! Edith, you must stop your brother from marrying Celeste!"

Edith was silent. The cold dark mask of reserve slipped over her face. Through its opaqueness she regarded Adelaide without speaking.

Adelaide sighed. Edith winced at the sound, but she did not move. Then Adelaide spoke again, in a low shaken voice:

"I've watched you a long time, Edith. I know you love Christopher. I know you think that by helping him you will

397

turn him to yourself. You think that Celeste is a very small thing to sacrifice for Christopher. You think even your brother is worth sacrificing, don't you?"

A dim pallor moved across Edith's face, she still did not speak. But her eyes dilated.

Adelaide stood up. She came across the room to Edith with quick feeble steps, and Edith, not moving, watched her come intently. Adelaide put her hand on Edith's unresponsive arm. She looked up into her eyes, not accusingly, not angrily, not with feverish importunity, but with understanding and pity and solemn earnestness.

"But, Edith, don't you know you are sacrificing Christopher, too? Don't you know that by helping him to get what he wants you will be helping him to destroy himself? If he succeeds in getting what he wants, that will be the end of him. Because of your selfish love for him, he'll have lost the last chance he has of becoming human again. Celeste is only a small part of all this. There's something greater going on in his mind, of which Celeste is only one part. The only hope for him is to be defeated. The only hope for all of us, and for yourself, is for him to be defeated. Edith, save my son! Help me to defeat him. Isn't he more important to you than yourself?"

A stark fixity made Edith's features like stone. Only her eyes, full of irony, were alive. "This is fantastic," she said at last. She looked away from Adelaide, across the room. "But suppose it were all true. What could I do about it?"

Adelaide seized her by both arms, as though she were trying to force the young woman to look at her. She succeeded. Now the irony was full of pain and uncertainty.

"Edith, it *is* true! And you *could* help me! You could speak to Christopher, or to your brother!"

Edith felt the thin old fingers bitting into her flesh. She looked down at the quivering face, the pathetically smiling lips, the old tears. She closed her eyes on an involuntary spasm, opened them.

"I don't know," she said sullenly. "I've got to think about it. I still think it is fantastic." With a light fierce brutality, she shook herself free of Adelaide's grasp. But Adelaide still stood before her, and her gaze held the younger woman in a grip stronger than that of hands.

"Please go way, Adelaide!" she cried, losing control of herself. "I tell you, I've got to think!" And then she went out of the room as though she were running away.

CHAPTER LV

HARDLY anyone is back in town," said Edith to her bother, as they ate dinner alone together. "But I'm glad of that. We can have a little peace. In two weeks this town will be a bedlam, with your happy nuptials and everything."

Henri drank his coffee and regarded his sister over the rim with some amusement. "You don't seem happy over the prospect," he answered, putting down his cup.

"I'm not," replied Edith, slowly. She averted her eyes. "I hate confusion. I wish, Henri, that we'd never come back here, after all."

He was surprised. "No? Why not?"

He thought she would shrug and answer offhandedly in her usual manner. But she said nothing for a full moment, and then he was more suprised than ever: "Because you wouldn't have seen Celeste."

He raised his eyebrows, and smiled. "Now, what's the matter with Celeste? You two never did seem to get along well with each other, I've noticed. But I thought you had become reconciled. After all," he added, his smile broadening to a grin, "you both love me."

Now she lifted her eyes, and he was startled at the dark passion in them. "No, Henri, you're mistaken. I'm the only one who loves you." When he did not speak, but only stared at her with a darkening expression, she added vehemently: "It's true, Henri! That silly little thing doesn't love you. She doesn't want you. Henri, she doesn't deserve you."

He was about to reply angrily and contemptuously, his face flushing, when he noticed, for the first time, that she looked ill and distraught, and that she had not touched the food on her plate. In the very midst of his anger, he was touched and concerned. His voice was much softer than she had expected, when he said:

"Oh, Edith, don't be ridiculous. What does that kid know about anything, anyway? Besides, I want her. And that's sufficient for me. That ought to be sufficient for you, too."

"No," she answered, very quietly, "it isn't sufficient. It's

399

never enough for only one to love. I don't want you to find out how true that is, Henri."

He was more touched than ever. He offered her a cigarette, and lit it for her. The drifting smoke seemed to enhance the strained tired look about her eyes and mouth. He thought: Poor Edith is a very plain woman, unfortunately. She resembles our father too much. He said: "Now, let's get down to candid facts, Edith. I've been around, among women. You know that. Celeste is no different from any other woman. She may not 'love' me, as you say so damned romantically. What the hell is love, anyway? My guess is as good as yours. And so I know that, though Celeste is a little ignoramus about the fine points of 'love,' no other man will ever satisfy her."

Edith colored faintly. The hand that stirred her coffee shook. He thought, watching her narrowly: She's too agitated for it to be only me. There's something else.

Finally she said, her voice trembling: "I wish we'd never come back. I wish we could go away, just you and I. We were so happy together, Henri, in England and France. We didn't seem to need anyone else but each other. We were friends, as well as just brother and sister."

He thought: She's jealous of Celeste! He was quite moved, and his face warmed with affection.

"Well, dear, we're still friends, aren't we? Oh, come, every sister thinks the woman her brother marries isn't good enough for him, or beautiful enough, or intelligent enough. In fact, God couldn't make a woman splendid enough. Don't let's be emotional about this, Edith."

She said, looking at him with gravity: "Henri, if you were sure that Celeste didn't want you, would you go ahead and marry her?"

Again he scowled at his sister, and answered. "Yes, I would. It's not what anyone else wants that bothers me. It is just what I want."

"Even if you wanted something that would be too terrible for you?"

He shouted with laughter, abrupt and brutal. "Nothing would be 'too terrible' for me, except not getting what I want."

They went into the drawing room. It was warm dusk, here. The French windows stood open. The sky beyond was the deep and brilliant blue of evening. In this passionate hushed light the autumn grass was vividly green, the trees still and washed in radiance. They could smell the warm wind, spiced and rich, full of the breath of distant harvests. A robin was singing his farewell song, his globed silver notes falling into the fulfilled quiet.

Edith sat down in the dusk, near a window. The diffused light made her plain clever face appear more haggard, less colorful than ever. Unhappiness was an aura about her. Henri, infected by her in spite of himself, stood at another window, smoking, pretending to be casually interested in scanning the sky. He was sorry for his sister, and impatient with her. She saw his profile, and thought, as hundreds had thought of his great-grandfather: His face is carved out with an ax.

"When you come back from your honeymoon, I won't be here, Henri," she said. There seemed to be a knot in her throat.

He turned to her, and smiled indulgently. "Now, don't be funny, Edith. Of course, you'll be here. This is your home, as well as mine. Besides, it wouldn't amount to anything without you. What does Celeste know of managing a house?" When she did not answer, he added in a gentler tone: "Besides, dear, I want you."

He waited. She still did not speak. He thought again: It's something else besides me. This annoyed and offended him vaguely.

She sighed at last, and repeated, as though talking to herself: "I won't be here."

He shrugged. "Have it your own way, then, Edith. You're hysterical. I'm surprised, too. I didn't think you had it in you." He paused. "Anything on for tonight? If not, I'll run over and see Celeste. They got in this morning, didn't they?"

Her voice was indifferent: "Yes, they got in. You don't need to run over. I thought I told you: Adelaide and Christopher and Celeste are all coming a little later. Just dropping in."

They came, Adelaide and her son and daughter, about nine o'clock. There was a change in Adelaide. She appeared quiet and firm, and much more composed than she had been for a long time. Celeste was serene. The little sparkle of gaiety which had always been present in her eyes, even when she was serious, was gone, and in its place was a restlessness. But otherwise, she was poised and casual, and apparently much older. Christopher was jocose. He greeted Henri with fraternal affability, held Edith's hand, and touched her cheek with the knuckles of his other hand. He saw that her expression was somewhat grim and hard, and wondered at it indifferently. And then, when her eyes touched his, they suddenly became suffused with a painful light, and she turned away.

The brilliance of the evening had gone. The air had become suddenly hot and sultry and sulphurous. Everyone was conscious that he had been making an effort at conversation, as though there were some psychic oppression in the air. They found themselves staring at each other apprehensively in the lamplight, and suddenly aware that no one had spoken for some moments. Eyes sought other eyes, searchingly. Christopher saw that Edith was deathly white, that her lips were set. He saw that Henri was uneasy and alert, as though conscious of imminent danger. He saw that Adelaide was wringing her hands in her lap, as though awaiting some expected and calamitous event. He saw that Celeste was affected by the atmosphere. She seemed frightened, turning her eyes slowly and questioningly from one to the other. Surely it was this psychic fright which made her young face so pale, and painted these dark shadows under her cheekbones, as though she had grown gaunt during the past few minutes. And then he remembered that he had been noticing these shadows very often lately, and had deliberately forced himself to forget them.

Christopher came back to Edith, and after he had scrutinized her for some time, he thought, with a quickening rise of wariness: She's up to something. He waited for her to speak, and when her lips parted he was suddenly dizzy with fear. But all she said, was: "There is going to be a storm. Does everybody feel as sticky and apprehensive as I do?"

Christopher heard his mother sigh. But Henri said quickly, as though he had been offered some escape: "Yes, I do! Let's go out and walk around a while. It can't be worse out there!"

They went out, Adelaide first, then Edith and Christopher, then Henri and Celeste. The hot darkness was intense, even in the open grassy spaces. It was even more intense in the smothering vacuums under the trees, which were pits of blackness. The profound and hollow silence was pierced through and through with the shrilling of autumn insects, a monotonous sound yet maddening. There was a portentousness in the air, an ominous waiting.

Adelaide sat down under a tree. Her heart was beating rapidly. The portentousness was part of herself. She had known about it, ever since Edith had called her abruptly that afternoon.

Christopher and Edith passed her so closely that she could have touched them, but though she saw them they did not see her. There was the faintest glimmer from the sky, and she could see how they walked, side by side, not touching, but emanating a private portentousness and danger. They were not speaking. Celeste and Henri passed. Celeste was laughing a little. The sound came mirthlessly to Adelaide's ears, a forced and artificial laughter. Then Adelaide was alone. She shrank, on her seat under the tree. She seemed to gather herself together for protection.

Christopher and Edith found their way to the rose garden. A few roses bloomed here still. They had a dry burning scent, without sweetness. Beyond them, the trees were nebulous shadows smudged faintly against a sky that glinted with pale lightning. It was too dark for either to see the other's face. Edith's voice, when she spoke, was very low, but the silence made it clear and sharp to Christopher's ears.

"I'm going away, Christopher, after Henri and Celeste are married."

"Going away?" His own voice was surprised, slightly edged with cautious concern. "You mean, for a trip, yourself?"

She was silent a moment, and then resumed even more quietly: "No. I'm not coming back."

Christopher was silent. She could barely see him. But she felt his imminence. Even in the darkness, she could feel this intense imminence, which was as strong as a pungent odor. The world, the garden, the night, outside him, became empty and presenceless before this imminence of his; they became without substance or living reality. The night, which made most men negligible, increased his ferine quality, as it increased that of the night-prowlers. His innate ferocity was enhanced in darkness, as his physical colorlessness was obscured. Quite irrelevantly and suddenly, Edith thought, with weariness: Oh, dear God! how much I'd like to know some 'nice' people for a change! Nice, safe, normal, kind people, dull people, stupid people, harmless people!

His threatening imminence became almost overpowering when he said: "You're not coming back? Why not? Don't you want to see me any more, Edith?" His voice was close, dangerously close to her, but, she thought, without warmth or passion. And yet it seemed to penetrate her very body.

"No," she said, stiffening her trembling lips. "No, Christopher, I don't want to see you any more."

And again he was silent. A dim murmur of thunder disturbed the air over the trees, and they whispered anxiously together, and then fell once more into their attitudes of immobile waiting. The dry burning scent of flowers blew into the darkness.

Then a rigor crept over Edith's flesh, for Christopher had put his arm about her. She kept herself rigid. His hand cupped her chin, lifted it. His mouth found hers. She stiffened backward, but he held her tightly. She seemed to smother; the trees swirled in a circle before her staring eyes, which were fixed beyond the vague outline of his head. His mouth, which always before had felt so dry and lifeless on hers, was warm now, and demanding. A sick pang ran through her. She thrust him from her violently, and cried out, careless of anyone who might be hearing: "Oh, go away! Leave me alone! You don't want me. You want—something else! And you can't have that and have me, too!"

He caught her arm savagely, and shook her. "Shut up, you idiot! You're making a fool out of yourself!"

She was sobbing dryly. She tried to release her arm. After a minor struggle, he let her go. Her sobs softened to smothered gasps. She could feel him trying to see her, and knew that he was no longer enraged, and even amused. She heard him laugh shortly. That sound cut her. She began to cry, silently.

"Edith, you're a simpleton. Do you know that? Making a scene like this. What's the matter with you? What do you want? Do you want me to make you a formal proposal of marriage?" He waited. She did not move or reply. He laughed again, put his arm about her. "All right, then. Will you marry me, Edith?"

He expected her to laugh, to surrender, to turn to him with eagerness and delight. But he had not expected her to stand like this, not moving, not agitated, and he had not expected her to say so quietly, so unemotionally: "No, I won't marry you, Christopher." And then, as he stood, dazed with amazement and affronted shock, she pushed his arm from her and stepped away from his side.

His sensations were furiously mixed: anger, humiliation, amusement, astonishment, confusion. She could feel his eyes searching for her as a wild beast searches. She wanted to run away, terrified lest she should betray herself, lest she should throw herself upon him, surrendering, lest she should cry out, or strike him. But she had something else to say, and had to remain to say it.

"I can't marry you," she repeated. "I couldn't bear to live with a man who was responsible for my brother's misery." She turned to him, and her voice rose with accusing passion: "Your own sister's misery doesn't mean anything to you! But my brother means more to me than anything else in the world. He'll be wretched, marrying your sister! And in spite

404

of knowing all this, you're pushing her at him, just for your own mean and wicked reasons!"

She panted. Tears and sweat mingled on her face. She waited for him to speak, but he did not. Yet even in the thick darkness she could feel the cold violence of him.

"Oh, go away," she said drearily. She left him, pushing her tear-blinded way through shrubbery and thicket. After a while she heard him following her without hurry. The house, which they were approaching now, was only a dim wall in which were inset triangles of yellow light.

Celeste and Henri had strolled slowly in a direction opposite to that taken by Edith and Christopher. They had talked lightly and casually at first, but now they were silent. When Celeste found herself in a grove of trees, she started uneasily, and then stopped. Her heart began to beat furiously, with a sort of dread and excitement. Henri, who had gone on a step or two, turned around and waited. But she did not follow. He turned back. "What's the matter, sweetheart?" he asked. He bent his head; his voice was close to her ear. She stepped back precipitately, and then stepped forward. "It's so dark and hot here, under these trees," she said. Now it was he who was following her. The night was laced with sparks and flashes before her frightened eyes. She had a horror that if he touched her she would cry out. And yet, more than anything else, she wanted him to touch her, bringing her the reassurance and forgetfulness she desperately craved.

They emerged into a narrow grassy area between two thick groves of trees. Here the air was cooler, freer. Celeste stopped, breathing unevenly. Henri was beside her now. "What's the matter, Celeste?" he repeated.

"Nothing. It is so hot and oppressive," she murmured. The smile which was so automatic and pathetic these days came again to her face, even though he could not see it. He stood beside her, not speaking, not touching her, not even turned to her. But he was thinking. He had had too much experience with women not to feel her disturbance, her distress, and fear.

He was thinking that some virtue in Celeste had been violated, some virtue which had drawn him to her from the very first. It had been a quality mixed of gaiety and steadfastness, purity and strength. Not only had it been violated, it had been destroyed. After a moment, he refused to accept this. Perhaps the virtue had been shaken, during the episode of Peter. But it would come back. Hadn't she, herself, told

405

him that she had made a "mistake" about Peter? Sometimes mistakes did shake the psychic equilibrium, but they never destroyed it. However, it needed time, and change.

He reached in the darkness and took her hand. At first she faintly resisted, then the hand remained in his, childishly warming, as though he had comforted her. He drew the hand forward, and then put his arms about her. He kissed her forehead, her cheeks, and then her mouth, very gently. Again she resisted, and then all at once, like a heartbroken child, she clung to him, silently, almost fiercely.

Tenderness was a new sensation for Henri Bouchard, and he was not yet used to its uniqueness. He could marvel objectively at the gentleness it gave his hands, the soft coolness it blew on desire, its warmth which was at once paternal and overwhelming. He thought: No matter how long I live, there'll never be anyone for me but this funny little girl. He was glad for this tenderness. He knew that Celeste's wounds would have borne no other handling, and would have opened more at the touch of exigency and passion.

After a time they went back to the house, their arms about each other. The deep diffused suffering which was an old familiar to Celeste had ebbed into a gray contentment and peace, as though she had taken a narcotic. When they reached the high level which dipped towards Robin's Nest, they saw Christopher and Edith entering through one of the lighted French windows. They followed. Unseen, unheard, Adelaide crept in behind them.

"Well," said Christopher, in a voice that sounded artificially loud and expansive, "I think we'd better be getting home. There's going to be a rumpus in half an hour. It's thundering already."

Henri glanced about the big room. His nostrils distended, like those of an animal scenting danger. He looked at his sister, so pale, her eyes glittering with tears. He looked at Christopher, the malignant light so vivid upon his narrow, bladelike face. He looked, now, at Adelaide, standing near a window, in an attitude of old fear, hardly breathing. He looked at Celeste, who stood like a child, uneasily aware of secret violence.

"Yes," said Henri, slowly, always watching, "perhaps you'd better hurry along. It looks like a hell of a storm."

He glanced at the window. Suddenly the whole scene outside, trees, grass, sky, terraces, flower-beds and groves, became a scene painted in grisaille, a thousand tints of spectral gray, evoked by the lightning. A moment or two later the deep hollow groaning of thunder rolled over the great house, accompanied by the dry rushing of the awakened wind. The room was filled, all at once, by a hundred disturbed odors of grass and earth and dust.

In the abrupt silence that followed the wind and thunder Edith spoke. Her voice was clear and calm, but singularly arresting. She spoke to her brother.

"Before they go, Henri, why don't you tell Christopher that you are not going to marry Celeste?"

No one moved. Everyone seemed petrified. Four pairs of dilated eyes fixed themselves with terrible intensity on Edith. No one made the slightest sound, not even Adelaide, at one of the windows. Outside, the wind rose again, with a louder voice, and filled the open room with a more insistent presence of disturbed earth and air.

Then Henri's face was suddenly suffused with a swelling scarlet. He regarded his sister with fury. "What's the matter with you?" he exclaimed. "Are you crazy?"

But she looked at him with passionate pleading. "Henri, can't you see what he is trying to do to you? He is trying to tie you, hand and foot. He is using you for his own advantage, not caring what it does to you or to his sister."

Adelaide, at the window, uttered a faint cry, and clasped her hands to her breast. Her brown eyes filled with tears. But no one heard or noticed her. Christopher's face was suddenly wizened, transformed to a wrinkled mask of evil, in which his eyes glinted. Celeste had turned white, her black hair spectacular against her forehead and cheeks. But Henri stood like an enraged bull, facing his sister, his head thrust forward and lowering. His face was swollen, and his inexorable eyes were baleful.

"Get out of this room," he said in a low and violent tone. "Go on, get out."

But she faced him without fear, only with steadfast grief and determination. "Henri, can't you see? He's afraid of you, even while he is using you. So he is using his sister like a rope, to tie you so you can't do anything." She turned to Christopher in sudden passion and thrilling accusation: "Why don't you lie? Why don't you tell him I'm a fool, or that I'm insane and ought to be locked up? Or why don't you tell your sister the truth, that you lied to her about Peter, and manipulated her into this engagement with my brother? Why don't you tell her that you are using both of them, because you are an inhuman monster who can think of nothing but your mean revenge on your brother? Why don't you tell her everything you have done to Peter, and herself, the lies you've told, the cruelties you've done?"

407

Christopher's shrunken lips parted; his teeth gleamed. He and Edith looked at each other across the room. She saw hatred and murder in his eyes, and a malevolence that was not human. She closed her own eyes on a spasm, unable to bear it, feeling that her heart was being torn and shattered in her breast. She thought to herself: It's all wasted. I've accomplished nothing, except to make him hate me. She felt herself seized by the arm and ferociously shaken. She felt the impact of someone's hand savagely against her cheek. She thought for a moment that she was going to faint, for everything became dim and confused, and the floor seemed to move under her feet. Nothing was clear to her but her own thoughts: He hates me. I've accomplished nothing. I'll never see him again.

She opened her eyes. In a gray fog she saw Henri's face, grotesquely and dimly enlarged, thrust towards her. She saw his lips moving, but could hear nothing. It was his hand which was shaking her, his hand which had struck her. She was faintly aware that her cheek was throbbing. There was a taste of blood in her mouth. She felt herself being propelled towards the door, towards darkness. Then she heard a voice, cutting through her confusion. It was Adelaide, who had left the window, and who was standing, now, before her stricken daughter, and pleading. "Celeste, my darling, it's true. Every word is true. Christopher lied to you about Peter. I don't know what he said, but it's a lie. From the very start, he's been using you. He's been pushing you at Henri; he's been working you into this marriage. Because he needed it. He needed it to revenge himself on Armand, because of your father's will."

"No!" cried Celeste, in a clear loud voice, an appalled voice, the voice of a child who, in terror, refuses to believe. Henri heard it, and forgot his sister, whose arm he dropped. He started back towards Celeste, who watched him come with blind and frantic eyes. He had almost reached her, when she saw him, and thrust out both her arms, stiffly, to keep him off. She seemed beside herself. Her expression, the look of her face, paralyzed him. He stopped abruptly, unable to move.

Adelaide turned to her son. She held out her hands. There was no condemnation in her face. Her hands were extended, as though she were praying to him. There was only compassion, only love, only sorrow, in her eyes.

"Christopher," she said. And that was all. But her eyes remained upon him, mutely, passionately pleading, not for her daughter, but for himself. All at once he remembered the

408

dream he had had of her, when she had pleaded for him like this.

The most frightful expression wrinkled his face, but it was only the vaguest shadow of the frightful sensations that went on inside himself. He could hardly endure the torture and madness that boiled in him, the hatred, the fury, the despair. He felt as though he stood in icy water, the sand sliding away under his feet. His hands moved futilely. He struggled appallingly in himself, to regain foothold, to regain what he was losing. He moved his head, as though he were strangling.

Then Celeste, with a rush, had flung herself upon him. Her hands tore at him. Bemused, he looked down at her frantic face, her staring desperate eyes. He listened to her cries. "Christopher, it isn't true! You didn't lie about Peter, did you? You didn't send him away, so that I'd marry Henri, because you had a reason for me to marry him? Christopher!" Her hands tore at him more and more. There was frenzy, futile panic, in her clutches, her drowning hands. "Christopher, you wouldn't do that to me, would you? You've always loved me, haven't you, Christopher? You wouldn't do this to me?"

He looked down at her, shaken by the desperate strength of her hands, his ears filled with her crying vehemence, seeing only her wounded eyes, eyes which begged him not to strike her down, which implored him not to destroy her belief in him, and so destroy herself. But he also saw, as in a terrible and clarified light, what he had done to her. He saw how thin she was, how feverish; he saw the lines of suffering in her young face. He saw her tears. And then, all at once, the pain that ran through him seemed mortal, beyond the endurance of flesh to withstand.

He sighed. He put his arms about her. He smiled. He pulled her head to his breast, in order that he might not have to see her eyes and her tears.

"Hush, darling. Hush, darling," he said tenderly, sheltering her head with his hand, holding her. "I was wrong, dear. I've just found out. I—I've talked to Francis. He explained everything. It was just a joke, those letters. It was a joke between him and Peter. I—I misunderstood Peter. He's everything you've ever thought him, my darling. I would have told you about it before, but I thought you had forgotten him. I even thought it was just an infatuation—I thought you had really returned to Henri——"

Her sobs became quieter. The pathetic tearing hands were still. She relaxed against him, her arms falling to her side. He held her tightly, kissing the top of her head. He did not hear

Adelaide's cry of joy, nor did he see her luminous look of compassionate understanding. He did not see Henri, standing in silence, biting his lower lip. He did not see Edith near the door, weeping. There was no one now, but Celeste, sighing, murmuring, relaxing against him.

"There, there," he said, more tenderly than ever. "Look, darling, I'll send for Peter, right away, tonight. Tomorrow he'll be here with you. There now, hush, my dear."

The next day Christopher received a short note from Henri:

"As we intended, the meeting we scheduled next week shall go ahead. What happened last night has had no effect on my plans. I am writing this to reassure you. Our business together is outside our private affairs, and I haven't changed my mind about anything."

CHAPTER LVI

WHEN Edith came into the breakfast room at the usual time, Henri was not there. She tired to eat. The food made her sick. Finally, she got up and went upstairs to Henri's rooms. He was sitting by a window, when she entered without knocking. He was wearing his dressing-gown, and had not touched the breakfast on the tray before him. He was smoking. Edith, with one swift glance, saw that the ashtray was full of cigarette ends, an occurrence unusual in itself, for her brother was a light smoker. With another glance, she learned that he had not slept. The bed was still smooth and untouched. Henri's chin was dark with stubble, his eyelids red-rimmed. He said nothing when his sister entered, merely regarding her fixedly with his light implacable eyes. His expression was inscrutable.

She sat down near him, still without speaking. She looked at the cold breakfast, the congealed eggs. She looked at the cold expressionless face. It seemed to her that her heart was being torn apart.

"You hate me, don't you, Henri?" she asked gravely.

He merely smoked in silence. She saw that his large strong fingers had a slight tremor. Her mouth contracted with pain.

410

She could hardly keep from bursting into tears, but her voice was quiet when she said: "Henri, I know you can't understand why I did it, even though I told you before that that ignorant child wasn't your kind. I know you think I was vicious and presumptuous. I know you think that I had some mean, jealous, and malicious reason, underneath what you would call my 'rationalization.' But that doesn't matter. I'm glad I did it. I would do it over again."

He spoke for the first time, indifferently: "I'm going to sell Robin's Nest. You can go where you want to. I'm leaving this afternoon."

She clenched her hands tightly together, but her eyes were sad and calm. "Henri, I can't bear to see you this way. I— I've loved you so much. You were the only thing I had in the world. You remember how Mother hated me, and was jealous of me if you even so much as gave me a civil word? You remember how she constantly saying to me: 'You are just like your father!' She couldn't bear to see us friends. She made so much trouble between us—" Her lips trembled, and it was a moment before she could continue: "I was glad when she died. I knew that you loved her, in spite of her malice, and her simpering, hard-hearted sentimentality, and her hypocrisy and tempers. I knew that she poisoned you against me, lied to you about me, found the dirtiest of motives under whatever I said or did. And so, because I loved you and was so terribly lonely, I was glad, terribly glad, when she died. You see, she couldn't bear in the least to see me happy. She alienated me from all my friends, made me ridiculous. Even you, who knew what a dreadful woman she was, finally felt sorry for me. For, underneath, you loved me, too."

She paused again. Henri's eyes seemed to bore into hers like cold steel. But they were a shade less implacable. After a moment, he looked away, gloomily. She leaned towards him, and her body vibrated with painful passion: "Henri, do you think I would have hurt you last night, deliberately? Do you think I did it out of Mother's own jealous viciousness and hate? Henri, believe me, I would have died rather than hurt you. But I had to do it. Believe me, I had to do it."

She gazed at him, pleadingly, her face stark and drawn. Then, when he did not look at her, or move, she put her hands suddenly over her face and sobbed aloud. His expression grew more and more gloomy. The cigarette burned down in his fingers. He listened to those harsh tearing sobs, and his brows drew together.

His mother's carping, jeering, silver-flute of a voice filled his mind. He saw her dark-blue eyes, glittering and dancing with malice. He saw her finger pointing at Edith. "She's up to something, the sly fox! She can't plot nice things, with that dark, ugly, sallow face of hers! She has to be clever, because she's so hideous! But I know all her tricks! Just a nasty old maid, who's trying to avenge herself on the world because she can't get a man, even with all her money!"

Henri's mouth tightened, then relaxed. In spite of himself, he could not keep from regarding his sister with furtive pity. He saw the tears between her thin dark fingers. "Oh, do stop, Edith," he said impatiently. He thought to himself, of his mother: She was really a damned bitch. He could not rid himself of the vision of young Edith, in London, in Paris, with her plain clever face and hurt proud eyes, and thin body; he could not stop hearing his mother's whining, petulant, hating persecution of the girl. He remembered that part of his old annoyance with Edith had been because his mother had made it uncomfortable to be friends with his sister. He recalled the furious physical battles he had had with Edith, after his mother had deliberately aroused him against her, and for one vivid moment he saw Alice's face, alight with sadistic glee, as he beat the girl. He said again, louder now, to shut out his mother's taunting voice: "For God's sake, stop crying! That's not going to mend anything. You've done the damage. No use wailing over it."

Edith wiped her eyes. She gazed at him imploringly. He could not meet her look, and again he turned away. "Forgive me, Henri," she said humbly.

He moved restlessly. "That's too much to ask. Yet, I suppose the best I can do is to try to believe that you had some altruistic motive behind your meddlesomeness. I've got to go away, for a long time. We'd better not write. We've got to leave it as it is."

She cried out, wildly: "You call it only 'meddlesomeness'! You don't know! You don't know that I gave up my whole life last night! My whole life! There's nothing left for me, nothing ever again!"

He stared at her, astounded. Her face was tragic, her eyes wild and wet with despair. "What's the matter with you? What do you mean?" he demanded roughly. He turned around to her, and faced her directly.

She struggled for self-control. Dry sobs pushed themselves through her lips; he saw the beating of her heart in her throat and temples. She said simply: "You see, it was all arranged, from the very beginning. He—Christopher—wanted you to marry—Celeste. For his own reasons. I didn't care so much, then. I thought perhaps she might be—decent—to you, after a while, when she realized what you were. I shut my eyes deliberately, even though I was sure, after a little, that you would be miserable with her. You see," she added, with the simplicity stark and touching in her voice and face and gesture, "I love Christopher. He promised that we would be married, after you and Celeste were married. Now he hates me. I'll never see him again."

He stared at her, more and more amazed and incredulous. His lip lifted in disbelief and distaste, and confusion. He rubbed his unshaved chin, and stared again. He muttered: "For Christ's sake!" And then was stupefied.

There was a long silence in the room. At last Henri began to laugh, without mirth, and with a somber cynicism: "Well, perhaps it's just as well. You save me, and I save you! From Christopher and Celeste. But you and Christopher! That Trappist snake! Why didn't you fall in love with the devil himself? You might just as well, you know. And so he was after your money, was he?"

"No! No!" she cried, passionately. "He wasn't! If he had been, he would have married me long ago. It wasn't money he was after. It wasn't money at all. It was what you could help him to do to Armand that he was thinking of——"

Henri pursed his lips with a curious smile. "Well, it may interest you to know that I've been playing a little trick or two of my own, and even if I had married Celeste it wouldn't have made any difference—in what I was going to do, and in what I'm still going to do. I'd like to tell that to his face." He added: "But it's funny about him not making a grab for you, when you offered. And you did offer, didn't you?"

Her wet face flushed scarlet, but she said simply: "Yes, I did. But he said he could only think of one thing at a time——"

His large brutal face lightened with pity for her. "Well, I'm not sorry, perhaps, for everything that's happened. You and Christopher. He would have made you dance! And so he won't look at you now, eh?"

She was silent. He reached over and awkwardly patted her knee. "Come on, the world's not ended yet, for either of us. Besides," he added with a cryptic smile, "I don't give up so easily. How about both of us going away, say in about a month? Together?"

She gazed at him humbly, her eyes slowly filling with smiles and tears. "Yes, Henri. Oh, yes, Henri!" And she knelt beside him, put her arms about his neck, and kissed him. His hand patted her shoulder mechanically. He frowned, thinking. Finally, his arm tightened about her, and he began to smile in a peculiar fashion. He rubbed his cheek against her hair, and his smile broadened as though he were enjoying some secret joke.

CHAPTER LVII

PETER had returned to Etienne's apartment in New York. Etienne was a vague fool, egotistic, unintelligent, pretentious, affected, tiresome and boring. But he was without malice. And so Peter came to him, feeling scratched and wrenched from all the malice and treachery in the world. It seemed to him that a friend without malice and treachery was the one thing he desired above anything else. Even Etienne's exclamations and lies and grandiose voice were comforting; they were like the gestures and words of children, without harm or cruelty. They were the quilts on the bed of an exhausted man, warm and secure.

Etienne was extremely disappointed, and tragic. He exclaimed constantly. He reviled Celeste in heroic and echoing periods. "Women!" he cried, with the posturings, the facial contortions, the breast-striking, of a tenth-rate early-Victorian tragedian. He struck a Macbeth attitude. Then he sighed deeply. He bunched his fingers together, touched them sorrowfully to his lips, shook off the kiss with a gesture of bitter renunciation. "Our hope and our despair! Life is death without them. But death is life, with them. What are we to do?" he demanded of Peter in accents of mournful dejection. He gazed at the younger man with an expression of calamity, the expression of a man who has known many women and is full of wounds, his big liquid eyes swimming in the water of sensibility and heartbroken sympathy.

Peter could not help smiling. He could hardly keep from laughing. "We could go to a monastery," he said.

Etienne sighed, shook his head with grief. He sat down. He folded his arms upon his bosom. He was Buddha, contemplating a world that had given him a distinct pain, especially the female portion of it. But he contemplated it more in sorrow than wrath. His large flabby features assumed an air of majesty and long-suffering. "A monastery," he murmured.

He lifted a hand, like one who calls attention to the distant shaking of temple bells. "Renunciation," he mourned, in a musical voice. "The things of the world forsaken for the wisdom of sadness. The cloister, the darkness, the pale torches." His eyes lighted with pleasure at his own words. His lips moved silently, as he repeated them to himself. He glowed. "A monastery. The idea appeals to me. I have often imagined the peace and mystery and sweet soul-satisfaction of the dim colonnades, and the monks at prayer."

Peter was entertained, in spite of his own misery. "But it would be duller than hell," he said. "No champagne, no first nights, no gardenias, no ladies. And what would you do without the women in New York, and what would they do without you, Etienne?"

The old actor's majestic expression softened. He smiled. He relaxed. He lifted his coat lapel and sniffed the gardenia on it with the delicacy and appreciation of a man with a soul. He confessed: "Well, I must admit that I've been told many times that I am the spirit of New York. They've even said a first night would be flat without me. As for the ladies— Ah, I really don't know!" He sighed, then resumed, becoming grave again: "I suppose one ought not to be selfish. It would be sweet to renounce the world, but one must consider whether that world would not suffer from this self-indulgence. One might even call it cowardice?"

"Yes," said Peter, without a smile, "I'm sure it would be called cowardice."

Etienne was relieved. He was as refreshed as though he had spent several years in a monastery and was just now returning to the world, bursting with excitement and eagerness. He glanced about him, proud and alight. "I'll give a party," he said. "The wit, the beauty, the grace, the genius, of New York. You'll enjoy it, Peter. As for myself, I prefer quiet contemplation. But I must remember that you have just suffered a great grief, and need distraction."

"Oh, for God's sake, don't bother about me!" exclaimed Peter, dismayed. "Frankly, I'd rather contemplate with you. I want to finish my book."

Etienne was cast down. He stroked his jewelled hand over his bald crown and flowing rear-locks. He was like a disappointed child who has just arisen from a sick-bed and has learned that promised delights are going to be withheld. He thought, after a man emerges from a monastery, even a spiritual monastery, he needs relaxation and brightness and gaiety about him. Peter saw his face, and said hastily: "Really, Etienne, I'd like a party, myself. But I didn't want to be selfish. I didn't want to impose upon you, and upset your quiet life."

So Etienne joyously gave a party. He told each guest, confidentially, that Peter had "a grief, a great grief," and must be diverted. As a result, Peter became uncomfortably aware of inquisitive and avid eyes, without knowing the reasons. He was completely wretched, anyway. He had an abhorrence for intellectuals, and Etienne seemed to know every outlandish, peculiar and moth-gnawed intellectual in Manhattan and its environs. He particularly seemed to know those of queer habits and large appetites and dirty collars and insulting mannerisms. Each one quarreled about his interpretation of "life," as though life belonged exclusively to him and the others were being extremely stuffy and presumptuous in claiming even the corners of it. There were mediocre writers there, who wrote novels full of obscene words and perverted situations, and carried clippings about them in which some reviewer spoke of their "robust and earthy style, and fresh strength," and "new, virile interpretations" of dirtiness as old as life and sin. "They go to the outhouses for their adjectives," thought Peter, disgusted.

There were "composers," who reviled the "decadence of modern music," and went into raptures about the fugues, scherzos, concertos and sonatas which they had written themselves. They were lofty about Bach and Brahms, conceding them "a certain harmony and nobility," which, however, were without "life." They wore their own poverty like banners, quoting that of Mozart and Beethoven with melancholy pride. One of the "composers" went to Etienne's carved grand piano and set it thundering in a frenzy. His longish locks flew; his fingers, with their dirty artistic rims, scampered up and down the jumping keys. Peter tried to find a solitary coherent theme in this frantic clamor of sharp and flat, this shattering, galloping discord, this marriage of the contorted musician with the tormented piano. Apparently, he thought, he was very stupid, for the others applauded vehemently, with cries of admiration.

There were poets there, too, and these Peter found the most intolerable of them all. Fixed upon their faces was a glazed look of ecstasy; their eyes were turned inward, as though contemplating subjective glories. But Peter noticed that, glories or no, visions or no, the poets had the appetites of trenchermen. They demolished trays upon trays of hors d' œuvres with amazing speed, drank cocktail after cocktail, and looked about them for more with sullen famished eyes. Their lyrical descriptions of some inanity that had lately impressed them were a little incoherent at times, as they kept glancing ravenously about for fresh trays of nourishment. There were actors, too, actors like Etienne, old men with sonorous voices and postures, and third-rate moving-picture "artists" with appetites and grudges and accounts of recent refusals to appear in productions that "violated the finest in them." There were singers in the Metropolitan chorus, who insisted upon rendering "Celeste Aida," and "Vesti la giubba" and "The Evening Star" in voices that might have lacked beauty but certainly did not lack strength. These artists also ate as though they had been on forty-day fasts.

He had met many real artists in Europe, and he knew that there were real artists in America. Unfortunately, poor Etienne knew none of them. He was blissfully convinced that the rabble that swarmed into his apartment and devoured his food and insulted him were the "soul" of the arts. He walked about with the sheepish prideful smile of an enraptured child. He accepted insults and ribaldry with gay indulgent laughter, and kept trying to catch Peter's admiring eye.

When Peter, who had never encountered specimens like these before, courteously asked writers and musicians if their last "works" were successes, he was greeted with stares of outrage and fury. He was informed, with elaborate sarcasm and contempt, that true artists were never successes. He was informed that only the "prostitutes" of the arts ever made any money. The degree of perfection, he learned, was the degree of emptiness of the artist's belly. The world never appreciated the truly great until they died.

Etienne had told them mysteriously that Peter was writing "a book." Some of the more courteous asked him about it. He was suddenly ashamed and angered. He felt degraded and humiliated, as though he had been discovered doing something meanly indecent. So he replied curtly, and walked away. The others let him go, for they were interested in no one but themselves. They stink, thought Peter with disgust. Later, he felt pity for them, these poor poseurs, these unclean worshippers, lingering in the outer colonnades of the temples, knowing in their hearts they would never be permitted to enter, and seeing only the distant glimmer of the altar fires.

He found an uninfested place in the hall and sat down, fuming with disgust and rage. It was some time before he could smile at his pettiness, and feel ashamed of himself. The telephone was near his hand, and he started violently when it rang. No one else heard it, for the uproar mounted as midnight passed.

He picked up the receiver, and was greeted by a man's

voice. "Peter? Well, I've had the devil of a time finding you. I've been paging you over two continents. This is Christopher."

Peter felt his heart shaking. He almost dropped the receiver. But he said, coldly: "Yes?" The uproar in the other rooms became a dim chaotic background.

Christopher laughed. "Don't be so cordial! The point is, when are you coming home?"

Peter was silent. His heart made a throbbing noise in his ears, like dynamos. He heard Christopher's sharp voice: "Peter? Hello, hello?" It was some moments before he could answer. "Yes. Yes."

"When are you coming home? Can you make it today? Tomorrow? Celeste wants you to come back, you know."

"Why doesn't she ask me herself, then?" He was amazed at the coldness of his own voice. Again Christopher laughed.

"Don't be stuffy. Come home. Perhaps she's ashamed to ask you. Look, I'm asking you. What more do you want?"

The voice was jovial, but Peter was suddenly swept with black hatred for the other man. He said quietly enough, however: "I'll be there tomorrow." And hung up.

He sat in rigid silence for a long time after that, his eyes staring sternly before him. Then all at once he was ablaze with joy, with incredulous excitement. Everything was forgotten but the fact that he was returning to Celeste. He got up, to tell Etienne, and his knees almost collapsed under him.

When he tried to go to bed, after the invading hordes had gone, leaving behind them ashes and cigarette-holes and demolished trays and assorted smells and dirty glasses, he found he could not sleep. The blood seemed to be bubbling and sparkling in his body; his heart kept throbbing with a rushing sound in his ears. Never had he been so awake, so stirred, so excited and alive. He got up and turned on the lamp at his side. He took out his almost completed manuscript. All at once he was filled with a sense of power and strength and potency. There was just the last chapter to do, and he would finish it now. Tomorrow, for many tomorrows thereafter, there would be no time, and there would be too much joy. Joy, like pain, had a certain anesthetic effect on the mind.

He wrote feverishly, until the hot gray September dawn filtered through the Venetian blinds, and the city accelerated its sleepless mutter into a confused and steady ululation. The last chapter, the last paragraphs, were completed with no slackening of passion, no diminution of power and strength.

"We know now that the world is in the hands of faithless, irresponsible and greedy men, who no longer pay even lip-service to honor and compassion and goodness. We know that they have dedicated themselves to the destruction of democracy and freedom, for they see in this destruction the final accomplishment of tyranny. They cannot use the juggernaut of religion again, for the people see the wheels and those who draw them. Therefore, with a brutality and cynicism never before witnessed in history, they will use force and cruelty.

"Prophesies are made and unfulfilled, and another will probably go unnoticed. But those who can see and hear know that in ten, in fifteen years, the oppressors will make one last effort to overthrow civilization, and destroy liberty and peace. They will use wars, and hatred, and the natural ignorance of men, and the masses' inability to think, and all the stupidity and lust-to-kill which afflicts the lower orders of society, all the beastlike prejudices and envy and madness of these lower orders, to overwhelm the enlightened peoples. An insanity is upon them, and a hatred for everything that is good and civilized, a loathing for everything which has urged man to stand on his hindlegs and liberate himself from his simian bondage. They cannot endure and flourish in a world of men. Therefore, they will try to overpower it and murder it, to roll it under, to flatten it out.

"They will use force, but greater than force, they will use words. They will set the ignorant and the fools to slaughtering each other. They will use the inferior and the dumb-minded masses to kill for them. Where the conspiracy will start, no one knows. Perhaps in Germany, already plotted against by the haters of men, perhaps in England, already enslaved and confused by its cowardly and treacherous ruling classes. Perhaps in Russia, already chaotic in the hands of the stupid. Perhaps in America, where the plot is already operating in the markets of speculation, and where plans are already made to paralyze industry and reduce the people to starvation. The plotters are still hidden, but those who can hear have even now heard their whisperings.

"Tyranny is old, cruelty is ancient, stupidity is immortal. Liberty, honor, self-control and dignity are all new in the history of men. They will be assaulted; many times they will be overcome; a thousand times all hope for them will be lost in the universal chaos of hatred and fear and blood and ruin and oppression.

"But they cannot die, for men have seen and heard them for the first time, and know what they are. No man will

419

completely abandon that which has once saved him and made him respect himself. The ruin will come, and the death and the despair, but out of it, out of the fury and darkness where the terrible struggle will take place, will come the final liberation, the final faith, the final democracy, the final peace of all men."

Surely, thought Peter, as he covered his typewriter, surely the spirit of Martin Barbour, assailed and wounded, thrown out and despised, ridiculed and forgotten, will be victor, at the last, over that of Ernest Barbour.

CHAPTER LVIII

ONE of the secret terrors of Peter's life, since the war, and his injuries, were periods when he was suddenly seized with a complete sense of unreality, of disorientation. It was not that he became confused, or lost sharpness of perception. Rather, his perception became abnormally clear and vivid, almost transfixed, like fluid water instantaneously stilled to crystal. But in the stilling, he lost the awareness of time and space, and there was only this transfixed clarity of perception, which was without meaning, without relation to past or present. He was absorbed by its petrified glitter, its aching projection into his mind, which was so tired, and which began, again, so desperately, its groping for memory and reality.

He never knew when this sense of unreality would come upon him, and he had learned to dread it, for through its petrified clarity values were lost, and the most important things lost significance. At one time he had suspected that he was losing his mind, and had consulted a psychiatrist, very cautiously. His discovery that disorientation was a symptom of dementia praecox did nothing to alleviate his sufferings. It had first come upon him when he had slowly recovered consciousness in a base hospital. His active consciousness was still dulled and floundering, but all at once the vivid perception of unreality had blown away consciousness, and he knew the horror of an unreality which was sharper and more tormenting than reality, and which left him, for days, with a sick wonder as to what was real, and what fantasy.

He flew from New York to Windsor the next afternoon after receiving Christopher's message. A storm had been rising all afternoon, and as Peter's plane rose into the oppressed air the storm broke. He did not like flying, for he feared height, and only resorted to it when his patience outstripped slower methods of travel. But his natural fear of flying was lost, all at once, in the terrible beauty of this celestial fury. The earth below was obliterated by a rushing sea of purple vapors, a sea of chaos, rolling over and over on itself. Above this sea, and close to the uneasy plane, flew thin clouds of radiant, streaming mauve, like banners. In the near distance turretted cities, medieval towers, arches and colonnades, seemingly formed of dark marble, were outlined in golden fire, against a chaotic sky of shifting bronze and scarlet, broken at intervals by colossal flames. They were hardly formed before tumbling into ruin, and dissolving into smoke that assumed grotesque shapes, or exploding into enormous silent mushrooms of gold and heliotrope. There was no sound, and the silence that accompanied all this tremendous exploding of vapor and fire and color seemed more awful than any uproar.

Then all at once the plane seemed boring into a universe composed only of blazing yellow smoke, enveloping and swirling. There was no earth, no sky, no reality. The dim bemusement which always preceded a period of disorientation suddenly fell over Peter, and he experienced the old sick dread. Celeste became a figure of glass, without body, without tint or meaning. There was only Christopher, and Peter was aware of this enemy, now disembodied, now a part of this horror of enormous furies, more potent, more universal, more imminent, than ever. He put his hands over his face; his senses were swirling like this yellow smoke that swirled about the plane. After a long period, full of torment and pain, he lifted his head and looked through the small window. A sky of unbelievable blue and brilliant rose dazzled his eyes. The earth was still lost in purple vapors, streaked with fire. But everywhere there was peace and majestic splendor, a pervading holiness of silence and unearthly beauty. The pain deepened in Peter's heart, but it was a sweet pain, and he thought: It is possible there might be a God.

Christopher, but not Celeste, met Peter at the Windsor airport. "She doesn't know you're here yet," said Christopher, with his smile, and extending his hand to the other man. Peter took his hand. He could feel its dry coolness, and his ancient aversion for Christopher Bouchard sharpened to loathing. He made himself smile, but could say nothing that would sound sensible or eager.

Christopher was everything that was humorous and light. But Peter saw the vindictiveness in his eyes, the endless hatred. He thought: There'll never be any peace between us. No matter how long we both live, there'll never be any peace. But something has happened. I'm not afraid of him. Something has defeated him. But I don't think it was Celeste, or myself. He has given up, but he was not forced to give up.

Peter sat beside his enemy as they were driven to Endur, and again he was conscious that the strongest reality of all was Christopher Bouchard, and that he would never be rid of this reality. He listened to the other man's light remarks, which were at once indulgent and friendly, and he knew something had happened which he might never know about, and which perhaps it was best for him not to know about. I've always had the damnable habit of taking things apart, he thought. I've always been a monkey, searching for fleas. I must stop it. I've got to stop it.

It was not until they were in actual sight of Endur that Christopher mentioned Celeste again. "Frankly," he said, pleasantly, "I didn't believe that Celeste really cared for you as she seems to do. After all, she is only a young girl, and without experience. However, I believe she knows what she wants, now. You seem to be what she wants, and Celeste's happiness has always been the most important thing in my life." And he smiled at Peter, as though sharing with him some amusement at a most delicious but somewhat absurd situation.

Peter's pale lips contracted. He had always hated this man, but now his former hatred seemed puny and childish compared with this sudden surge of fury that semed to burst his heart. He wanted to say something, but he knew, with bitter wisdom, that when a man did not speak Christopher was impotent against him. Christopher, the silent, was powerless before the silence of other men. So, instead of speaking, he looked fully at Christopher, and smiled, and after a moment Christopher's smile changed subtly, and they understood each other.

They reached Endur, and Christopher thought: With that face, he won't live long. The thought made his expression amiable, made his voice strong and gay as he called for his sister. Peter waited. He did not turn to the door through which Celeste would come, for now he knew that there were things greater than love, more significant and more terrible than desire. And he knew that Christopher Bouchard represented them, embodied them, and to the end, he, Peter, was dedicated to their destruction.

Celeste came in, white-lipped, her young face thin and tired and almost haggard. Peter turned to her, and he forgot everything that he knew he must remember later on. He saw her stop; she looked at him, and her eyes grew radiant. She said: "Peter," and came to him, and he held out his arms and took her. She leaned against him. Her body relaxed. She began to cry, and her hands tightened about his arms. She pressed her wet cheek against his neck. "Peter," she said again, and her voice was full of exhaustion.

"Yes, dear," he said, very gently, kissing her. He told himself that this was a child that had been tormented. And he knew who had tormented her. He looked over her head at Christopher.

But Christopher was looking only at Celeste, and for once Peter did not know what he was thinking.

CHAPTER LIX

EVEN in the "Jazz Era," with its paradoxical guardian angel, Calvin Coolidge, the breaking of the engagement between Celeste Bouchard, and her cousin, Henri, was a sensation. Celeste's face, six inches square, appeared on the front pages of every newspaper, accompanied by a smaller one of Henri. No one had been able to procure a photograph of Peter, and little information about him. But he was played up in some newspapers as a sort of Don Juan of irresistible fascination. His forthcoming exposé of the armaments industry, called *The Terrible Swift Sword,* was discussed. Editorial writers alternately condemned and praised the book, depending upon how much, or little, the owners had invested in Bouchard and Sons and its subsidiaries. Georges Bouchard's publishing house was deluged with advance orders, a fact which caused him no small gratification and amusement.

The sensation was no less profound, shattering, and delirious among the Bouchards themselves. Ann Richmond,

Peter's mother, was taken violently ill, but not before she gave an interview to the ladies and gentlemen of the avid press in which she hysterically denounced her youngest son in extravagant language. She would refuse to see him at any time, she cried. Francis, Hugo, Emile, swarmed upon Christopher, who seemed very calm and unconcerned. They were locked up with him for several hours, while the servants crept about and whispered. When they emerged, they were still pale and nervous, but considerably soothed. Armand's faction was jubilant. They went about, openly exulting. When they met the enemies of their faction they winked and grinned, and commiserated with them with a total lack of delicacy. Nicholas grunted with delight, and was so overpowered with gratification that he immediately decided to ask Edith to marry him, for was it not rumored that it was she who had so catastrophically upset the apple-cart? But Edith was not to be seen, and neither was her brother. The grounds swarmed with reporters and relatives. But still they were not to be found. Distant relatives from all over the country came, wailing, condemning, sniffing with curiosity. The telephones in Christopher's house and at Robin's Nest rang insistently with long-distance calls. But neither Celeste, nor Peter, who had returned, were to be found anywhere. Christopher gave out brief, composed statements, then shut all doors. Windsor seethed. Every inhabitant, down to the lowest wheelbarrow trundler in the mills, was wildly excited, and swollen with importance. To them it was an affair concerning them all. Intimate friends complained that they were kept out, and vented their sense of affront by freely giving their opinions to any reporter who happened to be cruising about. Christopher, often going in to console Peter and Celeste, hidden in rooms under the roof, took his last and final revenge on them. He did not spare them observing the throngs that had invaded the grounds. He let them hear the constant clamor of bells and telephones. He did not minimize the annoyance. Peter knew what he was doing, and hated Christopher the more for Celeste's pale face and sleepless eyes and frightened expression. He hated him to the last point of endurance when Christopher comforted the girl with a solicitude and affection which Peter himself had to admit were sincere. But this was his revenge for what they had done to him, and what he had allowed them to do.

One time he knocked discreetly on the door of the tiny servants' living-room where they sat together, and told Celeste that Henri wished to see her for a moment. He had fought his way through reporters outside and inside the grounds. Celeste, crying out faintly, said: "No! No!" and clung to Peter's hand. Christopher was very grave. Of course, he said, he agreed with Celeste that it was an awkward situation, and Henri had no right to come just at this time, but didn't she think she owed him this last little courtesy by returning his ring in person? To send it back by someone else would be an insult which no man could forgive. Besides, Henri had never done her any harm beyond that of asking her to marry him. At this, Christopher smiled, and regarded both his sister and Peter with a pale and venomous expression.

Peter stood up before Celeste, and said: "I'll take the ring to him." And the two men looked into each other's eyes with an eternal hatred and enmity. Then Christopher smiled indulgently, and said: "Well, now, isn't that just a trifle precious, Peter?" His manner implied that Peter had suggested something rather vulgar, something exceedingly improper, for which he, Christopher, was a little regretful.

Then Celeste, recovering from her first fright, and very resolute, said that her brother was right, and she would immediately return the ring to Henri herself. She owed him this, she said, her eyes pleading with Peter to understand, her lips trembling. He was touched, in spite of his perturbation and hatred for Christopher, and very gently he said: "Of course, dear, you must do what you think is best."

So Celeste, with her exhausted face and shaking lips, and her expression of delicate strength and resolution, went downstairs alone through the locked house, whose blinds, for the first time in history, were drawn. She went into the cool large living-room, with its bare furniture and glistening floors. Henri was waiting for her, and when he turned to her slowly as she entered she colored violently, and felt her heart heave. She had memorized a quiet little speech for him, expressing her regret and distress for him, a dignified little speech which would soothe him and explain everything. But when he turned to her, and she saw his large harsh face in the bright dimness of the room, and his eyes, she could not speak, and could not move. She could just stand in complete silence, staring at him with dilated blue eyes and parted lips, like a terrified child, her hands hanging by her sides, her whole body visibly trembling.

He came to her across the bare polished floor, his footsteps loud in the quiet. And then he was amused in spite of everything, for with a childish and frightened gesture she suddenly thrust out her hand to him, stiffly and convulsively. He thought it was a gesture to keep him off, and then he saw that in her small wet palm his ring sparkled and shimmered.

They both looked at the ring, Henri with an air of interest and detachment, Celeste as though it were some dangerous object which fascinated her, and from which she could not take her eyes. Then, after a long moment, Henri took the ring, but he also took with it the little tremulous hand. She stared somewhat wildly into his eyes. He smiled back at her reassuringly, and pressed the hand warmly and firmly.

"So, you're really kicking me out, Celeste?" he said. With his thumb he stroked the hand he held. He continued to smile at her. And very slowly she began to relax; the fear on her face diminished. Her trembling subsided. She smiled back at him uncertainly. Tears began to fill her eyes.

"I'm so sorry, Henri," she murmured, pleadingly.

He shrugged lightly. He looked at her lips and throat. He still stroked her hand. It was no longer rigid; it seemed to press against his, as though looking for comfort and protection.

"Well, don't be so upset about it, child. It happens every day, you know. It could have been worse. You might have found out after we were married. That would have been pretty bad, wouldn't it?"

She nodded, unable to speak. He saw that her fright had gone. She was comforted; she sighed, as though released from intolerable strain. Very gently, he let her hand go. Then, after a moment, during which they had regarded each other eloquently, he touched her cheek with his fingers. She sighed again, smiled, took one small step towards him, and then stopped.

"Good-bye, Celeste," he said gently.

"Good-bye, Henri," she whispered. Her smile disappeared. Something like dark confusion and distress rushed across her face, something bewildered and full of grief.

She watched him leave the room. She listened with pain to the last sound of his footsteps. She heard the distant door shut as he left the house. She stood in utter immobility for some moments. Then she rushed to a window, and oblivious to those outside, she rolled up a shade with frantic hands, and looked after him. Perhaps he felt her looking, for he glanced back. He stopped dead. He saw her white face pressed against the glass, her eyes. For a long time they gazed at each other, not moving. Then he lifted his hand lightly to her, and went on. She did not return the gesture. She did not move at all.

A little later, Adelaide heard Celeste running towards her room. She heard her cry out. A moment later the girl was sobbing in her arms, as though in terror and obscure sorrow.

Armand, on his way to the mountain resort where his ailing daughter was staying for a few weeks, relaxed in his private car, and smiled. He looked through the windows at the moving, rising countryside, and sighed deeply. At times he had to rise and walk up and down the car, as though he were too restless to sit. Then he would glance at his watch. He smiled again and again, and hummed to himself. He put his hands in his pockets, and slowly and deliciously jingled the coins in them.

CHAPTER LX

A RMAND watched them come in. He sat behind his desk, solid, impassive, untidy and inscrutable. His hand played with a pen, tapped it. One by one they came in, casually, talking together. Hugo and Nicholas, Jean and Emile, Francis and Christopher and Henri. Christopher and Henri were apparently the best of friends. The awkwardness of the broken engagement was not evident in their manner towards each other, which was easy and offhand. They greeted Armand, joked with him, helped themselves to his cigars. Hugo and Jean asked for a drink, and then filled their glasses generously with whiskey, adding soda.

Armand waited. That morning Christopher had come into his office and asked him if he had time for a little consultation. Armand had regarded him in silence for a moment or two, and then, in as indifferent a voice as Christopher's, he had said that he would have time. After Christopher had gone out, Armand had thought: They're going to show their hands. Somehow the thought did not agitate him as much as he had expected. He was even conscious of a little detached excitement. When he remembered the broken engagement, he smiled, and the smile was not pleasant.

He was curious about Henri, whom he had not seen since the engagement had been broken. But Henri appeared detached enough, and on good fraternal terms with his cousin, Christopher. In fact, they seated themselves side by side with affability. Christopher was exceedingly ingratiating to everyone, a fact which made Armand's spine tingle as though it moved in an atavistic raising of hair. Armand's heart began to beat thickly, and he was suddenly afraid.

"Well," said Jean, with a wink at Armand, "we're here, Chris, as you asked us to be. Go on with your plot. For you've got a plot, haven't you?"

"Yes, I have," replied Christopher agreeably, smiling from one to the other. "Or, I should say, *we* have. Henri, Emile, Hugo, Francis and I."

"I don't like the word 'plot,' " said Hugo, grinning. "The last time that was said of me in the papers I had to pay out fifty thousand dollars. Don't use 'plot,' anybody. I'm allergic to the word."

Armand said nothing. He watched them all from behind his desk, like a stout bear ready for anything, and wary.

Nicholas grunted. His small surly eyes roved about the room. "Well. Come to the point, Benedict Arnold," he said to Christopher. "We've known there was some stinky scheme. A long time ago. We thought perhaps something had come up to stop it." And now he grimaced maliciously at Henri. "But it looks as if I was premature. The plot goes on. Or does it?"

"It does," said Christopher, and there was something in his voice which made Armand sit up. The pen in his fingers tapped more rapidly, and his eyes pointed.

"What have you got on your mind?" he asked his brother.

"Pardon me, you should say, 'on our collective minds,' " Francis interposed amiably. "You see, Armand, we're all in it. Don't look so disturbed. This is a business conference, not a lynching bee."

Armand flushed. A sullen expression settled on his face. "Don't keep me in suspense," he said sardonically. "Come to the point. What've you all cooked up?" He did not look, now, at Christopher. He looked at dark, bloated Emile with his thick curly hair and ruddy complexion. Armand's quick glance became thoughtful, and lingering. His big fat-coated muscles tightened. All at once he smelled treachery and danger in the room. He had known they were there, but now he smelled them with his soul, and he could hear his heart throbbing heavily. Finally, he looked at Henri. The young man sat in complete and meditative silence, a silence that was both forbidding and strange. And now Armand saw that his face had the color and solidity of stone.

Emile lit one of his eternal cigarettes, and puffed at it impatiently. "All right, Chris," he said in a hard, irate voice. "Don't prolong the agony. Out with it." Armand, watching him, saw that he was perturbed, for his fingers dropped the

428

cigarette on the floor. He lit another. There was anger in his perturbation. Armand became more thoughtful than ever. He focussed all his attention on Christopher, and waited. The room seemed suddenly stifling to him. A gray September rain was washing down the windows, and a gray light suffused the air.

Christopher, the sadist, seemed in no particular hurry. He leisurely withdrew some sheets of paper from a brief-case; his motions were all delicate and careful. Henri turned his head slowly in his direction, and waited. There was something about him like the statue in Barbour Park, something as strongly immobile and expressionless and somber.

Armand said, his eye on the neat sheaf of papers in Christopher's hand: "Don't be too polite. You've been scheming for a long time, ever since our father died. You think you've finally succeeded. I've been waiting for this, a long time. You're not a fool. You don't strike until your object is in range. Like a snake."

The two factions, in spite of the fierce tension between them, could not help exchanging glances of amusement. They all hated Christopher, and none of them had any particular dislike for Armand. "I presume," Armand added, looking into his brother's motionless "Egyptian" eyes, "that your object is in range. And that I'm the object."

The mortal enmity and hatred of a lifetime were suddenly visible between them, like a virulent presence. Armand thought heavily: He would not come out in the open like this if he was not sure. He continued to look into Christopher's eyes, not with rage or detestation, but with sober weariness and despondency. He thought again: I wonder what it would have been like if we had been friends. His candid peasant blood, flowing from both Barbours and Bouchards, quickened with a passion for simplicity and honesty, for integrity and kindness, for goodness and peace. And as it quickened, his last enmity for Christopher dissolved in it, and he could even regard his brother with a sudden pity, a regret that he could so give himself over to worthless things like envy and malice and revenge. He saw the other's gloating, the balefulness of the triumph on his face, and he felt no fear or consternation, but only a sort of compassionate distaste and wonder.

"Yes," said Christopher, lightly, "you're the object." He glanced at his faction. But Francis was looking at Armand, and not at Christopher, and his expression was puzzled and a little ashamed. The others sipped their drinks and smoked, and waited.

Christopher laid the papers on Armand's desk, as an

executioner momentarily lays down his sword. "Let's talk a moment about Parsons Airplane," he said. "You own fifty-one per cent of that, don't you?"

Armand raised his brows without answering. His eyes narrowed.

Christopher quoted the market price of Parsons common stock. "However," he said, in the same light, almost jocose tone, "when it is known that Duval-Bonnet has secured the South American contracts, and the Russian contracts, not to speak of the French and the British and the Japanese, Parsons will drop out of sight."

Armand said slowly: "Yes? And have these contracts been secured?"

Christopher smiled. "The South American contracts are certain. Duval-Bonnet, on the strength of them, will compete with Parsons for the others."

"I see," said Armand thoughtfully. "This is very interesting. But would you mind telling me how this affects you, and what business you have with Duval-Bonnet?"

Christopher's smile widened into malignance. "Yes, I'll tell you. I'm Duval-Bonnet."

Armand's faction turned pale. One by one, each man turned to his neighbor and regarded him in speechless consternation and incredulity. One by one, each hand put down its cigar or drink. Christopher's faction exchanged glances, and then watched the effect on the others. Armand did not speak or change color. The hand that tapped the pen was motionless. Only his eyes showed any emotion, and they glittered. Henri hardly seemed concerned with what was going on. He sat in his silent and impassive statue-pose.

"The proof," said Christopher, laying his narrow fleshless hand on the papers, "is right here. Look at it, all of you."

Armand made no effort to touch the papers. He gazed only at his brother. But the others, with exclamations, seized the papers. They turned them over, examined them, and finally fell into a grim silence. Then Armand spoke, calmly and dispassionately: "What do you want?"

"I," said Christopher, slowly, watching him, "want to be president of Bouchard and Sons."

No one spoke. Armand's faction was too stunned, too shaken. Christopher's faction merely waited. Armand's eye travelled carefully from one to the other, and in spite of themselves, the eye of each man dropped away from him, even Emile's.

Armand said quietly: "Is that all you want? And if I say no?"

Christopher's faction was uneasy. They looked up, alertly, at him. They had expected Armand to be profoundly shocked, to threaten, to bluster, to be utterly overcome. They had not expected him to sit like this, unmoved, unagitated. They began to wonder if he had something up his sleeve.

"That's all," said Christopher genially. "Yes, that's all. And if you don't, Parsons is out of business, and you know what a loss that'll be to you. But I've got a bigger pressure than that." He glanced at Henri, and now for the first time Henri's implacable eyes lifted and riveted themselves on the other man with the coldest and most curious of expressions. "Yes," said Christopher, smiling at his cousin, "I've got a far bigger pressure. You've seen what a huge loan has been given us—twenty million dollars. Henri got it. He's majority stockholder, temporarily, in Duval-Bonnet. His stock is security for the loan, which will soon be repaid. We have discussed this matter carefully, and if you don't come to terms with us, he'll dump his Bouchard bonds on the Market, and we'll dump our Bouchard stock. And you know what that means, with a Sino-Japanese war in the offing within a year or two, and a European war within another few years. You know what that means in government contracts. You know what it means to the business of re-arming Germany, and what repercussions it will have on Robsons-Strong, Kronk, Schultz-Poiret, Robsons-Petrillo, and Skeda and Bedors. You know what it will do to any prospect we have of war. You know what it will do to our subsidiaries. You know what it will do to any hope of electing Hoover, or any other Republican, in 1928, and what success it will bring to the Democrats."

Jean and Nicholas stared at each other with the transfixation of horror. They were completely stunned. They swallowed dryly. Their eyes rolled upon Armand impotently and with something like disbelieving terror. Christopher's faction, recovering from their momentary shame and uneasiness, smiled. Emile's face was crimson. He regarded Armand with open enmity and cunning.

But Armand did not seem upset. His hand had begun its pen-tapping again, very softly, almost thoughtfully. He still did not seem to see anyone but his younger brother, and now there was curiosity in his eyes, an almost detached curiosity and inquiry.

Christopher spoke again: "Of course, we shall first expect you to sell me sufficient of your Bouchard stock to give me fifty-one per cent."

431

Armand said meditatively: "If I refuse, and you do what you threaten, you know what it will do to yourselves, as well as to me?"

Christopher shrugged. "We aren't too concerned. When the stock goes down we'll buy it up. We can wait. But you can't."

And now Armand smiled, as if involuntarily amused. He turned his head and again examined each member of Christopher's faction. He saw only enmity, and the defensive dislike of men caught in dirtiness. Francis tried to assume airiness, and succeeded only in appearing jejune. Hugo, fat and buff-colored and jovial, appeared to be only a sly cheap politician up to old tricks. Emile, more crimson than ever, looked back at him with violence. And then there was Henri, and it was upon Henri that Armand's interest centered. The young man had not spoken a word during all this, Armand commented to himself. He might have been a life-size image of himself, sitting in that chair, one arm over the back, his eyes fixed indifferently on the floor, his knees crossed.

Armand rubbed his chin. He said to them all: "You're a fine lot of skunks, aren't you?"

Christopher shrugged. He laughed. "No. Just business men, Armand. You know the tricks. We're quite impersonal though, I assure you. Dog eat dog. I've always wanted control of Bouchard. You know that, yourself. I think I'll do better than you. Yes, I've always wanted control, and now I've got it."

Armand said to Emile, ignoring Christopher: "Just as a matter of curiosity, what are you getting out of this?"

Emile did not answer him, but his bloated face swelled. Armand nodded. "Just more money, I suppose." He regarded Hugo thoughtfully. "More money, too. Duval stock will go very high. You're a rich man, but not rich enough, I presume, to be governor of the State. Bribes and campaigns come very high." He looked at Francis. "And money again. But of course, I'm being childish. It's always money. In your case, it's trickery also. You like trickery for itself." And then, at the last, he turned to Henri, and there was a little silence before he spoke, this time, almost regretfully, and with wonder.

"I always thought you lived up to the legend of your great-grandfather. I remember him very well. He played for big stakes. You play for peanuts. You've been used very cleverly. But Ernest Barbour was never used."

Henri lifted his head slowly and regarded Armand intently. The older man met the inexorable eyes; he saw the peculiar

432

smile. Henri removed the arm that had been swinging idly over the back of the chair. He straightened up. Suddenly his strong stocky body threw out an aura of power and exigency. Everyone felt it. Everyone looked at him with sharp alertness.

"Peanuts?" he repeated softly. "I don't think so. Seventy-five per cent of Duval stock isn't peanuts. Forty-five per cent of Bouchard stock isn't peanuts. Is it?"

An incredulous pit of stunned amazement opened in that room, filled, now that it was so deathly silent, with the rush and melancholy cataracting of the rain. They heard the loud clicking of typewriters in distant offices. A police siren screamed in the gray wet twilight. No man looked at his neighbor, but only at Henri Bouchard, and they could not look away. They waited, almost without breathing. Christopher's face had turned to a death-mask of itself.

"Forty-five per cent of Bouchard stock?" whispered Armand. He leaned across the desk towards Henri. Now, for the first time, sweat appeared on his forehead.

"Yes," said Henri, in a loud harsh voice. "You see, my friends here will sell me a lot of theirs, and you will sell me some of yours, and then I'll have forty-five per cent." He smiled at Armand. "You, of course, will keep your fifty-one per cent. Also the presidency of Bouchard and Sons."

And then Christopher cried out, just once, and then was silent again. Henri turned to him swiftly, and spoke only to him.

"Don't think things, Christopher," he said contemptuously. "I intended to do this, even if I had married Celeste. You see, I've always hated you very much. I hated your father, when I found out what he had done to us. You are the one most like him, so I suppose I came to dislike you the most. At any rate, I hated you from the start. From the very beginning, I came back to do this. I waited for someone to come to me; I knew he would come. You turned out to be the one who needed to use me. Instead, I used you."

No one moved or spoke. Everyone was transfixed. Only Henri had life, in this room of statues. And Henri and Christopher saw only each other. Lightning seemed to flash between them, the lightning of mortal hatred and understanding.

"Seventy-five per cent of Duval-Bonnet," said Henri, and now he smiled with the convulsive smile of Ernest Barbour. "It's mine. And you'll do as I say, Christopher. If you don't, there's no more Duval-Bonnet. Remember, I own a patent taken out before yours. You'll be ruined, Christopher. No matter how you try to squirm out of it, you will be ruined. And
433

all the other boys here, our friends, will lose a lot of money, too. They won't like that."

Still no one moved or spoke. The faces of Christopher's faction were white and drawn. But Jean and Nicholas had begun to smile.

"My bonds," said Henri, "will remain tucked away in their cosy little resting place in New York. And Armand is still president of Bouchard and Sons. I'm going to be part of it, too. I'm going to have the very biggest place in it, some day. For, you see," he added with infinite slowness and emphasis, "I'm going to marry Annette." And with a deep smile he turned slowly to Emile, and seemed to take pleasure in that man's sudden pallor and his expression of sickness.

But Armand was smiling. His eyes glistened, as though there were tears in them. With a slow movement, that yet had a quality of impulsiveness in it, he put his hand across his desk. Henri took it, and smiled back at him. "I made a mistake," said Armand, and his voice was somewhat hoarse. "You're just like your great-grandfather." His voice stopped abruptly, as though he could not go on.

Confusion broke out at last, and excitement. Jean and Nicholas laughed aloud with delight and glee. They insisted upon shaking hands vociferously with Henri, who had become very genial. They mocked Christopher's faction with ribald remarks and questions. But the spirit had gone out of Francis, Hugo and Emile. They sat, petrified, staring with rage and hatred at Christopher. Their faces were pale, their eyes evil and questioning. But he seemed unaware of them. For his life lay about him like a heap of scattered stones.

He sat motionless, looking at the ruin. It seemed to him that he was dying, for everything but the ruin was swirling in darkness. A horrible sickness was churning in his middle. A horrible pain was hammering in his head, and then outside his head, in the darkness, until there was nothing but that pain and that sickness. A paralysis lay all over his body, and an icy coldness like death. His flesh was numb. He seemed to see his father's face, satanic and smiling. You've won, he said helplessly to that face.

He heard someone speaking in the darkness and the pain, but he could not respond to it. It spoke again and again, insistently, and he heard, now, that it was the voice of his enemy, who had done this thing to him. He lifted his head, and the effort caused him agony. He looked through the mists, and saw Henri's eyes. He listened to what he was saying, though listening was an anguish in itself.

"—and so, it was my original intention, even if I had

married Celeste, to kick you completely out of Duval-Bonnet, too. I had decided that we'd all be better off without you. And then Edith told me that she wanted you, though God knows why. I'd rather have a wolf for a brother-in-law than you."

Edith. At that name Christopher felt a knife divide him. The mists cleared. He saw everything with merciless clarity. He saw the faces turned to him. Henri was regarding him with dark anger and contempt.

"Well, she can have you. God knows the poor girl's been kicked around enough, and never had anything she wanted. I suppose she'll regret it, but just now she thinks you have a sentimental yearning for her. She thinks you're not after her money! And so I've finally decided that though Windsor is no place for you, and there's no place in Bouchard and Sons for you any more, you can have Duval-Bonnet. You can come out in the open, now, and be Duval-Bonnet. You're president. I'm going to give Edith 40 per cent of my Duval stock, as a wedding present to you both. When you pay back half the loan, I'll return the other 35 per cent to you. I don't want any part of it."

He sighed with somber humor. "I don't know how Edith will like living in Florida. I'll miss her. But I think Florida will do your own health a lot of good."

CHAPTER LXI

EDITH sat on her heels as she packed one of her trunks with the assistance of her maid. The room was dark, and full of the sound of the wind and rain. The maid moved to and fro, her arms loaded with soft silks. In the midst of the heaps on the bed old Thomas Van Eyck sat in speechless and compassionate misery.

"We'll like it after a while, Father," said Edith, throwing him a kind and affectionate glance from her heavy-lidded dark eyes. "One can get used to not having a permanent home. Remember how you liked Torquay? We'll stay there for a while, and then we'll go down again to that little place in France. It's so warm and pleasant there. We'll be so happy, you and I. You'll see."

The old man's lip quivered, not with pity for himself, but only for Edith. "Oh, my darling," he murmured, wringing his hands together. "I won't mind where we live, if it'll make you happy."

Edith bent her head so that it was hidden by the streams of garments hanging over the side of the trunk. Her face was drawn and haggard, her lips pale. Tears ran down her cheeks. But her voice was cheerful and clear when she spoke. "Of course we'll be happy. You did like that place in France. I've got such ideas for improvements, too. Then we'll go to Paris, every Christmas. That ought to be very gay, don't you think?"

The old man nodded like a grief-stricken child who was resolutely trying to be good. "And then we'll come back sometimes, and visit here at Robin's Nest, with Henri and Annette," he said. He sighed. "She is such a lovely little thing, so good, too. They'll be happy together, I know."

"Yes," said Edith cheerily, "we'll come back often. And we'll make them name the first baby Thomas, too."

The old man wept silently to himself, though he smiled. He wiped his eyes with his handkerchief. His heart ached with a dull breaking pain.

They heard footsteps in the hall outside. "It's Henri," said Edith. She felt sick and old and tired, for she knew a great deal of what was taking place in Armand's office that day. Henri had told her about it. She could not bear to see her brother just now, she thought, after what he had done to Christopher. But she stood up, shaking, dry-lipped, suffering. There was no use in anything any more, not even in anger. And she could not afford to be too angry with Henri, for he was still all she had, and all she would ever have.

The door opened. But it was not Henri who stood there in the dim doorway. It was Christopher, with a face suddenly wizened and shrunken and terribly exhausted. She gazed at him, mutely, not breathing, the garments slipping slowly out of her hand, her heart bounding in her breast.

He was smiling. He held out his hands to her, and she thought wildly: He's come back. He loves me.

"Come here," he was saying. "I ought to break your neck. But come here, anyway."

She went to him, moving slowly across the floor, her eyes on his face. She felt his arms about her. Then suddenly she clung to him. "Christopher!" she cried, over and over, and all the pain went out of her heart with her tears.

THE Long Island home of Mr. Tom Butler, President of the Stock Exchange, was usually an extremely festive mansion. As a wag paraphrased it, illumination never set in it. Artificial light merged into daylight, and daylight into artificial light. Mr. Butler's wife, considerably younger than himself, was a gay piece, who forgot her husband's inadequacies in huge and illustrious, but by no means stodgy, parties.

There was an unusually brilliant party going on this particular mild May evening of 1928. It was warm enough for the big gardens to be included in the festivities. The French doors stood open, gushing forth blazing light onto the new green lawns, and touching the young leaves on the trees with restless gold. The music of a select Broadway band swelled over the sweeter and gentler noises of the night in a brassy flood. People strolled in and out through the windows, laughing, calling, murmuring.

The gay Mrs. Butler had been feeling slightly pettish tonight, however. Having been a Benson of Boston, socially secure for generations, she felt no particular need for surrounding herself with those of burnished names. She invited gay people like herself, some of them not socially acceptable at all, but guaranteed to be amusing, flippant, high-spirited and interesting. She invited curious fauna like authors, prizefighters, dancers, movie stars and other buffoons, not to mention gaudy criminals and radicals. Her taste was enchantingly catholic.

On this particular night she had invited the very cream of her miscellaneous and slightly reprehensible court, only to discover, with dismay, that her elderly husband had invited quite a few of his very uninspiring friends also. She was not impressed by the fact that one of them was Wilbert Ford, the great newspaper owner, whom she disarmingly called an "old bull," with naughty implications. Neither did she like Mr. Schultz, of the Pennsylvania Steel Company, or Mr. Burns, who was also vaguely connected with Steel. As for a Mr. Mitchell, of Milwaukee, she loathed him. (Mr. Mitchell was editor of a newspaper owned, body and soul, by a manufacturer noted for his meanness, egotism, piety and greed.) Mr. Mitchell, Mrs. Butler said of him candidly, was a witch-burner without any personal feelings against the witch being burned, or any true belief in her sorcery. He burned witches, she said, just for the fun of it, or the political expediency of it. Old Senator Ulster was there, and he was a creature whose opinions were invariably colored by the money of those who bought him. But he was a power in Washington, for he could orate, and he had a dry and humorous way of talking, all of which convinced the people that he was an honest man. Then there was Mr. Jay Regan, whose presence began to mollify young Mrs. Butler. She loved genial old men with paunches and twinkling eyes; she liked to tease them. And too, Mr. Regan exuded power. There were others who bored her: financiers, industrialists of various kinds, and politicians. She liked a few of them, such as Hugo Bouchard, the politician, who could tell such amusing stories, and Christopher Bouchard, who thrilled a woman with his indifference, and Francis Bouchard, who looked like a Connecticut Yankee. But she detested Emile, with his red-faced violence and tight black curling hair. There was a new Bouchard tonight, who greatly interested her, however. Young Henri Bouchard. She found herself excited by him. There was still another man, whom she disliked at first sight, a pale, silent Teutonic man, a Doctor Adolph Schacht, who seemed not to be connected with anything in particular.

After the dinner Mr. Butler carried all of his friends away with him to his own apartments upstairs, which threw Mrs. Butler into a pet.

For some time no one seemed disposed to open the subject uppermost in their minds. They all drank and smoked, shouted with laughter, talked at random. But each man was watching everyone else very closely. No one, except Mr. Butler, seemed to know why Doctor Schacht was there. Several of the politicians knew him slightly, but they had apparently forgotten their acquaintanceship. There was something elaborate in their innocence of his identity.

Mr. Butler asked in his kind lazy voice: "Well, there is no doubt that Hoover will defeat Smith, is there? We're all agreed on that?"

"Oh, perfectly," said Francis Bouchard. "The whispering campaign against Smith was excellent. 'First a Catholic in the White House, then a Jew.'"

"There was a time," said Christopher Bouchard, "when I

thought Hoover was going to make himself fatally disliked. That was when he tried to be a 'good fellow.' But he soon got over it. He confined himself to sensible, grave, high-sounding principles. There was a difficulty there, too. He lacked punch. What we've needed right along is a good slogan. 'Two chickens in every pot.' Very good. When it's a contest between a good slogan and economics, the slogan will usually win, with our dear public, but when a good slogan is combined with economics, the thing is irresistible."

"We've done a good job on Hoover," said Mr. Burns, chuckling. " 'American standards and American ideals.' Beautifully vague, and beautifully effective. That appeals to the middle class, as well as to the proletariat, for each man will believe that it covers all his pet phobias and prejudices and avarices. Gentlemen, the vaguer yet more dogmatic and bigoted an idea, the more it appeals to the people. In fact, I've recommended vagueness throughout our platform, and it has been successful."

"We've made Hoover the pure American fighting the alien hordes, the Jews, the Catholics, the gangsters, the rum-runners, the atheists, the radicals, and all the other riffraff," remarked Mr. Ford. "I tried a feeler, thinking to bring the Ku Klux Klan in, but that wasn't so good. Most of the people don't like the Klan, in spite of the nightshirts, the horsewhippings, and the torches. And when a people won't have anything to do with an organization, even with nightshirts, horsewhippings, and torches, then it's hopeless."

Mr. Mitchell said: "My good friend in Milwaukee asked me to suggest to you all that we ought to use a little more anti-Semitism. Mind you, I'm not personally advocating it, but I promised to put it before you."

"Quite impossible," said Christopher, with cool disdain. "Remember, the people have had it impressed upon them for at least twenty-five years that anti-Semitism is an immorality. Your friend, Mr. Mitchell, discovered that only a year or two ago, when millions of good Americans boycotted his —wares. However, I'm sure none of us will have any objection if it is very lightly done. I rely upon our clergy to do that, though. Nothing official."

Mr. Mitchell, smiled at the others. "Christopher," he said, "isn't particularly interested in anything except wars and profits. Of course, we sympathize with him, very much. Wars are our business, too, directly or indirectly. But one must sometimes be interested in other things." He glanced at young Henri Bouchard, who had been listening intently, without smiling, without speaking. Mr. Mitchell's eyes became tentative. He wondered just where this young man entered the scheme of things. Of course, he had married Annette Bouchard, daughter of the President of Bouchard and Sons— And it was understood that he was closely connected with the Company now.

"Christopher must be patient," said Senator Ulster. "We're doing all we can. He knows that. Patriotic organizations are receiving all the support necessary."

"Too much politics," said Christopher coolly. He glanced at Hugo, and grinned. "My father used to say that politics were the last refuge of the incompetent. No offense, Hugo. But politicians, thank God, go where we drive them. But there are so damned many of them! That's the trouble with democracies—too many politicians."

"Perhaps," said Mr. Butler softly, "we shall be able to dispense with all that, too." In a sudden silence, he turned to Doctor Schacht. "Perhaps Doctor Schacht can talk to us about this, in brief?"

In a silence that continued, the pale German rose and looked piercingly from one man to the other with his milk-blue eyes. Each man felt those eyes stabbing down to his heart and soul, and when they had passed on, he felt exposed and understood. Schacht smiled. He bent his head with Teutonic courtesy. His manner was compounded of arrogance, servility, respect, egotism and ruthlessness. The typical German manner, thought Christopher, who detested Germans.

"I," said Schacht, in his light, accented voice, "am founder and leader of the new Deutsch-Amerikaner Gemeinschaft, gentlemen. Perhaps you have heard of us?" No one answered him. Everyone stared at him intently. He lifted a delicate deprecating hand and let it drop. "It is a nationwide organization of Germans of American citizenship, either acquired or born. Its object is the preservation of 'American ideals.'" He smiled. Now everyone else in the room smiled, with the exception of Henri Bouchard, who seemed to see and understand everything. "Officially, our known members are less than fifty thousand. Unofficially, they number millions. In fact," he added with great and charming frankness, "I might include all of you."

The smiles became broader, more knowing. Schacht went on: "I have been accused of being a sentimentalist. But I am really a realist. It is as a realist that I am going to talk to you. I am sure that I have never had so sympathetic an audience. So, at the risk of being called a prophet, I shall speak to you openly.

"All of us know, in spite of America's present prosperity, that our system of government is really inoperable. Democracy is inoperable. It was staggering to its death in 1914, in every nation foolish enough to have tried it. The war was really a struggle between democracy and sensible autocratic government. Unfortunately, democracy won. Temporarily. Now, it is again staggering to its death. It was tried in post-war Italy. You saw the result. Communism and chaos. Mussolini stepped in, and saved Italy from the calamity of democracy and the final ruin of a people. And, very soon, a leader shall arise in Germany, and save her, too, from democracy. Just as America will need to be saved."

He paused. No one spoke. "Yes," he continued gently, "we still have a form of 'democracy' in America. But all of us know that within a very short time the prosperity we now have is doomed to disintegrate. Our system of production is far beyond the capacity of a whole world to absorb, let alone just America, herself. But we cannot destroy production and profits. We can't cut off toes just to fit a certain impossible shoe. We must rebuild the shoe. For, if we don't, we shall have Communism in America, and chaos, and confusion, and the downfall of capitalism and private property. Slogans are very good. But no man ever filled his belly with them.

"Of course, there are always wars. We shall have a war. If we can destroy a democracy which asserts that a man has the right to decide whether he shall fight what it is ordained for him to fight. If we don't destroy it, I can say, as a prophet without exaggeration, that democracy will degenerate into Communism. The capitalistic system, which is your life, and your power, will be destroyed, property confiscated, the natural rulers of the people massacred, and the rule of the proletariat established beyond uprooting. But you all know this! You have known it ever since the war. You have seen it coming.

"It lies with you industrialists, you law-makers, you financiers, you bankers and builders, to prevent this, to save yourselves from ruin and death, to rescue your people from Communism, and International Jewry, which is behind Communism, before it is too late, and ruin is upon you."

"Ah, yes, the Jews!" murmured Mr. Mitchell.

"The future of the world, the hope of the world, the life of the world, lies in that young spirit just awakening in Europe—fascism. It is not an Italian ideology, gentlemen. It is a universal ideology, squared with reality, profoundly tied up with the needs and the health of humanity. I am predicting that within five years it will be strong in Germany, that within ten years it will be all-powerful in Europe, that within fifteen years it will rule the earth. With your help. And only with your help. It is your life. You cannot turn aside from it.

"The first step in America must be the rousing of a 'folkic' spirit among the people. A national, militaristic spirit. America must have a vision! Patriotism, here, has still a sheepish and silly sound. It must be aroused, through your veterans' and other patriotic groups, to be a noble, a heroic, a passionate sound. War and pride must be its gods. The patriotic warlike spirit, the Nordic spirit, is splendid and majestic, and we must make the people understand this. Without patriotism, a nation must dwindle away into suspicious and futile alien groups, without a purpose, without virility and strength."

He waited. No one moved. But cigars turned to ash in fingers. Schacht smiled faintly. After a moment or two, he continued:

"The man in power who does not believe this is a fool. His folly can have only one result: the loss of his profits. And gentlemen, I am sure that when your profits are touched, your whole souls are touched."

There was a dim booming of laughter, then silence, as Schacht spoke again:

"This warlike—and profitable—spirit has a great and mortal enemy in every nation. The Jew. In every nation in which he takes up his parasitic abode, the Jew combats patriotism and the national spirit. He fights manly hatred, and calls it foolish and dangerous; he fights nationalism, saying it breeds wars, which of course it does! He slavers about brotherly love, which is a vicious and enfeebling doctrine, one that declares the weak and submerged have a right to live, which any man of sense declares they have not. The Jews believes in mercy, a vice rejected by nature, herself. He goes about, agitating speech, encouraging the worthless human cattle to strike against their lawful masters, stirring up the masses to demand a place in government. In short, he is the spirit of democracy, the destroyer of a strong, formidable and national spirit, which paralyzes heroism, the will-to-war and conquest, and replaces reality with enfeebling dreams."

Mr. Mitchell moved slightly. He lifted his eyes and fixed them coldly upon Schacht. "You know very well that it is impossible to have a true folkic spirit in America. Except

442

in a few Southern and Western States. As for the rest, they are permeated and riddled with all sorts of subversive races: the Irish, the Slavs, Italians, Poles, Hungarians. You can give them no common purpose that will bind them together, dissolve them into one powerful whole."

Schacht smiled. "Yes, you can. You can give them something to hate."

"What?"

"The Jews."

They regarded him thoughtfully. Some of them smiled. Christopher said: "Was she a very pretty Jewess, Doctor Schacht?"

They all shouted with laughter, the explosive laughter of relief, for every man had been listening with passionate intensity. And then they saw that Doctor Schacht had turned very pale. But he was also laughing. "Yes, Mr. Bouchard," he replied with charming frankness, "she was."

This disarmed them. They listened to him with more friendliness now. He went on: "Roman Catholicism is the next enemy to be destroyed. It must be destroyed in America, just as the Jew must be destroyed, for the Church is the enemy of true State domination. It must be destroyed, if we are to have a clean, strong, united and powerful nation. A Nordic nation, freed of Jewish decadence, criminal and fantastic democracy, Catholic perversion and humanitarian sentimentality."

He said: "I can see that some of you believe this will all be very difficult to bring about. It will be easier in America than in any other nation, for Americans, I say candidly, are mentally inferior to many other races. They believe everything they read in the papers, especially if it coincides with their prejudices. They'd rather see a baseball game than think; they prefer comedians to books. The Americans, in spite of their schools and their constant shouting about education, are the most illiterate people in the world. Why, our own German peasants have twice the intelligence, and three times the reasoning capacity! In Europe, the most stupid man has some idea of politics. In America, they elect the man with the pleasantest face and the nicest lies. And if he can remember more platitudes than his opponent, his constituents will rise up and call him blessed. In the most virtuous country in the world, virtue is the most despised. Americans, just now, ask only to be amused. Later, they will become restless. They will ask only to be given something to hate. If you don't give it to them, they will destroy you. The question is: will you give it to them?"

443

"You have a low opinion of us, Doctor Schacht," said Mr. Burns.

"No, merely a realistic one. Realizing facts is not depressing. It is life-saving."

He threw out his hands. "Will you live, or will you die? Will you prosper, or decay? Will you have heroic wars, or will you have decadent and gangrenous democracy? It is your choice. The world awaits your decision."

Again, they all looked at each other. Then Christopher said, with a slight smile: "Gentlemen, there is much in what our German friend has said. Suppose we allow him to leave, for no doubt he has many pressing engagements? We must give him a vote of thanks. Then, later, we can discuss this matter fully. Very, very fully."

But when Doctor Schacht had gone, no one seemed particularly anxious to discuss what he had said. Each man seemed to be thinking. He seemed to be surveying his own thoughts, about which he may have felt somewhat furtive. Then at last Mr. Mitchell said tentatively: "Of course, it's a little farfetched. Schacht is a zealot. Or is he?"

Christopher smiled. "A zealot? I wonder. I don't think there is such a thing. Certainly, Schacht with that face of his, and those eyes, is no real zealot."

"Nevertheless," said Mr. Burns, "we can at least—think —about what he's said. He strikes me as no fool."

Jay Regan spoke. He no longer had his usual good-natured and rollicking look. He surveyed his friends grimly. "There's a lot in what Schacht said. I, myself, think there's a day of reckoning, and so do you. But that day won't be caused by the Jews, or the Albanians, or the Catholics, or the Fuzzy-Wuzzies, or any other scapegoat to be used as an excuse for murder. It'll just be caused by you boys." He grunted. "It's a nice thing to think about. I'm glad we're all together. I've been wanting to talk to you for a long time.

"The nice, nationalistic, militaristic future so eagerly desired by Doctor Schacht, and by yourselves, for different motives, of course, doesn't interest me just at present. But I'm considerably goddamned interested in the mess you're cooking up to serve to America, and the rest of the world, within the next few months, or the next year.

"Just what the hell do you boys think you are doing, and where is this going to lead us? This orgy of pyramiding? This national speculation? You and I know that the fools are buying paper and a lot of water. You're encouraging the little man to think he's a financier, a big bold speculator, and a manipulator, by God! You've encouraged the ape-

444

greed in the paper-hanger, the shopgirl, the mechanic, the laborer, the little clerk. When they get scared, you talk of 'permanent prosperity,' and have your hired newspaper imbeciles to warn the people about 'selling America short.' In the meantime, a reckoning is bounding at your heels. You know that, in spite of all this 'prosperity,' unemployment is already ominously growing. You know that industry is already idling, in spite of a 'booming market.' Warehouses are already choked with enormous surpluses. I don't need to tell you this. We can no longer lend Europe the money to buy goods from us. We can, and will, lend money to Germany to accelerate her re-armament. The Bouchards, and their friends, are already arranging a little re-armament scheme for her. And a 'moratorium,' to help her 'starving peoples'; in other words, her starving armaments-makers. The other European nations can't even pay interest on our loans. We have already industrialized other nations, such as Japan, with our own money, so that they can now compete with us and cut our throats in the foreign markets.

"As our friend Schacht says, something is doomed, and maybe we are the marked cards. But it is certain that the things you are doing, the speculations you are encouraging, the vast surpluses you are piling up, the illusion of 'permanent prosperity' which you are feeding to the public, the contempt for thrift and saving and moderation you are artfully broadcasting, are rapidly bringing on a financial and economic collapse, and chaos. You know what's coming. The signs are already in the wind. You could stave it off. But you won't! And you know what the end will probably be: maybe a revolution, when the people get hungry enough."

Christopher said lightly: "When a man grows old, he becomes a philosopher. A full belly is the beginning of wisdom, and impotence the beginning of virtue. Don't be annoyed, Mr. Regan. I'm just quoting my father, who could turn out epigrams with a flick of his wrist. But when men speak of the 'crack of doom,' they've either got indigestion, or can't enjoy women any more.

"But suppose what you say is true: in that event, we'll have to do something. After we've gotten our profits. I grant you that. The re-armament of Europe is already under way. In the meantime, we're unloading stock, quite quietly and steadily. You're doing that, too." He smiled. The others smiled, all except Regan, who colored and swelled with anger.

Christopher continued: "When the 'crack of doom' comes,

we've still got war. War takes care of two surpluses: population and commodities. Or, if the worst comes to the worst—we've still got our Doctor Schachts, and we've still got our patriots, and our drums, and we've got various minorities we can hate and murder, to satisfy the people." He sniffed. "I can already smell the carrion!"

are you missing out on some great Pyramid books?

You can have any title in print at Pyramid delivered right to your door! To receive your Pyramid Paperback Catalog, fill in the label below (use a ball point pen please) and mail to Pyramid . . .